MY SECRET RADIO

A Novel

Michael Hallock

High on Loretta Press LLC

ISBN: 978-0-578-97429-3

For Carol, whose insights into this story always brought me closer to the heart of the matter.

It is playing a second time,
maybe a third.
Yes, a third time.
He remembers remembering it.

—from "All He Knows," by Leonard Cohen

CHAPTER ONE

"Idiot Wind"

Micanopy, Florida, 2016

Carl Decker, the best man at both of my weddings and current husband of my second wife, Linda, is getting out of prison. Or at least that's how I interpret Linda's nervous, halting message. She and I have been divorced for twenty-five years but have yet to recover our interpersonal equilibrium. Carl will be released soon, she says, but he's not— She pauses, reconsiders, then decides to leave it at that. "Call back Monday morning, Bill," she tells me finally, and hangs up.

Carl has served about half of his one-year sentence for consumer fraud shenanigans. I speculate that Florida's penal system is clearing space for more hardened criminals or, more likely, other inmates found Carl too annoying to endure. This last remark might sound tongue-in-cheek, but you don't know Carl.

No one knows Carl, I wager, as well as Linda and I. My father would've said I owe Carl several "horse whippings" for past betrayals. Still, if you squint a little looking at the same circumstances, you might imagine I owe Carl for my daughter Ramona, my career, my house, and even my illusion of freedom. Either way, it's for the best that a reasonable distance separates us on the days Carl isn't in prison. Once he's set free, he'll return to Tampa, 140 miles from my home in Micanopy (mick-a-NO-pee, not "my canopy"), a small town near Gainesville. Beyond its remoteness from Carl, Micanopy enjoys the virtue of nestling next to Payne's Prairie, a 21,000-acre nature preserve whose flourishing fauna include a bison herd, wild horses, sandhill cranes, countless gators, and, on rare occasion, those touchstones of my distant Georgia childhood, ruby-throated hummingbirds.

As magical as the Prairie is, however, living next door to a natural wonder had little to do with how I ended up in Micanopy. The town, you might say, came with the house, a sturdy, wood-framed relic I acquired when Linda and I divorced. To be clear, Linda and I spent our married years in a different, far more valuable house in Gainesville, but we sold that house to satisfy Carl's debts. Why did I allow that? Let's just say for now that my ex-wife possesses a genius for putting me on the spot.

More to the current point, when Linda and I divorced, our daughter Ramona was eleven. She is now in her mid-thirties, unhappily married herself and mother to sixteen-year-old Olivia, whom she finds moody and intractable. I, on the other hand, see Olivia as feisty, amusing, and appropriately alienated. Right now, I stand in my yard raking up spent cassia blossoms, waiting for Ramona to drop Olivia off for the Labor Day weekend. Dylan's sneering masterpiece, "Idiot Wind," seeps out through my open front window, the verse about ending up as a bloody corpse in a ditch catching my ear.

Thanks for the warning, Bob.

Meanwhile, tourist traffic—antique and pottery browsers mostly—already creeps slowly up and down Cholokka Boulevard, which is not only my street but Micanopy's lone commercial artery. Long ago, I could throw a baseball far enough to break the nearest storefront window. That store—the unfortunately named Harry's Pottery—now affects a vaguely nineteenth-century vintage ambiance, though I well remember it as a hippie head shop with a Peter Max paint job. And before that, I'm told, it served as an actual general store. And before that, something else or nothing else, but the point is that one tends to feel Micanopy moving backward because everywhere else lusts for the future by comparison.

William Bartram tells us in his illustrious *Travels* that he arrived at this precise location on the cusp of the Revolutionary War, visiting an Indian town called Cuscowilla to gather flower specimens for his patron in Philadelphia. His traveling party had a different purpose—to ratify the treaty of St. Augustine, establishing terms of peace "once and for all" between whites and Indians in Florida. We know how that turned out, but Bartram didn't. He happily collected his specimens, praised the "friendship" shown by Seminole women to white traders, feasted with his hosts on the choicest pieces of barbecued bullocks and tripe soup, and observed that the town stood "on the most pleasant situation that could well be imagined or desired."

Quite a claim, but who am I to say? These days, if not "the *most* pleasant situation," Micanopy is still pleasant—quite a feat in its own right. Local websites tout us as "the cutest town in America." As long as no one believes that, I will probably stay where I am.

My name, by the way, is William Davis Shaffer. My father had Jefferson Davis in mind, but I tell people my mother named me after Bette Davis. I am a slightly paunchy, retired teacher of philosophy (as opposed to a philosopher). My beard suggests an underfed Ernest Hemingway, and my voice conveys a faded deep-South twang salted with pretentious neo-hippie overtones. If you were to describe my academic career in baseball terms (what with the World Series coming up), I hit .239, mostly in the minors, except for a cup of coffee in the big show with a last-place team. What the "stats" *don't* show is how much I loved to play.

So far, I have lived about twenty-four thousand days; the first five thousand spent in the small south Georgia town of Hopperton—pine country—growing up in a well-respected, loving family. Despite these advantages, I acquired tastes and beliefs despised by almost everyone I knew. As for why I count my life in days, it helps me to imagine singular milestones for my otherwise prosaic existence:

"Philosopher William Shaffer Announces Discovery of Reality"

Conversely, lesser events, such as "**Local Man Discovers His Hair Is Falling Out**" never make the dailies at all. You will understand this explanation better if you know that I often regard my past as a terrible fire I have set, and from which, as this narrative will attest, I have deliberately rescued nothing but a few passionate love letters.

But back to Olivia's weekend visit. It frees Ramona to prepare for a court hearing Tuesday, the latest episode in the interminable dispute between her and her soon-to-be ex-husband, Antonio. Naturally, I'm sorry for Ramona's troubles, even a little sorry for golf pro Antonio, lately fired from a country club for (as I heard it) bedding one trophy wife too many (he claimed his only crime was disparaging the wrong backswing).

However this tidbit strikes you, I have seen too much to consider Ramona or Antonio the definitively injured party. I focus my loyalties on Olivia, who, of course, would rather die than admit she needs anything from me.

When Ramona pulls up in her overbearing Lincoln Navigator, whiter than anything in the natural world except perhaps bleached bones, she lowers her window but keeps the engine running. Olivia, bearing up Sherpa-like under her bulging backpack, climbs out and stalks past me on her way to the house, slowing down just enough to roll her eyes and emit a conspiratorial groan intended to remind me that her mother is an obsessed pain in the ass.

As are you, my dear, I say to myself.

As far as I can tell, both of them emerged from the womb thinking *this isn't funny* and still await a decent punch line. *My* first impression was probably *this isn't real,* which is no more likely to be accurate but at least permits me a laugh or two.

I watch Olivia disappear into the house, then look down absently at a pile of yellow cassia flowers into which a hint of amber sun has seeped, transmuting them to gold. Nearby, chameleons skitter in and out of the bromeliads that line my front walk.

"Dad, can you come over here?"

A bossy tone has overtaken Ramona since she became a critical care nurse, but I don't mind. I'm glad to see her, something I try to convey, hoping to undermine her wintry view of people. I drop my rake and walk over to her hulking vehicle.

"Hi, honey," I say. "Nice to see you. You look lovely." Cool, leather-scented air drifts from the Navigator's cabin.

"Okay, Dad," Ramona responds, continuing to grip the steering wheel and making it clear that she is hip to my game. I don't consider it a game, and in fact, Ramona does look lovely. In contrast to her mother and daughter—both dark-haired moon children—Ramona gleams like a surfer girl beneath a butterscotch-and-honey mane. And today she is very much put together in a satiny melon-green suit.

"Listen," Ramona says, pressing on, "I'm sorry to dump Olivia on you at the last minute, but this is the endgame. Antonio leaves for Spain soon, and when he's gone, he's gone. We've got to convince the court to freeze his assets before it's too late."

"We" comprise Ramona and her divorce lawyer, a handsome older man (according to his brochure portrait) who lives in Ocala and keeps racehorses who don't race. Ramona will spend the long weekend there, and I don't doubt they will discuss the case at some point. I wave her apology away and smile to myself at her use of the term "endgame." She and I played countless chess games before even that pastime became too frivolous for her sensibilities.

"It will be nice to get this behind you," I say.

"Only if I win."

"Speaking of winning, how's your mother?" Linda was once a shrewd property lawyer who only took slam-dunk wins to court. Ramona visited her in Tampa recently during a nurse's convention.

"Fine, if you overlook the fact that she's nearing the end, at least according to her."

"My God, is she sick?"

Ramona gives a cynical chuckle.

"Not exactly. Mom insists she's a 'crone' now and must accept a crone's destiny, which, according to her, means to speak a few prophecies and die. She swears one prediction has already come true, proving she might be close to her final days."

I thought back. In our very first conversation, Linda had claimed to be part witch. At the time, I chalked this up to the banter of strangers. But she was in earnest, as I would learn soon enough. Now, I don't want to imply she mixed potions or cast hexes; her "witchcraft" consisted, as far as I ever saw, of claiming "second sight" to demolish my interpretation of events. I wonder now if cronehood means further demolition is at hand.

"You mean crone as in an ugly old lady with a wart on her nose?"

Another weighty sigh from Ramona.

"Yes, absent the wart."

"Well, let's examine the premise. Does your mother *look* like a crone to you?"

"She's a little bit on the skin and bones side, but otherwise, no. Of course, she says the mirror tells a different story from what I can see with just my eyes."

"I hope she's a nice crone."

Ramona returns a rueful smile.

"Dad, you and I both know she's whatever kind of crone she wants to be."

I nod. As to whether magic or motive accounts for my ex-wife's newly acquired crone *persona*, I have my suspicions, but I'm confident she hasn't lost her mind. Her stellar defense of her miscreant husband Carl earlier this year marked her first and only case as a criminal attorney, undertaken some years after concluding her career in "immovable property" law—wrangling over easements, title clouds, rights of foreclosure, and boundary disputes. While nothing Linda knew about "open and notorious possession" as a trespassing defense could help her beat Carl's open-and-shut identity theft rap, she argued with rational grace before a female judge, making the best of a bad hand. Carl, of course, carped about his one-year slap-on-the-wrist sentence, but as I heard Linda chide him afterward, "The sisters of mercy have spared you. Show some speck of gratitude."

Ramona's cell phone makes a goofy jingle-jangle. She looks down, then up at me, her expression pleading for understanding.

"I know you have to get going," I say, "but I'm curious. What was your mother's prophecy, the one that came true?"

"You mean the one that *didn't* come true? Mom said, quote, 'Carl is on *his way home.*'"

"She said that to you in person, what, two weeks ago?"

"Those very words, Dad, I swear."

Ramona's tone suggests resignation to an unfortunate new truth about her mother's mental state. I am merely teetering into confusion.

"Interesting. I got a call from your mother this morning. It was a little cryptic, but I think she said Carl *is* getting an early release. It could be a coincidence, or she is an oracle, or she's pretending to be one for some weird reason. I take it you haven't talked to her since visiting Tampa?" Ramona shakes her head, her face a portrait of the last straw.

"She called me last night. Not a freaking word about Carl; just a wacky question about how much longer she would live, hypothetically, if she quit smoking right now." Ramona's exasperation with her mother persists like a low-grade fever. It gives me no joy and Ramona no peace.

"Let's hope we're just missing one little puzzle piece that snaps everything sanely into place."

"You need to get out of the sun, Dad."

"Point taken. Just trying to be open-minded. By the way, what did you tell your mother about cigarettes and death?"

"Well, first of all, Mom said she didn't see any point in quitting if it would only extend her life a few months on the average."

"And what did you say to that?"

"That she sounded like Carl, that averages didn't work the way she thought they did, and I had no intention of getting dragged into her bullshit."

"All of which she graciously accepted, no doubt."

"She told me to simplify my thoughts and have a good night. She wondered if I had a number for the Cancer Society. I said, 'no,' and we hung up."

I give a meaningless nod, suddenly longing for a stiff drink, groping for some light I can shed. "When I met your mother, she campaigned quite hard to convince me she would die young from diabetes and didn't care. The prospect of blindness, I imagine. Then she got pregnant and went to war against everything that was trying to take her down. Not a single cigarette for many years."

"Carl got her started up again."

I smile and shake my head. "I think she wants to deny life the satisfaction of finding out she cares all that much. Call it spiritual bravado in the face of, well…"

"Maybe that's what attracted you to her."

"You mean like she was a falling peach blossom in a Japanese poem?"

"Pretty much nothing like that."

As I fumble for more words to send Ramona off in decent spirits, Olivia shouts through my front window, asking if she can eat the leftover spaghetti. "Absolutely not," I shout back.

"I'm eating it," she screams, upping her volume, "and I'm turning off that shitty music." Then she's gone.

"Ah, youth," I say, trying to convey worldly tolerance. Ramona's having none of it.

"It's the opposite of youth. Olivia is a grumpy old lady. And I swear… Listen, Dad, she skulks around like she's up to no good. If she tells you something, you'll tell me, right?"

"If it's dire, sure."

"She'd rather live with you and visit me," Ramona observes as she slips the Navigator into gear

"That's what your mother said about you when we divorced. Pretty much word for word."

"And she was right."

"Apples and oranges. Olivia's just a typical teenage contrarian. She has a cushy life and the luxury of hating it. Who wouldn't want that deal?"

Ramona stares ahead as if looking out through some private window. "Nobody, until the bill arrives. Listen, Dad; I need to get going. How's the book coming, by the way?"

"It's getting there," I say.

"That's what you said a year ago."

"And it's even truer today. If thoughts would quit occurring to me, I could finish it tonight."

"Spoken like the slippery sophist you are. Anyway, I'll be back on Monday afternoon. Check on Mom, okay? I know you don't want to, but look at it as a chance to rise above."

"And I've done such a superb job so far."

Ramona, lovely Ramona, peers out with a wry grin and shakes her head.

"Quit fishing for compliments, Dad; it's beneath you."

CHAPTER TWO

"To Ramona"

"**A**re we getting this house when you die?" Olivia asks as she emerges from her bedroom, where she spends the first hour of every visit unpacking and probably hiding things she doesn't want me to see.

"Why, whatever makes you ask such an uplifting question?"

"It's kind of falling apart, that's all."

"Worried about your future home?"

"No way. Mom says we'll get more for the house if you keep it nicer."

"I'm touched by your concern."

Olivia continues to scan the room disparagingly, impervious to my sarcasm.

"What is that *thing*?" she asks, pointing to the old Philco radio sitting atop a twenty-five-dollar "antique" Victrola cabinet whose warped veneer the radio conceals. She's seen the Philco many times before but never deigned to acknowledge it.

"That's the magic box of my childhood," I say. "It sent me many secret messages when I was your age, including some from the ghost of a runaway slave. Well, it sent them to everyone, but I was the only one who listened."

"Quit talking like a crazy person and just tell me."

"It's a tube radio, a television without pictures."

She considers this absurdity for a moment, then remarks, "You need all new stuff."

I close the book I'm reading and give Olivia my full attention. Her T-shirt features a tombstone and the words *In Memory of When I Cared*. "Look," I say, "when I'm eighty and on my deathbed, you'll be thirty, living some life you can't even imagine now. This house and its contents will be far down on your list of concerns. But just to ease your mind, the house *isn't* falling apart. It's rock-solid with big rooms, and I don't have a lot of stuff to fill it up, which I prefer. I will admit the outside could stand a fresh paint job. Any suggestions for a color?"

"You'll pick white no matter what I say."

"White it is, then. Or maybe robin's-egg blue, like in the song."

"What song?"

"'Diamonds and Rust.' Bob Dylan's eye color reminds Joan Baez of beautiful blue eggs. Quite romantic."

"Whatever." Olivia refuses to humor my diversion. She flops down elaborately on the sofa, radiating boredom.

"Hey," I say, "be careful with Gibson. He was in storage for a long time, which is like a prison to a sofa."

"What?"

"I said you're sitting on Gibson, my prized arts and crafts sofa. I'm his godfather. Be gentle; he's had a hard life." I'm hoping Olivia will inquire into Gibson's origins (part of a story I will divulge later), but once again, she sneers at the bait.

"It's just a couch. It's dead."

Having failed to draw Olivia into discourse, I return to my book, *An American Tragedy* by Theodore Dreiser. Here are problems to make my issues slink away in shame. Dreiser's long, grim, meat-and-potatoes novel depicts in unsparing detail the moral collapse of one poor fellow, Clyde Griffiths, a lowly white-collar factory minion self-deluded into believing he could become a social dandy. The man who gave me the book didn't suggest I would end up in the electric chair like Clyde, only that I too risked choosing the wrong woman for reasons not much better than Clyde's. I read *An American Tragedy*, took offense at being compared to Clyde, and married the woman.

Well, regardless of whether or not what's in Dreiser's pages had anything to do with how *that* turned out, the chance of it brings me back every few years for another look. You're sure what's knocking isn't a ghost, all right, but what is it?

Almost immediately, Olivia springs back to life.

"Shit, this is big!" she cries. "Uncle Carl just texted me; he's *finally* getting out of prison."

"Finally? He's only been in a few months. Did he say why they're letting him go?"

"Nope. They probably figured out somebody framed him, just like he said."

A couple of things. First, the only "frame" around Carl consisted of incontrovertible audio surveillance authorized by a search warrant. And second, "Uncle Carl"—not me—is Ramona's biological father, and therefore Olivia's grandfather. I would be happy for Ramona and Olivia to know this, but Linda presses me to keep the secret—perhaps one family skeleton too many. I, for one, am not preoccupied with bloodlines. On the other hand, some societies throw away female infants because they don't carry the family name. Clearly, I don't run the show.

"Did he say when he's getting out?" I ask Olivia.

"Real soon, was all. Guards told him yesterday but didn't give him an exact day."

What legal sleight-of-hand, I wonder, has Linda been working behind the scenes? And why the guise of prophetic hag?

Olivia beams. Carl's text message seems to have flushed all the cynicism out of her system. I'm sure she finds it thrilling to be Carl's confidante, as I did when I first discovered he had fought the Vietcong and raced motorcycles.

"I take it you and Carl have been texting since he went to the big house?"

The question delights Olivia.

"Yeah. I never knew prisons had Wi-Fi. It feels illegal, but in an awesome way."

"It probably *is* illegal for Carl to have a cell phone, but guards pad their salaries by smuggling. Lucky for him, he's in a white-collar resort unit."

"*You* think he's lucky," Olivia retorts, "but I don't. Last week he told me jail gave him termites."

"What exactly is 'termites'—did he say?"

"No, he just said not to worry, he's seaworthy and can't wait to take me sailing. You know how he talks."

I nod; I know how he talks. Talking is why Carl is in prison. He called clients of a bank he no longer worked for and used his familiarity to elicit

11

confidential information. This much he admitted. What Carl denied were any bad intentions. After all, he only meant to offer the inside track on a can't-miss venture.

Imagine his horror, he told the court, when his "business partners" took out bogus loans in the names of his former bank customers. Carl's horror notwithstanding, the state's attorney had his calls, and down he went, though not as far as he deserved, thanks to Linda's legal acumen. Carl's sins were redacted and spun for Olivia's "sake," until they amounted to a mere wisp of guilt: Carl had "accidentally scammed" people. Olivia believes Carl was a pawn in the hands of bad people, in which she echoes Spinoza, who thought we were all pawns in the hands of divine law. Thus, said Spinoza, free will is an illusion. In Carl's case, the courts begged to disagree.

Once the Uncle Carl talk concludes, I lose Olivia to her phone. I return to *An American Tragedy*, where Clyde Griffiths mulls his desperately stupid decision to drown Roberta Alden, the factory girl whose pregnancy threatens to confound his future. Maybe this time Clyde will come to his senses (as I tell myself *I* would), marry Roberta, work his way up to assistant manager somewhere, and, as an existential bonus, avoid the death penalty. If only Clyde could have read his own story. Or is the book's whole uneasy point that Clyde *could* see his life—and chose to look away?

It takes about five minutes for Olivia to work up to another conversational gambit.

"Maybe I'll go to live with Dad in Spain," she muses. "Mom's probably going to marry her lawyer. He creeps me out."

Lacking a reassuring reply, I walk over to my record bin and pull out "Another Side of Bob Dylan."

"Olivia, listen to this song Bob Dylan wrote for your mother."

"Bullshit."

"True," I say, "but pretend it isn't. Listen to the song as if Dylan *did* write it to your mother."

Olivia's eyes narrow.

"What's the song called?"

"To Ramona."

Olivia's eyes become slits as if I am trying to sell her a used car she hates.

"That doesn't prove anything. There's a million Ramonas."

"There's a lot," I concede.

Then, to forestall further wrangling, I gently lower the turntable's tonearm onto the spinning black disk. Even to my receptive ears, what comes forth sounds cramped and primitive—hard jangly down strums in hurried waltz time, the nasal voice making no effort to caress the words, the slithering unmelodic harmonica. But each new stanza, filled with sad pangs, city flowers, and soulful magnetic alliteration, sews resplendent lyrical threads into ragged cloth.

As the song finishes, Olivia pulls a laptop from her bookbag and searches for "To Ramona" lyrics. She reads them avidly, amazed that Dylan's Ramona tries to cope with the dying just like her surgical-nurse mother, and that Dylan's serenaded Ramona is torn between staying and heading back south, just like her mother reluctantly returned to Florida after completing nursing school in Boston.

Utter bullshit has become magical truth in five minutes

"Is this the Ramona my mom was named after?" Olivia asks. I hint at *yes*, though Carl's mother was named Ramona, a wicked little fact I try to overlook.

YouTube predicts we'll also like "River" by Joni Mitchell, a song playing the first night I made love to the other woman I later married. I keep this anecdote to myself as Olivia—begrudgingly—taps "River" to life. The songs protagonist laments that she is difficult and sad, and wishes she could skate away on a frozen river.

"*I'm* hard to handle," Olivia points out, "but I'm not sad. Anyway, isn't this a Christmas song?"

"Well, the song takes place around Christmas, but it's really about people mistreating each other and feeling bad about it. It's like the song 'Imagine.' Everybody loves it, even though it's about how much better off we'd be without heaven or religion."

"I don't love it," Olivia says, refuting a point I wasn't making. She gets up, stretches like a cat, groans, and looks out the window, seeming to long for something important. That "something" turns out to be dinner at a local Thai place. We shoot for six to beat the promised rain. In the meantime, I head out back to my grape arbor, intending to repair bird netting and spread a wheelbarrow full of mulch. No need to water—grapevine roots need to sink deep and find their own. The main thing with a good arbor is pruning the canes, branches, and buds. Grapes only grow on one-year wood and can be finicky about overgrowth and bud counts. I learned from two failed marriages that sweetness depends on doing things that are not that hard to do—but are very easy *not* to do.

As I slip on garden gloves, Olivia appears at the window holding up her laptop.

"Oh my God," she cries, "they're hilarious; they look like miniature wooden science fiction church houses." I walk to the window for a closer look. Olivia has dug up a digital picture gallery of old tube radios, including one of my Philco's close relatives.

"Why are they so big," she asks, "if they don't have a picture?"

"They're full of tubes—glass gizmos with glowing wires inside—kind of like old-style light bulbs." I realize that she may not even understand my reference to "vintage" incandescent bulbs and find myself telling her far more than I intended about tubes and filaments, about how I cherished my old radio, how I tried to imagine voices flying through the air and somehow passing through those tubes and then into my ears, how I nagged my father to explain how vacuum tubes worked and how shocked I was that he couldn't.

"It all seemed so fantastically up-to-the-minute," I say, "but everything gets old-fashioned pretty quick. I mean, people have to hold cell phones in their hands, right? That's still pretty crude if you stop and think about it."

Olivia dismissed this heresy.

"Only old people have problems holding their phones," she says. Then, after a pause, she wonders if my old radio might be worth something on eBay.

"Not for sale," I say, recalling my return to Hopperton for my father's funeral, after which I lugged the radio back to Florida. I cherished that radio so much it inspired a terrible poem beginning:

sound waves lived in this box like fish in invisible water
no one noticed them but me.

"Why don't you come outside?" I ask Olivia, doing my best to shake off the past. I tell her I could use some help shoveling mulch, knowing full well this is the last thing she would do. "Or you could just sit on the back porch steps and soak up vitamin D. Unless you're a vampire, you need a little D to keep you from getting moody."

"Too late. Besides, the sun gives you cancer. All it takes is five sun-burns." She illustrates this truth by extending a pale hand out the open window and retracting it quickly before the cancer cells can form.

"The sun is your friend," I counter. "It makes photosynthesis possible and gives us a nice warm heater to orbit around in the otherwise cold blackness of space. Plus, there's sunscreen."

Olivia smirks triumphantly. "We studied photosynthesis in school; the sun doesn't need my help for that. Besides, I'm busy texting Uncle Carl for more info."

She drifts away from the window. I drop into a ratty old beach chair and contemplate a wheelbarrow piled with shredded bark. The words "termites" and "early release" stick in my mind. I hope Carl isn't dying; I don't bother to hope he repents. To paraphrase Dylan, Carl draws his own lines and casts his own curses. On the other hand, though he doesn't try to change, Carl does try to win you back. On his pre-prison trips to Gainesville to consummate the mom-and-pop drug deals he dabbled in to keep himself busy, he sometimes left exotic potted plants on my door-step. *Ready to be pals again whenever you are.* And Linda's calls to discuss Ramona's marital plight (twice a month) always include a plug for Carl, she being the one who selects the bird of paradise or white bat flower he deposits, and she being the one pointing out that Carl has made all the gestures of restitution anyone could ask.

"You're right," I tell her, "but it's not a matter of me forgiving Carl. It's just that things go to shit when he's around. Always have, always will. And as for restitution, well, that's a lawyer's word, right? I don't think the past owes me anything. I could well apologize to *it* for all the chances it gave me that I botched. But thanks for the flowers. They're beautiful, and besides, they remind me of my mother."

"Hey, old dude," Olivia calls, rousing me from my reveries.

"Hey, little diva," I say.

"Did you have a stroke or something? You're just sitting there like a zombie. You haven't touched that junk in your wheelbarrow."

"No stroke, just contemplating the universe."

"Just don't forget to contemplate dinner, okay? And wear something decent, not *too* embarrassing."

Olivia would perish to think how closely she echoes her mother as she chides me through the open window, managing reality as if from the mountaintop. I promise her I will wear clean clothes *without* patches, my slight sarcasm causing a crinkle of vexation to cross her delicate, heart-shaped face.

"Whatever. Just be ready. I'm so bored I washed your dishes."

"I know you hate to hear it," I say, "but you're in danger of becoming a good person."

"I'm already better than most," she retorts. "It's not that hard." Then she vanishes from sight, leaving me to wonder if everyone believes they are better than most.

"Give me an hour," I call after her.

It's not that hard. I repeat those words under my breath, meaning, in my case, the act of spreading mulch by hand so that my vines stay quenched and healthy. I stand still a moment, imbibing my arbor, its quivering leaves, its blind, inquisitive tendrils, and I marvel how, given only minerals, water, and sunlight, it wholeheartedly pursues its purpose. That's projection, of course. The arbor—I assume—lacks self-awareness. One thing I do know, it didn't choose, like many dead-set humans, to live in egotistical defiance of any purpose not dictated by their will. I gather a clump of mulch between my hands. When was I ever unequivocal in my actions in service of some higher purpose?

If my arbor weren't so busy being itself, it would probably tell me to shut the hell up and do something useful.

CHAPTER THREE

"Drift Away"

O livia has concealed a sleeveless black dress in her backpack. "Mom doesn't even know I own it," she announces proudly, adding an awkward twirl as she reveals her new self, liberated from glasses and signified by candy-apple red lipstick and matching nails, both fingers and toes. At least she's chosen sandals and not high heels.

"How do I look?" she asks. We both know it's not a question.

"Fantastic. People in the restaurant will think you're buying a homeless man a meal. Imagine their surprise when I pay."

Olivia nods without hearing, lost in self-delight at having transformed herself from a zinnia into an orchid. She pouts theatrically into her phone's camera until she traps the desired expression, then frees it into the wilderness of friends and friends of friends, not quite *ad infinitum* since her mother, she knows, will never come across this pixilated needle in a haystack.

How is it, I wonder, that what Olivia hides from her mother buoys her up, while what I hide weighs me down? Maybe this is a subject I can discuss with Hermine during some future stolen afternoon. Hermine Delaplaine is my long-time "paramour" and a psychiatrist. She claims my "fascinating plight" explains her attraction.

It crosses my mind that she is Ramona's new therapist.

"Let's get going," I say. "I need more fresh air and less thinking."

At the restaurant, Olivia chooses chicken on a skewer with peanut sauce, or, as she calls it, McNuggets and Jif. We sit in silence momentarily as Olivia pulls a Hillary campaign button from her purse and pins it to her dress.

"We're in public," she explains. "I have to represent."

"Have you gone big into politics?"

"Gone big?"

"As in 'go big or go home.'"

"*Nobody* says that, dude. And no, I hate politics. Plus, I can't vote anyway. I just want a woman president. As soon as we get one, I'm throwing away all my buttons and shit."

"Fair enough, but what you hate is not what I call politics."

The plum wine arrives, a full bottle with *ume* plum fruits nesting at the bottom. Olivia eyes the bottle covetously, but she has not lost track of my comment.

"What do you mean, 'not politics'?"

"I mean that 'politicking' isn't politics; it's just trying to get elected. Remember I told you about Socrates? He thought democracy was just a mob of gullible people who would support whoever told them the biggest lies. He favored rulers who were trained, like doctors in medical school. A lot of people back then disagreed, so they had public arguments—life-and-death arguments. *That* was politics. Not just goofballs looking for power they don't deserve."

"Isn't Socrates the guy who drank poison?"

"Yes, hemlock. Related to the carrot, by the way. Water hemlock grows all over Florida. One bite and you're dead, so watch out. Anyway, Socrates had what he called a daimon inside him, and…"

"A *demon*, like in *The Exorcist*?" Olivia leaned forward, hoping to be horrified.

"No, more like a spirit voice that advised him. It told him to drink the hemlock, and he always followed the daimon's advice. People back then took gods and goddesses and other unseen beings very seriously. I saw some spirits once in a root cellar."

"You're nuts, and Socrates should have split. It's not like he murdered somebody. I would have been *out* of there." Olivia stares at the plum wine bottle as if it were a crystal ball. "Mom and Dad are like that," she adds.

"Like what?"

"Like drinking poison because voices told them to."

"What voices?"

"Lawyers, other divorced people."

"Sounds about right for married couples."

"Mom saw a shrink. Now she wants me to 'open up,' but that's not going to happen."

"She'd just need more therapy after that, right?"

"Ha-ha."

"Speaking of poison, would you like me to sneak a little plum wine on your ice cream? It's a relatively harmless toxin, quite tasty."

"People shouldn't get married," Olivia concludes, simultaneously nodding *yes* to the wine. "They should just have sex and go back to their own houses."

A chipper young woman emanating potent waves of patchouli dispenses our food. I glance at the inevitable TV above the bar, hoping for baseball but finding close-ups of agitated faces at some campaign rally where sanity has taken the day off. The angry white faces remind me of the sixties and my rural southern hometown. Integration back then was the apocalypse and the Holocaust rolled into one. I hear complaints these days about crude campaign rhetoric, but the curses I heard in a Hopperton barbershop fifty years ago would melt our modern ears shut. In Hopperton, luckily, it was all talk, vile as it was. And the most despicable of those invectives, the ones involving hellfire and farm animals, did not target Negroes, but white traitors such as I had surreptitiously become.

Well, at least I didn't have to drink hemlock.

"Fuck those people," Olivia mutters, tugging me back from the TV, her chance to say "fuck" a blue-ribbon bonus.

"They can't hear you," I point out.

She shrugs. "I don't care; it still feels good to say it."

I can think of no uplifting counterpoint worth offering.

Olivia digs into her chicken sticks, and I test the pad Thai for heat—probably an eight, well beyond my comfort zone. I decide to anesthetize my mouth with several swallows of wine.

"Hey, don't forget to save some for my ice cream," Olivia cries. She stares at the bottle. "We get to keep the plums, right? You paid for them."

"Do you want one? The wide mouth on the bottle lets you fish them out."

Olivia wrinkles her nose. "I'm not sure. They kind of look like things in our biology lab specimen jars." She stares a moment longer, then breaks into a wide grin. "I'm a genius. I'll be an alien for Halloween, and these plums can be my eggs. Now I just need to find antennas on Amazon."

"I went as George Washington in high school; I was magnificent."

"Ugh," Olivia says, then nosedives into her phone. When dessert arrives, she tells me to save the plum wine bottle—she needs to preserve her offspring. "Since I'm never getting married, I'm never having real babies." She returns to her phone, confident she has explained everything.

We walk home through the tail end of windy twilight, the rain still holding off. Olivia's extraterrestrial offspring sleep safely in my jacket pocket. As she fiddles with her phone, I notice a store window displaying a telescope on a tripod. I remember looking through my father's as a boy, mostly at the moon, its magnified light focusing enough warmth to make my eye water. Back in the here and now, the moon is still too low to be visible, but a few twinkles dot the darkening sky. I recognize Mars and the ascendant stars of Sagittarius and pause to point them out to Olivia. She looks up mechanically, nods, then returns to her phone.

"I'm surprised the stars don't interest you, you being from outer space."

She shrugs. "There's an app on my phone that shows me where all the stars are if I need to know, which I doubt."

I stand there, remembering how I had talked about stars the first night I met Olivia's grandmother and how my father, on my boyhood hunting excursions, had lectured me on stars and seasons, adamant that I understand celestial reality as something far beyond twinkly decoration. His words had sunk in, even if I proved to be an atrocious hunter. "It's not just about where stars are," I say, trying against all odds to penetrate Olivia's dismissive crust, "it's *what* they are. Sure, the ancient Greeks—shepherds in the field with time on their hands, I'm thinking—connected star patterns to gods and animals, but they also figured out that stars might be chunks of burning metal or rocks, some further away than others. Very advanced thinking for their time. They didn't *know*, you see, so they were very curious, stretched their minds to understand. We, meaning scientists mostly, know what stars are right down to their subatomic gremlins. *We*, meaning the rest of us, no longer look at stars with fascination. The lack of mystery has taken the shine off, so to speak. Which is a shame. An appreciation of the stars might temper our pettiness."

Olivia looks up and sets me straight. "There's a lot more going on these days, a lot more stuff to look at than stars, which you can barely see anyway."

"A fair point, and one that raises an interesting philosophical question. Would you rather live in a cluttered house with mediocre "stuff" piled everywhere or a neat house with just a few exquisite things?"

Olivia pauses to eye me suspiciously. "We're still going shopping tomorrow, right?"

The front of my house includes a hand-built stone wall with a wrought iron gate. Inside the entrance, two smaller screened anterooms flank an open porch. I surmise those bookend retreats kept a happily married couple happy. When I open the gate, Olivia hurries inside to refrigerate her precious plums. I situate myself on one of the little screened retreats—the one where I stash my pot—and plan to do nothing for a while. I find age has intensified my interest in doing nothing, as if such sessions were shakedown cruises for the Eternal Nothing I've bought into as a nonbeliever. This particular session involves waiting for rain and watching car headlights shift shadows as they cruise down Cholokka.

Not really nothing, of course, this watching and waiting and remembering similar shape-shifting blocks of car light racing around my bedroom walls when I was a boy. I suddenly find myself inexpertly rolling a joint as I question how truly different I am from that boy.

Not very, I conclude. Still sad and uncertain, still unarmed in love, still grinding away at implications long after others have moved on, still the island no man is supposed to be. I drag on the joint, which pops and flares in protest, then hold my breath, giving the smoke enough time to deliver its parcels to my bloodstream.

As I wait for the world's strangeness to come out of hiding, I click on my porch radio—a little transistor set the size of a cigarette pack—and listen to the soul-freeing backbeat of "Drift Away."

Perfect. I wanna get lost in something too; I'm just not sure what. I close my eyes and begin to whisper-sing high harmonies along with the addictive hook.

"I smell weed." Olivia's voice, but in my altered state it seems as disembodied as a conscience.

"Where are you?" I call into the void. "And how do you know what weed smells like?"

"The bathroom at school. I bet half the kids smoke weed."

"Which half are you in?" I wait for an answer, but none comes. "Are you still there?" I finally ask.

"Yeah, I'm here, sitting on the swing. I'm barefoot, that's why you couldn't hear me. Are you coming out?"

"In a minute."

"Is that why Grandma divorced you, because you smoked weed?"

"She would've been more likely to divorce me for *not* smoking weed, and besides, Grandma didn't divorce me; we divorced each other."

"Mom told me Grandma divorced you."

"Your mom is flat wrong. Facts not in evidence."

"What about your first wife. Why did she divorce you?"

"Maybe I divorced her."

"Yeah, right."

"You never know."

"I know you shouldn't smoke when I'm with you."

"Then I won't, no problem."

"How old were you when you started on weed?"

"Hang on; I'm coming out. I have a right to face my accuser." I walk out and join Olivia on the swing. She's changed into sweats and scrubbed away all traces of novice *femme fatale*. "I've never been 'on weed,' but to answer your very loaded question, I think I first smoked in late 1967 or maybe early 1968. I was a senior in high school."

"Busted," she gloats.

"No, not 'busted'; I voluntarily confessed—a very different proposition. And trust me, I've done much worse." This gratuitous embellishment stokes the fires.

"Then why didn't you go to prison like Uncle Carl?" In the porch light, Olivia's eyes gleam with eagerness to know how I escaped justice.

"Sorry to disappoint you, but the things I did in my wasted youth weren't prison material."

"*Things?* Wow."

"Figure of speech."

Olivia pulls her knees up to her chin to help her focus on the nature of my transgressions.

"Let's say you killed somebody accidentally, like in a knife fight. They'd let you off if you were just a kid, right? If it was something like that, they'd probably just kick you out of town, right? Grandma said they kicked you out of town for something bad."

"It doesn't sound like Grandma told you what I did."

"Not exactly; she said you disgraced yourself."

"Good old Grandma."

"Well?"

"Well, no knife fight, sorry. And I was leaving town anyway, heading to college. As for what I *actually* did, I'll tell you this much: my misdemeanors involved an affair of the heart, mysterious violence, and an unexplained disappearance. And that—as they say —is *not* bullshit. As for why I did what I did—let's just say that when you're young, such as *you* are now, by the way, you tend to be selfish, for one thing, and for another, you do things and think things you shouldn't because you're, well, a dumbass."

Olivia jumped to her feet. "You said *you*. Are you talking about *me?*"

"No, unless it applies."

Olivia shoots me a haughty glare. "I plan to stay mad at you until you tell me *exactly* what you did."

I say nothing, relieved she is limiting her interrogation to my teenage years. She stares fiercely, hoping I'll crack, then grunts in frustration.

"I come from a family of criminals," she announces, then waits for a denial that isn't forthcoming. "This is *way* boring," she complains. "I'm going in. I have two shows to watch before I can crash; I better get started. I need energy for shopping tomorrow. Bye."

I return to the side porch and the facile comforts of classic rock. My little radio pumps out "Smoke on the Water" as a cold gust sifts through the porch screen, brushing past me like an itinerant specter. I look out at the street, watching for the first spatter of raindrops, and see a skinny, shirtless man walking rapidly, leaning forward as against a stiff wind, all the while contending loudly with someone unseen, presumably through some device, though possibly I am witnessing a cognitive duel between his reptilian and mammalian brains. The man stops suddenly to shake his fist. He is so desperately *sure* of something. I hear him yell what sounds like "Gorbachev" and then "Moldavian vineyards" and "authoritarian destruction of grafts." With a final "fucking commissar," he lifts his arms in frustration and passes rapidly out of sight.

I suddenly realize he must be one of the "laughing Russians" as I call them, my new neighbors who improvise at all possible hours a kind of conversational Cyrillic jazz within a classic trio of bass, sax, and piano—two male voices, one deep, one reedy and raspy, accompanied by a languorous, alto female voice. Their jam sessions emanate from somewhere beyond a hedge of bougainvillea and consist of what I assume are anecdotes, reminiscences, observations, and quips, all met by laughter-ridden replies or frenetic disputations. While it would be no remarkable feat to identify the participants, I prefer their disembodied voices, particularly the female voice, which reminds me of a girl I visited secretly, late at night, back when Russians were as alien as Martians.

Just as the ranting man disappears, a woman strides into view, hands on hips, seeming to stare after him. She doesn't speak or yell but shakes her head in eloquent resignation, embodying the way I imagine many women feel about many men.

She must be the "piano" of my imagined Russian trio, I think. Before long, she turns and walks away, leaving me with no company but occasional passing cars. As a boy back in Hopperton, I often sat on the front porch after school, listening for my father's '59 blue Cadillac, whose deep, formidable, pulsing throb I could distinguish from all other sounds. My mother always acknowledged its call by turning on the porch light. Soon I would spot the Caddy's gargantuan tail fins, and my father's return from work would signal the rightness and dependability of life.

And here I am again, just like in Hopperton, Georgia, 1967, sitting on a small-town porch near US Highway 441. I feel the past drawing me back and down into myself, like gravity drawing groundwater into the great Alachua sink.

I remember now. It *was* 1967 when I first smoked pot. Christmas Eve. With Wanda Grice. In her bedroom. Joy to the world and the last days of high school looming and starting to lengthen. Had I known what those days held, I would have walked back to September and started over.

CHAPTER FOUR

"Love Me Do"

Hopperton, Georgia, 1967

I won Hopperton Elementary's sixth-grade spelling bee, even though my best friend, Don Heffelfinger, was a far better speller. He spelled "maize" as "maze," despite being given its meaning as Indian corn. Unfair, he later insisted—he had given a correct spelling of the sound he heard. It was supposed to be a spelling bee, not a "definition bee." For a couple of weeks after that he barely spoke to me, as if I had rigged the competition. Unfair on his part, no doubt, if ingeniously so, but the point lies elsewhere. Once Don's indignation ran its course, he acquired a copy of *Franny and Zooey* and presented it to me at school. He knew I was a precocious reader and persuaded his father to buy the book on a business trip to Atlanta. Perhaps I wasn't ready yet for Salinger's irony, but the gesture touched me.

"This book is not an apology, Shaffer," he had insisted, "it's a peace offering." Don went on to explain that his father had taught him about "honor among men." I didn't care about honor; I was only looking forward to reading *Franny and Zooey*. But it did graze my consciousness that Don waded in deeper waters than I, an insight that to my childish mind made him both insufferable and invaluable.

By 1967, our senior year in high school, my friendship with Don resembled a blood-brotherhood, its vague vows unspoken, and certainly not based on like-mindedness, but still unbreakable. Elsewhere, the tantalizing Summer of Love had avoided pine-shrouded, God-fearing Hopperton by a dusty, rural Georgia country mile. Local boys would look in vain for a braless girl like those pictured in *Life* magazine.

Along the same lines, Hopperton's citizens, including its potential fodder, supported the Vietnam War, not that anyone used "fodder" to describe the local enlistees proudly pictured in the *Hopperton Herald*. Not war, but forced integration—"race mixing"—presented the not-so-distant doom threatening the hobbits of our particular shire, and one against which our town fathers, all businessmen, fought tooth and nail until Atlanta politicians threatened financial penalties.

If anyone in Hopperton other than myself opposed the war in Vietnam or supported integration, they matched me in secrecy. One thing I do know—that person *wasn't* my brilliantly misguided friend, Don Heffelfinger.

"Personally, I don't agree with the draft," Don announced at our lunch table on the first day of school. "We should be fighting communism because we *want* to, not because the government makes us do it. I mean, we say this is a free country, but how free is it if you have to do what the government dictates? Now me, I'm going to volunteer because I hate communism, but that's my choice, right?"

Tentative nods from other boys as Don paused to push his glasses tight against his shiny, avid face.

"It's like taxes. Everything should be an even trade. See, I tell the government what I want back for my tax money. We negotiate fair and square. If I'm selling you a car, I can't make you pay twice what you think it's worth, right? All I want the government to do is protect me against criminals, communists, and cheaters, so that's all I should have to pay for, right?"

Don holds up three pale, pudgy fingers and shows them around.

"If the government promises to do those three simple things and lives up to its promise, why, I'll wait in line to pay my fair share. But if the government sends troops against its own people to force the races to mix, should I have to pay for that?"

Heads shook. I held mine still.

"And look what happened when Lincoln tried to force us back into the Union. A lot of dead soldiers—and for what? It's a hundred years later, and how has the Negro progressed? Are we one big happy family?" Don let this last question hang melodramatically in the air.

I ventured a question. Invariably, I was the only one who did. "Weren't the Negroes forced to be slaves in the first place? Isn't that where the problem started?"

Don grinned triumphantly, as if he had trapped one of my pieces on a chessboard. "Bill asks a good, no, a *very* good question. The answer is that no man can be *forced* into slavery. Every man, including Negroes, has free will and reason. You can't enslave a man's mind unless he lets you. It was up to the Negro to free himself, don't you see? The North didn't free the Negroes; they only kept them from freeing themselves." Some heads turned to look at me, the hopeless underdog.

"What would have happened to any slave who told his master he refused to be a slave?" I inquired with what I hoped was devastating sarcasm. Don grinned again.

"What would have *happened* to that slave is that he would have been free, see?"

"What I *see* is that you can't be free if you're dead."

"No, Bill, you can't be free unless you're willing to risk your life for freedom. When I go to Vietnam, I will be risking my life for freedom."

"You're already free as a bird, Don, in case you hadn't noticed. You're not a Negro." A lone, uncertain titter from a listener. I tried to give my voice a scathing edge; Don countered with a saddened tone.

"I hope you're not defending what's going on in this country, Bill. I mean, it wouldn't make you a traitor—you're free to think what you want, but Christ, I hope you're on our side and not theirs."

I knew I would never outwit Don playing this particular game. Much later in life, I would teach at a small college and identify the remark I was about to make as a fallacy called *argumentum ad hominem*.

"You better start exercising, Don. I don't think the Vietcong is too scared right now."

Don blanched but recovered quickly, ignoring the smattering of laughs I had extracted. "Don't worry, Shaffer; I'll be ready to fight while you're hiding in a basement, praying I keep the red hordes out." Laughing and a few claps.

"Maybe I'll enlist just to watch you flunk basic training," I shot back.

"I'm not afraid to try, like a certain peacenik I know."

27

More laughs. Everyone knew Don and I traded barbs just to show off, without real venom. Or thought they knew.

Just then, I saw Sally Chiles hurry toward our table. Sally was the tallest girl in school, president of everything, and the conduit through which every bit of gossip flowed. She and I had been friends since we could barely speak, but only Sally had risen to Hopperton's social stratosphere.

"Did you hear?" she stage-whispered, "we're getting kids from over near Waycross."

"White or colored?"

This question came from Tommy Eddleston, who had wandered into earshot at Sally's approach. Tommy was our quarterback and our one faint hope for a decent season. I think most of us were expecting to hear "colored" from Sally since Georgia seemed to be fighting a losing if stubborn battle against federal school integration. Hopperton, so far, had managed to stay effectively segregated (we had *two* black students at Hopperton High) by relying on "neighborhood school" justifications and the attention we had *not* attracted as a small, insignificant rural town.

"White," Sally declared, as a crowd began to gather. "They're coming over to make sure there's no room for the coloreds. We don't have to take coloreds if we're already full up. That's the law. We're not supposed to let in kids from another county, but my mom says once they enroll, the state won't do a thing."

"We need football players, good ones," Tommy called.

"Cheerleaders. I vote for cheerleaders!" emanated from the small crowd gathering magnetically around Sally and Tommy.

"Shut up, pissant," Tommy growled.

Sally shook her head like a schoolmarm. "My lord, you boys are hopeless children." Cheerleading was a sore spot with Sally, who claimed a doctor in Macon had forbidden her to try out due to a mysterious spine ailment.

Sally's announcement trampled any interest in theories of slavery or Don's fitness to fight little men in black pajamas. And by tomorrow everyone would return to their cliques, depriving Don, probably for the entire school year, of the communal soapbox he craved. I felt bad for him, and turned to apologize for resorting to mockery, but he had left the lunchroom. When I saw him in history class later, he shrugged off the affront;

his attention now fixed on the rumored influx of "refugees" from Waycross.

"Well, Shaffer, here we are in history class, blindly ignoring the fact that *history* is happening to *us*. Big Brother is shifting us around like pawns. Another mad experiment on the huddled masses, the poor Southern stepchildren. We should be standing up on our hind legs and snarling rather than lying down and falling asleep, don't you think?"

"I think everyone should stand up, especially the Negroes. As far as I can tell, they're just freeing themselves like you suggested." To my shock, Don ignored this red flag waved in his face, intent instead on other students trickling in. When he spotted Clare Johnson, he grabbed my shoulder, turned me toward the windows, and spoke in a low, fierce voice.

"Listen, Shaffer, I offered to escort Clare to the dance, and she turned me down. What is it with these girls? I'll bet no one else asks her. Does she think I'm going to put the make on her or something? It's just a dance, not a love-in, for Chrissakes. And she *knows* I took Arthur Murray lessons over the summer." Don looked down at his shoes, black and shiny, as if they would testify on his behalf.

"Clare goes to my church, Don. She always wears gloves and a hat. She really prays when it's time to pray. I'm not sure her mother would—"

"Love, love, love. Damn the Beatles, Shaffer. It's all hogwash. These girls go crazy for the songs, but they don't want love. They don't understand love is *passion*. Not just sex, but placing real *value* on someone. Show a little passion, and they run off like scared chickens."

Don had leaned close, whispering as if in a confessional. I had no idea what the word *value* had to do with Clare Johnson.

"Clare's okay," I said. "She's the shy type, that's all. I don't think she's putting you down."

The truth was, girls disliked Don. He seemed to *demand* something from them. Don was smarter than I was, but at least girls talked to me; at least I knew enough to treat girls like they wanted to be treated, to let them talk about themselves. Sally and I would not kiss or even dance together, but that was beside the point. I would be there among girls, dancing and listening. In time, my strategy would pay off. Soon, I convinced myself, Don would be a virgin, and I would not. Then I would have an empirical sledgehammer with which to pulverize into irrelevancy (only if provoked, mind you) his precious theories.

"Take your seats, please."

Mr. Pee (Mr. Peebles, though students rarely used his full name) perched on his desk, crossed his short, fat legs, and sat balanced precariously on a single buttock. We boys relished the bathroom implications of "Pee" but did so with great fondness. Mr. Peebles was kind and gave us better grades than we could hope to deserve.

Clamping down on his angst over Clare Johnson, Don hurried to his front-row seat. Mr. Pee ranked second only to his father in Don's estimation. He called Don "Mr. Heffelfinger" in recognition of his showy schoolboy erudition.

"An item or two of interest," announced Mr. Pee, rocking gently atop his desk. "First, you may expect new classmates later this week, or so I'm told. If you have been talking to Miss Sally, then you probably know more than I do." The class tittered, and Sally preened in her seat.

"Also, Bill Shaffer is inaugurating a chess club each Friday afternoon in this classroom, which tempts me to a little linguistic diversion." Mr. Pee paused, maybe for dramatic effect, but since nobody knew what he was talking about, his silence only earned him a few blank stares. "Well," he continued undeterred, "surely you know that Donner and Blitzen are two of the nine reindeer. Does anyone know what their names mean?" Don itched to raise his hand, but he wasn't about to guess and lose face. "No one? They are the German words for thunder and lightning. From there, we deduce that blitzkrieg is German for "lightning war," which in turn tells us that Krieg means "war." Thus, when we hear that chess in German is "Kriegspiel," we can infer that the proper English translation is "war game," "Spiel" being therefore the German word for "game." Interesting chain of relations, don't you think? Especially given our present state of conflict in Indochina. Chess differs, of course, in that it offers a battle between two *equal* armies. If you lose, blame yourself. If you win, pat yourself on the back. Luck plays no part. Mr. Heffelfinger gave an excellent report last year explaining General Lee's daring maneuvers at Chancellorsville, splitting his army again and, yet again, driving Hooker back across the Rappahannock. You will find chess to be full of such stratagems. Perhaps there is a General Lee of chess among us."

Don raised an agitated hand. "Sir, how can chess be like war if there is no luck? Stonewall Jackson died from wounds inflicted accidentally by his own men. Without this terrible misfortune, surely the Confederacy would have prevailed. If Jackson had lived, the war would have lasted long enough for Lincoln to be executed by Booth. Then there would have been a treaty between two equal nations."

When Mr. Pee nodded, Don broke into a vindicated smile.

"And isn't it a pity, Mr. Heffelfinger, that we only live out a single strand of all possible histories? Perhaps I will assign a paper in which you propose an alternative outcome to the historical event of your choice." A mutinous groan rose against this terrible idea. "In any case," continued an unfazed Mr. Pee, "our young scholar has unwittingly made my point better than I did." He pushed himself nimbly off the desk and walked to the windows.

"Which is what, sir?" Traces of doubt and defiance colored Don's voice.

"Which is . . ." Mr. Pee paused and stared out windows where, as far as I knew, nothing of interest existed. He turned to the class. "Which is that chance is no man's friend—or enemy. Oh, it may *appear* otherwise at times, just like a stick thrust into the water appears to bend, but if you consider that *every event* could have turned out differently, is it fair to change only one thing, one general's regrettable death, to judge your luck?"

"How do you know every event could have turned out differently?" I called out without raising my hand, a significant breach of class decorum. Heads turned expectantly, but Mr. Pee let it pass.

"I don't *know* it, Bill, I only propose it as a possibility. Let's find a different possibility in your question. What if nothing can be changed? Are you then simply acting out a part written for you?"

"God has a plan for everyone." Had Clare Johnson ever spoken out in class before without being called on?

"Clare is no doubt right," Mr. Pee observed, "but are we required to follow the plan or free to refuse it?"

Don waved his hand wildly. "Sir, we are free to refuse anything opposed by our reason. If we follow any plan, it must be our choice. Otherwise, we are sheep."

"But are we not taught," Mr. Pee replied softly, "to obey God's laws precisely because reason is flawed and God is not?"

"Untrue, sir. Reason is not flawed. God's laws are words on a page until they are interpreted and understood by reason. Reason was—is— our greatest gift. *In the beginning was the Word.* Logos. Knowledge. And there can be no knowledge without reason. Don't you see?"

Mr. Pee smiled with serene good humor at this borderline heresy. "I do see, Mr. Heffelfinger, but I have also read the works of a brilliant thinker named Immanuel Kant, who points to many flaws in pure reason. I also see that God commands there to be no other God before Him, including reason. Qualities other than reason are needed to make a whole man—God's grace, for example. Don't *you* agree?"

I believe Don was close to tears. He was at least red-eyed and wincing, nervously pushing a lank black lock of hair back from his forehead. In retrospect, I would call his state of mind ecstatic frustration. He was in the arena with Mr. Peebles! But he was being outdueled, made to seem strident, defensive, as well as coming in a poor second to God. And, I will add, Mr. Pee had not raised his voice. Or insisted on any point of view. He had just chatted about chess, luck, and Chancellorsville and posed a few sensible questions.

It occurs to me now that I was attending my first philosophy class. There we were, even the devout Clare Johnson, discussing chance, determinism, divine intelligence. And there was Mr. Pee, postulating alternative hypotheses, giving us a glimpse of the small-town Socrates living inside him, giving us a taste of graceful thought.

Mr. Pee suddenly clapped his hands as if rousing a subject from hypnosis. I had seen him register Don's distress. "Ladies and gentlemen, back to reality and your reading assignment. Can anyone—besides the erudite Mr. Heffelfinger—tell me something interesting about Vladimir Lenin other than that he was a communist?"

CHAPTER FIVE

"Wayward Son"

A fter school, Don and I walked the mile to my house in a light, steady drizzle, hugging the sheltering maples. My mother no doubt awaited us on our porch with ham and tomato sandwiches and a pitcher of fresh-squeezed lemonade. The "veranda," as my mother insisted calling our wraparound porch, featured a filigreed balustrade somewhat at stylistic odds with our contemporary brick split-level house, but it suited her. From the veranda, whether hosting her many visitors or shucking peas, she could survey the comings and goings on Stagecoach Road, the name given to the short, brick-paved stretch of US Highway 441 which neatly divided Hopperton, and which happened to be our street of residence.

More generally, Highway 441 wends south from Rocky Top, Tennessee, on its way to sin-plagued Miami, carrying an inexhaustible stream of snowbirds, spring-breakers, theme park pilgrims, and sunseekers back and forth.

By 1967, however, most of that stream diverted around us via the Hopperton Circle, which allowed long-haul travelers to bypass the town, much as 441 itself bypassed the devilish muck of nearby Okefenokee Swamp. Only an occasional car or truck splashed past Don and me as we squabbled our way homeward, a routine essentially unchanged for a dozen years, give or take.

A few thousand people lived in and about Hopperton, whose layout resembled one of the pine trees that enveloped it. The trunk was

Stagecoach Road; the rest of the town branched off modestly to the east and west. For the most part, we had one business of each type—thus, *the* hardware store, *the* barbershop, *the* funeral home— though gas stations and ladies' apparel shops flourished in unaccountable abundance.

Don's house was beyond mine to the north, then a few blocks east along Woodbine to Lydia. As a rule, he lingered at my house as long as he could, not to avoid his home life, but to gorge on my mother's fare and bask in her affectionate regard. "You boys are treasures," she often remarked. "How lucky I am."

And I suppose she was, though I didn't consider myself the most compelling evidence. She had married well and presided over the Hopperton garden club, bridge club, book club, and the Timberland Methodist Church's Desdemona French women's circle. One fine day, my father often said, there would be a Maggie Shaffer circle of the TMC. Perhaps only winning the Pillsbury Bake-Off for her caramel apple pecan pie (and meeting TV host Bob Barker) could have given my mother more pleasure than my father's ecclesiastical praise. In any case, I believe Don *did* consider my mother lucky to have him. So, when he spotted her, he hustled ahead to grab a sandwich from the plate she held out, then sank, dripping rainwater, on the swing without a word of thanks. Had I been so rude, I would have felt my mother's reprimand, but Don, as her wayward son by proxy, merited tender indulgence. His birth mother had died or abandoned him or had been driven away or disposed of by Don's notoriously unpleasant father, depending on which story you heard at a church supper or family picnic. Don would not discuss his mother with me. "I swore to my dad," was all he would say.

By the time I reached the veranda, Don had already begun lecturing my mother on the "true meaning" of students migrating from Waycross. "They're bringing in white kids to crowd out the coloreds. It's a war played like a chess game. The Union overreaches. Lee bides his time at Appomattox. They make a move; then we make a move. Don't be surprised if you see federal troops in Hopperton. Then everyone will see their true colors."

I broke in.

"Mother, don't mind Don. He hasn't heard the Civil War is over. We're just getting some new kids from over near Waycross, that's all."

"*Just?* It's white kids from across the county line. It's a bold provocation. It means we're fighting them. And it makes them look bad to send soldiers against citizens. The country won't stand for that. There's no Lincoln this time."

My mother nodded as she folded pillowcases. Don might as well have been speaking Hungarian.

"Don, honey, when you're good and ready, why don't you ride Bill's bike home, just in case the skies open up again? I'll wrap up peach pie for you and your father."

Don managed an affirmative grunt. I watched him stare out at the trees and road which the warm, subsiding rain had cloaked in mist.

"Shaffer, can you come over to my house on Saturday? I have something to show you." Friday was the Kickoff Dance. Maybe Don wanted to know if Clare Johnson had come with a date. I looked at my mother.

"You go ahead, Bill. It's whitetail season; your father will be at his camp." My father hunted with a bow. He took me along a couple of times, but I showed little aptitude and less interest. If he was disappointed at first, I believe relief got the upper hand. He could go off and be himself, forget his duties as a father, husband, and—as he put it—the "beleaguered" manager of a turpentine plant.

"What do you want to show me, Don?" Maybe another Confederate uniform button. He prized a Sharps Cavalry bullet dug up, he swore, from the Shiloh battlefield.

"It's not anything like you'd expect" was all I could worm out of him. I didn't much care anyway. Going to Don's was preferable to whatever "hand me the hammer" chore my father and I would otherwise undertake.

The itch from my damp clothes claimed my attention as Don annoyed me further by attacking another sandwich. Even when I held up my end of an argument against him, Don made me feel like my mind was a cluttered junkpile, anything of value spotted by accident. Maybe college would clear away the clutter. I was headed for the University of Georgia next fall, my early acceptance already in hand. Don would join me, I supposed, once he quit bluffing about Vietnam.

When the rain stopped, he sailed off on my rusty old Schwinn, its basket stuffed with peach pie, ham, roast beef, and cornbread, all wrapped in an old tablecloth. He pedaled furiously—Miss Gulch in Dorothy's cyclonic dream—never looking back. My mother waved after him anyway.

"Bless his heart." She sighed. "I hope the storm relents; he could use a bit of mercy."

As Mr. Pee had assured the class earlier, luck is no man's friend or enemy, but who in their young heart believes that? As I watched Don turn right off Stagecoach, hunched over my Schwinn as if laboring up a steep hill, I counted myself lucky to be myself and not him. I turned to my mother to tell her this, intending to convey gratitude for her part in my superior fortune.

"Don's not going to the dance," I said instead.

"Why on earth?" my mother wondered as she fussed with recalcitrant bedsheets.

"I get along good with girls, but he doesn't. He just annoys them with his crazy ideas."

My mother looked up and regarded me with a flat stare, the perennial softness missing from her eyes. "It sounds to me, Bill, like you're climbing on Don's back to pick sweet apples for yourself." It took me a moment to translate my mother's country adage. Once I understood it, I burned with shame. She had seen me as I was. I had come to count on my mother's tenderhearted myopia to obscure my secret, heretical self, and here she was, seemingly keen-eyed as a red-tailed hawk. I bowed my head for effect.

"I didn't mean it that way, Mother; I don't think I'm better than Don." My mother smiled. Here was the son she knew, placed before her by the one she didn't. She bent down and took in the scent of fresh laundry as if inhaling goodness itself, then picked up the basket and started for the door. She turned before leaving.

"Some young lady will find Don exactly to her liking, as I'm quite sure some young lady has *already* found you." I made no protest, just a shake of my head. My mother chuckled softly and went inside, leaving me to stare at an inner vanishing point, glad to be free of human voices, not least of all my own. I reached my hand out beyond the eaves, feeling for the fine mist. It seemed to hover in the air like phantom smoke. I jumped down the steps and slid my bare feet across lush, wet grass as I had often done as a young boy. Then I stood and listened. Complicated birdsong rose up among the dripping oak leaves. Maybe a brown thrasher. Out on the road, the sweet groan of an old Chevy skillfully downshifted. I looked up to see a girl in a pink top waving to me from the back seat. A friend of Sally's. The dance tonight; I had better polish my shoes. I waved back and then practiced a couple of furtive waltz steps in the grass—steps Don had passed along from his Arthur Murray lessons. Maybe they would come in handy. Maybe Waycross girls liked to slow dance.

Saturday morning, my father left for his hunting camp long before sunrise. With me headed to Don's, my mother was free to enjoy her afternoon bridge social. When I walked into the kitchen, I found her humming a church hymn and filling the waffle iron with batter. A skillet of bacon sizzled on the stove and a glass of fresh-squeezed orange juice already sat waiting for me. She had made me a Sunday breakfast on Saturday, clear proof of her pleasure.

"Goodness," she exclaimed. "Look at you. Did you sleep in your clothes after the dance? Why aren't you in your Saturday dungarees?" I had indeed dressed strangely for a Saturday: creased cotton slacks; plaid, short-sleeve shirt neatly tucked in; polished penny loafers.

"Oh, you know how Don's dad is."

"He means no harm, dear. Try not to forget that he was a prisoner of war. I'm quite sure Mr. Heffelfinger is fond of you. He knows what a good friend you've been to Don."

I loved my mother, maybe more consciously, if not better, than most other boys. But Mary Magdalene was quite sure of many things I was not. I believed Mr. Heffelfinger was fond of almost nothing, and certainly not me. Despite hundreds of encounters, he still greeted me with a humorless smile, looking me up and down as if he were a drill sergeant conducting a close-arms inspection. I had the nagging suspicion that Mr. Heffelfinger could see into my soul and knew that he and I were deadly ideological adversaries. Nevertheless, I nodded acceptance of Mother's charitable take on Mr. Heffelfinger, seeing no point in disputing her well-meant counsel. She smiled.

"I'm proud to have raised such a nice young man. Now eat your breakfast and be on your way. Take that bag over there. I made peanut butter and jelly sandwiches for you boys. Call if you won't be home by good and dark."

I promised to call and, after stuffing myself with pecan waffles drowned in brown sugar syrup, headed out. From my house, situated on the left side of Stagecoach as you look north (known locally as "lakeside"), I crossed to "swampside," so-called because the Okefenokee Swamp officially began only a few miles due east through a marshy, overgrown stretch called the "slashes." Swampside was not the wrong side of the tracks exactly, but the term "lake people" was a social compliment. I was aware of such things but didn't care much. I liked the stretch leading to Don's house. Its modest wood-frame dwellings, while of lesser standing than my own sturdy brick home, were closer to the road, and I looked forward to hearing my name called out by older ladies rocking on their porches, ladies who would ask after my mother and offer a slice of pie. And while now and then a dog accosted me, I was old news—too familiar to bother biting.

The day exuded a serene quiet. I daydreamed about the new girls from Waycross at last night's dance. Sally and I fulfilled social technicalities by dancing the first dance—a lot of hopping around to "I'm A Believer"—but then we went our separate ways, occasionally reconnecting through smiles and eye contact. I danced with local girls devoid of romantic potential but could not summon the nerve to approach exotic newcomers. I spotted Clare Johnson among the unescorted "church girls" and started to ask for a dance, but she turned her head. I probably reminded her of Don. After that, I sat in the gym bleachers, snickering and whispering with a couple of other boys about *The Electric Kool-Aid Acid Test*. We had one dog-eared copy, which we passed back and forth like a skin magazine. None of us had ever seen a hippie or a Hell's Angel, much less dropped acid or joined in a free love fest. The book, along with lyrics we chanted from Jefferson Airplane's "White Rabbit" about body-altering hallucinogenic pills, was our barest nibble at psychedelic fruit.

After the dance, I walked Sally home. She was giddy with gossip. One of the girls from Waycross, she confided, had a baby already and gave it up for adoption. Sally had not interrogated the poor girl herself, but all the other girls from Waycross had confirmed the story. Kissing Sally was out of the question, but in her excitement, she gripped my arm at her door.

"Thanks for a super evening, Bill," she gushed.

I suspected she was thanking the pregnant girl, but I kept that to myself.

These reveries faded when Widow Mason's old brindle hound trotted out to sniff me, whining with pleasure. I scratched her head the way she liked. When she'd had her fill, she returned to her yard, rolled over onto her back, and wriggled furiously against the grass in celebration. This friendly ritual meant I was nearing Don's house, and while I would likely be pestered about the dance and have to extend fake politeness to Mr. Heffelfinger, at least I was free for a day, and Don had something to show me that just possibly might be cool.

Don and his father inhabited a drab concrete block bungalow doubling as a business office. A small sign reading "Farm Insur." pointed to a side entrance. The slope behind the house had been cleared and fenced; beyond the fence lay untouched woods. Nowadays, towns never seem to end, only thin out until the next one gradually thickens up again. In 1967, if you left the immediate environs of Hopperton, human artifacts were scarce, at least in the direction of the swamp. Nothing much out there but moonshine shacks and stills and the ghosts of primitive Baptist parishioners hanging around the charred remnants of an old church rumored to have burned down due to some unspoken sin.

I knocked without effect at Don's front door, then reluctantly walked around to the office entrance. Mr. Heffelfinger opened the door partway and examined me with a thin smile. "Well, well, if it isn't the lakeside boy come to visit the common folk." Mr. Heffelfinger then swung the door open, gesturing me in with a slight bow.

"Thank you, sir," I replied, meeting one falseness with another. I skirted uneasily around Mr. Heffelfinger and caught sight of Don at the far end of the office, holding up a crossbow.

"Look what my dad got me," he cried. "Isn't it fearsome-looking?" My father hunted with a compound bow, but some of his friends preferred crossbows, so I was familiar with them to the extent that I had cocked them and shot them at targets a few times. My poor results may help explain my father's willingness to forgo my rites of passage as a woodsman. As Don hoisted his prize, I could hear Mr. Heffelfinger's hoarse breathing behind me and the sound of a cigarette lighter being flipped open. He prodded my shoulder pretty hard.

"You know about them things?"

"Yes, sir, a little." I had long ago realized short answers were best with Mr. Heffelfinger.

"All right then, you boys go out and practice."

Don walked over to his father and spoke in a low voice, something about a book. While they were talking, I glanced at the Confederate flag hung behind Mr. Heffelfinger's desk and the pictures of Lee and Jackson flanking it.

"I hear Donald's teacher has no love for Stonewall Jackson." Mr. Heffelfinger's scornful tone suggested I tread carefully. I tried to recall Don and Mr. Pee's give-and-take about the Battle of Chancellorsville.

"Mr. Peebles just said if Jackson had lived, that was no guarantee the South would win."

Don broke in hotly.

"No, Dad, he said it was all a matter of chance, that it didn't matter if you had *right* on your side. He might as well have said that Jackson didn't matter, that the Southern cause didn't matter." Don and his father turned and stared at me as if I had killed Jackson myself.

"I honestly don't remember the conversation all that well," I mumbled. "Don may be right."

"I am right, absolutely," Don spoke with melodramatic vehemence. All the while, I watched Mr. Heffelfinger's face, a little out of self-preservation, but mostly noticing that it didn't look, to use Don's word, *right*. He was as naturally lean and leathery as Don was pudgy, but some of his ruddiness looked blanched away, and his skin drew tight to the bone. Of course, he knew that I was looking at him. He took a long, slow drag on his cigarette and stubbed the butt out in a brass ashtray which, he had once proudly told me, had once been the base of an unexploded Jap artillery shell.

"Look now, boy, when Gen'l Lee fought the Battle of the Wilderness, he *killed* more Yankees than was in his own entire army. Imagine if Stonewall Jackson had been there to help him for just a little bit longer . . ." Mr. Heffelfinger stared me down, daring me to draw a contrary conclusion. For all I knew, he was right. But even if he was, the fact remained that the South had lost the war, and I was glad. I silently projected that thought back at him as hard as I could.

"People don't know," he said suddenly. "Donald thinks he wants to go fight overseas. That's pure foolishness, but I can't tell him. It's his right to go kill hisself. Maybe you can tell him different, rich boy. I sure as hell know what you think. I can read your mind."

I went cold for a moment, more than half believing him.

"Come on now, Dad," Don said in a choked voice. "Bill's all right." Mr. Heffelfinger sank into his office chair.

"Sorry, boys, I've had a nip." He gave the desk a sharp, loud smack. "I keep a pint of Old Crow right here in my desk drawer. I guess my secret's out now." Something false rang in Mr. Heffelfinger's confession. Remorse that didn't fit. More likely, he *could* read my mind than he was drunk.

"Dad, we're going to my room for a second, then outside to practice the crossbow, okay?"

Mr. Heffelfinger nodded, then looked at me with a stiff smile.

"I'm a poor example today, Bill Shaffer. I don't suppose Ed Shaffer drinks at all, now does he?" An unpleasant implication about my father lurked in Mr. Heffelfinger's words, but I couldn't quite name it. I wanted to answer *none of your business* but ended up saying my mother mixed my father an occasional cocktail after work, and sometimes he drank beer on a hot day.

"A fortunate man, your father, to occupy such a strategic position in the community, and especially to be married to such a charitable woman, a true Lady of the South. Please remember to thank her on my behalf for the food she sends . . . to those in need."

"Yes, sir," I said, not knowing what to make of the forced smile Mr. Heffelfinger now wore. Were the Heffelfinger's "in need"? I had never thought of them that way. Don grabbed my arm and pulled me toward the door.

"Donald, don't kill yourself with that goddamned crossbow," called Mr. Heffelfinger as we left.

Don had a gift for me. A book. *Atlas Shrugged.* It was not new; it was a library book belonging to the Atlanta Public Library. Don claimed he'd waited at the library during one of his father's business trips, had looked at the check-out card and noticed hardly anyone had been reading it. Deciding that it was going to waste in that library, he had "rescued" it.

"Your dad didn't mind?"

"I guess he didn't notice." I doubted anything escaped Mr. Heffelfinger's notice. Don aimed the crossbow out his bedroom window at an imaginary target.

"Listen, Shaffer; we're at war. I know you don't see it, but this book explains it all: what the war's about, how we fight it. Everything that's going on in the world will make perfect sense to you after you read it. You won't be making fun of me about going to Vietnam; I promise you that."

In one sense, *Atlas Shrugged* was well-known to me. While I had never read it, I pretended otherwise to join pretentious schoolboy conversations.

I knew enough to say, "Who is John Galt?"—the book's enigmatic, recurring question—though I had no idea who John Galt was.

"I'll try it," I conceded, "but I like novels better."

"My God, Shaffer, it *is* a novel, for Chrissakes, the best one ever. And it's a vast *parable* to boot, just exactly like things are. That makes it even better than a novel."

"Okay, geez, I'll read it." I darned well knew Don hadn't dreamed up the phrase "vast parable," but since I couldn't precisely define parable myself, despite all those Bible classes, I kept my peace other than to ask Don if the book guided his father.

Don shook his head. "My dad doesn't need a guide; he already *knows* everything that's in the book."

I wasn't about to challenge Don on that. Instead, I asked why Mr. Heffelfinger seemed mad at me.

"Fear not, Shaffer, he's mad at *me*; he doesn't want me to fight for the government. I told him I was fighting for freedom, not the government, but he said I was a fool. You heard him. But then he got me this crossbow. I'm going to get good with it and prove to him that I can fight and not just talk. I think that's what he wants."

Just the opposite, I thought to myself. He wants you to see how terrible you are with a crossbow and come to your senses.

We took the crossbow and three short arrows, called bolts, and clambered over the back fence. I showed Don how to point the nose of the crossbow to the ground, step into the stirrup, brace the butt end of the stock against his belly and draw the bowstring smoothly upwards until it caught the triggering mechanism. Later, I learned that the draw on the bowstring was no more than eighty pounds, a relatively light draw that I handled without undue exertion. On the other hand, Don found all steps in the cocking process awkward and demanding; his body seemed to want to reject the crossbow as if it were a transplanted organ. Up among the pine tree branches, a crow cawed derisively.

"Shit," Don grunted, panting. "What the hell?" He could not draw the bowstring up far enough to latch.

"It just takes practice," I said. "You need to be able to draw the string up evenly with two fingers of each hand. Work on that, then I'll come back in a few days and we'll try shooting."

"Agreed, Shaffer, provided you agree to one shot. Can you cock it for me?" I cocked the crossbow, seated a bolt, and showed Don how to stand and use the sight. I had him stand no more than ten feet from the sacrificial loblolly. The bolt he fired posed the tree no danger, whizzing instead into the shadowy undergrowth beyond. We'd risked a lost bolt, but Don was in good humor nonetheless, having popped his cherry as a death-dealing warrior. I chose this time to tell him about the dance and seeing Clare. He waved the subject away, saying that *Atlas Shrugged* had shown him he needed a different kind of woman, the kind who did not run with a pack. I replied that the girls were hardly a pack, just some friends drinking punch, dancing, sharing company.

"They need to prop each other up," he said. *And who props you up*, I groused silently, *so you can shoot a lousy arrow we'll probably never find?* But I held my tongue and continued ferreting through the vines and needles. After a minute or two, I heard Don call out.

"Oh my God," he cried. "It stuck in a tree." The bolt had found its way deeper into the woods than I had thought possible, like a dropped coin found half a room away.

Impaling the wrong tree further elevated Don's sense of triumph. He beamed and muttered the word "omen" as we walked back. When I swung over the fence, I saw Mr. Heffelfinger at the window, exhaling cigarette smoke and nodding impassively at Don flourishing the crossbow.

Later, after eating my mother's sandwiches, Don and I pushed aside the dirty clothes that littered his bedroom floor and set up a chessboard in the cleared space. Chess, despite its strategic depths, was an easy game for bad players like Don and me. We pushed our pieces around and hurled insults, playing only to rub defeat into each other's faces. I think of us now as two harmless puppies snarling and biting, driven by nature to practice for fights ahead. On that day, I played even worse than usual, preoccupied with the sinister intimacy in Mr. Heffelfinger's voice and distracted by the trill of a pine warbler like the ones who took seed from my mother's feeder. *Go home*, it seemed to advise. I listened for Mr. Heffelfinger's footsteps or knock, the silence torture in its own right.

After a particularly suicidal game on my part, I made an excuse to go home early and help my mother shell pecans. Don grinned and hinted I was up to something else: at long last getting into Sally Chile's pants. "I wish," I replied, not particularly wishing it but glad to have my true motive misread.

"Quit wishing, Shaffer; it's time to *act*." Despite his nonexistent sexual history, Don had a point. My only erotic exploit was a slow dance with Emily Wheeler, during which my inner forearm might have grazed her breast.

"I have a girl in mind besides Sally," I said, having no one in mind since Emily had moved to Atlanta.

"And who, pray tell, would that be?"

"One of the Waycross girls I saw at the dance."

Again, not so. But, by the odd logic of magical thinking, I surmised that it could be true, or might later be true, and so was true enough.

"This *girl*, how about you point her out to me Monday at school, Shaffer? We'll introduce ourselves, ask her how she liked the dance, get to know her." Don smiled like a crocodile; clearly, he was trying to smoke me out.

"And let you scare her off with your crazy ideas? Not a chance."

"Okay, I get it. Maybe there's a girl, and maybe there isn't. But one thing I do know is that Sally likes you."

"We get along okay."

"No, moron; she has a big crush on you. See, you talk to girls and dance with girls, but I *study* them."

"You're nuts. Sally would never even let me touch her." *Was I right?*

Don shoved his king and queen into the center of the board, then stared at me, his eyes glistening with certainty. "Don't take this the wrong way, Shaffer, but sometimes I feel sorry for how dense you are. Yeah, maybe she's not ready for . . . you know. I thought maybe she was, but maybe not. But when she is ready, she wants it to be *you*. And she's pretty sure it *will* be you, the way you go around politely waiting for her to get in the mood."

"I'm not waiting for anything," I insisted archly. "I'm just trying to be nice."

"Oh, sad to say I believe you, dear boy. But have you let Sally in on that little fact? As far as she's concerned, when the time comes, she'll put the moves on you, and that will be that. Trust me, I've seen how she looks at you when you're not looking at her. She studies you like homework."

I didn't believe Don, but my vanity did. "Is Sally the only girl who 'studies' me?"

Don shrugged. "I heard a couple of girls say you were stuck up. I guess it's a compliment when girls talk about you."

"Which girls?"

"Give up, Shaffer, I'm never going to tell you. It's boring, anyway. But it does make me wonder. Would you rather have a girl who liked you but didn't like sex, or a girl who liked sex but didn't like you?"

"That's a dumb question. Why would a girl who didn't like you want to have sex with you?"

"Lots of reasons, Shaffer, but that's not the point. The point is that *you* would prefer the girl who liked sex. Don't bother denying it; it's simple self-interest. Sex is a necessity; being *liked* is a luxury. And besides, most people don't like each other when you get right down to it." Don concluded by tossing his queen into the air and letting it fall, clattering among my pieces. In the pocket of silence that followed, I thought I heard Mr. Heffelfinger's footsteps and stood up in nervous anticipation.

"Christ, Shaffer, why are you so jumpy?"

Instead of answering, I walked to the window and stared out at the sunbathed woods, seeking a transfusion of light and space. I felt like a stranger who had wandered into the wrong house. But despite my premonition, Mr. Heffelfinger failed to appear at the door.

"I need to get going, that's all," I said finally. And I did. I needed to distance myself from Don's brash opinions and his father's humorless, stricken smile. Despite the daylight remaining, Don did not object, other than to extract my promise to help him master the crossbow and to hand me *Atlas Shrugged*, wrapped in a paper bag. *Keep your precious stolen book,* I thought, but took it anyway. Then I left the house, walking away quickly, but not too quickly, like a prisoner escaping slowly enough to avoid notice. Mercifully, Widow Mason's hound trotted out to greet me again and break the malign spell I had cast on myself. By petting her, I recovered the pleasure of being alive and the illusions it permits. "Good girl," I crooned softly, then dawdled home, imagining Sally in love with me, along with other girls too.

CHAPTER SIX

"Purple Haze"

Back home, away from the harrowing Mr. Heffelfinger, my mother sat me at the kitchen table and fed me cold fried chicken and the creamy, butter-saturated mashed potatoes she called "Georgia ice cream." I related the crossbow story and wondered if she had heard anything about Mr. Heffelfinger.

"Why, Bill, what on earth do you think I might have heard?"

"I don't know. He just seemed different, like he might be sick or something."

My mother nodded and sighed as if I had confirmed a regrettable suspicion.

"Bill, dear, he has no wife, no church. Ladies Aid has visited his home, even offered to give it a good womanly cleaning, but he was not receptive. Mind you; we told him our offer was *not* charity, that he could contribute to the church, and that we only wished to provide a little spiritual and . . . maternal support. I believe he may well be suffering from common loneliness. And pride, may God open his eyes. But it's very kind of you, Bill, to be concerned about Mr. Heffelfinger."

My mother then rewarded my "kindness" with a tender squeeze of my arm. I accepted her gesture in guilty silence, knowing I had only inquired about Mr. Heffelfinger out of morbid curiosity and a nagging uncertainty—why had his praise of my father seemed like a bitter insult?

"He told me to thank you for your cooking, Mother, but I'm not sure he wants you to send any more food. We can just feed Don when he's here."

My mother gave a reluctant nod.

"That may be for the best," she conceded, "at least for now."

We watched *The Honeymooners* together. Ralph's get-rich-quick scheme backfired, but Alice saw through his fuming bluster to his good intentions and, as always, forgave him. "That woman is a saint," my mother murmured, as she did every week.

Later, while my mother watched *Lawrence Welk*, I listened to "Purple Haze" on an underground Atlanta station. Jimi's first album had come out over the summer—the vinyl equivalent of a supernova—but it had yet to be detected by Hopperton's only record store. My sole recourse was to listen at low volume on my Philco, which meant I could still hear the Lennon Sisters' genteel harmonies mingle with Jimi's distorted electric cascades. Out of this jarring dissonance I conjured Mr. Heffelfinger crouched outside my window, gathering evidence to confirm what he had suspected from his earlier forays into my guilty mind—that I was a nigger-loving communist. In a panic, I stood up, stretched theatrically, and edged toward my window. Nothing. Just the usual flickering pool of light gathered under the streetlamp out on Stagecoach.

Nonetheless, fear had primed me, and the wails Jimi extorted from his guitar suddenly afflicted me like human cries. Were they like the cries my mother made when she gave birth to me? I was aghast at my thought, as if someone had planted it in me like an insidious seed.

To calm myself, I silenced the radio and slipped *Atlas Shrugged* from its paper bag. As an accordion polka intruded from the living room, I lay down and opened the book. The first few pages concerned a man named Eddie giving a dime to a bum. The bum asked, "Who is John Galt?" which made no sense to Eddie. They were in a down-and-out big city, and for some reason which Eddie could not pinpoint, the outworn buildings, the bum, and the yellow twilight disturbed him. When Don gave me the book, I had brushed aside his wild claim that it contained all the answers, but now I felt Eddie's discomfort as my own and fell into the story as if Rand had written it for me. Yes, *Atlas Shrugged* went on about boring business affairs, but underneath, a battle raged between utterly noble people and utterly rotten people. I rooted for Dagny Taggart and Hank Reardon against their enemies like I rooted for the people of Middle Earth against the orcs. Never mind the steelmaking or skipped-over grim speeches about man's purpose. I read for a couple of hours. When I finally dropped the book, I dreamed of kissing Dagny and becoming a famous writer like Ayn Rand. As for Mr. Heffelfinger, I would face him down with an unflinching gaze, just like my newfound heroes.

I got up early Sunday and joined my mother for warmed-over biscuits and scrambled eggs. She had already set her hair and put on a yellow church dress. While I scanned the *Hopperton Herald* looking for the chess club notice Mr. Pee had placed, Mother concocted the sweet, pale coffee we both favored. I found the notice on page three, inserted between obituaries and family reunions, but saw no mention of my name or the fact that I had started a new club. *The high school chess club meets Fridays after school in room 109.* Hardly inviting. And football Friday, the only day available, was the worst possible time. I scanned the rest of the weekly without enthusiasm. It was a four-pager delivering "civic-minded, God-fearing, patriotic news since 1917." I didn't care about Baptist Centennials and Exchange Club meetings and FFA awards, and, as of yet, there were no football results to lament. I scorned an article by our local congressman supporting the newly proposed anti-ballistic missile system built, he opined, to foil Red Chinese ambitions. The congressman only wished the ABM system was vastly more comprehensive and immediate in its impact, shielding us from the Soviets as well. Like Don, the world at large obsessed over war. I only heard the word "peace" in church, where it's Prince was seemingly confined.

As I closed the paper, I happened to glance at the front page again and noticed an article entitled "Waycross Move Gets Local OK." The piece explained that the Hopperton planning commission had no objection to the influx of Waycross students and had petitioned the State Board of Education to approve their enrollment. Sally had given the impression that outsiders were enrolled surreptitiously and that everyone would simply turn a blind eye after the fact. But the article made it clear Hopperton coveted the state money attached to the transferring students and that getting the funds required official sanction. I knew firsthand from the dance that many Waycross kids were already in town and considered themselves students at our school; I assumed they would show up in my classes Monday. Perhaps the State Board of Education had privately given the OK in advance. Then I remembered Don calling our school's packing with white students an act of civil disobedience, a bizarre continuation of the Civil War. And yet to seek official approval did not seem disobedient to me. My father often spoke of "getting to the bottom of things." No doubt, he could provide a true picture of the situation. After all, he chaired the planning commission.

"Bill, eat that last biscuit," my mother insisted. "Waste is a sin. I'll go lay out your good blue suit; I just got it back from the cleaners."

Later, after church and the church social (during which Sally Chiles and Claire Johnson annoyed me by whispering together), in the waning hours of a mild, utopian afternoon that had swept Mr. Heffelfinger from my thoughts, my father returned from his hunting camp.

"Any venison, Edward?" called my mother from the veranda as my father exited his beloved blue Caddy. If he had bagged anything, the evidence would be elsewhere. No one would ever truss a deer carcass to the roof of *that* automobile.

"Sonofagun, I got one," my father shouted back with a grin. "You best believe that. The boys are brining and smoking it; should be a couple of days."

I walked over and took his keys. It was my customary job to retrieve his hunting bow from the trunk. But before getting the bow, I acted out of character by offering him a congratulatory handshake. He seemed to enjoy the gesture and held my grip long enough for me to smell cigar smoke and fried catfish in his clothes. I mumbled, "great job" and quickly busied myself getting the bow.

In truth, my handshake wasn't a tribute to father's deer stalking prowess. I didn't care much about that. But when I first saw him step out of the Caddy, I recalled Mr. Heffelfinger's wolfish smile from the day before, when he seemed to insinuate that Ed Shaffer built his life on false piety and sheer luck.

I knew better, and in that spirit shook my father's hand, imagining the gesture would vex Mr. Heffelfinger. It surely did not, but in remembering the handshake now, I remember why Mr. Heffelfinger misjudged my father.

To begin with, my father looked a bit like Humphrey Bogart. Both were short and favored hats; both had odd faces and voices that nevertheless exuded significance. In my father's case, his nose featured a dent from a baseball collision, and he always squinted when he looked at you as if trying to recollect your name. He spoke in a soft Southern growl, the words delivered with maddening deliberation. As his son, I did not enjoy being peered at with suspicion or waiting on his lagging pronouncements, but likely it helped him in his public life to put people on the spot and make them listen.

Not that my father's mannerisms were the wellspring of his authority. Hopperton sits in the heart of slash pine country, and therefore to manage a pine gum extraction plant for a turpentine distiller made my father an influential figure locally. Beyond that, I believe people ascribed to my father a shaman's gift for seeing the bigger picture. I often accompanied him around town from barbershop to hardware store. When other men spotted the snap-brim hat he wore tilted back slightly off his forehead, they, and not my father, would extend the first greeting: "Why hello, Ed" or simply a nod and "Mr. Shaffer." My father was not vain. I believe he saw himself as he was—a man of local importance who found it foolish to pretend otherwise. My mother was president of many clubs, my father of only one: the Exchange Club. It just so happened that the Exchange Club ran Hopperton (the malcontents joined the Lion's Club). Exchange had the more prosperous white businessmen, so—end of story.

As far as official town affairs were concerned, my father's chief responsibility on the planning commission (other than wielding the gavel) was upkeep of the municipal building, which had once been a county courthouse and featured the original turret, a clock tower, and Palladian windows. At my father's urging (to satisfy my mother as everyone knew), the commission approved an outdoor gazebo, and while rarely occupied, it did elevate local pride. I overheard one of my mother's bridge club members use the gazebo (she called it a pavilion) as an example of what mountains could be moved by husbands who *truly* love their wives.

Unofficially, given how I saw other white merchants and solid citizens show plain deference to my father, I believe his vote on contentious matters was the deciding one. Granted, Hopperton's controversies were seldom of earth-shattering proportions. Only occasionally, such as when surveyors found rich deposits of phosphates locally and the granting of leases required consideration, did my father's influence gain real significance. If the parent company of the plant my father managed obtained these leases for a favorable fee, that was no conflict of interest—that was smart; that was horse-trading; that was business. *That* helped keep a local plant open despite lower-priced turpentine competition down near Jacksonville, despite laborers preferring the less backbreaking jobs at wood pulp plants, and, as few people locally knew, despite competition from Portugal and Brazil that might, someday soon if we weren't careful, eradicate the domestic turpentine industry.

My father didn't hesitate to explain such things to me. Like certain philosophers, he believed the world was as it was, and it was no use pretending otherwise. If a man is wearing a hat, a man is wearing a hat, he was fond of saying, and only a fool would go out of his way to dispute that.

Only a fool.

Now, as much as I loved and respected my father (and despised Mr. Heffelfinger), here lay a problem. After Kennedy's election, my father remarked that only a fool could doubt that the Pope would soon be running the country. And only a fool could doubt our GIs would rout the Vietcong in short order. Nor would anyone but a fool think the country would ever stand for rock and roll, least of all endure Elvis Presley. And worst of all were the fools calling the shots in our country, Yankee fools who failed to see what was plain to see, who couldn't tell a hat from a bare head.

Given these plain facts, wasn't my father sometimes unable to tell a fedora from a crew cut? I concluded that, like any man, my father saw distant things less clearly than local ones. After all, no one knew whether Mars had little green people, but everyone knew when milk turned sour. And my father, however nearsighted, knew better than anyone "what was what" around Hopperton. He certainly knew better about all things— great and small—than the odious Mr. Heffelfinger.

That Sunday evening, in the wake of my father's venison conquest, my mother prepared a victory supper of ham, sweet potatoes, string beans, and biscuits with chicken gravy. She and I listened to my father recount how a whitetail wandered near where he perched quietly on the lower limb of a large oak tree and how the deer, once struck by his arrow, collapsed within his sight, a tribute to either his marksmanship or dumb luck, he could not honestly say which.

"Edward Shaffer, you know very well which one it was," my mother insisted, playing her little part in the ceremony.

"I had my eyes open," my father admitted with a grin. "That's as far as I'll go."

Indeed, my father had his eyes open. After dinner, I asked him why Waycross kids were already enrolled at Hopperton High if the state had not yet granted funding, as the newspaper seemed to indicate. And would the school keep them if the government failed to pay for them? I steered clear of questions about right and wrong. While my mother cleared the table for dessert, my father considered my questions as he lit a cigar and nursed a whiskey and soda.

"It's ticklish, Bill," he answered. "We must appear to be resisting by legal means, as we surely are. If a family from Waycross moves to Hopperton, why, they have every right to send their child to school here. But not all families can just pull up stakes like that. In those cases, transportation must be provided, and that is where it gets ticklish. Public school buses can't be used; that would tip everyone's hand and possibly lead to our schools falling directly under federal control, just like in the Soviet Union. So, we formed a committee to fund private buses while still petitioning the State. We believe Georgia will quietly give us its blessing, and because we're not using public school buses, we'll escape the notice of the do-gooders in Washington. Oh, there is some small risk, I suppose, but maintaining our way of life is worth that risk. Down the road, we expect the terrible examples of integration will force the government to come to its senses. In the meantime, we must offer what suitable resistance we can."

"Do you think things will go back to the way they were?" I was sure they would not but did my best to ask this question innocently.

My father puffed reflectively and shook his head.

"Not entirely. Funds should be more fairly appropriated to Negro schools. We must not repeat past mistakes. Negro children must be allowed to reach their full potential without holding white children back. We must be fair, but not by mixing children with vastly different intellectual capacities. That does a disservice to all concerned."

I had heard this very argument discussed on a Mutual Radio public affairs show.

"Our school doesn't separate the dumb kids from the smart kids," I said. "It sounds like you're saying they probably should."

My father chuckled. "Our taxpayers would never stand for that. Besides, most of your friends seem bright enough."

Besides Don, my father lacked any meaningful contact with my friends, much less their displays of "intellectual capacity." And I knew that

"Negro schools" no longer existed, as far as the courts were concerned. All in all, my father's views seemed only a little less unsatisfactory than Sally's and Don's.

"But what if the State doesn't pay for the Waycross kids?" I persisted. I had heard enough conversations between my father and his friends to know that money lay at the heart of almost every final decision.

"A good question, Bill, and one, Lord knows, I have asked myself. My answer is we will do what we always do—solve the problem." I nodded as if I understood my father's answer. Perhaps other people nodded the same way when they took his weightily delivered advice. After a pause, I changed topics.

"Don got a crossbow; I showed him how to shoot it."

"Good Lord, Bill. Where was Don's father?"

"Watching us from the window." I only assumed this to be true.

"A crossbow, an actual crossbow?" My father seemed dumbfounded, which pleased me no end.

"A Powermaster," I announced with facile authority.

My father practically reared up in consternation. "Now listen, Bill. That thing is a dime-store toy. The prod is pot metal. It's apt to snap and put an eye out while you're aiming the damned thing. Don will hang it on the wall and leave it there if he knows what's good for him." My father had spoken rapidly and cursed, both shocking events.

"Don only shot it once or twice," I cried, trying furiously to backpedal. "He needed me to cock it for him."

"Bill, I'm not angry at you, but I do wonder. I expect you to tell Don immediately what's what regarding that crossbow. I'll communicate the perils to Mr. Heffelfinger myself."

Having heard everything as she shuttled back and forth to the kitchen, my mother motioned me to keep my seat.

"Tomorrow will be fine, Bill; and Ed, from what both Bill and I have seen, Don's father is doing rather poorly. Can you find a business excuse to meet with him? I would appreciate a man's opinion as to his state of mind."

My father started to object, then wrenched himself into silence.

"If you promise," my mother added, smiling, "I will reward you with lemon meringue pie."

My father stared at her, then shook his head.

"I will call him Maggie, and that is all I will do."

"All right, Ed, but please be kind. Phillip Heffelfinger is a veteran and has no wife or church affiliation. I fear he is a lost soul." It was odd to hear Mother use Mr. Heffelfinger's first name. It had never occurred to me that she even knew it.

"I'll be kind—as I always am," my father said. "Now, can we move on to the pie?"

A raucous babble filled the lunchroom Monday—the social equivalent of a chemical reaction—as the kids from Waycross mixed in.

"Well, well," Don snickered. "Look at Mustang Sally in her new red dress, playing the queen bee for all its worth." Sally sat at another table, talking brightly to three girls I did not recognize.

"Listen, Don," I said. "We can psychoanalyze Sally later. My father swears he's gonna call your father about the crossbow, tell him it's junk, tell him the bow, the prod, will snap and kill you. When we get to my house after school, you have to tell my mother that you're never going to use that crossbow again. Then she'll tell my father, and he'll back off."

Don shook his head in vehement opposition. "Your dad must be thinking of a different model, Shaffer. Mine is a beauty. We shot it yesterday. I mean, I shot it; my dad cocked it. The bow part—what did you call it?"

"The prod."

"Right, right. Believe me, that thing is strong; no way it's going to break. My dad could barely cock it. And the arrow went into the tree like it was nothing!" As Don spoke, he waved his sandwich around like a white flag. I was sure he was embellishing his account; I had cocked that crossbow without strain. Doing so would hardly tax Mr. Heffelfinger. I concluded that Don was exaggerating to defend his crossbow. But that wasn't my main concern.

"Just tell my mother you won't use it, okay?" I was desperate to pacify my father before he talked to Mr. Heffelfinger. I had gotten it into my head that Mr. Heffelfinger would tell my father what he had seen in my mind.

Don, to my surprise, blithely accepted what he called "our little charade." I was relieved, but beyond that, I fervently wished Don would hang the damn crossbow on his wall and forget it.

"Put your eye out if you want, Don, but I bet you ten dollars my father is right." Don smiled tolerantly.

"Fear not, Shaffer. Once I can cock the beast and shoot it on my own, I'll be satisfied, and that will be that. You should fret about Sally and how jealous she's going to be when she unearths your mystery girl. Which one is she, by the way?"

I feigned my own mysterious smile. Later, a small, uneasy fib to my parents defused the crossbow controversy. In life at large, no football victory occurred that Friday or the next or the next, and the chess club sparked no interest. I crept ahead with the vastness of *Atlas Shrugged*, relishing how Dagny and Hank righteously crush one small-minded adversary after another, hardly caring *why*. Unlike Don however, I found no answers in the book. Its bleak world, populated only by the noble and the craven, bore no evocative resemblance to my own.

On the other hand, I drank in the main characters' heroic charisma and absurdly hoped to appear to my classmates as Hank appeared to me. I auditioned a piercing stare and no-nonsense tone, but no one seemed impressed. When Don took no notice and Sally wondered if I was sick, I slunk back to my colorless ways.

A few days later, as I sat on the veranda after supper reading *Atlas Shrugged*, I came across a passage where Dagny asks her childhood companion, Francisco, to describe the most depraved type of human being. Francisco answers: *The man without a purpose*. I was reading by the last good light, surrounded by the early murmur of insects, when Francisco's words struck me like a direct accusation. Francisco went on to tell Dagny that nothing in life mattered but *how well you do your work*. When it was finally too dark to read, I closed the book and tried to name my purpose or work, but I could think of nothing I wanted to invent or cure or construct. What I wanted, I realized with a stab of self-loathing, was to string together a long series of fascinating, comfortable days populated with pretty girls and friends who admired me. And more shameful yet, I didn't particularly like to work.

"Dagny," I whispered as if she were a real woman sitting close to me, "I will do something to amaze you, no matter what it takes." I felt a vague resolve well up in me—strong enough to convince me I had taken a bold step, but mild enough to require nothing immediate. I slept well that night, idolized as well as desired by my fantasy lovers.

Not long after, my mother passed down another family artifact, a Remington manual typewriter rendered dispensable by the IBM

Selectric she had acquired to lend polish to her countless church and club announcements.

I learned where to place my fingers and how to roll a sheet of paper into place. My mother said the cardinal rule was not to look at the keys once I had memorized their position. With that, my lessons came to an end. I punched at a few keys and sensed futility in the slowness of it all. Still, when I looked at the nonsensical printed letters—*gjkf*—I saw I had created, at least in form, elements filling the pages of *Atlas Shrugged*. And here, under my fingers, was the very same tool Ayn Rand used to do her *work* and fulfill her *purpose*! It could not be a coincidence. Shaking with excitement, I struck the keys again, this time with more intent—*b ill*. That was enough for now. I turned on my radio for the first time in days and lay down on my bed to think.

Later, after a handful of maddening sessions with the balky, finicky Remington, I managed (on my fourth or fifth try) to type without egregious error the following sentence: *My one regret in life is losing Delia Wingfoot, even though I know it was for the best.*

CHAPTER SEVEN

"Bad Blood"

Micanopy and Gainesville, Florida, 2016

The night Olivia acquires her plum wine alien eggs, I'm up until three thanks to the laughing Russians. Ranting-man and piano-woman seem to have patched up their differences. In the morning, I wake to remember a dream in which I am a boy swimming in Lonesome Pine Lake. Another boy taunts me in an unknown language, provoking me to smash his head against a dock piling. He sinks into the water, and I swim away. In the manner of dreams, people wonder where the boy is, but soon everyone moves on to whatever new absurdity I hatch in my subconscious.

I sit up in bed, still groggy, trying to remember swims I had with friends, and for a moment, suspect the dream is a real, repressed memory. No, that's just crazy. No boy ever went missing in Hopperton. It's just the disappearance that *did* happen, and that awful day at the quarry, bringing back old panic. Olivia's questions about the scope of my early misdeeds must have stirred up the mud.

It's only six o'clock. Christ. But I'm up now. I'll make coffee and open the pile of mail I've been avoiding like a trip to the dentist or urologist. Maybe that will send my subconscious packing. I get dressed, head for the kitchen, and fill my old tin percolator with spring water and home-ground Ethiopian beans. Once the coffee's bubbling, I tear open the first few envelopes. Reverse mortgage, term life—no physical required!—miracle hearing aid, UNICEF, college endowment. Then a handwritten envelope bearing no return address.

Inside I find an invitation to the Hopperton High fiftieth class reunion. Not the usual pre-printed one I toss away, but a hand-typed note on lilac-tinted paper. It reads *Bill; please come next year. Our 50th will be in late October. Sally.* The request perplexes me, and not only because it has been sent far in advance. One of those boyhood "crimes" I keep from Olivia caused a rift between me and Sally, a breach which seems destined never to heal.

Our mothers had been twin pillars of the Methodist church, regularly conferring on matters of charity, civic beautification, and, of course, religion—particularly the endless "revivals" needed to beat back human weakness—so both women were delighted to have the other's child to distract her own.

Consequently, Sally and I found ourselves in the preschool equivalent of an arranged marriage.

In the end, my affections for another girl led to our falling out, though Sally and I never carried on a romance, never sat starry-eyed sharing our hopes and dreams, and had only one problematic kiss. The details wait ahead in this narrative, but as I sit with the invitation, I'm not reliving those times; I'm only baffled by the urging in Sally's note. Has all been forgiven? Has something terrible happened? Or is she intimating a disclosure too vital to keep from me, despite her feelings? I've often imagined particular distant chickens coming home to roost, and no one would be more likely to spot them than Sally.

I tuck the invitation into a tattered paperback copy of Hermann Hesse's novel, *Siddhartha*, a book given to me the same year I last saw Sally. *Siddhartha* occupies a small shelf on my counter along with my family Bible, *Atlas Shrugged*, *Madame Bovary*, *Of Human Bondage*, and *Franny and Zooey*. Maybe Sally's intent will reveal itself, inspired by such august company.

In the meantime, I will be busy wrestling with Carl's suspect emancipation, Linda's emerging crone persona, and Olivia's unfettered avarice at the mall.

Rather than entering the kitchen at noon in a drowsy, grumpy slouch, Olivia bursts in at ten, waving her phone at me.

"Breaking news," she shouts. "Uncle Carl will be home Monday and wants us to be there for a meeting of the 'great powers,' whatever that means."

"Did he say *us?*"

"I'm going, dude. You can't put me in a kennel like a dog. Can you make me some scrambled eggs?"

"I'm aware of your human status, Olivia, *and* your tricks. Anyway, *if* I go, you can go. I never said otherwise." I feel fate dragging me to Tampa—no point in digging in my heels. Olivia grins, sensing my surrender.

"This is going to be freaking awesome," she proclaims, her teen indifference blown to smithereens. She has found a golden ticket in a Wonka Bar.

"For you, maybe." By now, I'm whisking a dollop of milk into the eggs.

"Anyway, get this: Uncle Carl says he has something important to give you."

I can't think of anything I want from Carl, but I can't help imagining a conversation where he offers to return Linda to me.

"No mention of what it is, I suppose?"

"Maybe he's dying and has a lot of money stashed away." Right to the mortal point again.

"If he did, he wouldn't give it to me."

"Maybe he needs you to get it." Unnervingly plausible. "Then you would get a cut," she muses, warming to the financial and movie plot possibilities.

As I stir eggs, I contemplate driving to Tampa, wondering if Olivia's presence will tamp down the craziness waiting at the other end or just rev it up. I also wonder if it was Carl's head I smashed against a dock piling in last night's dream. Maybe I'm more hostile than I know. I do admit the prospect of witnessing Carl and Linda's reunion makes me queasy. And no matter how I comport myself, it will appear to Linda that I am wearing a sign around my neck saying 'I told you so' in smug, iridescent letters. But I will go, regardless. Wronged or not, consciously or not, I participated in bringing these two bedraggled lovebirds together. Socrates would tell me to understand that and let the rest go. I will give it a shot, old boy.

Olivia interrupts me to plumb the mysteries of percolation. "Without a timer, how do you know when it's done?"

"By smell mostly and by the color of the water when it spurts up into the knob."

"You have to stick around and watch it? Sounds like a pain."

"It's a complete pleasure; that's the whole point."

Olivia is too happy to belittle my habits further. She is already else-where, texting her tribe, spreading the news. I turn down the heat on the eggs, grab a mason jar and hustle out back to harvest fruit from the Surinam cherry bushes along my back fence—a ritual that bears repeating every couple of days for best yield and for foiling pillaging crows, sparrows, and scrub jays. Outside, the air is fresh and inviting, the open sky dwarfing my petty thoughts. Cherries fall into the jar from the slightest touch, telling me that they are ripe for picking. Maybe all is not lost.

"Get in here, Grandpa," Olivia yells through the screen door. "I think your coffee pot is going to explode."

No explosion. Only good coffee and a pleasant breakfast of scrambled eggs and toast, with cherry jam from earlier harvests. Afterward, I clean up as Olivia prepares to meet her public. I finish long before Olivia and use the time to back my 1957 Studebaker Golden Hawk out of the garage and check its vital signs. They are probably better than mine since, unlike me, the Studebaker, with its massive Packard engine and resplendent eggcrate grill, has been fully restored, including an Apache-red paint job and killer sound system. Olivia predictably derides my car, whose cranked-down windows provide its only air-conditioning. Still, she can't hide her fascination with the primitive choreography of clutch, gas, and column shifter interacting somehow with hand and foot like some kind of ancient magic. She badly wants to give it a try. Soon her sixteenth birthday will arrive, and I have advised the Studebaker to gird itself.

The mall sits on the outskirts of Gainesville. It is Everymall—a place without local flavor, bright and bland, a hollowness shadowing voices and footsteps as they resound from unforgiving floors. Here, the acquisitive are happy, the rest of us resigned. Piped-in pop music mixes with the general murmur, the songs featuring young divas demonstrating colossal lung-power over intricate but mechanical backbeats. Some weird aroma mixing burnt popcorn and cheap air freshener assails me at intervals. Here and there, a weary husband sits and waits, a fellow stranger in this strange land.

Entering the mall, Olivia comes to life like house lights restored after a power failure. Here, she is a member of the dominant species: teen girls in shorts and bright layered tops, sporting clutch purses and earbuds, generally traveling in self-conscious packs. As we walk through the food court on our way to an escalator, two schoolmates of Olivia absorb her into their pack, and the three girls agree to shop in a clothing store called Hollister's, characterized by a cloying, perfume-like scent offered to the passing crowd like a fishing lure. A surprisingly comfy couch offers a line of sight to the store. I listen to background music for distraction, the song happening to be "Bad Blood" by Taylor Swift. Even I am familiar with this ubiquitous hit, but only now do I follow the words. In a nutshell, "Baby" turns mad love into bad blood by doing something, well, bad. The upshot: Baby becomes an enemy.

Ancient Greek healers recognized a similarly named condition called *dyscrasia*, or literally "bad mixture," in which the four bodily fluids or "humours" got out of whack. Coincidentally, the Greeks believed that blood was the strongest humour, the others being black bile, yellow bile, and phlegm. Each humour corresponded to one of the four elements: air, earth, water, and fire. Blood corresponded to air, which is an uncannily intuitive connection, considering that blood feeds air in the form of oxygen to the body's cells—a fact which the Greeks did not know. They would probably have diagnosed Taylor Swift's particular instance of bad blood as an excess of yellow bile, the "fire" humour, stored in the gallbladder and known to foment angry emotions. However, "Bad Blood" is a catchier song title than "Excessive Yellow Bile."

Less intriguing, but more to the point, I often heard the phrase "bad blood" during my Hopperton childhood, referring to the fluid circulating within former slaves. Unlike "white blood" (which is, in fact, red), whose deficiencies and poisonous excesses resulted from anomalous, foreign afflictions, Negro blood was bad in and of itself. When asked about such things, Mr. Pee told us a Negro's blood could save a white man's life, but beyond that, he was unqualified to say. One brave boy said he would rather die.

"And we would miss you," replied Mr. Pee.

The girls take their sweet time. The foot traffic flows past me like years, like the river Heraclitus claimed we never step in twice. Across from me, covering most of a store window, a poster displays the tightly bunched faces of three supermodels. Underneath their overwrought glamour, I read the phrase "beauty vs. the world." *Don't worry, girls*, I think, *you are in no danger*. It's a different kind of beauty the world is working hard to destroy. A brief pang of meaninglessness unsettles me. Despite or because of this, I find myself humming the insinuating refrain to "Bad Blood."

A woman separates from the throng and approaches me. It's Hermine Delaplaine, dressed in black capris and a man's white dress shirt tied at the midriff—my shirt. Despite confiscating my apparel, Hermine will not admit to being my girlfriend, preferring the term "paramour."

"Damn, Bill," she says, shaking her head, "you are the spitting image of a lonely old man." She purses her lips and sits down next to me. "It's not your best look."

"Olivia's shopping," I offer in my defense.

"Ah, you *are* a lonely old man. Mind if I wait here with you? I'd love to chat with Olivia. And my feet hurt. It's these sexy sandals." Hermine wiggles her toes vigorously. "What do you think of my pedicure? Too vain for an old woman?" The question is purely rhetorical; her glossily painted toes are perfect. All of Hermine glows with refined animal energy.

"I don't mind at all."

"Really? Even with me knowing all your secrets?" As she speaks, Hermine points insistently at her wriggling toes.

"You don't know all my secrets, but I will concede your toes look magnificent. And you smell delectably good."

Hermine smiles and pats my knee again.

"Well, they say you should wear your love like heaven, don't they?"

While we wait for Olivia to emerge, I catch Hermine up on developments with Carl. I am surprised that she approves of my proposed visit, including my willingness to bring Olivia along.

"Whatever plot Carl is hatching, Olivia will make it harder to pull off. Just don't let Carl take you aside for a private talk. Like I tell my patients, you *must* respect your weaknesses."

"I don't think he'll try to hypnotize me."

"Oh, but he will. He has some shiny thing swinging on a string. You just don't know what it is. You need to keep Olivia between you and Carl. Otherwise, you're screwed sideways."

"You're welcome to join us in Tampa; I'm sure Linda would embrace you like a sister."

"Sure, let's watch Carl try to get in my undies. That should be fun for you."

"I take that as a 'no'?"

Hermine doesn't bother to answer. Instead, she slips her arm through mine and shakes her head in rueful disregard. Eventually, Olivia emerges from Hollister's, laden with bags. When she sees how Hermine has latched on to me, she makes a grotesquely incredulous face. Then she whispers to her companions. They nod and wave to us as they walk away. As Hermine waves back, Olivia resumes her wary walk toward us.

"I can't remember your name," Olivia tells Hermine. Olivia has met Hermine at my house, treating her as one more faceless, sexless adult to ignore.

"Hermine. Your grandfather tells me you're a woman of strong opinions."

Olivia directs a token scowl at me.

"I guess."

"I'm that way myself," Hermine confesses ruefully. "I'm supposed to listen to my patients, not tell them what to think. But they're so thick-headed I have to help them see the light."

"Hermine is a psychiatrist," I explain.

Olivia stares at Hermine, her eyes peering shrewdly. "You're my mom's new shrink, right?"

"I'm not allowed to tell you; that's a professional secret. I *can* tell you that your grandfather is *not* my patient."

Olivia notices Hermine's free hand almost touching my knee. Her eyes widen, drawn to the possible palace intrigue fate has conjured out of thin air. She points at me. "Is he your *boyfriend?*"

Hermine shakes her head, slightly deflating me, but then continues. "The Spanish and Italians both use the incomparable word *simpatico* to describe what your grandfather and I share. I don't care for the term 'soul mates' since I have yet to detect my soul, but the idea is much the same. But I don't want to play dumb and pretend not to understand your question. I assume you are asking if we have sex. That is an *unprofessional* secret unless your grandfather chooses to tell you, which, given your evident maturity, he has my permission to do. Now, I understand you're going to visit your grandmother and your grandmother's husband?"

During her provocative soliloquy, Hermine glances my way as if to transmit a secret code whose meaning, I hope, is: *don't worry, I know what I'm doing.*

"Yeah, Uncle Carl is getting out of prison early. They found evidence to prove he was innocent."

Hermine assumes a puzzled face. "Uncle? I wasn't aware Bill—your grandfather—had any children other than your mother."

"Oh, he's not my real uncle. It's just what I call him. I've known him all my life."

Hermine smiles at Olivia's explanation and gives an understanding nod.

"Well, Olivia," she points out, "he *is* a relative if he's married to your grandmother, so…"

I feel the conversation veering toward dangerous territory. Hermine knows more than I'd like about Carl and my ex-wives, but nothing of his blood bond to Olivia.

"How did the shopping go?" I ask Oliva out of nowhere, sounding utterly fake to myself.

"Excellent," Hermine interjects before Olivia can answer. She then pulls a small box from her purse, opens it, and displays its contents specifically to Olivia.

"These earrings," she confides in a near whisper, "are *totems* carved from turquoise. They match my nails, and I took that as a sign. If you look closely, you'll see that each earring is a tiny tigress. Wearing them is supposed to give you the animal's power. I'm very skeptical by nature, but I have to admit I felt an undeniable *tingle* when I held them up to my ears."

As Olivia stares covetously at the earrings, Hermine turns to me.

"Bill dear, take Olivia down to Natural Magic and let her pick out a pair. A girl can never have too much power. And on that note, I've got to get going. Olivia, lovely to finally chat with you; enjoy your reunion with Uncle Carl. Both of you must be pleased to see an innocent man set free."

Hermine gives me a smile of wicked condescension as she utters this last remark, then rises to her feet, weaves herself gracefully into the passing humanity, and disappears.

As we drive home, Olivia alternates between fingering her turquoise tigress earrings and giving me disbelieving looks. Whatever else Hermine fomented, she elevated my standing with Olivia, who now must come to terms with my romantic prowess as well as my criminal past.

"You should definitely marry her," she announces just as we're pulling out onto 441.

"Why?" I ask.

Olivia gasps at my stupidity and proceeds to point out several salient and self-evident facts, among which are that Hermine did not ask her about school or tell her how cute she was. "If you married *her*," Olivia muses, "you would have somebody cool like Grandma has Uncle Carl; heck, maybe even cooler."

"Do you think she would say yes if I proposed?"

Olivia emits a deep sigh, as if under the burden of grave consideration. "Yeah, probably. I mean, she called you 'dear.' Buy her a super expensive necklace to go with her earrings. Like, I can tell she likes you, but get the necklace just to be sure. I'll start looking online tonight."

And I am left to ponder Hermine's assertion that a girl can never have too much power.

CHAPTER EIGHT

"The Ballad of Frankie Lee and Judas Priest"

Monday morning, as I am nursing my coffee and listening to St. Paul and the Broken Bones, Olivia emerges in all her groggy, rumpled glory for no other discernible purpose than to disparage my musical taste.

"What is *that?*" she asks, her contempt amplified by the general unfairness of ungodly hours.

"I believe they call it music. Rhythm and blues, to be precise. I'm sure you notice the debt owed to Otis Redding."

"No, I just want my coffee; we need to get going." Olivia's voice denounces any side trips into wit, irony, or edification—time to get real.

And so it is.

I stand up, put on an Etta James record, and begin concocting Olivia's milky, sugary brew of choice. "Do you like this singer better?" I ask, preferring Olivia's mean opinions to the kitchen table silence.

"She's okay. When are we leaving?"

"As soon as you're ready, princess. By the way, this is Etta James, recorded about 1960. She inspired Adele to be a singer."

"Adele is way better." Olivia refuses to ask how I know anything about Adele.

"Maybe," I concede, "but isn't it cool to see the connection, to *hear* the connection?" Olivia shrugs, unmoved. I would love her to be fascinated by the soulful flow from Otis to Aretha and Etta, and on to Mary J. Blige and Adele. I would love her to be fascinated by how the voices of Buddy Holly and Otis Redding, sharing the radio singer's wild blue curse, both crumpled to silence in the wreckage of small planes.

But Oliva merely shrugs, as she is entitled to do, slumped a little in preoccupation, blowing on her coffee, dismissing the past, waiting in the dull present for the prismatic future to *finally* get here. I smile, imagining her trying to beguile her uninterested children with affinities she's noticed, maybe between Romeo and Juliet and Adele's lyrics. Or perhaps she'll wake up some morning amazed that she's always lived in brick houses by a lake, just as I have lived in three towns on the same road. Maybe she'll ponder the meaning of such happenstance, as I have wondered why so many love triangles found me and chose me as the odd man out.

Olivia, oblivious to my increasingly maudlin speculations, makes short work of her liquid breakfast and departs to dress. While I'm waiting, I sit with Otis in the morning sun, humming my day-long lament to the ships as they come and go.

Olivia calls out, imploring me not to sing. Maybe someday I'll tell her about the time I sang the song a capella and how, without my absent-minded rendition and the conversation that followed, *she* might never have existed.

Linda is waiting beside the driveway when we arrive in Tampa. She maintains her slender frame and dyes her hair jet black, allowing her to look almost girlish from a distance, but she and I are the same age. When she squints in through the car window, her clouded eyes and lined, leathery skin say a great deal about time, diabetes, sun, cigarettes, and constant anxiety.

"This visit is my definition of a lousy idea," she snaps, "and I hope to God—" She spots Olivia, flinches as if slapped, then pastes on a smile. "I didn't see you there, honey. Why aren't you in school?"

"It's a holiday, Grandma."

"Holiday? Oh, right. Well, of course I'm happy to see you, but this may be a bit much for your uncle. He's—"

"He invited her, Linda."

"Well, you probably misunderstood."

"They text all the time. It's in black-and-white; hard to get that wrong."

"Uncle Carl didn't tell me *not* to come," Olivia puts in suddenly. "That's all I know."

Linda glares at me. "You took her word for it?"

"Yes, but—"

"Hey," Olivia shouts. "Can you guys argue inside? I need a cold drink; there's no AC in this so-called car. And Uncle Carl is in there waiting for us—especially for me."

Linda and I exchange a sheepish glance that recognizes our reflexive skirmish for what it is. Olivia gets out of the car, informing us that she brought her bathing suit for a dip in the pool just in case things get boring and that she could use a smoothie, too.

"Come on, honey," Linda says, putting her arm around Olivia. "I'll fix you up, then we'll find your uncle. Just remember to go easy on him; he's still a little shaky from his ordeal."

I trail behind, listening to Olivia embellish the encounter with Hermine that produced her tigress earrings. Linda takes a quick, suspicious look back at me as if I were following her down a deserted street. *I am the least of your problems*, I think back at her. Then I find myself alone in the living room, Carl being nowhere in sight. Following a hunch, I walk the length of the house to his back office, where I find him sprawled on a Lazy Boy, watching television. He waves me in without getting up.

"No games today, Professor. Florida State tonight, but that's it. Just my luck. All I can find is a Serbian cartoon movie and this *Law and Order* marathon. Pretty good, though."

I glance at the screen and see Mariska Hargitay, who plays a female cop, berating a suspect.

"That's Jayne Mansfield's daughter," I remark, equally apropos of nothing.

"She's one serious bitch on this show."

No welcome home, no acknowledgment of the years of estrangement, no mention of prison, no ritual inquiries into each other's general condition. And given what Carl and I know about each other, no inclination to do so. Instead, we stand there watching the TV show. He's barefoot, wearing a loud shirt and Bermuda shorts. His hair is still a thick shock—sandy blond mixed with steel gray—and the body of a high school tackle and Vietnam jungle fighter stubbornly asserts itself through the wear and tear of years.

"When Mansfield died in a car crash in 1967, she was in the back seat."

"Who?"

"That actress. Hargitay. They say the crash decapitated her mother."

"How do you remember that shit? Even the freaking year."

"I remember everything that happened in sixty-seven."

"That must be the year you lost your cherry."

"Yes, among other things." I make no effort to elaborate; Carl looks around to read my expression.

"Well, blow me down, you're serious. Okay, tell me something else cool that happened in sixty-seven."

I ponder a moment.

"Frankie Lee and Judas Priest."

"Wasn't Judas Priest some headbanger band?"

"Metal gods to their fans. But that's not where I'm headed. 'The Ballad of Frankie Lee and Judas Priest' is a Dylan song from an album released in nineteen sixty-seven. It's kind of about you and me."

Carl brightens like a kid. Nothing is easier than tickling his vanity.

"Which one am I?" he asks.

"Oh, you're Judas Priest, no doubt. He carries a big fat roll of bills and thinks he'll find paradise down the road. I'm Frankie Lee, the gambler. I see women's faces in every window."

Carl's eyes widen. "Wow, that's *us*. That nails us to the wall."

"Yeah, pretty much. And speaking of walls, here's a nugget you'll appreciate. Nineteen sixty-seven was the year Charles Manson got out of prison."

Carl eyes me suspiciously, then bursts out laughing.

"Me and Manson, huh?" He swings to his feet and shuts off the TV. "Now I'll tell *you* something, Billy boy. There sure as hell weren't any Mansons where I went, just crybabies. All they do is moan about their shitty lawyers, shitty wives, shitty breaks. I never *once* complained when I was in there."

No part of me believes that.

"Olivia's here, by the way. She thinks she's part of a crime family."

"What about Ramona?"

"She's out at her lawyer's horse farm plotting Antonio's doom."

"Fuck *all* lawyers," Carl growls.

"Thanks, darling."

I turn around to see Linda at the doorway, Olivia pressing in just behind her. Carl looks at me and smiles thinly.

"She hates it when I speak the truth."

"No, Carl," she says. "I hate it *whenever* you speak."

Carl grins. "It's good to be home."

Ignoring them, Olivia pushes her way to Carl and hugs him gingerly, the bodily equivalent of an air kiss. "You're a free man, Uncle Carl," she reminds him, favoring me with a reproachful glance. "Did you win an appeal or something?"

I watch Carl. My money is riding on "something." He surveys his audience and chuckles weakly. "Absolutely; my lawyer appealed right to the Supreme Court. No, sweetie, they let me out because I have this thing called HIV."

"We studied that in school," Olivia says to Carl, seemingly more impressed than distraught.

"Yeah, it's pretty famous. Can you believe it? Nothing to worry about though, just take a few pills. But boy, the minute the good old Department of Corrections heard 'HIV positive,' I was a hot potato—a very expensive hot potato they weren't about to pony up for. 'Surprise, you're free,' they told me. Free to die on somebody else's dime."

"Carl, that's not—" Linda is an old hand at debunking his explanations, but Carl has the inside track and presses indignantly on.

"They let Linda think she sprung me for humanitarian reasons, but I saw their faces, and whatever else I don't know, I know people."

Linda gives an arid chuckle. "Carl wants me to appeal his release, get him reincarcerated."

Carl throws up his hands and mock-collapses into the Lazy Boy in the manner of a man eternally misunderstood. As he stares mutely at the blank TV, Olivia seizes the opening.

"How did you *get* HIV, Uncle Carl?" she asks, barreling past indiscretion. Carl looks at Linda, perhaps expecting her to swoop in with a courtroom objection, but when she doesn't, he smiles and shakes his head back and forth several times.

"Well now, that's the mystery, isn't it?" He leans his head back and looks up as if in rapt contemplation. "It's something to do with blood; that's all I know. I haven't had any transfusions, but I give blood; maybe something bad happened there with a needle. I mean, I'm not gay, so we can rule that out, right?"

The Taylor Swift song pops out of hiding. Bad blood, indeed. We're way past irony now. *How about unprotected sex with prostitutes?* This thought begs me to speak it, but I settle for hurling it wordlessly into the ether with as much psychic force as I can muster.

"Fascinating, Carl," Linda says, "but we're not going to solve your little *mystery* standing here, are we? I'm going to the patio for fresh air and drinks. See you there." Before anyone can respond, she turns and walks briskly down the hall—no looking back this time.

Olivia waves me away. "Go ahead, dude. I have *interesting* things to tell Uncle Carl."

"As you wish," I answer, adding a small bow.

On my way to the patio, I stop in the living room, not anxious to catch up with Linda. Carl's father furnished the house back in the late fifties, in mid-century *au courant* style, and as he envisioned it, it mostly remains. Still in place are sunburst copper mirrors, floor lamps evoking atomic geometry, bright yellow armless vinyl chairs on spiky chrome tripods, Scandinavian screens, cork parquet, and floor-to-ceiling curtainless windows. Neither Carl nor Linda evince any need to depart from this vision. A plastic, boomerang-shaped coffee table still sits precisely where it sat forty-something years ago. Its only accessories are a massive, spotless cobalt-blue ashtray and a sailing magazine that, I note, dates from July 1979. A sleek leather couch, uncharacteristically new, faces the table, its leather fabric stained a color I would call—of course—ox-blood red.

I sit on the couch, recalling what my mentor Gibson Levine once said—that the universe is an answerless question—and contemplate the time I sat here beside Gibson's stepdaughter and my future wife, Karen, ecstatically bewildered by how swiftly the distance between us had vanished that day on Carl's sailboat. Carl's dad had plied us with his specialty—"little rum boogies" as he called them—and played Sinatra through the towering Klipschorn speakers, even now standing guard across the room from me, still wired to the holy electronic trinity of their heyday: amp, pre-amp, and tuner. And each of those components, formidably encased in its vintage silver shell, still sits on a custom shelf, waiting in the cool museum quiet.

Had Karen coveted this house and had it been *my* family home rather than Carl's—who knows? Now I wonder, absurdly, if the Decker house even remembers Karen, who passed a little time here with Carl as she reconfigured a future always meant to occur elsewhere. For that matter, I wonder if the house notices Linda now, who seems to regard it as a vacation rental, kept tidy for the sake of a security deposit. Well, we're all trying to hold on to summer a little longer, aren't we?

As I stand up, I glance at the sailing magazine again. July 1979. The month Carl's dad died. The year I met Linda. I stand there motionless for a long moment, trying to remember. It finally comes to me that Carl's father was named Albert. I feel guilty about having forgotten and speak the words "Albert Decker" out loud to join the reverberant acoustic ghosts who live here. Then, fortifying myself with a sigh, I head for the patio.

Linda lounges by the pool, a tall, frosty glass in hand, staring up at a palm frond fragment fallen on the overhead screening. A thread of smoke wends upward from an ashtray on her lap. I pick up the pool skimmer and gently nudge the offending flora edgeward.

"You'll tear the screen," Linda says. "Sit down and have a cocktail for God's sake."

Knowing what I know about Linda and myself, I put the skimmer down, pour myself a glass of whatever golden elixir fills a Kool-Aid pitcher nearby—mango juice and vodka, I think—and sink into an adjacent lounge chair. Across the patio, I spot a wooden table with a small, brightly lit, artificial Christmas tree perched on it.

"Wow. Is that the same tree from … before?"

"Yes. I never turn it off anymore, except when I move it. I keep it going like a prayer wheel. The newfangled lights would make my life easier— they last a billion hours, as if anyone is counting—but maybe the tree would lose its … mojo. I tell people it wards off evil spirits, but I make it sound like a joke, you know? I don't want to freak them out."

Linda runs her fingers compulsively through her hair, and I notice that her nails are unpainted. No lipstick either. No makeup of any kind. It is as if she sacrificed her hues to the technicolor Christmas tree, leaving me to ponder what she keeps for herself. Even the mutable green of her eyes vanishes as she slides sunglasses down from her forehead and mutters, "Shit." Without knowing what she's referring to, I know the feeling.

"I like the tree," I tell her, understanding now as I never did when we were married the virtue of simple praise.

Linda taps her cigarette several more times than necessary, then turns to me, lifts her sunglasses, and makes rare eye contact. "That's a nice thing to say," she replies, surprising me further by leaving it at that. I nod and return to sipping my drink, hoping to wait in peaceable silence until Carl and Olivia appear. Linda, however, seems to be studying me.

"Bill, I'll tell you a story about the tree, but first tell me if you hate me."

I make eye contact now, trying to discern if I have wandered even deeper into the haunted forest than I had expected.

"That's an easy one. No."

"Don't you think about what happened? How can you *not* hate me a little?" Linda continues to tap her cigarette free of phantom ashes as I weigh the question.

"*If* I hate you a little," I say, "it's because I hate everything a little. I suppose I hate flowers and stars a little because I can't enjoy them for that much longer. So maybe there's some hatefulness I wake up with every morning, you know, like cosmic background radiation. But otherwise, no, I don't hate you. I mean, it's a nice day, nice house, both of us somewhat intact, so how bad could things have been if we ended up here?"

"Wow, that's convoluted even for a philosophy teacher."

"I know. Does that mean I don't have to hear about the tree?"

Linda smiles.

"Oh, no. I'm like, *totally* buying what you said. But I don't suppose it matters anyway. I spent all those years in courtrooms and deposition hearings, coping with lies I heard and lies I had to tell. I guess I can cope with your crap if that's what you're handing me. Anyway, Carl and I fought a couple of years ago—about sex."

"This better get back to the tree real fast."

Linda looks up through the patio screen as if imploring the gods to strike one of us down, but then continues. "See, *that's* why I needed to know if you hate me. I know you think I went to Carl for sex."

"You did."

Linda's face twists in frustration. "How about if I don't try to change your mind, and you let me tell my story?"

"Fair enough, up to a point."

"Anyway, it's true that right after I married Carl, we, you know, 'did it' like crazy for maybe a couple of weeks, but then, boom—it was over. At least for me. I about died from embarrassment. Everything fizzled out, and there we were. I apologized to Carl. I offered to move to another state. Write a letter he could show people to prove I was no good, a slut, a gold digger, whatever. Anything to avoid just calling it off and imagining the smug—no offense—look on your face. But Carl had the same problem. If I left him, even if it was all my fault, it still ended up looking like he fucked you over for no good reason, scamming you to get that money from selling our house. He couldn't stand to lose *all* your respect. Shit, other than that first time, we never had sex again until after we were married. He refused to commit adultery, not that I asked him to. That was Carl."

"Yes. I've always been grateful that he fucked me over for a good reason."

"Excuse me for not wanting those Cuban maniacs to kill him. You know very well that Carl just went along with my plan. The point is we decided to stay married. Agreed to a 'don't ask-don't tell' sexual etiquette. And up until a couple of years ago, it wasn't that bad. This house, even a cleaning service. Nice restaurants. Carl's buddies threw legal work my way. And you know Carl. Right now, I bet there's a couple hundred thousand squirreled away in the house."

Linda's version makes complete sense. I'm shocked never to have considered it.

"All right, you came to an understanding. Very adult. What happened?"

"As I said, we fought—summer before last, as I recall. Out of the blue, Carl said he loved me. That was okay, but then he said he wanted to resume marital intimacy. I said no. He got mad and, for spite, said he couldn't sleep with the Christmas tree lights on anymore. 'Either turn them off,' he said, 'or I'm sleeping in another bedroom.'" This was a potent threat in Linda's eyes since she hated to sleep alone.

"Couldn't you just keep the tree on in another room?"

"That's what I did, and that's when things started going to rack and ruin: the bogus bank shit, prison. One day I looked pretty good; the next day, I was an old crone. See, evil spirits attack you where you're weak, and Carl and I were very weak in the bedroom from our previous selfish ways and sleeping like strangers. But once Carl got incarcerated, I set the tree right back beside the bed. The tree wasted no time sending me a message about death and Carl getting out. I figured it was *my* death, lung cancer probably, but now, with Carl infected, I'm thinking magic is just as fickle as reality."

"So, what you told Ramona about Carl getting out was an actual … premonition, not something you had in the works?" I do my best to keep incredulity from creeping into my voice.

"Oh, I had stuff in the works: a couple of garden-variety appeals going nowhere. They had nothing to do with what the tree told me. So, yeah, I got a strong message."

Spirit trees and prophecies, Olivia's tiger-powered earrings, Sally's reunion letter. I remember how my boyhood radio, my incandescent Philco, found stations inaccessible to lesser models. Maybe I'm a cheap radio as far as magic is concerned, I surmise, unable to catch the signal. Then again, as every self-respecting mage and sorceress knows, even in magic, there's no free lunch. Once your love potion forces a woman to love you forever, it's a safe bet she'll become disfigured or insane pretty soon thereafter. Looking at Linda makes me feel overmatched by fate, so I close my eyes and listen to the low hum of the pool pump and distant thumps and shouts emanating from what is probably driveway basketball. I remember something else then, something from high school, a kind of riddle about how girls either like you or want to have sex with you, but never both.

"Since we're asking, Linda, do you like *me*?"

Linda sighs as if pained by a question she had hoped never to answer. "When we were married, I had you *and* Carl. Now I only have Carl, assuming he manages to stay out of prison. When you and I split up, I thought you'd stay mad for a few months and then we'd be friends again. You were always sweet that way. And I still miss our conversations. You talking about stars, French music, Plato, stuff like that. Carl talks about himself, and he's not as interesting as he thinks he is."

"I take it that's a yes?"

Linda takes in and expels a long, thoughtful drag of cigarette smoke, seemingly amused by a private thought. "It's weird, isn't it" she says, "how everything's about sex in the beginning; pursuit of the holy orgasm. Now I prefer conversation."

"Well, what with his condition, I don't suppose Carl will be pressing the sex issue."

Linda jabs out her cigarette, her face betraying a flicker of devastation. "Let's not jump off that particular bridge, okay?"

"Anyway, it's pretty peaceful here."

"Not peaceful. Dead. This neighborhood is a dreary snowbird ghetto." Linda gets up, walks to the patio screening, and looks out at the sun-flecked canal. In silhouette, there seems little of her to spare. High above the channel, I see what appears to be an osprey hovering. I happen to catch both its freefall plummet toward some hapless fish and its stuttering ascension as it tries to eat and fly simultaneously.

"Listen, Bill," Linda says, turning with hands on hips as if to face a jury. "Since you're here and being suspiciously nice, this must be the appointed time. What I mean is, it's time to tell Ramona Carl is her father, and I need you to tell her. I'm under some heavy, heavy shadows, as you know, so I can't do it. But roads have to meet; I see that now. What I just told you, I mean, you feel the forces at play, don't you? I know how sensitive you can be. That's why I laid myself open to you, Bill, and I hope … I hope you won't point any fingers."

"No," I said, "and I agree roads should meet. *Should* have met when Ramona was twelve or thirteen, around the age of accountability, if I remember my Bible school lessons."

"I know what you think, Bill. I'm only asking…"

"Don't worry; I'm not going to blame you for not telling her. Just be ready for a little roadkill coming your way. And speaking of carnage, she wondered why you brought up cancer and cigarettes the other day."

Linda shook her head. "That girl is strung tight as piano wire. You ask her one simple statistical question based on a powerful premonition, and she loses her mind. Frankly, Bill, I'm worried about her."

We both turn to the sound of the patio door sliding open. Olivia fairly bursts through in her bathing suit. "I told Uncle Carl about your girlfriend," she announces breathlessly. "We think she might be a white witch."

"Well shit, Bill," Linda says. "You've got a type."

Olivia cannonballs into the pool. A second later, Carl steps through the door in baggy surfer swim trunks, his torso covered with a veritable pelt of gray and white hair. He heads straight for me, clearly relishing my sudden romantic notoriety.

"Amazing, Billy Bob, the women you attract. You're like—what's it called—a lodestone?"

"Attracts and ultimately repels," I answer. Carl chortles, takes a seat beside me, and flashes Linda a peace sign.

"Neither one of you ever brought me a minute's peace," she says, lifting a single finger. Carl bellows like a drunk at a comedy club.

"Let's ease on down to the dock, Professor. Linda can get her precious peace, and you and I can parley." As he speaks, Carl looks pointedly at his hand, drawing my attention to a small box.

"I'm going too," Olivia shouts between splashes.

"Give us a head start, honey, fifteen, twenty minutes. I'll give you a holler when I'm done with the professor."

"You can come with us now," I call to Olivia. "We'll wait."

"No, no, Bill," Carl says in a hush-hush voice. "This is big stuff Olivia might not be ready for."

I see Linda walk over to check on her totem tree. And Olivia hauling herself eagerly from the pool, little semi-precious turquoise tigresses dangling from her ears. And I imagine Hermine watching, listening, as I give Carl a fatherly pat on the arm.

"You just went to prison, my friend, for saying stuff you didn't want anyone else to hear. If Olivia shouldn't hear it, then maybe you shouldn't say it. See what I mean?"

Carl nods. "Sure, sure, I get it, but this is personal between you and me; nothing shady."

The box. *Uncle Carl has something to give you,* Olivia had told me. *He has a shiny thing on a string,* Hermine had warned, *ready to hypnotize you.*

"Whatever it is, Olivia needs to start seeing us for who we are. If I go, she goes." Carl shoots me a long stare, trying to figure my angle. What he concludes seems to amuse him.

"Okay, Professor. I see everyone has gone nuts while I was away. You win." He is already on his feet, calling Olivia. "Get a move on, sweetie pie. Let's get this party started."

Party. Hardly the word of a chastened man, but perfect for Carl. As he saunters away, I see Linda flagging me down with her eyes, reminding me of what I must do, and Olivia seizing a towel, ready for anything. I suddenly wonder how we even coexist, each of us seemingly a different species. And *that*, as both Carl and Hermine would point out, is your problem—wasting time wondering about useless shit.

"Sharks," Linda calls to Olivia, as if the word requires no explanation. Maybe someone spotted a shark in the channel, or maybe Linda wants to warn Olivia about the company she keeps.

CHAPTER NINE

"Dock of the Bay"

Gainesville, Florida, 1979

One late summer evening in 1979, I found myself sitting on Carl Decker's dock singing "Dock of the Bay" over the muted din of his housewarming party, which was still going strong past midnight. Beyond the dock appeared no Frisco Bay, just a small, tranquil lake nestled on Gainesville's outer margin—no tide to roll away. But *I left my home in Georgia* was accurate enough for both Otis and me.

An unknown creature splashed in the weedy shallows to my left: frog, fish, coot, egret, even a gator maybe. Anything was possible. Here I was, after all, attending a party hosted by a friend who had slept with my former wife, Karen, just a few days after our divorce. I suppose not technically adultery, but in spirit, Carl had broken the male code's first commandment.

So why the hell was I here?

For one thing, Carl's father, Albert Decker, who stood high in my affections, had died earlier in '79 of a heart attack on the heels of my own father's death a year earlier. Accordingly, I felt the need to pay respects beyond the formalities of a funeral where Carl and I barely spoke. For another thing, one of Carl's acquaintances had rigged the hiring decision responsible for my current employment. I had applied to the college without much hope, then received a call two weeks ago telling me I had the job: no face-to-face interview, no drug test. Elated, I accepted on the spot. Carl called the next day, making no secret of his thumb on the scale. "Come on, Professor, let's bury the old hatchet; it's been three years." Putting aside the virtue of forgiveness, Carl had me. Renouncing him meant rejecting a plum job, and I wasn't about to do that. In the end, I conceded as little as possible by promising him, "I won't act like an enemy." Of course, I had no enemies list and no appetite for starting one with Carl's name, which brings me to the other reason I came to Carl's party: the ten-year friendship we shared before he bedded Karen.

A good deal of what remains in this narrative concerns Carl, but for now, I'll just mention that Carl was a newly returning Vietnam vet when I met him in a philosophy class at the University of Florida in 1969. The mentally broken, chemically poisoned soldier returning from that war became a terrible cliché, but Carl appeared to be anything but damaged goods. Back then, he had the look of a "jungle warrior," as he called himself, all wiry muscle and skinned to the scalp. You may reasonably picture me at the time as the classic bookish introvert yanked out of his existential doldrums by a cocky, charismatic, pot-smoking badass. In any case, our friendship took hold, and as far as I could tell on the evening of Carl's party, some tenacious fragments of it had survived.

Our initial encounter at the housewarming party lacked drama. Carl greeted me as one more in a steady stream of guests; no moment of truth, just a wink. Since his father's funeral, his frame had thickened, and he'd grown a lush, reddish beard; his sun-streaked hair had fallen to shoulder-length, like an extra in a Viking movie.

After exiting Carl's reception line, I wound through animated clusters of grad students and young professional types with ritual beer bottles in hand. My momentum carried me past the spacious, tastefully furnished, arts-and-craftsy living room and out through expansive glass doors opening on a dock and small lake beyond a lush lawn. The noise of revelers behind me pushed me down to the lake, sky, trees, and other hidden life, life with no opinions to consider—a respite from the hit-and-miss improvisations of human crowds. I love people, but only certain people at certain times.

On the other hand, I never tire of trees and massed water and the wheeling expanse above parading its innumerable, scattered clumps of burning gases. The poet Gerard Manley Hopkins thought of stars as "firefolk" clustering in galactic towns and suburbs, and I suppose if God is alive and purposefully afoot; then *everything* could well be alive, including stars. Anyway, similarly starstruck, I sank into a rickety Adirondack chair and began singing "Dock of the Bay." As a bonus, out in the sky beyond the lake, lightning flickered like an erratic lighthouse.

As I sang to myself, I heard someone approach, a woman with a glass in one hand and either a cigarette or a joint in the other. I suspected Carl had sent her my way as a step in the peace process. She plopped down in the chair next to me with a groan and handed me the glass. Her face wore what I would call a pleasant sneer, as if she had witnessed a few beguiling things within a generally distasteful life.

"Oh cool, heat lightning," she said.

"That's a misnomer; it's just lightning too far away for us to hear the thunder."

"Damn. Now I'm going deaf too."

"Too?"

"Sorry. Bad joke. I tend toward self-pity. I'm diabetic, and I'm not supposed to drink. But I do. My eyes are going. The doctor says I'll be blind in a few years if I don't straighten up."

"Maybe you should straighten up."

"Pretty soon. I'm trying to switch to pot."

"I'm sure your eyes will thank you."

The woman was trim, pale, and short-haired. She looked a little like a prettier Edith Piaf. I stared at her a bit more than politeness would allow, hoping she would not notice me trying to decide if she was beautiful. Her besieged eyes were inaccessible in the minimal light.

"That's Jim Beam and ice," she said, confirming my suspicion. She was Carl's emissary.

"And I'm Linda," she added, offering me what was now obviously not a cigarette.

"I'm Bill." I declined the joint, eliciting a shrug.

"Carl told me. By the way, what were you just singing? It sounded familiar."

"Otis Redding. 'Sittin on the Dock of the Bay.' An all-time favorite of mine."

"And here you are. It must be a sign."

"I hope not. It's a killer tune, but the words are depressing as hell. Nothing to live for and so forth."

"Finally, an honest song." Linda put her bare feet up on a tackle box as if she intended to stay awhile. She wore black capris and an unadorned black T-shirt. Androgynous but not mannish. A tortured artist, maybe. "I was all about country music back in the day," she mused. "'Ring of Fire.' 'Stand by Your Man.' Patsy Cline. Maybe 'Wichita Lineman' if I was desperate. Stuff like that."

"Well, 'Dock of the Bay' isn't country by a long shot, but it does have that 'poor lonesome me' feel. Otis died in a plane crash just after recording it. Maybe the lyrics were premonitory."

"My goodness. How you talk. When was that?"

"Nineteen sixty-seven. December. I was a senior in high school."

"You remember that?"

"Clear as day. Otis and I are both from Georgia. I used to listen to R&B stations out of Atlanta late at night when I should have been asleep. I'd heard of him because he wrote 'Respect.' You know, the Aretha Franklin song."

"I know that one. R-E-S-P-E-C-T."

"Aretha added that."

"Good to know."

Out of words, I sipped Jim Beam.

"Tired of the party?" Linda asked.

"No, the party's fine. I just like it out here."

She flipped the dead remnant of a joint into the lake and shook her head. "Is it the bugs or the humidity you like best?"

"Neither. Although both are big bonuses." I waved my arms. "It's the cosmic view. You can peer as far out into the universe as your senses will take you. See the Big Dipper up there?"

She looked up, squinting. "It's pretty fuzzy, but maybe."

"Well, anyway, the ancient Greeks called it The Great Bear. Homer mentions it in the *Odyssey*. He says Odysseus kept those same stars to his left-hand side as he sailed east, trying to get home after the witch Calypso set him free. The point being I can sit here, put the Great Bear to my left, and imagine I'm sailing with Odysseus. Of course, he had the goddess Athena conjuring up favorable winds. I seem to be on my own."

"Not entirely; I'm a goddess-witch myself."

"How about stirring us up a cool breeze then?"

"Not my specialty. But I'm excellent at confusing people."

"Speaking of confusion, see the water out there?"

"Hey, I'm not blind yet."

"Sorry. The point is that water hasn't worn out in all the eons since it became water. It might evaporate, but it rains itself back into a lake or river or swimming pool sooner or later. It doesn't die or lose its liquidity, at least not in any time frame we can grasp. And we're mostly water, right? Don't you find it ironic that we're made of this indestructible stuff, and yet we're very fragile? I can sit here and think about the fact that I'm evaporating and immortal at the same time. How's that for confusing?"

Linda continued to peer starward while I was talking. Now she looked at me, sizing me up as far as I could tell in the available light.

"Well, well," she said, "Carl warned me you were 'out there.' A philosophy teacher, right?"

"We'll see. My next class in about a week and a half will be my first. I'm not sure how much wisdom anyone can love at eight o'clock in the morning."

"Love? I never had to love anything in my law classes. Not even the damn law. I didn't know how easy I had it."

"Figure of speech. I don't plan on asking my students to love anything either. I'll just say 'pass all your tests, and you'll get a B. If you can figure out your part in everything that has ever happened to you, then convince me in five hundred words or less that you succeeded, you'll get an A.' Very fair, I think. Open book test, just like life."

Linda shook her head. "Horrible idea. Doomed to failure. What other skills do you have to fall back on?"

"Welder, loan shark, disc jockey. Some combination of those. Carl could bankroll me."

"As his lawyer, I'm going to advise him against that."

"Wow. Carl has a *consigliere*. You're Tom from *The Godfather*."

"No, alas, I'm the barely-scraping-by lawyer who kept him from getting screwed when he sold his father's business and bought this little corner of paradise, which I furnished by the way. Now he thinks if he runs into trouble with his weed farm, I'll keep his ass out of jail. I keep telling him I'm not that kind of lawyer. I hope he doesn't have to find out the hard way. The one thing they forget to tell you in law school is not to have any friends."

"Weed farm?"

"You didn't know? Good. Maybe the narcs don't either. Yeah, it's out near an abandoned quarry. Carl bought this house so he could keep an eye on his operation. One of his best customers got you your job, by the way."

"Great; more karmic debt. And from the look on your face I'll bet you couldn't wait to tell me that."

"Wicked pleasures *are* the best, I'll admit."

"Speaking of pleasures, does Carl still have his Tampa house?"

"He'll never sell that. I can see why. It would be a perfect house to go blind in. One floor. Easy to get around in. Steady breeze off the water."

"So, you've been there. I kind of fell in love in that house one night."

Linda gives a like-minded nod. "It's definitely got that vibe."

Carl's women, as I remembered, tended blond and energetic, hardly a description of Linda. I had a hunch that Linda and Carl had not slept together but was appalled to be venturing a guess at all. My thoughts, like raindrops returning to a lake, seemed to be seeking their lowest level.

"I know that quarry; I fell off Carl's motorcycle and broke my arm there."

"Hmm. Now that you know where Carl grows his weed, I guess that makes you an accessory after the fact."

"You're the one facilitating a criminal enterprise."

"True," Linda said, "but Carl's been nice as pie to me. And he pays me. A decent retainer. As long as being a criminal is his only tragic flaw…"

Linda seemed to be waiting for me to add another.

I gave a shrug I hoped seemed enigmatic.

"Ah," she said, "so we're cagey about Carl. I wonder what that means."

"Nothing," I answered, a little more darkly than I intended.

Linda exhaled a cloud of pot smoke toward the stars.

"'Nothing comes from nothing,'" she recited. "Speak again."

"What?"

"I think it's a line from Shakespeare. But whatever, you get the point."

"My wife—ex-wife—used to call me Shakespeare because of my name. You know, William Shaffer. Plus, I had a pretentious vocabulary even back then. Anyway, to blazes with Carl and nothingness. Let's get back to enjoying the bugs."

"Hold that magnificent thought, Bill. I need a drink. And you need another one. I'll be right back."

I turned to watch her step gingerly up the dark slope and into the frame of bright windows. Suddenly restless, I stood up, walked to the end of the dock, sat back down, and dangled my shoes, not quite brushing the skin of the lake. Off to my right, I noticed Carl's little Sunfish rocking gently, and given past events, I saw not just a boat, but the pattern it completed—me, Carl, a sailboat, and a woman.

In the first instance, as previously noted, that woman was my ex-wife, Karen Levine, and the configuration she and I had formed with Carl and his sailboat led to love, betrayal, divorce, and so forth. Now I wondered how paranoid I would be to see the Sunfish and Linda as new elements in a recurring pattern? A "true" pattern?

Permit me to digress and explain what I mean by a "true pattern."

First, Karen "borrowed" the last name Levine from her stepfather, Gibson Levine, to help him facilitate the covert transfer of certain assets should the IRS finally make their move. My full dealings with the Levines will find their place later in this account, but for now, it's enough to know that Gibson Levine, a sports bookie who "retired" to Florida, took me under his wing for a time.

In any case, Gibson had used what he called "true patterns"—such as a team's batting average against left-handed pitchers—to separate gamblers from their money. This type of pattern recognition, he explained, was just smart. However, to be wise, you had to discern and cope with the "false patterns" invented by your desires.

"You do understand, do you not, that constellation you call the Great Bear does not resemble a bear?" By chance, Levine had invoked stars beloved to me; stars Odysseus had followed home to Ithaca. Having piqued my interest, he went on to describe something called "apophenia," an obsessive inclination to see meaningful connections between unrelated things. In the worst case, he said, it led to schizophrenia. In the case of hunch gamblers—his steady customers—it usually led to poverty.

"And likewise," he had continued, "I trust you understand that my niece Karen, or rather the version of her you are amorously inventing, may not resemble the young woman herself?"

When I argued that patterns and resemblances rooted in love, and not logic, might be valid, Levine had not bothered to disagree.

"Yes, of course, William," was his surprising reply as he shuffled and dealt cribbage cards. Picking up my hand, I felt I had scored a point to compensate for my woeful showing at cribbage. Levine, looking tired, glanced up at me and ventured one more question.

"How much more time, William, do you suppose the average human being spends obsessing about what they *desire*, as opposed to understanding their part in everything that happens to them?" Levine didn't bother to wait for the obvious answer but proceeded to trounce me again at cribbage.

"Oh shit."

I turned to see Linda approaching the dock, teetering, holding glasses aloft in each hand like a circus acrobat. I scrambled to help her.

"Oh my God," she gasped. "I almost fell."

"What happened?"

"Nothing. Just a little woozy."

"There's that nothing again," I said. "Quite a little pest, isn't it?" Linda laughed weakly. I grabbed the glasses and guided her into her chair, fearing a diabetic collapse. Her plight brought to mind my mother's friend back in Hopperton, Mrs. Gracewell, a very fat woman with an opulent flower garden. As a boy, I often accompanied my mother on her visits to Mrs. Gracewell, knowing I would consume butter cookies and sweet tea. Her garden was a paradise for ruby-throated hummingbirds who, like me, came for the nectar. I also remembered Mrs. Gracewell blithely injecting herself with insulin in front of us and the dread that arose in me as I watched. A little of that dread reentered me now.

"I'll drink these; you need a break." Linda tilted her head back and closed her eyes, offering no objection. Mrs. Gracewell had entered a diabetic coma and passed away that same night. Linda was neither fat nor old, but my apprehension heightened a little nevertheless.

"What I need," Linda said, after a few seconds of silence, "is your pancreas. Can I have it?"

"As soon as I'm done with it, sure."

She managed the barest chuckle. "Don't think I haven't heard that one before."

We lapsed into recuperative silence. Leaning back, I saw the moon near its zenith, a white balloon leaking a little air. Four days past full. My father, who hunted at night, had insisted I learn to "mark the moon." I had kept the habit, and therefore knew the moon had slipped the modern mind; no one knew her phases anymore, her tidal eminence, except maybe a few retrograde poets. How I felt about the moon mirrored how Carl felt about sailing winds and how my restless, ambitious ex-wife viewed the future. Look at *this*, we all say, all pointing at different phenomena. I suddenly wondered where Linda's troubled eyes were looking. I turned and asked if she was okay. She nodded.

"I think I'm back to my normal rate of deterioration."

We chatted a bit more. Linda lived in Micanopy, known to me then as a hip little tourist town selling anything secondhand under the rubric of "antique." I lived in Gainesville proper, near (but not in) the relatively ritzy "Duck Pond" neighborhood, in a little apartment over a perpetually empty garage.

"What the hell?" Carl's voice boomed from up the slope. Moments later, he strode onto the dock and glared at us with mock sternness, as if we were naughty children.

"There is no hell, Carl," Linda countered pleasantly. "I thought we'd been over that."

"For what I'm paying you, you'd better be right." Carl's face radiated delight at the badinage.

"Absolutely," Linda said. "An airtight case."

I noticed Carl was carrying a cigar box.

"What's with the humidor?"

Carl looked puzzled. "Humidor?"

"Cigar box, Carl. Did some lucky woman have your baby?"

He snickered at the thought. "No man, you know better than that. And what's in here is much better than cigars." Carl, who had rappelled from helicopters and fought hand-to-hand in Vietnam, opened the lid on what appeared to be a collection of dried human ears. A thrill of horror passed through me.

"Magic mushrooms!" Linda cried, clapping her hands. "Instant philosophy!" She reached into the box and grabbed a few "ears."

"I'm no match for these now," she told Carl, "but can I take them for later?"

"Help yourself. We found a bunch of 'shrooms in a pasture near power lines. Maybe they're supercharged." As Carl extolled his psychedelic treasure chest, Linda looked around like she'd lost something.

"Shit," she muttered, "I don't have a purse. Bill, do you have an extra pocket, and can you give me a ride? I'm in no shape to drive. Oh, and Carl, we'll need a baggie. If these babies mix with Bill's sweat, he'll be flying."

Carl acquiesced with a smirk, clearly relishing developments. He had worn the same wolfish expression while arranging the sailboat excursion that sealed my fate with my former wife, Karen.

"I'll drive you home, but you carry the contraband. As I said, I don't need a lawyer, and I'd like to keep it that way."

CHAPTER TEN

"Angel of the Morning"

W e walked up to the house, Linda weaving ahead to visit the
powder room.
"She's a mess," Carl said.
"Thanks."

He clapped me on the back.

"Hey, if she's too much for you, just drop her off and come back. You
can crash here. I'm heading out to the quarry tomorrow; you should come."
His voice rang with smooth, familiar warmth. I had come to his party—
what more did he need to know? I realized then that Carl would offer no
further *mea culpa* about sleeping with Karen.

Here's the old friendship—take it or leave it.

"What's at the quarry?" I asked, playing dumb.

"Wild blackberries, like before, only millions of them. I fertilized a
little. Now I'm thinking about marketing Uncle Carl's Blackberry Jam."

In fact, "Uncle Carl's" sold a shitpot of jam over the next few years, a
few actual jars and thousands more according to invoices paid with laun-
dered marijuana dollars.

"Is it safe out there?" If Carl sensed what I was getting at, he didn't
show it.

"Safe? From who? It's just scrubland, dude, palmetto, worthless trees. I
guess a wild pig could get you if you weren't careful. In case anyone gets too
curious, I put up a big sign announcing plans to reopen the quarry, no date.
Come to think of it; I might just do that." He chuckled at his boldness.

Look, Carl, I could have said, you dallied with my wife and sell weed. Thanks for a lovely evening, but I won't be back.

"Do you still ride out there?" I asked instead. Up until my broken arm and concussion, Carl and I had ridden his Husqvarna 250 motocross bike around a slick, crash-prone, rock-strewn loop he had laid out inside the quarry.

"Yeah, I ride sometimes, but not there; noise attracts attention. Also, it traumatizes the plants."

"Bad for the blackberries?"

Carl smirked. "Yeah, the fucking blackberries."

I flipped on the Studebaker's radio (tinkered back to life by Carl's father) to blot out Linda's snoring. The college DJ spoke in secretive half-whispers as if he and his listeners were sharing songs banned by the government. At some point, he played "Broken Arrow" by Buffalo Springfield, a song I'd first heard in late 1967, lying in bed, waiting for midnight to cover my forbidden visits to a girl named Wanda Grice.

Broken arrow.

I had no idea what the song meant, something about weddings and funerals and Indians waving from riverbanks, but Neil Young's mournful falsetto matched my memories of Don Heffelfinger and his crossbow, and all that followed, like a deliberate soundtrack. Not able to help myself, I cranked up the volume.

Linda groaned, sat up, and after a long silence, wondered if she'd died and come back to life or whether she was still dreaming.

"Out of one dream and into another," I ventured.

"No," she insisted. "I lost myself on the frozen road."

The "frozen road," wherever it led, turned out to be a thoroughfare created by the magic mushroom Linda had eaten in Carl's bathroom.

"I took one big bite," she confessed. "It was so bitter I thought I'd pass out, but I kept it down. Now it's all shining in there."

As Linda luminesced, we followed 441 past Payne's Prairie, south to Micanopy, entering through a tunnel of live oaks and drooping Spanish moss made horror-movie eerie by our shape-shifting headlights. We pulled up and parked on the main street, directly in front of the Cholokka Vintage Emporium. Linda lived above the store in an apartment reached by a side stairway. She insisted I come up.

"I have something to show you," she said, grabbing my arm and grinning with madcap insinuation. Up we went. Linda ordered me to wait, then went inside.

"Now come in," she called, beckoning me into darkness. As I stepped inside, she switched on the lights of a small tabletop Christmas tree.

"That's my happiness." She pointed to the tree. "We should always try to be happy, right?"

No argument. The tree was artificial but lushly branched, strung with multicolored bulbs and topped with a woven straw angel playing a straw guitar. As I stood contemplating the effect, Linda stashed her mushrooms in a drawer of the tree's supporting table, then sank into the shadows of her couch with an eloquent moan. The tree offered enough light to show a small, spare living room with a tiny alcove kitchen off to the left. I noticed a shelf of fat books above a desk, probably law books. I stood with arms folded, awaiting developments that took their sweet time.

"So that's what happiness looks like," I commented finally. "I'm glad somebody knows."

"I only know what *my* undersized happiness looks like. That's why—" Linda stopped herself and groaned in dismay, apparently at some inner obstacle. "Shit, this is weird," she muttered, then fixed me with an odd stare. "You have to answer a question first, Bill."

"First before what?"

She tranced for a second, maybe resting at a psychedelic oasis. I waited some more.

"Carl said you would be good for me. Is that true?"

I assumed she'd invited me up for sex, or at least to test the waters, but Linda's use of the phrase "good for me" gave me pause. That and the intense stare she leveled at me as she spoke.

"What do you mean by 'good'?"

"I'll tell you if you sit down. I can't think with you hovering over me like a cop." I sank onto the small couch, trying to ignore the fact that our thighs were touching. Linda attacked my question the second I was off my feet.

"Well, not 'good for me' as in the opposite of evil. More like good for me as in a month's vacation. Or better yet, good for me like a man for all seasons." She offered me a lopsided smile.

"Wow. And Carl claimed I fit that description?"

"No. That's my embarrassing romance novel fantasy. He just said you'd be good for me."

"He prescribed me like medicine?"

"I suppose. Are you good medicine?" The sheer eccentricity of the question demanded an answer.

"Well, let's see. I have a poor track record with women and relationships in general. My first wife divorced me based on an unpromising non-career. And I can't even say I *want* to be good for anyone—no offense—it sounds too much like a job. How am I doing so far?"

Linda emitted a weird bleat of frustration and banged her head against the back of the couch.

"Okay, you don't think I'm sexy. That's cool, neither do I. It's just not in my bag of tricks."

I felt bad to have my words taken as rejection, thereby breaking the quirky spell trying to capture me. "Look," I said, "you're incredibly attractive, but let's take a break from trying to figure each other out. Got any beer?"

"As you wish, sir." Linda got up and feigned a little curtsy. I suspected I would be leaving soon.

But Linda put *Electric Ladyland* on her portable record player, smiled, and handed me a Corona from the fridge. She mouthed a line from "Watchtower" about a kindly thief and resumed our close quarters. I drank my beer, glad to have a use for my hands.

Maybe thirty seconds passed before Linda jumped up and walked over to the lone window facing the street. She appeared to be weighing things by a private algorithm. Then she went over to her desk, pulled out a large book, and brought it back to the couch. After turning on a nearby floor lamp, she held the book up. Its title, embossed in understated gold letters on a dark red cover, was *The Female Orgasm*. Linda opened the book and riffled through onionskin-thin pages typical of bibles. She tapped the cover.

"*This* is what I wanted to show you, which I find myself doing despite your somewhat shitty attitude." She displayed the book in one hand, using a finger of her other hand like a teacher's pointer to highlight the word "Orgasm." I had to believe she was still under the influence of that magic mushroom.

"I've never had one of *these*, Bill. This book didn't help. Shit, it's over a thousand pages. It made things worse. It shouldn't matter that much, but

I've got it into my head that I'm, like, eating and not swallowing. I tried a couple of black guys because, you know, they're bigger, but that didn't do the trick. And my diabetes is worse than I told you before because I can't stop drinking from worrying about my diabetes and going blind and never having an orgasm. I'm fucked, but not in a good way." She forced a ragged laugh, looked at me, and waited.

"When you say 'good for me,' you mean…" Seeing that I seemed more curious than appalled, Linda perked up, eager to elaborate.

"I mean, I don't think expertise or size is the problem. *I'm* the problem. I need to relax, to be with someone *nice* who I can maybe get a crush on. That's how Carl described you. Anyway, if I'm freaking you out, we can go get my car right now."

"Not necessary. I'm only *slightly* freaking out, and I haven't finished my beer." Not that I'd admit it, but Linda's radical honesty had won me over. I recognized us now, sex or not, as natives of the same bewildered tribe.

Linda reshelved the orgasm book, then walked over to the Christmas tree table and opened its drawer. *Please*, I thought, *no more mushrooms*.

"I keep spare bulbs in here," she explained. "None of the lights on the tree are the original ones. I just keep replacing them, keep the tree going, keep myself going. I'm only in my thirties, but I already think of myself as running out of spare parts. It's ridiculous. It makes me do ridiculous things. I tell myself I need to get a grip, but I don't change inside. Do you know what I mean?" She turned for an answer, weirdly aglow in the multifarious hues of Christmas lights.

"Nobody's got anything but spare parts," I said. "Every cell you were born with is long dead. Given that fact, some deep thinkers say the *idea* of you—Linda—must have existed before you did, maybe in God's brain. Anyway, according to them, the idea of "Linda" is eternal and will continue *ad infinitum* after your physical body finally exhausts its supply of Christmas lights."

Linda brightened, warming to the implications of my garden-variety philosophizing. "Even after I die," she realized with a kind of simmering glee, "even *if* there's no heaven or hell to take me in, I'll still be floating around *out there*, waiting to hitch a ride on another body when it becomes available."

"Well," I said, "not to burst your bubble, but technically it will only be the *idea* of you floating around. Nothing to write home about from a human-interest perspective."

Linda fairly scurried back to the couch. "That's got to be it," she exclaimed, squeezing my knee in a manner reminiscent of Sally Chiles in the Hopperton High lunchroom. "*That's* why I don't change much inside." She was breathing fast, searching my eyes for confirmation.

What followed wasn't the best kiss I'd ever been a party to, a little bitter-tasting and hesitant, yet it brought on life's pent-up sweetness in full flood, a sweetness painful in its rarity, a sweetness that beckoned love, whether it came or not. Far too soon, Linda sat back, groaned, and put her hands over her face.

"It's that mushroom," she moaned. "Why did I eat it?"

"Don't blame the mushroom. As far as that goes, why blame anything? Wasn't our … entanglement, shall we say, the idea all along?"

"I guess, but I'm usually all theory, all talk. Now it's way past bizarre."

"How ironic; I'm just starting to get comfortable."

Linda studied me for a moment. "It's probably the mushroom talking, but you have a nice blue aura now that I swear wasn't there before." With that, she got up and replaced Hendrix with a scratchy Hank Williams record, while I scoured her refrigerator and found the makings for scrambled eggs and cheese toast. As Hank applied his twangy genius to lovelorn self-pity, Linda attacked my makeshift breakfast with the crude gusto of someone alone and starving. Finally, she looked up, made an impish face, and said, "I feel a little closer to that orgasm already."

I laughed like I hadn't for a long time.

But despite the joke, we agreed it was too soon and too contrived to pursue that particular ambition. And anyway, neither one of us had condoms. I slept on the couch, waking early, cramped and sore. When I peeked into Linda's bedroom, she was sleeping naked on her stomach. Not to make too much of it now, but a shaft of light from the window fell across the bed, across her back and bottom, and I couldn't look away. I gazed in silence for a long, breathless moment, and with a purer admiration than I could plausibly explain, because there would never be another first time to see her this way. Finally, I closed her door as far as I could without risking a sound and made my way out, passing the dormant Christmas tree. It seemed only right to illuminate it before I left.

In one of my undergraduate philosophy classes, we got onto the topic of infinite parallel universes. Walking out of Linda's apartment, wearing clothes I had slept in, having (I thought) agreed to an as-yet-unspecified ritual of sexual healing *a la* Marvin Gaye, I felt I had shifted two or three universes away—not a large number when compared to infinity, but still an unnerving sidestep.

I hoped this universe offered coffee and pancakes. Happily, within a block, I stood outside a bistro of sorts called, I swear, Out of Tyme. Inside, old photographs covered the walls, many of bygone travelers posing next to stagecoaches. A sign above the diner-style counter read "Any picture $25."

Since I grew up on Stagecoach Road in a town also along 441, I wondered idly if the same stagecoach had stopped both here and there. The particular picture I studied featured a man clutching a carpetbag, staring into the camera with a look that managed to be both hopeful and doleful at the same time, an expression I suspected I conveyed. Was he meeting his mail-order bride or running from the law? Was he a field hand hoping to get hired by a Chicago timber speculator? Was I, in horror movie fashion, looking at an earlier incarnation of myself?

A young waitress in pigtails, flannel shirt, and candy-apple red lipstick set a cup of hazelnut coffee in front of me, then moved on to another customer without speaking. She was a prototype grunge-angel well before Nirvana, wearing world-weariness like jewelry.

I tried to make eye contact, but she wasn't having it. Our universes may have been parallel, but they definitely were not touching. *Buckwheat pancakes, free refills, and a good tip*, she signaled with a capitalistic smile. *Let's leave it at that.*

The buckwheat pancakes were gritty but filling. Not wishing to acknowledge her effect on me, I left my waitress a scrupulous 15 percent tip. On a whim, I bought the stagecoach picture, stuck it in the Studebaker's trunk, then called Carl from a pay phone. No answer. Had I agreed to the quarry excursion? I couldn't remember. I decided to go home (*tiny garage apartment*), clean up, then head over to Carl's. Linda could sleep. Carl would have her phone number; I didn't even know her last name. We would get her car to her later. Then I could go home, back to my solitary state, and shake off the dream I seemed to have entered. Except, of course, it wasn't a dream. Sleep all you want; you wake up to where your life left off, only with less time to change it.

CHAPTER ELEVEN

"Killing Me Softly"

I didn't worry about Carl heading to the quarry without me. The morning sun, as far as I knew, never touched him unless he was sailing. And sure enough, I found him sprawled on a recliner, still in his bathrobe, reading the newspaper; I hadn't bothered to knock.

"Well," he asked without looking up, "did you get in her pants?"

"Linda can fill you in at your next briefing," I said. "I'd hate to spoil the surprise."

"Nothing to spoil, amigo," Carl said, flinging the paper aside. "She already spilled the beans. She called, wondering where the hell you are. She needs her car, man."

"If you know what happened, why ask?"

"Yeah, well, you get in the habit of suspecting everything in my line of work, no offense."

"Since when is trust fund baby a line of work?"

Carl wagged his finger at me. "Sticks and stones, Professor. I'm just playing the hand I was dealt and playing it way better than *some* people I know."

"You're right, Carl," I admitted. "Forget what I just said. Let's face it; I'm not that good at being a wiseass. And if your point is that you've outsmarted life and life has outsmarted me, what can I say? But the last time I checked—and I've checked pretty often— pride still goeth before a fall, no matter how smart you are."

"It's funny how you atheists always sound religious. Linda's got a saying about rich people, camels, needles in a haystack, and missing out on heaven if you hang onto your money. But I don't see her turning down her paycheck."

"I grant you we're all hypocrites—stop the presses. But even a liar can speak the truth. And speaking of truth, what exactly did Linda say when she 'spilled the beans'?"

Carl stretched grandiloquently. "I thought we might get back to that little topic. Can't remember it word for word, but she spouted some crazy bullshit about you being the best piece of ass she "might" ever have because you were nice to her tree. She sounded high as a kite and half-asleep. Like I told you before, she's a crazy bitch. So, how was *she* in the sack?"

Carl had missed the evasion in Linda's answer. I answered in the same spirit: "Lovely, especially in the morning light."

Carl headed for the shower, barking "quarry at fourteen hundred hours." I dropped into his recliner and began to reassemble the *Gainesville Sun*, noticing in passing that he had circled several menial jobs in the help wanted section. Well, an answer to *that* puzzlement would have to wait.

The quarry road lay some distance out Archer Road, a few miles past Lake Kanapaha, a watering hole where William Bartram had camped two centuries ago under live oaks that still stand. Of course, in so-called modern times, you're unlikely to see black wolves feeding on a horse's carcass. What you will see is fences, the promise of future developers to gorge on the land itself.

As we drove along, I asked Carl about the help wanted ads he had circled in the paper. "Codes, no shit. I got the idea from a spy novel. I place ads to tell certain people certain things about my business. They place ads to let me know they got the message. Shit gets done, and nobody's hung out to dry. No names or phone numbers, just PO boxes. It's totally foolproof." This scheme was Carl outsmarting life, as was a ragged red bandanna innocently tied to a strand of fencing to mark an otherwise invisible shortcut to the quarry. That path had once been an asphalt road, now reduced to ruts, with chunks of asphalt embedded in it like chocolate chips in ice cream.

The pleasant morning weather persisted into the afternoon. Gathering clouds seemed likely to fall short of a storm. Carl inhaled two joints as we drove along, seemingly unaffected. I took a courtesy toke, which transformed me into a baffled zombie. No matter. When ragged foliage suddenly gave way to the quarry clearing, my reborn memory likewise burned the marijuana fog away. We parked and stood at the rim of a deep, rocky hole about a football field across. Weeds, erosion, and a handful of years had obscured the course we used to circle on Carl's motocross bike, but its singular landmark, a massive central boulder which had snapped my right forearm back in the day, shone in the sun like a crudely polished jewel.

Carl cautioned me not to trip over a rusty iron spike that had been driven into the earth near me to align with a second red bandanna visible across the chasm. "If you follow their line straight back," he said, "you'll find a bright yellow cannabis bandanna. Quite a coincidence, huh?"

"Amazing. What about the blackberries? Is there a black bandanna somewhere?" Carl stared at me with drug-brightened glee. "No, but sure as shit, there will be soon." He then did a full 360-degree rotation, seeming to signify the vastness of some unspoken plan. "Hey, Professor, would you mind moving the truck over by the sign?" The sign stood to the left, across the clearing. It announced the quarry's reopening in the near, unspecified future by an entity known as "Decker Brothers, Inc." I called to Carl, asking about his heretofore unmentioned brother. "Don't have one," he called back. "It just sounds more ... more..."

"Dishonest? Bogus? Impressive?" I suggested.

"That's exactly it!" he cried. "Wright brothers, Parker brothers, Marx brothers. You get the picture. Shit, you could be a Decker brother yourself. Who'd know the difference?"

As I was about to point out that *I'd* know the difference, a black Lincoln Continental entered the clearing by the public road and parked next to the Datsun. Its passengers, I hoped, were Carl's reason for coming to the quarry, not the premature burial of my career in the person of agents from the ATF, FBI—what difference did it make what acronym was on the badge? Then the driver's window slid down, and a lumpy man challenging the elasticity of a stained purple polo shirt muttered something unintelligible—until the last word: "Daker," as in "faker." Relieved, I looked around to where Carl had been standing, but "Daker" was nowhere in sight. I shouted for him. No answer. He had to have heard me. I shouted again. Again, no answer. A second large man, wearing a powder blue suit and an incompatible Panama hat, emerged from the Lincoln's passenger side and strolled nonchalantly toward the quarry. The polo-shirted man directed the single word "stay" toward me in a tired voice and reached for the glove compartment. This gesture induced in me a state of fear toward which I had been inching since the second man began his unhurried walk to the quarry. Mercifully, what the driver fished from the glove compartment was a bag of pork rinds. On the other hand, when he shifted his bulk to secure his snack, the gun tucked against his outer thigh came briefly into view.

I looked away and leaned back against the Datsun with my arms crossed, trying to make a show of my apathy toward a trite situation, the likes of which I'd encountered countless times before.

"Keys," the driver grunted, holding out a greasy palm. I shook my head at the silliness of it all but complied, tossing the keys with as much unconcern as I could muster.

By now, his partner's Panama hat was beginning its descent beyond the quarry's rim. I thought about death then, the quick and businesslike way (in my bit-player case) it would probably come about, and the likelihood my remains would remain undiscovered, much to the dismay of very few. I spent the next few minutes trying to convert such thoughts into the conviction that being dead wasn't all that bad.

Then a single shout echoed up from the quarry, followed by palpable silence. The Lincoln driver and I looked at each other. Neither one of us knew who had shouted. The driver heaved himself up out of the car, probably to hear better, and for this reason, I suppose, left his gun laying on the seat. We stood side by side, waiting. After a couple of minutes, another shout. This one I recognized as Carl's, but in a stroke of desperation, I turned to my companion and shouted, "What did your friend say?"

He muttered something profane-sounding and stepped forward a few paces. I reached in through the Lincoln's open window, grabbed the gun, and tossed it as far into the bushes as my terror-heightened strength would propel it. One salient fact, and only one, had convinced me to commit this apparent act of bravery: I knew I could outrun the fat asshole if it came to that. And indeed, in the time it took him to wheel, peer into the Lincoln, and figure out what happened, I had moved to the car's opposite side, the sure winner of any ring-around-the-rosy chase.

"He doesn't have a gun, Carl," I shouted. To my infinite chagrin, Carl didn't reply. But at least his antagonist didn't either. The driver, of course, was also busy assessing the situation. Perhaps he believed both parties in the quarry were equally incapacitated. Or that both shouts had come from his wounded but triumphant partner. In any case, he turned to me, smiled, and fake shot me with his index finger. Then, having come to some private conclusion, he lumbered off toward the quarry. It occurred to me then that hanging onto the gun might have been a beneficial refinement of my plan.

Fortunately, my tactical shortcomings were matched by my purple-shirted adversary's. Yes, he had my keys, but *his* keys hung from the Lincoln's ignition. Once he was halfway to the quarry's edge, I grabbed the keys, popped the Datsun's hood, and ripped out a handful of wires, which I then tossed into the trunk of the Lincoln, noting with dread the shovel, rope, and roll of plastic already there. The man turned and watched me for a few seconds, yelled, shot me a bird, then resumed his plodding steps. Now I was probably safe. I could drive away in the Lincoln, call the police, and let justice prevail—except that I didn't trust justice half as far as I could throw a handgun. I saw myself taking the rap for murder, car theft, and drug distribution, what with Carl being dead and the two living occupants of the Lincoln being flush with cash and lawyered-up to the hilt. Better to at least take a peek into Paradise Lost (as I had just named the quarry) by driving the Lincoln to its rim and using the car's massive door as a shield against the gun Mr. Panama Hat must have been packing.

Pretty good protection, but not perfect. It *had* been Carl's voice I last heard, hadn't it? Now I wasn't sure, so I decided on a slight change in plans. Rather than pausing at the quarry's edge, I eased past at school zone speed and glanced down into the pit. I thought I saw the gunless driver taking a piss against the boulder that had insulted my arm. Was he so sure of how things stood that he could afford this self-indulgence? I took another pass and noted that he had not moved. The third time, I braked to a fearful halt. For a good while I did nothing but stare at the man, suspecting masterful chicanery on his part while at the same time knowing better. As I was about to chance a shout to Carl, he stepped out from behind the boulder, wearing a Panama hat, its previous owner draped across his shoulders. The purple-shirted man seemed to take no notice.

Carl saw me and yelled, "Get your ass down here, pronto. I need help with these bodies."

Bodies.

The "help" I provided Carl was as little as possible, and then a bit less. Nor did I bother to ask Carl whether we should go to the police. We inferred from their passports and driver's licenses that the two dead men were from Serbian Yugoslavia, had spent considerable time in Milan, then came to the United States two years ago on long-expired tourist visas. Carl knew the men as customers, ones with whom he exchanged codes through want ads, given their sizable purchases. The men had even been at his party, but regrettably for them, out of earshot when he provided the gory details of his jungle warfare skills. Nor had he arranged to meet them at the quarry, the reddest of flags.

According to Carl, the same instinct questioning whether I'd coupled with Linda told him the two men had come to murder him as soon as their bloated automobile appeared.

"You saved my life, Billy boy," Carl said as he lugged the first man to the surface. "They split up on account of you." Carl groaned and dropped the body like a sack of cornmeal when he reached level ground, adding, "Man, I'm getting too old for this shit."

Unlike Carl, I was new at lethal mayhem, and it must've shown. "Throw up if you need to, my friend," Carl advised, with evident compassion. "I find it's good for the soul." I doubted if anything would have helped my soul right then. I settled for hurrying away to retrieve the shovel from the Lincoln's trunk, then following the bandanna line out beyond the marijuana crop and digging for all I was worth, all following Carl's plan. Way too soon, he brought me the first installment of the "goods," as he called them. The second ensued just as I was scattering leaves and weeds over packed earth.

"I'm digging my way to hell," I told Carl and myself. I stared at the second corpse, still horrifying under the haze of rope-bound plastic.

"Fuck that," Carl said, spitting for effect. "You didn't kill anybody; you tossed the gun into the damn bushes. A stupid move, by the way. And while we're at it, when you yelled that your guy didn't have a gun, how did I know he wasn't making you say that?"

I sat down, deciding the rest was worth the argument. "Well," I countered, "when you yelled that second time, I told the driver it was *his* buddy yelling, even though I knew it was *you*. That's why he moved away from his gun, to hear his buddy better."

"It *was* his 'buddy,' genius. I made him yell 'come quick' to lure the fat guy down, though I couldn't be sure that's what he said. After that, I broke his neck. It couldn't be helped. Maybe your guy had a gun; maybe he didn't. One problem at a time." Carl shrugged philosophically.

"What about Panama Hat?" I demanded. "Didn't he have a gun?" For the first time in my life, I had nicknamed a corpse.

"No, just a knife. I think Panama thought I was a pussy just because I invited him to my party. Man, was he surprised."

"Let me get this straight. If I'd kept the gun of the guy I just buried, I could've walked him over to the quarry and nobody would have died."

Carl seemed to give my logic some hard thought, then nodded his head. "Come to think of it, that's exactly right. I mean, we'd have the drop on them, so what could these dead assholes do but get in their car and drive off with their tails between their legs, never giving another thought to revenge?"

A brief staring contest commenced between Carl and me. I lost.

"Don't feel bad, amigo. What is it they say at recruiting stations? 'Sign up and see the world?' Well, I saw the world, and trust me, this shit ain't nothing. And didn't Linda tell us there's no hell?"

"It's 'join the Navy and see the world,' Carl. It isn't 'join the Army and kill the world.'"

He snorted.

"I see you're still chock-full of useless crap. Anyway, when I tell Linda about this little drama, I'll make you look like a hero. That should keep the ball rolling."

"Tell Linda? Listen, Carl. I've seen her when she's high. She's liable to say anything to anybody. You might as well just put one of your stupid ads in the paper with a map to the bodies."

"Well, the ads are a problem. I'll give you that. But don't worry, man, Linda's cool when she has to be. Besides, she's my lawyer; she can't say shit."

"Except, *except*, if she knows of a *crime*. Then she *has* to go to the police."

Carl made a peace sign and shook his head tolerantly as if a small child had told him Batman would make sure all the bad people went to jail.

"First of all, what crime? And second, Linda's been out here; she knows the whole layout. She sure as hell digs the product, right? But let's say she loses her grip and your little paranoid fantasy comes true. All of a sudden, no paycheck for Linda. See?" Carl sat cross-legged, extending his arms to the sides, palms up, Buddha with a much harsher take on enlightenment.

Equal truth.

I would have to go with that for now.

After pulling myself up by the shovel handle like an invalid pulling himself up by a crutch, I started wordlessly digging again. "Hey, listen, Professor, let me take over here. You go find that gun you chucked into the bushes. We need to get rid of those damn bandannas too. I gotta cancel the ads. Go mom-and-pop again. Luckily there's no blood with broken necks. Now, like I said, you saved my life. But next time, wait until the second guy is down in the quarry *before* screaming that you swiped his gun. That way, I know he hasn't got you by the balls."

Of course, after we had gotten on the same page about what would happen "next time," there was still the matter of the Lincoln. As Carl so eloquently put it, "We sure as shit aren't going to bury it." I drove the re-wired Datsun back to Carl's house, then picked him up near campus, where he had parked the Lincoln on the street, not too far from Leonardo's pizza joint. Then we called Linda. Getting no answer, I drove her VW bug to Micanopy and parked it in front of her apartment. Carl followed in the Datsun. Linda wasn't at home, so we left a note on the VW, making no mention of dead men. A couple of days later, Carl and I drove by the abandoned Lincoln, and to Carl's delight, there were tickets on the windshield. Carl hopped out and drove off in the Lincoln. I returned to Carl's, switched from Datsun to Studebaker, and headed for my apartment. Carl had wanted the Lincoln last officially seen far from the quarry. Now, with his ruse in meter-maid writing, he (somehow) dumped the titanic Continental into a Hogtown Prairie swamp hole, then hitchhiked back into Gainesville, where I met him at Mama Lo's for beer, barbecue goat, and—at Carl's insistence—"a powwow on keeping our stories straight" in case we'd missed something.

My candidate for what we might have "missed"—since I had thought of nothing else for the last few days, thrown up a couple of times, and smoked what seemed like a garbage bag of pot to fend off multiple panic attacks—was two dead bodies next to Carl's illegal marijuana crop. "Don't worry," Carl reassured me amid the racket of blues music, inebriated hilarity, and clacking billiard balls. "Those guys are a long way from the quarry now." Exactly where Carl wouldn't say. That way, I suppose, I couldn't crack under police interrogation. Anyway, Carl's concern observed the crime movie conceit that criminals (us) *always* miss something. Consequently, our versions of what "went down" at the quarry had to match perfectly. And the truth wouldn't do. There had to have been two guns, one being held to my head, creating a "Mexican standoff" when Carl disarmed Panama Hat. Eventually, an uneasy truce allowed all four of us to survive, the evil foreigners screaming unintelligible curses as they roared away in their big black Lincoln. "Worst case, there's a pot bust charge," Carl assured me. "And trust me," he continued, patting my arm, "Linda can handle that in her sleep."

In her sleep. That's how I had last seen Linda, with a very different future in prospect. Shortly after the Mama Lo's summit, I got the guts to call her, but she already knew everything. "Listen, Bill, when I told you I was half witch, I wasn't kidding. Those guys *earned* their destiny—you just witnessed it playing itself out. You weren't any more to blame than one of those trees out there. And one more thing you should understand. Yes, in a sense, you saved Carl's life by being present and muddying the water for those idiots. And he did say you handled yourself pretty well. But *everything* Carl did, the way he dealt with the situation, was to protect you."

Linda's summation-to-the-jury tone precluded objection. All I could slip in was "How do you mean?"

"If he'd answered you when you first called out, they'd most likely have shot you on the spot and double-teamed him. As long as they didn't *know* he was down in that godforsaken quarry, you might be useful alive. I suppose they could've tied you up and gone down together, but they were dumb and cocky. Carl knew it was only one guy because they weren't talking. People can't help talking. The way the guy tried to knife him was a joke. He also—"

"Wait a minute, are you taking Carl's word for all this?"

"No. I'm taking what Carl told me and drawing my own picture—the way it *had* to happen for you to get out alive."

"Based on *what?* No offense, but you're a real estate lawyer, not a nineteen forties hard-boiled detective."

"No offense, Bill, but *you* think like a harmless philosophy professor. The way I look at it, there are four people, two cars, a hole in the ground, and a big rock to hide behind. You know what two of the people want. It's like a chess game. You look at the board and figure out the moves you need to win. Christ, it's not that hard."

I pictured Linda at home, drawing a diagram on a sheet of paper—stick men, rectangles for cars, and a big circle with a little circle inside. "It seemed hard at the time," I said.

"It was," she conceded, "but Carl figured it out. That's the point. Don't forget; he won a war. Not the whole war, but his part of it. Look, he knew from prior dealings that *his* guy was the boss. He kept him alive in a choke-hold and made him order the other guy down. Perfectly logical. When you yelled something about the gun, Carl didn't answer, right? He didn't want your guy to think he was still alive. He just hoped he would follow his boss's orders rather than decide to kill you first. What happened out there combined skill, luck, love, and destiny. Carl's skill and love for you led him to make the right decisions; luck and destiny did the rest."

I might have reminded Linda that Carl, being unarmed, did well to hide whether I was there or not. I might have pointed out that however shrewdly Carl interpreted my shout about the gun, I was the one who got rid of it.

Instead, I praised her powers of deduction, whether rooted in witchery or chessboard logic. Privately, I had a different theory: she was trying to cement brotherly love between Carl and me. Exactly why, I was still working out.

"Bill, it's okay if you don't believe me. People these days are full of shit. Like that Japanese movie where everybody tells a bogus story about what they saw?"

"*Rashomon*," I said, a little startled that the movie had just crossed my mind.

"Yeah, that's it."

"The bandit, the wife, the Samurai, and the woodcutter. Came out about the time I was born. I get the connection, but all those people were lying. I don't think you're lying."

"Except maybe to myself, right?"

"No more than anyone else, including me."

Linda laughed and said, "Well, this is fun. Let's agree that Carl needs to change his ways. How about that?"

"Sounds good."

"Excellent. Moving on, are you going to help me with my orgasm problem or not?"

CHAPTER TWELVE

"Ne Me Quitte Pas"

As I mentioned, I began writing a novel in my teens whose opening line ran as follows: *My one regret in life is losing Delia Wingfoot, even though I know it was for the best.*

Of course, if my beloved literary relic were actually to appear these days in a "hip" novel, an editor would probably pare it down to *Delia left.* I mean, we all have regrets, we all have illusions, so why "go there?"

Likewise, I could try to explain why I decided to help Linda tackle her "orgasm problem," but why go there? I *can* say that "easy" sex wasn't my reason. I sensed—I *knew*—nothing concerning Linda was heading toward easy. Whatever my motives, I can report that Linda's "happy ending" manifested itself, though not in the classic manner I anticipated. Without belaboring the particulars (as if anyone these days is unsure about what bodies look like having sex), Linda and I began sleeping together. After a couple of "sessions," one thing became clear to me: mountains were not going to move for Linda—to put it plainly—until she forgot why we were copulating. And that wouldn't happen unless she wanted *me*—not just an orgasm. So, I cooked for her, commiserated with her, inquired at length about white witchcraft and property law. I can't prove my strategy worked; all I know is one night she cried, "Oh, *Bill*, I feel something." While the sensation didn't quite turn Linda into a butterfly right then, it pointed her to the sky. "I see how to get there," she exclaimed afterward, brimming with elation. "Oh my God, Bill, you can't know until you know, but once you do, I swear, it's a piece of cake."

"Sounds delicious, but can we postpone dessert until tomorrow night? I have to get some sleep for my day job."

That job—the one finagled by Carl—took me to Sea Island College, a small, liberal arts school housed back then primarily in a collection of repurposed old homes near Newberry, a town uncomfortably close to Carl's quarry. On the other hand, the college stood nowhere near a sea island. Instead, the name was chosen because Gainesville, back in the 1800s, was the primary distribution point in Florida for sea island cotton.

The school had only recently come into existence, owing to a wealthy Newberry resident's death a few years earlier and the endowment he bestowed. He had envisioned a liberal arts oasis, harking back to a time when philosophy, art history, Greek, Latin, and classic literature were prerequisites of an enlightened mind. And while Sea Island offered a Classical Studies major (the endowment otherwise rescinded), the school's *living* administrators had other fish to fry.

To be frank, they envisioned the school as a five-star diploma mill, a pedagogic cash cow with "high tuition and low expectations," as a colleague put it, offering a soft curriculum to indolent rich kids. Business Management, for instance, became a popular major as word of its nonexistent rigor spread among students. One contrary fact of life faced Sea Island's bureaucrats, however. The school's beloved founder had stipulated a host of full scholarships be doled out annually to the disadvantaged and dark-skinned. The school became, like the nation it occupied, a conflicted experiment teetering between cynicism and idealism.

That suited me fine. I looked at my student's motley makeup as the ragged embodiment of "thesis, antithesis, and synthesis," a popular philosophical concept misattributed to Hegel but first mentioned by Fichte in his *Grundriss des Eigentümlichen der Wissenschaftslehre, in Rücksicht auf das theoretische Vermögen* (1795), a fact I wickedly assured my students would be on some future test. At any rate, and analogous to Linda's erotic "piece of cake," I found teaching philosophy satisfying and easy; satisfying because I could wallow in my passion and maybe win over a convert or two, and easy because, for most of my students, my class served as both the on-ramp and dead end of their philosophical road. I wasn't the Calc I prof berated by the Calc II prof for not adequately covering the sandwich theorem of limits. Absent student complaints, I had no one to please but myself.

And to scotch complaints, I began to emulate Mr. Pee, the hero of my high school days, by baldly assuring my students that they would get better grades than they deserved. To my knowledge, no one ever ratted me out to the administration.

And it didn't hurt that philosophy was a lazy lesson planner's dream, conveniently divided into disciplines and "isms"—metaphysics, epistemology, materialism, rationalism—while providing a well-accepted list of brain-twisting questions with no clear right or wrong answers, such as how something (like Linda's Christmas tree) can keep changing yet remain itself, or what a number is, or what our thoughts might have to do with what's "out there." Add a few ridiculously easy multiple-choice tests and you paint the picture of an unambitious, low-level minion of higher education, trying to get by.

But this wasn't the whole story. My students, rich or poor, were far more often the local deep-South types than the up-from-Miami hip-to-the-zeitgeist types populating the University of Florida. And keep in mind, this was 1979—no cell phones. Even good old DOS for computers was only a year old. So, other than a few pampered know-it-alls, my kids tended to be Christian, conventional, and passive, empty vessels hardly imagining anything should be expected to pour *out* of them. In the larger world, the Iran hostage crisis was center stage, its ramifications unimaginable. My charges were too young to feel much angst about that and too old to care that McDonald's had just introduced the Happy Meal.

So how to get them, like Linda, to relax into inspiration? How to get them beyond their fears of judgment, embodied in that first inevitable question: *how will we be tested?*

"Life will test you," I would tell them, "certainly not me. All I'll ask of you is obvious answers to straightforward questions. Until you die happy, or at least with your curiosity satisfied, you won't know if you passed life's 'test.'" Groans and boos, but they'd see I was smiling and perk up. One canny young woman did ask me if I thought *my* life was heading toward a passing grade, her question earning her an A for indifferent work. By the way, I answered that I would find it a hard slog to raise my life-grade to a C-minus (and, yes, I will regret it if it ends that way).

I remember best from my first class asking someone to define philosophy and seeing the first brave soul, a thin, hawk-nosed boy in a Led Zeppelin T-shirt, finally raise his hand.

"It's asking what reality is, isn't it?" he ventured, expecting to be wrong.

"Yes. To quote Plato, 'Those whose hearts are fixed on reality itself deserve the title of philosophers.' Anyone else?" I waited, but having heard the right answer, the class had completed their job.

Thankfully, as I was about to launch into a soul-killing explanation of Platonic Idealism, a young woman shot up her hand. "Don't scientists know what reality is? I thought they knew what everything was down to the atom."

"They have a pretty good idea of what physical reality is, but pretty good isn't the same as perfect or complete. And besides, scientists can only know about things they can measure. Anybody in here ever had their thoughts measured?" A sprinkle of laughter. Then, another young woman in the back, overdressed in a floral, skirted suit and speaking in a soft drawl, said, "God can hear all our thoughts."

A shiver of *déjà vu* shot through me. Clare Johnson, one of the "church girls" back in Hopperton, had said much the same in Mr. Pee's class. "*God has a plan for everyone*," she had proclaimed with much the same quiet certainty. Don Heffelfinger had defended Godless Reason to the point of tears. And how had Mr. Pee handled it?

"Very likely, but scientists, philosophers, all of us mere mortals, have to figure things out *without* that power as best we can." I went to the blackboard as behind me arose a soft cacophony of notebook openings and pen clicks. I wrote *reason, logic,* and *theories* under philosophy; and, after hesitating, *scripture, prayer,* and *faith* under religion. Then, turning to the floral girl, I said, "As you can see, young lady, philosophy does not challenge religion any more than a car mechanic challenges a brain surgeon just because they both use tools."

She sat very still for a moment, then smiled. "Yes, I see, but you left off the best tool of all—our Lord and Savior, Jesus Christ."

"Ah," I said as if just recognizing the omission. "Well, that's because we're using religion here as something Aristotle invented, called a *category*, a term of general classification. And that's because there are many religions, some of which ... have not yet discovered Jesus. But all religions, as best I can recall, have holy books, prayers, and belief in ... a divine spirit." *But not a personal god*, I thought to myself, hoping that nuance would pass unnoticed.

The young woman, if not satisfied, at least took no offense. However, someone else stirred the pot by asking if God could make a rock so big He couldn't move it.

"Very provocative, but there is an answer, at least according to philosophy. And the answer is that your question isn't a real question."

"Sure, it is," a muscular young man had the guts to fire back. "Either He can or He can't."

"I admit your words about God and the rock are in the form of a question, but the contradiction they introduce denies them the status of a *true* question. They are, to put it nicely, nonsense. If I write one equals two on the blackboard, does the fact that I can write it make it true? Likewise, stringing together words that end in a question mark doesn't make them a question. Do you see?"

"Not exactly."

"Good for you. That means you haven't given up thinking about it. Kierkegaard, a very religious philosopher, believed that contemplating contradictions, or paradoxes—as he preferred to call them—created the passion needed for deep thinking." I pointed to the questioner and said, "Maybe we've found our first secret philosopher."

The class laughed, the husky fellow blushed, pleased with the attention, and off we went. *This is going to be okay*, I thought, awash in gratitude to whatever or whoever made it so. I hoisted myself up onto my desk (table actually), sketched a misleading, tawdry-free version of my previous life, and told them about Mr. Pee, and how, by questioning the nature of luck, he became my first Socrates. They didn't care much about that, except the indelicate nickname. In due time I became "Mr. Bill," so-called after an unfortunate clay-figure character on *Saturday Night Live* who suffered undeserved mutilation episode after episode at the hands of Sluggo, a sadistic clay nemesis. Occasionally in class I would hear a high-pitched "oh noooooo" in imitation of Mr. Bill's trademark wail of dismay. I took that sound as a favorable sign to the extent that I didn't share Mr. Bill's fate.

So, all in all, as those early days passed, I took increasing heart. A Leonard Cohen song suggests only a joyous few see Jesus in his proper light. Similarly, I found lurking among my students a joyous few eager to confront the antipodes of essence and existence, noumena and phenomena, appearance and reality, free will and determinism. Aiming my words at these intrepid souls, I ad-libbed in step with their impulsive curiosities, creating a kind of drunkard's walk through ideas and personages: Heidegger celebrated the purity of human existence, thought Hitler had beautiful hands and joined the Nazi party; Leibniz proposed the digital computer back in the 1600s, consoling himself with the pinwheel calculator and inventing calculus; Nietzsche believed the countless shuffling of chaos would bring us all around again at some future time. I presented strange and exquisite ideas with deliberate and—I hoped—disarming nonchalance. I covered what I covered, curriculum be damned, trying to mine a few diamonds rather than dig a large hole, and no one, outside of an occasional protégé, was any the wiser.

But to return to the day after Linda's erogenous epiphany, I called her in good spirits, confident, finally, that some administrator would not spot me as a fraud and unceremoniously toss me out of the college. To my chagrin, she sounded muffled and weary.

"I'm drooping, Bill. This easement case is kicking my ass. And I think I need a short, sexless vacation to recharge."

"Okay," I said, leaving it at that. Linda would tell me only what she wanted to tell me; no need—or use—to try and ferret anything out. *She* was the lawyer. And I didn't mind the vacation. I'd stroll down to the university's student union and maybe catch a game of chess.

"Last night was great," she assured me. "Life-changing. Don't read anything into my shitty mood."

"I'm not. Just take care of yourself. It sounds like you're getting a summer cold."

"Summer?"

"Yeah, we're still a few days away from the equinox."

"Oh, that. You and your stargazing."

"Not really, it's on the calendar by your fridge."

"Oh, well, you know me."

"Yes, I do."

I waited, listening to Linda breathe. "Look," I said finally, "I think we should put this conversation out of its misery and let you get some rest. How's your sugar?"

"Not too sweet, but I'm making it."

"Well, let me know when you're up for a visit. We can go dancing in a honkytonk if you want."

"Thanks, Bill. I'll call you soon."

"Soon" turned out to be a week, an interval which found me about three days into anxiety over her silence. If I weren't in love with Linda— had I made it a point *not* to be in love with her? —how could I deny that she filled my life with *interest?* Waif, witch, tough cookie, *willing* conversationalist (until that last phone call) on just about any subject.

And a sexual mountain climber with her loyal Sherpa.

"Bill?" she questioned when I said hello, as if she might have dialed the wrong number.

"Yes, I still am."

"Oh, you sounded funny, that's all."

"No, I'm still unfunny. How are you?"

"Good. I finally settled that damn case."

"Wonderful." I considered asking her how her "vacation" went but thought better of it.

"I was thinking of coming over tonight. Are you busy?" Linda's apartment, and far superior bed, had been home base before now.

"You honor me. What time?"

"After dinner. I've got documents to deliver."

"Okay, see you then." I hung up feeling good. With Karen, I had never learned to fight for equal footing. Maybe with Linda I could master the art of it.

Linda arrived at about nine. She wanted to smoke, tobacco and otherwise, so I kept the front window open. We sat in my one common room at a flea market café table—umbrella hole and all—as Jacques Brel sang songs from *Ne Me Quite Pas* over the whoosh of traffic. Linda hadn't eaten; she nibbled fitfully at a wedge of Jarlsberg cheese, emanating tension like a minor force field. Even a single week apart had estranged us in some indefinable way. I speculated it had something to do with Carl and the quarry fiasco's aftermath. I asked if she'd heard anything through the legal grapevine.

"Oh, yeah, they found the car."

A kind of prickling numbness passed through my body as I tried to make sense of Linda's casual tone. "Don't you think that little bombshell deserves more than an 'oh yeah'?" I couched my words as mildly as I could.

"Sorry. I know it sounds scary, but the police have no idea what it means. The car's just one piece of the puzzle, and they probably need four or five more pieces to get anywhere."

"Like the bodies."

"Yeah, and they'll never get those."

We stared at each other in silence for half a minute.

"I don't suppose you're guessing," I said finally.

Linda shrugged, crossed her arms, and expelled a voluminous puff of marijuana smoke into the laggard, wobbly blades of the ceiling fan. "Bill, I think you *are* a man for all seasons, or at least most of them. I think we should be friends forever. We can sleep together if we want to, but not like before. I don't need you to make me climax. I figured that out this week on my own." I recall expecting a sheepish grin to accompany her revelation rather than what resembled somber contrition.

"That's something I should have told you right away," she continued, "but I thought it might hurt your feelings. I'm sorry."

"Not to miss the main point—and congratulations, by the way—but don't you want to find out if you can 'get there' with an actual partner?"

"Oh, of course, of course, and I'm sure that will happen. But we don't have to work at it like a job. I would love to stay here and sleep with you tonight without going for sex. Do you realize we've never done that?"

And she was right. "Why, Linda, is this some sneaky trick to become my girlfriend?"

She got up and came around to kiss me. Then she drew back a step. "No, not girlfriend; it's way too late for that." As movie-perfect as this sounded, I couldn't unravel on the spot what she meant. Given the mood, I didn't want to ask. Instead, I nodded as if I understood perfectly.

Linda walked closer to the speakers and listened intently. Brel was singing "Ne Me Quitte Pas," the title song.

"What is he saying?"

"He's beseeching a woman not to leave him, not to quit him. He's begging her not to forget all they had."

"It's very intimate, almost like we shouldn't be listening."

"Yeah, the French are all about the *cri de coeur*, the cry of the heart. I thought you looked French when I first saw you. Here, let me show you something." I walked over to a small bookcase near where Linda stood, pulled out *The Vagabond* by Colette, and showed her the cover drawing of a dark-haired, introspective woman.

"My God," Linda gasped, "that's me."

"I thought so too. Did you ever perform in a traveling music-hall revue?"

"Maybe in a past life. I am a great singer and dancer."

"Well then, this probably *is* you."

We reveled together in that thought, the camaraderie chasing off my sense of disaffection. "Wait here," I said, then went into the bedroom to retrieve something I kept on my night table. I returned and handed a thin, yellowish book to Linda. "It's a poetry journal," I explained. "Pretty old, a first edition. I found it in an old bookstore when I was living in Lake City a few years ago. I bought it because it featured a piece written by a sci-fi writer I like, but that's not what I wanted to show you."

Linda stared at the cover, a weird drawing suggestive of an ancient map to some mythical place. "What does 'ephemeris' mean?" she asked, referring to the journal's title.

"An ephemeris is a printed table showing the positions of celestial objects at various times. The ancient Babylonians and Persians used them, the Mayans too. Christopher Columbus used one to predict a lunar eclipse to natives he met. I also assume it implies transience, evanescence, the fact that nothing lasts."

"Truer words. Now, what was it you wanted to show me?"

"I wanted you to hear something that reminded me of you." I opened the journal and recited a poem: "As happiness takes off the tie it borrowed from me and gets into bed…"

When I finished, Linda gave me a tender, dubious look. "Like my Christmas tree, my happiness. Same idea, right?"

"Exactly. Well, not exactly. This guy's happiness is someone climbing into bed with him, but the idea's there—happiness captured like a genie in a bottle. Anyway, that line reminded me of you."

"Is that how you spend your time, looking through old books for things that remind you of me?"

I took a moment to consider her question, even if she meant it in a teasing fashion. "I wasn't looking for them; I just came across them. But I did notice the connection, so I guess that means you're fascinating."

"Bill," she said, patting my cheek, "few people are as excellently full of shit as you are."

When I climbed into bed with Linda that night, putting aside whether I was her happiness or not, it felt lovely, a promise of pleasant dreams. And as the days passed, we continued to sleep together, mostly at my place now, sometimes with sex, sometimes without, but often enough for my contentment. And despite myself, I took particular pride in—and credit for—Linda's occasional ecstatic cries.

CHAPTER THIRTEEN

"God Bless the Child"

Early in 1980, just after a Super Bowl won by the menacing Pittsburgh Steelers (and shown, in a grimly surreal touch, to the hostages in Iran), Carl stopped by. Since the quarry, he had steered clear of me, any news of him coming through Linda, who used those scattered reports to push for reconciliation. She wanted me to think of Carl as my wayward brother-in-arms rather than my antagonist, and while I balked at this revision, her campaign had its effect. So, when Carl showed up, I let him in, if only to mollify Linda.

"Sorry to neglect you, amigo," he said while thrusting a bottle of cognac at me, "but I've been over in Tampa on business."

"Cognac. Wow. Very provocative." Carl brought cognac once before to the cottage where my first wife Karen and I began our romance. The three of us finished off the bottle that night, forming an inseparable trio on our way to becoming a wretched triangle. Carl surely remembered.

"Yeah, I know what you're thinking, but how about we let the good times kick the bad times' ass tonight?"

I ignored the offer. "When you say you've been away on business, I assume you mean sailing, not to mention laying low."

"Sure, sure," he said, "but no shit, I was having this bitching *arroz con pollo* over in Ybor City, and I ran into a couple of guys. Get this; they'll buy my weed at a decent price, upfront, then take it back to Tampa and sell it. Boom, I'll practically be home free, legal-wise. And no more Yugoslavian assholes to worry about."

"Just Cuban assholes."

"Right! That's just the kind of thinking I need to hear. I'm having them checked out like I read your mind."

"Start with reading my face."

"Okay, okay, I get it. Now, can we just crack this freaking bottle open and sit down? If I'm going to take your shit, I need to be drinking."

I poured two hefty cognacs into cheap wine glasses, then rested the bowl of one in the palm of my hand and swirled it around.

"Stirred, not shaken," Carl announced in poor theatrical British.

"That's Bond's martini. You don't stir or shake cognac; just swirl it to warm it up."

"Like old times; still pompous as ever." He downed the contents of the glass before any warming could occur. The cognac's power showed on Carl's face; his eyes went wide.

"Shit, those guys were right."

"Who?"

"Those Cuban guys. They gave me this stuff, swore it was the tears of angels."

I nodded, finding nothing to say. Carl, too, seemed at an impasse, his eyes darting around the room, looking for anything to inspire commentary. "What's that book?" he settled on, pointing to the one by my elbow.

"Spinoza's *Ethics*; I'm boning up for class."

"Yeah, I think you wrote me a paper on Spinoza back in the day. Wasn't he the triangle guy?"

"He was 'a' triangle guy, Carl, the smart kind, not the home-wrecking kind. Maybe I'll use that tomorrow. I was looking for a simple way to explain his excommunication." Spinoza had said that if a triangle could think, it would describe God as an omnipotent triangle. Spinoza's contemporaries did not take kindly to such insulting impieties.

"He was kicked out of the church for talking about triangles?"

"Not the church, the synagogue. He was Jewish. His community had taken refuge in Holland during the Spanish Inquisition, and Spinoza's opinions offended the locals. He believed the natural world was the body of God, for example, and this"—I raised my glass of cognac and took a cautious sip—"couldn't be the tears of the angels, according to Spinoza, because angels were a fantasy." The cognac spread through me like a warm fog.

"Good thing we're not religious, Shaffer; we'd both be out the door."

Maybe it was the cognac, or Carl evoking Don Heffelfinger by calling me Shaffer, or Linda's peace initiatives, but a barrier in me gave way.

"Here's to being out the door, Carl," I called, raising my glass for a toast.

"Fucking right," Carl answered with a broad smile.

After that, we reminisced about Carl's father, Albert—his legendary cookouts and cocktails, his genius with electronics, his nautical mastery, and his goodwill, which you would have to work hard to lose. "Girls liked to come over to my house because my dad was so damn charming," Carl said at one point, "but it worked out; no complaints." I knew those girls would have come anyway. Yes, Carl had good looks, but it was his energy that set him apart as if the sun shone from him, not on him.

And here I was, living in a garret like Spinoza, the only difference being that he was creating possibly the most influential treatise in modern philosophy, while I was grading papers and had yet to write the book I had been contemplating and notebook-filling and postponing since high school.

We whittled the cognac down. Carl wanted to know how things stood with Linda and, oddly, how my Studebaker was running. "Linda swore she and I would be friends forever, which was nice. She stays over when she's in the mood. I can't say yet where we're headed; I'm a long way from figuring her out."

"Friends, huh? Does that mean there's not much happening in the bedroom?"

"Everything's fine. Do I look deprived?"

"No, no, Professor, I just remember what she said on the phone about you maybe turning into a primo lay. Any improvement?" Carl added a genial leer.

Vanity prevented me from ignoring his question. "I believe so," I said, "but I can't speak for Linda."

"Wouldn't expect you to, you being such a Southern gent." After this oblique comment, Carl downed his cognac and refilled it. Then he reiterated his question about my Studebaker.

"It's running," I said. "Could use new tires, I guess."

Carl was wearing a leather bomber jacket impossible not to covet. He fished into its inner breast pocket, produced a bundle of bills, and dropped it on the table. "Here," he said. "Use this to fix up your Model T."

"What's this?"

"It's five grand, all legit. I pawned off some of Dad's shitty inventory while I was in Tampa. And don't even think about turning it down. The only reason I took you out to the quarry was to show off—to prove what a big operator I am. Linda said I need to make, and I quote, 'a concrete gesture of humility' to teach myself a lesson. She said you might not want the money, but if I told you my reasons, you'd take it. What do you say?"

"I say it's the second time in my life somebody handed me a wad of cash." (The first "wad" was actually neat piles sent to me by my Aunt Miriam in the bottom of a candy sampler—more on that later).I considered my options. While five grand wouldn't enable any vast scheme, I didn't have one anyway. On the other hand, I imagined buying better clothes, affording better haircuts, a matched set of dishes, even a rare book or two—as well as a paint job and overhaul for the Studebaker. And yes, Linda had undoubtedly stage-managed this proposition, but her intentions were benign as far as I could tell.

"How much did you pay for that jacket?" I asked.

"What the fuck?"

"Humor me, Carl, and I'll give you an answer right now."

He shrugged. "Okay, let's see, I think about six hundred."

Not exorbitant, but more than my entire wardrobe. "Okay, I'll take the money. But listen, I went to the quarry knowing you grew more than blackberries out there. I'm not asking you to feel guilty. Feel what you want; do what you want. Let's just call it good and keep our business separate from now on, deal?" It had crossed my mind earlier to harry Carl about his evil ways and suggest he reopen his father's stereo business. But maybe I was becoming a determinist like Spinoza. Carl could zigzag his sailboat through capricious winds and outfox the local fuzz, but wasn't he still in the grip of unbreakable cosmic law? The one he could never see *because* he couldn't break it?

And did it matter how long I lay in bed trying to figure out Linda, or Karen before her, or the high school girl in Hopperton who first possessed me, and whose bright yellow hair kept blazing back into memory like a lit flare? Would the solving of fantasy puzzles make me the master of anything? Carl extended his hand, smiling with boyish hope, accepting my "terms" for taking the cash. And he would keep to them, I knew, until some mysterious law neither of us could see dictated otherwise.

"Amigos?"

"Until the end," I affirmed, grasping his hand. Then I added, "Which will be here soon if we don't mend our ways."

"Okay, Professor, you start mending. Once I take care of a few things, I'll try and catch up."

After Carl left, I stashed my windfall of fifty-dollar bills in the hand-made Cuban humidor bestowed on me by my ex-wife's stepfather, the aforementioned Gibson Levine. The key to the lock was lost, but what would that matter if Carl's schemes brought irate Yugoslavians or Cubans to my door? "Not *remotely* plausible," I lectured aloud to myself, shaking my head violently as if shedding a bad dream. The day at the quarry still owned me, still cried for its pound of flesh. I went to the sink, splashed cold water on my face, then sat back down and opened Spinoza's *Ethics*. He asserted our only hope of freedom lay in making peace with eternal laws and expressing our passions in concert with them. Only our best, most poised thinking could imagine a *likely* future, one towards which we could profitably bend our efforts.

I poured myself a little more cognac. It might only provide the illusion of poise, but, for the moment, it burned the darkest futures away.

One Saturday afternoon in late March, a couple of months after Carl's cognac-and-cash visit, Linda stopped by unannounced. Her visit was more surprising than Carl's since she had become a stickler for firm arrangements. As I once told her, she could have taught Mussolini a thing or two about keeping the trains running on time. Nevertheless, there she stood, pale and fashionably austere in black shirt and pants, apparently indulging an impulsive wave of affection for me. I certainly took it that way.

She came in, or should I say stalked in, not that carrying herself this way was unusual. Linda often entered exuding agitation and a tendency to look around as if checking for an intruder. But then, after a little wine or a puff or two of Carl's "Gainesville Green," she usually morphed into excellent company. That day, however, she declined all mood modifiers and, after acceding to a brief, distracted hug, headed into my bedroom and toppled onto the mattress. I followed her in and sat down gingerly on the bed's edge. "What's up?" I asked.

"You know my last name, right?"

"I assume that's a rhetorical question, but yes, it's Featherstone."

Linda nodded, continuing to stare at the ceiling.

"I always thought my last name was a cool combination of light and heavy, but Featherstone is just a town in England, and the 'feather' part is just a mispronunciation of an old word meaning 'four.' I'm really 'Linda Four Stones.'" Her tone of voice suggested despondency. I clearly was missing something.

"Your name is great, whatever its—"

As I searched for the word "provenance," Linda broke in.

"I found out the truth about my name two weeks ago. The next day I found out I was pregnant—*heavy* with child. That *can't* be a coincidence."

I raced past the wild desire to correct Linda's misunderstanding of coincidence. "How great with child are you?" I asked, stunned because we had used both physical and hormonal protection. And doubly stunned because, unknown to anyone outside my hometown of Hopperton, a similar disclosure confronted me during my senior year of high school. I would have married the young woman, but it never came to that. Doubts and strange claims arose, leaving me with no clear truth to tell myself or anyone else. Later on, I will do my best to explain all this, but for now, just know that the shock of Linda's words carried a painful echo only I could hear.

"I'm not *very* great," she said, laughing through sniffles at her self-appraisal, "but I'm definitely a *little* great. Early Christmas present on the way."

I groped for supportive platitudes, but none came. Instead, questions crowded in. Linda answered one of them immediately.

"I *have* to have this baby," she whispered. "I've been *told*." By whom she didn't say.

"Can I get you anything?" I asked, trying to fill the precarious silence.

"Christ, no!" she cried. "I can't drink or smoke *anything*. I'm basically a nun for the foreseeable future."

"How about a glass of water?"

She nodded. "And a couple of aspirins if you have them."

Out in the kitchen, the other inevitable question surfaced: *Am I the father?* Circumstances would say so, but I prayed Linda would confirm this unequivocally and without prodding. As I rummaged around for aspirin, she came out and sat at the café table.

"I was at a real estate seminar earlier today," she began, her tone suggesting the last few minutes had not occurred. "I'm getting my license. The university's growing like crazy, and Gainesville's a boomtown in the making. Even Micanopy's picking up." She went on to think aloud about the flexibility real estate would provide her and how it dovetailed with property law. I felt I understood Linda's abrupt change of topic: human beings operated that way, defending themselves against their own thoughts, buying time to devise counterattacks against not-so-simple twists of fate. And from my side of the table, what good could come from pressing the issue? Time would furnish plenty of insistence on its own. The question of paternal certainty would *have* to arise. For the moment, I took the hand Linda extended as she talked. For the moment, I followed her, like Hansel being led by Gretel through pathless woods.

Linda woke me up at five a.m. the next morning. I opened my eyes to see her standing over me, fully dressed. "Listen, Bill; you won't see me for a while. I need to get away, go on a pilgrimage." She spoke in a low, confiding voice as if strangers might overhear.

"What?" I mumbled, half-convinced I was dreaming.

"I'll be out of town, but don't worry. When I get back, we'll talk about *everything*, I promise."

"Wait, where are you going?"

She bent down, kissed me on the forehead, and then retreated to the doorway.

"Somewhere quiet."

I groped for an objection, but none came. "Okay, I'll be here."

"I know."

I didn't answer, waiting, I suppose, for further expression of tenderness and appreciation. Instead, Linda said, "Carl won't know where I am either, in case you're wondering." I hadn't wondered at all about Carl, but about his five-grand bequest and all the pleasurable things it was now unlikely to buy.

I waited most of a harrowing, sleepless month. Finally, I broke down and called Carl. "Good timing, Professor; Linda just showed up at my house. Maybe she knew I was about to fire her ass."

Three years or so would pass before I fully decoded Linda's "pilgrimage." However, one purpose became immediately evident on her return: she had managed, more or less cold turkey, to quit all stimulants and sedatives, as well as the malevolent comfort of cigarettes. She had also adopted brown rice, miso soup, and steamed vegetables as her entire diet.

I discovered all this the evening of the day I finally called Carl, as I sat in his great room, listening to Linda explain her new self. "And my eyes," she exulted, "are already better. It's like clouds clearing after a storm."

Carl sat in his recliner, smiling and nodding a bit idiotically I thought. Linda and I occupied opposite ends of a plush gray couch. As happy as I was to see her, the whole scene annoyed me to no end, and I fought the urge to get up and leave without explanation. She hadn't mentioned the baby, and what were we doing at Carl's anyway? Did he even know Linda was pregnant?

I stared at Linda, willing her to intuit my discontent. "I'm glad you're doing so well. Come by and we'll catch up. I'll leave you and Carl to do the same. Early class tomorrow; I've got to get home." I stood up and started for the door.

"Hold up, Wild Bill Hiccup," Carl said. "We haven't even got to the main point of this powwow."

"Okay," I said, "I'm listening." I heard the disdain in my voice as I stood, unmoving, waiting.

"Bill, I didn't intend to get into this tonight. I only came by to deliver legal papers. But Carl knows I'm pregnant. I didn't see any point in hiding it. He thinks you and I should get married."

"*He* thinks. Why should I care what he thinks? Is Carl Decker your new guru?" I felt trapped in the jaws of some wicked circumstantial bear trap. I could spew indignation until the cows came home, but Linda would still be carrying my child.

"*You* shouldn't care," Linda said with maddening calm, "but he knows you better than I do. I wanted to hear what he had to say before—"

"Before what?"

"Before I proposed."

I sat for a moment, trying to summon up a credible reply. "I'm flattered, but forgive me if this doesn't seem like a very happy occasion."

"That's on you, Billy boy," Carl put in. "You're crazy about Linda, you like kids, and I sure as shit know you have money for a ring."

"Forget Carl," Linda shouted in exasperation. "He's an asshole. All I wanted to know is whether you'd be happy with me. He said yes. He might be wrong, but I don't think he's lying. And I don't need a ring. I need … shit, sanity, I guess. You're the only one in this room who has it, and I do love you."

And I do *love you.* Not an afterthought, but not the screaming head-line either.

"Linda, I'll be honest. Marriage has not fared well in my company. And nothing I've heard tonight makes me feel any better about that. Something tells me I'm not even the father." There it was. Linda looked down and closed her eyes as if mastering herself before replying.

"You're the father, Bill," she said in a low, pained voice. "You're the only man I'd *want* to be the father."

"All right," I said gruffly, trying to hold my ground. "But I need time. Maybe not thirty mysterious days, but time. Come over in a couple of weeks and we'll talk things over. And don't bring Carl."

"We can have the wedding here," Carl offered, unfazed. "It's on the house. All I need is a date."

CHAPTER FOURTEEN

"Gimme Shelter"

I took the next couple of days off and holed up like a film-noir gumshoe brooding over a case: *was the gorgeous dame who hired me to find her husband on the up and up?* Given Linda's month-long disappearance, any hard-boiled dick worth his salt would smell a rat. But since I wasn't Sam Spade in a trench coat, I lurched back and forth between doubt and faith as I washed down cheese toast with the remnants of Carl's cognac. Still baffled at the end of my brief sabbatical, I wrote to my old teacher, Mr. Pee, for advice. He and I exchanged friendly postcards now and then, his greetings mailed from northern California, where he had "retired in rural splendor."

Here's his reply:

Dear Bill,
Recalling the circumstances under which you left Hopperton, I grasp the irony of your present predicament. That said, I don't believe your history reveals a road map. Too much has changed, within and without. I once told you that "chance favors no man." To that, I would now add "but that doesn't mean chance treats all men equally." We get the life we get; we get the luck we get. Little use to complain. I cannot tell you concretely what to do. However, if my memory serves, you have an affinity for Buddhist wisdom. Therefore, you might keep in mind that if you don't know where

you are going, all roads serve equally well. (*Or equally poorly, I thought to myself*) To put it less arcanely, I don't think you can decide wrongly if your heart is in the right place. My new cat sits by the window carrying on the work of my old cat. That's the sum and substance of <u>my</u> news.

With warmest regards, Hiram Peebles

For all his pertinent insights, Mr. Pee replied (to my dismay) like a kindly doctor who sympathizes with your illness but refuses to write a prescription. Still, waiting for his answer prolonged my separation from Linda, throwing into stark relief my longing for her company, if not her hand in marriage. In that respect, his note served its purpose. I called Linda the day it arrived.

"Is your offer still open?"

"I assume this is Bill?"

"Yes."

"Well, Bill, my answer depends on your answer. Why are you asking?"

"I like your captivating company. I'm happier when I'm with you."

"And that's it?"

"You know damn well all the moral reasons, practical reasons. Why recite them?"

"Okay, fair enough. Do you love me?"

"Yes," I said, still far from knowing what I meant.

"You sound sincere, which is good because we were always going to get married. Lord help you, white man, if you speak with forked tongue."

And on that romantic note, the die was cast.

Two months later, we held our inadvertent June wedding in Carl's living room. Linda's sister Anita flew in from Colorado to serve as the maid of honor. I didn't know about Anita beforehand. For the most part, Linda acted like she didn't have a past. For her, it was all about maneuvering the present moment to advantage—nothing untoward about that in my view; a pretty garden-variety way to live. Thus, her law practice. Thus, her hot pursuit of the momentary carnal ultimate. Anyway, Anita, a gregarious woman with a henna-tinted pixie cut, laughed loudly at everything Carl said and postponed her departure for several days. For my second consecutive wedding, Carl served as both the best man and financier, Linda's sapphire engagement ring gouging a large hole in his $5000 "grant". Sapphire,

Linda insisted, repelled misfortune and guaranteed a healthy baby. And, as a bonus, it changed colors if its wearer proved unfaithful. Carl doubled as our wedding planner, hiring a photographer and supplementing the handful of souls Linda and I invited with "extras" from his drug-widened circle. Someone, he insisted, had to consume the catered feast guaranteed to feed 100 guests.

The ceremony took place in front of Linda's illuminated Christmas tree. She wore a vivid violet sheath dress deemphasizing her baby bump and freeing me to wear a department store gray suit instead of a tux. A colleague of mine, a Latin professor, conducted the service. While he held no religious office, he was a Notary Public and perfectly qualified to marry people in Florida. He presided on condition that we took our secular vows a second time in Latin: *William, vis accípere Linda, hic præséntem in tuam legítimam uxórem iuxta ritum sanctæ matris Ecclésiæ?* I suspected we had thereby drawn God in as an observer, but I didn't mind that. *Volo.* I do. My mother wasn't there, but when I wrote her with the news, I could speak with a clear conscience of a marriage blessed by the Creator.

That night, as we watched a small horde of strangers jump around to "Sympathy for the Devil," Linda and I decided to forgo a honeymoon, given her quickening condition and the fact that our inaugural sexual foray could hardly be topped. Instead, after a day of rest, we consolidated our holdings by transferring my scant possessions to Micanopy: my Philco radio, clothes, chess set, houseplants, books and records, tin percolator, and keyless Cuban humidor encompassing most of them. Carl supplied his Datsun pickup, complete with stoic, grizzled, anonymous driver. Clumps of soil littered the truck's cargo bed, and while the driver spread canvas before loading, I couldn't help scanning the rubble for traces of blood. Yes, the two Yugoslavians had suffered bloodless deaths at Carl's hands, but who could say what disinterment might do?

Whatever the truth, I saw nothing, smelled nothing, sensed nothing—no Lady Macbeth moment. The real trauma came later that day. It had taken maybe ninety minutes to blend my belongings with Linda's, the apartment suffering no noticeable shift in ambiance. Afterward, we sat drinking oolong tea and listening to *Tapestry.* At some point during "It's Too Late," Linda moaned, "This isn't going to work," fixing me simultaneously with a fatalistic stare.

I gaped, coldcocked with disbelief. "Holy hell," I cried, "did you have to wait until I moved all my shit?"

"Very hilarious, dumbass. I mean this *place* won't work. We need a house, a big one. Otherwise, blood *will* be spilled."

I stood up abruptly, appalled with myself, then walked to the window, pretending to look out so I wouldn't face Linda. "I wish I could paint," I said, wildly changing the subject to cover my tracks. "I would love to paint you."

Linda pulled at her dark tangles. "That's very sweet, Bill— strange, but sweet. I tell you what. Once we're in our new house, I'll pose for you, nude, if you prefer."

I confessed how I'd watched her that first morning as she lay sleeping.

"I wasn't asleep, but I didn't mind. I do remember you stood there for an indecently long time."

"I'm only human."

"Well, dear Bill, I'm a bit more than human, but we can work around that, I'm sure. Now, I'm about to buy us a great house; I was thinking out near your college. Make sense?"

Linda later claimed she had been looking for a house near Newberry since well before her pregnancy. A premonition involving me "and possibly another."

"And was that possible other a child?" I asked.

"I wouldn't go that far," she replied, smiling. "Just a third presence."

This isn't going to work.

While I berated myself for misreading Linda's comment and for lacking marital faith, she busied herself locating a beautiful home in Newberry clearly beyond our means. It sat on five grassy acres, artfully situated among mature mossy oaks. A single-story brick affair well over 3000 square feet, it seemed to stretch forever. The view from the back patio included a white-fenced field crying out for polo. Oak floors exuded an opulent glow aided by soft light streaming in through many large windows.

Linda stood with arms folded over her rounded belly as we stared together at this low-slung castle.

"It's magnificent, but we can't afford it."

"That's true, but we need to live in it worse than we need to afford it."

"Okay, if you can finagle a deal that doesn't land us in debtor's prison or sell our souls to Carl Decker, have at it."

Linda smiled, gave me a reassuring pat, but agreed to nothing. "We could raise a couple of white goats on the back forty," she speculated. "That would be cool."

We managed to move in around Halloween, just a month before Ramona was born. The seller, a visiting Marxist professor, had returned to Argentina prematurely, pining, as Linda had somehow discovered, for his showgirl mistress. Linda made an insulting lowball offer halfway between the asking price and the mortgage balance, which was more or less accepted after a token tug-of-war. Carl's banker (at least not Carl's money) granted us a feasible monthly outlay in exchange for a catastrophic balloon payment looming ten years down the road.

"Don't fret," Linda told me. "We'll own this sucker free and clear in five years."

Four years. Linda's renunciation of intoxicants liberated frenetic energy, which she poured into what would later be called "house flipping." Besides Carl's dubious dealings, she put her law practice on hold, having discovered a more lucrative use of her talents. She had a nose for the housing market and, inexplicably, an equal knack for ferreting out gossip about the private lives of transactional adversaries and their corresponding pressure points. She also discovered the personal computer and the strategic edge provided by spreadsheets and databases. It was as if people played poker against her with their cards face up. Oddly, she didn't try to make a killing on any one deal, relying instead on many modest chunks of profit, all of which she applied to our mortgage principal at the expense of household furnishings, new cars, vacations, and other manifestations of the good life. However, since in real estate (as Hamlet put it, albeit regarding death), "the readiness is all," Linda hired a nanny and housekeeper not long after we moved in to guarantee her constant availability. They were sisters from the Dominican Republic, unshakably dependable, with deeply etched, kind, shy faces.

"Eridania and Awilda are Spirit women," Linda confided, "true down to their bones." And loving caretakers of Ramona, along with Thelema and Tanith, effervescent white, long-eared goats Linda bought as a Christmas present to herself.

But to return to Ramona's birth, we were still unpacking when she arrived. Since I had been single, meager in possessions, and lucky to be working six months before, her existence astonished me all the more. And yet here we were, eternally bound together, living well up the totem pole of American status.

When I got home from the college, I went immediately to Ramona's crib and peered closely, looking for the slightest signs of flux—a new kick or gurgle, a hint of growing recognition. Linda regarded my examinations with amusement, choosing to take her living handiwork more in stride. "Ramona's perfect," she would say. "Don't be such a worrywart."

I wasn't worried. I was in love, a love that hit me with the physiological impact of a teenage crush. Not that little Ramona mirrored my delight. She met my smiles with speculative neutrality, saving her loud, contentious opinions for Linda, who, after all, originated and sustained her existence. For her part, Linda expected Ramona to be rational from the start. If her mewling or fussing continued too long, Linda would say, "Here, Bill, see if you can *reason* with her." I would take Ramona, bounce her gently, murmuring assurances until she tired of fretting, or Linda would retrieve her, having recovered her patience. I would resume my lowly place in the domestic pecking order.

It was all part of an idyllic period following Ramona's birth, with the grotesque exception of losing John Lennon. *I heard the news today, oh shit.* Heard it on the Philco I still clicked on from time to time, listening for the sweeter part of my past. I called off that day, too angry and shaken to function. Like John, I had been touched by the deadly combination of crazy and guns—in the quarry, and one other time in Hopperton. Either time it could have done me in. Random or not, chance is an unrighteous bitch.

Eridania and Awilda, unencumbered by grieving over John Lennon, established a new domestic order by the spring of '81, overthrowing their employers in a bloodless coup. Awilda planted a summer garden of okra, eggplant, black-eyed peas, sweet potatoes, herbs, and myriad hot peppers, tending it with open contempt for the midday sun. Eridania's phlegmatic ways suited Ramona, neither of them requiring the other to smile vapidly. Linda and I excelled professionally. Kids packed my classes, and Linda collected her retainer from Carl while bluffing, wheedling, outsmarting, and outworking her way from one profitable real estate deal to the next. And not to forget, the goats prospered. I built them a shady lean-to, and Eridania's dexterous hand accomplished the daily milkings.

Elsewhere, the Iran hostages started home soon after the old, soft-spoken actor became president. Double-digit inflation slowly eased and the space shuttle *Columbia* completed its maiden voyage. As if to vindicate Don Heffelfinger and Ayn Rand, the federal government would henceforward restrict itself to protecting us against the Evil Empire and quit running our lives. It was high time to stop pussyfooting around and proclaim ourselves the all-time greatest country. And anyone who felt different could take their Summers of Love and shove them up their ass.

Which brings me to those summer nights Linda and I sat outside in cushioned Adirondack chairs under skies still peppered with stars city dwellers no longer see. We always talked first about Ramona's progress, aghast at her stubborn ways, amazed that she never whined, assured of her superiority. Then Linda, like a CFO reporting to the board, would assess our holdings, spicing up the numbers by reveling in the stratagems behind her latest real estate coup.

One evening, as I smoked a nostalgic joint, Linda concluded her financial analysis with that most ancient of insights—people are dumb.

"You remind me of my father," I said. "His word of choice was 'fool.'" I spoke absently, with no particular interest in pursuing the comparison. The pot was kicking in, turning the goats in their shelter into a rudimentary nativity scene, the singular brightness of Venus off to the west completing the effect.

"Smart man," Linda said.

"Yeah, but sometimes when it counted, fools got the best of him. Go figure."

"Hence the term 'dumb luck.'"

"Hence the term 'hubris.' My father assumed that if someone had a foolish purpose, they would use foolish means. It doesn't work that way. I don't happen to think most people are dumb. They're just finite, that's all—too little time to wise up about everything. Say, for instance, a guy comes to fix your washing machine. He makes a simple but costly repair, then leaves shaking his head because you're too dumb and lazy to figure anything out for yourself. Is he right?"

"No, because my warranty covered the repair. And he's making a third of what I'm making if he's lucky. And he just happened to run into a wolf among sheep."

"Okay, wolf lady. Just don't forget to factor in dumb luck—and especially people *playing* dumb—when you're wheeling and dealing."

"Are *you* playing dumb?" Linda trotted out her cross-examination tone

"Don't worry; *not* catching on is my specialty."

"So you say," she murmured, staring into the falling dark as if straining for a last glimpse of a vanishing detail.

"Your Christmas tree has company," I said, casting about for a new subject.

"What?"

I gestured toward the goats resting next to their feeding trough. "There's our stable complete with a manger. And Ramona being born. Clearly another sign." I paused, waiting for Linda to absorb my discernment.

"Another oracle in the family; maybe you *are* catching on, Bill. I better start paying attention." All I could read into her tone was restlessness. She stood up and faced the house, probably looking at her tree. "Tell me, Bill, what does it signify when the Virgin Mary wants a cigarette so bad she can taste it?"

I lingered a bit after Linda went in, waiting to spot a shooting star before turning in, imagining it shot from the celestial bow of Sagittarius, the Archer, then enjoying summer prominence. As it happened, three meteors fell in quick succession. "Surely an omen," I muttered aloud, sarcastically dismissing the possibility. Bad enough that I let flashes in the sky tell me when to go to bed.

Linda, who never fell asleep without me beside her, murmured that I preferred the stars to her body.

"No, just taking the universe in before it's gone." I stripped down to match her nakedness. "Anyway, thinking gives me a headache, and staring at the sky cures it." I slipped in beside her and rolled close, the first touch of her skin, as always, a sweet shock.

"How's Ramona?" I asked.

"Sleeping like a baby. Did you figure it out?"

"Figure what out?"

"Whatever was giving you the headache."

"No, but at least I quit trying."

"That's my boy," she whispered. "Now shut up and hibernate." She held my hand to her breast as she turned away, bringing our bodies into the position she desired. Her breathing slowed before long, and I tried to match its rhythm, but a phrase she had used earlier—"so you say"—lingered in my mind. Don Heffelfinger had used that phrase countless times during our high school arguments. I could claim our friendship ended because Don disappeared from Hopperton, but he could make the identical claim about me. We shared a great childhood, a moment of notoriety, then nothing. My father would say we "let go of the rope." No, the rope got cut. My letters were refused.

Futile ruminations led me back to another nagging unknown: where had Linda gone for a month after telling me she was pregnant? She had never told me. And I had never pursued the question, hoping she would remember her promise.

And where was Carl keeping himself? A less fraught question, no doubt answerable by Linda, who cashed his retainer checks. I was reminding myself to ask both questions when sleep finally had its way with me, luring me into a dream where I hammered on Hopperton doors, trying to find shelter from whoever was chasing me with a crossbow. No one would let me in, but on the other hand, you never die in dreams, do you?

CHAPTER FIFTEEN

"Get Together"

"He's around," Linda replied to my Carl inquiry. I nodded and let the subject go. We were enjoying a weekend breakfast of Jinotega coffee, fresh-squeezed orange juice, and *arepas*—white corn cakes stuffed with black beans, beef, plantains, and salty cheese—from which Ramona in her highchair gouged fistfuls for the apparent benefit of the terra-cotta tiles below.

As I proffered a bean for Ramona to disdain, Linda returned to Carl. "He comes by once in a while to sign papers and sample Awilda's cooking. You're always at school, so…" She let the last word hang in silence as if only one conclusion could follow.

"I'm at school less than forty hours out of one hundred sixty-eight," I countered. "Carl's very unlucky to have missed me." Ramona wrenched her head aside and grimaced, repudiating the bean.

"He feels he's a bad influence on you. He doesn't want to be the reason you screw up fatherhood."

"What reason would he prefer?"

"He doesn't care, as long as it isn't him."

"And I don't care if he comes by when I'm here, as long as the feds don't bust in after him, traumatizing the womenfolk."

Linda snickered. "If cops showed up, Ramona would hold off pissing her pants longer than you would. Anyway, from what I hear, none of the narcs have mentioned Carl's name, which is as close to a stay-out-of-jail card as you're gonna get." By now, Ramona was pulverizing her *arepa*, perhaps trying to absorb nutrition through the pores of her palms.

"Okay, I'll chance a Carl sighting, but I think it's *you* he comes to see anyway. You two think disturbingly alike."

"Yeah, Carl's just like me, a drug-free, law-abiding homebody."

"Don't get me wrong," I added, sensing umbrage, "you're wonderful. But you have to admit that neither of you is happy unless you're outsmarting one poor sap or another."

Linda gave a dismissive shrug. "Everybody's like that; it's called survival of the fittest. Some people are better at it, that's all."

"If by 'like that' you mean everybody wants to survive, sure. But just to play the devil's advocate, biologists say cooperation often helps you survive better than competition."

"You mean like that hippie song where we get together in a big pile and love each other?" Linda sang a line or two of "Get Together" with skill and feeling despite her ironic intent.

"More like John Stuart Mill's theory of sympathetic affection, but you're on the right track. And by the way, Linda, you should be in a band." Ramona had demolished her *arepa* and pounded on plastic like a judge demanding order in the court.

"I *was* in a band, in high school. I was the Grace Slick of Alamosa, Colorado."

"What kind of band?"

"We called ourselves My Weekly Bath if that gives you any idea."

"The mind reels."

"Yeah."

"Since we're so chatty, are you ready to tell me where you went for a month?"

"As I promised, right?"

"Well, yes, but I like to think I'm not asking in a coercive spirit."

"In which case, you won't be upset if I don't tell you."

"Meaning you're *not* going to tell me?"

"That was my plan, for entirely benevolent motives."

"I don't suppose Carl knows."

"Carl doesn't know much of anything." Linda sipped her coffee and yawned a bit conveniently, I thought. "And even if he does," she added, "you're far too cool to ask him, aren't you?"

"I'm not going to ask him; I'm asking you. It's not life or death. If—"

"If we're still married in ten years, I'll tell you, Bill, I swear. Now you have a *raison d'etre*." Linda gave me her best crooked, skinny-French-actress smile.

"Okay, asked and answered, peace restored, the need for secrets admitted. We *all* have them." I failed to sound provocative and mysterious.

"You don't mind Carl coming over tonight?"

"No, not that I'm stupid enough to think my objection would keep him away. He's like a weed with a taproot you're never going to dig out. Especially when your wife thinks it's a beautiful flower."

"More like a cash crop, but otherwise a pretty smart take."

I had to admit Carl livened things up. He flirted with "the Latin ladies," as he called Awilda and Eridania, via the scraps of Spanish he picked up hanging out with his Cuban middlemen in Ybor City. Even the stoic Eridania fell prey to his advances, exhibiting a smile usually reserved for the goats. When he wasn't talking up the ladies, he doted on Ramona, undeterred by her deadpan stare. Then, a few Sundays into his string of visits, an odd eruption. Carl sat with Ramona on his lap, feeding her Cheerios and bits of spicy pork, providing a nonstop fuming commentary on a rerun of *Columbo*, explaining why he would have foiled the rumpled LA police detective. "Any idiot can tell he's just pretending to be confused. What bullshit."

Linda, curled up cat-like on the loveseat and seemingly half-asleep, was listening closely enough to inject her mantra: "People are dumb, Carl, and people who don't *get that* are even dumber." Carl chuckled, then leaned down and stage-whispered to Ramona. "Did you hear that, honey? Take my advice and don't be a bitch like your mother when you grow up. Be nice to people like Bill. Like your good old dad."

Linda sprang to her feet and snatched Ramona out of Carl's lap, scattering Cheerios and pork. As Ramona wailed her displeasure, Linda faced her daughter toward us. "See those two beady-eyed creatures over there, Mona? They're called *men*. You will do a lot of screaming and crying because of them; you might as well get used to it."

At this point, Eridania appeared in the hallway. When we looked at her, she didn't say anything, but she didn't retreat either. She just folded her arms and watched, clearly intending, like a fraternity mother, to stay put until the foolishness subsided. Linda marched over to her and transferred

Ramona into her arms, muttering something that sounded like "disaster." Then she stalked down the hall toward our bedroom.

Eridania could not possibly know who or what had instigated the quarrel, but she, like Linda, knew we were men—more than enough explanation. After one last impassive stare, she too turned and disappeared down the hall with a suddenly quiescent Ramona in tow.

"On the rag," Carl concluded, turning his attention back to *Columbo*.

"You or Linda?" I started collecting strewn food.

"Good one, Professor. Yeah, I guess I fucked up your happy home. It won't happen again."

With that, Carl returned to *Columbo*, leaving me to wonder about the skirmish; not the ho-hum exchange of insults, but the simmering discord they laid bare. Perhaps a battle of wills related to Carl's illegal dealings. But then where did I fit in? Maybe when she declared people were dumb, she meant *men* were dumb. Hadn't she warned Ramona that all men were versions of the lowdown cheating skunks in a Bessie Smith blues? Yet before tonight, she never railed against men—even those who failed her quest for the sexual holy grail.

Well, as Don Heffelfinger's father once told me, *Boy, you don't know shit from Shinola.* And he was right. Chasing people's motives back then only served to get me lost. Why would I think Linda was a maze I could solve now? And besides, what could the cheese at the end of that maze possibly be?

As I kept myself busy overthinking, Carl gestured and swore at the TV, his dustup with Linda seemingly forgotten. I saw his point. In an alternate universe, one in which I could forget he slept with Karen, I might break out the Jack Daniels and relive some fragment of college camaraderie—tubing the Ichetucknee wrecked on hashish or catching Mudcrutch (Tom Petty's old band) out at the Stone Castle, where passing cars often pulled off the road to listen. And sweetest of all would be reviving the early days after Karen came along, days when the three of us felt happier together than any two of us alone, sitting in lawn chairs outside Karen's cottage, talking about jack shit, "Brown Sugar" blasting from speakers slid to the open front door.

And I knew I could break the seal on those righteous days anytime I wished by clicking off *Columbo* and offering some recollection to

Carl—maybe Karen, drunk on apple wine, ripping the veil off human weakness by trying to sing along with Joni Mitchell. He wouldn't give a hang *why* Karen was no longer a *verboten* topic. No, he'd take my change of heart in stride, eyes gleaming, fixed on the promising road ahead.

Maybe someday I would achieve the Buddha-like detachment necessary to treat chunks of my past like episodes of *Columbo*—self-contained and solved.

Maybe, but not that Sunday night.

"Gotta work tomorrow, Carl; I'm turning in."

Carl nodded, absorbed in some sneaky interrogation by Peter Falk. He would turn off the TV and the lights—or he wouldn't—no great matter.

"Just shut the front door; we never lock it."

In the bedroom, as always, Linda pulled me close.

"Life is horrible," she said, offering no example. And I felt no impulse to ask for one.

By the summer of '82, the year of Ramona's second birthday, the Equal Rights Amendment was ratified by thirty-five of the thirty-eight states needed for passage. It didn't pass in large part because antifeminist women opposed it: women would have to fight wars, take jobs, and do all sorts of other unwomanly things. This treasonous sabotage infuriated Linda, who revealed that Phyllis Schlafly, the ringleader, was a black witch.

As a white witch, Linda assured me, she would know.

And indeed, Linda's real estate success bordered on the uncanny. She reaped a steady stream of commissions and profits, making short shrift of our mortgage principal. Sooner than seemed possible, we owned more of the house than the bank. Linda reveled in this state of affairs as if it were a victory over fate itself, but her giddy triumph (like in countless novels) left unintended consequences swirling in its wake.

Late that summer, thanks to a colleague, I received an unexpected job offer from a Miami college, promising better pay and sabbaticals. We could profitably sell our house, Awilda and Eridania could embrace more of their native culture, and Linda could hook bigger fish in a bigger housing pond.

But when I broached the subject, Linda reacted with a bleak stare, as if I had suggested we move to Kazakhstan and become potato farmers. "This is where we need to be," she insisted, her tone prophetic, hinting that her words arose from otherworldly sources.

"Fair enough—you've certainly been right about a lot of things—but do you mind telling me why?"

Linda sighed and sank into thought, apparently contemplating how best to translate to the uninitiated. As I waited, I looked around. Amber light suffused the living room where we sat savoring Irish coffee. The Latin ladies, with Ramona as their understudy, worked outside, gardening and goat herding. Our furnishings were still sparse but quite lovely, mostly Ethan Allen pieces Linda had extracted from a house she flipped. Admittedly, our current domicile provided a life of beauty and order anyone might regret abandoning. One of the new furnishings, a Federal-style inlaid mahogany sideboard, supported Linda's Christmas tree, now backed by a large mirror to multiply its varicolored prismatic aura. Over time I had stopped paying the tree any special notice. Now, I found myself staring at it, suspecting its influence over Linda, that suspicion itself seeming more neurotic to me, more preposterous than any of Linda's supernatural claims.

"Our life here is in balance," Linda finally answered. "If we move, it will come crashing down."

"Isn't that a bit dramatic? People move all the time without disastrous consequences. What's special about us?"

Linda, dressed in a dark blouse and pants, slim and porcelain pale as always, leaned back into the corner of our plump gray couch. As if summoned by a painter to shade the portrait of a mysterious woman, passing clouds subtracted color from the room light, transforming Linda into a study in black-and-white, an effect intensified by her stillness. I remembered my wish to paint her and her lighthearted promise to bare her body in fulfillment. But here was the pose I would ask of her now, knowing that anyone who could capture her haunted expression would create a masterpiece.

"We're not special," she pronounced with a certain bleakness. "It's just that I married us to this place."

"How?" I demanded, fighting to keep incredulity from creeping into my voice.

"I took a vow to care for it as long as it cared for us. Why do you think everything's gone so well?"

"To be honest, I gave *us* credit for living right. Anyway, couldn't you make the same vow with a house in Coconut Grove?"

139

"Maybe. But that's not the point. To move, we would have to *divorce* this house. Then all the misfortune it held at bay might be released."

"It sounds like you made more of a Faustian bargain than a marriage vow. What about us innocent bystanders?"

"I did it for Ramona *because* she's innocent."

"I don't doubt your good intentions, but if we're stuck here forever, beholding to the house, I'm sorry, but it reminds me of a horror movie."

"It's not like that. This property is our Garden of Eden. It won't *punish* us if we leave; it just won't protect us anymore."

"I seem to recall a snake in the Garden of Eden."

"That's Christian propaganda, Bill. I could just as easily have called it Shangri-La, or Utopia, or Atlantis—whatever—you get the point."

"Okay, forget the snake. I guess my question is, what are you afraid of out there? What exactly is the house protecting us *from?*"

"The quarry," she said, folding her arms tightly. "And before you freak out, I'm not talking about that pissant hole in the ground. I'm talking about a very unpleasant world that's hard as hell to steer clear of." Linda paused, leaned forward, then made sweeping gestures with her hands, as if summoning our surroundings into existence. "Ask yourself, dear Bill, how many happy stories do you tell yourself when you daydream about the past? How do they compare to the life you have now?" Her expression suggested a great deal depended on my answer.

Something compelled me to get up, walk over to the Christmas tree, and stare at myself in the mirror behind it. Thinning hair, patchy beard, an average face in the first of its timeworn stages. "Believe me; I know how good we have it here," I said, speaking to myself and Linda and some invisible crowd of listeners.

"But not quite good enough, right?" When I faced Linda, she wore the bitter smile of someone who had leaped to a very unflattering conclusion.

"Okay, Linda, why don't you tell *me* what my motives are for considering a move? I thought I'd outlined logical advantages, but apparently, I'm nursing some secret grievance. Go ahead; I'm all ears."

Linda looked down, shaking her head, announcing her reluctance to say what she was about to say. "All right, sometimes I feel you resent that I made all this happen."

"Resent? You wanted to do it, and I didn't. Do you resent that I understand Schopenhauer and you don't? And besides, you didn't make *all* this happen. I made half of Ramona, and what's more important than that?"

"Nothing, 'Professor,' unless you screw things up by dragging her down to godforsaken Miami."

As it happened, Awilda and Eridania preferred to stay put. Their closest relatives lived in Orlando, an easy drive down 441 in the used Ford station wagon Linda bought for them (and wrote off as a business expense). Sea Island also helped Linda's cause by bumping my salary, probably having gotten wind of the Miami offer. And anyway, as the only man in a pro-ERA household, no good would come from putting my foot down like some biblical patriarch. You can't expect to win with a half-hearted bluff.

In the end, after a couple of days of private grousing, I turned down the Miami job and put it behind me, finding it too abstract to pine over, like a delicious dessert you've heard about but never tasted. Linda, on the other hand, appeared permanently shaken by my disloyalty to our homestead. Her nervous glances seemed to accuse me in advance of further rash attempts to upset the apple cart. Ramona suddenly found it necessary to wriggle free of her mother's protective embraces. At night Linda still needed me near, but now she groaned and shifted before sinking into sleep, reluctant to give up some ghost of apprehension.

In response, I went about my business, trying to embody a steadfast demeanor that would give Linda's fears no perching spot. And in an alternate reality where coincidence, witch magic, accident, karma, and guilt didn't exist, my laissez-faire strategy probably would have worked.

However, a few days after the Miami dustup, the sapphire stone from Linda's wedding ring dislodged from its setting. Linda believed the stone had fallen out as she chased Ramona, who had been "herding" baby goats around the pasture. All five household members combed the grass for an entire afternoon without success. On the one hand, Linda's distress touched me; on the other hand, as in the case of the Miami job offer, she ascribed tragic dimensions to a loss I would call regrettable. Putting aside sentimental attachment, finding a deep blue sapphire of equal quality would not be difficult.

I made this argument to her as she sat on the edge of our bed, hanging her head, looking sick at heart.

"We can't find the old one. Buying a new stone won't change that."

"No," I conceded, "but it also won't change anything for the worse."

Linda looked up at me balefully, and I braced myself for some scathing riposte.

Instead, she replied in a soft, sad voice, "The sapphire doesn't *want* to be found, Bill. It knows everything is out of … cosmic balance."

I resisted pointing out the inanimate nature of sapphires or the hyperbole of "everything."

"Anything I can do?" I offered.

"Sure, if you're an idiot. But I doubt if I'll ask you, so don't worry about it."

"I'm only worried because you told me not to worry."

"Okay, Bill, let me put it this way. Either everything is fucked up, or nothing is fucked up. I'll know which one it is in a couple of days; leave it alone in the meantime. Can you do that?"

I nodded. "You do know that I'm on your side, right?"

Linda fell back on the bed and put her hands over her face. "I know you *think* you are."

Emotional algebra with too many unknowns to solve. I hoped I wouldn't have to wait ten years for the answer to this unknown.

CHAPTER SIXTEEN

"Instant Karma"

Two evenings later, Carl showed up with more cognac—a fresh supply of angel tears. Other than this evocative offering, his visit was routine, the friction between him and Linda lately smoothed over, or at least simmering beneath the boiling point. The cognac drew Carl and me to the kitchen table instead of the TV couch, and to my surprise, Linda joined us. Karen, Carl, and I had happily gathered like this many times during our college years to share a bottle of convenience store wine, and I found the parallel comforting. Maybe a distant cousin of that camaraderie could reincarnate from time to time.

Despite her war on diabetes, Linda accepted a token pour and sat in silence as Carl recounted an anecdote from his days as a drug kingpin. I didn't buy his latest tall tale, but it was lively talk, and anyway, this wasn't a symposium on Hegel.

As Carl went on, Linda began to shift around in her chair and grimace as if in physical distress, until she more or less shouted, "Carl, what the fuck? Are we going to do this or what?"

Carl threw up his hands in mock defeat.

"Sure, might as well go for the throat, right?"

I imagined they were about to thrash out their mutual grievances in a verbal free-for-all. Instead, Linda turned to me.

"Bill, I never believed I cheated on you, but I guess I did."

"You *guess?*" I felt a cold wind sweep through me. Carl sitting there could only mean one thing. One crushingly obvious thing.

"Just listen, Bill. I spent all day yesterday looking for that damn sapphire. I know it's out there, but it's not blue anymore. That's how I know I cheated. Not now, but before. I thought I saw my ring start to fade when you wanted to move to Miami. It was warning me—time for Carl and me to confess. And you must try and understand. Otherwise, Ramona's going to have the same horrible life we're having."

"Hey," Carl protested. "My life isn't horrible, and I sure as hell didn't screw your lovely *wife* here." I said nothing, forcing him to hear his own words. Desperate to lose the spotlight, he glared at Linda and growled, "Tell him, dammit!"

I downed half my cognac, hoping to burn away the sick feeling in my gut, all of Linda and Carl's words but "cheated on you" and "tell him" forgotten.

"Go ahead, Linda, tell me. Whatever you say is just window dressing anyway. It's not like I'd be shocked to think you and Carl, or myself for that matter, aren't good people."

She stared in dismay. No doubt, she had imagined how things would unfold—everyone does. Now she—and I—knew better.

"God, Bill, just the other day you swore you were on my side. What the fuck?"

"Trust me," I said, "we're on the same side. It's just not a very admirable side."

Carl smacked the table with his glass like a judge with a gavel. "I swear to God, you two are my favorite idiots in the world. You both think you're heavyweights, but you're just a couple of nine-year-olds. Listen, Bill, Linda thinks I'm Ramona's dad. I probably am."

Linda tried to intervene.

"Shut up," Carl barked. "You'll get your chance. The truth, Professor, is that good old Linda and I had sex without protection back in the day, and from what I'm told, you were always a *gentleman*. The sex was her idea, but I didn't exactly fight her off. Nobody was married to anybody then. Hell, nobody was even going steady, according to Linda. She swore you wouldn't care. She swore I would be doing you both a favor, something to do with 'taking the pressure off.' We did it twice. After the second time, she was all happy and said we should call it off. Too complicated or something. As far as being Ramona's dad is concerned, I'm good with the way things are. You are *Father Knows Best* material, and I'm the friendly uncle type.

Just pretend you adopted her if it makes you feel better. And if you want to go crazy and divorce Linda over this bullshit, go ahead. You can still be Ramona's dad; I won't blow your cover. I sure as shit don't want to marry Linda and take your place."

Carl's pared-down version of events rang true. Linda *hadn't* "reached the mountaintop" by herself. Nothing like a little icing on the world's shittiest cake. I turned to Linda, who sat with arms folded, thin-lipped, shaking her head.

"That night at Carl's when you proposed; why did you tell me I was Ramona's father?"

"That was a spirit-truth. A truth to come. That's why I told it in front of Carl. That's why I told you I didn't want anyone else to be the father. I felt love for you. You felt some kind of love for me. You *are* the father."

"Shit," Carl said. "How long did it take you to write that?"

"Fuck you, Carl."

"Sorry, honey, that ship has sailed."

I tried to stare holes through Linda. "I appreciate you lying for my benefit like that. Very enlightened. And when you told Carl I wouldn't care, how did you know that? Spirit voices? I don't recall you asking me if I minded you screwing Carl."

"I honestly didn't think you would. We weren't *in* love, or are you going to suddenly tell me we were?"

"No, I'm just going to tell you that I don't believe you."

"Why the hell not?" Linda mustered up as much defiance as battle weariness would allow. She shook the foot of her crossed leg violently.

"Simple. You told me you solved your sex problem yourself. Solo. You talked Carl into giving me five thousand dollars. That's classic consciousness of guilt, counselor. Then that crap about not moving to Miami to appease a house god. I don't suppose that had anything to do with papa Carl's secret visitation rights?" I glanced at Carl. He nodded, clearly unsurprised.

"Yeah, I told Miss Featherstone to stay put if she wanted her big fat retainer and certain other real estate perks she might not have in Miami."

"Miss Featherstone?" I turned back to Linda.

"Come on, Bill. It's good for business if men think I'm single, that's all. The sapphire helps too. Men think all wedding rings are diamonds. It's pathetic."

"Yes, pathetic."

"Look, Carl didn't blackmail me into staying—"

"Forget it, Linda; as Awilda says, *no importa*. It's true; it isn't true. I'll never know anyway, whatever you say. I do know that Carl is the only person who would strike me as a deliberately wicked choice. The night we met, you said he wanted something from you he was never going to get. If I thought you were attracted to Carl, I'd have told you to walk home from that lousy party."

"I'm not attracted to Carl. He was just handy at the wrong time. Sorry, Carl, but that's the truth."

"No problem," he answered, smiling languidly. "You weren't that special either. But that was funny, Bill, that shit about me being a wicked choice. Wicked choice—wicked witch. Hilarious."

"Bill, I only went to anyone besides you to get that last little bit of excitement I needed. I wasn't unhappy with you. Just the opposite—"

"Where the hell did you disappear to after you got pregnant? Your ten years are up."

Linda gave Carl a forlorn glance. His shrug conveyed an explicit message: *it's your mess, baby.*

"I went to Carl's house in Tampa."

"Ah."

"By myself."

"And Carl never happened to stop by?"

Linda looked miserable, as everyone does who's trapped by the truth.

"Of course he did. It's his house."

"And you slept in separate beds?"

"No, but we didn't have sex. A warm body helps me sleep; you know that."

"I do, but I don't know why you went to Carl's house."

Linda smiled. "It's a nice house. No one was living there. It's by the water; you can feel the wind. I needed to feel the wind to regain my true direction."

"And your true direction was to marry a man who *wasn't* your baby's father?"

"Yes."

"Why not Carl?"

She fixed her gaze on him before answering.

"Because he's a lunatic destined for prison."

Carl replied with a scoffing jeer. "The way you operate *your* business, you'll get there way before I do."

"I'm clean, Carl, and you know it."

"Like I said before, sweetheart, act like a bitch, and sooner or later, people will take you down. That's why I told Ramona to be more like her good old dad, and I wasn't talking about me." Carl raised a toast in my direction, causing Linda to fix me with a speculative stare.

"Can I ask *you* a question, Bill?"

"Shoot." Had there been any decent excuse to say no, I would have used it.

"Why did you agree to marry me? Why not just be the baby's father and leave it at that?"

"Let me turn the question around. What justification could I have given for *not* marrying you? That you were an unlovable person and bad company? That arranged marriages lack 'true love'? They can't work any worse than the free-for-all, merry-go-round system *we* use. And mating in pairs seems to be nature's preferred way for humans to raise their young. It all made sense to me at the time. Now, of course—"

Carl slammed his hand down on the table. "Damn, Bill," he shouted. "I know you fancy yourself as a deep thinker, but you swung and missed on this one. When Linda popped the question, did you think you could do better than her in a million years? No offense, but that's a joke." Carl gave her an admiring glance, followed by a sly grin. "But come to think of it, she's stuck with us, so how wonderful can she really be?"

Linda's stare bored into Carl. "I'm wonderful enough to *never* be in love with either one of you as long as I live. I see now I can't have love *and* my powers. And believe me, I prefer my powers. Don't worry, Carl; you're safe from me."

Carl burst out laughing. "Me? Damn, Linda, your husband's sitting right there. Isn't he the one who should worry about being safe from you and your badass powers?"

Linda flinched a little at this and looked at me. "I'm sorry about this, Bill, I really am."

I threw up my hands in resignation. "You're sorry, I'm sorry, Carl probably isn't. Anything more we need to decide before I go to bed and hope to wake up as somebody else?" I contemplated moving out, weighing the pain of separation from Ramona.

"Holy fuck, this is weird," Carl said, downing his cognac like lemonade. "Anyway, I say we sleep on it for a year or two, then have another one of these delightful meetings. And in the meantime, here's one more brilliant idea. You lovebirds buy another magical sapphire and see if *it* turns black or yellow or green, you know, like a mood ring. Since you're both batshit crazy, you might as well go all the way."

Well, if nothing else, Carl was practical, laying out the cold-blooded facts, eliminating Lord knows how much tiptoeing and mumbo jumbo. Maybe he inadvertently liberated Linda and me from fictions of undying love and spared Ramona from whatever dire fate Linda had glimpsed in her witchy visions.

Maybe.

The words Carl, Linda, and I wielded against each other that night hovered inside me, waiting for a judgment I couldn't hand down. I couldn't go back and revisit the events each of us purported to describe—I couldn't go back in time—least of all through my porous, revisionist memories. Yes, I had been wronged. But how purposely?

And what now? Were my indignities sufficient to curse Ramona with a broken home?

I found myself taking Carl's advice and "sleeping on it" for far more than a single night, waiting, I suppose, for the past to return of its own accord, ready at last to explain itself.

It took its sweet time.

Meanwhile, Carl kept showing up like nothing had happened, affably daring me to prove otherwise. Linda relaxed now that she felt we'd cleared the air sufficiently to save Ramona from karmic doom. And with "love" off the table, she and I even had occasional sex, though not the sweetest kind where you lose yourself. We sought relief, not satisfaction, and in my case, the propitiation of some god I continued to offend, probably because I couldn't shake the feeling that Linda was faithless, even if her body wasn't. In that ignominious spirit, I monitored her new sapphire, watching for changes in its lustrous blue character.

On the one hand, the stone maintained its hue. On the other hand, it made no promises.

Despite the famous catchphrase of Reagan's reelection campaign, it was never quite "morning in America" during the '80s. We had the usual recessions, market crashes, scandals, tax increases, deficit increases—all the icky stuff that accompanied our enjoyment of the fruits of cutthroat capitalism. Real Americans headed for the Sunbelt, leaving the urban wastelands behind, consigning them to the Blacks, the Browns, and whatever other wastrels chose to scavenge the ruins. Government was now the problem, and rugged individualism was the solution.

Perhaps to punish me for my unhealthy liberalism and Linda for the legal shenanigans Carl had hinted at, something—maybe the Jedi force—regressed her real estate profits to the mean and beyond, Lotus 123 and an IBM PC notwithstanding, welcoming us into the plight of average, struggling Americans. We didn't have to make radical sacrifices, but we weren't socking away a cushy future either. Carl, I suppose, was doing okay since he opened a savings account for Ramona into which he made regular, substantial deposits. Beyond that, he asserted no parental rights, choosing to regard her fondly from an avuncular distance. "She's sober as a judge," he would say as he watched her concentrate at the chessboard. I had taught her the game when she was six. I didn't care for Carl's reference to the penal system, but he was undoubtedly right. She took inordinate time with her moves and never looked up afterward for my approval, never lamented her losses, just requested another game until she grew tired of playing.

I situate these games in late, sun-dappled Saturday afternoons, Ramona and I sitting on the patio through timeless hours, Linda coming and going like one of those Prufrock women, while the Latin ladies, our multiplying goat herd, and soft rock on the boombox each add something sweet and essential to the memory.

So, we went along, me teaching my holy trinity of Plato, Spinoza and Heidegger, Linda and Carl shaking the coin-operated machine known as capitalism as hard as they dared, and Ramona growing up skinny and deadpan, with the long blonde hair of a heroine in a book.

When she was ten, I began taking Ramona to grapefruit league spring training—the Dodgers in Vero Beach, the Yankees in Fort Lauderdale, the Pirates in Bradenton, the Red Sox in Winter Haven, the Tigers in Lakeland. We would set out in the Studebaker, be gone a day or two, and come back with Ramona the proud possessor of impeccable scorecards and autographed baseballs from the likes of Barry Bonds, Wade Boggs, Jack Morris, and Eddie Murray. I wonder now what she and I talked about on those long rides. I know I told a few baseball stories—Babe Ruth traded from the Red Sox to the Yankees, creating the curse of the Bambino, Lou Gehrig's Luckiest Man on the Face of the Earth speech, Mazeroski's long drive sailing over Yogi Berra's head in game seven of the 1960 meta-dramatic World Series. And I remember Ramona pouring forth endless questions, looking for facts and numbers, goading me to learn the names of palm varieties passed along the way—cabbage palm, queen, royal, Chilean wine, coconut, Canary Island date, Chinese fan, windmill, fishtail, and many others now fled from memory. Did she ask me about marriage, the future, the meaning of life? I only remember one such question, posed by Ramona out of nowhere as we idled at a railway crossing near Bradenton, waiting for innumerable boxcars of the Tropicana juice train to pass: "Why do we *have* to die, Dad?"

Oddly enough, I had never considered her question beyond the answer I had once given while drunk in a bar: that death gives the minions of heaven and hell material to work with.

"Sweetheart," I shouted through the clanging, flashing, clacking, and rumbling, "we have to die to make room for the new people being born."

Ramona mulled my answer until the train passed, waiting to reply until she could do so softly.

"Why don't we just keep the people we have and quit making new people?"

We had a solid three-hour drive back home. "If we quit making new people (I wasn't about to explain why that would be a hard sell), we would still die, and then we wouldn't have *any* people. See, millions of years ago, nature designed people to die. It's way too late now to change nature's mind. You'll study evolution in school, survival of the fittest; it'll all make sense then."

We drove along in silence for a while, Ramona caught up in crossing the Skyway Bridge, no seat belt, sticking her head—blonde hair whipping—out the Studebaker's window. Like all traffic, we traveled the northern span, the southern span having collapsed a decade back, now only a very expensive fishing pier. A freighter caught in a seventy-knot squall had struck a main support column, plunging cars, trucks, and a Greyhound bus into Tampa Bay—thirty-five lives lost. Two grown men I know won't cross the towering span at all, beaten by their phobias. While Ramona consumed the vertiginous view, I considered survival of the fittest, remembering from my college science requirement that "fitness," in the final analysis, meant creating children to keep your bloodline going. Carl had done that *and* found a surrogate father, freeing him up for who knew how many additional inseminations.

Nevertheless, I instinctively reached over and grabbed Ramona's shirt as she leaned outward, not dragging her back from the open window, just holding her steady. Nature be damned. It shouldn't have given me self-awareness if it didn't want me to love this child.

"Big trees don't die," Ramona proposed as we cleared the bridge.

"They do die. Trees just live a lot longer than we do."

"I'd rather be a big tree."

Ramona didn't laugh a lot or need much provocation to get stubborn. But she was nobody's fool.

CHAPTER SEVENTEEN

"Take Me Out
to the Ballgame"

Gainesville, Florida, March 1991

An unusually long trip took Ramona and me down to Fort Lauderdale, then across to Dunedin on the Gulf Coast to check out the Toronto Blue Jays new stadium and, since we were nearby, horned owls and nesting ospreys on Honeymoon Island. When we returned late one night, I noticed Carl's Corvette. I glanced through the lit kitchen window to see Carl and Linda sitting quietly at the kitchen table, a scene unpleasantly reminiscent of our infamous meeting ten years back, but otherwise typical enough. The closing car door brought Awilda out to take custody of a sleepy Ramona. I headed for the kitchen, intending to pay my respects then tumble into bed as quickly as possible.

Carl and Linda turned to look at me with identical grim expressions. "Who died?" I asked, instantly regretting my choice of words. My mother was seventy-six.

"Nobody yet," Carl said, trying—and failing—to form a grin.

"And nobody's going to, Carl," Linda snapped, fixing him with a withering stare.

"Well," I said, "I'm not planning to kill anybody, so what depressing shit are you guys talking about?"

"Sit down, Bill; this is kind of complicated."

There was no cognac, just coffee. No amused detachment from Carl. After pouring myself a cup, I took a seat, waiting to hear how he had botched something that would require my forbearance. *So*, I thought, *what else is new?*

"First of all," Linda said, "the narcs found Carl's weed farm. They know he owns the property, but that doesn't prove anything. His bank records, his taxes, all in perfect legal shape thanks to me. There *was* lots of cash, but that's gone with the wind." She glared at Carl. "I *think* he won't get busted. Anyway, that's the least of our problems."

"*Our* problems?"

"Come on, Bill, I'm Carl's attorney, remember? But like I was trying to say, the main problem is not the legal system; it's Carl's business associates."

"You mean the Cubans, or is it somebody else now, maybe the Mafia?"

"Yeah," Carl admitted, "it's the Cubans, the same guys you had me check out way back when. They checked out, by the way, and it's been smooth sailing up to now."

"Then what's the problem? The Cubans can't possibly blame you for having your weed discovered."

"No, you're right, you're dead-on right. Except that I owe them a lot of money, and I was going to pay them in product."

"Wait, that doesn't make sense. They pay *you* for the weed; how can you owe the Cubans money?"

Carl looked beseechingly at Linda.

"Carl borrowed money from them to finance an investment."

I waited for someone to elaborate. The two of them exchanged a nervous glance, each, it seemed, trying to outwait the other. *Our problem.* A wave of dread passed through me.

"You're the lawyer, Linda," I said. "You'll probably do a better job of explaining this 'investment' to me."

I'll give Linda credit. She did an excellent job of explaining. "Carl invested in a real estate project I brought to his attention, an apartment complex. The project is on hold right now. It will ultimately be a great success, but a couple of prospective investors got cold feet, so we're looking for new investors. Typical stuff."

"Do *we* have money tied up in this investment?"

"Not a lot," Linda said, "but that's not the point. The point is the Cubans want their money back."

"How much money?"

"Four, maybe five hundred thousand with interest."

I shook my head. "Carl owns two homes. You're a real estate agent. Get him a good price, lesson learned, and he can recoup his money when the project pays off."

Now it was Carl's turn. "Sorry, man, both of my houses are mortgaged to the hilt. I'm gonna let the bank take the Gainesville house. That's more or less a done deal."

"I thought you were swimming in money. All those killer drug profits. Where did they go?"

Carl shrugged and grinned weakly.

"I spent it, you know, living. Keeping the new boat in Tampa up to snuff. At least it's paid for. But just maintaining it is a bitch."

"Well, since the real estate project is on hold, can't you just back out? Retrieve your investment?"

Back to Linda. "We paid that money out. The project is well underway. Foundations poured, framing, and so forth. We're just on standby for a little while." A pause followed, leading up to a conclusion I couldn't quite spot yet.

"Do you think the Cubans would take Carl's stake in the project as payment? Maybe you could convince them to diversify their business approach."

"Hey," Carl objected, "I'm not letting those dudes anywhere near Linda. Forget that shit."

"All right," I said in exasperation. "What's *your* plan? Beg for mercy?"

Linda interrupted. "I have two plans. The first is to empty Ramona's savings account. After all, it's Carl's money. That would cover close to half of the principal, and maybe Carl could sweet-talk them into taking a stake in the apartment project, leaving me out of it. You can call that my backup plan."

"Okay, let's hear your major-league plan."

Linda stood up, paced around for half a minute, stared out the window. "We sell this house."

I knew at once this had been the idea all along. Maybe the facts mustered against my suggestions were valid, but make no mistake, here was the garden path down which my companions had led me.

"Carl's sins nail *us* to the cross. How does that make sense? And what do we do without a house?"

"Actually, I'm the one getting crucified," Linda answered without turning.

"How so?" An icy fury seized me. Nothing but black selfishness could justify Linda's words. Still, I had spoken softly, and she turned with an equivalent calm.

"You said it yourself, Bill. I got us this house, this nice life. If anyone's losing what belongs to them, it's me."

"That's probably the shittiest thing I've ever heard anyone say. But I'm glad you said it. Now I don't feel bad pointing out that my name is on the deed." I turned to Carl. "I'm guessing you know what that means."

"From the look on your face, I'd say I'm a dead man. Got any whiskey?" Maybe resignation had restored Carl's spirits. In any case, he smiled and slapped my shoulder—pure Carl and maddeningly sincere. Linda found the Crown Royal and brought it to the table.

"Look, Bill, you haven't heard the rest of my plan. It's not going to make you feel any better or hate me any less, but it might persuade you to let me sell the house."

"Say what you have to say, and make it quick. I'm going to bed soon, and right now, my answer is go fuck yourselves."

Linda bowed her head before speaking, as if summoning up her last reserve of will. "Okay, here it is. There's this house in Micanopy, a nice old house I bought to resell. I'll deed it over to you. You can assume the mortgage, which is only a few hundred a month. I got the house for a song; you'll have it paid off in no time."

"Be real, Linda, what does it matter who owns the house? We're still giving up our life here. Frankly, I don't trust anything the two of you said tonight. If that's the best you've got, I'm turning in."

"Bill, I'm not going to be living in that house with you. I'm going to Tampa and live with Carl. If you help us out, you get a house, Ramona keeps her college money, and Carl stays alive—maybe both of us for all I know. Otherwise, it's all misery. You may not believe in my powers, but that little prediction is a sure bet."

There it was.

I glanced at Linda's replacement sapphire ring—still sarcastically blue—then I looked at Carl. "I distinctly remember you saying that Linda was nothing special in the sack. And I believe she returned the compliment. But I suppose practice makes perfect, right?"

"Hey now," he protested. "We haven't done anything since the old days. Swear to God. And unless you and Linda split up, we never will."

"What the hell, Carl," Linda cried. "Are you *trying* to get yourself killed?"

Something—absurdity, I suppose—forced me to my feet. "No, it's fine, Linda. I should be shocked as shit that you want to live with Carl, but I'm not. You'll have some slick little justification that I won't want to hear and sure as hell won't believe. Let's not bother with that. Like I said a long time ago, you're not good people. Not to say I am. Just stating the obvious."

Linda's face had become a stony, shadowed mask. "Bill, I can't afford to care what you think right now. I just need an answer."

"If we divorce, what happens to Ramona?"

"I won't fight you for custody," she replied in a flat, rehearsed voice. "She'd rather live with you anyway."

Carl nodded. Were they making a necessary sacrifice or palming her off? I noticed then how bad Linda looked, gray-faced and disheveled, like someone sitting up in a sickbed.

My gut told me to close the deal and be done with it.

"Linda, if she stays with me, she can see you anytime she feels like it. How soon can we move into our wonderful new house?"

"I'll figure it out," Linda muttered grimly, producing a cigarette from behind her ear. As far as I knew, she hadn't smoked since her pregnancy.

She got up, lit the cigarette on the stove, then stood with her arms crossed, watching Carl and me. Nobody said anything for a while. Then I heard her cigarette hiss when it hit her coffee cup.

At that point, I knew the die was cast. When I got up to leave, Carl grabbed my arm. "You're right, Professor, what you said about bad people. I'm no great shakes. But I didn't wreck your happy home this time. It—"

I shook free.

"Did you try to save my life at the quarry, Carl? Or were you hiding and it just worked out that way?"

His face contorted in puzzlement, but he answered.

"I was trying to kill those motherfuckers. That's all I was thinking about. Things happened the way they happened, and I took care of business. I lived, you lived. Great. What the hell is your point?"

"My point is that you're off the hook about my happy home. I know *you* didn't mastermind this little travesty. And I think in your own screwed-up, misguided way you try to be my friend. But our friendship is a catastrophe. I'm calling it off like I tried and failed to do before. It's been interesting knowing you." I extended my hand.

"Fuck that," Carl spat.

Linda tried to weigh in. "Listen, Bill, you—"

"No, no 'listen Bill' tonight. Or ever again. I think 'listen Bill' is what got me into this mess. My fault, not yours, Linda. Now I'm going to sleep in the spare bedroom. Oh, and when a real attorney *proves* the house in Micanopy is mine, I'll deed this one over. Better get busy."

"Shit, Bill," Carl said, gesturing at Linda, unable to let it go. "We're not even in *love*. It just has to be this way."

"Come on, Carl. No love, no sex—what's the payoff? If you want somebody to cook and clean, you'd be better off marrying Awilda."

Linda had busied herself rinsing out her coffee cup and refilling it. Now she faced us, a freshly burning cigarette in hand. "Carl's right; we're not in love. But I'm essential to Carl. Have been since he bought that first house. I'm strictly optional to you, Bill. You chose to marry me. But that's all it was—a choice. It's not like you couldn't live without me. Maybe Carl's headed to prison, but if he isn't, it'll probably be because of me." After a pause, her voice softened. "And if Ramona lives a good life, it'll probably be because of you."

I'd be lying if I said that last remark didn't get to me. Still, I had to ask. "It sounds like everybody's getting 'paid' but you. Or am I missing something?"

Linda dunked another cigarette into her coffee before answering. Then she looked up, favoring me with a faint smile. "You know I've always loved Carl's house. And the sea breeze. I feel like it's sending me messages from the great beyond."

"Well, they've certainly steered you right so far."

I headed for the bedroom to lick my wounds in peace. As I undressed, it hit me that Carl's pricey sailboat—a Beneteau 405—was paid for, yet not a word about selling it to settle with the Cubans. I fought a momentary temptation to confront him. But Linda would have an answer—fine print I couldn't foresee or challenge—check and mate.

Instead, I lay down naked and spread-eagle like da Vinci's famous drawing. At least sleeping alone offered freedom of movement. I wiggled my toes and muttered, "Fuck."

Fuck. *That*, I thought, *is an ironic choice of words for a man in my position.*

I got up, turned out the lights, returned to bed, and, with no one to object, relieved my frustration. With this last philosophical homage completed, I went to sleep.

Once houses and money got shuffled around according to Linda's plan—"slick and quick," to use Carl's term—taciturn nephews of the Latin ladies showed up to tie the goats into the beds of two dusty old pickups and haul them to Apopka, a small town outside Orlando. The Latin ladies followed in the station wagon Linda had titled to them. They were sad to leave Ramona, but not, I think, surprised at what happens when you work for foolish white people. Awilda gave Ramona a *chanchito*, a lucky three-legged clay pig from her dead husband's Chilean village. Ramona accepted it with a solemn "*Gracias, senora*" and clutched it in her hand all the rest of that day. She keeps it in her purse even now, her one concession to the supernatural.

Linda told Ramona that Carl had many terrible problems and needed her to help him. Of course, Ramona shed tears at her mother's departure, but she didn't beg her to stay. And she didn't ask unanswerable questions about why people are the way they are. She wondered if she could choose her bedroom, where she would go to school, and how she would get there. She liked the house in Micanopy, especially its proximity to stores. Proprietors seemed fond of her solitary visits and her questions about antique dolls, bright silk kites, and, as I imagined it, vintage radios.

Whereas Ramona's enlightened consent to a shifting reality would have made Buddha jealous, I seethed with enmity. I fantasized *schadenfreude*, praying Carl's boat would sink about the same time Linda got disbarred. Forced to sell their house, they would rent a small apartment, even shittier than the dump Karen and I had occupied before *our* divorce. Delicious thoughts, yes—just like lollipops are delicious to a four-year-old but lethal as a steady diet. So, after a month of vengeful brooding, I switched to the lesser vice of imagining Linda and Carl's daily routine. Sure, Linda was legally indispensable to Carl, but what about the other hundreds of hours a month? A constant carousel of sex and sailing? Not likely. Linda would never suffer a fool gladly, and Carl could never resist being one for very long. Be that as it may, I couldn't summon a vision detailed and unpleasant enough to intrigue me. I would have to take their mutual misery on faith.

Besides, considering the "prizes" available, hadn't I *won?* Ramona, the house in Micanopy, a decent career, a mind freed from the torturous quandaries of uncertain love. Since my current hypothesis was "life is cruel and unjust," it seemed plausible to give "I won" a shot. Happily, in the days and weeks that passed, no one stepped forward to object.

I started my victory march by stringing galvanized wire across reinforced posts on my way to creating a viable backyard grape arbor. Ramona was my inspiration, or rather the fact that I spotted her trying to read *The Grapes of Wrath* at the tender age of ten.

So I began the quarter-century between my second divorce in 1991 and Carl's AIDS-induced release from prison in 2016. As it happens, events I have yet to describe for this narrative to make sense require me to jump back in time—to my last hurrah in Hopperton and beyond—then return to developments after Carl's release. Of course, a great deal happened between '91 and '16, not the least of which is that computers stopped working for humans and we started working for them as data delivery slaves. Mr. Pee passed away, followed by my mother, and finally, at the far reaches of a cigarette-rich old age, Aunt Miriam. Mr. Pee's last, brief note read: "William, I am on the cancerous cusp between trying to live and trying to die. It is a tricky perch, but the view is rather interesting. All is indeed well. Yours in philosophical affinity, Hiram Peebles."

My mother's passing, or more precisely her behavior in the time preceding it, compelled me write the one short story I ever published, a tale about the dying days of a masterful sneak thief named Ethan Matheny. While Ethan hardly resembled my mother in character, I created him to emulate her in one respect: to mirror how she chose to spend her last weeks—in solitary pursuit of some final goal, some final understanding, free from the distractions of futile medical attention and awkward well-wishing.

Aunt Miriam sat with me on the veranda before the funeral, a glowering storm gathering above us as if on cue. She described how my mother took to her bed one day without warning, declaring she needed a "good long rest," after a lifetime of "doing and doing." She didn't complain about pain or debilitation, and the doctor Aunt Miriam called in against my mother's wishes found nothing worrisome in her vital signs.

The days passed. My mother spent most of her time in bed, though sometimes venturing out to the veranda at twilight. She radiated an odd contentment, seeming, as Aunt Miriam put it, "to be in this world but not of it." Near the end, my mother claimed to have known all along that she was dying, telling her sister she had chosen to be alone with her thoughts rather than pursue medical intervention. "She needed time to remember things as she saw them, and to pray, and to reconcile herself to her failings," Aunt Miriam said, as the first fat raindrops spattered down and a gray mist overtook Stagecoach Road. "Then she told me not to worry; that her memories were beautiful."

My aunt's voice grew choked with feeling, and she shook her head, as if renouncing what could not be denied. We sat in silence after that.

Reconcile. Look back and balance the books—or cook the books if necessary—to find, in fair hope or desperation, that we lived at a profit, or at least broke even. Personally, I was not looking forward to that calculation.

In any case, we buried my good mother and I returned to Micanopy. The word "reconcile" nagged me like a bad cold all the way back, an unwanted bonus tacked on to the guilt I felt at surely being one of why mother's so-called "failings." So, you will not be surprised that my story about the sneak thief, Ethan Matheny, concerns his late and strange attempt to not merely excuse his criminal career, but to glorify it.

Faced with a terminal brain tumor, he carries a lifetime of loot—jewelry mostly—to the police station and turns himself in. "I didn't want to die without people knowing how great an artist I was," he says. The burglary detective, a jaded veteran with a withered arm, rolls a cigarette with his good hand and says, "I get your point, but your crimes amount to a shit pile of paperwork for me. Why don't you sell that junk and hire yourself a ghostwriter to tell your life story?" The thief runs an ad and receives a call from such a person, a young woman. He invites her over and is taken by her strikingly alert green eyes (the rarest eye color). They remind him of a chrome tourmaline he stole from a house in Schenectady. He tells her about his futile encounter with the police. "Can you tell my story?" he asks. "I can probably make you famous," she answers, accepting the project and arranging to meet him at her office for the first recorded interview. He shows up, but no such address exists. Assuming he got the address wrong, he returns home to contact the woman.

Meanwhile, the old detective has told the sneak thief's story to an ambitious rookie, who takes it upon himself to get a search warrant for the sneak thief's home. The thief returns from his fruitless errand to find the police waiting. Combing the thief's apartment, they find his stash in a battered cigar humidor—except that there is no stash, only a note from the woman with green eyes. Her message reads: "Based on your cache, I'd say you're as great a thief as you claim. As professionals ourselves, my boyfriend and I admire your work. People will hear about you for a long time to come if we have anything to say about it." The note proves nothing, of course, and the overzealous detective stalks out, empty-handed and fuming. The thief is overjoyed. He still has his freedom, short-lived as it might be, and the likelihood he will become a legend among his peers. He sits down, chases a pain pill with a beer, and smiles. He never liked books anyway.

I suppose you could say I gave my story a "happy ending" in psychic self-defense. Not that writing it helped me understand the machinery of fate any better. But publication did stroke my ego and kept me writing—"gathering material" as we star-crossed pretenders call it. Back in mundane reality, I raised Ramona until she began rearing me. At Sea Island, I evolved from "Mr. Bill" to Professor Shaffer, my female graduate students bothering less and less over time with office conferences and speculative glances.

Not that they were ever really within reach of an average-looking, unfashionable, balding, middle-aged man driving an absurdly old car. And given that unmarried women near my age seemed disinterested, virginal, or afraid to relive past heartache, I endured lengthy spells of circumstantial celibacy.

Then, sometime shortly after the millennium, a woman who'd been auditing my class approached with brisk strides. She may not have been young and pink, but she was assuredly sleek and expensive looking in a tailored gray suit and matching pumps.

"You're confusing those sweet young things," she advised without preliminaries. "The next thing you know, they'll be needing a psychiatrist."

"My brother's a psychiatrist," I retorted, gathering my wits. "We have an arrangement."

The woman raised a perfect eyebrow. "Oh? I don't believe I know a Doctor Shaffer."

"I don't really have a brother," I mock-confessed.

Yes, I got that. Did you get that I *am* a psychiatrist?"

"Seriously?"

"Well, yes and no. I am a psychiatrist, but not seriously. My patients take themselves so seriously that I hate to pile on. I find mocking them the best approach."

"I find that entirely credible." The woman's look was all country club fundraiser except for the small gold ring piercing her left eyebrow. I found her immensely appealing. She had sad eyes, a full mouth, and delicate crinkles at the corners of her eyes.

She waved a manicured hand. "My derisive tendencies mean nothing, just a bad habit. I *sincerely* enjoy your class. I want to invite you to a party. My friends have terrible ideas, and they're always invoking this or that philosopher. I'm dying to find out what they'll say in front of you. Will you come?"

"Maybe. If I can. When is it?"

"Well, I would've preferred 'yes,' but here's my card. Hermine Delaplaine. Call me; I'll fill you in."

Since college life now claimed Ramona, I attended the party. Hermine's friends behaved pleasantly, conversed sensibly, and never once quoted a philosopher.

So began my affair with Dr. Delaplaine, which to date has endured longer than both my marriages combined. Hermine's acerbic, supercilious inclinations may explain why she was not "taken" when I met her. Like Carl's cognac, she is a potent distillation, an acquired taste. To paraphrase a poem, her "mean opinions" would bend a tenpenny nail. But here's the saving paradox: while she does indeed hold a low opinion of many people, patients and otherwise, she wishes them well and tries valiantly to help them through what she calls "overdue confrontation" (not fun, as I can attest). And, by the way, Hermine glitters with brilliant observations, cooks like Escoffier, and excels in the sack.

One more profound benefit to me of courting Dr. Hermine Delaplaine came to pass inadvertently. "I will continue to enjoy your company," she said one evening early on, "as long as we play together like children." Her ultimatum struck a chord. Later, as I leafed through a notebook full of descriptions, observations, and snippets of conversation I had amassed, I realized I had *worked* at writing but never played at it. Shit, no wonder it seemed so hard. I wrote a page for the fun of it, indifferent to quality, putting on paper the crude beginnings of the novel I suddenly knew how to pursue. While Ramona, Olivia, and Hermine occupied centerstage of my post-marital life, writing was finally savoring the footlights—no longer merely a source of wishful angst. As for Linda and Carl, I never opposed any contact Ramona sought with her blood parents and *never* involved myself in their lives. When the three of us attended one of Ramona's rites of passage—graduation, recital, softball game, chess tourney—I did my best to clamber up above the fray, sagely withholding my opinions. When Linda began to call me a few years back, I put that insight back into practice, steering clear of advice and fulsome commiseration, offering an ear and nothing more. Linda knew what I was up to but kept calling anyway, which brings me back to the call instigating this narrative about Carl getting out of prison and the egregious violations of my noninvolvement rule which followed.

Well, we don't know what we were, what we are, or what we will be later. And no rule or philosophy will ever change that. So just finish the freaking story, Shaffer, and get back to your grapes.

CHAPTER EIGHTEEN

"Mack the Knife"

Hopperton, Georgia, circa 1960

My parents moved our tabletop parlor radio into my bedroom around my tenth birthday, supplanting it with a mammoth console television. The Philco endured the further insult of replacement by a $39.95 transistor radio capable of accompanying my mother from room to room, ensuring a constant gospel serenade. Alone all day now, ignored at night, the Philco waited in stoic silence on a table near my bed.

One night, bored with math homework, I turned my chair to the radio, rotated its station knob to the lowest frequency, and clicked it on. A robust hum arose that I had never noticed in the parlor, suggesting a mysterious life force. I grasped the station knob again and worked my way slowly up the dial.

A couple of years earlier, I might have found *The Lone Ranger* or *Amos n Andy*, but 1959 happened to be the year radio's golden age played out for good. *The Lone Ranger* had ridden off in a cloud of dust and a hearty "hi-yo television," and society had finally noticed *Amos n Andy's* racial caricatures after thirty years and over four thousand episodes. The last of the live radio soaps, *Our Gal Sunday* and *Young Doctor Malone*, played their final organ licks and plotted their final cliffhangers. No more Tommy Dorsey live from Casino Gardens; farewell to the pride of Wistful Vista—*Fibber McGee and Molly*.

What I did find as I rolled the radio's indicator needle up the AM band were mostly flavors of static mixed with the garble of overlapping signals, crooners unwittingly emoting together in competing keys and tempos, whistling feedback, deep male voices delivering unintelligible news, Spanish-sounding ululations—in short, a cacophonous metaphor for the turmoil of desires beyond our reach.

The first clear signal I caught arrived from a distant city. This minor miracle sped my heartbeat. It might have been Cincinnati Top 40 or Chicago classical, or maybe a Cleveland Indians baseball game (I do remember that Cleveland's right fielder, Rocky Colavito, hit four home runs in one game that season, only to be summarily traded to the Tigers for his troubles).

Whatever the city, whatever the sound, I was hooked. Coaxing voices from distant places into my bedroom seemed outright magic to a dreamy only child more interested in observing life than living it. In nights to come, thrilled by illusory eavesdropping, I sat with my ear close to the radio speaker, turning the channel knob slowly like a safecracker listening for combination lock tumblers. I "cracked" "The Legend"—WSM in Nashville, home of *The Grand Ole Opry*—as well as stations in Louisville, Ft. Worth, New York, Boston (folk music, and ultimately its apostate high priest, Bob Dylan), Pittsburgh, Philadelphia, Charlotte, St. Louis, Richmond, and even WCCO from Coon Rapids, Minnesota, where I once heard short stories read over the air.

I occasionally encountered jazz, though I was too young for its sublime speculations. Only Brubeck's "Take Five," played on jazz stations with reverential repetition, stuck in my mind. I heard Miles Davis and John Coltrane spoken of as jazz deities, but I could not find their churches through labyrinths of stilted tempos and frenetic alien scales. Besides, what chance did jazz have against the powder keg energy of Chuck Berry, Fats Domino, Screamin' Jay Hawkins, and Jerry Lee Lewis? Those guys pumped out ecstatic *excitement* about something—something that hadn't made its way to Hopperton, where men talking loud after a few beers at my father's fish camp passed for exhilaration.

Later, I listened to Jack Kennedy's campaign speeches, played on the radio in their entirety. That voice, with its eloquent turn of phrase and exotic accent, entered me like music. No one could speak that well and not be *right*. I began reading the local paper for stories about Kennedy and discovered the editors hated him. They called Kennedy a "papist" who sympathized with Negro insurrection and was soft on Communism. I immediately hated the editors, going so far as to write an anonymous letter (unpublished) condemning Nixon as a Quaker—whatever that was. The election (stolen by the unions, my father claimed) came and went. I was careful not to exult since people might rightly conclude I had embraced the Negro cause, among other heresies, in which case I could pack my bags for military school.

How to explain my radical change of heart? Maybe it was just the radio's effect on a susceptible kid stranded in his pliable mind. Perhaps I had absorbed more than my share of guilt and compassion from the collective unconscious.

I don't know.

I do know my secret radio didn't change my outward life much, if at all. You see, I liked my life, my family, my school, my pleasant home, my good friend Don, the long sandlot summers, my friendly town. In church, I silently prevailed upon God to forgive everyone for their misguided beliefs. I could do or say no more, I told myself, given how hamstrung I was by circumstances.

Then, one weekend night when I was twelve, a New York City DJ brought up a stabbing somehow connected to "Mack the Knife," a mainstream hit for Bobby Darin a few years back. The DJ went so far as to interview a college professor about violent lyrics, impressionable delinquents, and society sliding into chaos. The professor, grasping the unlikely opportunity with both hands, explained that "Mack the Knife" referred to a criminal character named MacHeath from something called *The Threepenny Opera*, which, according to the expert, was not an opera but a German play with music, a "beggar's opera" about workers forced to grovel at the feet of their capitalist masters. And the song "Mack the Knife" was a bloody warning to greedy rich people that they were next. As for the women mentioned in the song—Suke Tawdry, Lucy Brown—they were lovers of MacHeath who sometimes sold him to the gallows for money, sometimes bribed or broke him out of prison, depending on whether desperate love or desperate poverty held the upper hand at that moment.

Now, I had heard "Mack the Knife" dozens of times on Top 40 radio. Darin sang it in a jaunty, sassy, jazzy style, and whoever Mack the Knife was, he seemed like a cool guy committing heinous violence in a spirit of winking fun. And while I could not define capitalism, I knew it crowned our way of life, and besides, who cared what Germans thought about it. We knew what Germans were, didn't we? Except for my father, of course, whose own father was born in Heidelberg and spelled our last name "Schaeffer." And as for beggars, only shell shock from the war or laziness explained them. No need to be *that* poor; even my covert liberalism had its limits. Finally, tiring of the talk, I turned off the radio and peeked behind to watch its bright tubes dim to nothing. Then, with "Mack the Knife" running through my head, I lay down and, like cooling radio tubes, faded out.

Waking the next morning, I gave no more thought to the radio saga of *Threepenny Opera* than to a mostly forgotten dream. But, of course, a forgotten thing does not necessarily cease to exist. A couple of weeks later, toward the end of a long summer's afternoon, my mother and I returned from church to find our "yard help"—an old black man—standing in the shade of an oak tree, waiting. My mother spoke to him with commendable Christian warmth, thanking him for his work and asking him if he was thirsty.

"No, ma'am," he said. "I've been drinking from the hose."

Then my mother dropped a few coins into the palm of his hand. I knew he had been helping her all weekend, and he showed it, sweat-soaked and sagging, with a dried trickle of blood along his arm where rose thorns had probably scratched him. He didn't look at the money, or precisely at my mother either, but just mumbled something, gave an awkward approximation of a bow, and turned to the road.

The look on my face must have moved my mother to justification. I had spoken nothing aloud.

"Those people can't do right with money," she advised in a low voice, "so there's no use giving them too much."

I glanced apprehensively at the departing yardman, fearing he had overheard, but his slow, bent walk told me nothing. One thing I knew—my mother had treated him like a beggar, not a man earning his daily bread. I remembered the phrase "beggar's opera" then, and somehow the menace of Mack the Knife seemed connected to the harmless old man walking away. *Three* penny opera—now it made sense. My mother murmured "well," as if to say "that's done with." I nodded, not wishing her to feel bad. If she was anything, my mother was *good*, so the fault for her wrongful words and miserly action must lie elsewhere. Something was amiss in the world. My mother, had she felt what I felt, would have called it the devil.

"Where does he live?" I asked. My mother peered at me from under her floppy straw hat.

"Goodness, Bill, I don't know. Edge of town, I imagine. Ask your father. He went there to hire Cato."

Cato. Not a name I had heard before, though I would later come across it in history books—Cato the Younger and Elder, Cato the Wise—Roman statesmen of considerable fame. Cato, I came to find out, was also a slave name in Georgia and the other slave states, presumably assigned by high-minded plantation owners. Generational math suggests our yardman's grandfather had been a slave. What's certain is that I took over Cato's duties a couple of years later in exchange for an allowance doled out in dollar bills, not coins. Among my first purchases with that money were replacement tubes for my radio. And it was as if my Philco, in appreciation, gave me a gift in return. For now, on my late-night forays across the frequency band, I began finding the voices of Phil Ochs and Pete Seeger, and other witnesses to far worse than what I had seen transpire between my mother and Cato, as he stood there, dead tired and bleeding from her roses.

CHAPTER NINETEEN

"Bali Hai"

Hopperton, Georgis, 1967

I met Wanda Grice on Friday the 13th, October 1967, after school at the Hopperton High chess club. Later that night, in gallant defiance of superstition, our Panthers, otherwise a winless football team, beat the Valdosta B squad eight to seven on a late safety, the opposing punter bending to tie a shoelace when the ball was hiked past him and on through the back of his end zone. Our team tied laces around their wrists for the rest of the season, to no avail.

But back to Wanda. I knew her first name and scrutinized her from a distance, as I did every new Waycross girl. After all, she and her counterparts were "city girls," likely open to behavior too bold for locals. While Wanda was technically among the nonpopular like myself, even below me since I enjoyed the good graces of Sally Chiles, her gender elevated her far above me according to my private caste system. And within that system, Wanda stood above many popular girls because her skirts were exactly as short as school policy allowed. Almost as crucial to her privileged status was her hair, a careless yellow mop failing to hide—even seeming to flaunt—black roots. And when I say yellow, I don't mean dyed blond, but rather the effect of having painted her hair with yellow house paint the color of American cheese.

No other girl in school dared to wear her hair like that, like a bright, brave, strange flag of self.

When Wanda paused at the classroom door, I dropped *Atlas Shrugged* like a hot potato and scrambled to my feet. In my flustered state, I adopted the officious tone of a bank clerk.

"Can I help you?"

"Help me? No. I'm fine." She stepped inside the room and spotted the lone slightly warped cardboard chessboard.

"Where are the pieces?" she inquired with apparent suspicion. I grabbed a cigar box from the bookshelf behind me and flipped it open for her inspection. She peered dubiously at the jumble of hollow plastic chess pieces.

"Do you even have all the … guys?"

I knew many girls. Other than the "church girls," most of them were in the mold of Sally Chiles—cheerful and oddly dramatic about the least little thing, anxious to be seen in a particular effervescent light. Such was my admittedly superficial impression—that girls *presented* themselves, a bit like the actresses they worshipped.

Wanda, I sensed, was having none of that.

She stirred the pieces with her finger and sniffed. "I don't see a black queen."

"See that wooden bishop? Use it," I said. Wanda's face suggested she was proceeding against her better judgment.

"Well, let's see what happens. I'm not very good. I'm just warning you." She sat down across from me and began setting up pieces, taking the white ones for herself, sticking me with the mismatched queen. I could smell her fruity gum.

True to her word, Wanda was a poor player. She invariably moved the one pawn necessary to free her queen for doomed excursions, her remaining forces rarely leaving their starting squares. Even my meager skills went untested. I won a couple of games as politely and as slowly as I could, but seeing that Wanda neither wished to quit or change her futile strategy, I risked the moment, my heart thudding.

"Would you mind a suggestion?"

"What about?" She eyed me narrowly.

"Your queen. You need to use your other pieces to help her. Get your knights and bishops out first. Once they get the attack going, then bring your queen out."

Wanda stared at the board. I braced myself for rebuke.

"What's your name?" she asked, looking up.

"Bill Shaffer."

"Do you know my name?"

"No."

She eyed me again. I didn't know her *full* name.

"In case you're not lying, it's Wanda. Now you know. What about these guys in the corners? What good are they?" She was pointing to her rooks.

"You usually have to trade pawns to get them out."

"What if the other player doesn't want to trade?"

I had never thought about chess motives, but Wanda, I felt in my bones, required a plausible answer. "If he doesn't trade, then you trade. And then you find out whether it was a good trade or bad trade. Anyway, people want to trade. Otherwise, nobody wins."

"We can move our pieces around without trading and the game can go on forever, right?" Wanda looked at me as if she caught my king in a trap.

"Sure," I said, "if we're both crazy."

"Don't you want your life to go on forever? Do you think *that's* crazy?"

"That's not the same," I protested. "A game is just a game. A life is… I mean, you're trying to get somewhere."

Wanda stared down at the jumbled remnants on the chessboard. "Yeah, maybe. To me, people just try to keep their lives going. My mom goes to work, comes home, cooks dinner, talks to me, smokes cigarettes, looks through mail-order catalogs. I bet she'd be happy doing that forever. Well, maybe not happy exactly, but okay with it. And I'm not saying that's bad, wanting to live just to live, but is that getting somewhere?"

Don was always ready with traps of logic and final answers, and Wanda, after all, was only asking—*musing*, if you will—but her question seemed far more to the point that my wordy clashes with my friend.

"Well," I ventured, "I feel like *I'm* trying to get somewhere. At least that's my opinion."

"A wise girl holds no opinions," Wanda pronounced. She reached over, picked up *Atlas Shrugged*, and held it in both hands as if weighing it.

"What do you mean, 'no opinions'?"

Wanda put the book down, taking her time before answering.

"When my father died, my Uncle Daniel from Detroit came down for the funeral. He's the one who taught me chess. He's a Buddhist, and my aunt is a Baptist. My mom says they only got married because they're both hard of hearing. Anyway, Uncle Daniel said your mind is a teacup full of yesterday's bitter tea. Meaning your crap opinions. You have to pour the old tea down the drain and start over with a fresh pot. A wise person thinks about what they hear but never accepts it. Once you accept stuff, you quit thinking. That makes sense to me."

No reply came to mind. Wanda waited a moment, then pointed to *Atlas Shrugged*. "My dad had that book."

"Did you read it?"

"Some. I quit because nobody in it laughed; nobody had a good time."

Nobody laughed. Nobody had a good time.

That was it! The book's great failing. Heroes and villains, everyone was miserable. Who would want to live in a world like that? Only Mr. Heffelfinger, I thought. I tried to stare at Wanda by looking away, astounded to have fallen into the company of the perfect girl. "I thought wise girls didn't have opinions," I objected, hoping to hide my adoration.

Wanda began setting up the chess pieces and didn't answer until she finished.

"I don't have an opinion about *Atlas Shrugged*, just a feeling. Maybe it's a great book; I don't know."

I nodded, impressed by her answer and happy to let the subject go. What did it matter if Wanda liked *Atlas Shrugged*? She advanced a knight and looked up at me.

"Good move," I said and pushed a pawn forward. We played in silence while I gathered courage for my question.

"What happened to your dad?"

To my relief, Wanda didn't mind me asking. And instead of a brief, sorrowful answer blaming a heart attack or car wreck, she gave a calm, expansive account of the fatal incident. Her father's job in a textile mill had required him to sit on a high stool. One day he leaned too far forward, the stool tipped over, and he fell into his machine. He didn't die right away but contracted a terrible infection that ultimately killed him. According to Wanda, even in light of the accident, people in the factory protested when their high stools disappeared, forcing them to stand. Afterward, she and her mother moved to Waycross from North Carolina, seeking a fresh start.

"We were sad for a long time," Wanda said, "but then my mom started reading the Bible and got a lot better. I'm half Buddhist and half atheist, but that's my little secret."

I hung on her words since this allowed me to study her openly. Her face put me in mind of a pretty Indian squaw in TV Westerns. She would later claim Cherokee blood, a fad back then, but bloodlines aside, there was an air of the medicine woman about her. When she later offered me marijuana, she took the occasion seriously.

"I don't know what I am," I said. "My mother is Methodist, my father's Baptist. I usually go to church with my mother, but that doesn't mean I'm more Methodist than Baptist. I guess I believe in Jesus; I mean he was a real person, that's a proven historical fact."

I was just talking now, thinking about going to the game tonight with my father, though I hadn't promised I would. I could get home late without causing trouble for myself. My mother knew where I was and admired my interest in chess. She admired me generally; considered me the quintessential Good Son. So my thoughts ran, without any particular purpose, other than a baseless hope to need an excuse for being late.

Wanda looked in the direction of the window, clearly restless.

"I have to go home," she announced with what might have been a reluctant tone.

"Where do you live?"

"Barlow. Three streets over."

"Yeah. I walk that way when I miss the last bus."

"Bullshit," she said, using a word I had never before heard spoken by a female. And no one but my mother had ever called me out on a fib. I blushed fiercely, preparing to offer some lame defense, but Wanda let me off the hook. "Come on; you can walk me home. We have to finish this brilliant conversation."

When we got to Wanda's house, a small, typical wood-frame box with faded white paint and a scant, patchy yard, she invited me in to meet her mother. We found Mrs. Grice on the screen porch, rocking and smoking, a pack of Pall Mall cigarettes perched precariously on the arm of the rocker. She wore a waitress outfit, including a bright green hairnet.

"This is Bill, Mom," Wanda said. "We were playing chess." I waited for questions about my family—the time-honored way to establish my place in the social scheme of things—but Mrs. Grice just smiled, seeming to take my arrival for granted.

"Chess, huh? Way over my head. Nice to meet you, Bill. Honey, get Bill some iced coffee. I would, but I have to go in. That new girl quit—the second day of all things. I should be home by ten. I made potato salad with celery." Mrs. Grice had Wanda's cheekbones, though hidden under considerable flesh. Her eyes seemed kind and hard at the same time.

"Okay, Mom, we're going to listen to music. See you after work."

"All right, honey. Don't forget that coffee."

Had *my* mother known I was alone in the house of a friendly young woman, coffee, iced or not, would have escaped her concern. Feeling as if I were floundering in deep water, I made an excuse to call my mother, who answered promptly and greeted my voice with warmth and trust. "Yes, dear, of course your father will be disappointed if you miss the game. But he knows your studies come first. You boys try to make good use of your time." I nodded into the phone without speaking, then told my mother I wouldn't be home all that late.

I hung up, then turned around to find Wanda gone. I glanced around, noticing the absence of adornment that was my mother's strong suit: no flowers, no polished china closet, no bright hooked rugs. Everything looked worn, chipped, or faded, but neat and clean. Then I heard Wanda call from another room.

"Leave your stuff on the kitchen table and come in here." The kitchen was spartan as well, everything put away but a battered tin coffee percolator on the stove.

"Here" turned out to be Wanda's bedroom, which, like Don's, looked like a burglar might have ransacked it. Despite that, it smelled sweet, like a garden flower I couldn't name. She had taped up a couple of movie posters—Clint Eastwood in a poncho; Raquel Welch in a prehistoric bathing suit—along with thumbtacked scrolls inscribed with Chinese or Japanese writing and painted with unrealistic, snowy mountains.

Wanda sat on her tousled sheets, looking through a stack of record albums. The nerve to sit beside her was well beyond me. I stood petrified in her doorway until I spotted a desk chair piled with clothes.

"Just toss them anywhere," Wanda said.

I stood a moment, overcoming the sense that I was violating some taboo by touching her garments. Finally, I grabbed them in a clump and dropped them gingerly on the corner of the bed farthest from Wanda. Then I sat down, my heart pounding, not expecting anything in particular, just awash in a momentous sense of occasion—I had entered a girl's bedroom.

Wanda swung her legs onto the bed and propped herself up on pillows and wadded clothes. Ingrained propriety caused me to turn my head as she lay back, which caused me to notice the phrase *drinking green tea I ended the war* handwritten on the wall.

"Do you like music?" Wanda called.

I longed to tell her that I was Hopperton's high priest of music. I wanted to boast that I knew all the hit tunes, plus underground songs of sex, poetry, government hatred, mockery, and hallucination, sometimes all of those things mixed up dreamlike in seven-minute anthems.

But whatever Wanda wanted to show me—because she wanted to show me—mattered more.

"Sure," I said.

"This is my *favorite* music," she cried, waving an album cover. "It's the soundtrack from *South Pacific*. Do you mind if I play it?"

Even with my limited wiles, I knew enough not to mind.

"Great," Wanda said, beaming. "Let's go."

I realized with dismay—mixed with relief—that we were leaving the bedroom. Before following Wanda, I paused to fix details in my mind: the chaotic bed, the cardboard box of *Seventeen* magazines, the off-kilter floor lamp. I wanted to see the room clearly when I thought about it later—when I imagined what *could* have happened.

The record player rested on a worn tiger-oak dresser in the living room. Wanda gestured me to the sofa facing it, then explained like a teacher to her class that *South Pacific* was a Broadway musical and a *divine* movie. I already knew this but listened obediently anyway. Satisfied, Wanda lowered the needle. When the music began, she turned to me with a delighted smile and pretended to conduct for a few seconds.

"This is just the overture," she explained. "I have time to get you Mama's special iced coffee." She ran out and came back quickly, carrying two metal tumblers chiming with ice.

I sipped the liquorishly strong brew as Wanda stood poised by the record player. When the overture ended and the first song began, she sang along in a soft, tremulous soprano. The voices she accompanied were children singing in a foreign language, and the simple tune reminded me of nursery school. Wanda closed her eyes as she sang, sometimes swaying, sometimes rising on tiptoes, often making small theatrical gestures with her hands, seeming to inhabit a distant idyllic place. I sat transfixed in fascination, disbelieving her uninhibited aura. What kind of girl felt no need to hide from a strange boy?

After the song finished, Wanda lifted the needle and sank to the sofa beside me with a deep, dramatic exhalation, seeking my eyes, my reaction. Seeing what she'd hoped for, she smiled happily.

"They're singing French," she confided. "This boy asks a girl why life is beautiful. He wants to know if it's because she loves him."

"What does she say?"

"The song is just him asking. But you kind of know her answer anyway." Wanda leaned a little closer, eager to share her joy, tempting me to imagine I brought the feeling on.

"I liked your singing," I said, liking her nearness even more.

"Thanks. I sing *all* the songs, mostly without the record. Would you like me to do one by myself?"

At my nod, Wanda sprang up to sing "Happy Talk," a capella, complete with hand gestures of bird, lily, and moon, copied, she would afterward tell me, from the movie. As I watched her mimicry, a memory came to me of a repeated dream in which I came home to a family of strangers. In the dream, they know me, but I don't know them. They're all kind to me, mother, father, and children, and I have little choice but to accept them and live the surreal new life I have entered. This encounter with Wanda belonged in that dream or the other way around. I thought about my real home, the game tonight, and felt an absurd, momentary fear that I would find them changed once I left Wanda's house.

I clapped when the song was over; the sound seemed to chase my presentiments away. Wanda laughed and bowed.

"*Merci.*"

Wanda recounted the song, the love affair between Liat and Lieutenant Cable, and Cable's tragic wartime fate. At the mention of a war, I remembered something I wanted to ask Wanda.

"Did you write that saying about green tea and war on your wall?"

"Yeah. My Buddhist uncle told me to look at those words every day until they made sense. I wrote them up there so I wouldn't forget. He said people in other countries think making tea is a holy thing, kind of like communion. I guess if you're taking communion, you're not thinking about fighting in a war. That's what I think it means. But my uncle also says it might mean different things at different times and not to worry about it because not understanding is kind of the point. It's very confusing."

I raised my drink as if toasting some grand occasion and took a sizable swig. "Do any other drinks end the war?" I asked, trying to sound witty. Wanda rewarded my effort with a smile.

"I don't think my mom's coffee will do the trick; she's all for the war. She hates communists. She thinks unions are a little communist, but she loves them anyway because my dad did. It's just one more thing I can't figure out."

"I'm against the war," I blurted, emboldened by the conversational flow to utter that phrase out loud for the first time. Even with Don, I had only argued that total victory, complete with Hanoi's surrender, was not predestined. Wanda drew back in mock horror.

"Good grief, you're a pacifist. I might have known the way you play chess. You were almost too nice to beat me."

"Peacenik. That's what Don calls me. Are you *for* the war? What about green tea?"

Wanda shook her head as if I had entirely missed some vast point.

"Wise girls hold no opinions, remember? Hey, is Don a chubby, nervous guy who talks fast?"

"Sounds like him."

"He talked to me the other day. He said that by me moving here, I was 'part of history,' something about the coloreds and the government. I didn't say much, so he turned kind of red in the face and walked away. I felt bad, to tell you the truth, but I wasn't mean to him, I swear."

"I'll tell you about Don and girls if you want. He's not exactly a smooth operator."

"He seems very smart," Wanda observed, passing up the chance to delve into Don's shortcomings. I felt a pang of shame. Had Wanda encouraged me, I would have poured out anecdotes describing Don's social gaffes.

"He's probably a genius," I said, trying to atone. "We've been friends since the first grade."

"Lucky," Wanda murmured, half to herself.

"I guess, but he's been a pain lately; he got this crummy crossbow to make himself into a warrior and kill Vietcong. Plus, he and his dad are still mad about losing the Civil War, like it happened to them personally a couple of weeks ago. Then Don gives me *Atlas Shrugged*, begging me to read it, practically telling me it puts the Bible to shame. It's like he's gone crazy."

"It sounds to me like he's scared of something."

Scared of something. I often grumbled to myself about Don's peculiar moods and ways, but I never thought to explain them. Don was Don, and up to this moment, the question of *why* Don was Don had never occurred to me. As in the chess club, Wanda had spoken with casual intuition. But I was already thinking of what Don might be scared of. Fighting a war? His father? The exposure of a dreadful secret concerning his mother? Then I remembered how he had come close to tears when Mr. Pee had seemed to diminish Stonewall Jackson. Maybe Don was just afraid of being wrong.

"Don lives with his father," I explained. "Nobody's sure what happened to his mother." I wasn't sure how this answered Wanda's speculation, but she nodded as if she knew.

We subsided into small talk after that, but in my mind, our love affair had irrevocably begun. Wanda went on a bit more about *South Pacific* and her old school and how she occasionally swiped one of her mother's cigarettes. I tried to listen, but the future had seized me, the one where I saw Wanda again, the one where I could tell from her eyes whether our day together had faded or brightened in her recollection. And I was growing restless, not tired of Wanda's company, but vaguely anxious, like a child in a fairy tale who had wandered too far from the family cottage. To ease my departure, I told the slight untruth that I had promised to meet my father at the game.

Wanda jumped up, disappeared into her room, then reemerged, waving a slender book. "You can borrow this," she said breathlessly. "I can't let you have *South Pacific*, though. I'd die if anything happened to it."

Wanda handed me a book called *Siddhartha*. She explained that its author wrote *Steppenwolf*. She expected me to recognize *that* book, but I knew its title only as the name of a rock band famous for "Born to be Wild" and "Magic Carpet Ride." Nevertheless, I nodded sagely and took the book in hand with what I hoped was an air of casual reverence.

Siddhartha's cover displayed a feminine-looking man, his head ringed by a halo of light, but from his garments clearly not Jesus. The man sat under a tree in golden robes, his eyes closed, smiling as if he possessed the world's juiciest secret. Rabbits and squirrels sat in the grass near him, seemingly basking in his presence. The colors of the cover picture were weirdly bright, like a holy Disney cartoon. Trying not to sound dubious, I asked Wanda if *Siddhartha* was a religious book.

"Well, it's not about God, so I guess not. But it's cool; my Uncle Daniel gave it to me. It's about enlightenment; you know, seeing what's really there and all that crap, excuse my French."

Whatever was in the book, I could tell Wanda didn't think it was crap. I looked down at where *Atlas Shrugged* lay fat and heavy on the sofa cushion. On a rash impulse, I offered it in exchange, suggesting we swap back later. I knew the book wasn't mine to lend, not to mention Wanda's low opinion of it, but offering it at least fulfilled the letter of an improvised law I felt the moment demanded. To assuage my guilt as I handed it to her, I reminded myself that Don had stolen it himself. Still, I felt him standing nearby, glaring at me with outrage.

And finally, the matter of leaving. At the door, utterly at sea, I extended my hand.

"It's been a pleasure to meet you," I said. Wanda gave me a long, bemused look and, rather than shaking my hand, swatted her head softly with *Atlas Shrugged*.

"Off you go then," she answered, in a voice at once friendly and dismissive. I turned to the street and heard the door shut firmly behind me.

A short stroll through breezy twilight would bring me to Stagecoach Road. I started down Barlow, whose houses mostly had porch lights lit and dark windows. Everyone was heading to the game. I could dimly hear the dogged blare of our marching band and, for a moment, saw myself in the stands, sitting with my father, hollering and munching on salty popcorn. Or I could turn left at Stagecoach and pour whatever version of the day's events I chose into my mother's sympathetic ear.

At that moment, I caught a whiff of sweet clematis and turned toward its redolence, a white profusion stretched along the fence of a nearby house. I sat by the fence, fell back on my elbows, and took in the sky, which was no longer a background of blue or black or reddish gray but seemed to recede into its colorless, speculative depths. I closed my eyes, trying to find a safer place than memory to keep the day. How long I searched is lost to me, perhaps because the search has never concluded. In any case, it was nearly dark when I got up and started home. I walked half a block before hurrying back to the flowered fence to pick up the precious book Wanda had given me.

CHAPTER TWENTY

"Twelfth of Never"

"I talked to a Waycross girl, the one I told you about." I spoke this half-truth to Don as we walked to school Monday, sure that a barrage of excited questions would follow, allowing me to unfold my unprecedented hours with Wanda. Instead, Don merely nodded. And when football victory shouts came from a passing car, he shook his head as if dismissing frivolous fuss.

"Winning that game was blind luck," Don insisted morosely. "Even Mr. Pee would have to agree with that."

"Christ, Don, you sound sorry we won."

"Not so, Shaffer, merely devoid of triumph. Do you have a contrary assessment?"

"Like I said, I was too busy talking to a Waycross girl." A second chance for Don to beg for details.

"Making out under the bleachers, no doubt."

"No, we weren't at the game, and besides, she's not that type."

I then wandered off into thoughts about the goodbye kiss that did not happen but might have. What else could account for *off you go then?* At school, probably today, I would encounter Wanda in the hall. A look would pass between us. I quailed at the implications of that look. And even more fateful was the possibility that we might talk. To prepare, I had gotten a few pages of *Siddhartha* under my belt. The book began in a flowery make-believe land where Siddhartha is this perfect boy who, for some strange reason, the girls love because of his "slim hips." Everyone, I mean everyone, adores Siddhartha, but he doesn't adore himself. Something is missing, and after a long, tedious section where he questions everything, you find out that what he's missing is the location of his soul, which Christians never talk about; the point being what does it matter exactly where your soul is as long as you have one and you save it from hell? My familiarity with such conjecture, I felt, would carry the day with Wanda.

"I may be leaving Hopperton, Shaffer."

I turned with a start to see Don staring vaguely ahead.

"What do you mean 'leaving'?" I demanded. "Is it that stupid Army thing?"

"Wake up, Shaffer. I'm not even eighteen yet. No, it's my dad, his job; he's seeking greener pastures." *Atlas Shrugged* was full of talk about business, factories, production, finances, but I had understood almost none of it. Maybe the Heffelfinger's *were* poor.

"When are you leaving?" I didn't want to know.

"I ... I'm not sure. My dad said it would take at least a month to make arrangements. He packed a couple of boxes a week ago, then stopped. Since then, when I ask him where we're going, he says it's too soon to say but probably not far."

We dragged our steps; other kids passed us, boisterous, keyed up about the game. Ahead, trees shimmered in the restive air. I stared past them into the blank sky. *Shit*, I thought, *I have to get* Atlas Shrugged *back from Wanda before Don asks for it*. In my mind's eye, I saw her, unsmiling, tossing the book to me, saying, "Off you go then."

My mind seemed to be setting traps for itself.

"Hey Don," I called, grabbing his arm. "Maybe your dad will let you live with us until you graduate."

Don shook his head.

"That's not in the cards, Shaffer. You can't tell anyone about this. Top secret."

He didn't say why, but I knew the matter was closed for now. I sought out Wanda's shock of hair between classes, but to no avail. The school day passed. On the way home, Don kept glancing at me, maybe mistrusting me to keep his secret or maybe for reassurance, I couldn't tell. In any case, he seemed to have forgotten about the Waycross girl. We sat on the veranda with my mother; Don kept his eyes on her as if he might never see her again. The next day Don missed school for the first time in memory.

By chance, but feeling preordained, Wanda appeared out of nowhere to ask me if the chess club met every week. She was friendly enough, but in a way that intimated nothing. "Maybe I'll see you Friday," I said, making no mention of *Atlas Shrugged* lest it upset our precarious bond. Wanda dared a quick peace sign and hurried off.

Don showed up for school again Wednesday and resembled his old self. He hinted proudly at a shrewd delay in his father's plans. "We're both thinking things through, Shaffer, like a military campaign."

Wednesday night, I decided to "think things through" about Wanda. After dinner and homework, I stretched out on my bed, *Siddhartha* resting on my chest like a talisman. I had read far enough to know that looking for your soul was like looking for a needle in a haystack because of all the distractions: people, work, sights, and noises, pretty much the whole pile of straw. Siddhartha decided to become a beggar and quit wanting or looking at anything. He kept talking about emptiness like it was a compliment. Being a beggar was a noble occupation in his world, and people were happy to fill your bowl with food as you went door to door. In *Atlas Shrugged*, beggars were the worst of the worst—parasites. In *Threepenny Opera*, beggars were mistreated and dangerous. Rather than intrigued, I was merely annoyed by these discrepancies. My thinking would have to do.

Just as well, since I had a definite notion of thinking things through, namely, to endlessly relive last Friday's hours with Wanda until all my mistakes dissolved into fantasy.

Two things became clear to me : First, I should have kissed Wanda at the door—a brief, tender kiss, confident but not overdone. Second, I should have said or done *something* to present myself as remarkable, as she had done by swaying before me dreamlike to that children's song from *South Pacific*. I decided I had missed my chance when we exchanged books. That would have been the time to offhandedly say, "I wish I could give you my novel, but I haven't finished it yet."

"A novel?" Wanda's voice would fail to conceal her doubt.

I would put it to rest by speaking the novel's first line: "My one regret in life is losing Delia Wingfoot, even though I know it was for the best."

If only I had recited that line! And then, with Wanda under my spell, sketched the story of how a young Southern college student named John Freeman Kent uncovers a secret Confederate army headquartered in his small, rural hometown in 1961. The army's leader calls himself General Richmond Newlee and is itching to fight the Civil War again, 100 years later. Nobody believes Kent's story about a brewing war. Then, one day while he is walking through the Okefenokee Swamp collecting herbs (he is an amateur botanist), he encounters an ancient Negro man who is part ghost of a runaway slave, part witch doctor, and part expert in hand-to-hand combat as a result of fighting gators and other swamp creatures for the last century. Kent proves himself in ritual battle with the Dark Warrior (narrowly losing), so they form an alliance, and soon Kent can fight as well as his unearthly instructor, needing no weapons but his hands and feet.

Also, Kent's radio back home can receive messages from the Dark Warrior—advice, tips, warnings, and so forth, including instructions to contact a certain young woman named Delia Wingfoot, who is a crop duster of unmatched skill and daring. She becomes the young man's paramour and plays a vital role in the story's final confrontation due to her flair for aerial bombardment. The story ends as a heartbroken Delia tears herself away from Kent, then flies off to work as a secret agent and protector for the handsome young president (saving him and changing history), which explains Kent's mysterious opening remark.

That's how my last few minutes with Wanda should have unfolded.

And a few days later (no matter how), she would have ended up *here*, sitting on my bed as she had on her own, wantonly nonchalant, reading pages of *The Dark Warrior* as they poured from my Remington, loving them, loving me, and like Delia Wingfoot, devastated to think of leaving her lover, even to save the nation.

After this reverie ran its course, I sat up, causing *Siddhartha* to slide to the floor and splay open like a tiny tent. I picked it up and found a small rip in one of the pages. Appalled by my clumsiness, I placed the book on my desk and covered it with my dictionary to shield it and to flatten the damaged page.. My typing was equally appalling, mostly a matter of dislodging jammed keys, bringing *The Dark Warrior* no closer to life. I wondered glumly if these mishaps presaged my luck with the real Wanda, the one who sang with her eyes closed as if I weren't there.

Thursday at lunch, I saw Wanda standing at the cafeteria's entrance, talking to another Waycross girl.

"That's her," I blurted out to Don.

Don looked at the two girls for a long moment. "By 'her,' I assume you mean Wanda." Don paused long enough to note my surprise, then gave me a grim, knowing smile. "I'm *very* familiar with Wanda," he smirked. "I gather she's the one you've been pining for?"

True, Wanda had mentioned speaking to Don, but his emphasis on *very* carried despicable implications. Moments before, I had relished laying my encounter with Wanda before Don like a banquet feast. Now, a few heartbeats later, death would take me first. I stared down at my tray of meatloaf and parsley potatoes, trying to hide my red face. Part of Don, I decided, was downright rotten. And that smile, that was his father's smile. How had I not seen that before?

"I'm not *pining* for anybody, Don. That's your department. And I doubt you've been *very* familiar with any girl." I reinforced my retort with a contemptuous stare, expecting Don to wither.

Instead, he seemed happy, as if I had praised him, and began speaking with rapid-fire glee.

"So you say, Shaffer, so you say. I happen to know better on both counts, but I don't expect you to believe me. Anyway, I see the attraction. A girl from another planet, right? The crazy hairdo. But there's nothing to it, trust me. She doesn't have a clue about history, about how she's part of it. Notice that she doesn't eat in the cafeteria? Well, I do notice; I notice a lot. Certain things that are said. Not that I care. But like my dad says, a good general notices the big picture *and* the little things, like whether his soldiers wash their faces. Battles are won or lost before the first shot is fired, as they say, right, Shaffer?"

"I think *you've* lost it, Don." I shook my head, trying to project cold indifference. But I had keenly heard *certain things that are said* and remembered Sally's gossip about a Waycross girl who had given a baby up for adoption, and the odd question Wanda had asked me in the chess club—whether or not I knew her name. A shadow of doubt crept over me, bringing with it a dull but desperately intense pain. I watched Wanda with her friend, watched her push nervous fingers through that shock of hair, and I wondered. But then Wanda spotted me and motioned me over with a broad smile. Faith restored. I gave Don a triumphant smirk and got up.

Wanda introduced me to Betty Jean, who was doing poorly in algebra. Would it be okay if Betty Jean came to the chess club Friday and I tutored her instead of playing chess? "Sure," I said, utterly deflated, unable to even ask Wanda if she would be there. Betty Jean thanked me, and the girls left. Back at the table, I sat down without comment and pointedly returned to my lunch, determined to leave Don hanging. A couple of minutes passed before he finally spoke.

"She's watching you like a hawk," he whispered.

Flushed with confusion, I looked around to where Wanda no longer stood.

"Not her, you moron. *Sally.*"

Betty Jean came alone to the chess club; I gave her a bright, prepared smile. She was a quiet, wide-eyed girl who smelled like baby powder. We went over a recent test she had failed, and for an hour and a half, I lost myself in unmasking exponential trickery and tracking down elusive unknowns. In the end, Betty Jean seemed happy and graced me with a look that seemed to say *I like you.* I did my best to return the look in kind, manfully desisting from grilling her about Wanda.

Betty Jean left at a little past five. Tonight was another home football game, this one against a Clinch County team of regional renown. Last week's shoelace victory had whipped up ridiculous local hopes, but I knew better and had no appetite for another letdown. Don was moving away, Wanda was an undermined fantasy, and the Remington typewriter was sluggish and intractable, refusing my words so insidiously that I forgot them. Who needed another kick in the rear?

Well, I had one bright spot at hand—Wanda's book, *Siddhartha*. I suddenly realized that I wanted to keep this book, finish it, then demand that Don, with all his smug opinions, read it much as I had practically been *forced* to read *Atlas Shrugged.*

Which brought me back, helplessly, to Wanda. I left the school just before six and called my mother from the pay phone outside, reminding her that I was helping a classmate with algebra and might miss the start of the game. My father, I told her, should go on ahead. My mother compared me to the Good Samaritan and promised to keep a homemade pot pie warm in the oven. I thanked her too profusely and hung up.

I stood a moment, watching the usual stream of headlights proceed slowly up Stagecoach through the pregame dusk. *It's like a funeral procession,* I thought perversely as I began walking in the opposite direction. At the first corner, I turned left to avoid running into my father and continued to Wanda's house. I rehearsed what I would say at the door, how I was sorry to show up like this, but I had forgotten to ask for Don's book at school and I had promised to return it right away since he and his dad might be leaving any time.

"Good evening, Mrs. Grice," I said as Wanda's mother squinted at me through the screen door. To my surprise, she immediately broke into a friendly smile.

"Why you're that boy from before, aren't you? Wanda will be happy to see you. Come on in, and I'll go get her." Mrs. Grice pushed the screen door open for me and called to Wanda, saying "that boy" was here. Wanda yelled back something unintelligible.

"I'm Bill," I reminded Mrs. Grice.

"Bill. I'll remember next time. Wanda allowed that you favored my iced coffee. Are you two studying, Bill, or is this a social call?" The house smelled pleasantly of fried food; I remembered I hadn't eaten dinner. Mrs. Grice stood there in a pink housecoat, arms folded, waiting.

"Oh, I just stopped by with a quick question." Mrs. Grice gave me a look of kindly disbelief and shook her head.

"Lord, young man, if there's anything Wanda isn't, it's quick. You best make your peace with that now." She chuckled. "Take a seat on the sofa. I'll get you some refreshments. Just made a pitcher of Kool-Aid."

Several minutes passed before Wanda emerged in red pedal pushers and a girlish white blouse at odds with the borderline defiance of her usual school dress. I suppose I gaped as I jumped to my feet. I certainly noticed the lipstick she never wore at school.

"Sorry to disturb you," I said, "but I need to get Don's book." Wanda stopped short and gave me a puzzled look.

"You mean *Atlas Shrugged*? He already has it. I brought it to school Monday to give to you, but he saw me with it in the hall and promised he'd pass it along. I tried to read it, but it was way worse than I remembered."

I stood frozen. Don's sidelong glances after school Monday made sense now. But why not scold me outright, knowing I had forsaken his precious book? Why no mention all week?

"Are you in a hurry or something?" Detecting irritation in Wanda's voice, I realized I was standing like a fool, shook my head, and sat down on the sofa.

"No, no," I stammered. "I just… I mean, how did Don notice you had the book?"

"He always notices me."

Wanda sat down next to me without further elaboration. She smelled a little like the clematis I had passed but more like gardenias, and whatever she wore had been boldly applied. Harsh light from a naked ceiling fixture emphasized small pits in her cheeks, but every excess, every flaw, distinguished her favorably from all other girls. If only Don and his deliberate silence, his damned book, and the suspected meaning of his "notices me" remark would fade from my thoughts. Vague worries roiled around in my brain like one of those algebra problems Betty Jean had struggled with earlier.

"Did Don tell you he's moving?" I asked.

Wanda shook her head.

"He was so excited thinking his book was *my* book that I thought he'd pee his pants. When I told him it was his, he got serious like he was on TV or something. He wanted to know how I got it, if I liked it, did I understand its philosophy, all that garbage. When I told him I wasn't crazy about the book, he said something about destiny and how if 'things worked out,' he would change my mind. He didn't mention moving."

Then, as I groped in vain for a lucid train of thought, Mrs. Grice called from the kitchen, announcing she was making a big batch of pigs in a blanket.

"He's staying," Wanda decreed. She looked at me as if daring me to disagree. Eight o'clock, I guessed, was the absolute latest I could stay and still walk to the game in time to find my father—a bit over an hour. Any later and he was apt to have left in disgust at the score.

"Thanks, Mrs. Grice," I called back.

"I'll put on a record," Wanda chirped happily like a small child with an unexpected playmate, the lightness of her voice lifting me out of my conflicts.

"How about rock and roll?" I suggested. Wanda turned to me from her bedroom door. "Sorry; my house, my music. You can play that crud for me at your house if you want to."

Rather than the expected *South Pacific*, Wanda put on *Parsley, Sage, Rosemary and Thyme*, sang the Garfunkel harmonies passably well, then switched to an album by Pete Seeger, during which Mrs. Grice, smoking incessantly, sat with us as we snacked on Vienna sausages "blanketed" by globs of burnt biscuit dough and sipped cold, sweet coffee. She asked after my "people" and wondered whether I would "sign up" after high school. Maybe after college, I told her. In her day, she said—what with the war— all the boys signed up. I nodded, politely taking her meaning.

Wanda paid little mind as Mrs. Grice measured me and prodded me toward my patriotic duty. Instead, she joined Seeger at intervals on "Guantanamera" and "We Shall Overcome." I sat in the vocal crossfire between mother and daughter, watching the time approach, attain, then narrowly surpass, eight o'clock. Now, at best, I would have to rush to the football field at a steady trot to rendezvous with my father. And that would only be possible if I jumped up and bid good night in the truncated fashion of a restless, captive guest. Instead, I displayed prolonged scrutiny of my watch.

"Are we keeping you, Bill?" Mrs. Grice inquired with amusement.

"Oh no, it's just that I'm expected home by nine; that's all." My words had a galvanizing effect. Mrs. Grice exchanged a single glance with Wanda, then got to her feet.

"Lord, but I'm tired," she proclaimed. "Time to quit pestering you children and go to bed." I stood up to shake hands, causing Mrs. Grice to observe that such courtesies were beyond those "heathen" boys over in Waycross. I could only hope her mother's praise was not a black mark in Wanda's eyes.

The moment her mother disappeared, Wanda scooted over and tugged my arm. "Come with me while I clean up." With the imprint of her touch ecstatically persistent, I sat at the kitchen table, facing her backside as she swabbed and rinsed, the view blotting out worries tied to Don, my waiting father, and the precious minutes blurring past.

"I guess you miss your friends," I said, thinking about Wanda's no doubt numerous heathen boyfriends.

Wanda snickered and shook her head. "What friends? I was new at the Waycross school. The girls didn't like me. They whispered mean things like I moved there on account of giving up a baby in another town. I was 'Wanda, the girl who had a baby.' That's why I wondered if you knew my name. Some of those girls transferred to Hopperton too. Just my luck."

"I never heard anything about you,"

Wanda turned around, the water still running. "Do you want to know what I heard about *you?*"

We spend thousands of hours contemplating other people's flawed lives. Still, the other side of that counterfeit coin always comes as a shock.

"Sure, why not?" I shrugged, masking my apprehension.

"I heard that Sally Chiles is your girlfriend and that you're two-timing her with me."

"Who told you that?" I yelped, my face already beginning to burn.

"Betty Jean."

"How—"

"She heard it from other girls."

"That's crazy. I never said one word to anyone about you." Except for Don. And what had I really told him? I saw in a heartbeat my sin was handing his book to Wanda. But in the next moment, I concluded that Don's blabbing—a greater sin—forgave mine. In any case, Wanda seemed to accept my lavish denial at face value.

"People probably saw us talking by the cafeteria. Anyway, *is* Sally Childs your girlfriend?" Wanda, to my surprise, seemed more curious than accusatory.

"No, definitely not. We're just friends. We grew up together, go to the same church, that's all. I take her to school dances, stuff like that. Just to be nice. We don't ... do anything." I hated myself instantly for uttering this last, awful, disloyal sentence.

"Does Sally *think* you're her boyfriend?"

"We don't even sit together at lunch. How could she think that?"

Wanda smiled at my simplicity.

"Not all girls are wise girls who hold no opinion. And no offense, but boys are dumb about girls. I just thought you should know what I heard in case nobody else told you."

I managed a barely audible thanks. Mercifully, Wanda turned back to the sink to dry the dishes. For a time, I sat alone with an immense awkwardness that blocked all possible ways forward. I looked around at standalone white metal cabinets spotted with rust and then at my watch—twenty minutes to nine.

"All done," Wanda cried with startling cheer, tossing her apron aside. "Come on; one more song, then you can go." The song was "Twelfth of Never" by Johnny Mathis. Once again, Wanda closed her eyes and sang along, the lyrics imploring someone to hold her forever. Then she played the song again, this time making me slip off my loafers and dance with her. She wrapped her arms around me as forbidden by school chaperones, and continued to sing—barely above a whisper—about loving someone until long after bluebells have forgotten how to bloom.

Bluebells grew all over Hopperton, making it seem the words came fresh from Wanda herself. I pressed my hands into the small of her back, and the slight closing of space between us was enough to amplify my sense of her a hundredfold. She was warm and sturdy; I felt her ribs distinct against my palms, an exquisite intimacy. As we swayed, my hand brushed against her bra strap, and I half expected a protest. None came. I slid my hand along her back, intending, if not executing, a caress.

But it was enough. Wanda stopped singing, turned her face upward, and drew me down for a kiss.

I complied, and yes, the moment held genuine romance, and yes, the fact of the kiss flooded me with fearful delight. But actual kissing was a skill I hadn't practiced. I moved my lips on Wanda's lips, uncertain of pressure, technique, duration. Fortunately, she came to my defense.

"Stick your tongue in my mouth," she murmured.

Again, I complied and understood, really for the first time, why people kissed at length. As Johnny sang to us in his weird, wobbling falsetto, we kept kissing, and I suppose I would have continued indefinitely, out of both desire and ignorance of the etiquette of stopping, had Wanda not pushed me away.

"I guess what they said about us is true," she said, wearing a defiant grin rather than the glaze of sensual bliss I had imagined, but I would sort that out later. At present, I needed to say something cool.

"I'm writing a book, and you're in it," I exclaimed. "You have a different name, but she's just like you."

Wanda had turned to lift the needle and silence Johnny Mathis. Now she turned back, eyeing me, her arms crossed in a classic skeptic's pose. "What kind of book?"

"A story, a made-up story, you know, a novel. Your name in the book is Delia Wingfoot, and you save the country."

"Me? With what? My good looks?" Wanda twirled sarcastically.

I explained Delia's aeronautical prowess to her, how the hero loved her madly but let her go, like Rick in *Casablanca*, so she could keep JFK from being assassinated. I would have been hard-pressed to tell her how Delia was "just like her," but Wanda was preoccupied repeating the name Delia Wingfoot to herself as if she was considering adopting it.

"It sounds wild. Can I read it?" Wanda had taken a restless perch on the sofa's arm. She radiated eagerness, the lion's share aimed at my book.

"It's mostly in my head," I admitted. "I have an old typewriter, but it takes me about an hour for every word."

Hearing this, Wanda slid down and shifted closer to where I sat, putting on my shoes.

"I'm a good typist. I got an A in advanced typing. You dictate, and I'll type. It'll be fun, and I can make sure you say the right things about good old gorgeous Delia."

And hadn't that been my fantasy? Wanda in my bedroom? But that ecstatic vignette had floated free of my actual life, my mother's scrutiny, for example. And as I spoke my outward delight at her offer, I wondered what pretexts I could create to export my typewriter to *Wanda's* bedroom.

At the door, Wanda bestowed a grazing kiss. No more "making out," she said, her smile promising other nights. About a block away, I turned around and saw that her porch light was still on. I took this as a sign. Surely Wanda's truth would leave Delia Wingfoot's fiction in the dust. Nine o'clock. I could still make plausible excuses. As I approached Stagecoach, I saw dim figures heading home from the football game. I hurried along, learning the game's wretched outcome from those I passed. My parents greeted me as always, my mother solicitous, my father too disgusted with the game to pay me much mind.

Relief flooded me—no house of strangers from a dream. I let my mother coax me into the second piece of peach cobbler. "Tomorrow," my father warned, "we're scraping and painting the shed before the weather sets in for good."

I nodded agreeably, truly not minding. For the moment, I didn't mind anything.

CHAPTER TWENTY-ONE

"Court and Spark"

Tampa, Florida, Labor Day Weekend, 2016

Olivia scurries down the steps winding from Carl and Linda's house to the walkway along the canal, leaving me to fend for myself against Carl's ploys, unlikely as they are to unfold just now. Surely a legal beatdown, coupled with an influx of microscopic viral terrorists—not to mention a wife hovering between black and white magic—must have dampened his scheming spirits. But in case I'm wrong, I follow Hermine's advice that I not speak meaningfully to Carl when we are alone. On cue, he stops me halfway down the slope to point out the tile inlaid in the concrete steps.

"One thing I learned in that shithole," he says, "is to notice things more. For instance, that tile down there is from Morocco. Who cares, right? I mean, I had to look on a map to see where Morocco is. But I met this old guy inside who was doing a few months for so-called tax fraud, as if taxes weren't a fraud to begin with. Anyway, I passed him a hundred times—nothing. Then, one day I decided to notice him, like the tile, out of boredom maybe, and we got to talking about how our not-worth-a-shit banks and government are why we're locked up. He gave me the inside scoop on cryptocurrency, which is what they call computer money. No banks; hell, it's safer than banks, and no government snooping. I looked it up. Totally legit, invented by some Japanese super-nerd. And if you have a good computer, you can mine for this stuff like gold. Pretty soon, this is how everyone will buy and sell everything. Then demand will skyrocket and drive the price up. But, like the old guy said, you have to see the little things other people don't see. You can't just jump in. If you do, you end up flapping your gums with a fellow convict, wondering what hit you."

I'm not sure where Carl's prison wisdom is heading, but I don't intend to go there.

"First of all, nothing hit you; you hit yourself. And second of all, I read about Bitcoin," I say. "It's probably a bubble, like the mortgage meltdown. And remember all those cassette recorders your dad couldn't give away?"

Olivia beckons frantically from Carl's fishing boat. Carl waves back, his unbuttoned Hawaiian shirt billowing weirdly in the bay breeze.

"Yeah, that's it, Bitcoin," Carl says with undimmed enthusiasm. "Glad you've heard of it. Maybe you can advise me. I'm going to be getting into it, maybe set up an exchange myself, make a fee for my trouble."

Hey Carl, let's you and I live our lives over and do better. That's what I'd advise, but not what I say. "Carl, all I heard just then was the word 'trouble'—speaking of noticing things."

Carl replies with an impenetrable grin.

"Hey, Professor, what's the name of that philosophy, the one that says life is just a bunch of surprises that kick your ass?"

"It doesn't ring a bell."

"That's because I just made it up." Carl hooted and down we went, treading on one lovely, pointless Moroccan pattern after another.

Ramona will be late coming back from her divorce lawyer's digs. This is the "great news" behind Olivia's frantic signals. Now there's time for a boat ride out into the channel, maybe even the Bay. Carl's fishing boat is a vintage sixteen-foot Starcraft, plenty comfy for three but leaving little room for conversational escape. "No hat," I say, a last-ditch ploy, but Carl digs a bucket hat out of a storage bin. Olivia has borrowed a wrap from Linda, and the sun has already done its "worst" to Carl—an unblemished leathery tan.

We ease down the canal past cookie-cutter docks and low-slung homes in flamingo pink and aquamarine, pastel repositories of the good life. Olivia quizzes Carl about prison as if it were a theme park she's anxious to visit. At first, I resist the outing, but eventually, the outboard's drone and the hypnotic glitter of open water overtake me, instilling in me that rarest of feelings—peaceful indifference.

As we clear the channel, Carl suggests we head for a dockside pub, not too near, not too far, where we can reinvigorate ourselves with crab cakes and cold drinks. We all buy in, and in the wake of this harmonious interlude, Olivia remembers something.

"Hey, Uncle Carl, you texted that you had something to give Grandpa. Is it cool? Can I see it?"

"Keep your shirt on," Carl says, looking back from the wheel with a grin. "I'm just waiting for the perfect moment."

"That moment better include me," Olivia threatens. "I'm the one who tricked Grandpa into driving over."

She's drunk on tigress earring power, I think, not minding. At least she's out, prowling and growling, not hiding, lying in wait.

"It won't be so easy next time," I say, trying to inject quiet menace into my tone. Olivia cackles at my toothless threat.

"What's the verdict, Professor?" Carl shouts over the wind and Evinrude. "Should we let Olivia in on the classified material?"

"Okay," I say, "as long as it isn't drugs or a dead person's finger."

Carl whistles in mock amazement.

"Wow," he says. "Damn close in a weird way, but I'm pretty sure 'Liv can handle it."

"I can handle anything," Olivia insists. "It just better be something good."

We dock at the Drop Anchor pub. It's packed with holiday pleasure boaters—a multitude of apparently happy, prosperous, carefree souls. I see many spotless deck shoes and loud Bermuda shorts on people just past their midlife crises. Carl and I finish one round of Dos Equis as we stand at a fake tiki bar waiting for a table. Olivia's eyes gleam with liberation. She is sufficiently emboldened to supplement her virgin pina colada with furtive sips from Carl's beer. I tolerate this, unsure how to put the cat back in the bag. Carl is busy telling a not-quite-young, overtanned woman in a banana-yellow sundress that his sailboat will soon be out of drydock and she's welcome to come aboard, even bring a friend. It's all so natural and friendly, utterly beyond my social means. I turn back to Olivia. For the moment, she's preoccupied with her cell phone, and seeing that, an obvious question occurs to me.

"Olivia, whose idea was it for your mother to pick you up late?"

"Busted," she crows, grinning just like Carl.

We eventually perch at a high table, from which we order crab cake platters and begin filling up on salty tortilla chips and acrid salsa. As Olivia and Carl chat about sailing to the Keys, I stare at Olivia's earrings. Five Chinese tigers hold the world up, she had informed me on the trip to Tampa. Two rings, she had mused, and maybe a tattoo would complete her five. I related to her the misconception that Atlas held up the earth (as punishment for rebellion against the Olympians) when the sky was actually his burden—the celestial sphere. After all, I told her, where would Atlas stand to hold up the earth?

"It's magic, dude," she retorted. "Get a life."

More drinks arrive, rousing me from my reverie; nothing to do but await the magic to come.

"Let's see it, let's see it," Olivia cries, meaning whatever mysterious token Carl has procured on my behalf. I can't imagine, but at the last second, I am uneasy remembering Hermine's characterization of Carl as a sinister hypnotist.

Carl holds up a small, glittery object—a ring that fails to stir in me any pang of memory or sentiment.

"Don't you recognize it, Professor?"

"I recognize it as a ring; otherwise, no."

Carl gives his head a sad, theatrical shake. Olivia, with the swiftness of a striking cobra, grabs the ring from Carl's hand, then peers at it like she imagines a jeweler might.

"It looks like an engagement ring," she announces.

"Bingo," Carl says. He looks at me expectantly, sure the light will soon dawn. But I am drawing a cosmic blank.

"Is it Grandma's?" Olivia asks.

"Not the one I gave her," I say. "She wanted a sapphire stone; swore it would protect her and keep her *pure*."

My comment draws a sheepish glance from Carl. Olivia turns to him, offering back the ring. He finishes a prolonged swig of Dos Equis, takes the ring, then holds it up like a priest with a communion wafer.

"This is your ring, Bill," he says. "The one you gave Karen."

I can think of no way for this to be true. Still, when Carl hands me the ring, I note how meager the diamond is—just as the stone in Karen's ring would have been.

"Karen?" Olivia says. "Who's Karen?"

"My first wife," I say.

"Oh right," Olivia says. "I forgot."

"No reason you should remember."

I look at the ring again. Maybe Karen has kept in touch with Carl and undergone some late-life change of heart. Our divorce had stepped on the heels of our wedding day, so the ring's return had been in play. But at a contentious point, Karen had promised to sell it to pay for the divorce. The contradictions baffle me.

But no such incongruities slow Olivia down.

"How did *you* get the ring, Uncle Carl?"

"Well, honey, technically, I stole it."

At once, Carl's claim makes no sense and explains everything. Whatever the truth is, he seems to be enjoying himself.

"Aren't you afraid of going back to jail?" Olivia asks. She doesn't ask how he could have stolen the ring. Or why.

"Not likely, considering I snatched it, what, forty years ago? Right out of that bitch's bedroom." This garish confession, seething with unintended consequences and delivered like the pivotal line of a B-movie, is Carl's real surprise, not the ring itself.

Before I can respond, Olivia jumps in.

"Oh my god, Uncle Carl, you did *not* say that."

"Excuse my language, sweetheart, but I swear—"

"You called Grandpa's wife the *b-word*."

In time Olivia would probably contemplate the nagging implications of Carl having known both my wives, having stolen the wedding ring from the bedroom of one and married the other. But right now, *b-word* is the centerpiece of her teenage shock and awe.

"Okay," Carl says, "forget that word. I take it back, but listen—"

Now it's my turn to interrupt. "The cops never called me, and don't they say it's always the husband? I should've been their prime suspect, right?"

"Right," Carl says. "But see, Karen never called the cops. For starters, she wasn't positive somebody stole it. I mean, she *thought* she knew where she put it. And to be honest, the ring wasn't exactly a priceless family heirloom." Carl turns to Olivia before continuing. "See, 'Liv, your grandpa was poor back then. I bought the ring for him—just for the ceremony. Nothing fancy, as you can see…"

"I think it's gorgeous," Olivia says, her voice soft, her crusty exterior cast aside.

"Oh, definitely," Carl says. "Just not worth a lot of money. Not worth a cop visit. And besides, Karen knew young Bill hadn't taken it because he didn't know where she was."

"Was she hiding from him?" Olivia gives me a dark look.

"No, no, he thought she had moved up north, but she was at my dad's house taking care of business affairs. I didn't say anything to your grandpa. I didn't want to stir things up. Anyway, I heard her brag to my dad about keeping the ring. Like I said, I bought that damn ring, chauffeured her ass to the wedding, played the best man, all that stuff. I got pissed and took it. I was gonna give it to Bill here right away, but we didn't see each other for a while, then I forgot I had it, and then he and your grandmother had *their* problems, so the time never seemed right."

Olivia nodded as if she understood perfectly, then added, "You shouldn't cuss so much, Uncle Carl."

Carl's self-serving mishmash of lies and misleading truths satisfies Olivia's curiosity. But the Carl I know could never have withheld the ring story for all these years. The plot is too juicy, too perfect, especially with him as its avenging antihero protagonist.

While I chase this suspicion, Carl glances at me to confirm what Olivia must *not* hear about Karen and him. Hardly a worry since Olivia is gawking at the ring like Gollum at his "precious." I look at our fellow patrons, then close my eyes to focus on the collective babble. Is intimate angst like ours unfolding at other tables? Are we all just here to hide our fears in a festive herd? Or is it just me, my thoughts fermenting in the bright afternoon, making too much of the world?

"Hey," Carl says, "do you want this or not?" When I open my eyes, he is amiably extending the ring to me. I take it and, without thinking, wiggle it around to catch the sun.

"Let *me* do that," Olivia cries.

I am happy to hand her the ring, which she moves about until little flecks of brightness find her face. Then she slips the ring on her finger—the proper one at that.

"Why did *this* wife leave you?" she asks.

"The usual; I smoked too much weed."

"Very funny."

"Yeah," Carl says, "funny since both of them out-smoked Billy boy by a long shot. No, this particular wife wanted a rich husband, private-jet rich."

Now that Olivia knows a salacious explanation isn't forthcoming, she loses interest and starts taking selfies of her bejeweled hand. Carl works on his beer and orders another. I get up to buy a six-pack for the next leg of the complicated voyage home. As I squeeze past Olivia, an impulse strikes me.

"Do you want the ring?" I ask her.

"Seriously?" she says.

"Sure, I think my marrying days are behind me. And I don't imagine Uncle Carl will mind. Right?"

Carl eyes the ring before answering. "Keep it, honey, but don't lose it. You wouldn't want to get on my bad side."

Olivia displays the ring triumphantly. "Her hands must have been tiny," she says. "It almost fits."

I try to remember Karen's hands. All I can see is her nails, chipped and bitten to the quick.

On the way to buy beer, I pass a sign that says "unattended children will receive a double espresso and a small kitten." The moral equivalent, I suspect, of giving Olivia tigress earrings and Karen's tiny diamond.

We pass the homeward leg of our excursion without conversation, surrendering to the outboard's drone and the hull slapping against a light chop. As we enter the canal, Carl throttles down to barely above an idle and points to where the low sun has added breathtaking shades of coral, smoky raspberry, and amaretto to cloudbanks hovering gulfward. In response, Olivia stands up and stretches her left hand to catch the sunset's colors in what she calls her "unwedding" ring. When Carl gooses the engine slightly, Olivia's higher center of gravity topples her into the canal. I yell at Carl as Olivia screeches. A frantic splash, more screaming. Carl cuts the engine to make sure Olivia's wrap doesn't tangle in the prop, then has me hold his belt as he leans out to grab a floundering arm and, without seeming effort, lifts his secret granddaughter into the boat.

"Are you trying to *murder* me?" she cries, wrenching herself free.

"No, 'Liv," he says. "I only murder people for insurance money."

"Not funny," she spits out in fury as she yanks at her soaked wrap. Even as a shivering waif with plastered hair, she tries to recover as much of the traumatic upper hand as possible. "You're the worst boat driver ever," she shoots at Carl, at the same time flinging me her wrap to wring out over the side.

"Yeah," Carl says, "but I saved your life."

I hear Olivia hotly dispute this claim as I squeeze the soggy garment. *Nothing terrible has happened*, I think to myself. *That's the main thing.* When I turn around, Carl is draping Olivia's shoulders with a beach towel as she alternates between sniffles and moans of self-pity. Anything I say will provoke an outburst, so I busy myself spreading the wrap on a footlocker to dry. Before I can finish, Olivia emits a despairing howl.

"My ring," she wails. "Where's my ring?"

Carl and I look at each other. We both know, more or less, where the ring is. Still, we conduct a scrupulous search of the boat, fending off the evil hour. As I comb the deck, I can't help seeing the scene in *Lord of the Rings* where a troublesome gold band sinks to the murky bottom of the Gladden River. And wasn't I just reading that pivotal episode in *An American Tragedy* where a young woman falls from a boat and drowns? These echoes, hinting at hidden meanings, pester me as I rummage among life vests for a ring I won't find.

Take me home, I pray to no deity in particular. *Let me sit there by myself and listen to Marlene Dietrich sing "Where Have All the Flowers Gone?"—in perfect French, mind you—four or five times, or until this fiasco fades like a bad dream.*

After a fruitless quarter hour, Olivia makes her inevitable pitch—Carl and I should dive in and find the ring. Carl points out the canal is now in complete shadow, but *maybe* at high noon tomorrow he can come back with his snorkel gear and catch a sparkle. To prove his sincerity, he takes a hatchet he keeps on board to cut moorings quickly during a storm and hacks a divot in the canal wall to mark the spot. I sweeten the deal by promising a return trip to the mall to buy her a matching tigress necklace. Olivia takes her profit with a grin, her trauma suddenly undetectable.

At the house, after a hot shower, I sit in a semidaze on the ox-blood couch, drinking wine and listening to "Whatever Lola Wants" by Sarah Vaughan. I can see Olivia gesticulating on the twilit patio, illustrating the day's reversals and counter-reversals of fortune to Linda. I imagine Linda absorbing Olivia's account of the diamond ring caper and, being the canny litigator she is, later worming out of Carl details of his dalliance with my *first* ex-wife.

Then there's the daunting prospect of telling Ramona Carl is her "real" father. Not that I exactly promised Linda I would do it, but haven't I been lobbying for a clean breast since back in the day?

"Tempranillo," Carl cries out, flourishing a bottle as he enters the living room in clean clothes, smelling of good cologne.

"What?"

"The wine. Spanish. Comes from a black grape. Good with pizza."

"Very pleasant," I say. "Too pleasant, considering the drive ahead of me. Better make it coffee."

"Okay, message received. I'll whip up some *cafecito*. Hang loose for a sec." Carl heads for the kitchen then reappears a few minutes later on the patio. I see him talk to Olivia, after which she hugs him for the second time in one day, undoubtedly a record. He comes back a little later with steaming Cuban coffee and a shot glass filled with sweet cream.

"I hope to God I can find that ring," Carl says. "I know where to look, but sunlight and water can play tricks."

"Funny you should say that. Galileo described wine as 'sunlight, held together by water.' Maybe that's a sign you'll find the ring."

"*Not* funny, Professor. And what genius talks about wine and doesn't mention grapes? How does that make sense?"

"He probably thought the grapes were too obvious to bother with."

Carl shakes his head. "It's the shit people *don't* mention that —for instance—get you thrown in jail."

I nod, sipping my coffee in place of a futile reply. Sarah Vaughan has moved on to "My Funny Valentine." Linda and Olivia are still chatting against a sky taking on deep russet tints. To fill the conversational void, Carl pulls what appears to be a fountain pen from his pocket. He holds it up theatrically and presses it with his free thumb. Blue light flashes briefly from the pen.

"Okay, I'll bite," I say. "The light is a low ink indicator, right?"

Carl chortles. "Strike three, Mickey Mantle. It's a fucking weed pipe. I got it inside. An old jailbird was using it for cancer pain until he passed. I bought it, along with his stash. Legal pot. It's some kind of goop. You dip this wick in it, and boom, a battery heats it up. That light tells you how long you have to take a drag. No smoke, either."

"Are you taking it for pain?"

"Rotator cuff. But this magic goop is the whole enchilada. ESP pot. Euphoria, sleep, *and* pain." Carl takes a long drag and coughs out a bit of steamy vapor. He presses the pen again and extends it to me in a high-tech variation of the classic pipe-passing gesture.

"None for me, thanks."

Carl shrugs and takes my turn. Then we sit saying nothing, me staring at the hi-fi lights, Carl with his head bowed, as if waiting for reality to readjust itself to its new inner surroundings. Finally, he sighs and looks up.

"Listen, man, I *did* steal the ring; that's no bullshit. And Karen pitched a fit. But I just stonewalled her. What could she do—call the cops on Dad and me?" The memory seems to bring Carl some substitute for pleasure.

"I'm not surprised you got away with it," I reply, "but why do it?"

Carl drains his wine glass, pours it full again, then looks out to make sure Linda and Olivia are still preoccupied.

"After we slept together, she told me sex with you was better. I guess I bugged her to tell me; I can't remember. Anyway, she knew the two of you weren't going to make it, so she gave me a try. It's human nature, right? She was bound to wonder—the three of us hanging out. And I had a boat, a house. That definitely interested her; you know how she was. But it turns out I wasn't *that* rich, and I just didn't do it for her in the sack. And like I said, I dug her, even down to the cold bitch act she trotted out at the end. I probably dug her more than you ever did. I guess when she changed her mind and decided to hang on to the fucking ring as a 'keepsake,' it pissed me off."

Carl stops then and looks at me like a kid who's picked a fight and waits for the first punch.

"Carl, this may shock you, but I'm happy to stipulate—to use Linda's term—that you loved Karen, and I only thought I did. Trust me; it's crossed my mind. I propose we let it go. My life is damn sweet in many ways, and you're a free man. You stay in your sandbox, and I'll stay in mine. Why push our luck?"

Without answering, Carl gets up and replaces Sarah on the turntable with Joni Mitchell's *Court and Spark*. One of Karen's favorites.

As Joni's first jazzy plaint begins to fill the room, he sits back down with a grunt and looks at me with an expression both schoolboy-sheepish and sad. "Shit, Bill, I have this damn virus, and I got it in my head that it's connected to me keeping the ring. I think Linda's getting to me with all her haunted Christmas tree craziness. All that shit is why I decided to give the ring back. Fucked up, huh?"

I shrugged. "Thinking the ring caused AIDS is a *little* fucked up, but in a way, it's no different than pushing the elevator button a bunch of times to make the elevator come quicker. It's what they call magical thinking. Everybody does it, one way or another."

"Yeah, but pushing an elevator button doesn't give you AIDS."

"Not as far as we know. Anyway, better to focus on getting well, maybe reopen your dad's stereo business; all that vintage gear is making a comeback."

Carl jumps to his feet and paces around, the soothing marijuana no match for him. He glances a few times toward Linda and Olivia on the patio, their silhouettes blending into the dusk.

"The past is a can of worms, dude," he says. "Nobody ever looks back and says, 'Hey, let me tell you about all the great decisions I made.' Whatever I do, it won't be going back to a place with a dead-end sign built in."

"Okay," I conceded, "no more advice. I haven't exactly knocked it out of the park myself. But listen, speaking of the past, Linda wants me to tell Ramona you're her father. Mystically clear the air. What do you think about that?"

He stares glumly at his wine.

"I think she'll wish it was anyone but me. But do what you gotta do."

"Carl, Ramona dislikes most people. She acts like a hanging judge. I mean, I'm in the doghouse as often as not. But she comes around if you take her as she is."

"Professor, I think that ship has sailed. I've dropped her a few hints over the years, but she'd rather drink a bucket of warm spit than get personal with me."

"Why don't you write her a letter, explain everything, give her something to mull over?"

Carl seems to hold this option in suspension through a couple of sips of wine, then breaks into a smile.

"Not a bad idea. Maybe you could help me with the wording."

Somewhere between Tampa and Micanopy, Olivia wonders if Hermine can meet us at the mall to help her pick out her spirit animal necklace. "I'll ask," I tell her. After a few silent miles (other than wind battering and whipping through the cracked windows), Olivia offers an observation.

"You old people are way more messed up than I thought."

All I could think of to say was "Lord knows we try."

CHAPTER TWENTY-TWO

"Everybody's Somebody's Fool"

Hopperton, Georgia, Fall 1967

The Saturday morning after I kissed Wanda, ordinary life resumed with a breakfast of venison bacon, eggs, and cold pear slices. I helped my mother set up card tables for her bridge social, then began my weekend chore—squatting beneath our shade oak on an overturned washtub and scraping defeated paint from the woodshed. I hated repetitious tasks, but the day promised freedom beyond a couple of hours in gloomy shadows, and besides, chores at least left me alone with my thoughts of Wanda. While I prized the forbidden wisdom captured by my Philco, those signals seemed faint, ambiguous, almost irrelevant now. Wanda's emanations overpowered them. Her kiss, her words, her defiant hair, all desirably illicit, seemed to subvert, even refute, my tranquil life. As I alternated between jabs at stubborn olive-drab paint flakes and distant stares at hummingbirds hovering and darting around a trellis of trumpet flowers, I was elsewhere—watching Wanda type the last page of my novel, undress, then fall into bed with me. And in the way of such daydreams, she was suddenly both herself and my novel's heroine, Delia Wingfoot, bathing in a hidden grotto, purifying herself before battle. I shivered pleasurably at the thought of writing such a scene and watching Wanda read it.

I heard footsteps and looked up to see my father walking toward me, frowning, his hat jammed down on his head rather than perched at its usual jaunty angle. To my relief, he had not come to criticize my work habits but only to tell me a fistfight had broken out at the plant and he needed to settle matters. I asked him what happened, sure he would tell me nothing. To my surprise, he glanced back at the house, then leaned down and whispered two words with evident disgust.

"A woman."

As my father stood up, I nodded as if I completely understood. He nodded back and glanced at the woodshed.

"Keep your mind on your work," he admonished, fixing me with an intense stare, "not on foolishness."

Flinching at the word *foolishness*, I tried to think of nothing, fearing that my father, like the leering Mr. Heffelfinger, could read my mind. But of course, it was only the plant scuffle he was thinking about, two men fighting over a woman, likely a loose woman if I rightly understood why he had whispered. I could well imagine what he would think of Wanda.

"I'll try," I said, unwilling to bend any closer to my father's advice.

In the early afternoon, he returned and released me from my chore. He'd sent a man packing, a deed long overdue. But he looked more sad than resolute in the telling, and I guessed he had hated to do it. As he was about to leave, he turned and said, "The path's always too narrow for some fellows, no matter how wide it is." I was downright shocked to hear my father philosophize, especially with pithy eloquence. He smiled at my surprise and clapped me on the shoulder. "That's enough, scraping; you can go about your business. I'm going in to finally smoke my morning cigar."

Set free, I hurried to the porch swing, making myself visible to Wanda in case she walked by, although she never had before. I waited a while, but no one appeared except an old man in dungarees, trailed by a dispirited collie. Eventually, my mother came out to bring me iced tea and two dollars for the movies, a small bribe to clear the decks for her bridge social. I took the money, happy to go. I might see Wanda. And anyway, I loved Westerns. Bad men getting the sneers wiped off their faces, and the other kind of story—a washed-up gunfighter saving the rancher's family before dying in the saloon girl's arms, hearing her swear she *did* love him.

The Rialto was Hopperton's only movie theater. Most of the seats were broken down and spewing padding; boys were known to bring a two-by-four to prop them up. The floors were both slick *and* sticky from the constant assault of Jujubes and butter grease. Adults, for the most part, avoided the Rialto, preferring the Dreamland Drive-In's outdated first-run movies. Sci-fi and horror B movies typified the Rialto's fare, except on Saturdays when it catered to younger kids (who called it the "Rat Hole") by running two vintage cowboy movies from open to close. Fifty cents bought an all-day ticket; starting times were irrelevant.

In prior years I had enacted the ritual: stay as long as possible, act up, trade catcalls, throw popcorn, and hop from seat to seat as your friends came and went. But that Saturday, I sat in the far back, happy to occupy an intact seat and watch a movie I had never seen before, a Seventh Cavalry versus Indians story called *Bugles in the Afternoon*. I was strangely taken by the movie because, like the scuffle at my father's plant, the plot involved two soldiers fighting over a woman. One soldier, an officer, was bad; the other, unjustly demoted, was good, but the woman didn't know that until the wicked soldier got his just deserts from an Indian arrow after Custer's Last Stand and the truth came out. When the movie ended, I sat for a moment wondering if the truth had come out at my father's plant. What if he had fired the wrong man? This uneasy thought made me restless, and I stood up. A few lights came on to facilitate snack runs; I took an idle look around.

Down front, the usual clump of fidgety, boisterous kids. To the right, halfway, a couple. And one of them, her beacon of yellow hair blazing in the dimness, was Wanda. The other was a boy from school, Bobby Heatwole. They sat there, Wanda nodding, Bobby talking. I watched them with morbid concentration, trying not to move, like a spy whose life is forfeit if he's spotted. When the lights dimmed, I bent over to ease the wrenching pain in my gut and groaned aloud despite myself. Fearing discovery, I fled the Rialto in a despairing panic, fled it like the cursed and crumbling place it was, swearing as I exited never to watch another movie there again.

Back home, I paid my required respects to the bridge ladies (choking out admiration for their fancy hats) before imprisoning myself in my room to wallow in unprecedented misery.

Wanda was faithless.

I stared at my radio, then my typewriter. They sat there like genie bottles bereft of wishes. I cursed the world, then gazed out my window, wanting to see Wanda standing there, alone, staring remorsefully at my house. But my yard and street stood empty; nothing to see but the long shadow of a dogwood fighting the burnished light of the late afternoon.

Nothing to see.

I stared anyway. A rattletrap Ford F-100, mottled with brick-red primer, the cab blue, the bed green, rolled slowly by with three kids hollering and waving wildly from the pickup's bed. The truck passed, exhaust billowing in its wake, the merriment of its cargo deepening my misery. To think that I intended to shape Delia Wingfoot in the image of Wanda Grice! "Only a fool," my father would say. "Don't you see?" Don would say. "Well, fuck you all," I muttered, determined to turn a hardened face to fickle girls and cheap advice. And one thing I knew: Delia Wingfoot's hair would *not* be a "sun-colored nimbus."

I stood there, fists clenched, trying to pull myself up on righteous bootstraps, seeking the happiness of unhappy people: self-justification. But as I walked to my desk, ready to write the cold note I would leave in Wanda's mailbox, a pain welled up in my chest, extorting from me an image of her in the darkened Rialto, necking with Bobby Heatwole. Every vindictive atom in my body marshaled itself against that image, but it did no good. I cast myself down on my bed and sobbed until Mother called me for dinner.

I ate salty shepherd's pie in silence until my father, perhaps sensing something, asked how I was "faring." I told him, with involuntary sarcasm, that I had never been better in my life.

"I hope you mean that, son." He put his fork down and fixed me with a flat stare. I had blundered into a minefield and mere backtracking would not be enough. Eager to escape, I shook my head and sacrificed my promise to Don.

"Don is moving away."

"Heavens no," my mother cried. "Whatever for?"

Her shock swept my impertinence aside.

"His dad's business, that's all I know. And I wasn't supposed to tell you; please don't mention it to Don." As far as that went, Don had not stopped at my house after school for the last few days, sulking, I assumed, about Wanda and his precious *Atlas Shrugged*. He had told my mother a different story: new chores had fallen on his shoulders in light of his father's "all-consuming" business affairs. Either way, his absence served the moment's ragged cause.

Hearing the news, my mother folded her hands as if in prayer and eyed my father. "Ed, did you speak with Philip Heffelfinger as you promised?"

"Yes, Maggie, I did. I told him I had plant equipment to insure. He didn't buy it; I can tell you that. I did manage to work things around to the crossbow, but he laughed it off, said his son had already lost interest."

"Thank you, Ed, but what about his state of mind? Did he mention moving?"

"No, but I can't fault a fellow in his line of work for wanting to swim in a bigger pond."

"Of course not, Ed, but did he seem *right* to you? You know what he's been through."

"Maggie, I was falsely polite with him; he was the same with me. I don't honestly know what to make of the man."

My mother, distraught, unsatisfied, turned to me, her eyes moist and glittering. "Rest assured, I will keep your confidence, Bill, but I intend to make inquiries."

My mother's threatened "inquiries" terrorized me. I imagined Mr. Heffelfinger, like a telepathic bloodhound, tracing my mother's well-intended snooping back to my craven disclosure of his travel plans. Amid this dread, gaping at my mother's words, I spotted an unpleasant pattern: I had played fast and loose with Don's cherished book; I had spilled the beans tonight to save my hide; worst yet, I had long seen myself as Don's better. Wanda, no doubt, was my punishment for conceiving a selfish, erroneous view of life. Well, Peter had denied Jesus to the Romans but made up for it later. How exactly had that happened? I couldn't remember but resolved to look it up. In the meantime, I knew it was pointless to contest my mother's plans. The best thing I could do was get back in Don's good graces. Agreeing with one of his crazy ideas was the most straightforward way. Then I would become the kind of friend he deserved.

After dinner, I walked over to the gazebo. With its fluted pillars lost in climbing vines, I had long ago recast it as an elven temple from *Lord of the Rings*. That evening, misty dusk and choral pulses of cricket song deepened the illusion. I sat in morose meditation, perched on the railing, trying to pinpoint the cause of my life's collapse. Was it perverse luck, like a Rebel rifle ball finding Stonewall Jackson at Chancellorsville? I thought back. What bad thing had ever happened to me in my whole life before now? I strained to think of one. Nothing came. A bitter laugh escaped me, forced out by the premonition that Trouble—having spotted me at last—was eager to make up for lost time. Don's mother was gone, likewise

Wanda's father. I stared out into an expanse filling with darkness. How terrible would things have to get to balance out my undeservedly soft life?

In the middle-distance, now that the sun had given way, I could make out the postage-stamp glow from my bedroom window, along with a few stars. And that was part of it too, wasn't it? The light of one thing hiding another. And something—some harsh truth, I felt sure—had been hiding in the light of my complacent happiness. I needed to wise up, toughen up, cut the crap. I contemplated how I planned to begin *The Dark Warrior* in 1961 on an abandoned Georgia farm where a ragtag rebel army was re-forming. But what did I know about armies or even the farms that ringed Hopperton? I needed to visit farms and *listen* to the rambling hymns of praise Don offered to confederate stratagems. I needed to reacquire *Atlas Shrugged*, which bristled with descriptions of buildings and machines, and make my observations sound like Ayn Rand's. But most of all, I needed to become the new, unsmiling me, the one with hard, skeptical eyes who could shrug off Wanda's fickle ways like so much dandelion fluff. Grasping a post, I leaned recklessly back to scan the emerging stars. *They're still there*, my father reminded me more than once, *even at noontime on a summer day.* Still there.

Wanda's book, *Siddhartha*, still sat in Mr. Pee's classroom, tucked under the cigar box of mismatched chess pieces that began the whole thing. *This world would make short work of good old Siddhartha*, I told myself.

At that moment, a low voice drifted in from the near darkness. I pulled myself upright to see on the sidewalk below the dim shape of a man who, as he walked along, seemed to be talking tenderly and at length to his dog. It was the man who had passed my house earlier in the afternoon as I foolishly waited for the off chance of Wanda's appearance. On impulse, I called out. "Sir, you're welcome to sit here with your dog; I'm just leaving." The man didn't speak but paused and bent down as if consulting with his dog about whether to accept my offer. Moments later, they headed up the rise. "Ain't this private property?" the man called as he approached.

"No, anybody can sit here,"

"Well, damnation. Come on, Dixie girl. Let's go live like proper folks."

The man wasn't old, just a little bent, sunken-eyed, and slow-moving. He dropped down with a pleasurable groan, plucked papers and tobacco from his overalls, and began relating the details of his day as people do, assuming a sympathetic ear. Dixie preferred sniffing bushes to listening, but

I felt relief, even comfort in hearing about experiences less harrowing than my own. The man told me he'd been out visiting his sister, a "farm widow" living a couple of miles north of town. He'd replaced porch boards, scythed down overgrowth, then played Monopoly to please her. After a fried chicken dinner, they enjoyed the reborn porch while talking about bygone days and wondering where the traffic crawling along nearby 441 was trying to get to.

"I had a terrible day," I blurted out.

"Yep," he grunted, lighting up. "Plenty of those to be had." He scrutinized the gazebo, then gave me a speculative squint. "Was this here your rendezvous point?"

"What?"

"Rendezvous point. That's what they was always telling my platoon in France: rendezvous here or there with another outfit, but I'll be damned if they ever showed up, kilt or lost or some such. I thought maybe you were waiting hereabouts for some girl you were sweet on."

"She's not coming—ever."

Rather than scoffing at my self-pity, the man nodded in commiseration.

"Men do the chasing, but women do the picking and choosing. That's how God set things up. You'll get picked soon enough. Someone fancy from the looks of you." Dixie came back then, panting and wagging. She sat down next to her master and laid her chin on his knee. He smoked and smiled at me like a weather-beaten oracle.

"Got to push off," he said. "What's your name, son?"

"Bill Shaffer."

"You Boss Shaffer's boy?" I had never heard my father called that, but I had no doubt who the man meant.

"My father works at the turpentine plant."

"Be damned. Tell your old man Tom Fields hopes he gets his just due. Good luck to you, son."

I stood up, shook hands, and watched Fields amble away, feeling that he, like everyone else, knew things I should have known but didn't.

Sally came to church Sunday sporting a new fall dress, green, as I remember, sprinkled with little white flowers. As if summoned, Tom Fields's "fancy girl" sat down next to me: white gloves, wide-brimmed hat, and the faintest possible hint of womanly perfume. No fruity gum, no vanilla-scented body oil, certainly no welcoming of a strange boy into her bedroom.

And no "rendezvous" with Bobby Heatwole in the dim, dank decrepitude of the Rialto Theatre.

I stole glances at Sally throughout the service, trying to be taken with her. Boys I knew favored the perky, dimpled cuteness exemplified by girls in the beach party movies all the rage back then. Sally was more the Katherine Hepburn type, her face angular and striking rather than pretty, her aura far more assertive than compliant. Wanda belonged to neither kind. I scrutinized Sally one last time and sighed. Her looks wouldn't tilt the balance between us one way or the other. Understanding this and keeping with my avowed rebirth as a man of action, I hit on a tactic to lure the murky nature of whatever we meant to each other into the open.

In the meantime, Reverend Farrior sermonized about parables in the Bible—the Good Samaritan, the Prodigal Son—thundering on about how they were not just uplifting stories but divine instructions we must follow lest we perish. Shit. A feeling swept through me like a biting wind. I suppose you could call it a privileged young man's version of grief and terror. Without thinking, I took Sally's hand and stared hard at a nearby window of stained glass, wishing I could see through its kaleidoscopic mosaic to the pure blue sky. Sally squeezed my hand, released it, then gave me an affectionate pat on the arm. She seemed unfazed, as if what I had done fit into a familiar pattern. Before long, we stood and sang "The Old Rugged Cross" and "How Great Thou Art" and "Onward Christian Soldiers," Sally and I sharing a hymn book, though we had long known the words by heart.

Monday morning, I slipped into Mr. Pee's classroom and recovered *Siddhartha*, intending to return it to Wanda with a telling lack of explanation. Lunch period, however, brought no sign of her—just the reek of fatty meatloaf and Don hunched at our usual table, greeting me with an agitated wave. "Good. There you are, Shaffer."

"Here I am," I conceded with all the pained ennui I could muster.

Don rushed ahead, unaffected, an odd, rehearsed quality to his speech. "As I suspect you know, Shaffer, *someone* returned *Atlas Shrugged* to me. I would like to put that comedy of errors behind us. More important matters are at hand. I see now how fickle a mistress my crossbow is, and I wish to enlist you to refresh me on the technique for cocking it."

"I suppose I could, but since we're being honest, I only gave your book to Wanda for a few days, and she hated it. And I don't like hanging around your father; I think he hates me."

Rather than protesting, Don smiled as if I had fallen into another cunning trap. "A false theory about my dad, Shaffer, but I'm not surprised to hear it. You fail to grasp that Philip Heffelfinger is a *philosopher*. Petty hatreds are beneath him. Oh, I know how things might look from where you stand, but there is a different explanation than hostility for my dad's . . . demeanor. He's preoccupied with a great undertaking, and certain roadblocks frustrate him, so you see—"

"See what? What are you talking about?"

Don leaned close and whispered fiercely, "I'm sworn to secrecy; you must swear the same. Otherwise, I can't tell you."

"I swear, sure."

Don feigned a hard stare as if weighing my words, but I knew better. He was desperate to tell me something.

"Okay, Shaffer, here it is in a nutshell. My dad has *proof* that the Civil War, as you call it, was arranged by a divine intelligence to teach us what happens when one force tries to overpower its opposite. It's like matter and energy; we need them both, right? People say we don't need hate, only love, but don't we have to hate injustice? When Lee surrendered because he loved his men, the world got thrown out of balance, which explains the terrible shape we're in."

Don may as well have been speaking Hungarian. "Sounds deep," I said, "but what's that got to do with your father acting like he hates me?"

"He likes you, Shaffer, a lot. He's just grumpy because when he tries to write his theories down, he . . . he's a thinker, not a writer, and it drives him crazy. I've been trying to help him after school, writing down what he says, but he tells me it's not going near fast enough. 'Time is not our friend, Donald,' is how he puts it."

Mr. Heffelfinger's gaunt, drawn face came forcibly to mind. "Is he sick?" I asked.

Don paled, convincing me I'd hit the mark. At that moment, I couldn't help picturing an old dog crawling off to die.

"No, no, nothing like that."

People are, for the most part, much worse liars than they think they are. "Your father is okay?" I demanded, fixing Don with my best unflinching gaze.

"Good god, Shaffer, he works hard, he's had a nagging cold, and he can barely hold a pen since the war. But he's quite alive, thank you. Anyway, he's got business in Atlanta this weekend, and since you delight in misunderstanding him, the coast is clear for a crossbow session. And you can recount the ridiculous doings at the Harvest Hop—this Friday, is it not? And I presume you're squiring Sally?"

"Yeah, we're going as George and Martha Washington; it's embarrassing. My mother is making my costume out of this shiny blue stuff. I have to wear a wig too."

Don brightened, his old self returning.

"How interesting that you're going as a *married* couple." He grinned wickedly. "But I will say no more. My dad tells me I provoke without cause. He says only rash fools act that way."

The words "only" and "fools"—from my father's pet phrase—brought Wanda miserably to mind. I glanced around and spotted Bobby Heatwole at a back-corner table among a clump of boys beneath consideration for popularity. I tried for contempt but found only a vile, poisonous taste. *Let him have her.*

When I turned around, Don was examining *Siddhartha*. "That's Wanda's book, the one I swapped for yours. It's short, but it's cosmic as all get-out, and every bit as good as *Atlas Shrugged*." Don dropped the book with scorn.

"I'm going to assume you said that for the sake of controversy, Shaffer, but let me tell you, only *history* judges books, and I'm quite sure of where history is headed. I'm quite sure where *you're* headed. Life is less mysterious than people like to think." Don paused to shovel in mouthfuls of meatloaf and mashed potatoes.

"Bullshit, as usual, *Heffelfinger*."

"Okay, Shaffer, here's what I see in my crystal ball. You get a law degree from Georgia, bottom third of your class, then come back to Hopperton to defend the pitiful and weak. You marry Sally, who's the principal of good old Hopperton High. You two chaperone the Harvest Hop every year. A couple of kids. Life is complete. The end."

Don's prediction struck me as both insulting and eerily plausible. "That's crap, Don; I'm headed for New York or Chicago, places where people use their brains."

"Shaffer, you're no match for those hyenas up north; they will pick your bones clean."

"And you're no match for the Vietcong, Don. I guess we're even."

"Evenly doomed, it would seem. But in the meantime, I can't let that wretched crossbow get the best of me, don't you see?"

For once, I did see. "I'll do my best to come Saturday."

Don beamed like a kid walking into a county fair. "You rescue me, Shaffer, and perhaps I'll return the favor."

CHAPTER TWENTY-THREE

"Monster Mash"

T he holidays were upon us. My father commented, as he did every year, that my mother's vast preparations eclipsed the Normandy Invasion. The days were finally cool enough for girls to show off beaded pastel sweaters, the Hopperton High football team limped into the mercy of a bye week, and Aunt Miriam, my mother's older sister, arrived for her holiday visit. My aunt was a frequent houseguest from Birmingham and the only person who ever ventured criticism of my mother within my hearing—scolding her gently for being "full of herself." Aunt Miriam had run off just after the war with a professional gambler named George Harrison. When a massive heart attack killed him at the apex of a high-stakes winning streak, she paid in advance for a year's lodging at the Ideal Hotel in downtown Birmingham. Before the year was up, she became the hotel's manager and maintained that role for most of her remaining life.

Aunt Miriam's visits were cautionary adventures. Within the spare bedroom set aside solely for her occupancy, she chain-smoked unfiltered Pall Malls, applied lipstick, removed her wig, poured whiskey into her iced tea, and occasionally cursed as she paced around in red silk pajamas and a sweeping black robe. I witnessed these activities firsthand since neither of my parents would venture into the room and Aunt Miriam required a listener. Curiously, my mother encouraged these tête-à-tête's, despite their dissolute aspects.

"You are a good influence on my dear sister," she once told me. "Perhaps, through God's good graces, you can do for her what I cannot." I didn't think Aunt Miriam needed correction or improvement, and maybe my unconditional admiration was precisely the balm my mother had in mind. In any case, Aunt Miriam certainly improved *me*, with twenty-dollar bills and shocking maxims to mull over. "You are the luckiest boy in the world to start your life in this sweet little town," she advised me one afternoon as we sat on her bed playing gin rummy. "But you will be the unluckiest boy if you finish it here." When I asked why, she said, "People in this town walk through life backward like they're afraid they dropped something."

I agreed with her, not knowing why, persuading myself I knew what she meant. "Move back," I begged. "My mother cries every time you leave." Aunt Miriam just shook her head and dealt a new hand.

"She'll be fine, Billy. She'd cry a lot more if I stayed here all the time. Just be grateful you have the best mother in the world." Then she leaned down, kissed me on the cheek, and whispered, "When you're older, you can come to Birmingham and I'll buy you a Delmonico steak and tell you stories to curl your hair."

Other than pal around with Aunt Miriam, I did little else but rehearse my next conversation with Wanda, putting the kind of abject words in her mouth that wounded people hope for but never hear, reserving for myself a fiery and indignant upper hand.

Yet when I encountered her Monday between classes, I could only revert with a thudding heart and sheepish falsity to the passive, pleasant Bill Shaffer I now despised. And to deepen my torment, Wanda seemed happier. Most days at school, she wore skepticism like a uniform, but *something* had softened her up. I remembered how, after our kiss Friday night, she seemed jumpy, as if shying away from a static shock. Maybe another kiss had met with less resistance. As I wallowed in this speculative futility, Wanda mentioned the Harvest Hop. I froze between morbid curiosity and outright fear.

"Are you going?" I stammered.

"Ugh, dances. Are you taking 'Miss Sally'?"

"Yeah." I lacked the heart to elaborate.

Wanda shook her head. "You're doomed, Bill."

Doomed. First Don, now Wanda.

"*You* would know," I said with more bitterness and less mystery than I had intended, but Wanda was too cheery to follow me down that rabbit hole.

"*Anyone* would know, but have fun anyway."

216

Where was the dark drama of my rehearsals? I managed a pitiful banality. "Do you want your book back?" I asked, holding up *Siddhartha* like a shield between us.

"You read it, huh?" She smiled a satisfied smile like the guy on the cover. "Keep it for now. Bring it by my house after school, and we'll discuss it." Mercifully, the day was left unspecified.

I tracked Wanda's bright yellow beacon as long as I could through the babbling traffic, dismayed not to have detected in her even a furtive flicker of guilt. I stood there for a moment like a small child lost in a crowded store, then headed for Physics with old lady Gaffney, who wore a red wig and stank of stale cigarette smoke, but who, like Mister Pee, seemed to have dug up a few philosophical nuggets.

As she informed us between hacking coughs, one of them was that everything—from "our mortal bodies to the immortal stars" —sooner or later runs out of gas. She swept her arm around the room to indicate the building we inhabited, warning us that the atoms clinging to each other for dear life to keep our beloved school upright would eventually release their grips and all would fall to dust. And not by happenstance, but in obedience to a *law*, a law of nature, and therefore, like gravity and the speed of light, an expression of God's law. This law, called entropy, served to remind us (Miss Gaffney surmised) that God wished everyone and everything to return to him innocent of desire and complication, as it was in the Garden before the Fall. What then, or who, I wondered as I trudged to class, was out there trying to keep it complicated? And why did the very *best* things—books and girls, for example—take you down such twisted paths? I thought about posing this question to Miss Gaffney, but I figured she would bring the devil into the picture, and I didn't want to hear that.

My mother owned a small cherry bookcase populated by classic novels like *Moll Flanders*, *Tristam Shandy*, *Vanity Fair*, and *Ivanhoe*. I doubt my mother knew these books were full of sex and irreverence, but I had opened them and knew they were as racy as *Playboy* magazine. Women in those old books were "comely" if they had sex appeal. When I saw Sally Chiles in her rose-pink satin, floor-length colonial Halloween costume, I saw her as "comely" for perhaps the first time. Her dress featured a bodice which, for all its modesty, emphasized the breasts it covered. Sally registered my appraisal with satisfaction, but I wondered in passing what she thought of her looks. As far as I knew, she had never had a real date—a "rendezvous," ill-fated or otherwise. I also wondered what she made of the rumors about Wanda and me. She had replaced them, I supposed with gloomy logic, with gossip about Bobby and Wanda.

"You look beautiful, Martha," I offered, determined to be bold.

"Well, it's about time somebody noticed," she replied with good-natured indignation, clearly pleased. On the Chiles' sweeping lawn, Sally's mother snapped pictures against the backdrop of their pillared entranceway. Sally warned that we better win the best costume prize or someone would be sorry.

The gym was awash in black and orange crepe bunting. A trove of construction paper skeletons and leering pumpkins from prior years plastered every surface. As a backdrop for photos, the decorating committee had created a giant web of fuzzy yarn, inhabited by a man-size stuffed spider with red eyes blinking like turn signals.

Sally barely noticed, too busy scouting costume competition. "They're all copycat hippies," she whispered scornfully. "You're not going to win with bell bottoms and a headband." Only Myla Farmer, busy blessing everyone with a sparkly wand (Glinda the Good Witch), worried Sally. As Sally fretted about Myla, I fended off insults about my sissy costume from a football player whose entire ensemble was plastic fangs as strains of "Monster Mash" reached me through lulls in the chatter. So it went, until Betty Jean, dressed as Little Red Riding Hood, appeared accompanied by a boy wearing a cheap Wolf Man mask, but otherwise dressed in nondescript street clothes.

When the boy flipped up his mask, I recognized him as a lunchroom tablemate of Bobby Heatwole. I couldn't remember his name but knew him as a rough, touchy kid known for winning playground scuffles. Betty Jean and the wolf boy looked around, ill at ease and improbably paired. I had momentarily forgotten about Wanda and Bobby, but here they were in the guise of their stand-ins, seemingly sent to goad my wounded pride. Then, as if on cue, the boy pointed toward me and laughed. I rushed over, glared silently at Betty Jean, then turned to the boy, standing closer than custom permitted.

"What's so funny, asshole?" I spat out.

"Piss off, sissy." He seemed more amused than threatened.

"My goodness, Bill," Betty Jean added. "Are you drunk?" They both knew I was bluffing, even if I didn't. The rout was on.

"A little," I mumbled, then drew back, croaking out "sorry" as I lurched away.

Later, standing in front of the blinking spider with Sally, receiving to the barest applause our preordained best costume prizes, I spotted Betty Jean on the far side of the gym watching the ceremony, wolf boy nowhere in sight. I ventured a conciliatory wave, hoping to elicit a smile, hoping for it like a saving grace, but she just stood there, maybe noticing, maybe not; I couldn't tell.

On the walk home, Sally glanced at me appraisingly a few times. Eyewitness accounts of my confrontation would have flowed to her like mountain streams to the river below. Seemingly in passing, she identified the boy with Betty Jean as Abel Theroux. His mother, a widow, worked for Sally's father as a legal secretary. Abel had found "every sort of trouble," according to Sally. That's why all the girls steered clear.

"Anybody but a low-class Waycross girl would know better than to go out with Abel Theroux," she proclaimed. Was this a backhanded swipe at Wanda?

"Isn't he good friends with Bobby Heatwole?" I asked, my voice sounding thick and false.

Before answering, Sally stopped and looked up at the moon, just a bit on the far side of full. "How perfect; a harvest moon for the Harvest Hop."

"It's not a harvest moon; that was last month. This is a hunter's moon." Sally shook her head.

"Goodness, Mr. Know-It-All, where's the poetry in your soul?"

"It's in there," I said. "I listen to poetry on the radio."

One time, for five dreary, uncomprehending minutes.

"You've done no such thing," Sally chided, "but regardless, why on earth would you ask about Bobby Heatwole?"

My answer took the form of an inspired lie.

"I ran into him at the Rialto. He seemed a little off in the head."

And if he had that reputation, Sally would know.

"Well, I wouldn't be surprised," she said, her opinion based on the rumor that his body was "covered with scars" from a fire when he was a little kid. Opinion, she confided, was split among Hopperton girls regarding their eagerness to see the terrible damage. So far, no girl had. And Bobby was excused from gym, meaning no boy had either. Sally's recital, lurid as it was, cast Bobby in a sympathetic light, and I had been cravenly hoping to tarnish his reputation.

"Maybe he doesn't have any scars," I suggested as Sally finished her account.

She gave me an exasperated glance.

"Lord, Bill, how would such a story get started if it wasn't true?" There were a thousand ways, I knew, but none came quickly to mind.

A chilly breeze kicked up as we turned off Stagecoach and headed down Apalachee Trace, the freshly bricked road meandering a mile to Sally's lakeside house. On both the road's borders, precise rows of sycamore, sweetbay, and tupelo swayed and wound hypnotically into darkness.

"This road could be a poem," I said, only half out of mischief, hoping to draw Sally into any kind of conversation to divert me from imagining Wanda touching Bobby Heatwole's scars. But Sally declined to rhapsodize about the road. She countered instead with a small wail of despair at having left her good cashmere shawl at the dance, while at the same time hugging herself dramatically against the wind's bite. I put my arm around her, thinking myself gallant.

"That's sweet, Bill, but it doesn't help."

I knew with stinging certainty that she didn't find my gesture "sweet." I dropped my arm, halted my steps, and said, "Sally, can I ask you a question?" using for the first time in my life that put-upon tone indispensable to marital skirmishing.

"And I want to ask *you* one. Bill Shaffer, have you been drinking? Everyone at the dance tonight said so, but I hardly believed it." She hesitated, then added, "And I've heard other things about you too." She stood in the moonlit space between two restless arboreal shadows, waiting for my answer. I noticed she had raised pale fingers to fidget with the strand of pearls she had earlier taken pains to announce was genuine.

"Not a drop, I swear. What other lies have you heard?"

Sally gave me a long, dubious look, ignoring my question for the moment. She had placed her faith in drinking to explain my peculiar behavior and now decided to test that faith before casting it aside. "Let me smell your breath," she said, stepping gingerly forward.

When I kissed her, she startled like a deer, causing white pellets from her broken necklace to rain down on the pavement. I watched them bound away helter-skelter with mad, supernatural energy. "Shit," I said, kneeling to recover the wayward orbs, expecting Sally to do the same while berating me on any one of several fronts. Instead, she sighed and spoke quietly. "Don't bother with the silly pearls; they're from Woolworths." My costume had no pockets; I clutched the few pellets I had apprehended and stood up.

"Why did you do that, Bill?" Not a question—a sad accusation.

"Why do you think?" Neither one of us invoked the word "kiss." Instead, we eyed each other across a weird, invisible no-man's-land.

"Honestly, I haven't the faintest idea. You've never shown the least interest in me before, and from what I've heard … well, never mind that. Lord forgive me for being a doubting Thomas, but I'm not sure I believe you haven't been drinking."

"Well, I haven't, and from what I've heard, boys get drunk at your swimming parties all the time. The parties I'm never invited to."

"Those boys are the sons of whoever my father invites. It's how he does his business. I don't care what those fools do."

"Well, anyway, *you're* the liar; you said these were real." I held out the fake pearls I had rescued.

"My goodness, that was one little fib, just for fun. How can you be so mean?"

I let the pearls dribble off my palm and clatter against the brick. "I don't care about those or your stupid parties. And don't worry; I won't torture you with any more kisses. People kept telling me you like me. I decided to find out if you did. Now I know."

These last three words changed Sally. "Yes, now you know," she whispered, her face darkening, "and aren't you glad?"

I should have said, *No, I'm not glad. Any boy in his right mind would want you to like him.* I should have used those words, even if I wasn't that boy myself. Instead, I said, "If you say so."

"Well, I do, and that's that," Sally replied with the barest tremor bleeding through her officious tone. "Now, Bill, if you'll help me pick up the pearls. I wouldn't want birds to choke on them."

The next day, keeping my promise to help Don "master" the crossbow, I approached his house warily, looking for Mr. Heffelfinger's pickup truck, ready to turn tail home if I spotted it. I was miserable enough already. As if Sally's rebuke wasn't sufficient, I had stripped more paint from the utility shed that morning and gouged my knuckles into dry, splintery wood. Now my bandage seeped blood. Misery had decided to open a new front seeing that it had me on the run. But at least the truck was gone. On cue, Don emerged, waving his crossbow. He had been watching for me.

As we passed through the house on our way to taking potshots at unsuspecting pine trees, I was shocked to see the living room in a shamble, as if Don's bedroom had become contagious. Books, *Atlas Shrugged* among them, lay splayed open on the floor next to scattered piles of papers and yellow legal pads. Dirty dishes and wadded clothing decorated the furniture. A faintly organic smell permeated the air, like garbage neglected but not yet stinking outright. This state of affairs, intolerable to the Mr. Heffelfinger I knew and feared, told me Don was not expecting him back anytime soon. It even crossed my mind that he had died, the pickup hidden somewhere by Don to conceal the fact.

Then there was my mother, who, when I left the house, threatened a visit to the Heffelfinger's herself, pending my report on their "state of affairs." She had "looked into the matter" of their pending departure without much luck, given Mr. Heffelfinger's radical privacy. As far as I knew, my account of the day was all that barred her from a firsthand appraisal.

I would have to lie. Despite my mother's refinement and good intentions, she was still an adult full of implacable opinions, sure to barge into the Heffelfinger's lives like a ship ramming into a channel mine.

"Where's your father?" I asked as we paused in the kitchen while Don fished something out of the icebox. He turned, beaming with delight, flourishing a forbidden bottle of beer.

"He found an answer, Shaffer. Not *the* answer, mind you, but a cure for his illness, which will give him the time he needs to *elucidate* his findings. He sees the linchpin, Shaffer, I'm sure of it. He just needs time to bring it into focus. And now he has it."

My hunch about Don's father had been right.

Don took a swig of beer, then another, grimaced happily, and passed me the bottle to likewise toast the good news, but I couldn't manage it. Maybe it was just my soured outlook, but at that moment, I had more faith in my lunchroom vision of Mr. Heffelfinger slinking off to die than in Don's rosy prognosis.

"What's wrong with him?" I hunted up a spot for the bottle among dirty dishes.

"Lung cancer, but it will soon be routed. He's in Atlanta now, taking his second treatment in absolute secrecy. He'll be back Tuesday, utterly cleansed. You know I'm not a religious fellow, but when Dad came home from his first treatment, he was a man reborn. It was as if the biblical Jesus had laid hands upon him. In this case, of course, science has provided the miracle, so don't imagine I'm endorsing the notion of a literal miracle, per se."

Maybe Mr. Heffelfinger wasn't dying. Don had witnessed his father's progress. And wasn't the TV news full of stories about miracle drugs and transplanted hearts? "That's great," I said, reconsidering the beer. "Does that mean you're staying in Hopperton?"

Don's eyes lowered before he answered.

"As you know, Shaffer, great forces are at work in this country. My dad confided that we might be called upon to play a part, here or elsewhere."

Don's answer was vague, pretentious, probably bullshit, and yet... Play a part in what? Was Mr. Heffelfinger even sick at all? Was he off plotting a rebel uprising, like in *The Dark Warrior*? Had I absorbed the plot of my book from Mr. Heffelfinger, who had so convincingly claimed to read my mind? All crazy, I knew, but I took a shot anyway. "Don, if this is a secret thing, like with your mother, you don't have to tell me."

"I *can't* tell you, Shaffer. But it's the strangest thing. My dad is *different*, not just feeling better. The treatment may be ridding him of more than cancer. There may soon be no need for secrets."

"Amen to that," I shouted, hoisting the beer bottle to what I wasn't exactly sure, but taking a long, sour swallow anyway. "And speaking of secrets, I kissed Sally."

I waited then, hoping to savor Don's astonishment, but instead heard this: "And?"

"And what?"

"And did that kiss lead to further sex?"

"Kissing isn't sex." In saying this, I felt the shine beginning to rub off the moment.

"Ah, but it is. It opens the door, Shaffer. Without kissing, the door stays closed, locked. Why do you think girls are so damn hard to kiss? They know. You can bet Sally knows. But I'm getting ahead of myself. You kissed Sally, and from your face, I'm assuming no further sex occurred. What did occur, pray tell?"

I told him, working my way back from the pearls to Abel Theroux. "Her pearls were paste," Don said. "How rich, how very rich. Why, don't you see, Shaffer? She's the girl in the riddle, the one who likes you but doesn't like sex. And make no mistake, she adores you. But you still want the *other* girl, the one who's bound to despise you, despite great sex, just like I predicted." Don smiled, his pale, plump cheeks reddened by triumph and alcohol, framed by the same window through which Mr. Heffelfinger had stared at me after the first crossbow shoot.

"Sally hates me, and there is no other girl, but you got everything else right." I picked up the crossbow and headed out the back door. Outside, I aimed it at a fence post, checking the sight. Tarnish, I noticed, had dulled the prod, the flexible metal crosspiece which flung the bolts.

"I see my little riddle got under your skin," Don called from the doorway.

"No," I answered. "To be honest, it smells bad in your house; that's all." I lowered the crossbow and turned around. "I like the riddle. Even though it isn't a riddle. I mean, you can't solve it, right? It's more like one of those Zen things, like saying that you can end a war if you drink green tea. You think about it, and it supposedly makes you wise."

Don snorted. "Zen? Buddhists are pacifists, defeatists. What major war have they ever won?"

"I don't know, but from what I heard on the radio, a lot of Vietcong are Buddhists. I guess you'll find out firsthand how good they fight." Don gave the world-weary groan of someone correcting a mistake for the thousandth time.

"Killed in action, right, by the first starving communist peasant who comes along? You and my dad are already picturing me in a body bag."

"No, Don, I picture you behind a typewriter if, by some miracle, you make it through basic training." Don stared at me, no doubt mortally offended. He grabbed the uncocked crossbow, sighted it at some invisible star, then swung around to aim where I stood. Harmless, but still, I shied away. To my surprise, when I looked back, Don was beaming.

"You're right, Shaffer. The weapon must fit the man. I have been wasting my time with this . . . accursed thing. But were I to master the *typewriter*, then the Army could assign me to explain the Eastern mind and its inability to sustain *active* resistance."

"No offense, Don, but how many books have you read about the 'Eastern mind'?"

He rolled his eyes at this petty quibble.

"None directly, but *many* through discussions with my father. His philosophy deals quite effectively with these cult religions."

"You should read the book Wanda gave me. This guy, Siddhartha, is a Buddhist. He becomes enlightened because he thinks *his* thoughts, not his father's thoughts."

I think this stung Don a little. He made a sweeping gesture toward the trees and sky.

"How can anyone be enlightened who thinks this *very real* world is an illusion? And mind my words—*my* words, Shaffer—people will only fight so long for an illusion."

I looked out at the vista Don had invoked.

"Everything out there looks like a painting from here, but I guess it's real."

"You *guess*?" Don fixed me with an incredulous squint.

"Well, anyway," I said, flexing the crossbow's prod with my bandaged hand, "I was going to tell you to keep an eye out for rust on this thing."

"Christ, Shaffer, what happened to your hand?" In the unfolding strangeness of the last half hour, I had forgotten about my injury. I stared at the bloodstained bandage covering my knuckles and joked, "I hurt it punching Abel Theroux," half believing it myself.

For perhaps an eye blink, Don took me at my word, then recovered. "I think not, old boy. I rather suspect Sally stomped on your hand as you crawled around hunting for her pearls." Bolstered by half a beer each, Don and I giggled like toddlers, causing a dog somewhere to bark at the ruckus, maybe the widow's brindle hound snuffling around for anything to get worked up over.

"False alarm," I shouted to the dog, and to myself, *No one's dying here from cancer or jungle mayhem or the cruelty of girls.* I dropped the crossbow on the nearby weather-warped picnic table, probably waiting for its first picnic, then turned to watch Don, who had removed his glasses, daub at them with his grimy T-shirt, thus exposing a swath of white belly.

"I'll help you clean up," I offered, surprised to hear a fondness in my voice that had been missing for a good while.

"Thanks, Shaffer. I was resigned to bearing that cross alone. And speaking of crosses, would you mind cocking that damned thing one more time?" I cocked and loaded the crossbow and handed it to Don. He tilted it upwards, grunting and muttering, and sent a bolt arcing into the woods. Afterward, he made no effort to retrieve the projectile. Instead, he turned to me, his face grim. "Shaffer, there's some bit of history I must relate to you about Abel Theroux."

My heart thudded, all reassurances about false alarms chased away, sure that Don was about to connect Abel to Bobby Heatwole and Bobby to Wanda, confirming soul-deadening truths—truths Don had probably learned from Wanda's lips.

"What is it?" I managed to get out.

"Well, now, perhaps I'm wrong, but based on his past behavior, and how you challenged him, I believe Abel will find you after school and beat you up."

When I left for home, I heard the dog again—a deep growl emanating from an unkempt pasture just north of Don's house. I turned to see a burly and collarless black hound standing in chickweed, looking my way. I would not have stopped to watch the dog—an act likely to heighten any hostility it might harbor—had I not been imagining the ways Abel Theroux might ambush me. As it was, the dog and I locked onto each other like two gunfighters. After a few seconds, the dog realized *I* wasn't going to charge and lowered its head to retrieve something, in this case, a small, furry carcass, probably a young rabbit. It had only been warning me off its prize.

"Git!" I shouted, stomping my foot, well aware that I was plenty close enough to Don's front door to escape an attack. The dog didn't advance, but it didn't "git" either. It simply ignored me and sank to enjoy its kill, just as I would expect from a blood brother to Abel Theroux. And what was *I* to Abel? Not a boy stomping and shouting from a safe distance. I was the rabbit.

CHAPTER TWENTY-FOUR

"Just My Imagination"

I provided my mother a report calculated to relieve her worries—assurance that the Heffelfingers weren't moving after all. Not necessarily true, of course, but it was the best and least lie I had, and, I felt, as *apt* to be as accurate as Mr. Heffelfinger's fatal illness, harrowing ordeal, and miraculous recovery. And anyway, telling *that* story to my mother, true or not, was out of the question. Mister Heffelfinger would then become a *cause célèbre*, galvanizing the Methodist Ladies Auxiliary into irresistible and catastrophic action. His privacy obliterated, Mr. Heffelfinger would turn his terrible eye on me like the Eye of Sauron fixing on Frodo. Then Abel Theroux's punch would become the least of my problems.

At first, my mother nodded along as she chopped and breaded okra. Then I heard her sigh impatiently. "Bill, dear, of course I'm overjoyed to hear Don is staying, but we're not one step closer to getting to the *why* of things. Now, you have a good heart, and you're young enough to take people at face value, but I'm sad to report that as folks grow older, they may collect troubles and secrets and do foolish things that cause harm to themselves. Why you yourself noticed something amiss with Philip ... Mr. Heffelfinger ... a few weeks ago. Bearing that in mind—"

I broke in then in a high-pitched voice. No good could come from letting my mother complete her thought.

"Mr. Heffelfinger wasn't there, Mother, but Don was happy as a lark. He's sure everything is going to be fine."

"Why then," my mother said, "there's no reason in all creation he can't come by here for a sandwich and chat after school like he has since the beginning of time, now is there?" She gave me a lawyerly once-over and waited.

"Well, I don't know. Don's real busy helping his father with his book. He wants to borrow my typewriter." True, but only now, under duress, did I decide in his favor.

"A *book?*" my mother scoffed. "Why, Phillip Heffelfinger speaks fewer words than any person in Hopperton. And don't tell me it's another war story. That's the last thing Donald needs to hear about." My mother's eyes blazed dangerously. I could *feel* her urge to drop the paring knife, cast off her apron, and march over to the Heffelfinger house.

"No, no, it's nothing like that. It's a philosophy book. And you're right; Mr. Heffelfinger hardly says anything. But he has these genius ideas, according to Don. The way it works is Don helps his father find the right words for his . . . his treatise, I think it's called. And I think maybe they were going to move just to get help with the book, but Don changed his mind about going to Vietnam, so he'll be around to help his father, so . . ." I trailed off, worried I had already stumbled into treacherous terrain from which there was no return.

"Philosophy," my mother murmured, turning the word over in her mind. "Well, that's better than many other topics, I suppose." She gave me a suddenly tender, searching look. "And I'm sorry if I tempted you to say more than you intended, but you would need to explain the missing typewriter sooner or later." She smiled. "Or didn't you think of that, my dear son?" I shook my head, happy to admit my short-sightedness, only caring that the Remington had miraculously bumped Mr. Heffelfinger off center stage.

While my mother fried okra, I fetched pickled beets from my father's root cellar under the shed. As I stood in the cellar's creepy dimness, peering at dusty jars, I brooded over the tangle of disclosures, deceptions, betrayals, and doubts suddenly ensnaring my life. A kind of hallucination took hold of me—a memory of a memory, a vision, a waking dream—call it what you will. Whatever its nature, I "saw" a circle of grinning skeletons surrounding me, holding hands. I might have run screaming from the cellar had I not seen the skeletons before, in an early boyhood dream one Christmas Eve, maybe the psychic residue of a 1950s cartoon show. In any case, back then, the skeletons had delighted me, seeming to cavort for my pleasure. Now they only scared the bejesus out of me, delivering a paralyzing, icy shock and hemming me in with ghastly intent like the plights that had befallen my life since the school year began. I grabbed a jar and hustled upward, seeking my mother's company like the lost little kid I suddenly was.

"Goodness, Bill," she exclaimed as I handed her the beets. "You need more exercise if a trip to the root cellar shortens your breath."

My father's Lions Club meeting ran late, but he more than atoned by announcing that he had "strong-armed the boys" into funding a fountain and extra benches for the gazebo park. "Ed, you're a miracle worker," my mother praised, covering his hand with hers. When I saw this, my usual disdain gave way. Despite myself, I *felt* their affection and sensed, maybe for the first time, the bargain they kept behind it. I felt an overpowering need to be a part of that bargain.

"Speaking of the gazebo, Father, I met a man up there who worked for you."

"And who might that be?"

"I think his name was Tom Fields. Anyway, he sends his regards."

My father's indulgent smile fell away. "Tom Fields of all people. He's just the sort of fellow I was telling you about, Bill, the kind you can't do enough good for."

"What do you mean?"

"He worked for me alright, and I can't say he was a bad worker, but he complained about everything—the hours, the pay, right down to the gloves and masks we gave him. I never saw the like of it. Finally, one day it got too much, and I had to let him go." My father shook his head at some inward thought, then grilled me about "how in the devil" Tom Fields knew I was his son. The word *devil* told me this conversation was not—as I had hoped—pressing me closer to my family's warm bosom, but rather back into the root cellar.

"Our last name, I guess. We introduced ourselves as he passed by, walking his dog. See, his sister lives outside of town. He goes there to help her." Something told me not to mention that I had pointed out our house to Mr. Fields, or that he hoped Ed Shaffer got his "just due."

My father pointed his porkchop-laden fork at me. "There's a knack to it, Bill, how to stay a bit shy of strangers without being unfriendly."

I gave a hangdog nod, barely listening, thinking instead of my father driving away in his Caddy to settle that fracas at the plant the morning of the Rialto horror, then coming back having "let go" a man who, like Tom Fields, couldn't keep to the path.

Any more than I could.

"At ease, soldier," my father said, chuckling. "I know you meant well, and I know you have a sharp mind that will understand when I tell you some people do *not* mean well. Very few by count, I'm sure, as your mother will insist, but those few can be most troublesome. Something to file away, right?"

"Yes, sir."

My mother smiled, pleased by my father's tempered approach.

"Good . . . good," he said, a brief hesitance undercutting his conviction. Then he continued. "You see, Bill, some bureaucrat up in Atlanta, some fan of Lyndon Johnson I warrant, is proving quite troublesome in the matter of our good students from Waycross. We are being put through a trial by paperwork to prove the legitimacy of their enrollment. As it turns out, the sovereign state of Georgia is terrified the federal boys will seize upon some technicality to swoop down or, perish the thought, withhold funds. Bud Folmar, I, and others have been going through parental affidavits with a fine-tooth comb to make sure they pass muster. It is amazing what this life puts you through in the service of the greater good."

It turned out that Georgia wanted proof of residency in the form of sworn statements. The fact that the state was willing to take people at their word indicated to my father that the request for proof was a formality to placate the fools in Washington. Still, it paid to be cautious, so my father and his cronies doctored and crafted parental statements to indicate *intention* to move from Waycross to Hopperton, giving a variety of excuses for the delay such as aging relatives, real estate closings, and pending job applications. My father explained all this to me matter-of-factly and in detail, assuming I was, in spirit at least, a co-conspirator. I was hardly that, but I *was* fascinated to see stratagems laid bare and risks calculated. I also saw my father only feigning to walk a path higher authority demanded of him.

In this, at least, I was my father's son.

My mother busied herself with tangible tasks—dishes and leftovers, her bountiful hair pinned up—leaving her "menfolk" to plot control of events they could not possibly control. She made no mention of Don's likely return to the fold, despite its uppermost importance to her: Ed Shaffer wasn't keen on the topic.

And I wasn't about to mention my root cellar vision, certain my father would ferret out the tangle of fears, conundrums, and secrets it embodied. I listened absently to his soft, persuasive baritone like it was a Top 40 song I had heard too many times on the radio. Inwardly I indulged a dark, guilty thrill of realization: I hoped someone uncovered my father's school enrollment deception and, while I was at it, hoped we lost the war in Vietnam. Not for a moment did I hope to see *my* deceptions exposed or *my* battles lost.

"Well," my mother put in at some point, turning from the sink and fixing my father with an unwavering stare. "I'm praying for *all* concerned in this dreadful school business *and* for all who bear false witness." My father flushed, having forgotten my mother was listening.

"That's why wives are our better half, Bill. In your mother's case, the North Star to us lesser lights." He chuckled without much heart. My mother did not reply.

"Put away the dishes, Bill," she said, the usual lilt absent from her voice.

At church, Sally and her mother gave me looks halfway between polite and the evil eye. Sally conceded to hold my hand during hymns but only through the barrier of a thick, unfashionable winter glove. I remembered Don's riddle and his insistence that kissing was sex. Did Sally like me while hating the kiss, or hate me because my kiss wasn't real? I closed my eyes in self-defense as Reverend Farrior berated his flock for paying lip service to the Lord. Maybe Sally would think I was praying for forgiveness. Maybe I was. Or if not forgiveness, at least the restoration of an amicable alliance based on taking each other for granted.

I went to school Monday, expecting to be pummeled or otherwise afflicted, but Monday rolled into Tuesday and Wednesday without incident. Furthermore, Mr. Heffelfinger did return as promised, his cancer, as Don put it Wednesday after school, "burned away" through a "trial by fire." Don compared his father to a soldier too noble to speak about his wounds and suffering. I didn't quite believe any of it, the cancer or the recovery, preferring to imagine Mr. Heffelfinger had been away on nefarious paramilitary excursions. But to cover my tracks, it was Don's version I would publicly profess, a nonbeliever mouthing the Apostles Creed. Don, buoyed by his father being made whole, agreed to walk to my house as before, a prodigal returning to my mother's sandwiches and affection.

On the way to my house, Don told me he had arranged with Bubba Pridemore to transport my typewriter—Don wasn't about to lug it himself—in Bubba's rust-eaten Dodge hot rod, the two-dollar fee proffered by the reborn Mr. Heffelfinger. To hold up my end of the chattering, I recreated my root cellar visitation of dancing bones.

"Good grief, Shaffer, it's like Scrooge and the Christmas ghosts. We better keep our eyes peeled."

As we talked, we huddled closer, presumably against the biting, swirling wind. Don was beside himself with supernatural speculation as I humbly downplayed it all. Then, as my house was about to come into view, Abel Theroux and Bobby Heatwole loomed before us with spectral and prophetic suddenness. Actually, only Abel loomed, leering above crossed arms, while Bobby shrank back a bit, seemingly the reluctant sidekick. I was both dumbstruck and distracted by a dust devil frantically traversing Stagecoach Road.

"What's up, Shaff-hole?" Theroux's voice was a menacing bray.

"Nothing." My tough-guy intentions evaporated instantly. Theroux snickered and took a step forward. At the same time, Don advanced, putting him even with Theroux's left side, and thrust the bottom of his foot karate-style into the side of the other boy's knee. Theroux buckled and howled, spit out a chaw of black tobacco, then collapsed into a babbling litany of "motherfucker" alternating with "I'll kill you."

I looked at Bobby Heatwole. To my consternation, he was already hot with tears. Pointing a shaking finger at Don, he sobbed, "You're gonna go to jail for this."

Don didn't reply to Bobby. Instead, he looked down at Theroux and addressed him in a weirdly dispassionate voice. "You left your flank exposed, you dumb shit." I suppose, robbed of Vietnam, Don needed his warrior moment, but that's hindsight. At the time, I was busy wondering what Wanda saw in Bobby Heatwole as, in the back of my mind, I began forming the lie I would need to tell to defend Don as he had defended me.

"You have to go to my house and bring help, Don, *now*." Probably numbed by the shock of his deed, he mutely complied, walking as if his steps dragged in invisible mud. By then, Theroux had shifted from threatening Don to moaning laments of "oh shit." "Take it easy," I said. "My mother will know what to do." Then I added an unconvincing, "You'll be okay."

"The hell I will," he muttered.

His retort, understandable as it was, incensed me. "What were you assholes doing here anyway?" I demanded. Theroux shot me a defiant bird. I glared at Bobby, then hissed, "You jumped *us*. You're the ones going to jail."

"That's a lie," Bobby shouted. "Abel just wanted to warn you not to mess with us. He wasn't going to do anything. He knows your dad is a big shot."

"You're crazy," I screamed. "I never did a lousy thing to either one of you."

"Liar," Bobby shot back. "You know what you said to Abel at the dance, and why you said it." He was beginning to sob again. "I hate you," he cried, then sank beside Theroux and waited.

Friday morning came, and no arrests. A fight among high school boys was not a police matter in Hopperton. It was a matter for parents to sort through and mete out whatever justice lurked among conflicting accounts, denials, cross-accusations, and stubborn silences. In the present altercation, none of the four boys could, or would, pinpoint the cause of the fight or admit to bad blood. *They* had started it—with a taunt, a kick, or a threat, take your pick.

Don's father ultimately paid "reparations" to the tune of one hundred dollars, probably because Mrs. Theroux worked for a lawyer. I played dumb with my parents, though in truth, it wasn't entirely an act. My remarks to Abel at the harvest dance had infuriated Bobby, something tangled up with Wanda, no doubt, but that *something* eluded me.

By lunchtime at school Thursday, Don, nicely recovered, had risen from tolerated eccentric to celebrity. He theorized to an uncomprehending circle of onlookers that the incident was a manifestation of the fight for the soul of the world (as prophesied by *Atlas Shrugged*). I was present at Don's bizarre recounting, acting as a kind of prop owing to my now publicized "prophetic vision" in the root cellar—and of course, Sally was there, neither one of us saying much of anything or trading our customary amused glances: no playing the foil, no bubbling commentary. Abel, Bobby, and Wanda were offstage. A few people ventured questions, but I gave nothing up, keeping my jumbled puzzle of personal intrigue to myself.

Anyway, *Don Heffelfinger kicked Theroux's ass* was the startling center-piece. The rest was window dressing.

Friday after school, and before intending to accompany my father to the football team's final defeat, I went back to Mr. Pee's classroom to put the chess club out of its misery, an act accomplished by tucking a cigar box and warped chessboard under my arm. As I turned to leave, I saw Wanda standing in the doorway, fixing me with an unrelenting stare. The shock of seeing her sent cold static through me, and whatever upper hand I hoped to hold folded without a bet. Her hair was a softer amber now, which may explain why I never spotted her in the hallway. In this muted state, she seemed more vulnerable, more attainable, less the counterpart of her mythic familiar, Delia Wingfoot. At the same time, her gaze promised no apology, no explanation, no flustered cheeks. I fumbled in contradiction, lost to speech, only able to manage a timorous "hello."

Wanda said nothing at first, looking instead at the chess paraphernalia under my arm, then up into my eyes. "Too busy with Sally for chess?"

I didn't see the point of such a question or the venomous smile that accompanied it, but started to answer anyway. "No, Sally is . . ."

"I hear you tried to kiss her, and she slapped you. Quite the Romeo, aren't you?"

By this taunt, I knew that Sally had gossiped about me and that Wanda could mock without mercy. For all I knew, Bobby Heatwole was just out of sight, listening. "No, she didn't slap me, and it wasn't that kind of kiss." *Not like our kiss,* I wanted to say but would be damned first. "And no, I didn't do anything to Abel Theroux or make that asshole Bobby Heatwole cry like he probably told you."

Wanda flushed. "He's not an asshole. He thought you— "

I took her reply as an intimate knowledge of Bobby's nature, proof of my worst suspicions. No profit in holding back now. "I don't care what he thought, and anyway, why would I come to your house?"

"Wow," she said, shaking her head, her voice quavering. "I thought you were trying to be my boyfriend, but I guess you were just adding a kiss to your collection."

"Me? You're the one"—I fumbled around for a phrase—"*loving it up* with Bobby Heatwole."

Wanda gave me an incredulous stare. "Who told you that?" she demanded.

"I saw you two sitting together at the Rialto."

"So?"

With that one word and the contemptuous way Wanda delivered it, a horrible suspicion dawned on me. "Why were you with him?" I managed, already more or less guessing the disastrous answer.

"I wasn't *with* him," she retorted. "We just met in the lobby and decided to sit together. He's in my English class." A pause ensued, a giant sinkhole of a pause. Then: "I can't believe you were spying on me, Bill."

I hadn't been, but I let the accusation pass. Wanda continued, her voice thickening with emotion.

"My uncle warned me. He said expecting anything from people was like fishing for the moon in water." With that, she turned and stomped away.

Later, only a few intrepid stars shone above the football field where the game, its conclusion forgone, seemed more like an excuse to be out in unseasonably pleasant weather than a proving ground of young warriors. I sat with my father, nodding at his time-honored, detailed critique of the team's misaligned defense, wondering if anything I saw appeared as it was or if it was all painted over by an invisible, ever-present veneer composed of my stupidity. The lopsided score had quelled the crowd, and I was able to locate a pocket of laughter centered around Sally Chiles. Whatever harm our spat had done seemed undone now, her exhilaration on full display, ribbons of red and white, our school colors, woven into her hair. *Good*, I thought, *maybe we can be pals again.* As I watched her, the field lights suddenly went out, raising an *ooh* from the crowd and allowing a host of new stars to enter the sky. In later years, I daydreamed about watching a movie of my life and counting my mistakes, from forgetting to put the milk back in the fridge to dreaming up the nonexistent romance between Wanda and Bobby Heatwole and other blunders of all types numerous enough to rival the dumbfounding haze of stars on a moonless night. But outside of fantasy, one gets tired of counting, and there are too many things to count anyway, whether we're talking about stars or mistakes. In time, the lights, as they did that night in 1967, come back on, the stars go home, and the game, lost as it may be, continues.

CHAPTER TWENTY-FIVE

"Will You Still Love Me Tomorrow?"

Mrs. Grice frowned at me through the screen door as if I were a door-to-door salesman interrupting her nap. I waited silently, hoping for my identity to dawn on her. Finally, after a long moment, she flipped on the porch light and nodded in what I took to be resigned recognition. It was about dusk on Saturday following the last football game, but Mrs. Grice was already in curlers and a pink chenille robe. I was about to apologize and walk away when she turned and called out loudly, "Wanda, get out here. I think it's that first boy."

I expected to hear *tell him to go away* but heard only the rapid thump of footfalls, probably Wanda sprinting for her bedroom. Mrs. Grice did not invite me in but looked back over her shoulder as we waited. The message was clear: I was Wanda's problem.

"Wanda," Mrs. Grice reiterated to the emptiness behind her, "get out here *now*. I'm not decent, and I'm worn to a frazzle."

"It's okay," I said. "I—"

Mrs. Grice turned and shook her head emphatically.

"Son, you stay right there. At least you're polite and quiet when you come calling. Now I'm going to take some headache powders and go to bed, but don't you dare leave until Wanda comes out, do you hear?"

"Yes, ma'am." I thought to keep my promise for no more than five minutes.

As she left, Mrs. Grice called out one last time. "He's still here, Wanda, and he ain't leaving."

I felt like a fool but conceded ten minutes to Mrs. Grice since I had a porch chair to sit in and she'd left the light on. Before long, Wanda came out and took the other chair.

"That chair is rusty; it'll ruin your clothes." I stood up and tried not to either gawk at her or cravenly look away. She was barefooted, wearing pedal pushers and a sweatshirt saying *Yankee go home.*

"I wanted to give you my chess set and return your book. I read about half of it. I liked it."

"Why on earth are you giving me your chess set?"

"I'm giving up all my stuff, just like Siddhartha."

"Great. What else have you got for me? Money? Precious jewels?"

An odd sense of liberation swept over me. An illusion I had been clutching winked out of existence, taking with it a fraction of my jealousy. Whether it was Wanda's reviving humor, or her hippie book, or my anxieties collapsing under their own weight, I wasn't sure. "I have a two-dollar bill in my wallet," I offered.

"Cool. Fork it over."

"Your feet look cold."

"Yeah, I'm going in." Wanda picked up the cigar box and chessboard from a fraying rattan serving table. She opened the screen door halfway and looked at me. "You can come in for a minute," she said. "I have a question to ask you. But then you have to leave. I have two or three other boys coming over."

Wanda's living room suddenly felt like the shabby set of a great movie, down to the gleaming rip in a tasseled lampshade. The air smelled strongly of fish sticks and boiled greens. As I got my bearings, Wanda slipped a booklet from the waistband of her pedal pushers.

"My horoscope," she said. "I have to check it."

I waited. When the time came, Wanda read her astral advice out loud. "'Anything is possible now. You may remember this day for years to come.'"

"Sounds dramatic."

Wanda shrugged. "Yeah. Some days it's like 'good time to organize your clothes.'"

I waited again, not daring to suggest myself as the basis for the stars' extravagant guidance.

"Why were you spying on me, Bill? That's totally creepy."

"I wasn't. I was just there to watch a movie."

Wanda sprung her trap. "What movie?"

"*Bugles in the Afternoon.*"

"Who's in it, and what's it about?" I told her, down to the fact that George Reeves of TV *Superman* fame had a small part. She tucked her booklet away and flopped down on the couch, reconsidering. I kept standing, like a job applicant waiting to be offered a chair. "What about you kissing Sally? That little story is practically in the Hopperton Hall of Fame."

"She got on my nerves, smelling my breath for liquor. So I kissed her."

Wanda scoffed. "Yeah, sure, like we got on each other's nerves the last time you were here."

I shook my head, trying not to bite into that particular apple. "I was sick of wondering what she wanted from me. That's all."

To my surprise, Wanda seemed to get my point, even if I wasn't sure I had made one. "Yeah, I used to think guys all want the same thing, but that's crap. Just because guys want sex, it doesn't mean that's *all* they want. Sometimes sex isn't even the main thing they want."

"Well, at least girls get to know one thing guys want. I have no idea what Sally's after, and we played in a sandbox together."

"Sally's okay; she's just playing a part she got from her mother and magazines."

I stared at Wanda with surreptitious awe. Once again, her casual analysis rang truer than anything I'd come up with.

"What's the story on your hair?" I asked, daring to ease down onto the far end of the couch.

"My mother has the black-ass on my account. That's what my dad used to call it. I thought the new look might calm her down."

"What's her problem?"

"Oh, you know, grades and Bobby coming over to cry on my shoulder—stuff like that."

"Did he tell you he cried for real when Don kicked Abel? Then he screamed at me like *I'd* kicked Abel and yelled something nuts about me trying to ruin his life."

"I know. See..." Wanda paused to chew on a nail. "Okay, I guess I have to tell you," she said, making an incorrect sign of the cross as she looked up and whispered, "Promise broken, sorry." Then she looked back at me.

"See, Bobby likes *boys*"—Wanda paused to make sure I understood the hyper-scandalous implication —"so when you asked Abel about him at the dance, he thought you'd found out. That scared him shitless."

My mind stumbled, trying to catch up. "Is Abel his…"

"Boyfriend? No, Bobby's never *done* anything. Abel's just his protector. He doesn't even know. They've been friends forever, like you and Don. He thinks Bobby is a sissy, but that doesn't stop Abel from looking out for him. He thought you guys were picking on Bobby."

I swore to Wanda I would keep Bobby's secret, winning a delicious hug from her. In the aftermath, I felt free to indulge my morbid curiosity.

"Are Bobby's legs really burned?"

Wanda scooted closer as if to foil prying ears. "Well, a little bit, but not all scarred or anything. He begged his folks not to make him go to gym class, and they went along."

Nodding sagely, I claimed to have figured it was something like that. After that, the Bobby conversation lapsed. Wanda leaned forward and pointed to her neck. "Smell my new fragrance," she offered. The scent seemed less like perfume than something pleasantly familiar but hard to name. "It's called Arrowhead; I wear it in honor of my Cherokee blood. It's got burnt root in it that makes it smell like a campfire. And vanilla too. Can you smell them both?"

"I think so," I said, though what I thought I detected was charred honeysuckle flowers. And the word "arrowhead" made me recall Don's abandoned crossbow bolt and wonder whether I should go find it.

"Oh shit," Wanda groaned, pulling my head down and burying it against her neck. I was instantly erect, given over to whatever might follow, nuzzling her neck in the meantime.

"Wait," Wanda whispered urgently. "I have to tell you something."

Hearing "wait" rather than "stop," I reckoned on a short delay to discuss particulars of sexual procedure. *Probably just as well,* I thought and sat up.

"Someone might be coming over," she said in a pained voice.

"Bobby?" I surmised. Wanda gave a downcast shake of her head.

"Don."

"Don *Heffelfinger?*" Perhaps the stupidest question of my life, but Wanda's hangdog demeanor had provoked it.

Wanda galled me further with a gesture to keep my voice down. "He comes over a lot, but he hasn't … I mean, I would never let him *do* anything.

He talks about his theories and how terrible the world is. He even tries to talk to my mother. It drives her crazy and—"

Inside me, competing outrages battled for supremacy. "Don tells me he's home every night helping his father," I spat out. "That's why he couldn't stop at my house. What a liar. Anyway, why do you let him come over if you hate it that much?"

Wanda closed her eyes as if the answer would appear behind them. "I don't know, I just—"

"*I* know; Don's in love with you, right? And I guess you like to hear that."

"No, what I *like* is that Don is totally dumb about girls. He doesn't have any tricks. When I told him I had a crush on another boy, he didn't get mad or gloomy. He said it was 'honorable' of me to tell him. He didn't bug me about who the boy was. Instead, he said I had a 'fascinating mind' and a 'mysterious soul.'"

"He already *knew* who the other boy was," I hissed in an overheated whisper. "He told me bad stuff about you; he wants you all to himself."

"What bad stuff?"

"I can't remember, just crap about you being trouble."

"I *am* trouble. I steal boyfriends and have their babies." Wanda gave me a hard, hurt look, then fell back with an anguished "Shit."

In the ensuing silence, I regarded the *Yankee go home* slogan on Wanda's sweatshirt. "I don't think you're trouble, but I do think Don will try tobrainwash you." I pointed to her chest. "Do you want all the Yankees to go home? That's Don's dream come true."

"Oh my God," Wanda said, rolling her eyes. "I got this shirt in Detroit when I visited my uncle. The 'Yankees' are imperialist *gringos* who should mind their own business. Yes, I know stuff like that, believe it or not—ugly Americans and all that garbage. Don is maybe the biggest *gringo* on the planet, but it's all from books. He wouldn't hurt a fly unless he talked it to death."

"Yeah? What about breaking Abel Theroux's leg?"

Wanda smiled knowingly. "*You're* the one Don loves. I don't mean he's like Bobby, but I guarantee he wouldn't break Abel's leg for me."

I got up and paced around to shake off my agitation, my erection long gone back to sleep. "Sit down, Bill," Wanda pleaded.

In reply, I dropped into a battered, overstuffed chair facing the door. "I'll wait here."

"Wait for what?"

"For Don."

"Come on; he might not even show up." Wanda got up and peeked out through the side of the front window shade.

"What's the latest he would get here?"

"Eight, eight thirty, I don't know."

"I'll wait until then, and if he doesn't show up, I'll leave."

"I wish you'd leave now, Bill," Wanda said in a pleading whisper. "My mother's already on my case, and I can't stand this jealousy shit." An uninvited moment of truth had arrived ahead of Don.

"I'm not jealous," I growled, both lying and bluffing, "but if you kick me out, I'm never coming back."

"Crap," Wanda muttered as she peered outside again. Then she lay back down on the couch without addressing my threat and put a throw pillow over her face. We went on this way for an impossibly long time. Finally, Wanda got up, looked at the mantle clock and, without a word, went into her bedroom and shut the door. Faint country music emanated from another part of the house. Mrs. Grice, no doubt, drowning out the foolishness.

At eight thirty, I stood up and walked over to Wanda's door. No music, no crying, no nothing. I waited for a few seconds, then sat back down. I remembered what Don said before Abel and Bobby accosted us about my root cellar vision being like Scrooge and his Christmas ghosts. Here I was, Wanda silent as a ghost, and me waiting for the knock of another one. If I weren't such an idiot, I thought, I'd rouse myself and walk to the midterm study party that had been my pretext for going out—even if Sally would be there.

I heard Wanda's door creak open and glanced at my watch— nine thirty. I hurried to my feet as she emerged, wrapped in a black robe with gold trim at the cuffs and hem. She made me think of Kemala, Siddhartha's lover, during the years the world of pleasures and possessions had captured him.

"You're still here," Wanda whispered, her voice hoarse from sleepiness or sadness; I couldn't tell which.

241

"Yeah," I answered, "it looks like no fight to the death tonight."

"My feet are getting cold again; if you're not leaving, turn out the lights and come into my room so my mother will go to sleep." Wanda's somber tone, far from enticing me, caused me to hesitate. She sensed this, shook her head, and walked back into her room, leaving the door slightly ajar. I turned out the lights and stood in the darkened room, feeling foolish, out-maneuvered, and wretched with need. Finally, I resigned myself to some final rebuke, made my way to her bedroom, and peered in to see her blanketed shape on the far side of the bed. "Close the door and lie down, Bill. I'm tired. But take off your shoes first."

Shoes, not clothes.

I honored Wanda's terms and lay down on top of the covers like someone perched on a precarious ledge. With no further course mapped out, I listened intently, trying to decipher her feelings. But no clues came, no quickening of breath, only an inkling that Wanda was thinking hard and nowhere near sleep—or seduction. Words came to me, but they all seemed apt to ruin everything.

"Why did you say Delia Wingfoot is like me?" Wanda asked in an imploring whisper. "I mean, *how* is she like me?"

Of course, Delia was, in a sense, no more. I had sent her into exile along with my typewriter, as Wanda had done to her blazing yellow hair.

"She doesn't care what people think," I offered.

"I cared if you liked my singing," she countered. "If you didn't, I would have died."

"Well, Delia's brave. And you were brave enough to sing in front of me."

My logic seemed irrefutable, but Wanda wouldn't have it. "I was too chicken to make you leave tonight."

Not a point I wished to debate.

"Delia Wingfoot is just somebody I made up. I mean, real people can't save the world all by themselves. She's like you, but she's not you."

"I couldn't even save my dad," Wanda said in a choked wail. We had drifted into bottomless waters.

"Maybe Delia Wingfoot's dad died too," I ventured, "and maybe she couldn't save him, and that's why she's trying to save the world." My words felt meager to me, lines from a movie I might've seen, but they seemed to reach Wanda. She rolled over to face me.

"Say 'Kiss me, Delia,'" she whispered. And with that, as it happens in lives from time to time, if not often enough to suit us, fiction became a reality. Wanda would tell me later that she always slept naked, that she wasn't precisely a virgin or a Cherokee princess for that matter. But that's just history, paling before the wonder of first touching a woman's nipples.

As I made my way home much later, drunk with wonderment, I noticed the smell of chimney smoke and stood a moment to breathe it in as deeply as I could. Lovemaking with Wanda had intensified the hint of embers promised by her perfume, and I wanted to shout *holy shit* at the top of my lungs in recognition of this astonishing coincidence. Amazement saturated everything—the air itself seemed glossy with vapor. At one point, when a gray cat scrutinized me from a lamplit doorway, I stopped to return the favor out of sheer absurd joy. After a brief standoff, the cat bolted into shadow. With Don, I thought things would go much the same. After all, any battle over Wanda was part of a war I had already won. I smiled to myself, waved to the shrouded cat, and marveled at my new, unclouded vision of the human race and the true meaning of my root cellar vision. *I had nothing to fear!* I did feel a brief pang of regret at having left *Siddhartha* at Wanda's, wishing to have its few unread pages for company. Oh well, no doubt its tortured namesake would keep looking for what he could never find.

And besides, what happy person frets over a forgotten book?

Before I left, Wanda had begged me not to confront Don. I protested just for effect, which may explain why I suddenly wished Don well. If anything, he seemed more of a brother to me now, his deceptions, frailties, and appetites justifying my own. Could I blame him for desiring Wanda, the girl who didn't "run with the pack," the girl who not only didn't shun him but welcomed him and his precious ideas into her home again and again! Wanda, I surmised, would eventually become Don's cross to bear, but that was for him to sort out.

My cross, as invisible to me as Don's was visible, began taking shape during the subsequent nights I snuck out to lie with Wanda in her bed. I would wait for the witching hour, slip through my window, then walk (never once accosted, never once even seeing another living soul) the back way over to Barlow. Wanda left her window open, happy to see me if not willing to "go all the way" again. Short of that, she enjoyed my caresses, though she wanted something in exchange for them: my willingness to let intimacies be part of the fantasies that gripped her, to let her respond to me as Delia Wingfoot, or a Cherokee princess, or Liat or Nellie Forbush from *South Pacific*.

I was happy to comply. I didn't even mind her reluctance to consummate since I regarded myself as a sexual pretender, probably hurting my standing by doing it all wrong. I fretted far more about my dubious skills as a lover than the appalling consequences of being caught. I concluded via adolescent logic that because I needed to evade detection, I would. Mrs. Grice would not barge in unannounced; why would she? No one would bring my peculiar late-night wanderings to the county sheriff's attention, and if they did, I would provide a (yet to be devised) perfectly logical explanation. And as for my parents discovering my illicit activities, that possibility was simply too dire for contemplation. Only lousy luck would do me in, and hadn't Mr. Pee proved that luck, if no man's friend, was equally no man's sworn enemy?

CHAPTER TWENTY-SIX

"We Three Kings"

I n early December, I found out through my secret radio that Otis Redding had died in a plane crash. I had heard Otis on Atlanta R&B stations, where they referred to him as "the madman of Macon," and I knew he appeared at the Monterey Pop Festival along with Janis and Jimi. The news hit me hard; Otis was only nine years older than I was, and shared my Georgia roots. I contemplated adding a bard to *The Dark Warrior* in his honor, a magic minstrel singing spells to shield my hero and heroine from evil.

I told Don about Otis over a lunchroom murmur that had risen to near exultation over the looming Christmas break. He peered at me through the smoke of fried fish hazing the air. "My sympathies, Shaffer, though I fail to understand your affection for a minor singer you've never met."

"I've heard his voice; that's kind of like meeting him. And besides, you love Robert E. Lee, and you've never met him."

"Granted, Shaffer, but I've met his *exploits*, which, unlike your Negro singer, are unparalleled. But I don't wish to quibble about that. You are entitled to your feelings. And despite what you may think, I do believe *all* men are created equal. I simply observe that they don't *remain* equal."

I shrugged and picked at greasy fish breading. "I like music; you like history." On an impulse, I turned and looked at Sally, who was chatting merrily with several girls. "And Sally likes attention."

Don chuckled. "Wake up, old boy. She's just keeping herself busy until you come around. Get down on one knee, beg her forgiveness, and she'll fall into your arms."

"You got it backward, Don. She needs to beg my forgiveness. And anyway, I don't want her in my arms."

"So you say, Shaffer, but I suspect otherwise." Don's sly grin told me that he thought he *knew* otherwise. I wanted to put an end to the Sally business once and for all.

"Speaking of arms," I said, "have you seen Wanda lately?"

Don looked down, as if into a deep, dark well. When he looked up, he said, "It's too noisy here among the rabble; I can't hear myself think."

We took our trays out into the small courtyard behind the school and sat on a dusty bench among ragged azaleas. Don shielded his eyes and looked up toward the sun. "Thank God the days will soon be getting longer, Shaffer. I'm not at my best right now. My father's trials. It could've been him rather than that Otis fellow, do you see? As for Wanda, I must make amends to you. I warned you against her, yet I have taken her on as my protégé, even visiting her occasionally when you might have thought I was home acting as a scribe for my father. You once said of Sally that she requires attention. Wanda, you see, requires a *teacher*. She has quite a thirst for knowledge. The whole thing is remarkable, quite an eye-opener."

"So why did you warn me about her?"

"Oh, I'd truly heard stories. I assumed your interest was romantic, so I—"

"You weren't jealous; you were just looking out for me, right?"

Don looked miserable. "Yes, I suppose. But see, I'm trying to wipe the slate clean, and—"

"It's clean, Don, clean as a whistle if you pipe down about Sally. And I promise to shut up about Wanda. Deal?"

Don grimaced, laboring to weigh my terms. Finally, something seemed to click. He smiled like a happy baby.

"Of course, Shaffer! What's past is prologue, as they say." Don picked up half of a hefty slab of catfish, took a cheerful, ravenous bite, then pushed his grease-smeared glasses back up his nose. "Now that we've cleared the air, I feel I can venture a proposal. My father wishes you to visit him—us—after Christmas. He wants to atone for any unfriendly treatment he gave you on account of his illness. What do you say?"

Only the words *Don, I'm sleeping with Wanda* and *I never hope to see your terrible father again* would truly clear the air. Otherwise, this conversational blind alley left me only one way out.

"Well, I'll be pretty busy with my family, but..."

Hearing "but," Don knew he had won the day *and* salved his conscience. "You will see, Shaffer, that my dad is a true gentleman of the South—mark my words." Don beamed, his spirits "knee-deep in high cotton," as my father would say. All I could do was offer him my uneaten catfish and regret not wearing a coat to school. The azaleas, trembling in the biting wind, seemed to share my regret.

Aunt Miriam, just arrived for the holidays, sat on her bed, still in her shiny blue traveling dress. As I confided in her about Wanda—or all I could dare—she listened quietly, smoking a long, thin filter cigarette and tapping the ashes into a knobby glass ashtray balanced on her lap.

"Well, well," she said, releasing an eloquent cloud of smoke.

I had expected congratulations from my aunt, not this equivocal murmur.

"So, your young woman resides on Barlow," she continued in a speculative tone. "May we expect her for dinner some night? Is she from a family I might recall?" Aunt Miriam knew better. No family of substance lived on Barlow.

"No, she's ... not from around here."

"Ah. I take it you haven't had a chance to introduce her to your parents?"

"No."

"Bill dear, one more simple question. Is this young woman from a poor family?"

"Her mother is a widow."

Aunt Miriam nodded and patted the bed beside her. I sat down, expecting a lecture or sympathetic platitudes. Instead, she said, "Christmas is coming. Have you given any thought to her gift?" I hadn't, to my sudden shame. When I admitted this, Aunt Miriam clucked and retrieved her purse. "Poor girls especially need nice gifts. They need to know they are worthy of them."

Aunt Miriam then proffered a fifty-dollar bill. I gaped at it, trying to muster an adequate reply. In the meantime, she stood up and paced around. "No," she muttered, "that won't do. There's no place in this town to buy decent jewelry, and it *must* be jewelry." She seemed to ponder the matter, then reached behind her neck to unfasten her necklace. "This should suffice," she concluded, handing me a delicate chain with a small red stone attached. "It's a rather nice ruby. It was given to me by a man. Even at my age. You fellows can't help yourselves, can you? In any case, I have lots of such things, so don't make a fuss. Use the money to buy a gift for your parents, an antique vase perhaps, a token of your affection before you go off to college."

I floated through the days before Christmas, unruffled even by Mr. Heffelfinger's invitation. Sally had thawed a bit too. At home, we feasted on ham and venison and whipped sweet potatoes drenched in brown sugar and butter. My father had an extra drink or two and told fish camp stories of no interest to anyone but himself, everyone listening and laughing anyway.

Just after midnight on Christmas Day, I slipped out and walked to Wanda's through a foggy chill, the ruby necklace in a small, brightly wrapped box compliments of Aunt Miriam. We had planned this rendezvous, so Wanda waited to raise the window. Once I climbed in, she drew the shade and, to my surprise, turned on her floor lamp, lending the room a dim, amber glow. Before tonight, she had always insisted on darkness. To keep light from leaking out, she had stretched a bath towel across the bottom of her door.

The lamp allowed me to see Wanda. She wore an embroidered white nightgown belonging, I imagined, to olden times. Her eyes were red and heavy lidded as if I had dragged her from sleep, but she moved with eager energy to hug me and whisper that she wanted me to "try something." Without waiting for an answer, she grabbed a small brass pipe from her nightstand and sat on the bed to fill its bowl with vegetation from a cellophane bag. An Indian peace pipe? Her ritual baffled me, but I just waited, fearing to appear ignorant.

Once she'd finished filling the pipe, Wanda confided, "It's a present from Abel Theroux for me being nice to Bobby. It gives you a real mellow high."

The word "high" swept away my stupidity. "You smoke *pot?*"

"Yeah, sorry, I figured you did too since you knew about sex."

"Okay," I said, not about to deny erotic expertise.

"I tried it last year with my Uncle Daniel, the Buddhist, remember? He looked after me to make sure I didn't freak out. It's good to have a spirit guide. I can be yours."

"I don't know," I said. "Will I be able to get home?" She giggled as if I'd said the silliest thing possible.

"Don't worry; you *have* to try it." Given the risks I'd already taken, on what grounds could I refuse? And weren't we outlaws already? Bonnie and Clyde without the bad intentions?

"Okay," I conceded, "just a little."

She held the match to the bowl and instructed me to draw the smoke in *gently* and *hold* it. I tried to obey, but once inside me, the smoke fought like a demon to get out. I coughed and gasped, tears filling my eyes. Wanda covered my mouth to silence me and buried her face against my shoulder to muffle her laughter. "Lie on the bed," she said. "Close your eyes, don't fight it. It's awesome once you catch on."

Within seconds I had "caught on." By chemical chance, I was putty in the hands of marijuana. I had never felt my body before, or its connection to a world I barely recognized. When Wanda spoke, her words trailed off before I could translate them. "I can't talk," I croaked, my utterance proof that I could. This paradox struck me as profound and hilarious. I gazed up at cracks, ridges, and stains of the ceiling—an ancient map. I knew its contours, a world from a previous life. When Wanda lay down, we fell into lovemaking, swept along by marijuana. Maybe I resisted my body's demands for release a handful of minutes, but probably no longer.

Afterward, once she'd reclaimed her nightgown against the cold, Wanda sat cross-legged, watching me. She drew her breath in sharply a couple of times before finally speaking. "Bill, I'm a terrible girlfriend, but I do love the shit out of you." Ignoring whatever private, peculiar notion of love Wanda might possess, I concluded she was *mine*, the word "shit" making it undeniable, the words "terrible girlfriend" a touching apology I didn't deserve. When I managed to get "I love you too" past my thickened tongue, it sounded passionless and polite compared to her brave declaration.

Fortunately, I had the necklace.

After dressing, I fished the ring box out of my pants pocket and silently offered it to Wanda. She stared, not yet reaching for the box.

"It's not a ring, is it?"

"A *wedding* ring?" I blurted before I could catch myself.

"No, moron, one of those rings boys give girls to wear around their neck like they own them."

"Slavery is Don's department," I said. "Anyway, it's not a ring."

"Hand it over then," Wanda demanded gleefully, ignoring my dig at Don. She snatched the box, tore off the wrapping paper, and peered inside, regarding the necklace for a long, subdued moment.

"What is it?"

"A necklace."

"No, what is *that*?" She pointed to the ruby pendant.

"It's a ruby."

"A *real* ruby?"

"I think so. I mean—"

"Where did you get it, Bill?" Wanda's tone intimated at foul play. I explained about Aunt Miriam, omitting the part about poor girls needing rich girl gifts.

"She wanted you to have it. Otherwise, it would probably just sit in a drawer. She's loaded. She has lots of jewelry." Not quite what Aunt Miriam had said, but close enough.

"This blows my mind." Wanda put on the necklace. Bewitched by the marijuana, the red stone, lustrous against the white of her nightgown, inspired me. Delia Wingfoot, my literary heroine, would draw magic power from such a stone while maneuvering her bomb-laden crop duster in the pitch-black sky. Woe to the bloodthirsty Southern insurrectionists below...

I broke from my pipe dream to see Wanda trembling, fidgeting with the pendant.

"It's crazy," she said. "After my father died, Uncle Daniel wished he had a ruby to give me because each one of Buddha's tears was a ruby." Wanda's eyes glistened, and my skin prickled.

"Does it make you sad?" I pointed at the stone. Wanda shook her head.

"My uncle told me Buddha was sad for everyone, so we have to be sad too. Not gloomy, but sorry for people's hard lives, and not just at their funeral when they die. Like, I know you hate Don coming to see me and lying to you. But I can't say no to him. Or Bobby Heatwole. Their lives are ten times harder than yours or mine. Anyway, I love the necklace, I swear. I'll keep it forever."

Keep it forever.

I felt against all logic that Aunt Miriam had foreseen this moment. "It was meant for you," I whispered, "since the beginning of time."

Wanda didn't mock my romantic excess. Instead, she gazed at me with somber speculation, as if I too needed her sorrow. Then she reached for something on her nightstand—a book that she handed to me. "It's *Siddhartha*. You should keep it. I know it by heart."

"Thanks, it's a cool book." I opened the cover and saw that Wanda had already written *to Bill from Wanda, 1967*.

"How far did you read?" she asked.

"Let's see, Siddhartha was getting rich and having a big romance with Kemala."

Wanda smiled. "In the shady grove by her big house. In her pleasure garden."

"Yeah, he traded her poems for kisses, I think."

"At first, but then her kisses got more expensive; he had to get a job."

"I have to go to college first." Wanda didn't react.

"Do you know what happened to Kemala?"

"No, I didn't get that far. Did she die?"

"No, they stayed together for a long time."

"Did they get married?"

"Of course not, Bill. Kemala was a . . . courtesan. Siddhartha was just one of her lovers."

I had naïvely remembered them as boyfriend and girlfriend. "Oh, right. What did happen to her?"

"I won't spoil it for you. But it's never what you think."

As I leaned away to put the book in my jacket pocket, I heard Wanda behind me murmur the words, "This is my pleasure garden." I turned back with a grin, understanding the connection but brutally missing the point.

"I don't want to be Kemala," she said. "I don't want a boy sneaking over to have sex with me, bringing me gifts like in the book." Wanda had the face of a miserable child.

"I didn't give you the necklace to get sex," I cried, close to grief at being so misunderstood.

"I'm sorry, Bill, I know. Please quit yelling; you'll wake my mom. I'm just saying I want to go to the movies or have a picnic, stuff like that. Not this."

And with *not this*, my career as a midnight Casanova came—as my mother would say—to a screeching halt. You might think I erupted in protest, but I had squandered a lifetime of indignation on the Bobby Heatwole fiasco and simply didn't have it in me.

And besides, Wanda was right.

"I'm not mad, Wanda, but I think I'll go home. It would be crazy if I got caught tonight of all nights."

I hugged her at the window, making as little fuss about my eviction as possible, promising a Rialto date over the holidays. Once I had clambered out into the chilly darkness, a weird lightheartedness overtook me. I had proven myself as a lover. I had skirted great danger. I had smoked pot. And Wanda was still mine. Occasions for sex would arise, surely. In the meantime, the sharp stars above Hopperton drew me out of myself as I hurried along. At this late hour, the kings of Sheba, Arabia, and Egypt—the three wise men, as my mother called Orion's belt—had long disappeared to the west, with only Sirius, the star of stars at which they eternally pointed, still visible. Many good Christians in the little town of Hopperton could name Gaspar, Melchior, and Balthazar as the three wise men. But owing to my father, I could name the three stars from which (some say) their legend arose: Mintaka, Alnilam, Alnitak—Arabic words neither my father nor I understood.

I did remember from Bible school that the three Kings grew wise from watching the stars and noting their position relative to earthly events such as the flooding of the Nile. By signs and observations never explained, they also knew a prophesied child was coming.

As was daylight in a few short hours, and there would be no sleeping in. I broke into a brisk trot, slowing only when I caught sight of my somnolent house. The prodigal son returned, and no one knew he had ever left.

Christmas day fell on Monday. Sally stopped by after church with gifts; for me, gold cuff links featuring little white crosses. My mother "found" my gift to Sally—a string of pearls purchased without my knowledge—from the pile under a tree groaning with ornaments, meticulous tinsel, and multicolored bubble lights. It seemed our mothers still saw Sally and me as a good and likely match. What Sally thought I couldn't tell; she spent her brief visit chatting with Aunt Miriam about clothes, then after a cheery, impersonal goodbye, left to "make her rounds."

"What a lovely girl," Aunt Miriam announced. "The best this town has to offer."

"Amen," my mother added, hearing *the best* and not *this town*.

"Raised right," my father threw in, an eloquent editorial coming from him.

I contributed a final "she's great," after which my mother considered the matter happily closed. My father's cigar smoke mingled with aromas of evergreen resin and browning pie crusts. My mother expressed enchantment at the vase I had found, a delicate specimen painted with waterfalls and cherry trees and snowy mountains, much like the scrolls tacked up on Wanda's bedroom walls. "It's perfect," she said.

"And so few things are," Aunt Miriam put in.

"Goodness, sister," my mother replied. "Isn't that a bit jaded for Christmas day?"

"Oh, I don't suppose there's any harm in saying what's true. If many things were perfect, how could we possibly learn God's hard lessons?"

"It's *we* who are imperfect, Miriam."

"Yes, Mary. In any case, your son has rare taste for such a young man, does he not?"

"The vase was Aunt Miriam's idea," I said, hating the praise, feeling I would be more at home with Wanda and her bone-tired mother, drinking iced coffee and eating Aunt Jemima pancakes from mismatched crockery.

"It was," Aunt Miriam admitted, "but Bill chose a lovely vase from among many unsightly ones."

"Pure luck," I muttered.

"Why, Bill, that's not like you," my mother chided.

A chill swept through me. I'd almost forgotten to present the boy my mother knew.

"It's manhood creeping into him," Aunt Miriam said with a resigned sigh. "There is no help for it."

"At a snail's pace." My father chuckled at his wit. "Nevertheless," he continued, "we have one more gift for you." With that, he reached into his breast pocket and pulled out a small box. It contained a Swiss watch—a Titoni Airmaster—a thing gleaming with expense and status to my young eyes. I wore it to bed that night, listening to it chip away at time.

Now, at least, I had something better than a crossbow to bedazzle Don.

CHAPTER TWENTY-SEVEN

"He Ain't Heavy;
He's My Brother"

The Saturday after Christmas, my father dropped me off at Don's house on his way to the plant for the "annual song and dance with the bigwigs," as he put it. Once again, I had to knock at Mr. Heffelfinger's business entrance. On my third knock, the door opened a few inches and no further. I could see a sliver of Mr. Heffelfinger's gaunt face and the fact that behind him, the room was dim, with no sign of Don. "I'm sorry," I stammered, "I thought…"

"No need for sorrow," he said with a raspy chuckle. "You are expected and, I might say, gallant to accept my invitation. I own that I am hard to like and confess that I have put you on the spot without adequate reason. Not to say without *any* reason, but none for which you are accountable." At that, Mr. Heffelfinger released the door and walked—shambled really— over to his desk, leaving me to push my way in. Once inside, I found the shades drawn and smelled an odd, fallow odor of confinement. Seating himself with a groan, Mr. Heffelfinger called to Don in a weak voice, the effort forcing him to stifle a cough.

I stood pretending interest in a photograph of Robert E. Lee, pleading silently for Don to show up. Surely Mr. Heffelfinger was drunk.

"Matthew Brady took that one, young Mr. Shaffer. He mostly photographed Yankee rabble, but even he knew a great man when he saw one." These few words wracked him with a prolonged spasm. When it subsided, he slapped his desk hard. "A man walks through the fires of hell to cure himself, and I'll be damned if God doesn't reward him with the worst cold of his lifetime. And yes, Mr. Shaffer, I am cured; don't feel obliged to act the innocent. Donald tells you everything, does he not?"

"He said a doctor in Atlanta got rid of your cancer."

"That doctor and I fought as comrades in arms, young man, and despite cowardly opinions to the contrary, war is humanity's greatest achievement, its greatest art form, its greatest teacher. War is suffering and genius on the grand scale. Suffering drives humanity onward, but only genius makes the effort worth a plug nickel. Gen'l Lee wept for his dead boys, doubted himself like Jesus on the cross, I'm sure, but his battle plans will last through the ages, and his nobility put the North to eternal shame. All men die, but a few men's ideas and examples live on, do you see? It's all of a piece. My battle against death brought forth ideas I doubted I could ever conceive. But Donald has served as my loyal adjutant, helping me commit those ideas to paper…"

Mr. Heffelfinger interrupted himself. "No need to stand on ceremony, Mr. Shaffer; that settee behind you belonged to my wife. It's dusty but quite comfortable. Sit down, sir. Donald is typing a summary of my manifesto. I wanted you to have a copy. Perhaps we can discuss it down the road. Donald reveres your mental powers and your sincerity."

"Okay." I made my way to the settee with rude haste, glad to be out of conversational range. When I turned around, Mr. Heffelfinger was bent over his desk, writing so slowly that he seemed to be inscribing. In the meantime, I tried to absorb the shock of his sudden "regard" for me— either a sly charade or a miracle. And he had mentioned his fabled wife! But in the past tense. She was probably dead, and Don sworn to never speak of it! As for his love of war, well, he didn't want Don to go to Vietnam, did he? That hypocrisy proved his ideas were bankrupt—no need to give them any further thought. I sat surmising like this for a few minutes, occasionally peering at a preoccupied Mr. Heffelfinger through the gloom. At our last encounter he looked unwell; now, he looked ravaged. Maybe he *was* returning from death's door, but it was still swinging shut behind him. Watching him felt like watching the boring part of a horror movie. When I finally heard Don's footsteps, Mr. Heffelfinger looked up, smiled, and called to me. "Please raise the lights, Mr. Shaffer; my eyes are rested now."

Don came in, waving a sheet of paper and exclaiming, "It's great, Dad." When he spotted me, he cried, "Christ, Shaffer, you're here. Perfect. This document is my dad's statement of principles. You've arrived on a historic day."

Mr. Heffelfinger took the paper and chuckled. "Donald's prone to overstatement. You boys catch up now while I read this. If it passes muster, you may keep this copy, Mr. Shaffer. My scribe there can produce others." Don beamed. The funereal air dissipated. I showed off my new Swiss watch to Don as his father scrutinized the document. Finally, Mr. Heffelfinger nodded his approval and folded his manifesto into an envelope. "Please do not fail to read this, Mr. Shaffer, preferably in the quiet of your home. While I know we are not like-minded, I know you are Donald's friend, and his handiwork touches these affairs as well."

I solemnly agreed and tucked the envelope into the breast pocket of my coat.

Mr. Heffelfinger dealt with another coughing spasm, at the end of which I assumed he would dismiss Don and me. Instead, he announced that the paper he had given me was not the promised conciliatory gift. "During those dark days in Atlanta, I came across an item for you boys to share. I ordered it, and it just arrived at our post office. What do you say we drive over and pick it up? I put blankets down in the bed of my truck."

"Sure," I said, glad to escape the sickroom feel of the house. I would ask Mr. Heffelfinger to drop me off at home after the post office, planning to plead a raft of nonexistent chores. Don and I could easily make other plans, and maybe by then, Wanda would get up the nerve to set him romantically straight.

We headed out along a backstreet parallel to Stagecoach, Don and I hollering with childish glee at the cold wind, the jostling bumps and unencumbered vision of ordinary things made enjoyable by rushing past them. We waved and called out to dogs and two girls holding hands and a woman hanging bedsheets to dry. If we had turned right after about a mile, we would have pulled up next to the post office. Instead, we veered left, following a dirt road that wandered through the barrier of slash pine that hid the Okefenokee Swamp.

"Where's your father going?" I yelled to Don over the pickup's jouncing racket.

"Probably thought of another errand. He likes moonshine," Don called. Likely enough, I thought; there's nothing else out this way.

I looked back at the sun, flickering like a candle through the shifting trees. We passed the skeletal remains of an old Missionary Baptist church and bumped over defunct railroad tracks once used by cypress loggers. At one point, we crossed a paved road bearing southeast. I didn't care much. The rhythms of travel soothed me, made my concerns seem small. I was content to float along on someone else's purpose.

Nothing but twin cairns of rocks half hidden in weeds marked the swamp's edge. The road soon became a boggy path through waters so still and darkened by tannins that they shone like black, polished stone. I looked for gators but saw none; just occasional wading birds among water lilies—eerie white statues fishing the gloomy shallows. Moss-draped cypress and blackgum tupelo trees rose above lush ferns and other vegetation that climbed and twined and pushed its way into every square inch. It came to me with a jolt then, my secret meaning for this place. I kicked Don gently to get his attention.

"Hey, do you know the legend of the Dark Warrior?" Mr. Heffelfinger had slowed the truck to a crawl, probably scouting for his moonshiners; Don and I could converse easily.

"Some local nonsense, I presume."

"Sort of. Supposedly the ghost of a runaway slave haunts the swamp, bringing justice to evil men."

Don scoffed. "White men, no doubt."

"If you say so," I answered. "The story just says the Dark Warrior *made* himself a free man. Nobody helped him. His spirit got so strong that he's still here. He fights with his bare hands and sees into people's hearts."

Don considered my depiction for a moment, then smiled. "If he made himself into a free man, then I applaud him. As you can see, Shaffer, I hold no grudge against the Negro."

If Don suspected the origin of the Dark Warrior's "legend," he hid it well. "Then I guess you're safe out here, Don," I said. About then, Mr. Heffelfinger stopped the truck. I looked for a shack or a still, but we were water-bound on both sides of the path. Mr. Heffelfinger climbed down from the cab, walked to a cypress tree, sat down, and leaned back against its base, groaning loudly like a wounded beast. Don gave an alarmed cry and tried to leap from the truck. He caught his foot and cartwheeled to the ground. Fortunately, the "ground" was peat—centuries worth of vegetation rot—far more forgiving than solid earth. The cypress tree quivered in response to Don's impact, but he staggered to his feet and hurried over to his father. I hung back, absurdly noting the resemblance between Mr. Heffelfinger sitting at the base of a tree and Buddha sitting likewise on *Siddhartha's* cover.

Mr. Heffelfinger seemed to wave away Don's concern. At that, I hopped from the pickup and ventured over. "You boys help me up," he said, breathing hard. "Then go take a piss if you need to. Ain't nobody gonna see you but a bear or a bobcat." The power of suggestion sent us to separate spots. When we returned to the pickup, Mr. Heffelfinger stood there, bathed in sweat, holding Don's crossbow. He held it out to me and said, "Here, lakeside boy, you take this. A little surprise for you. I'm going back to sit under that tree, and I advise both of you to come over and listen to what I have to say."

Before long, Don and I were quite literally sitting at Mr. Heffelfinger's feet on the cold, damp, spongy rot, waiting for a revelation more terrible than I could imagine. He lit a cigarette, winced deeply at the first inhalation, then looked up at a sky he probably couldn't see. Don cried, "Dad," and got no further.

"Be quiet, Donald," his father demanded. "That's an order." Don hung his head and said nothing more. I was too nauseous with apprehension to venture a word.

"Boys, here on earth, we are all defeated. Our so-called savior got strung up, General Lee surrendered his sword, and I too have been defeated, though I don't presume to stand in such eminent company. The fact is when my cancer was discovered, it was already well beyond the reach of medical science. I spent precious time in Atlanta beating my thick head against that truth, but I did find a sympathetic doctor of like mind who gave me enough morphine and laudanum to last through my final days."

Don was crying now, and Mr. Heffelfinger did not try to stop him. Instead, he addressed his remarks directly to me. "I lied to Donald, hoping we could discover together the key to what I've been seeking, a completed battle map showing every human being how to win the war they must fight. Lee's strategies and maneuvers are the codes, but I have failed to decipher them entirely. You, Mr. Shaffer, doubt me. And what galls me is that you doubt me because you don't like me. You are a boy trapped in his petty emotions who has experienced nothing. By comparison, I am a man who has experienced everything. Do you see?"

I stared ahead, not about to risk the wrong answer. The crossbow lay across my lap, pressing down with a force well beyond its weight.

"Oh, don't worry, Mr. Shaffer. I've made my peace with this life, including how little you see. What matters is that Donald embraces you with brotherly love, a far nobler form of love than rutting with females. Therefore, you must play your part." Mr. Heffelfinger took another painful drag and tossed his cigarette into the swamp. Then he reached into the breast pocket of his coat, took out a vial, removed the cap, and emptied the contents into his mouth. He grimaced, then produced a small flask from another pocket and washed the pills down. A slight shudder convulsed him. After it subsided, he offered the container to me. "Go ahead, Mr. Shaffer; you will likely need this." I shook my head.

"Very well. Then down to business. All that I require of you, all that Donald requires of you, is to cock that crossbow. Don will then fire it into my heart, an act that will transform him into the man he must become."

"You're crazy," I shouted. "I'm not doing that." Don's face made it clear he wasn't a willing party to his father's plan.

"I believe you will," Mr. Heffelfinger said with a weak smile. He forced himself to his feet, grunting and gasping, and drew a pistol from the rear of his waistband. I went from fear to paralytic terror. Don wailed in distress and scrambled toward his father in a blind attempt to wrest the gun away. Mr. Heffelfinger calmly raised the weapon out of reach. "Get ahold of yourself, Donald. Time to claim your manhood. The gun is for your benefit; to prove coercion to the authorities. I *hope* to harm no one but myself." He turned to me then. "You take my meaning, lakeside boy? Now, I'm going to point this gun at you and request that you turn facing the truck, cock that goddamned crossbow, and hand it to Donald. If you turn around with it cocked and loaded, I will shoot you."

I quaked, close to fainting, but managed to obey. My face must have shown my silent prayer: *Shoot the bastard.* A white-faced Don shook his head as I lay the crossbow in his arms.

"Now, Donald," Mr. Heffelfinger gasped in a slurred voice as he slid down the tree, "there's no life insurance this way, but there is money. I've arranged for that. And I left a confession. When I'm dead, leave my body and go straight to the sheriff. And for God's sake, don't touch the gun." He closed his eyes for a long moment, and I hoped they might not open on account of the pills. But they did open; he patted his chest above his heart. "Come on, son, help me find a measure of *peace*." He looked at me as he spoke this last bit, making the word peace sound like an epithet.

Don sobbed and trembled, unable to raise the crossbow to a level position. And Mr. Heffelfinger was noticeably fading. I stood there, rooting hard for the impasse to continue. But Mr. Heffelfinger wasn't having it.

"Donald, what I'm about to say is for your own good; God's truth. If you don't put me out of my misery, I'm going to shoot Ed Shaffer's son, and soon. Then you will hate me and probably kill me anyway."

Don gave me a beseeching look, begging me to defend him somehow as he had defended me against Abel Theroux. I don't know what my face signified to him, but with a despairing cry, he whirled and fired the crossbow, the bolt passing well wide of his father and the cypress tree, landing somewhere in the dark waters, beyond retrieval.

Mr. Heffelfinger smiled and croaked out, "Well done, Donald." He then pointed the gun at me with deliberate aim and whispered in a dead voice, "Once again, lakeside boy." I grabbed the crossbow from Don, stepped into it, and yanked the bowstring upward with murderous violence. At that point, I discovered my father was right. The metal crosspiece of the bow gave way, the freed chunk of it whizzing past my head. I looked at Mr. Heffelfinger, raising the ruined crossbow to shield myself.

"Well, goddam," he muttered, shaking his head and lowering the pistol to his lap.

"Can we go home now, Dad?"

These days I wonder at such love and forgiveness. Back then, I confess, I found Don's words monumentally stupid.

"Best not," Mr. Heffelfinger said, utterly changed, his malevolent ferocity replaced with resignation in the space of a heartbeat. "You boys git along; that means you too Donald, and no backtalk. Bring back grown men and an ambulance. Bouncing around in that old truck would more likely kill me than some gator. I'll rest under this tree. I got this pistol and anyway I best be alone to reconcile myself to what I put you boys through." He added a small, gasping laugh. Then to me: "Can you drive that truck? Don't lie." I nodded. I'd learned in our old throwaway Dodge, shifting gears for hours out in a hardpan field.

Still, it took me fifteen lurching minutes to turn around. Don stayed with his father throughout, shouting occasional warnings to me about submerging the truck. Before we left, Don covered his father with a blanket from the pickup's bed.

"We'll bring you food and water," he called out as we pulled away. I stayed in second gear, fearing to downshift and stall out, focusing with heart and soul on the center of the path.

"This explains everything," Don exclaimed at the first permissible moment. "A great man at the end of his rope. Can you imagine what those pills must have done to him?"

"He'll go to jail if he doesn't die first," I said.

"Good God, Shaffer, why? Nothing happened."

I was too offended to answer, leaving Don to stew in his preposterous remark.

"My dad had no intention of harming you. He assured me of that while you were maneuvering the truck. A strategic ploy, don't you see?"

"No."

After about a quarter mile of silence, Don pleaded, "Can't you drive any faster?"

I sped up once we cleared the swamp's overgrowth. The pickup bucked and bogged when I had to downshift ineptly, but we made it to my house without real incident. Don bolted from the truck and headed inside, calling out to my mother in alarm. I followed at a fast walk out of duty, not eagerness. When I stepped inside, I heard Don explaining to my parents that his father had suffered an "attack." No mention of crossbow, pistol, or lethal threats. I decided to follow suit for the moment, not wishing to pile more troubles on my friend. My mother had the phone to her ear, summoning help. My father stood with his arms folded, listing to Don's panicky, circuitous narrative. He greeted me with a searching look, which I answered with a quick shake of my head. Well, no matter what Don claimed, people in charge would see for themselves.

When Don went to the kitchen for water, my father took me aside. "Why on earth didn't you bring the man back?" he demanded.

"He wouldn't come. He said he'd be okay until we got grown-ups to help him."

"You drove that truck here from the swamp?" I nodded; my father nodded back.

261

Assistance arrived in due time, and a small caravan headed back to the swamp. My father and I led the way in Mr. Heffelfinger's truck. Don followed in the sheriff's car, with an ambulance bringing up the rear. No sirens and breakneck speed, though my father did drive in haste, asking me along the way for a "sane explanation" of our venture into the swamp.

"Moonshine, I guess. We were supposed to be going to the post office." My father pushed his hat back off his forehead and fixed me with a hard squint.

"Until I see for myself, I'll pretend to believe your friend's cock-and-bull story. But sometime soon, young man, I'm going to expect the truth from you. For your mother's sake, I didn't say anything back there, but that boy is a bad liar as sure as I'm a bad dancer."

"Mr. Heffelfinger is crazy," I said, expecting demand for elaboration, but my father only muttered, "Now we're getting somewhere."

Once in the swamp proper, we eased our way toward Mr. Heffelfinger like a funeral procession. I almost begged my father to stop the truck so I could get out and vomit, but my dread of early winter sundown stopped me. We finally came to the landmark cypress but drove slightly past it before I told my father to stop. It *had* to be the right tree, yet Mr. Heffelfinger was nowhere in sight. "That's where he was, I swear."

I searched for the damaged crossbow to verify my instinct. No crossbow. Everyone was exiting the other vehicles. I walked to the tree as if by staring at it, I could make Mr. Heffelfinger materialize. "Look," I said, pointing to a lone cigarette butt. Behind me, I heard Don cry, "Dad, where are you?" The men hunted around, exchanging dubious glances. My father knelt, picked up the butt, then showed it to the sheriff. The sheriff squinted at it, then spat. "Don't prove nothing, Ed."

To my mind, it proved everything, including that only a *fool* would ignore evidence screaming Mr. Heffelfinger's name.

"Well, Clarence," my father pointed out in his soft, persuasive public voice, "it got here one way or another."

"That's the kind my dad smokes," Don wailed.

Clarence took the butt delicately from my father and put his hand on Don's shoulder. "Now listen, son. This here's nothing but white paper and tobacco. Do you even know what brand your old man favors?"

Don did not.

"Camels," I said. "Can we look around for an empty pack?"

262

"Humor the boys, Clarence; I'm going to scout ahead a bit. Won't be but a minute." The better part of a half hour passed before my father returned—empty-handed. No further physical evidence ever appeared concerning Mr. Heffelfinger's disappearance. I suspect he waded off into the blackwater, incriminating crossbow in hand, the gun jammed under his belt until the pills he swallowed or his illness felled him. In any case, local authorities weren't about to drag the swamp to find out. They did grant *something* had happened. After all, the man never showed up again. But how his disappearance fit in with the unsubstantiated story of two boys was hard to say. So hard, in fact, that it seemed best to move on.

Well, not *precisely* move on. Mr. Heffelfinger's financial affairs were not in order. He had cleaned out his accounts and left unpaid debts. Merchants placed liens against his house. Don came to live with us, occupying the spare bedroom usually reserved for Aunt Miriam. And around that time, I told my father the outlandish truth. He sat with a cocktail and a pungent cigar, nodding his head from time to time as if everything I related confirmed his general view of humankind—and "two-dollar crossbows."

"Your mother has a soft spot for war vets," he said, "so let's keep this under our hats. At least the man had the good graces to clean up his mess and shut the damned door behind him."

CHAPTER TWENTY-EIGHT

"It's the End of the World as We Know It"

Mr. Heffelfinger's confession also remained under a hat—mine—and has remained there to the present day. He left it with me in the same envelope as his manifesto. Here is the end of his statement:

Whether I am living or dead as you read this,
I wish only one thing to be known. Under no
circumstances would I have visited harm upon
anyone but myself. Whatever threats I made
to ensure my demise were empty, as
my unloaded firearm proves. My sincerest
apologies extend to Mary Magdalene, whose
son played an unwitting part. He is a decent boy
who cannot be blamed for believing the weak-
kneed lies of a deceitful world. I urge that world,
for the sake of its salvation, to heed my son,
Donald. There is no God, but on Earth there is
Hell. Against it, war must be waged. If you will
only care for Donald, he will someday
be for this world what Lee was for the South.

Dulce et decorum est pro patria mori

Yours in truth,

Phillip Friedrich Heffelfinger

I hated every last word. The deliberate omission of my mother's last name. My characterization as a naïve fool. Don compared to Robert E. Lee! The notion that an *empty* gun made everything okay. I wasn't about to give anyone the chance to believe that crap, especially not Don. And after all, we didn't need the letter to prove our innocence. No one accused us. My father had praised Mr. Heffelfinger's choice to disappear. I imagined the Dark Warrior found him under the tree, confiscated the bow, and forced him and his (probably loaded) pistol to flee deep into unforgiving waters.

I phoned Wanda to tell her Mr. Heffelfinger had disappeared. "Yeah, I just heard. It's terrible." Not much else got disclosed since we were sure to be overheard on our party line. Innocuous to anyone but me, the words *I just heard* rang like a fire bell. Don had borrowed my Schwinn, announcing during breakfast that he needed to visit his house alone in case his father "returned or left spiritual clues in the manner of Houdini."

He had gone to see Wanda, no doubt eager to relate shameless, self-serving lies about what happened in the swamp. I'd bet my life on it. And given his animated disposition today, Wanda had *not* named me as "the boy she liked." I sat in the little cane chair my mother kept by the phone, muttering "fuck" under my breath, the beginning of a lifelong habit. Wanda was a pushover, and Don was possibly more underhanded than I was. Worse yet, Mr. Heffelfinger had chosen me to protect Don's interests, a burden I suddenly despised almost to the point of relinquishing.

Almost.

Mr. Heffelfinger's envelope contained not only the confession and manifesto Don had typed but also a name and address in Concord, New Hampshire, above a short message: *Please write to my sister Greta Miller and tell her the deed is done. If you are a true friend to Donald, you will do this.* It seemed beyond implication that Mr. Heffelfinger had a Confederate who knew of his twisted plan and who comprehended the ghastly meaning residing in "the deed is done." Incredible! A mystery too intriguing to abandon, especially since I had become a pivotal figure in its unfolding.

I deduced the bank money had gone to Don's Aunt Greta. Probably as cash in a box disguised as a Christmas present. However it happened, I wanted Don to have that money, not greedy men in suits—no matter how cravenly he had schemed to see Wanda. So, I wrote to Aunt Greta, sketching out the bare facts and providing my name and address (I didn't risk my phone number), along with assurances that all secrets were safe with me. I walked my letter to the post office, escorting it as far along its route as I possibly could. The ancient clerk reeked of gardenias. She took my letter without interest and handed me a package meant for the Heffelfinger address.

"The boy stays at your place, don't he?"

I nodded.

The cumbersome package was addressed to "Master Donald Heffelfinger and Friend." I shook it gingerly, with great perplexity, but it gave nothing away. The post office had just been an excuse to lure us into the swamp. Why send a real package? Maybe Don was right. Maybe Mr. Heffelfinger's scheme had not yet played itself out. I didn't doubt his body was rotting out there, probably no more than a football field from the cypress tree, but he still seemed hell-bent on having his say.

"Jesus Christ," I exclaimed aloud.

"Here now," the clerk said, glaring. "Take the mail or don't, but I'll have no more of that."

I had made love, risked gunfire, and now joined a conspiracy by mailing a letter. No old biddy would cow me today. I tucked the package under my arm and loudly proclaimed, "It's a free country." For good measure, I made a flamboyant peace sign as I exited the door. Outside, a cold, punishing rain had crept in, compliments of God, or Mr. Heffelfinger, or no one at all. I used the maples for cover as best I could and headed home.

Mr. Heffelfinger had mail-ordered a wooden chess set nestled in a velvet-lined, lacquered wooden box with a gold latch. The classic Staunton pieces had been painted Confederate gray and Union blue. Don exulted in the symbolism and begged to play, but I refused. It smacked of honoring his father. I declined to discuss Mr. Heffelfinger at all, and given his status as Don's only topic, we reached a conversational impasse for the first time in our young lives. Ordinarily, I could have relied on my father to minutely rehash the swamp catastrophe "to get to the bottom of things" and make sure I'd learned all possible lessons. But to my surprise, he accepted my version at face value and found little to criticize in my conduct. Erratic, troubled men, he observed, were not news to him—just thank the Lord the poor fellow didn't take anyone with him. No use wasting brain cells on the inner workings of Phil Heffelfinger, he opined. They were unknowable and probably not worth knowing anyway.

I felt flattered, briefly, until it turned out Ed Shaffer's peculiar brevity had nothing to do with my faultless conduct. He simply had bigger fish to fry. One evening after dinner, as he sat on the veranda with a second cocktail, I stood by the screen door and heard him tell my mother about his meeting with the plant owners. "The top brass doesn't want to hear it, Maggie, but it's God's truth. Not one man out of a hundred, colored *or* white, will put up with the wages we pay for the work we ask. We're cutting our own throats. They expect me to run the plant with a poorhouse skeleton crew. You know what happened to Larry. And things are worse now. I still don't have a safety manager. All I can do is put up posters and give the men free coffee and doughnuts for weeks without accidents."

As my mother offered sympathy and confidence, I tried to remember Larry, but nothing came. I knew from my father that tapping loblolly pines and lugging buckets of resin all day was no picnic. And distilling turpentine put men at close quarters with fumes and scalding steam. Maybe Larry had gotten burned. Well, at least my father wished his men got paid better. And at least I understood the preoccupation that made him terse.

Settling for these facile conclusions, I opened the door and walked out. "Where's Don?" my mother called.

"I don't know," I replied, affecting an air of deliberate indifference; Don and I were barely speaking.

But that would soon change.

The Saturday after Mr. Heffelfinger's disappearance, the *Hopperton Weekly* reported it—after a fashion. The paper's headline announced "Lions Club Hosts a Christmas Party for Youths." The article about Mr. Heffelfinger (half of a narrow column in the lower section of the front page) read:

Local Man Missing

A local man is missing after hiking near the 3rd Rd. entrance
to the swamp, according to Dep.
C. Dixon. Philip R. Hefelfinger,
a veteran, was reported missing
by his son and another boy. The
young men claimed Mr. Hefelfinger may have fallen ill and
wandered off. A search is underway, according to Dixon. Anyone
with knowledge of Hefelfinger's
whereabouts should contact the
sheriff's office.

Our shared outrage at this false account closed the breach between
Don and me, especially after my father shrugged off its inaccuracies. "Don,
they got the word out that your father is missing; that's what matters. We
all pray he turns up, but we don't have the means to search the swamp.
What Clarence says here is just a courtesy statement."

"But sir," Don stammered, "don't Christians hold that the truth makes
you free?"

"Yes, son," my father replied with surprising tenderness, "and the truth
is your father is missing and not likely to return, I'm afraid. I wish I did
not have to speak so frankly and do so only out of concern. It's a damned
shame you have to grow up too soon, but there it is."

Don blinked at his welling tears and shoved his glasses tight against
his face. "The . . . the . . . likelihood of my dad's return is unknown, sir."

"Only God knows," my mother put in, "and I for one trust that He is
merciful."

After chores, Don and I hurried to the gazebo to vent out of earshot.
My father and mother had pointed Don toward acceptance, but he had
another destination in mind. "It's quite breathtaking here, isn't it, Shaffer?
Not a cloud. You wouldn't know what nature has in mind for us. Or what
crap human beings will accept. When I read that newspaper article and
listened to your well-meaning parents, I felt exactly like Hank Reardon in
Atlas Shrugged, do you see? All around me calls to accept lies, to surrender,

to sacrifice myself to the so-called common good. But I am more awake now than ever."

"My father's got problems at work," I offered, willing to go no further in defending him.

"No, your father opened my eyes. If there are men like fat Clarence Dixon, perhaps there are a few like Hank Reardon as well."

I suddenly needed to tell Don everything I'd kept from him.

"Do you know your Aunt Greta?" I asked, choosing to start there and work my way to Wanda Grice.

Don startled at the name. "That's . . . what did my dad say to you?"

"Nothing. Your father left me her name in case something . . . happened to him. He said if I was your friend, I'd write to her. I guess he thought you'd be too upset. He made it sound like life or death, so I sent her a letter. I guess it was part of his plan."

Don was beside himself with welling emotion. "*Now* you know why my dad trusts *you*. Not some hopeless fool like Clarence Dixon. He sees what I see!"

I shrugged. "I still don't think he liked me. He just figured I'd stick up for you. I mean, he knew I owed you one for Abel Theroux."

"Perhaps," Don conceded as he cleaned his glasses with his shirttail, "though I received a stiff reprimand for attacking without first discerning Abel's intentions. My dad *volunteered* the one-hundred-dollar reparation well before any demand. And he was *not*, as I may have let on, proud of my actions."

"Well, you tried to do the right thing."

Don said nothing for a while, working at his glasses as if he meant to regrind the lenses. I stepped out to look at the weathervane. The January wind cut steadily across the rise.

"Let's not refight old battles, Shaffer," Don called. "What matters is that my dad brought you inside the circle."

"The what?"

Don put on his glasses and fixed me with a fervent smile. "However peculiar I seem to you, Bill, I'm quite aware of who I am. Do you see? I called you Bill, not Shaffer. Furthermore, I recognize that my dad may be dead, and I'll bet you're the boy Wanda likes. Do I deny reality as you probably think? No, I simply address it on my terms—the same as you.

Sally got a glimpse of the real you when you tried to kiss her, didn't she? Imagine if everyone knew you favor integration and oppose the war! And do you suppose I care? Why should I? History is the clash of opposites. So you see, I don't need to restart the Civil War as my counterpart in your novel does—yes, I know about that too. No, the "circle" I refer to is just the keeping of a particular secret. Now I can share it with you if you want to know. What do you say, Shaffer?"

History, Don's secret, even his acknowledgment of my heresies, waited in line behind the phrase "I'll bet you're the boy Wanda likes" and mention of my novel. I blundered ahead.

"Don't worry; you're not in my book. Nobody real is in it. I don't know why Wanda told you that. But yeah, she likes me. She wants to hold hands and go to the movies, stuff like that. Then you come over for deep conversations. I guess I'm supposed to be jealous, or you are. I don't know. You probably have a theory. Heck, you're probably a genius. But I always wonder if you believe half the crazy stuff you say or if you're just waiting for me to catch on to the joke. I mean, people write history *after* it happens, not before, right? I bet that in twenty years, you'll be sitting somewhere thinking, 'Why did I believe all that crap that never happened?' But if you still want to tell me your secret, go ahead. I won't tell anybody."

I stared at the blank blue sky as I talked, getting it all out before facing Don's wrath or sputtering indignation, whatever it might be. But when I turned, he seemed delighted, as if I'd just announced his name for some award.

"This is fantastic, Shaffer. Do you remember my conundrum about preferring a girl who liked you but didn't like sex, or liked sex but not you? I believe Wanda provides the answer. She is *both* girls, don't you see? I am a boy she likes, and you are the sex. Oh, not literally. But holding hands, just like kissing, *is* sex. For *you*, she is the girl who likes sex, just as I predicted."

Don's theory was too breathtakingly off base for argument. "You might be right," I told him.

"Yes. And about history too. Nineteen eighty-four is *less* than twenty years away."

"Whatever, Don. Let's hear your big secret."

Don leaned close, too excited to be put off by my sneering skepticism.

"Put simply, Shaffer, Greta Miller is my *mother*. After they liberated my dad from the POW camp, he met a German woman. They wrote letters, and four years later, he went back to Germany and married her. They came back to Georgia and lived over near Cairo. Great, except that the day they got there, she told my dad she was pregnant by a terrible man back in Germany—a Nazi! She had only lied to escape. My dad forgave her but couldn't trust her, do you see? And nobody in Cairo wanted a German woman around. So my mother left the baby—me—with my dad and moved up North to be around other German people."

Don spoke matter-of-factly, as if relating the plot of a spy novel. If anything, he radiated pride in his origins.

"Why did your father want me to write to *her*? Isn't she out of the picture by now?"

"The picture is *history*, Shaffer. The very thing you mock. The war. It created her destiny. My dad understood that. The war turned Greta Mueller into Greta Miller. The war created *me*, Donald Heffelfinger. Think where I'd be if I'd been born in Germany! Perhaps now you can begin to see the roots of my dad's philosophy."

I couldn't.

"It was nice of him to raise you. I guess he kept in touch with your mom."

Don gave a hesitant nod. "He . . . he wrote to her about me once a year. You see, she didn't want a divorce. She was sure they'd deport her. My father acted with honor and accepted her wishes. But that deprived me of a mother. And my father wanted—"

"A real wife."

Don gave me an odd stare before nodding again.

"Yes. My dad told me . . . personal things when he came back from Atlanta. He said I should understand his life. I guess he knew he couldn't tell me later."

"Maybe she'll want to see you."

Don responded with a wretched smile, then gazed back at my house.

"I have a . . . more than adequate mother, though I make no claim. And besides, I will achieve legal manhood quite soon. My fate will be my own. No, I will be busy taking steps to redeem my father, not finding a new mother."

Added to events that passed all believing, Don's revelations felt like final proof that my life had become extraordinary. Granted, it was Don's life, not mine, that had been brutally upended, but *I* had written the letter to Greta Miller, *I* had set things in motion, and surely fascination repercussions would soon show themselves. But Greta Miller failed to answer me over the next couple of weeks. The weather turned sharply colder, frosting lawns and slowing life to an uneventful crawl. I began to feel fate was bluffing, despite the chaos, forgetting that cause and effect still ground on behind the scenes.

In early February, as I shared Saturday morning coffee with my mother, I came across two startling articles in the same issue of the *Hopperton Herald* (I read the paper with cynical attention now, knowing its editors to be incompetent).

The first article was prominent and starkly headlined: "Legislators Say Pine Gum Industry Faces Extinction." It didn't escape me that "extinction" included my father's plant. Without state subsidies, the article claimed, 30,000 turpentine workers, mostly Negroes, would lose their jobs, swelling the relief rolls with catastrophic economic consequences. The politicians called on the state to save "a historic and respected" industry. Reinforced by my father's frustrated remarks about wages at his plant, their warnings rang like a dire prophecy. I looked up at my mother. She talked to herself softly as she composed a shopping list. If I told her what I'd read, she'd say not to worry, maybe quote a verse about the lilies of the field. I didn't think parables would help me right then, so I kept my peace and went back to reading.

A lengthier article filled the bottom of the page: "Ware County Says No to Funding." Ware County wasn't our county, and its business could not have been less meaningful to me. But the word "Waycross" in the article's first sentence caught my eye, and I started reading.

The article revealed that Ware County had refused our county's recent request for Ware to fund Waycross students at Hopperton High. "We" were educating their kids, after all. But Ware officials argued that "adequate" schools existed in their county, even if "integrated" went hand in hand with adequate. I surmised our county had gone begging because the state had not come through with promised money, but the article said Georgia officials had turned down our funding request *in June of last year*. We had petitioned for reconsideration, only to be rebuffed again by the state, which feared the wrath of a federal agency called HEW if they violated federal integration guidelines.

I remembered my father gathering and doctoring statements from Waycross parents to assure funding. But he'd never mentioned the first unfavorable ruling, leaving me with the impression that the parental affidavits were nothing more than missing paperwork. The article finished by hinting that our county might end up financially crippled, pointing to an unnamed Hopperton official's absurd suggestion that county lines be changed to circumvent the state's ruling.

I saw then how false a face the world put on. And that my clandestine visits to Wanda were cut from the same cloth as my father's ploys to exclude Negroes, except that my visits hurt no one. *This will be the last year for my father's plant*, I thought. *Georgia will never give out money for turpentine or Negroes.* I moped around in oracular gloom most of the day, keeping my thoughts to myself—at least until dinner.

After the pork chops and collard greens had been passed around, I mentioned the article in which Ware County refused to fund the Waycross kids. I intended to give the issue of pine gum "extinction" a wide berth. My father replied that a new, more legally forceful petition to Ware County was "in the works." I nodded, feeling the futility of reply, but after sitting there a moment, I succumbed to frustration and said, "It's not going to stop integration."

My father gave me a look indicative of someone who wouldn't put up with much. "And what, precisely, isn't going to stop integration, young man?"

"Anything. They've already integrated a lot of schools. Hopperton's getting Negro teachers next year; it's all set. I read about it in the paper."

"'Read about it,' you say? Well, that settles that, doesn't it? Never mind that it's cowardly to give up your beliefs because others oppose you. Do you think your mother would surrender her Christianity to godless communism?"

"No, Dad, but is segregation something a person *believes* in, like a religion? Isn't it just something people ... want?"

"I don't care about segregation," Don interjected, unable to resist. "I just don't want to be ruled by the weak."

"Oh, for— Maggie, what does the Bible say about mixing races?"

My mother looked dismayed; she had no interest in refereeing this debate. "Why, I'm not sure, Ed. Of course, the tribes of Israel scattered, and Jews were forbidden to marry Gentiles, and Noah cursed Ham, who is reputed to have fathered the dark Egyptian people, so it does seem God wished different peoples to stay separate from one another ..."

"Sir, sir," Don called. "Those stories concern marriage and breeding. While I'm opposed to *forced* integration, surely the Bible isn't opposed to a mere arrangement of consolidated education."

My father gave Don a withering, incredulous stare to which Don, I believe, was oblivious. I would have laughed, had I dared.

"The Good Book isn't 'stories,' son. I suggest you—"

"Donald has never attended church before now, Ed; let's not lose sight of that." At these irreproachably soft words from my mother, my father looked back and forth at the three of us, weighing the least of three evils, and settled on me.

"Bill, I believe the races should live apart for their own good, not out of hate. Negroes are among my best workers. And mark my words, unless we fight the government, they won't stop at school integration. They won't be satisfied until they rip our whole way of life off the hinges."

"Okay, but like I always tell Don, the South lost the Civil War. We got rid of slavery. Did that make our way of life worse?"

"We only lost a *battle*," Don argued hotly. "And most men are slaves to this very day."

"And will be," my mother said, "until God forgives original sin and those sins we've heaped upon ourselves. Ed, I'm sure we are all thankful for what a wonderful provider you are, aren't we, boys?"

"Yes, ma'am. Mr. Shaffer prolonged the search for my father that first day in the swamp." Then Don looked at my father. "I am in your debt, sir."

"No payment required, son. Best you show your gratitude to Mrs. Shaffer by eating her fine dinner before it gets cold."

"You didn't answer my question, Father," I said, my heart cold to the trouble I worsened for myself. "If we're better off without slavery, isn't it possible we'd be better off without segregated schools?"

"Anything is possible, Bill. But I have to live according to what is likely. And only a fool does otherwise."

My father's tone put an end to the conversation. But we both knew it wasn't the end of our unfolding battle.

CHAPTER TWENTY-NINE

"Subterranean Homesick Blues"

S nowflakes stinging the tongues of overjoyed kids offset the frigid days dogging February. Likewise, my Rialto date with Wanda momentarily squared accounts between the heartless world and me. I even managed to stay chipper when Don lobbied to "tag along," swearing he would not interfere with my "impersonation of Casanova."

"The idea is to get *away* from you," I bantered, still offering up a grain of truth. We sat on the veranda drinking syrupy hot cocoa.

"Very droll, Shaffer. What's playing?"

"*The Man Who Shot Liberty Valance* and *A Fistful of Dollars.*"

"Ah, let's see . . . John Wayne, Jimmy Stewart, Clint Eastwood. Giants of the silver screen. Perhaps I'll go on my own. It's still a free country, if not for much longer."

"If you stay home, it's still a free country. And you'll still have a friend."

Don cackled. "Christ, Shaffer, there's no need to resort to empty threats. I hereby retire from the field in favor of your mother's coconut cake." He stood up, gave me a movie-Nazi bow, and goose-stepped his way to the kitchen.

Wanda reveled in the outing: no more shielding Don and me from each other, no intimacies to fend off or surrender to, buttered popcorn, escape to the Old West, and the sheer fact of getting out of the house—all these reliefs and delights put her in a buoyant mood, suppressed only by an apparent cold. The absence of visiting boys had calmed her mother down, and Wanda loved her new hair color, an odd red somewhere between orange clay and cherry soda.

We sat in the otherwise vacant balcony. Since Wanda's sniffles discouraged making out, I alternated between spoiling the movie plots and reliving the swamp drama. I couldn't shut up. At home, my words raised a stream of objections, corrections, and object lessons. Wanda, on the other hand, nodded, exclaimed "wow," and devoured popcorn, pointing out not a single error in my thinking. Walking home, drunk on my newfound authority, I further prophesied the turpentine industry's collapse, the return to Ware County of most Waycross kids except her (since her mother was locally employed), and, at best, a draw for the US against the Vietcong. I kept news of Don's mother to myself, not wishing his affairs to take center stage. Wanda interrupted here and there to point out the waxing half-moon, or our frosty breath, or how a TV set flickered through someone's front window.

At one point, an old bloodhound loped out to the sidewalk to grace us with a gruff hello. Wanda reciprocated by kneeling and speaking to it in a soft voice. The hound whined as if in confirmation. She whispered to him, then stood up. "He used to be a person," she explained, "but he wasn't loyal. That's why he's a bloodhound this time around. He'll be a person next time. I think he's learned his lesson."

"How do you know?"

"I don't. It's just a feeling. All I know is everything goes in a circle. Look at the earth, the moon, even the Milky Way is spinning. It's like they say in *Siddhartha*, everyone plays with life like a toy, over and over again through many lives, until they decide to get serious, you know, get enlightened. Mr. Heffelfinger died, so I guess there's a baby, a creature or a person, carrying his soul."

"A water moccasin."

"That's mean, Bill."

"Sorry. I think *you'd* come back as you."

Wanda stood up and hugged me.

"Now *that's* sweet, but I'm coming back as a ballerina with perfect skin."

The glow cast by my perfect date, indeed the most flawless moment of my young life, didn't last long. Once again, the *Hopperton Herald* bore the bad tidings:

Elixapine Sued for Death

The family of Lawrence Lasker
intends to sue Elixapine for damages,
claiming his death in a plant accident resulted from company
ignoring safety procedures. Atty.
Lothrop, representing the family,
said witnesses would bear this out.
Elixapine manager Edward "Ed"
Shaffer offered no comment. No
date has been set for trial as of yet.

"They're going to say we murdered the man." My father fumed and
paced around the kitchen, his celebrated voice of reason nowhere to be
found. "I know the witnesses, men like Tom Fields. They won't think of
all the families the plant has provided for over the years, just their pound
of flesh."

"Sir," Don said, "if the company compensates the family without being
forced to, won't it appear honorable and perhaps pay far less what a jury
might award? That was my dad's thinking after I assaulted Abel Theroux."

"That's right on the mark, son—*appear honorable*. Elixapine will offer
a pittance. Lothrop—who's hooked up to a big Atlanta outfit—will spit
on it. Sooner or later, they'll settle on a number. The fool who let this
terrible thing happened will be fired, probably long before the settlement.
Not long afterward, the plant will shut down unless Elixapine throws in
the towel and declares bankruptcy just for spite."

"Sir, why don't you fire the person responsible right now?"

My father imitated a smile. "Well, Donald, you can't very well fire
yourself, now can you?"

The next week the city fathers of Hopperton received a letter from the
State Board of Education stating that no further petitions would be considered pertaining to the question of relocating Ware County students.
Further, the Board found "irregularities" in petitioning parents' affidavits,
which would otherwise be investigated had the underlying request not
been denied. The Hopperton paper ran an editorial praising the doomed
attempt and supporting a *temporary* property tax surcharge to cover the

school budget shortfall. But enough's enough, they concluded. Lesson learned; medicine taken.

The editorial said nothing about whether the Waycross kids would stay put through the school year.

It turned out they would. Dances and tests were at hand, and an entire summer stood between now and next school year. Don ranted, of course, but his classmates only shook their heads at his tired act. I felt I understood (and cared about) how the Waycross migration unfolded beyond any of my peers, including Don. Accordingly, I lingered after class to ask Mr. Pee what he thought. He perched on his desk and gave me a long look, knowing full well who my father was.

"Have you formed an opinion, Bill?"

"I'm for civil rights and against the war." No need to hold back now.

Mr. Pee raised an eyebrow and smiled. "You have wandered into the wrong town. But since you are forthright, I will return the favor to the extent I'm permitted. This country is not a melting pot, as folks often claim. It is a pot of stew that people fail to enjoy because they are too busy bickering over the ingredients. Some people go so far as to want separate pots. I don't believe that's going to happen, so..." Mr. Pee paused to size me up, to see if I'd grasped his point.

"My father says we're fighting for our way of life."

"And who isn't? If not the one we have, then the one we want. I certainly don't blame your father for that. Nor any of the citizens he opposes. Or myself." He paused, taking his characteristic look out the window into the empty distance. "You'll be the first to know that I'm leaving Hopperton."

"Why?" I'm sure my voice croaked with dismay.

"Just say that I'm an awkward ingredient in this particular stew."

"Where are you going, sir?"

"I'm not sure. I have friends in Northern California. In any event, a poet named Rilke advised that we let ourselves be conquered by the great storm of life to become someone greater, someone who no longer even needs a name. Or color, or ... well now I've gone too far afield."

I may have missed Mr. Pee's final point, but I knew I felt like crying.

"And Bill, please don't tell anyone, especially young Mr. Heffelfinger. He's suffered enough losses recently."

At home, two more doorstep arrivals rattled my family life. First, a letter from Greta Miller announced her intention to come to Hopperton and requested lodging suggestions. After telling my mother Greta Miller was a new pen pal, I called Aunt Miriam, who got the unvarnished truth.

"I'll put her up here at the hotel, Bill. I can arrange for flights to Birmingham if she's not driving. I'd like to meet her, see what she's about, for Donald's sake. She can take the bus from here just as easily as Atlanta. If she chooses to stay in Hopperton a while, I'll trade favors and find her a place. And by the way, how's your young lady? Does she still prize her necklace?"

"She loves it. She thinks it has some Buddhist magic."

"Well, the man who bestowed it on me *was* quiet and eccentric. Also, he wore a hairpiece."

"Anyway, you're the best, Aunt Miriam."

"Why yes, I believe I am."

Agents from the Georgia Bureau of Investigation comprised the second doorstep arrival—two younger, easygoing, athletic, close-shaven men in suits looking for a chat with Ed Shaffer. They had badges and guns visibly holstered on their belts. My mother entertained them like old friends passing through town, wanting to hear about their families. Ed, she assured them, would be right along. I assumed their visit pertained to the "irregularities" mentioned in the State Board of Education's last letter. Don introduced himself, shook their hands, praised them for the dedication he had no obvious way to judge. I felt neither my mother's equanimity nor Don's effusiveness—only scared-shitless nausea in my gut.

When my father arrived, the three of them retired to the den. After half an hour, my father came out and motioned for me to join them. He looked fit to be tied but not scared. I went in to find the two agents smoking cigars; one of them wrote in a notepad.

"Now, Bill," the other agent said, "you're not in any trouble. I'm Agent Lassiter, and this is Agent Feeney. We just want to know to the best of your recollection what happened the day Philip Heffelfinger disappeared."

They weren't here to arrest my father! With a sense of relief bordering on elation, I revisited that day in detail, withholding only the personal documents Mr. Heffelfinger had entrusted to me (I trotted out his public manifesto with a flourish). I told the agents about his post office ploy, pistol, death threat, and weird, drug-distorted confession. And, of course, the crossbow. When I finished, the agents exchanged an enigmatic glance, then looked at my father, who nodded. "Okay, son," Agent Lassiter said, apparently satisfied, "what happened when you brought the authorities back to the scene?"

"Mr. Heffelfinger was gone. The paper said we reported him as missing, but we didn't. I don't think the sheriff believed us. My father searched up ahead but didn't find anything. I guess Don's father headed off into the swamp to die on his own."

"Did you hear any talk about a search party?"

"No, the sheriff said it was too hard; the swamp was too big."

Lassiter nodded without comment, then turned to my father. "What was the thinking on the search party, Mr. Shaffer? I understand you weren't in charge, but if you recall…"

"We didn't have the manpower at hand, and we didn't have a clear idea of what happened. The man's son—Donald—was in a panic and saying all manner of wild things that didn't sound right."

"Was a search party ever organized, Mr. Shaffer, as far as you know?"

"I think Charlie is still looking at the case from all angles."

"Well," Lassiter said, stubbing out his cigar, "we received a letter from your . . . houseguest alleging police misconduct in this case, including negligence and conspiracy between the press and local government. He suggested we contact you, Mr. Shaffer, not only because you were an eyewitness, but because of your high character." Agent Feeney handed his partner a newspaper clipping as if by prearrangement. "Other than this initial report, sir, have you seen any follow-up articles in the paper? Has the sheriff shared with you his thinking about whether Mr. Heffelfinger's status will remain unknown for the foreseeable future? Any plans for a limited search around the point of disappearance?"

My father shook his head to all these questions. I wondered if he would order Don out of the house today. Maybe Don could live with Aunt Miriam and finish school in Birmingham.

"One other thing," the agent continued. "Do either of you have suspicions that Mr. Heffelfinger was engaged in subversive activities?"

"You mean, was he a communist?" my father inquired with grim amusement.

"Let's say anti-government," the agent responded.

"I didn't know the man. He sold insurance. Kept to himself. Not a churchgoer."

"All he talked about was the Civil War," I offered. "I think he hates communists."

My father stood up. "Listen, gents; there's no conspiracy. Our sin is living in a small town and shying away from big decisions. I'll give you that. But if you poke Charlie, he'll step up to the plate. The Exchange Club will help with a search; you have my word. By the way, that must've been one doozy of a letter to get you boys to come down here."

Lassiter chuckled. "He sent copies to Governor Maddox and on up to Washington DC. We figured him for a grown man."

My father gave a rueful nod. "For a fact, he surely thinks he is."

After the agents left, ushered out in the friendliest possible way, my father spoke to Don. "Listen, son, if you're going to go off on another wild tangent, kindly let me know. Otherwise, it's going to get too wet to plow. Now you boys go far away and stay there."

My father, to his great credit and my great surprise, appreciated Don's position. The promised search materialized, but nothing turned up. I suppose the crossbow lies submerged out there somewhere, or at least the broken prod. Aluminum may be terrible for crossbows, but at least it doesn't rust.

CHAPTER THIRTY

"Dover Beach"

My mother and I sat together on the veranda during a warming Saturday twilight just before the Ides of March. She busied herself crocheting a rag rug from strips of her old dresses as I reread *Mother Night* by Kurt Vonnegut, a book set during World War II with German women like Greta Miller as characters. One of them married Howard Campbell, an American man posing as a Nazi but acting as a double agent for the allies. Her sister was a white supremacist who betrayed him. I read as long as light permitted, egged on by loose parallels between real life and the book's plot, hoping, I suppose, for a lurid epiphany.

I finally closed the book, leaving Campbell in an Israeli prison, and watched late sunlight play along the tops of westward pines. Then I noticed two people walking from the direction of town, a man in a white shirt gesturing grandly and a woman in a church dress. I recognized most passersby even at a dim distance, but not these two. Idle curiosity prompted me to track them. At about a block's distance, the man spotted me and waved. I looked hard then. I had assumed Don was in his room, but here he came, with Wanda beside him dressed just like girls she loved to mock.

Before I could do anything, Don hurried to within calling distance, Wanda trailing, not attempting to greet me. "Mrs. Shaffer," Don shouted, "let me introduce my good friend Wanda Grice. She moved here recently from Waycross with her widowed mother."

I glared at Don to no effect. My mother welcomed Wanda, who looked exactly like her notion of a proper young woman, right down to a tamed hairdo, its usual bristling energy drained away.

"Hello," I managed, and Wanda, in keeping with her "good-girl" disguise, replied as if she barely knew me.

I fumed in silence as my mother served peach pie and milk, gently interrogating Wanda in the process. Before long, she knew how Wanda's father died, where her mother worked, even her exact address.

"There are many nice houses out that way," my mother offered.

"Ours isn't that nice," Wanda said, "but it's okay."

"I'm sure it's nice," my mother replied. "Tell me, dear, what church do you attend?"

"Crossroads Baptist." I knew Wanda had never set foot in her mother's church. I also knew she'd won my mother over with her humble replies, all of them true until that last answer. As *Don's* friend, and no rival to Sally, Wanda would be welcomed into the fold. But I wasn't about to stand for such a charade.

And Don would know that soon enough.

But the moment the screen door closed behind my mother, Don spoke in a whisper louder than his usual speaking voice. "This was Wanda's doing, Shaffer. Except for the dress. That was my inspiration."

"Which I hate," Wanda hissed, her old self wasting no time resurfacing. She pointed to the gazebo, kept visible by the rising moon. "Can we go up there where it's private?"

My heart sank, suspecting Wanda was leaving Hopperton. And my conviction deepened on the walk over, as Don furnished a running commentary on the "Waycross mess," especially praising my father, whose doctoring of parental statements he saw as civil disobedience.

"No, Don. Wrong. Negroes protest in the open. They're proud of their cause. They get beaten, go to jail. That's brave. *That's* civil disobedience. My father wasn't brave. He tried to sneak everything through and not get caught."

"I admire your father. I—"

"You both make me want to scream," Wanda snapped. After that, we climbed the slope in silence. I regretted agreeing to this godforsaken trek. I felt jealous, put-upon, and pissed off. No matter why we were here, I vowed, I would make a show of not caring too much. But when we reached the gazebo, the wind fluttered Wanda's dress and carried her floral scent my way, raising an ache in my chest that felt permanent.

Once we sat down, Wanda said, "I like your house."

"Yeah, it's nice. Why did you come over like you were Don's girlfriend?" Maybe I would be pleasant after we cut to the chase.

Don started to talk, but Wanda stopped him.

"I think I'm going to have a baby."

Don's face sagged with shock. My own body seemed to flush every available chemical into its bloodstream, and for a second, my vision went away. Then I looked back and forth at the two of them, and dark thoughts came to me.

"Why is *he* here?" I demanded.

Wanda shot me a cold stare. "Is that all you can think about, Bill? Whether I had sex with Don? Well, I'm not a whore, and Don isn't like you. He'd never try to make me do that."

"*Make* you?"

"That first night you said if I sent you home, you'd never come back, remember?"

I was dumbstruck. "It wasn't like that at all, and you know it," I cried. "I was ready to leave, and you invited me into your room." I looked at Don in the absurd hope that he would take my side. Instead, he piled on.

"My father was right about you, Shaffer."

"That's a laugh," I shouted. "Your father's never been right about any-thing, and neither have you."

Don responded with maddening calm. "So you say, but I'm proud to be my father's son, unlike you, and as such prepared to help Wanda despite her lies."

"What lies?" I croaked, unable to stop myself.

"That she loved me but wanted to remain a virgin until marriage."

"I wish I *was* a virgin," Wanda moaned, letting Don's accusations stand. She looked close to tears.

"I bet even Shaffer wishes that," Don dared to say. I didn't challenge him. Disillusionment owned me. Betrayal and blame owned us all. I can still see the three of us sitting at roughly equidistant points around the gazebo's circling bench, each no doubt believing themselves to be the mistreated apex of our forlorn triangle, Don and I each protecting Wanda against the other, and both of us together offering her nothing but company for her misery.

"Our parents will kill us."

"I have no parents," Don said. "I can be the baby's father. The disgrace means nothing to me."

"I'm sorry about your dad, Don, but I don't want to marry you," Wanda spat out through clenched jaws. "I don't want to marry *anybody*."

"Yes, of course," Don said, his voice carrying an odd hint of excitement. "But don't you see? Your mother despises me. She'll place the blame entirely on my shoulders. We can marry and divorce quickly. The child will have a legal father. And Bill can continue his role as a dutiful son."

"Leave Bill alone," Wanda said. "You're just jealous." Don gave a manic shake of his head, clearly stung.

"On the contrary. As you said, I'm not like—"

"I say a lot of things. Especially when I'm knocked up."

"Are you sure you *are* pregnant?" I asked, bracing for furious indignation. But Wanda simply shrugged.

"I'm pretty sure. I missed my period, and my whole body feels weird all the time."

"Did you tell your mother? Maybe she knows some foolproof way to check."

She shook her head mournfully. "I'll try to tell her tomorrow." With that, she pulled something out of her dress pocket and stuck it between her lips. Cupping a match against a whipping wind, she ignited what looked like a skinny white twig.

"Christ," Don muttered. "Isn't that a federal crime?"

"Call the FBI," Wanda retorted, expelling a massive cloud of smoke. Don batted at the pot haze like it was a reeking death fog, loudly lamenting the "stench."

"It's not the FBI," Don sputtered. "It's the GBI, a *state* bureau."

Wanda, shaking her head, extended the joint to me, and when I declined, offered it to Don, who found no humor in the black joke and stared in horror. I wondered how many illusions about Wanda he had left.

"I think I'll have the baby," Wanda announced in a musing tone as if deciding between harmless alternatives. "My mom and I can go back to

Burlington. When she gets over being mad, she'll love the baby. We'll say its father died or something."

"I, I believe that's wrong," Don stammered. "A father—"

"Shit," Wanda said. "Sorry, Don." She took a last drag, then flipped the still burning remnant into the darkness with one final comment: "This sucks."

No one disagreed, and no one had anything to add. I stepped into the breach with a non sequitur. "Don's mother is coming to Hopperton. It's supposed to be a surprise, but I think—"

"A *surprise*, Shaffer?" Don shouted, lurching to his feet. "What makes you think I want her here? Who else is in on this conspiracy? I demand to know."

"Your father told me to write to her; you can blame him."

"My father?" Don protested in a strangled falsetto. "Why, what possible—"

"Don't crap your pants, Don, I'll tell you later."

"I need you little boys to take me home," Wanda said. "I think I'm too stoned to find my house."

Don and I flanked her like a sullen ceremonial guard to her front gate, as close as we dared get to Mrs. Grice, her movements easily seen through thin window curtains. Wanda "swore to God" she'd talk to her mother, a promise I found equally hateful whether she kept it or not. In any case, we agreed to reconvene at the gazebo Monday evening after dinner; to what end, no one seemed clear.

Without any real farewell, Wanda turned in a kind of sad trance and started toward her door. Right then, I felt worse for her than for myself; the fact that her body carried a growing child, while I bore nothing more than a fear of consequences. But empathy is a far cry from courage, and only much later did it occur to me that I should never have let Wanda walk into that house alone.

On the way home, anxiety coursed through me like a spiking electric current, my state of mind making Don's badgering about his mother intolerable. "The South lost the Civil War," I said finally. "That's my answer to all your questions until we get home."

"Very well, Shaffer, I'll confine myself to statements, such as observing that cause and effect has no definitive beginning or end. Logically, it's impossible to say 'the South lost the Civil War' until the consequences of that war are exhausted. And as you see firsthand, the conflict goes on even in our very school."

"Which you're also losing, and dishonorably at that."

Don vented his offended feelings as I watched clouds hustle across the moon. I remembered the night Sally's necklace broke and how the little moon-like pearls had bounded away like living things trying to escape. Sally had made a point to tell me later that she had gone back and picked up the ones we missed owing to darkness. I imagined her kneeling to retrieve them, wondering glumly what I had become. Now she would know. I realized I would sooner confess Wanda to my mother and father than to Sally, who'd scorned my kiss and now, in the scathing light of day, would see the wisdom of her refusal.

"Cripes, Shaffer," Don exclaimed at one point, "you look like you're heading for the gallows."

"Great. I guess that makes you the hangman."

"On the contrary. I'm the priest trying to save your soul."

So it went between us until we sat down at the kitchen table, the theme song from *Petticoat Junction* leaking in from the parlor. "Here," I said, handing Don the note from Mr. Heffelfinger instructing me to contact his "sister," Greta Miller. He held the paper close to his face, his stubby fingers trembling.

"It says here 'the deed is done,' Shaffer. I hope you told her I didn't murder my dad with the crossbow."

"Holy crap, man, why would she even *think* that? I just told her he disappeared in the swamp. Anyway, she's coming. Then you'll have two mothers, and I'll have *zero*—once mine disowns me." I spoke in a vexed whisper, guilt convincing me my mother might overhear. Don, staring avidly at the note, had probably not heard me at all.

"May I keep this, Shaffer?"

"Sure."

Don folded the note with reverent care and tucked it into his wallet. "Thank you. Now, as to your mother disowning you, perhaps you recall my comment earlier about cause and effect. Whatever your opinion on the fate of the South, you can hardly deny the principle, which is that our personal histories began, in a very real sense, before we were born, do you see?" He paused, waiting for me to catch up, his tone giving the impression of a rehearsed speech.

"Pretty obvious, Don. What's your point?"

"My *obvious* point is that events which began long ago, events you never knew about, shed light on why you and I are sitting here together." Don leaned forward and lowered his voice before continuing. "You see, Mary Carstairs was my father's first love."

I blanked for a second, too lost in my dilemma to recall my mother's maiden name. Then Don's words rushed into focus, his claim of "first love" between his father and my mother eliciting unthinkable images drawn from my own "first love" with Wanda. I couldn't yell with my mother close at hand, so I hissed "you're dead" with all the menace I could muster.

Don waved dismissively and smiled.

"Oh, don't worry, Shaffer, nothing happened. Your mother wrote to my dad during the war, that's all. One of her last letters disclosed that she had a 'beau'—*your* dad. That was that; my dad married Greta Mueller. He told me all about it after he came back from Atlanta that last time. Think of how perfectly cause and effect worked it out! We were both born and became friends. And now we're both in love with Wanda. And you appear destined to win her just as your dad won your mom. It's almost mathematical. And who knows what the next effect is, do you see?"

What I couldn't grasp was Don's cheerfulness. For him, having lost his father and Wanda, the future still promised irrepressible hope. I just didn't buy it.

"'Win Wanda?' I'd be happy to trade places with you," I growled. "I should've gone to the game after I met her in the chess club instead of following her home like a puppy dog. And just so you know, I didn't seduce her. If anything, it was the other way around."

Don kept smiling, irritating me to no end.

"I believe you, Shaffer. I'm beginning to see that it doesn't matter whether *you* prefer a woman who likes you for yourself or sex. What matters is what *she* prefers. My god, think of it, *Atlas Shrugged* was written by a *woman*."

"Whatever, Don. Right now, I don't give a damn."

"Go ahead and pretend not to care; I'm guilty of the same thing. I'm dying to know what sex is like, but do you suppose I'll ever ask you?"

"I wouldn't tell you if you did. And quit gossiping about my mother or I'll punch you in the face. I'm not mad—I know how you love your precious theories. Just a friendly warning, okay?"

All things considered, we headed to our bedrooms on good terms. I could hardly doubt that Philip Heffelfinger might have been in love with my mother or that she wrote to him during the war out of kindness. Evidence remained in how they spoke about each other. And it made sense that Mr. Heffelfinger sought a poor substitute for Mary Shaffer in a German woman. The cosmic twist was Mary Shaffer becoming Don's "true" spiritual mother, completing a weird circle of sorts. But Don spoke about me loving and winning Wanda as if it widened this circle, fulfilling some predetermined pattern. That might be true if Wanda and I were meant for each other, but were we? Even asking the question, I felt, amounted to a discouraging answer. Unable to sleep, I turned on my Philco. An underground Atlanta station played "Dover Beach" by the Fugs, a song whose lyrics were lifted from a poem by Matthew Arnold (which I happened to remember from English class). The song ended like a haunting lullaby with hypnotic repetitions of the poem's famous line:

> Ah Love, let us be true to one another
> Ah Love, let us be true to one another...

How beautiful, I thought as I drifted off. Maybe that was what a good life amounted to—repeating and believing those words, forgetting (if I ever knew) the exquisite pessimism at the heart of the poem:

> ...For the world, which seems
> To lie before us like a land of dreams,
> So various, so beautiful, so new,
> Hath really neither joy, nor love, nor light,
> Nor certitude, nor peace, nor help for pain;
> And we are here as on a darkling plain
> Swept with confused alarms of struggle and flight,
> Where ignorant armies clash by night.

I woke to my secret radio emitting its own version of confused alarms, a turbulent static that scraped away any comfort sleep had provided. Sunday. My trusting mother. Church. Sally Chiles. And the unshakable feeling as I showered, dressed, and walked to the kitchen for pecan waffles that my steps led me to a modern version of the guillotine. And yet the day, blind to my plight, unfolded on the pleasant side of average. Sally's smile suggested that all might be forgiven soon. Don seemed outright happy, accompanying my mother and me to church (only once reasserting his atheism) and peppering me throughout with reassuring glances based on nothing I could detect.

For better or worse, I had my misery to myself. After dinner, I sat on the veranda, watching the low, coloring sky and breathing in the musty scents of rain. Church bells called from all directions. Exactly when, I wondered, does day become night, does *just barely* light become *just barely* dark? The first stars were no help; a few barged into the last faint glow before their time. And as for the sky itself, its sunset's final rays fell unseen behind distant pines. I tried staring at a vase of yellow roses on the table beside me and watched for the instant I could no longer detect its hues. I focused as firmly as I could, but in the end, when only the dark shapes of roses remained, I felt the change had slipped past me, maybe when I had blinked or strayed to a passing thought.

It's easy now to say to my younger self from half a century's distance that one can't see a boundary that's not there; to say that light offers its intensity only as a continuum, without demarcation. But back then, I desperately needed lines to be drawn—unwilled fatherhood or not; married or not; disowned or not—failing to realize that those lines would dissolve as soon as I crossed them, the choice *never* amounting to one thing or another, but just more blurred circumstances on the other side.

What I thought at the time, of course, lacked all philosophical distance and ran more along the lines of *Tuesday's coming like a freight train, and I'm a dead man.*

Then, out in what the vase of roses told me was technically the darkness, I saw two figures walking my way in uneasy mimicry of Don and Wanda the day before, except now it was two women, and surely nothing to do with me. But they held my attention anyway, since they walked through the rain under one umbrella with energetic purpose, unlike typical twilight strollers. When they approached my house, one of them pointed at it, and the other said, "You sure both of them boys are in there?"

CHAPTER THIRTY-ONE

"American Woman"

Mrs. Grice's voice, outraged and implacable, terrorized me, I swear, worse than Mr. Heffelfinger's gun. I stepped back into the darkest corner of the veranda and waited. Mrs. Grice, somehow made more formidable by her green hairnet, stormed to the front door and knocked hard, too intent to notice me. When the porch light came on and Wanda saw me, she raised her hands in a classic helpless gesture. Then I saw her mouth a single, illuminating word—*Don*.

When my mother opened the door, Mrs. Grice softened like butter in the sun. Sensing this (and having no other choice), I stepped forward to muddy the water a little longer, saying, "Good evening, Mrs. Grice. Nice to see you." She spared me an annoyed glance and turned back to my mother.

"Sorry to disturb you on God's holy day," she said in a now deferential, rehearsed voice. "I'm Clarinda Grice, and I guess you know Wanda."

"Why yes," my mother replied. "Don's friend."

"That's a sweet way to put it," Mrs. Grice muttered, beginning to remember why she was here.

"Well, do come in Clarinda, and you too, Wanda. And Bill, please set their umbrella where it won't blow away. I'll put on a pot of tea." I took far longer with the umbrella than needed, awash in Mrs. Grice's potent fragrance, hoping my absence would magically immunize me against the lethal disclosures waiting inside. When I finally went in, my mother was just making her way from the kitchen to the parlor, where Mrs. Grice and

Wanda were seated on the divan. Most horrible of all, I saw my father standing by the piano, making easygoing small talk with Mrs. Grice. Don, on the other hand, remained conspicuously absent. Wanda wore the same dress as yesterday, but the rain and wind had freed her hair from its tidy disguise. She stared blankly ahead like a defendant brought before a judge for sentencing.

"The tea will be right along," my mother said as she sat down on the piano bench. "But in the meantime, Mrs. Grice, what do we owe the pleasure of your visit?" My mother smiled warmly and openly, exhibiting no apprehension about the unexpected guests. After all, she was quite accustomed to extending a helping hand to those in need.

"Where's the other boy?" Mrs. Grice demanded.

"Bill, dear, please go find Donald and tell him he has visitors."

Don wasn't hard to find; he stood in the hall listening. I pointed toward the parlor, not seeing the need to say anything. He didn't say anything either. The weird, silent standoff continued until, to my shock, he turned tail and headed back to his room. I went back to the parlor. "He's getting dressed; he'll be right out."

My father locked eyes with me but spoke to Mrs. Grice.

"I take it you know my son," he said, nodding toward me.

"Him? Yes, he's been by a few times. The polite one, I call him."

My father chuckled without mirth.

"Well, Maggie gets credit for that. And I suppose it's a quality every mother looks for in a young man who's courting her daughter."

"It's a start, sure enough," Mrs. Grice conceded, trapped into confirming my father's suspicions.

"So, Mrs. Grice," my father continued in his calmest, most disarming voice, "matters in addition to neighborliness sent you out into the rain, I suspect."

She nodded. "You might say, you might say. See, that other boy stopped me on the way home from church and told me Wanda was *expecting*, and he was the daddy. But Wanda said that wasn't true."

"Excuse me," my mother interjected. "What wasn't true?" As she asked, she crossed her legs and leaned forward to hug her knees. I'd never seen her do that before.

"That's what *I* wanted to know, particularly since Wanda has all the signs. Her titties are sore, and she's warm to the touch."

"I never even kissed Don; he's a liar."

"In that case," my mother said, "perhaps a doctor's examination—"

"I'm most likely pregnant, Mrs. Shaffer. I've even got blood spots."

My mother turned to Mrs. Grice and said, "What help would you like us to offer? My church—"

"What help? Lord in heaven, what kind of question is that?"

My father stared me down again as he spoke. "Maggie means well, ma'am. No one means better. She is simply confused, as you might imagine. Perhaps Bill can clear up the confusion."

I stood there, paralyzed with dread, my gaze fixed on the piano keys behind my father, my mind idiotically counting them. Before long, I would have to speak, but not yet.

"Mr. Shaffer, sir," Don called unexpectedly from behind me. "I'm the baby's father. *Miss* Grice will deny it because she's in love with Bill. But *Mrs.* Grice knows who visits Wanda, isn't that right, ma'am?" I suppose the only lawyers I knew about back then were Clarence Darrow and Atticus Finch, but Don certainly shared their gift. Mrs. Grice nodded and jabbed her finger at Don.

"That one comes at all hours and never stops talking; he would try the patience of Job."

"Mom, like I told you, we never did anything *but* talk." Wanda looked at me, still stopping tortuously short of naming me as the father. I knew she was waiting for me to accuse myself.

"It's me," I whispered, feeling I had just placed a curse on my mother, nullifying all the goodness in her life. My father's opinion of me would sink but had not nearly as far to fall.

"Sir," Don cried. "Bill is only confessing that he *could* be the father. Maybe that's true, or maybe he's just trying to protect me as a loyal friend would do. Either way, I'm prepared to swear on my father's honor that I'm the child's likely father."

"He's crazy," Wanda shouted.

"Now, now," Mrs. Grice said, patting Wanda's leg. "Let's ask the *gentleman* how we go about finding out." She gave my father a shrewd look.

"I assume you mean verify paternity," my father replied. "As far as I know, there's no sure way."

"What about their blood?"

"Again, I assume both of them have red blood."

"It doesn't matter," Wanda said. "I'm *not* getting married. You have to love somebody to get married. If you don't, *that's* a sin." She'd been sitting forward, chewing gum nervously. Now she threw herself back with defiant force and folded her hands across her belly. My mother looked at me then, appraising. If Wanda wasn't in love with me or looking to trap a husband, then what motive did she have but the truth to name me as the father?

"Whichever one of these fools is the culprit," my father said, "they live under my roof. Either way, I'm responsible. So—"

Mrs. Grice jumped in. "We'd appreciate a little bit of money now and then; you can use my brother's address in North Carolina. We mean to say the baby's daddy died fighting overseas."

"Lying about death brings death," Don called out, invoking a superstition I knew he just invented and didn't believe.

"Wanda," my mother said, her voice more delicate and serene than I could have imagined, "I wouldn't expect you to marry my son or anyone if you felt it trapped you in sin. I would only ask you to pray on that notion, perhaps talk to a clergyman. I see that Bill has sinned against you, but we all fall short, as I have in guiding him. He's a good young man, as I'm sure you know in your heart."

"I never claimed Bill sinned against me. He's sweet. He gave me this beautiful necklace. But when people get married, they have babies, maybe a whole passel of them. After I have this one, that's it for a long, long time."

"We have as many as God grants us," my mother replied. "Bill is our only child, but he is a wonderful blessing."

Mrs. Grice made a noise approaching a snicker as she fumbled open the clasp of her large purse, pulled out a pack of Pall Malls, and looked around for a nonexistent ashtray. "*That* boy," she said, pointing her cigarette at Don, "told me different. He accused your boy; said he was a communist and believed in race mixing."

Before I could reply to these indictments, Don rushed forward with an ashtray for Mrs. Grice, adroitly keeping his back to me.

"Now, ma'am, I only meant to say Bill was sympathetic to integration and the so-called peace movement. I admit he's a federalist and weak on individualism, but that's quite separate from issues of character..." Mrs. Grice drew back as if Don had rampant leprosy.

"Whoa, Nellie," my father called. "Mrs. Grice, how about you, Maggie, and me going to my study for a short business meeting? You want to smoke, and I need a cigar and strong Georgia tea. And you three"—he fixed me like a target as he spoke, glowering with disgust—"sit here and stew in your juices. We're not done with you."

"Yes, sir," I said with ritual meekness, my attention fixed on my mother as she scrutinized Wanda's ruby necklace. Yet more hell to pay, I knew, after my mother telephoned Aunt Miriam wondering if she was missing any jewelry, only to find that her sister conspired with her wayward son in furtherance of his clandestine romance.

"Stick to your guns, Wanda," Mrs. Grice admonished as she lumbered out. "Don't listen to no devilish ideas."

I sat down on the far end of the sofa from Wanda, her mother's artificial scent floating between us like a miasma. Don paced as if to present a moving target and, before accusations could fly, began a rapid-fire justification of his Sunday morning encounter with Mrs. Grice, explaining it in military terms such as "divide and conquer" and "strategic diversion." This went on for maybe a minute before Wanda interrupted with a loud, caustic cackle. "A wise boy knows the smell of his own shit, Don. I can smell it over here." As Don translated Wanda's words from her dialect into his, I could see the bravado draining out of him. He slumped, took his glasses off, and wiped his sleeve across his eyes. A verbal duel with me was one thing; facing genuine derision from Wanda was quite another.

"Your . . . your mother misinterpreted my—"

"You talked Bill down; you showed your tail." Wanda leaned forward and checked the door before continuing in a low voice. "Your karma is way, way worse than bad. And if you blab about me at school, I'll make Abel Theroux kill you, which he might do anyway."

Don blinked, reddened, backed into the furthest chair available. A glum silence overtook us, a perverse circle of sorts completed: nature had punished Wanda, my father would punish me, and now Wanda had punished Don. Accusations, confessions, betrayals, denials, lies and truths, conscious and unconscious motives, writhed inside me like a mental snake pit, impossible to untangle or escape. I thought about *The Dark Warrior*. My novel couldn't be just battles. My hero, John Freeman Kent would have a half-brother, also in love with Delia Wingfoot. A perfect name for him would be Kyle Knight Kent.

My father sat me down in a hard arrow-back chair across from his leather smoking recliner and explained there would be no punishment. There would, however, be consequences. "I paid Mrs. Grice a lump sum to close the books on the matter," he explained. I dreaded his businesslike voice worse than a raging scold. "The amount was fair but substantial. Since the plant is closing at the end of the year, as I have just been informed, your mother and I are in no position to fund your college expenses in the immediate future. Besides, further schooling would be a waste until you grow up and acquire a solid character. Your mother will want you close by, working in town, but I believe you would fare better elsewhere. People hereabouts will wonder why you're not off to college or the armed services, and they will know soon enough unless we keep Donald in his room with duct tape over his mouth."

"Don won't say a word; he promised Wanda he'd rather die than lose her . . . blow his chances with her."

My father chuckled at this optimistic absurdity. "Don is an excitable boy with a big mouth. He won't keep quiet, and he won't die as a consequence. You must know that."

Rather than concede the point, as honesty demanded, I changed the subject. "Is the plant closing because of the dead guy?"

"'Dead guy' is disrespectful, Bill. Larry Lasker was one of my best men."

I nodded but said nothing, letting my question stand. My father sat very still in his recliner, deciding, I suppose, if I merited an answer. "The plant's closing because it's no longer a going concern, Bill. Elixapine itself will follow suit in short order unless I miss my guess. And after that, well, there will be little enough work for Americans since people in less fortunate countries will work for nothing."

"Don's mother is coming to Hopperton," I informed him. My father would have to fix the crosshairs on me; I wasn't about to do it for him.

"Yes. Donald told me. Out of earshot from your mother. Another mess you're mixed up in unless the boy is lying."

"Don never lies. He just always gets the story wrong."

"Well, *someone's* been lying, Bill. Are you a Negro sympathizer who runs with the peace crowd, or aren't you?"

I had expected this question and tried to sound offhand.

"I just think all men are created equal, like it says in the Declaration of Independence. And I guess I go along with the Bible when it says blessed are the peacemakers."

My father gave a dry chuckle and shook his head. "How you ever came to think integration and appeasement lead to peace and equality I'll never know. If it's peace you want, go back to before all this race nonsense started. And I'm all for equal Negro schools, but our taxpayers squeal already, and there's likely to be one wage earner less pretty soon."

"If segregation was so great, you wouldn't need to lie to keep it." A trace of venom leaked into my tone.

My father looked hard at me then but recovered enough to speak evenly.

"I take your point. And without college studies to interfere, you'll have plenty of time to make that point as often as you please. Who knows? You may even run across a man who isn't a liar." He tapped his ashes into the old beer stein handed down from his father, and I felt him recede into private thoughts. "But listen, Bill, we mustn't let your mother hear such talk, agreed?"

"Yes, sir." My gut turned sick and cold at the thought of facing her alone over morning coffee.

My father dismissed me without mentioning Wanda. He did reach into his wallet and hand me ten dollars. "Here, buy yourself some rubbers."

To my undeserved relief, my mother laid it all at the feet of God and His plan, according to which Wanda and I had succumbed to the serpent, like modern-day Adam and Eve. While wistful about what might have been, she didn't resist removing her possible grandchild to a distant state, and I wondered (without evidence either way) if seeing Sally and Mrs. Chiles in church every week influenced her outlook. Despite Wanda's rebuke, Don still pressed his paternal claim, hinting at a brilliant and mysterious motive. Wanda quit school, her reason camouflaged by other absent Waycross students who had relied on now-canceled bus service. I imagined daring her window one more time, not for sex, but to say something eloquent that would make her at least regret her decision to leave. I didn't, of course, but in any case, such fantasies got shoved aside when Greta Miller arrived, chauffeured from Birmingham by Aunt Miriam in a rented gold Chrysler Imperial.

I happened to be alone on the veranda when Greta Miller stepped out of the Chrysler, needing only uniformed ushers to complete the illusion of a movie star attending a Hollywood premiere. She and the Chrysler comprised, in fact, the two most expensive-looking things I ever saw in Hopperton. I stood and advanced toward a tall, deeply tanned woman surefooted on shiny high heels. She wore oversized sunglasses and wrapped herself in an opulent fur shawl later identified as sable. She lowered her glasses to greet me, revealing soul-melting blue eyes and a smile that put to rest any aloof Garbo comparison.

"You are the young Herr Shaffer," she declared, her accent —devoid of the barking gutturals I associated with German—caressing perfect English. As I groped for a less than fatuous reply, I heard the screen door swing open and saw Greta Miller's face erupt with joy. "And you," she trumpeted, "are my Donald." She brushed past me then, leaving me face to face with Aunt Miriam, who looked frazzled and spoke without her usual courtesies.

"Bill, I'm sorry about the mess you're in, but before I set foot in that house and confront my sister, I need to know if you gave that girl my necklace to get sex."

"No ma'am, I swear."

"You had . . . prior experiences?"

I nodded with averted eyes.

"If you're lying, you'll go to hell and probably drag me down with you."

"I'm telling the truth." For once, I was.

"And when were you going to tell your poor mother about Frau Miller, as she calls herself? Don't you think she's had enough surprises?"

"Shit," I mumbled.

"Yes, that's exactly what you've done. But don't worry; I warned Mary." She shook her head and motioned toward the reuniting pair on the veranda. "Two of the strangest peas you'll ever find in a pod." I turned to see Don and Greta Miller entering the house, laughing together like old friends. At what I could not imagine.

By the time Aunt Miriam and I joined the gathering inside, my mother had already uncorked a bottle of holiday wine for "Margarethe," who answered to Greta but preferred "Gigi," and insisted on pouring a glass of wine for everyone to toast Don's new life of private schools and skiing lessons. "Bill's only exposure to wine is taking communion," my mother said, in the end allowing me a "small glass as a tonic." During the toast, she raised her glass without drinking. Afterward, she confronted

"Gigi" with the last question I expected. "Am I to take it you are still Mrs. Heffelfinger?"

Don's mother, in the manner of a politician, answered what had not been asked.

"I have always been Donald's mother, but—life is cruel. Best to accept the truth and go forward, *nein*? Miriam tells me motherhood has been cruel to you recently. We understand each other, yes?"

"I wish we did," my mother replied, "but I've only just met you. And I'm not sure what cruelty you speak of." She didn't bother to spare a glance toward Aunt Miriam. "As for my question, I am admittedly curious about your . . . lengthy absence. Not to condemn you but, as you say, to understand you."

"She wasn't welcome here!" Don cried. "My dad said people treated her like a *Nazi*."

"No, Donald," his mother corrected, "that is ridiculous. You must not believe so easily." She swung around to face my mother, tapping cigarette ashes delicately into the ashtray left from Clarinda Grice's visit. "Since you do not understand me, I will explain. Philip had written to me from America to propose. I believed myself pregnant by a bad German man, so I accepted. Do you see? Of course, I was not honest. I waited to reach America before confessing my condition. Philip was furious. He found revenge by telling me he loved an American woman who had married while he was a prisoner of war. He admitted he settled for *me* out of loneliness. We could not forgive each other, so after Donald was born, I left. Philip wished to raise Donald, to teach him certain beliefs filled with false pride. Since I knew we would only fight about this, I stayed away. For Donald's sake as I saw it. But perhaps I was wrong." She paused then, shrugged philosophically, took a swallow of wine, and continued to fix her gaze on my mother, who must have known, if Greta Miller did not, that she was the "American woman."

"Thank you," my mother said, betraying nothing. I watched Don, whose face had been afflicted with distress since his mother accused his father of "false pride." God only knew what he might blurt out.

Aunt Miriam spoke then. "Yes, thank you. It's quite bracing to hear such honesty. We Southerners tend to tiptoe politely around personal matters. You'd almost think such things didn't happen down here."

"Is Donald to finish school in Hopperton?" my mother inquired. "Perhaps there are legalities to consider. We know a fine lawyer." Sally's father, who would tell Sally everything.

"I have my papers." Greta Miller tapped her large, shiny black purse.

"She has my dad's letters," Don added. "Once we talk to Wanda and Mrs. Grice tomorrow, I'll decide about staying."

Before anyone could conjure up a reply, Greta Miller said, "Donald's first words to me were to insist I meet this young woman." My mother met these words with an unaccustomed force.

"Mrs.— Gigi, Donald has an imaginative attraction to Wanda, but I'm not sure—"

"It's not imaginary," Don said hotly. "She may be having my child."

"Gigi," my mother said, "I'm not suggesting Donald is making things up. But I feel obliged to tell you that my husband made financial arrangements on behalf of Wanda and her child that do not concern your son. You may speak to the Grices, of course, but please be prepared to replace our arrangement with one of your own."

Greta Miller gave a knowing smile mingling respect and amusement. "Frau Shaffer," she said, "in a different life, you and I would have been best friends."

CHAPTER THIRTY-TWO

"Nowhere Man"

The Heffelfingers, mother and son, motored off the next morning (chauffeured by an eye-rolling Aunt Miriam) on their bizarre pilgrimage to the Grice household, Don waving triumphantly at me as they pulled away. I felt he'd gone slightly mad or, emboldened by Greta Miller's appearance, had taken the brakes off the looniness he'd always possessed. Either way, I was thrilled to have no part to play in his ludicrous excursion. I had enough drama as it was, dominated by the premonition that I would be leaving town soon, never to return. My mother behaved even more tenderly to me now that she knew she was losing me. She cooked my favorite foods—stuffed pork chops and fried chicken with biscuits and gravy—acts of love which nevertheless made me feel like a prisoner eating his last meal.

As soon as the mammoth Chrysler pulled away, a despairing restlessness seized me. Without any particular destination in mind, I set out toward the other end of town, paying acute attention to the people I passed: older ladies in modest print dresses buttressed by sweaters and hats; younger women in bright skirts and blouses, most still sporting country music singer hairdos on the wane in hipper parts of the country; men either neatly dressed in pressed pants and shirts or, oblivious to matters of style, in worn farm overalls. Some I knew and greeted briefly. Two were classmates I had no appetite to encounter. All of them seemed at peace with themselves, free from the inner torment and outward disgrace bedeviling my ruined life. At the Rialto's dilapidated marquee (*Drums in*

301

the *Deep South* paired with *Bikini Beach*), I ran out of emotional gas. I stopped dead, half expecting someone to approach me and demand an explanation. For what I couldn't say. Had I known where Mr. Pee lived, I might have walked there. Instead, I headed back to my house, but without any sense of homecoming. I stopped across from the gazebo and watched two doves on a fence rail flutter against each other for a few seconds, then perch motionless, one tucking itself under its companion's breast. Even when I passed them on my way up the slope, they failed to take wing, as if love protected them against all dangers.

I sat in the gazebo with my back to the lovestruck doves, staring at clouds piling toward a thunderstorm. Amid this meager reverie, Wanda called out from behind me.

"It's me, Bill. I was on my way to the Piggly Wiggly and saw you." She sounded forlorn, vulnerable, tired.

"Hi," I said. Wanda sat down next to me rather than across from me.

"Hi."

She smelled like the summer lilies my mother grew. "Why were you walking to the store?" I asked for want of a better question. I had no stomach to hear about her meeting with Don and his mother, though I knew with a sinking heart that I would.

"Mom took our Mercury to a garage. It needs a rebuilt carburetor fixed before we leave. I need stuff for my stomach, so…"

"Are you sick?"

"Not exactly. My mom says it's for in case I puke."

"Do you want me to walk with you?"

Wanda made a small sound that might have been a laugh but wasn't. "Like you're helping an old lady cross the street?"

"No."

After a pause, she said, "Don's leaving town with his mother. I guess you knew that."

"No, I didn't. Shit. Right away? Is that why he came over? To tell you that?"

"No. It was crazy. Don's mom dressed like a movie star. Red lipstick to make her lips look big. She went on about how Don wasn't the baby's father, how he was a brilliant young man with terrible ideas. I thought he would crap in his pants when he heard this. He started to talk, but she shushed him. She apologized for his 'strange behavior' and—get

302

this—gave my mom *five hundred dollars* for the trouble he caused. I felt sorry for him. I know he ratted on you to my mother, and that was shitty, but I mean, he didn't cause me any trouble that wasn't coming anyway, right? When I said I wasn't mad at him, my mom freaked out. I guess she wanted that money. She swore he caused *her* a lot of headaches, acted like he ruined her life. Grown-ups are *so* full of it."

"His mother's smart. She wants to make sure Don's off the hook. I guess it worked."

"Yeah."

"How do you know he's leaving town? Wasn't he pissed at his mother?"

"Maybe at first. He kept wanting to talk, and finally, she said, 'Only if you're truthful, Donald.' She sounded scary with her German accent, you know? And she stared him down like a cop or something. He kept looking back and forth between her and me. Then he cracked and admitted, 'Okay, maybe I'm not the baby's father, but she'—meaning me—'agreed to have sex,' which meant I *wanted* him to be the father. Like I said—crazy."

"He came right out and said you agreed to have sex with him? Don tells fibs sometimes, but damn."

Wanda grimaced and shifted around as if in physical discomfort.

"Well, he kept bugging me all those times he came over, wouldn't give it a rest. Finally, one time I called his bluff, that's all. As soon as I said 'yes,' he said 'no'; he just wanted me to *prove* my love. He never even tried to kiss me. I don't know if he prefers boys, you know, like Bobby Heatwole, or whether he's more like, you know, a priest. But I never would have done it anyway, Bill, I swear."

"That's about what I figured," I lied.

"Anyway," she continued, "after his little confession, he smiled at his mother like she was an angel from heaven. Then we ate molasses cookies, and they left. At the door, Don told me my baby was the last link in a long chain and destined to do great things. It made no sense, but at least it was nice." At that, Wanda leaned her head on my shoulder. I felt any sense of grievance between us melt away, leaving me with an unbearable tenderness.

"I guess you're leaving," I said as gruffly as I could manage.

"As soon as the car's fixed."

"Why did you say you loved the shit out of me? I'm not saying you should, but I was just wondering."

She didn't answer directly but patted her belly instead. "I can't believe your baby is growing in me. If it's a boy, I'll name it after you if my mom lets me. What's your middle name?"

"Jefferson."

"Maybe I'll try to name it Jeff."

"I hope it's a girl."

"A *wise* girl, way wiser than me. I was thinking of naming her Delia if you promise me one thing."

"What?"

"That you'll keep me in your book like you said. Remember? That first night we . . . made out."

"I remember. It was my first time. You were my first time for everything."

"Do you promise?"

"I swear. I'll make you famous."

"In that case, I *do* love the shit out of you. But it's not the right kind of love for marriage. Someday you'll thank me for setting you free."

I didn't argue but had my doubts, as I do to this day. It's possible I would have been happier with Wanda than with the very different life I happened to lead, one in which no one ever again professed to love the shit out of me, despite public vows to that effect.

I walked Wanda to the store, never thinking to confess I loved the shit out of *her*. She let me carry her grocery sack of Alka-Seltzer, Milk of Magnesia, Jell-O, Pop-Tarts, Lipton soup mix, sour cream, and *Seventeen* magazine. I could not forget those items if I wished to. We didn't say much. Neither the past nor the future cried out for discussion. I wanted to hold hands, but that didn't happen until the last block before Wanda's house, when she grabbed mine and squeezed hard, like someone taking off in a plane for the first time.

"I don't know your address," she said. "Give it to Betty Jean at school, and I'll write to you." She told me where I'd most likely run into Betty Jean and what was wrong with the Mercury, which got us to her front door. The sack of groceries stood absurdly in the way of any romantic farewell, but I doubt I'd have held up my end of it anyway. After a quick kiss and "Goodbye, Bill," Wanda took her groceries and turned without looking back. I watched until the screen slapped closed behind her.

"Off you go then," I said under my breath. It hit me then that I'd forgotten to talk to her about *Siddhartha*. It seemed a great pity to have missed that chance.

"Fuck me," I muttered, then headed home.

With one notable exception, Don verified Wanda's version of his visit as we sat on the veranda feasting for the last time on my mother's ham and tomato sandwiches.

"When Wanda said 'yes,' Shaffer, I didn't say 'no' as she claims. I simply couldn't *perform*, Shaffer, a blow to my pride like no other, I tell you. That's why I needed to be the father, as my mother explained to me, and it makes perfect sense."

"You told your *mother* what? That you couldn't get a hard-on?"

"She has a way of getting to the bottom of things. It's uncanny. She says she understands me better than I understand myself. Not my theories, mind you, but my 'personal outlook' as she calls it. She wants to *invest* in me. A physical fitness trainer. Psychoanalysis. I've decided it's *auf wiedersehen* and *semper amici*, Shaffer." He raised a glass of tea in salute, but to what I had no idea.

"Speak English, Don," I grumbled, unable not to wonder how naked or clothed Wanda had been when Don called a halt to the proceedings. Had she scared him off by reaching for a button? Or had his flesh, confronted with her emerging nakedness, failed the spirit? Or had he recreated the whole event in his distorted image? At the time, I would've given up a year of life to know. Nowadays, I want the years back I spent grinding away at unanswerable questions like those.

"Oh, that means 'goodbye' and 'friends forever,'" Don explained. "But rest assured, I will write to you from New Hampshire. And I'm leaving you my copy of *Atlas Shrugged* for old time's sake. My mother has promised me a hardback copy! Its truth—its *Wahrheit*—is waiting for you when you're ready."

Don's cheery, pompous air annoyed me to no end. He had bought into his mother's nonsense, worshiping her on sight, adding her to the holy trinity completed by Ayn Rand and his father. Worse yet, my importance to him was fading by the hour.

"You should keep your father's chess set," I said. "I don't think I'll be playing much from now on."

In the next couple of days, Don and Wanda withdrew from school, Wanda's departure blending in with other withdrawals by Waycross kids—mainly those now deprived by politics of a free bus ride. Without my companions, I walked the Hopperton High corridors like a dazed ghost. I wanted to talk to Sally, but my clumsy kiss and her broken pearls—or rather my reenactment of those disasters—barred the way. At home, I sensed a struggle between my mother and father for the fate of my soul. Ordinarily, I would bet on my mother, but my instincts told me the tide was turning otherwise. None of my words or deeds lately, other than driving Mr. Heffelfinger's pickup truck under duress, sat well with my father. I wondered what had gone his way recently; precious little, I imagined. He wasn't smiling much, and he holed up in his study with his cigars more often than I could ever remember. Not a recipe for magnanimity.

One event that did coax a smile from him occurred when Greta Miller—squeezing his arm like Sally used to squeeze mine—convinced him to handle any remaining affairs concerning her missing husband. He likely didn't know that Philip Heffelfinger was Mary Carstairs's early, passionate admirer and wartime pen pal. But I felt dead sure Greta Miller had learned it during her "glorious reunion" with big-mouth Don. In any case, she fawned over my father until he agreed.

"Why, Ed," Aunt Miriam commented with the devil's own grin. "That's the most Christian thing I've ever known you to do."

A day soon came when Don and I played our last chess game. His victory, he proclaimed, foreshadowed "the shape of things to come." The next day he left, bound for Birmingham in a golden automotive chariot equipped with *two* air conditioners, on his way to living among Yankee carpetbaggers. He and I were boys; our goodbye wasn't much. It didn't help that I blamed him for leaving or that he could barely bother with acknowledging it, given the intrigue of his "rebirth." For me, sentiment set in later, and I suppose this account is proof of that. My mother's kindness forbade her to cling to him or to remind him of any obligation. She made a basket of food for the trip: roast beef sandwiches, potato salad, peach cobbler. Aunt Miriam hugged my mother a long time before pulling out onto Stagecoach Road to pick up 441.

My mother waved and said, "I do hope…" After which, her voice trailed off. A few minutes later, I found the chess set and *Atlas Shrugged* on my dresser with a note: "My mother says chess is a Russian game and wishes me to abandon it. It's the least I can do in return. I will write to Ayn Rand to ask her opinion on this. Quite fascinating! Warmest regards, Don H."

Wanda left not long after. On her way out of town, she called me from a pay phone to say goodbye. I felt horrible, like I'd buried her and her baby in an unmarked grave. At home, I made no mention, listening instead to my father remind me that my eighteenth birthday and the end of high school were less than two months away, after which I needed to become gainfully employed or otherwise account for myself through my efforts.

"We've tried raising you your mother's way," he told me one morning as we transplanted a dogwood. I'm sure those words had long been stuck in his craw and probably deserved to be said. But I found them unforgivable, denigrating my mother and proving that my father never loved me. I suppose Freud would say the icy abyss I then placed between myself and my father constituted classic Oedipal behavior. A cruder way to say it is that things got where they were going, and neither my father nor I knew how to stop them.

"Don't worry; I'll be leaving soon," I retorted, not bothering to stop shoveling and taking a fierce, dark pleasure in uttering the words.

"Well," he replied, unmoved by my declaration, "I don't doubt you'll do what you want to do, come hell or high water. I've spent my whole life around men like that." I had joined their ranks in my father's eyes—men like Tom Fields, the troublemaking malcontent, or the man he'd fired that day for fighting over a woman.

"I'll do better than anybody in this town. Way better."

"Could be, just a bunch of country folks hereabouts. Shouldn't be that hard."

As busy as I kept myself afterward trying to hate my father, our dogwood quarrel would seem like a pleasant prelude compared to what followed. Don had heeded Wanda's demand that he keep his mouth shut about her condition, but Wanda had not. She told Betty Jean everything, the same Betty Jean I appalled at the Harvest Hop with my "drunken" behavior, the same Betty Jean who had stopped smiling at me or asking me to tutor her in math, the same Betty Jean needed to forward my address to Wanda. As soon as Wanda left, Betty Jean began enthusiastically airing the dirty linen she had inherited, starting with Sally Chiles. Sally later confided to me how the scandal erupted, bringing it full circle. By the end of the school day, only kids too strange or unpopular to have friends were in the dark about how Bill Shaffer had gotten a girl pregnant, forced her to leave town, and gone his merry way afterward as if nothing had happened. Within another twenty-four hours, every influential adult in Hopperton had heard the same story—meaning every friend and business associate of my parents. It hardly mattered that Bill Shaffer had *not* forced a girl to leave town, or that his "way" felt anything but merry. The "pregnant" part tended to overshadow those nuances.

The dam broke in the form of phone calls to my mother beginning about five o'clock the day after Betty Jean spread the news like a raging virus. Of course, I could only hear my mother's "half" of the conversations: "yes, it's terrible," "thank you for your prayers," "at the young woman's house, I suppose," and, in a vain attempt to save me, "Bill's very sorry she refused to marry him." At six, about the time my father usually got home, my mother took the phone off the hook, sank into her favorite parlor chair, and wept softly.

I saw all this and approached her, close to tears myself, and tried to stammer out words equal to my remorse. She waved me away, saying, "No, Bill, this is not the time."

I understood—maybe better than my mother. Any apology that mattered lay behind us now—and no road back. My father would be home tonight to find no dinner waiting for perhaps the first time in his married life. I left my mother to her sorrow and sat on the veranda to intercept him. When the blue Caddy rumbled into the driveway, I stood up. My father saw me but didn't wave. "Everybody knows," I stammered when he reached the steps, unable to look at him. "And Mother's been crying."

"The buzzards are circling," he said. "Well, let's go in and sort this out. I'll not have Maggie Shaffer hung on somebody else's cross." He had not only seen a public scandal coming but had also devised a counterattack. After comforting my mother and exchanging words with her in a low, tense voice, he called Mr. Lipscomb, the high school principal, and confirmed that I'd already met the graduation requirements. After that, he called Sally's father, not bothering to shield the conversation from me.

"Tubby," he thundered, "I'm sure you know my boy got a girl pregnant. I wonder if you could have your missus call the other biddies and tell them we're sending Bill to military school and to please quit calling here. Poor Maggie doesn't know anything. Bill and that girl did their business in secret. We sure as perdition weren't invited to *that* party."

CHAPTER THIRTY-THREE

"Dixie"

My father decided the military school fiction made a better story than the truth: a job waiting for me in Lake City, Florida, working in a friendly competitor's turpentine plant, which, my father made a point to emphasize, I was free to turn down if I had a more high-minded path to pursue. "Either way, don't worry about going to school tomorrow," he declared. "You'll get your diploma, but *you're done.*" Then he set my eighteenth birthday, coming up in mid-April, as my day of decision. In the meantime, I could do as I liked—as if Hopperton offered anything now I was apt to enjoy doing.

And what did Hopperton offer my father, I wondered? His face showed sadness and wear on my account, certainly, but the Waycross school business and Elixapine's demise had taken their toll as well. I had a vague sense of our parallel undoing and asked, "What are *you* going to do?"

His eyes widened at the nerve of my question, but he answered. "I'm going to close down the plant, hope there's still a pension waiting, then take your mother on a nice long vacation, maybe New Mexico. I heard you can get a good look at the stars out there, even see a flying saucer. Then we'll come back, and if my pension falls through, I'll work somewhere until I drop dead."

I sat there under my father's baleful gaze, nodding stupidly, thinking about the stars and flying saucers over New Mexico I would never see.

The next evening, when the bell rang during dinner, my father jumped up, usurping my mother's role as greeter. She and I sat in silence, listening.

I expected to hear my father shoo away a nosy member of one of my mother's clubs, but instead, I heard Mr. Pee introduce himself as Hiram Peebles, "Master Shaffer's" history teacher.

"Bill's not playing hooky," my father said gruffly. "He's off to military school." I got up and walked to the foyer, making sure Mr. Pee could see me.

"Ah, Bill," Mr. Pee said. "Good, I see you haven't left yet." Then to my father: "Bill is my shining star. His new school will be lucky to have him." Mr. Pee, dressed in a rumpled blue suit and clashing plaid vest, then stood to wait for my father to acknowledge the compliment.

"I guess you know the circumstances," my father growled, intent on putting a stop to any cheery nonsense.

"Circumstances? No, not at all. It would be disingenuous of me to say I hadn't heard rumors, but none of them featured any circumstances." My father grimaced at this undue bit of subtlety. Mr. Pee, with a book tucked under one arm and a bowler hat cradled in the other, kept beaming at my father, waiting for a reply. My father had nothing to say, only wishing to bid this oddly dressed interloper good night. Fortunately, my mother's appearance broke the impasse. Seeing her, my father crossed his arms and shifted as if to intercept contact between her and Mr. Pee.

"Why hello, Mr. Peebles," my mother said, a little light reentering her face. "I remember you from PTA meetings. Won't you come in?"

Mr. Pee glanced at my father, then said, "Alas, Mrs. Shaffer, I'm on my way to a function, but I wanted to bid farewell to my prize student and present him with a parting gift." Satisfied now that Mr. Pee represented neither threat nor extreme bother, my father offered a stiff goodnight and returned to his pot roast and baked potato. As soon as he faced away from them, I saw my mother and Mr. Pee exchange a look of mutual sympathy, telling me that Mr. Pee knew more of "circumstances" than he professed to my father. And beyond any doubt, my mother knew that Don—not me—was Mr. Pee's "prize student." But things stood as they stood, and in a moment, after exchanging courtesies with my mother, Mr. Pee turned to me and said, "Bill, do you mind walking me out? The book I have for you requires a short but tedious explanation."

We stepped outside. I gulped air free of cooking smells and cigar smoke, free of reproachful, disappointed faces, and imagined leaving prison after an unjust sentence. Mr. Pee handed me a thick book—*The Story of Philosophy* by Will Durant. "It's a history of sorts," he elaborated,

"but of ideas, not kings and wars. I worry there might be educational deficiencies in your new school."

"There's no new school. I'm getting kicked out. That's all."

"Ah. Well, you and I have much in common. Read this book and try
not to feel sorry for yourself. At your age, you should be looking out, not
in. *Quo vadis?* as they say, not *in quo et vos?*" Mr. Pee caught my blank
stare and said, "Forgive me, Bill; I attended Catholic school all through
my youth. We were required to attend mass, cultivate cursive handwriting,
and learn Latin. It pops out from time to time of its own accord. 'Whither
goest thou?' I mean to say, is more important than 'where didst thou go?'"

I nodded, not minding *his* foreign words, only wishing to seem worthy
of such erudition. "Sir, someone told me that a wise girl holds no opinion.
What do you think of that?"

Mr. Pee put on his hat and swatted at an erratic moth.

"An ancient thought, quite out of fashion. But one I happen to endorse.
Opinions dam the river that carries you onward. And I would further say
that whatever young woman told you that probably has no future in this
town either."

Either.

"She's already gone," I said, guessing Mr. Pee had deciphered my connection to the "wise girl."

"I'm sorry, Bill. But as I told young Mr. Heffelfinger, luck is as likely
to favor you from time to time as not. Either way"—he tapped the book I
held—"these thinkers may help you . . . live beyond the easy reach of luck
and make the best of exile."

"I'll read every word of it; I swear." The guilty thought crossed my
mind that I placed more faith in Mr. Pee and his book than I ever had in
God and *His* book. Then, not knowing how to end things, I said, "I guess
you're off to a meeting."

"No, that was a ruse of the moment. I'm just going home to talk to
my old black cat. She makes many demands, but requiring me to lie is not
one of them."

Cars slowed down now when they passed our house. My mother would've
perished to know I waved back at them as I sat defiantly on the veranda
reading Mr. Pee's book. Still, she surely sensed a change in me beyond
the scandal's effect. The morning after Mr. Pee's visit, I mentioned to my

mother at breakfast that "Negro news" in the Hopperton paper never exceeded a small paragraph. And why, I wondered, did they separate Negro news from other news in the first place? "It says here Lucille Jones died, what church she attended, and that she left behind a husband and four children. Why does it matter whether she's a Negro or not? Is it so white people don't have to care?"

"Why, Bill, what a terrible thing to say!" My mother dropped her fork and stared at me in shock.

"Why is it terrible, Mother?"

"Why? Because you are assuming the worst of people. I believe you are placing your troubled thoughts into other hearts. You are a good person, Bill, something I fear you no longer believe."

"I believe I'm better than a *lot* of folks in Hopperton; at least I don't hate colored people."

My mother paled but didn't speak to my accusation. Instead, she retrieved the family Bible from the parlor and presented it to me. "Bill, I confess before God that I have felt sorrier for myself than for you, and I have refused to submit to whatever He has in mind for you. I hope you will forgive me and take this with you."

With you. Now I knew the last door had locked behind me.

I accepted the cumbersome book, the words OUR HOLY BIBLE lovingly carved into its wooden cover. "Nobody needs my forgiveness," I said, "except maybe Mr. Heffelfinger for pointing a gun at me."

"I don't believe he . . . well, promise to read from this book every day, and I will sleep better at night."

After I promised, my mother spoke a verse to me, which I later found was Corinthians 10, verse 13: "*There hath no temptation taken you but such as is common to man; but God is faithful, who will not suffer you to be tempted above that ye are able, but will with the temptation also make a way to escape, that ye may be able to bear it.*"

I did not take much comfort from the prospect of bearable suffering, but I thanked my mother anyway and put the Bible in my room, next to my secret radio.

A couple of days after Mr. Pee's visit, my mother answered the phone, listened at length, then handed the receiver to me without a word, her gaze intimating that another chicken was about to come home to roost.

"Hello?" I asked gingerly as if the phone might erupt in curses.

Bill," Sally said in an odd, shaky whisper and without preliminaries, "I want you to know I didn't tell anybody. Betty Jean told me *and* everybody else."

"Okay."

She waited for me to demand justification of some sort, but when I didn't, she implored me to believe her.

"Sure. Why wouldn't I?"

"Because you've hated me ever since the Harvest Hop."

"No, I just realized we weren't friends. Probably never were."

"How . . . how can you say something so mean?"

"Let's face it, Sally, we've been stuck with each other because our mothers were friends. They had a half-assed fantasy about us getting married. I tried to kiss you, and you about threw up."

"That's not true. You . . . hardly meant it, and I could tell. You had another girl; you were just playing with me."

"That's crap. You couldn't tell anything. If you could, you'd know I wasn't with Wanda then." I had been arguing with Don for a decade, and Sally had never been crossed or called out in any serious way. In this one respect, I was out of her league. Still, she had one last rock to throw.

"You ruined everything, you . . . stupid boy!"

"I guess," I said. "I got kicked out of my house, and I can't go to college. And trust me, there's no military school. That's bullshit my father made up. He makes up a lot of stuff. And by the way, Bobby Heatwole doesn't have burns all over his body, and no Waycross girl got pregnant before she came to Hopperton. Just more rotten gossip spread by certain people. Certain people who didn't mind whatever lies kept colored people out of our school."

"I hate you," Sally sobbed, then hung up. I went to my room, sick at heart, and packed my suitcase, leaving it sitting in plain sight on the hope chest at the bottom of my bed. Yet through all my misery, I knew that Don had been right. Sally had feelings for me. You hardly ever hate a person you didn't love before.

I took the job in Lake City after talking to Aunt Miriam. "Go down there, young man," she ordered. "Open a bank account; I will send you three thousand dollars. Don't spend it if you can help it. Get a Florida driver's license right away. Establish residency. At some point, you will be eligible for in-state tuition. You will need a good trade to provide for yourself. If you ever do come back to Hopperton, you want to be on top of the world."

"Why would I ever go back to Hopperton?"

"Shall I tell your mother you asked me that? Now listen, Bill, you *must* grow up. If you get mixed up with another girl, don't come crawling to me for help, understand?"

I did. Three thousand times better than five minutes before. Aunt Miriam would later admit she could've sent me considerably more without batting an eye but decided three grand would get my attention without ruining me. "One other thing. My hotel detective is looking to see where Wanda and her mother set up housekeeping. If you're any kind of man, you'll care to know."

Two more deaths—assuming Mr. Heffelfinger's demise—punctuated my last days in Hopperton. Neither victim was a local person, and each stood at an opposite end of history's bell curve, as humans calculate such things. In the first case, I had settled on the veranda the day after talking to Sally, alternating between Mr. Pee's philosophy book and wallowing in a mood I would call defiant guilt. Nature didn't care, producing a sublime, temperate day for those with a sense to appreciate it. Yes, a spring rain was in the offing, but you knew it would be brief. Hearing shuffling steps, I looked up to see Tom Fields heading for his sister's place, gripping a suitcase in each hand. "Mr. Fields," I called, "hold up." I intended to offer him water, even respite on our property. My father's potential objection hardly mattered now.

Fields stopped, put his suitcases down, and looked my way. He didn't move or wave or smile, so I got up and walked closer, assuming he hadn't recognized me. When I got close enough for us to speak without raising our voices, he said, "They killed Dixie."

I'm sure I gaped in shock. *They* killed Dixie. Not "Dixie died" or "someone killed Dixie." And "they" had to be Elixapine in retribution. I felt terrible for Tom Fields, and almost as bad for myself, fearing that he blamed my father and hated me by extension.

"That's awful," I said. "What happened?"

"They shot her. Thirty aught six. Old-style bullet, like maybe from a World War II rifle. Didn't wanna leave no doubt. Middle of the night. Guess I'm deafer than I thought."

I went cold, remembering my father had such a rifle. Not the one he carried during the war, but the same model, bought afterward. Tom Fields shielded his eyes against the sun and sized me up.

"It weren't your old man," he said. "He's got rough spots but nothing like that. Only a shyster or a bad neighbor would think up mischief that spiteful, and I ain't got no real neighbors."

"Shit," I said.

Tom Fields spat in acknowledgment.

"My sister's taking me in. We'll get in each other's hair, but there's nothing for it."

I didn't ask why he needed to move or mention my imminent exile. "Can I get you a glass of water or little shade?"

"Naw."

"How far to your sister's place?"

"A good stretch. Best be at it."

"Mind if I walk with you? I've never been out that way except on a Sunday drive."

"You in trouble, boy?" Tom Fields squinted into my soul, at least a little ways.

"Not police trouble."

"I recollect now. You were waiting for your sweetheart up on the hill."

"She moved away."

He nodded as if he had all the pieces of the puzzle he needed. "Well, if you're coming, may as well make yourself useful." He pointed to a scarred leather suitcase. When I lifted it, it felt empty, as if its owner had tossed in nothing more than a change of clothes. "That's the suitcase I took to Fort Benning in 1942; never thought I'd live to need it in such a spot."

Pelting rain caught us the better part of an hour later, just as we turned left down an unmarked path thick with pine straw. I took my cue from my companion and plodded on through the downpour with manly stoicism. Don and I would have chattered and griped, I knew, our tribulations soon to be remedied by sandwiches and a sheltered porch. But this was different, a sad procession, too real for small talk.

After a twenty-minute trek that wound through dripping loblolly forest, we arrived at Tom Fields's sister's place, a rugged cabin with a sharecropper's shack behind it like a kind of outbuilding. The two structures stood in a well-tended clearing, a sizable spring garden adjacent to the rough but well-maintained pair. Two wicker chairs sat out front of the cabin, the porch beneath them a patchwork of old and new lumber. I doubted Tom would remember my first name, but he did. He introduced me to his sister, Alma Fields, a beautiful woman with darker skin than any white woman I had ever seen and a prodigious mass of gray-blonde hair secured by what seemed to be hand-carved wooden combs.

Alma greeted me warmly, extending her hand to shake. I might as well have squeezed a cast-iron pump handle, for all the give in her grip. She didn't inquire about who I might be in the scheme of things, contenting herself to invite me in and seat me at a sturdy three-legged stool from which I could survey the cabin's one room. With one exception, there wasn't much to see: a quilted brass bed, a table with three arrowback chairs, a porcelain sink, a noisy old icebox. But on the floor lay a polar bear rug, its glassy eyes and snarl fixed on me, its clawed feet and paws spreadeagle, intact.

"Drink, son," Alma said, interrupting my uneasy communion with the bear's predatory remnant to hand me a milk bottle filled with cold water. As I drank, Tom told his sister what he knew and what he suspected concerning Dixie's murder. Alma listened, shaking her head in stoic sorrow. "Damn shame," she said, making no effort to seek out further grisly details. When I handed Tom the milk bottle, he downed its contents in one long swallow, grimacing afterwards as if he'd tasted something bitter.

Within a couple of minutes, brother and sister had settled their new living arrangements. Unlike me, they seemed to regard misfortune as something too ordinary to belabor. Alma served biscuits, squash soup, and a salad of lemony lettuce, spring onions, and radishes hot enough to bring a tear. "We" talked about gardening and the weather, meaning I ate and contributed nothing much. I occupied myself by taking a hypothetical mental walk with *my* suitcase to some grim boardinghouse room, compared to which the Field's humble homestead felt like paradise. After the meal, the two thanked me and sent me home—no last-minute advice from Tom Fields, no mention if Dixie, only the story of how he haggled for the polar bear rug with a Russian soldier, surrendering his cigarette lighter in exchange. I walked back to the main road as slowly as I could, kicking idly at pinecones and breathing the rain-cleansed air, trying to keep my future at bay as long as possible.

My father's Remington rifle hung high in his study; its stock covered with unmolested dust. Only after taking note of this did I tell him about Tom Fields's dog. I couldn't bear to face him with doubt in my mind. He groaned, then looked skyward, shaking his head. He asked me how I knew what I knew; I told him, including my walk with Tom Fields.

"Did you talk about Elixapine?"

"No. Not a word. All he said was he didn't think you shot his dog."

"How could he…?" my father started in protest before stopping short of the self-evident answer.

"I won't say anything to Mother." My father nodded, and—to his credit—placed the angry phone call I heard minutes later, during which he too invoked the word "shyster." In any case, a *Hopperton Herald* I received from my mother a few months later reported that Elixapine, as my father had predicted, went belly up, all creditors unsatisfied.

The second death was that of Dr. Martin Luther King Jr. on April 4, a Thursday. I got the bulletin over the radio, shortly before dinnertime, then ran out and turned on the TV. After a few minutes, the sound drew my mother from the kitchen. She watched for a moment, drying her hands repeatedly on her apron, then wondered, "What kind of person shoots a man of God?"

"A white man, they think," I replied. "A young white guy was seen running away."

I'm sure my answer missed the intent of my mother's question, but she accepted it without comment and sat down. We watched TV together until my father got home. He had already heard the news on his car radio and dropped into his chair with a fatalistic grunt. "That fool has started a war unless I miss my guess," he said.

I had heard "race war" talk at the Heffelfingers and in the barbershop. As far as I knew, Negroes were vastly outnumbered and possessed no means of organizing and raising an army. Most white men in Hopperton had multiple rifles and shotguns for various types of hunting. I had never seen a Negro with a gun. Therefore, I assumed "race war" meant shooting Negroes until they quit making a fuss.

But I was sick of fruitless arguments, and given my looming departure, I kept this assessment to myself.

Dr. King was shot with a thirty-aught-six slug, the same caliber used to kill Tom Fields's dog. This coincidence is unremarkable in itself, since that caliber, as my father informed me, was as "common as ticks in a hound's ear." And while James Earl Ray used a Remington like my father's,

Ray's rifle employed pump action rather than bolt action, allowing for more destructive impact. Still, these loosely related facts, along with my exposure to Philip Heffelfinger, persuaded my young, distressed mind to further lump Southern white men into a cabal born of hate and ignorance.

I now know that hateful, stupid people constitute a minority scattered among all demographics. Still, back in 1968, Dr. King's death convinced me that being a pariah among backwoods Georgians was a badge of honor. Yes, I was leaving under a cloud of scandal, but now, I told myself, Hopperton's complicity in Dr. King's death dwarfed my disgrace and justified me in saying "good riddance" to the benighted town.

Doubtless, my pride would've found another crutch if the bullet had missed Dr. King, but in any case, when, just after my birthday, I boarded the Greyhound bus to Lake City, accompanied by two suitcases just like Tom Fields, righteousness kept me from crying.

"I'll be fine," I assured my weeping mother. My father stood by, shifting from one foot to the other, unsure whether to hold his hat or wear it. "Goodbye, sir," I said, releasing my mother and shaking hands with excessive formality, determined to hold my ground—as was my father. I did not tell him he would find my prized Swiss Airmaster watch on the desk in his study.

We stood silent for a moment; then, my father had the last word. "Put a mind to your business, son, and you might go far."

CHAPTER THIRTY-FOUR

"Hello, Goodbye"

Lake City and Gainesville Florida, from May 1968

The Greyhound from Hopperton left the highway every few miles to stop at a rural gas station or post office, where mostly no one got on or off. I stared out at nondescript countryside through a dirty window reflecting the spectral image of a sailor in dress blues across the aisle from me sprawled out and incessantly smoking, lighting each cigarette off the one before.

At one point, I dozed off and dreamed I had lost my wallet and faced the prospect of begging like some desperate character in *Threepenny Opera*. I woke in a panic, took out my wallet, and felt for the bills inside. My father had allotted $200 to tide me over until my first paycheck, to which my mother had quietly added $400. To my relief, my bankroll was intact. And Aunt Miriam's $3000 would arrive once I had a mailing address. To calm myself, I took further stock: I had clothes, toiletries, a few books, including the family Bible, and Mr. Heffelfinger's chess set, along with the intention—withheld from my father with righteous pleasure—to never set foot in the turpentine plant where I'd been sent to slave, as I saw it, as an indentured servant; Joseph sold into Egyptian bondage.

But rejecting the turpentine job also meant losing access to the board-inghouse run for plant workers. So, when I finally stepped off the bus in Lake City and stood blinking in the humid glare, I took note of a long, dirty pink building facing the highway and about an outfielder's throw from the depot. Its badly weathered wooden sign said "Alligator Motel— Best Rates day or week." *Well*, I thought, *a person can't do any better than "best."*

After reclaiming my baggage, I walked over and boldly rented a room at the weekly rate of seventy-five dollars, asking in passing about the help wanted sign in the window. The man who hired me on the spot, Tillson (no first name, no "Mr."— just Tillson), sported an enormous belly supported by double suspenders that brought to mind a well-endowed woman's bra straps. But physique and pungent onion odor aside, Tillson was okay, throwing in a free room at the motel (a concession comprising my entire benefits package). My interview lasted five minutes and involved no resume or paperwork. I agreed to start right away, my job training occurring on the spot: prices, guest register, room keys, cash register. Swimming pool maintenance instructions would come later. "Keep the radio low in the office," Tillson said, "and look alive. Motel clerks tend to let themselves go," he lamented.

I took a day to get my bearings; that is, to call Aunt Miriam from a pay phone and give her a place to send $3000, find a bank, and sample waffles at the tiny Waffle House. Otherwise, Lake City, with its omni-present churches, failed to win me over. The last thing I wanted was a larger version of Hopperton. I unpacked back in my room, lay down in a lumpy, unsteady bed, turned on a dim lamp useless for reading, and opened Mr. Pee's book to the next chapter on Elizabethan philosopher Francis Bacon. Bacon said that most people just *imagine* the world, never looking past the mirror of their mind. I shut the book, pained to have come face to face with the sin that landed me in this mess—trusting my treacherous brain and the slippery world. I would start over tomorrow, calling bullshit on everything and everyone, including myself, until, like doubting Thomas, I had the bloody proof at my fingertips. Groaning and close to tears despite my hard-boiled resolution, I closed my eyes and breathed in dankness fit for an ancient cave, a residue that would never abandon that unloved room. According to Bacon, real knowledge could only arise by accurately comparing one thing to another: my mother's hand-ironed pillowcases smelled of sunlight; the scratchy fabric beside my cheek reeked of unrinsed bleach.

I groaned in anguish, tossed the offending pillow against the far wall, then put the accursed philosophy book in a drawer next to the Bible. Where were the ideas that made you *happy*? Restlessness and hunger compounded this piteous question. I had nothing to do and no means to cook. At a nearby store called Quik-Tote, I bought Peter Pan peanut butter, bread, and a Pepsi, and would have added a *Penthouse* magazine if the clerk had not been a woman. Instead, I settled for a book of crossword puzzles and a couple of sci-fi and crime paperbacks. Then I sat by the empty Alligator Motel pool until darkness and stars pushed the last gasp of sunset from the sky. Tomorrow would begin my first shift: ten p.m. to six a.m.. A grotesque caricature of manhood fast approached, and I didn't even own a coffee pot.

For the first couple of days, my "post" in the narrow space behind the motel office counter had its charms. Other than checking in an occasional late-night straggler resorting to the Alligator Motel out of exhausted desperation or a furtive couple finally taking the sexual plunge, I was free of the world's scrutiny. I listened to an underground college station from Gainesville, partially completed a few crosswords, and fantasized about lonely college girls stopping for the night, hungry for companionship. When these diversions palled, I decided to write Don a letter, using a dusty yellow legal pad for stationery. I happen to write swiftly, in a passable cursive, and as I began filling him in on recent events, an urge gripped me to recount our last year of high school, as if the entire year composed a single entity living in my brain and scratching to get out. Over two nights, I wrote twenty pages, beginning with our slavery debate that first day in the lunchroom and ending with Dr. King's death, which, I told Don, proved that many wished that slavery still existed. Wanda and Mr. Heffelfinger emerged as central characters, embodiments of light and dark: the girl with hair like the sun, the man in dark eclipse. I knew Don would hate much of what I said, but at least he would know I cared enough to remember.

At my first opportunity, I mailed the bulky sheaf to Don's new address, relishing in advance his (no doubt) rich, astonished reply. The next night at work, I tried to write a similar letter to Wanda, but the well ran dry. It wasn't the same. Our hours together, however poignant, provoked no narrative. I settled instead for this poem:

your wings
your bright yellow hair
your tilted quizzical smile
your beautiful secret opinions
what you showed me
what you hid from me
what you sang with your eyes closed
what you said looking right at me
even the band-aid on your arm
this is what I remember
except for the wings
i put them there myself

It would have to do. Hopefully, the lack of capital letters would make it cool, along with the wings thing, like Delia Wingfoot. I would write it out carefully on nice paper and send it, once I knew where.

With my writing projects behind me and nothing in particular ahead, I sat staring out from a space smaller than what I imagined could hold a death row cell. Two frames hung on the wall behind me. One informed the public that Alligator had been the original name of Lake City. The other announced that the largest Florida battle of the Civil War had been fought here, won by the South. Otherwise—nothing.

Shit, I thought with a shiver, *this is no good, no damn good at all.*

Aunt Miriam's money came a couple of days later, hidden under the chocolates of a Whitman Sampler box—thirty $100 bills spread across the bottom. Here is her letter, which to this day sits folded up in a Cuban humidor:

Dear Bill,

First, the nuts and bolts. Put *every dime* of this in the bank. Don't go hog wild. Don't be an idiot. Get your Florida driver's license now. Don't quit your job, which I imagine you will find terrible before long. That's normal. Now, to the news, which, I warn you, is upsetting and confusing. Please do not share any of this with your parents. Wanda and her mother have fallen off the face of the earth as far as my house detective can tell. Their people in North Carolina tell different stories. Some say Wanda lost the baby. Some say no; the Grices just don't want to be found. One cousin who didn't like Mrs. Grice said there never was a baby and that the whole sorry business was just like Clarinda Grice.

You need to know this, Bill, for better or worse. If any truth comes to light, I'll pass it along. Life is not what we think it is when we're young, but I guess you're figuring that out on your own.

Love, Aunt Miriam

I read the letter outside in the bright, hot sun, then stared into the pool's concrete void, sorrow and outrage slugging it out. The only clear thought I could summon concerned the need to take the assorted chocolates inside before they melted on my money. As I flopped down on my shitty bed (finding a cherry center on my third chocolate morsel), I remembered that I'd never finished reading my Christmas gift from Wanda—her prized copy of *Siddhartha*. I dug it out of my suitcase and found where I left off, the point where Siddhartha not only parts ways with his lover Kemala but with his town, his job, *everything*. The parallels to my plight became downright and deliberately eerie when a little later in the story, Kemala turns out to be pregnant by Siddhartha. I read avidly then, hoping for a happy, helpful ending. But soon, Kemala died of a snakebite and Siddhartha's new, pain-in-the-ass son ran off. Granted, by the book's end, Siddhartha figured it all out, but he was really old then, and besides, I wasn't sure what he'd figured out anyway. Something about everything being true sooner or later; just take it all in. It hardly seemed fair, waiting until you were practically dead to finally "get it." I lay in gloom for a long time, devastated to think that Wanda would never read my poem.

Over the next couple of days, I auditioned explanations until I found one that cast Wanda in the best possible light: she had mistakenly thought herself pregnant and had been forced by her mother to maintain the fiction for monetary gain. After all, hadn't Clarinda Grice taken Greta Mueller's $500 *on top of* my college tuition? And wouldn't Wanda have married me if she'd indeed been pregnant? At work that night, as a slowing southbound Greyhound passed the office window, I decided Aunt Miriam's letter had freed me from disgrace and my hellish job. Wanda, I daydreamed, would escape her mother's clutches and find me, if for no other reason than to apologize and admit her abiding love. In the meantime, I needed to attend to Aunt Miriam's "nuts and bolts" and escape Lake City. All signs pointed to Gainesville, less than fifty miles down 441 and home to the University of Florida. Yes, as a Georgia football fan, I'd always hated the Gators, but if it would get me out of the godforsaken Alligator Motel, I'd learn to love them.

Taking the driver's test required a car. Luckily, I had landed squarely on Tillson's good side and passed my test maneuvering his extra car, his "beater," a faded electric-blue '58 Bonneville convertible. Now that I had a license, he mused, I could be his errand boy and, who knows, work my way up to assistant manager and a day shift. Accordingly, I picked up bundles of toilet paper on my own time, acquiring tacit rights to the Bonneville as long as I paid for the gas. Tillson clapped me on the shoulder from time to time, feeling his plans for me coming to fruition. Well, I had my own plans, and I suppose that pretty much accounts for the plot of every novel ever written.

My next off day shone blue and cloudless. I told Tillson I planned to take a friendly young bank teller on a picnic and instead set out for Gainesville with the Bonneville's balky ragtop retracted. I drove in fear of highway death past scrubby cow pastures, dilapidated gas stations, and a couple of barbecue joints, the speedometer's needle barely touching forty. Eventually, the road bent hard right and passed a charmless cinderblock, its sign containing the incredible word "topless." I pulled into the deserted parking lot to make sure I hadn't imagined it.

No, the word was still there. Along with "miniskirt contest" and "live bands." My heart pounded at the mere possibility of entering a breast-baring roadhouse, a "sinners paradise" to use my father's words. Well, I was old enough to die in Vietnam, wasn't I? Having pushed my father's spirit away with this logic, I drove on, charged like a battery.

Highway 441 splits Gainesville down the middle—just as it divides Hopperton. Gawking my way along what is locally called Thirteenth Street, I saw hippies and a cluster of orange-robed people with bald heads, women included, all peacefully intermingled with people dressed just like Hopperton High kids. Along the side wall of a bookstore, someone had painted "HELL NO, WE WON'T GO!" in foot-high letters, the words attracting less notice than I did in the open convertible. I felt I had stumbled into Utopia, its liberated inhabitants sure to embrace me. I drove south until Thirteenth Street reverted to the highway, then turned around, noting a couple of rundown motels like the Alligator, yet somehow more inviting. At a drive-in called Chandler's, I bought a sack of undersized burgers. I devoured them as I drove back to Lake City, savoring the whipping wind, my fear of highway death replaced by one-handed steering bravado.

See you later, Alligator.

Tillson took my departure in fatalistic stride, asking me not to bother him with my "sorry explanation," only hoping I'd stick around for a few days until he could find "a body with a pulse." That body belonged to a retiree from a Goodrich tire plant in Akron, Ohio, with poor hearing and a noticeable tremor in his left hand. During our brief friendship (a couple of shifts to make sure he survived them), he insisted I call him "old man Stebbins," like he worked the next farm over. Stebbins went on about Japanese tire companies, their existence in the USA proving that Japan had gotten the last laugh and might as well have won the war. The fact that Hirohito, a god in Japan, had surrendered proved that he'd cut a deal with the Freemasons. Bridgestone, he said, was Jap code for world domination.

None of it made any sense to me except for the underlying notion, echoed by my father, that America would be out of business soon if we weren't careful. I didn't care. Some asshole, probably a Republican, just shot Bobby Kennedy. America *deserved* to be out of business. And someday, my novels would expose the evil that brought us to our knees. Sure, I told Stebbins, I'll buy Goodrich tires. Why the hell not? The next day I boarded a Greyhound for the short ride south.

I paid dearly for a month at the Bambi Motel, called Tillson to forward my mail, then announced my move to Gainesville via palm-and-sunset postcards. That same afternoon, I hitchhiked to campus, impersonating a student by carrying Mr. Pee's philosophy book. A Bambi clerk had told me about an area across from the university called the "student ghetto," where cheap housing should be plentiful, especially with summer coming.

The "ghetto's" dwellings, arrayed along sleepy, dusty, narrow streets, consisted mostly of single-family homes chopped up for student use. In style, the houses differed little from swampside houses in Hopperton, except for ubiquitous bikes, blacklight posters in windows, and an amicable seediness that would've instigated widespread gossip back home.

I ended up renting an upstairs room in a large, primer-gray, wooden firetrap called the Mango Lodge for fifty dollars a month. Other than a drawerless desk and army cot, the space was utterly bare. No hotplate allowed (everyone, it turned out, had one). Communal bathroom down the hall. No screen on the lone window. I leaned out its opening and peered down, satisfied I would survive the drop in the likely event of a fire. The old lady who ran the place lived in an adjacent house, its cool, antique-laden interior a mocking contrast to my new abode. I gave the lady fifty dollars, signed a piece of paper, then left feeling self-satisfied and hungry. Chandler's Hamburgers, where I'd stopped after my first foray from Lake City, sat just a few blocks away. I had lunch there and filled out a job application. "Call back in a couple of days," the burly, harried manager said.

By the next week, I'd become a grill cook, sweating heavily, mass-producing hamburgers and cheeseburgers.

During my remaining paid-up days at the air-conditioned Bambi, my letter to Don came back marked "return to sender"—no further details given.

Greta Miller. *Frau Mueller*. She was the culprit.

As I stood in the motel lobby, grumbling to myself, I overheard the pretty clerk talking on the phone. "God, Vicki," she said, "he's such a creep." She nuzzled the phone as she spoke into it, indifferent to my glance.

"Maybe Vicki's a creep too," I said, the thought becoming words before I could stop it.

"What?" The clerk shielded the phone and glared.

"Sorry. I mean, we're all creeps; what's the point of saying it?" I grinned to cover my tracks. For a long time now, I realized with a sinking heart, most of my conversations had been arguments. Now I was starved enough for company to contradict strangers. The young woman whispered into the phone, hung up, then began dialing another number. I stammered the word "peace" and backed out, not waiting to critique her next exchange of views. A hard truth washed through me as I left: Gainesville was not Hopperton, but I was still Bill Shaffer.

Not long after I decamped to the Mango Lodge, Mr. Pee's postcard made its way to me from Philo, California. *I love the town*, he wrote, *named after an ancient philosopher. Smaller than Hopperton. Vineyards and hippie crops are creeping in hereabouts. Sheep farmers are leaving. My black cat sits by the window, looking out. I trust you are "looking out" as well. Quo vadis? Regards, Hiram Peebles.*

Look outward, look inward. Which was it?

Mother's postal offerings continued, including the Hopperton paper, which reported integration's intrusion with bare-bone sullenness. Still, I could detect no appetite in its rhetoric, despite Don's prophecies, for reigniting the Civil War. The names and beaming images of my old schoolmates popped up everywhere. Their exploits in sports, 4-H, beauty pageants, and church activities, as well as the commitment of young men to fight the Vietcong, stood at the heart of town pride. Sally won awards for citizenship, stooping slightly in the pictures to shake hands with grown-ups, her smile less effusive than I remembered.

I worked at Chandler's as a fry cook until the fall of 1969, the smell of reconstituted onions clinging to my fingers for months afterward. As for my "social" life, a nervous, female coworker invited me to her apartment once, telling me frankly that intercourse would betray her boyfriend in Vietnam but that she needed "something" short of penetration to keep from going crazy. I obliged her, but I never managed a return engagement since she quit a few days later. Greta Miller spurned my (brief) second letter to Don as she had the first. Aunt Miriam wrote that Wanda's trail had gone cold for now, but that she'd sprinkled around a little money to keep eyes and ears open. Her letter concluded with precise instructions for gaining admission to the University. "If I have to come down and help you," she said, "I will be most annoyed."

The University accepted me without fuss or fanfare. Aunt Miriam's money would cover all four years' tuition, with a chunk left over. My father got hired by the timber outfit thirty miles from Hopperton as a shift supervisor, rotating between day and night shifts. I quit Chandler's and got a work-study job in the library. Most of my freshman classes were requirements, except for one elective. So, not long after Labor Day, 1969, I walked into the Basics of Philosophy and met Carl Decker.

CHAPTER THIRTY-FIVE

"Born to be Wild"

Gainesville, Florida, 1969

As my fellow University of Florida freshmen and I shuffled to our seats in silence, one lean, muscular male student bantered with the girl next to him, bestowing a booming laugh on the room at large. I took the empty seat closest to him to get a better look at his tattoo, a skull clenching a knife in its teeth, the word "Ranger" bannered above. His tattoo, his faint fuzz of scalp hair, and a tight olive-drab T-shirt all proclaimed him as a Vietnam vet, a self-marked man in light of college antiwar sentiment. Still, he exuded good cheer, showing no battle scars, physical or otherwise.

Maybe he felt my scrutiny. Anyway, he swung around my way and said, "Do you know anything about philosophy? I don't know shit." Before I could answer, he looked at a list of words on the blackboard. "What the fuck is ethics?"

I happened to know, from reading Mr. Pee's book. "It's theories about what's good or bad. Like, is an action good because it's useful? Or because it feels good? What if something helps me but hurts everybody else? Is that good or bad? Stuff like that."

"Very deep." He grinned and rubbed his head. "What's your name, deep thinker?"

"Bill."

"I'm Carl Decker.'Decker the Wrecker' they called me over in Nam. Which is a fucked-up place. We're getting our ass kicked, by the way. And we deserve it. They wanted me to re-up. Gave me some 'my country 'tis of thee' bullshit. Fuck that." Then he shrugged. "But if somebody wants to die a hero, it's a free country."

"Dying for the greater good."

"What?"

"It's an ethical theory. What's good is what's best for the greatest number of people, regardless of how it affects any one person."

Decker the Wrecker snickered. "Yeah, and 'me fuck you a *long* time,' soldier.'"

After class, he collared me, gripped my shoulder in an amicable vise, and insisted on treating me to pizza at Leonardo's. We sat at a café table outside so Carl could take in the passersby. He watched them with an amused smirk. At one point, he said, "Six to four, more loose tits than bras. I'd rather write a paper on that." Despite the survey, his attention shifted abruptly when the pizza came.

"Listen, Bill; I didn't understand *shit* in that class. I think you were the only one who did."

"A smart man gave me a philosophy book. I read it a couple of times, that's all."

"Whatever. You're the class brain, and I want an A in philosophy to blow my old man's mind."

I sensed some sort of devil's bargain coming my way. "You want me to tutor you?"

"No, fuck no. I want you to write my papers. Yeah, okay, you can tutor me too so that I won't look like too big a dumbass in class, but papers are the main fucking thing, right? See, I have a nice apartment, car, motorcycle, and a boat over in Tampa that I sail on the weekends. I won the war, my part of it anyway. Burn the flag; I don't give a crap. I'm flush. I'm set to take over my old man's hi-fi business. What's left but figuring out the meaning of life, right?" As if he just closed a big sale, Carl leaned back in triumph, arms folded, tilting his chair back on two legs.

"Well, falling in love would be high on most people's list."

"Forget that one. You know why? Because it's too damn easy. Fall out of a boat and you'll hit the water. That's about how hard it is to fall in love.

Anyway, write my papers and I'll pay you pretty good. And if I get my A I'll take you sailing, help you get laid."

"I can get myself laid."

"Really? I figured you for a virgin all the way."

"Well, I'm not."

"Yeah? You act all scrawny and harmless and brilliant, and the next thing they know, they're flat on their back. Is that how you do it?"

Carl's status as near-stranger liberated me. I gave a just-short-of-lurid account of my affair with Wanda, detouring along the way to provide a self-glorifying version of the swamp fiasco, alluding as often as possible to crossbows, pistols, and drugs.

"I'll be damned; you might have a kid out there," he mused. "Welcome to the club." He made no mention of my brush-with-death exploits, to my intense irritation.

"Tell you what," I said. "I'll write your papers for twenty-five dollars a page on one condition: you come to all the classes."

Rather than rejecting my outrageous terms, he pointed his pizza slice at me and growled with false menace. "Okay, but you better be fucking Shakespeare for that price."

"Listen, I have to write my paper, your paper, make them sound like two different people, and not make you seem a lot smarter than the professor thinks you are. The smarter you act in class, the better paper you'll get. And you'll have to read the paper I write for you and understand it, in case the professor asks you about it."

"Fuck. Vietnam was easier than this bullshit."

We kept to our deal, netting me $200 and Carl's company for more or less the rest of my life. I suppose our sailing excursions sealed my fate. We'd leave Gainesville Friday after classes and head for Tampa in Carl's rust-eaten but sexy red Mercedes. His father, Albert, would welcome us with steaks on the grill and Sinatra on the hi-fi, standards like "Night and Day" and "Begin the Beguine" pouring like honey from enormous speakers. Unlike my father, Albert Decker exuded optimism. While both of them were interested in business, Albert countered my father's pessimism with a view of the future as one big, fat, juicy opportunity. There would be no end to the country's hunger for the state-of-the-art stereo equipment he sold. Too bad about my father's job, of course, but the antiquated had to make way for the modern. And I had to admit I found the Decker house airy and wonderfully stylish. Maybe Albert was right.

And maybe, Carl pointed out cheerfully, his father was full of shit. "There are people out there, old man, working hard to fuck up wet dreams like yours. Matter of fact, I've killed a few of them. But the greedy fuckers back here running the bomb factories are worse and harder to kill. You're small potatoes. If hi-fi gets big like you say, you'll have to sell your fancy shit at a loss or sell out to Sam Goody's. You should be adding those cheap-ass Jap receivers to your inventory and hope nobody notices you're making money."

Mr. Decker, physically fit, deliberately unshaven, and eternally good-looking like certain male actors, sat in a loud, unbuttoned shirt, sipping his cocktail and chuckling, taking no offense. "Carl knows how to fight and curse and sail. Watch out if he opens his big mouth about anything else."

I soaked it in, envying the natural give-and-take I'd missed with my father. And tomorrow I'd go sailing, "bottle sailing" as Carl called it, with a lazarette full of cold beer.

One such Saturday, as Carl and I returned to port at dusk, he noticed the full moon rising and wondered "why that son-of-a-bitch doesn't spin and show us its backside?"

"First of all," I said, "the moon is a woman—Luna—and second of all, she *does* spin." I demonstrated this by circling Carl while always facing him, pointing out my passage through all four quarters of the wind—proof that I had spun. My father and I had performed the same choreography with roles reversed, causing me to wonder then how the moon *knew* to turn just enough to keep itself half hidden. My high school science teacher, Mrs. Gaffney, had assured me that the moon knew nothing but only bent to gravity's demand that any orbiting body eventually matches its period of rotation to its period of revolution. She gave me a rare smile when I asked why, briefly revealing her infamous, nicotine-stained dentures. "You're a smart boy, Bill, but not *that* smart."

Fortunately, Carl didn't question the moon's implausible compliance. "Damn, Professor," he said instead, using that sobriquet for the first time, "you know some *useless* shit."

Other than sailing, the "useful shit" Carl offered in return included the chance to navigate his 250 cc Husqvarna motocross bike. Motocross racing swept the country around this time, and Husqvarna motorcycles were the kings of the track. Carl raved about Torsten Hallman and Bengt Aberg and Stirling shocks and Bing carburetors and Swedish supremacy and finally persuaded me to accompany him to an abandoned limestone quarry and, if nothing else, sit on the "live" bike and savor its engine's glorious rumble.

We entered through a gate whose chain had rusted away. Carl left the gate open and drove through a narrow path in the overgrowth to a yawning, weedy, irregularly gouged, oval pit, maybe a football field long.

"It's a played-out limestone quarry. No one comes out here; trust me."

I didn't trust him but nodded anyway. We unstrapped the bike from its trailer, and before long, I found myself sitting astride it, listening to the engine Carl had kick-started. A glistening red gas tank formed the centerpiece of the machine's undeniable coolness. I had no problem understanding throttle and clutch, brake and shifter, all analogous to Mr. Heffelfinger's pickup, which I drove so admirably the day he disappeared.

"Ease on the throttle just a hair," Carl instructed, "and ride it up to that tree stump. Don't worry about shifting gears. You won't be going fast enough to bother. When you get to the stump, release the throttle and use the handbrake." Carl grinned. "Then you can tell girls you're into dirt bikes. Guaranteed poontang." When Carl extended his helmet to me, I shook my head. The tree stump stood a bare twenty yards away along a relatively smooth path leading to the open gate.

"I'll be fine," I said.

I "eased" on the gas with several times the required force, causing the bike to leap forward with a raging snarl, its front tire rearing skyward. Panic froze my hands to the grips. I did manage to roll back the throttle, but when the front tire slammed to earth, the shock caused me to wrench the throttle forward again, rocketing me toward the open gate and the public road just beyond. Had I been unlucky, a junk collector's truck would have smashed me dead, but I made it across the empty highway, where my senses suddenly returned, and I came to a serene stop. Carl shouted and waved as he ran toward the gate. I waved back, caught between trembling weakness and the exhilaration of cheating death. After a few deep breaths, I cautiously eased the throttle and maneuvered the Husqvarna to the highway and across.

"No reason to get excited," I called to Carl.

"Yeah, except that was the funniest fucking thing I ever saw." Carl's amusement seemed untouched by the sort of contempt I'd felt watching Don struggle with his crossbow, tipping the moral scales unexpectedly Carl's way, edging him closer to lovable scoundrel and away from outright scoundrel. He asked me if I wanted "another ticket to the rodeo."

"Not just now," I told him.

"My turn then," he crowed with little-boy glee, hopping on the Husky and heading for the quarry, leaving me to watch for vehicles and calculate just how lucky I'd been not to become roadkill. I counted three cars and two trucks in half an hour.

Hard to say, I told myself, *maybe fifteen or twenty-to-one in my favor.* Better odds than Carl had faced every day in Vietnam, no doubt, but DNA had built us differently. Carl had a knack for moving on. I would waste the next few weeks seeing myself walloped by a station wagon and wondering about the moment just before oblivion.

Despite this brush with outright psychosis, I no longer feared the Husqvarna itself and, within a couple of weeks, powered it around the rubble-strewn quarry course with unwarranted aplomb until it spit me off a berm and flung me into the unsympathetic, bone-snapping boulder.

In the final analysis, I retired from motocross racing and Carl got a B- in philosophy. The professor, a cadaverous old gentleman and unapologetic atheist, would have smelled a rat if Carl's papers had proceeded too smoothly. On one occasion, Carl interrupted him to say that God must exist because so many people believed in him, the very essence of the *argumentum ad populum* fallacy we had just covered. Unable to write logically on Carl's behalf, I produced passionate papers, hoping to convey, if nothing else, supreme effort. Not that it mattered. Carl had moved on from philosophy well before grades came out, starting to dabble in weed dealing for a little "freaking excitement for God's sake." He considered us blood brothers when he was around but reserved the right to disappear for long periods without explanation. I would find afterward that he had holed up with a new "sun bunny," or gone blue water sailing, or, in one case, driven to Michigan to "meet a man." I stayed put, grinding my way through undergraduate studies in three years, pausing only to attend protests against Vietnam's deadly fiasco. In May of 1972, with the war widely understood to be unwinnable, Nixon mined Haiphong Harbor—among other brutal, futile escalations—reigniting student protests nationwide. In

Gainesville, students, including myself in my one act of physical defiance, erected a barricade across—where else?—US Highway 441. I got a good whiff of teargas, but at least I wasn't beaten, as many were, by vigilantes from surrounding counties on hand for a little hippie-kicking fun.

Maybe short hair, clothing from Sears, and glasses saved me.

Carl watched the fray from the second-story window of a nearby frat house while smoking marijuana with a customer. Afterward, he came to my room to scold me. "Listen, Professor, you are looking at a *great* fucking soldier, but I sure as shit didn't go out of my way to get killed. This garbage by Nixon is his last big sale before going out of business. No point letting yourself get taken down with him."

He stretched out on my cot—hard to call it a bed. I sat in my one wobbly chair, looking out at trees and sky and deceptively peaceful bungalows, remembering. "The greater good," I said, leaving it at that.

"Yeah, you hit me with it the first day I met you. It's a cool thought as long as you're around to think it."

Point taken, leading to one of philosophy's favorite, conveniently unanswerable questions: do we create reality, or does reality create us? Either way, I continued to exist and graduated *magna cum laude*, plunging ahead for my master's in the fall of '74. Saigon wouldn't fall until the next spring, but at least I had the consolation of watching Nixon slip on his self-created banana peel. Nothing on Wanda or Don, nothing new at home, other than Sally (still unmarried) becoming vice principal of Hopperton High in partial fulfillment of Don's prophecy. My path back to Hopperton became a trail of disappearing breadcrumbs. My mother kept writing, kept sending the Hopperton paper with its editorials sorrowing *not* about the war deaths of local boys, but the disgrace of American defeat. As for the other "defeat"—school integration —the editors now kept their opinions to themselves. The carpetbagging federal wolves were not just at the door; they were in the house, fangs bared. The paper resigned itself to factual news about the misbegotten experiment of race mixing, even showing a couple of pictures of Negro teachers standing next to white teachers. I had put *The Dark Warrior* behind me a while back, embarrassed by its preposterous "second Civil War" plot. Still, when I recalled how Hopperton whites spoke privately about black people, I had to wonder where all their rage, all their defiant, chest-thumping pride, was hiding.

CHAPTER THIRTY-SIX

"Psycho Killer"

Micanopy, Florida, Labor Day Weekend 2016

We leave Tampa in the early dark. Olivia shouts at Carl as we pull away, reminding him to rescue "her" diamond engagement ring from its watery grave. I see Linda on the patio watching with her arms folded, her Christmas lights reduced to a gleaming multicolored blob behind her. As I seek the ramp to I-75, Olivia is full of giddy chatter, like a gambler on a winning streak. I pretend to listen, feeling the return of a sensation I last felt while in the throes of my original severance from Linda and Carl; namely, that life is a soap opera. What else to make of Carl's return from prison, complete with dread disease and my first wife's wedding ring? Or Linda regaling me with her bewitched sexual autobiography? And now, I head home to initiate a bloodline confession reminiscent of a made-for-TV movie about babies switched at birth. As I rehearse what I might say to Ramona about fatherhood, Olivia fixates on "hitting" the mall next weekend to acquire more magic jewelry. She suggests I let Hermine take her. That way, I can stay home and fix up my dilapidated house.

Back home, Ramona is waiting. She puts down a magazine with a horse on its cover and indulges Olivia's breathless depiction of the weekend's awesomeness with a smile I don't trust.

And sure enough, as soon as Olivia goes to her room to pack, Ramona turns her humorless face my way. "Did you buy her that black dress?" she demands.

"Yes," I lie. "Did you snoop through her things?"

"Yes. Did you get her those earrings too?"

"At Hermine's suggestion."

"Well, I would be furious, but Earl and I figured out how to fix Antonio's wagon."

"That sounds vindictive rather than fair," I say.

"It's fair, trust me."

"Forgive me if I don't trust you, just this once."

"I forgive you; I always do, Dad. And speaking of forgiveness, how's Mom? She just called me, sounding spooky and nervous. She said you have something 'pivotal'—of all things— to tell me."

I take a seat in my reading chair, stalling for time. "Well," I say finally, "maybe more like a question to ask. Is there anything you know about Carl that I might not think you know?" I glanced toward Olivia's door, making sure it was closed.

Ramona caught my glance and gave a disbelieving chuckle.

"Wow, Dad. You're one subtle dude. Do you mean about Carl being my so-called *real* father? That's old news. I've pretty much known for years. I mean, I guess I owe him a debt of gratitude for accidentally knocking Mom up, but that's about it. I could've had one of those 'talks' with you, but I didn't see the point. Have you watched TV lately? Everybody's part of a family they didn't start with. It's like a cliché anymore. You can tell Mom to relax. Is she still into that crone thing?"

I can't believe that in a heartbeat or two, Ramona has glossed over a first-magnitude family secret that's been eating at me for decades and blithely changed the subject. I'm too stunned to do anything but play along.

"I don't think your mom literally believes she's a crone. It's more like a metaphor that works for her. I mean, what's a crone but an old woman full of hunches, intuitions, what have you? We had a long, weird talk about stuff I'd rather not know, but she's not crazy, I promise you that."

Ramona leans back, elegantly overdressed in a blue suit. "That's a charitable take, but I'll accept it anyway."

"You're decked out. Has Earl cast a spell over you? Maybe he's a warlock."

Ramona ignores my dig and says, "What's with Carl? Olivia mentioned 'termites,' of all things."

"Prison doctors found out Carl contracted HIV. He made light of it, of course. Acted like his release was a scam so the state could dodge paying his medical bills."

Ramona—a nurse after all—frowns at the mention of HIV and leans forward, tossing her magazine aside.

"Shit, Dad," she says. "Is he sick?"

"Not that I could see. He said he had the virus but not the disease."

"He *said*. Well, that settles it. Fuck. Now I have to drive over to Tampa. Whether he has AIDS or not, I'm going to nail him to the wall. Check out his meds. God knows what he'll tell Mom."

"Okay, am I to understand this whole biological fatherhood thing is a closed book now? Just like that?"

Olivia comes out then, probably sensing exciting strife. "Olivia," Ramona says, "do you know who got your grandmother pregnant with me?"

"Uncle Carl."

"And who is your grandfather?"

"Him," Olivia says, pointing at me absently before returning to her phone.

"And one last question," Ramona says. "You've been acting sneaky lately, so I went through your belongings looking for drugs. How did you get that black dress?"

"Him." Olivia indicates, pointing at me, not bothering with indignation, her fib flowing smoothly from either eavesdropping or teen instincts.

"Fine," Ramona says. "Enjoy looking at it, and don't grow too much because you're forbidden to wear it until you're eighteen." Olivia pouts for effect, a conspiratorial flicker of a grin sent my way. "And listen, Liv," Ramona adds, "you're staying with your grandpa another day. I've got sorry business in Tampa."

Olivia lights up like a beacon, not diluting her delight by asking why she's staying. "Okay, but I can't go to school. No clothes —except for the dress."

Ramona glares at me, not Olivia, as if I spent the weekend orchestrating her daughter's ruination. "I'll be back before dark tomorrow, Dad. Swear to me you won't buy her anything before then."

I give a *pro forma* nod, but I'm thinking about the juicy details Olivia may demand now that the sexual degeneracy of her already criminal family is out in the open.

"I'm surprised, Dad," Ramona says on her way out, clearly amused. "I thought a philosophy professor would know all the ancient truths."

"Which one did I miss?"

"It's always best to assume that everyone knows everything."

The next morning, I call Olivia's school, then have breakfast alone (fake eggs from a little milk carton), trying not to think about the exposé she's dispatching to her social network. During my third cup of coffee, I hear a sharp knock at my door. I open it, expecting to find that Ramona has reconsidered her merciless errand. Instead, a strange woman stands there, a woman with coal-black hair, lilac lipstick, a long, electric-blue skirt, and a translucent, sequined blouse seemingly designed to highlight a black bra underneath. She is somewhere between forty-five and sixty and attractive in a voluptuously lean and hungry kind of way.

"Hello," I say, my stare no doubt borderline rude.

"Excuse me, please, but I seek my brother."

I know immediately she's the female Laughing Russian—the piano— probably the woman I'd seen Friday calling after the shirtless, shouting man.

"He's not here. Is something wrong?"

She sighs and closes her eyes, emphasizing the extraordinary length of her eyelashes.

"Everything is wrong."

"I'm sorry," I say. "I often feel that way myself. Is there any specific wrong I can help you with?"

The woman gives stone-faced consideration to my question, then sniffs me like a bloodhound. "Do you have coffee, maybe espresso?"

With that, she appropriates my kitchen, drinking coffee she finds tasteless, explaining that the man I saw was her drunken brother, prone to wander off in rages. The third member of the Laughing Russian trio is her ex-husband, who lives with them because he has nowhere else to go, no money, no ambition, and no sight out of one eye owing to a fistfight between him and her brother. She is a proud citizen, she proclaims. They are not. They are children trembling behind their mother's skirt.

"I looked in your yard," she tells me. "I saw the grapes, and I thought my brother might be sleeping there. Some commissar cheated him out of a vineyard back in Russia."

"Ah, that explains his . . . protest in the street."

"You saw that? Why didn't you call the police?"

"He wasn't hurting anybody."

"Just me," she said, her accent making a sad comment seem tragic.

"Sorry."

She shrugs. "I am Natalya Rozetka. Who are you?"

For some stupid reason, I make a slight bow of the head and say, "I am William Shaffer, a retired philosophy professor."

"This is your house, William?"

"Yep. Call me Bill."

She wrinkles her nose.

"I will call you William." With that, she stands up and walks to the cupboard where I keep my books. "I see you know Alisa Rosenbaum."

"Who?"

"She hides behind the name Ayn Rand. I must respect her success, but she was a romantic psychopath. Do you follow her philosophy?" I feel Natalya's stock rising, and my pulse quickens.

"No, but the book is precious to me, a gift from a childhood friend. Ayn Rand was his . . . goddess."

"An aspiring *Übermensch*, no doubt; a common mistake at that age," she says, picking up *Atlas Shrugged* and turning it over in her hands like evidence in a crime. "You see," she continues, "Alisa had her private god—a murderer. Many years ago, just after she came to this country, she reads of man who kidnapped girl, strangled her, cut her up, gave her body to father for $1500. When police captured him, the man behaved like monster. Said if State could do as it wished, so could he. Alisa admired this man. She hated the State, the Bolsheviks who stole her father's business, men like the commissars who stole my brother's vineyard. This, I understand. But she supported this Nickerson, who was cruel. Like State. This I cannot accept. How could evil in State become good in this terrible man? No, it cannot be right. And her books? Her characters are cruel and cold. No souls."

Wanda had called Rand's characters humorless—close enough for a pang of old heartache. Then an image of Don Heffelfinger arguing with my formidable Russian visitor came to me and with it an intuition. "Did you *know* Ayn Rand?"

Before answering, Natalya uses a napkin to wipe the lipstick from the rim of her coffee cup. Her smile suggests she's been hoping for this question. "I know her soul, William. I met her in 1976 at book signing in New York. I felt joy when she signed my copy of *The Fountainhead*. Later I sold silly book for much money."

Natalya stands up and wanders into the living room, peering here and there like a customer browsing in a store. After a brief appraisal, she heads for the picture I bought the morning after I first slept at Linda's house—the old black-and-white photo of a man standing by a stagecoach. "Is this you?" she asks.

"No," I say, "that's from . . . long ago; it just reminds me of me."

"He is sad, as are you, but not so sad as that man."

"Well, that brightens my day," I reply, noticing that Natalya is wearing stiletto heels well before noon.

"Yes." She peers out a window. "A bright day, many bees."

"Bees?" I say, assuming I misheard.

"My brother tells me, how you say, bees are 'heading for exit.' Soon, no more bees, no more food, so I watch for bees."

Having cleared up this mystery, Natalya notices my blue and gray chess set sitting nearby. "*Shakhmaty.*" She speaks the Russian word for chess with particular fervor. Without hesitating, she walks over to the board and pushes the gray king's pawn two squares. I join her and push the blue queen's bishop pawn two squares. A few moves later, she blithely surrenders a knight for a mere pawn. I accept the gift, only to be checkmated by a series of moves she makes instantly, having foreseen a chain of events utterly opaque to me. Natalya, it turns out, is an international chess master, deriving the income with which she supports her brother and ex-husband from a Facebook website where she plays amateurs for a small fee.

"Parasites," she mutters with contempt, not making it clear who she means. But it does become clear soon afterward that she's in no hurry to leave my house and return to her freeloading entourage. She takes a seat on my sofa and wonders if I have any vodka.

"No," I say, not mentioning any other intoxicants I do possess. I am still weighing the pleasure of Natalya versus the risk of acquiring her menfolk in the bargain. She screws her face up in disapproval.

"Please, more coffee then, twice as strong. After that, I will help you."

"Help me?"

"You must not play the Sicilian defense. It is too complex for you. I will teach you the Petroff. Very simple, very good."

"Thank you, but I don't play much anymore. Just once in a while with my girlfriend."

Natalya smiles, waves away my comment with lilac-tipped fingers. "Coffee, please; I will teach you."

About then, Olivia emerges, spots Natalya, and cries, "Hermine!" She rushes toward the sofa, no doubt bursting with remarkable revelations, then stops short. "Shit, who are *you*?"

Instead of answering, Natalya shoots me a speculative stare. Surely she doesn't think Olivia is the girlfriend I mentioned.

"This is my neighbor, Natalya. Natalya, this is Olivia, my granddaughter."

"Greetings, little dove," Natalya croons. "You have such big, lovely eyes." Inside five minutes, after gushing over Natalya's clothes and accent, Olivia launches into a loud, lurid, inaccurate synopsis of her weekend and, by extension, my marital history, encouraged by questions from Natalya I can't quite overhear. When I serve the coffee, it's apparent I'm momentarily superfluous.

"I'm going to my room to write," I say. "Nice to meet you, Natalya. Good luck finding your brother."

"Yes, William, good luck to you." I notice she has kicked off her stilettos and tucked her legs up underneath her as if settling in to watch a movie on HBO.

I do go to my room, but not to write. Maybe if I lie down and empty my mind as the compassionate Buddha taught, some of the weekend's bewilderments will dissipate. Oddly, when I close my eyes, the one voice that will not shut up is Carl's, insisting he loved my first wife more than I did. Logic would rank this claim as the least of my concerns. After all, if Ramona's paternity is "old news," then "Karen and Carl and me" is ancient history whose only artifact rests at the bottom of a Tampa canal. But logic plays all sorts of nonsensical pranks. I used to ask my students why, if a man can dig a hole in sixty seconds, sixty men can't dig that hole in one second? You'd be astonished at how hard it was for them to pinpoint the reason. I find myself doing just as poorly trying to figure out why Carl's claim rankles me now, a day after I made a show of shrugging it off with indifference.

As I close my eyes, muttering a couple of profanities, Olivia's loud giggles and Natalya's baritone chuckles reach me from the living room. They are pals already, a knack I envy. And it strikes me that I envy Carl's feelings for Karen more than I resent them. The truth is, I don't think about Karen much. Far less than Wanda Grice, with whom I only spent a relative handful of days and nights fifty years ago.

Bothered by this, by not knowing why I have let Karen drift into a caricature of memory, I summon her face and body as best I can. Pain washes through me at the effort. Not because the true memory of her repels me, but because portions of it are too lovely to bear.

CHAPTER THIRTY-SEVEN

"Heart of Gold"

Gainesville, Florida, Fall 1975

"I miss Brooklyn," Karen Levine sighed one evening while fitfully twirling in her chair. She stopped revolving to look at me, waiting for encouragement. I froze, lacking a map for this new, relatively intimate territory. Karen and I were work-study employees, part of the University library night crew, and up to now, she had treated me with the arm's-length friendliness males get from disinterested females.

"I've never been there," I replied finally. "My father used to say politicians were trying to sell him the Brooklyn Bridge, and I think Sandy Koufax, you know, the Dodger pitcher, comes from Brooklyn, but I never thought about what it's like to live there. Lots of people crammed together is what I picture."

I heard Karen laugh for the first time. Nothing remarkable, but I took it as a small affinity. "People picture tenements with fat housewives hanging out the wash," she said, "kids playing in the streets, saying *youse guys*." She shook her head. "We had a regular house in Bay Ridge, a yard, nice trees. And nice schools, nice stores, nice friends," she added wistfully. "Yes," she admitted, "there were problems when the Puerto Ricans started moving in, but don't believe *West Side Story*."

I nodded along, delighted that listening gave me the right to look. Karen wore what amounted to her uniform: polo shirt, tight jeans, and Keds, with jet-black hair piled ingeniously atop her head and secured with tortoise combs and colored bobby pins. As she talked, she squinted at tiny phantom flaws in her skin. Behind gold wire-rim glasses, her face radiated a delicate quiver, as if she were barely suppressing a shocking secret. I imagined her leaning close, ineffably scented, whispering the secret to me, the secret being nothing, the whisper being everything.

For something to say, I inquired about Flatbush, Ebbets Field—the Dodgers old stomping grounds. Privately I indulged the not very high-minded thought that Karen was the best-looking woman I could ever hope to attract. Flatbush wasn't her neighborhood, she said, but pretty close. She smiled to herself, remembering. I knew her smile wasn't for me, but that didn't matter. It fell on me like warm sunlight.

Her awakened nostalgia and my attention provided as good an explanation as any for Karen's decision to begin unfolding her life's story in nightly reminiscences, like episodes of a TV show. Her narrative sketched a journey from idyllic Brooklyn to Cleveland's west side in the aftermath of "family problems." There, her house sat directly beneath the glide path of approaching airport jets, whose whining roar rattled crockery and caused Karen to duck her head uselessly. Next, an "emergency" migration to Florida during her early teenage years. She left vague the varieties of distress that led to her eventual southern exile, and I didn't press the issue. It was enough to know we had distress and exile in common. Now I could add kinship to the lust and loneliness that drew me to her.

In any case, Karen's "family problems" didn't remain mysterious for long. Because baseball had come up in our early conversations, Karen made a point to explain that she acquired her last name from Gibson Levine, her stepfather, a white man named after legendary Negro League catcher and power hitter Josh Gibson, who happened to be a hero of mine.

"I use Gibson's last name, but I'm not adopted," she told me one night between bites of cold pizza. "My mother wants me to use his name for legal reasons." Karen seemed to need this clearly understood. She went on to explain that Levine had been a sports bookie in Cleveland, and when the IRS came calling, he married Karen's mother, bought a trailer park in her name, and used it to launder his money; his reward for being on the smart side of people's dumb bets. Karen's mother had long since divorced Karen's birth father, a feckless Manhattan cabbie. Mrs. Levine now ran the trailer park located in Lake Lucinda, a little retirement haven about an hour east of Tampa.

"Gibson owes the feds about seven million dollars, and he's technically under house arrest," Karen confided another evening as we were shelving an assortment of gorgeous art books.

"Technically?"

"Well, they don't want to put him in jail until they get their money. They think he'll lead them to it sooner or later." Karen leaned closer and whispered, though the library was otherwise deserted, "He stashes it in the Cayman Islands. He even goes down there, but the feds never catch on."

The "feds." I remembered my father referring to cock-and-bull stories. Whether Karen's story fit the bill or not, her telling of it brought her near enough to drop pleasant hints of vanilla and bring nights with Wanda acutely to mind.

"I'd like to meet this guy," I ventured, the words seeming to slip out against my will.

Karen rubbed her nose forcibly, suggesting I'd blundered and put her on the spot, endangering a possibility that hung in the balance.

"Actually," I reconsidered, "maybe that's not a good idea. I've already had a guy pull a gun on me out in a swamp. The guy disappeared. The cops got involved. Everything went to shit after that." I tried to sound fearless and fascinating.

Karen dropped her books on the cart. "Are you saying you *killed* the guy?" To my surprise, she seemed far more curious than horrified at the idea.

"No. I escaped, and when I came back with the sheriff, he had vanished. Never seen again. Probably snakes and alligators got him." In time, I would furnish Karen with most details of the Heffelfinger saga, only omitting any mention of Wanda and possible fatherhood.

"How did things go to . . . shit?" Karen asked, standing still and staring at me.

"The FBI came and questioned me. Thought he was maybe a white version of the Black Panthers."

Okay, I told myself, *that's enough bragging.*

Karen measured me with a newfound glimmer of respect. "Don't worry, Gibson's not that kind of criminal. He's a teddy bear."

Several days later, as we left the library, Karen tugged at my arm. "Bill, I'm going to see my mom tomorrow. Do you want to tag along and meet the notorious Gibson Levine?"

A mild jolt passed through me; I may have even flushed red. Gibson Levine hadn't come up again after his first mention. I assumed Karen had spotted my interest in Levine as a tacky ploy aimed at her seduction. To save face against that probability, I had consigned him to the realm of fiction. Given Karen's current offer, I had gotten something wrong, but what was the nature of my error? Too late to figure that out. But by chance, two nearby male students were arguing loudly about an upcoming fight between Joe Frazier and Mohammed Ali, masking my hesitation. When Karen turned back from glaring at them, I managed to fake an offhand answer. "Sounds interesting; are you sure I won't be in the way?"

"I'm sure. Anyway, Mom always says she wants to meet my friends. Let's see, how about the library parking lot at nine? Look for a dark green Barracuda."

I tried without success to hear intrigue in her voice, then headed for Mango Lodge to heat canned tamales on my clandestine hotplate. After considering an all-nighter to eliminate the chance of oversleeping, I ultimately decided to smoke a lot of pot, go to bed early, and set my alarm clock for five a.m. I woke up as planned and raised the shade. Below lay Dylan's empty streets—way too dead for anything but dreaming at this hour, especially in a hung-over Southern college town.

I got up, showered with unprecedented leisure in the communal bathroom, then donned my one clean, collared shirt along with khakis whose wrinkles would probably smooth out after a bit of walking. With my heart beating briskly in anticipation and a bit more pot in my system, I set out for the Mini Mart, seeking coffee and two apple turnovers. It was not quite seven o'clock when I finished breakfast sitting on the curb outside the store. The walk to the library parking lot would consume another ten minutes. If only I'd kept the beautiful Swiss watch I left in Hopperton out of spite!

A rational young man would have waited near a clock in the air-conditioned library, but somehow, I chose the parking lot's grassy border, where I placed my back against a pine tree and tried unsuccessfully not to doze off. Luckily, general activity woke me in plenty of time to see a green Barracuda enter the parking lot. I bolted to my feet like a soldier coming to attention, then overcorrected my impulses by walking too slowly toward the car.

Karen stepped out to greet me and maybe to show off her black sundress speckled with pink stars. I'd never beheld her in sunlit feminine regalia, and the effect on me, deliberate or not, was incandescent.

"Where's the party?" I called, trying to mimic an unimpressed Carl Decker.

Karen laughed. "You don't know my mom."

October had arrived, but the Sunshine State held fast to summer glamour. We headed down I-75, past the flat expanse of Paine's Prairie, home, Karen informed me, to countless drowsing gators and a buffalo herd. We were on our way to 301, then somewhere east. Karen drove and talked fast, choosing her best friend's troubled love life as a topic of conversation. I supposed she was forestalling an unpredictable silence; otherwise, she sounded a lot like Sally Chiles.

"I adore Nancy, but she is such a fool to get mixed up with this guy. I think he's married. Drives a Buick, definitely a married guy's car."

To show interest, I added my innocuous two cents' worth. "Well, maybe it will turn out all right. Things don't always go to rack and ruin."

Karen grew silent, seeming to give my words profound consideration. "I need to tell you something, Bill, before you meet my mom."

I said "okay," then waited, half expecting Karen to confess a previously unmentioned boyfriend, squelching any chance of a romance between us.

"See, I had an older sister, Marie, who died. She was hiking with her fiancé. They say she slipped and fell on some rocks, but my mom knew the kid Marie was engaged to, knew his family from the neighborhood, and swears it was no accident. I don't know about that. But, I mean, my mom has had a hard life and thinks the worst of people sometimes, but she's brilliant about, you know, surviving."

By warning me that her mother would probably despise me, Karen had also exposed intimate sorrows. A double whammy. I suddenly suspected I belonged back at Mango Lodge, sleeping in with all the other wasted youths. It hit me, as only the obvious can, that Karen and I were pretty much strangers. "God, Karen, I'm so sorry about your sister. How terrible for you. And listen, I'll try not to say anything to upset your mother."

She gave me a grateful smile. "Thanks, but don't worry. Nobody's upset my mom in a long time. She does the upsetting. Just don't freak out if you get the evil eye. And it's okay about my sister, I mean not okay, but I guess I mean I'm okay."

I could only blame myself for envisioning a weekend lark with erotic overtones. All Karen offered was a chance to meet Gibson Levine. How much longer, I wondered, would I let my fantasies drag me around by the nose? As I brooded, Karen resumed her storytelling. She explained that Marie had been a beauty queen with a bad temper—Miss Parma, Ohio, among her crowns—who attracted men with her looks then berated them with her vicious tongue. Anything was possible with Marie. Maybe her boyfriend killed her out there on that hiking trail, or maybe she just got so wound up in a quarrel that she fell.

"That's what drives people crazy," I said.

"What?"

"Being aware that anything is possible, having to deal with all the whacko stuff that jumps out of the bushes. It's a miracle we're not all in mental hospitals."

"God, Bill, you're worse than me."

"The very worst," I admitted. Karen seemed pleased that my pessimism surpassed hers. She leaned back and slowed the car a little. *Well*, I thought, *whatever the wrong thing to say was, I didn't say it.*

After about an hour, we traded the main roads for a winding asphalt ribbon passing through a procession of picturesque lakes, marine repair shops, the inevitable barbecue joints, countless antennae-laden trailers, and one elongated shack whose enormous sign offered BARSTOOLS, PET SUPPLIES, CLEAN FILL. Finally, after barreling through one last single-minded spate of rain, we coasted past a gilded cast-iron gate whose sign identified Hibiscus Shores Community Park. Underneath the name a little reassurance: "Relax, You're Home."

The Levine's combination residence and business office sprawled in vaguely Mediterranean splendor behind leaning palms and a webwork of bright flowering tropicals. Inlaid with pentagons of blue tile, the walkway wended through a shadowy profusion of ferns and bromeliads. A ceramic castle with minarets hung over a pond exhibiting reddish-gold fish with rippling fins. Exotic opulence intensified my fear of Mrs. Levine, and I slowed to let Karen reach the door before me.

Mrs. Levine greeted us in a dark pants suit. *Definitely a carpetbagger*, I judged uncharitably, Don Heffelfinger's old insult coming in handy at last. She and Karen looked alike, though Mrs. Levine emitted a potent formality alien to Karen and wore her hair in a stiff amber globe. As I barely squeezed her hand, I reminded myself of her dead daughter and of my need to maintain proper decorum. I had been raised with "manners" as they are understood in southern Georgia—opening doors, giving up seats, waiting to be invited—and hoped they would carry the day.

Mrs. Levine, as if to confound my preconceptions, insisted I call her Dorothy, a request I mostly forgot to honor. She and Karen hugged and exchanged inaudible confidences. I stood aside, noticing the dim, somehow subterranean coolness pervading the interior, an ambience eerily reminiscent of the root cellar back home. After a few moments we proceeded down a long hall into a chandeliered, moorishly dark living room. There, at the foot of a cordovan leather sectional, lay a full-grown, unfettered, very-much-alive cheetah.

"That's Delilah," Karen said. "She's a nice old girl. Poor thing. She needs dental work." As Karen and her mother took seats on the couch, Delilah gathered herself, rose to her feet and padded toward me with what struck me as an equivocal rumble in her throat.

"She likes you," Mrs. Levine observed, looking up with the barest flicker of amusement. "Otherwise she'd ignore you." I beseeched Karen for confirmation, but she was busy pouring coffee from a sleek carafe.

"Pet her, Bill; she just wants a little love."

I tentatively leaned down and stroked Delilah's bristle-brush coat. She shifted closer, and her rumble quickened. I read that after Stalin gave a speech, guards shot the first person to stop clapping for showing counter-revolutionary tendencies. Fearing a similar dynamic at work, I continued stroking Delilah's pelt until she yawned and ambled around the coffee table to sniff Karen's sandals. I seized the moment and sat down. "Go away," Karen ordered, kicking the great cat gently in the nose. Delilah meekly accepted this rebuke and consoled herself by licking her paws.

Mrs. Levine—Dorothy—watched this interaction with a fond smile. Mother, daughter, and cheetah were briefly bunched together like an absurdist Norman Rockwell painting. Behind them, filtered sunlight fell through curtained patio doors and floor-length shaded windows, backlighting the scene. A wave of estrangement joined the fatigue that had been sneaking up on me all day. I didn't feel mistreated, ignored, unwelcome—merely extraneous. *Why was I here?* Get a grip, I told myself. Benign, ordinary explanations sufficed. Karen seemed happy, at ease. "Relax, You're Home," the sign out front had advised. I needed to take its suggestion to heart.

Mrs. Levine chose this moment to offer me coffee. When I accepted, she—not Karen—got up and brought it over to me. After I took the cup, she sat down close to me to me—too close. Her perfume reminded me of Hopperton church ladies. Nothing else about her reminded me of them.

"Karen tells me you're pursuing an academic career," she said. I thought she attached a certain asperity to the word "academic," but I wasn't sure.

"I'm finishing up my master's degree in philosophy this year."

Mrs. Levine took a thoughtful sip of coffee. "Bill, I've always been curious. What exactly is it philosophers *do*?"

"They think, Mom," Karen put in.

"And what do the rest of us do, my dear?" I had to admire the question, though I knew damn well Dorothy Levine had *never* been curious about philosophy until ten seconds ago. "It's a different kind of thinking. Way different." Karen didn't elaborate. No matter, she had defended me. I tried to weigh in.

"It's not that different, really, except that philosophers write books to explain what they think and why other philosophers are wrong. It's true that hardly anybody reads these books, but say you're a rodeo clown. Rodeos are cool to you. Even if everybody else you know hates them. Philosophy is kind of like that. But if you're asking what philosophers do for a living, they usually teach at colleges, hope people buy their books, that sort of thing."

"I see. Might I ask if being a philosopher is an alternative to an occupation . . . less unusual?"

"Well, my father's turpentine business was a possibility, but all those jobs went overseas. Now he's in the paper business. I suppose that's an option." I hoped repeating the word "business" would mollify Mrs. Levine. Mercifully, Karen interrupted my cross-examination.

"Mom, this is boring. Let's show Bill around. I think the rain let up."

"Of course, dear. Bill and I can continue our chat later." Mrs. Levine patted my leg. "But I can't go far with my old bones. And Bill, do you like okra? It's good for osteoporosis." I nodded, happy to assure her pot roast and fried okra were mainstays of my childhood dinners.

We strolled out into the trailer park. Delilah was left to doze on the patio. Old couples were out, holding hands and walking small dogs. I envisioned Mrs. Levine strolling with Delilah and wondered whether people would run screaming into their aluminum homes or take the sight in accustomed stride. Boisterous boys came by on undersized bikes with absurdly high seats. Here and there, dragonflies hovered, their wings making a dry rattle.

"It's not that different from a village in the old days," Karen observed. I found her comment agreeably optimistic and democratic. Whatever my status here, the day undeniably had its novel pleasures. As we walked, Mrs. Levine gave me a brief statistical rundown on the park, its size, rental rates, and so forth. She extolled its profitability with unconcealed pride. And, I thought, a hint of condescension. I did my best to appear interested until Karen interposed.

"By the way, Mom, where is Gibson? Is he in hiding? Bill came all this way to talk to him about baseball."

Mrs. Levine smiled at her daughter's take on my motives.

"Of course not, dear. He'll join us now that Delilah is out on the patio. I'll tell him you're here with a guest. I also need to let Bona know the count for dinner."

After Mrs. Levine departed, I followed Karen to a spot of emerald, lacework shade across from a shiny hump of a trailer. She took my hand to seat herself. *She is a Renoir*, I thought, as she spread her skirt out like a flower. We chatted about Janis Joplin, Al Pacino, Charles Manson. Karen pretended to worry I was mad about Delilah, but she knew better. For a few minutes, we swayed comfortably in the penumbra between intimacy and awkwardness, then walked back to the house.

At the risk of melodrama, I can honestly say Gibson Levine emerged out of the shadows, in this case, a dim hallway off the living room. Like a creature coming out of hibernation, he came forward hesitantly, looking around the room as if struggling to remember it. Levine was slight and dapper in high-waisted, pleated ivory slacks and a billowy soft-green shirt. His face was narrow, with a neat mustache, his sparse, sandy hair swept back. He reminded me of pictures I had seen of famous old actors on vacation. Karen introduced us, mentioning philosophy and baseball as possible common interests.

Levine clasped his hands behind his back, closed his eyes, and shook his head. "My interest in baseball, in sports, is mathematical, numerical, not nostalgic. My birth name was not Gibson, but rather Avraham. But

Josh Gibson and I were born on the same day of the same year; I changed my name motivated by superstition, a weakness. Forgive me if I cannot muster up adulation for physical prowess, although I do find its consequences interesting in the aggregate. As for philosophy, I wonder if you know of one that would assist me in reading men's minds?" He opened his eyes and looked at me with what appeared to be absolute sincerity.

"Well, philosophy might help you understand men's minds, but probably not read them."

"Unfortunate," Levine replied. "While I have found an attunement to human nature to possess utility, it fails to provide specific assurances when conducting . . . well, critical affairs. Whereas one wishes not to rely on a single past example to predict the outcome of a sporting contest, one would very much wish to extract a single thought from the cognitive morass in certain moments of truth—if you see what I mean."

On the one hand, no one had ever spoken to me as Levine spoke. On the other hand, I understood him.

"I see your point, sir, but philosophy's specialty is asking questions that have no answers, like why is there something rather than nothing? Or, since you mentioned mathematics, consider that a number isn't a thing out there you can touch. On the other hand, a number isn't a thought since two plus two equals four, whether you think it or not. So, what is it?

"Ah, quandaries to contemplate in the absence of real problems. A pleasant thought."

"You can't have real problems until you figure out what's real."

Levine gave the slightest shrug of dismissal, a gesture I would learn to know well. "When Allied soldiers overran German positions at Normandy, a combatant famously said that they found the stench of three things: death, sausage, and German philosophy. I take it you believe the Holocaust was real?"

"Yes, which proves, by your own words, that philosophy is powerful."

Levine favored me with the thinnest possible smile. "Alas, it's only a club where a scalpel is needed."

Bona, the cook, came in scowling and muttering something to Mrs. Levine, who announced, "We are short of catfish. Bona is from Poland and does not drive. Karen and I will not be gone long. Gibson, please be a good host."

Karen added with exuberant good humor, "I'm sorry to miss the clash of brains. No fistfights, please."

Levine and I were soon alone. I expected him to excuse himself and melt back into the dim hallway. Instead, he asked if I played cards.

"For money?"

Levine saw through the question. "I take it, William, you know more of my history than I of yours. Rest assured your funds are safe."

"Okay, well, I know bridge and pinochle, but not much beyond the rules. That's about it."

"Your father learned pinochle in the Navy, no doubt."

"That's right."

"An inelegant number of cards, but otherwise a worthy game. Are you familiar with cribbage?"

"Is that the game with pegs?"

"It is." Levine waved a delicate hand. "Learning the game is a matter of moments. Come with me." We proceeded to Levine's study, its walls adorned with photographs, mostly in black-and-white, of boxers, race-horses, and baseball players. Some of the pictures were autographed. I recognized Rocky Marciano and Bob Feller.

The room smelled not unpleasantly of cologne and cigars. A large, burnished wooden box sat on Levine's desk. A card table sat by the window, already equipped with playing cards and what I presumed was a cribbage board. Several yellow legal pads sat in a stack nearby. I walked over to fireballer Bob Feller's picture, indeed autographed, but not to Gibson Levine. "Commodities of business transactions," Levine clarified, confirming my suspicion. He then added, "I do enjoy them; I think of them as trophies."

Before joining me at the card table, he stopped at his desk, opened the large box, and removed an old, zippered bank deposit bag. He then sat opposite me, unzipped the bag, and pulled out a small bundle of dollar bills. "I keep them in my humidor with my Montecristo premiums," Levine explained. "I rarely light a cigar, but they are good company. Cigar smoking traces its roots back as least as far as the tenth century. It appears in Guatemalan art of that period."

"My father loves cigars," I said, almost adding "more than me." I stared at the dollar bills.

"This constitutes my bankroll," Levine explained as he riffled the bills by his ear. "When we play, I will bet my real dollars against your imaginary or, if you wish, *philosophical* dollars. When my bankroll is exhausted, I will quit the game. I feel good sportsmanship demands I inform you in advance."

I could have believed I was a character in a play, Gibson Levine playing the eccentric sage to my clueless acolyte. "It sounds like you're rigging the game in my favor," I said. "Anyway, why bet? Why not just keep score? I don't even know how to play yet."

"I do not 'rig' the game," Levine replied archly, "only the betting terms. Much as the game uses pegs, I use these dollars to keep personal score, not to manipulate."

I had seen a cribbage set in the Hopperton barbershop: a small, unadorned, hinged box with space for pegs inside. Levine's set was an actual board, maybe a foot long and covered with burnished copper intricately etched with floral designs. The copper rested on four layers of wood constructed to create a stairstep effect. The pegs were copper as well, with tiny bits of purple glass, or genuine amethyst for all I knew, crowning each peg. Sure, Levine was hustling me, but I saw no harm and quickly learned the rules. We played. I won an occasional hand, but Levine kept his dollars. I wondered how long he had held on to those very same bills. Finally, I heard voices and Karen's chiming laughter. Levine turned his cards face up, ending whatever this was—passing of time, contest, object lesson, philosophical debate, exorcism of loneliness. He wrote on a legal pad, then regarded me for a long moment. "Tell me, William, how far advanced is your embroilment with Karen?" An odd, irritating choice of words.

Still, I answered.

"We're just friends. She invited me to meet you."

"Because, I suppose, I am a colorful criminal with an peculiar first name?"

"She made you sound interesting, not criminal."

Levine tucked his dollar bills away with loving care, musing throughout. "I am simply a person who scoffs at certain laws. Criminals—the Mafia and their warring rivals—drove me out of Cleveland more surely than the IRS. Mobsters in that fair city tend to resolve their differences with car bombs. As for Karen, she is a fine, even admirable, young woman, cast in the same mold as her mother. I observed today that she looks at you fondly; I have long observed that she knows what she wants."

Levine, done with his task, regarded me like a professor staring at an unprepared student. "Now, William, based on the way you play cribbage, let me advise you. As much as Mrs. Levine's feline companion unnerves me, that cat is the most harmless female in this house. Please do not take this as a warning; consider it information, like remembering your discards in cribbage. You do tend to forget them, you know."

CHAPTER THIRTY-EIGHT

"It's All in the Game"

We feasted on batter-fried catfish and okra; everyone but Gibson, who stuck to Bona's cabbage and sorrel soup. Mrs. Levine's offhandedly posed questions pointed toward my financial future like a compass toward a lodestone. I parried politely, longing to tell her Karen wasn't my type and I'd just come along for a free meal. After dinner, as we sat in the living room sipping coffee, Karen informed me we were staying for the night.

"Bona fixed you a bed in the vacant trailer, Bill. It's air-conditioned; you'll like it." She beamed like she'd won something. Maybe her two worlds had collided more gently than she expected. Delilah padded in and sat at my feet, offering herself for duly delivered caresses. Up until then, Gibson had been sitting quietly, reading. Seeing Delilah, he stood up and pronounced with cryptic elegance, "She and I have too much in common. It unnerves me." Mrs. Levine departed too, but not exactly with him.

"They have separate master bedrooms, separate bathrooms," Karen confided. "I've never seen them kiss or fight," she said. "It's weird."

A bit later, she walked me to the trailer but didn't come in. I lay down on an excellent bed, knowing sleep would find me as soon as I closed my eyes. I postponed that moment, wondering if I might later hear a soft knock at the door. No, I decided that would *not* happen. And I was right.

And I continued being right when Karen and I returned to Gainesville, our breezy camaraderie standing pat. Yet, in some indefinable sense, she had claimed me. I was "Billy" now.

I filled Carl in when he passed through town on his way to Key West for "serious sex and deep-sea fishing." "She invited you to her mother's house but not *her* pad," he took pains to point out, lightly salting my emotional wounds. We sat in the Cin City Lounge, shouting over KC and the Sunshine Band, or maybe the Average White Band. Disco had befallen us, even if no one called it disco yet.

"Her sister was killed by a jealous boyfriend. You can't blame her for being cautious."

Carl let out a derisive bellow. "Yeah, that's it, Professor, she's worried you'll murder her. Interesting. Maybe she invited you to her mother's house so you could murder her mother."

"Funny."

"Here's the truth." Carl leaned forward like he was bestowing the secret of all existence. "You want a golden doorknob, and she's giving you a bucket of cowshit. She expects you to earn that doorknob. Fuck that. You need to grab it and turn it. *Comprende?*"

I understood Carl's advice in theory. In practice, I had nary a clue. By Thanksgiving, my intimacy with Karen hadn't progressed even a single hug beyond the word "Billy." She drove back to Hibiscus Shores for the holiday weekend; I splurged on a turkey dinner at the Holiday Inn. When we reconvened at the library, Karen seemed restless and disinclined to discuss her excursion. She glanced at me a few times, unsmiling, leading me to imagine she was reconsidering even our limited personal standing. Then, just before closing, I felt a gentle kick on my leg.

"I have a huge favor to ask you," Karen said. "Come with me to the trailer park for Christmas. I need someone normal to talk to. Thanksgiving was gloomy. I swear Gibson was mad I didn't bring you. Last time, you balanced things out. Unless you have other plans?"

Carl's warning came to mind. Was this the golden doorknob or the bucket of cowshit?

"My friend Carl invited me to Tampa, and anyway, are you sure I'm doing you a favor? Your mother's not my biggest fan."

Karen drooped a little in her swivel chair. "I'll be honest, Billy. If I bring you again, Mom will think we're about to get married, and I'll have to have a "talk" with her, which I hate. But see, Delilah likes you, and I think you're literally the only person other than Mom or me that Gibson talks to. And we can't talk to him the way you do. Please, come with me. I'll owe you one."

We each speak a different language, our words attached to images, memories, associations unique to us. And we hear each other's languages through an interpreter which we assume is us, but isn't. It's our feelings doing the translating, feelings we pass through like that cloudburst Karen and I passed through on our first drive together.

"I'll do it, but please don't 'owe me one.' I hate that shit," I growled. My last bit of dark vehemence seemed to come of its own accord, and neither of us knew what to make of it. I ventured a compensatory smile.

"Okay." Karen shrugged. "No favors for you. Better for me, I guess."

I refused to hope I was anything more than a fourth for bridge when one of my mother's club ladies failed to show. But that didn't mean I wasn't going to go.

Glittering red ribbon adorned the park's arched entrance in candy cane fashion. However, inside the Levine's house, neither Christmas tree, nor nativity scene, nor gaily wrapped gifts held sway—adornment stopped at the burning of silver tapers. Did the candles burn for the lost or simply stand as an aesthetic rejoinder to Hibiscus Shore's paying residents and their haphazardly strung lights and inflatable Santas? I didn't care much, too caught up in wanting Karen to feel differently about me. Alas, nothing pointed that way. Mrs. Levine took my presence in unruffled stride, suggesting confidence that I played no part in her daughter's future. So, as she and Karen communed, I spent my time reading *The Day of the Jackal* on the patio, hanging out with Delilah. Her amiable nature was nearer a certainty than anything else I had concluded about the Levines.

Gibson postponed his emergence until he and I were alone in the house, Bona being away, visiting her daughter in Miami, the other women shopping, and Delilah snoozing in the shade of a vast, potted fig. The Jackal was methodically killing people to maintain secrecy.

"Ah, William, back for more, I see." I looked up. Gibson had somehow opened the patio door noiselessly and stood at the entrance impeccable and still. I could now hear music emanate from his study, a jazzy combo several decades out of style—frantic, haunting. When I glanced toward the sound, Gibson explained, "Django Reinhardt, a Gypsy guitarist of considerable fame, undeterred by two useless, burned fingers. They say he avoided the death camps because a Nazi officer was enamored of jazz. May I ask what you're reading?"

"Nothing deep; just one of those spy thrillers."

He sidled closer; peered at the back-cover summary. "A man avenging betrayal. Betrayal is how certain elements in France saw DeGaulle's surrender of Algeria."

"You read the book?"

"Oh, no, no." Gibson waved away the very possibility. "I am simply a fan of revenge, of history, more or less the same phenomenon. Such an attempt on DeGaulle's life was indeed set in motion. Churchill was booted out after the war. Political revenge, very personal. And speaking of history, how far have you advanced your cause with Karen?"

I feigned a shrug of indifference. "There's no cause to advance."

"I see. Then I take it you're not in love with her?"

From what I could tell, Levine was not trying to catch me in a contradiction but merely following a line of thought to its conclusion. I tried to answer in the same spirit. "I have thought about being in love with her. Does that count?"

"Yes and no. It doesn't precisely answer the question, but it helps me understand you. You see, there are two kinds of people, and you—"

"Everybody says that," I objected, "but it's never the same two kinds."

"True," he replied, "but not germane. Now, as I said, there are two kinds of people: the strategic and the improvisational. You are of the latter sort. The universe, as it happens, is on the fence about which it prefers. On the one hand, a few strategic underpinnings, such as gravity and the speed of light, point to a certain constancy in the space-time continuum, if you will. On the other hand, houses become messier with neglect, not more orderly, do you see? A room *improvises* its appearance in the absence of constant effort to the contrary. You, William, have yet to discover your unbreakable laws, so you improvise, you tolerate ambiguity. You tend to forgive what you don't understand. Not an altogether reprehensible trait, I assure you."

"I guess you're the strategic type, not the forgiving type," I replied with a bit of resentment.

"Perhaps, although improvisational hand gestures always seem to accompany my words. That contradiction aside, shall we return to your question of whether contemplating love signifies love?" Gibson sat down, despite Delilah, to provide an answer.

"Well," he continued, "I suppose love is only a thought after all. As you surely know, plants form from air, water, and a pinch of minerals. But within each seed is a thought of growth. That thought is the *sine qua non* of vegetation, is it not? Hence, I do not disparage your amorous thought, insufficient as it may be without air, water, and so forth."

"Air and water?"

Levine smiled, almost with mischief. "Their equivalent, if you will, in matters of the heart."

"Which are?"

"The hours from noon to noon, or midnight to midnight, as you prefer."

Cribbage, I decided, was less disquieting than a conversation with Gibson. We played as before, Gibson excusing himself periodically to refresh the turntable, every record introduced: "This is Sonny Rollins, very hard bebop sax, incarcerated for armed robbery, his both precise *and* improvisational message not yet completely deciphered by yours truly." As for Cribbage, I *had* begun to decipher the game, gaining a feel for crib tosses and pegging strategies, as well as an awareness of Levine's predilections, including his dubious fondness for tossing pairs into his crib. I won my share of skirmishes, even pressed close to winning matches, but found myself irked to fall short inevitably. And the more of Levine's searing, buttery Napoleon brandy I drank, the closer I came to rash words.

"What the hell did you mean earlier by 'back for more'?" I demanded. "Was that your gentlemanly way of telling me I'm a fool?"

Levine looked up from his legal pad, tapped his pen, and considered. "You heard provocation? Perhaps even derision? Emotional conjecture on your part, but not irrational. 'More,' I assure you, referred only to the eccentricities of these surroundings, and of course Karen's desirable company."

"Desirable? Last time you warned me she was more dangerous than Delilah."

"I recall saying less harmless, not more dangerous. And since you long for clarification, I will explain. At this moment, Karen and my wife are somewhere buying tea towels, but what they are actually doing is weighing strategies, making judgments, formulating roles for me, for you, wondering how, if at all, we fit into their futures. They do this without malice, but not without, shall we say, repercussions. On the other hand, we are here weighing the merits of random playing cards and how to wield them. In *my* defense, such calculations assist me in my profession. In your case, you are, and forgive me here, merely *diverted* by the problem of Cribbage, and expect no solution."

"Are you advising me not to play? Also, how can a game of chance be 'solved'?"

"There are ninety-one meaningful discard combinations in Cribbage. One can know the average point value of each. I know them all, drawing me closer to a solution." He shrugged imperceptibly. "Calculus solves many problems by approaching limits that cannot be reached. Thus, I am hopeful. As to your playing, entirely credible on infrequent and brief occasions. Diversions must be seen in the light of whatever path they depart, you see. Leave the path too long, and you lose your way. This presupposes a path, of course. Consider Delilah, how domestication has deflected her from her nature, her killing power. She stalks nothing now. Do you think I am afraid of her? Not at all. I find her fate perverse, and therefore avoid her."

"She seems pretty happy; *she* doesn't know she has a fate, a path, whatever. Maybe you're projecting your issues on her."

"Certainly, I am. My own life is . . . compromised."

"So how. . .?"

"Can I judge? My 'right to judge' is precisely my kinship with Delilah. Rest assured, I am working on her behalf as well as my own to obviate our compromises."

Whatever his last comment meant, it bothered me to find that Levine's respect for our discussion seemed superior to mine. I tried to do better. "Mr. Levine, you know many things that I don't. As far as *I* know, Karen invited me along as a friend to . . . to make things easier for her."

Levine got up, lifted a record from the turntable with the utmost delicacy, dusted it with a fine brush, and slid it into its sleeve. Only afterward did he reply.

"You are here, yes, yes, to occupy me, to play a part in lifting the pall of tragedy. All of that." He paused again to return his dollars to the humidor. "But do you believe Karen had no other motive?" He sighed. "I suppose all philosophers try to pare things to their alleged essence. Notice that music does not; art does not. They express some fragment of the inexpressible and leave it at that. Imagine trying to reduce impressionism to a blob of paint. Surely multiplicity and doubt play a central role in philosophy."

"I believe Karen will return with multiple pizzas. I doubt they will be all that good. And I don't say that to mock you or dismiss your question. It's just that I'm hungry, tired, and my head is spinning. Maybe it will all sink in later."

"Fair enough, William. The code that creates the lilac is not the lilac. From time to time I lose sight of that."

After pizza, the Levines talked park business in low, pragmatic voices, freeing Karen and me to migrate to the patio. Delilah parked herself between us, emitting an occasional rumbling purr, as if to hold up her end of the conversation.

A few Christmas lights, a few stars, as the day faded.

"I miss Christmas," Karen murmured. "We weren't religious, but we were Christmas people when my dad was around. Now, with Gibson here, and my sister . . ."

"You're not Jewish?"

"Nope, not by a long shot. My old name was Covolo. We still have relatives in Tuscany. Mom says we're temporarily Jewish. How about you?"

"I'm waiting for one of those stars up there to show me a sign."

"How will you know?"

"Good question. Maybe I've already missed it."

"Oh, don't worry. I believe what Gibson says, that patterns repeat. If you divide the number eleven into the number one, you get the number point-zero-nine repeating forever. In a way, we *can* see the future."

"And *what* would you divide into *what* to see a person's future?" I asked.

"The universe does the dividing. It's a big calculator. That's why physical laws repeat. Everything is information, which boils down to numbers. We're expressions of laws and numbers, right? So, *we* repeat, making us and our futures predictable. That's why I'm a math major. That's where the action is."

Karen's calculator theory struck me as reductive, but it did suggest that she was smart enough to plan my fate if she put her mind to it. Well, I was my own man, so let her try. And besides, I had no evidence that she wished anything but the best for me. I sat for a moment taking in Karen's loveliness, the irresistible upturn at the corners of her mouth. Then I closed my eyes and silently whispered my desires into the paling ether.

Overall, Christmas with the Levines went "tolerably well," as my father would say. Observing that Karen and I never kissed, embraced, or held hands, Mrs. Levine insinuating questions ceased. And if a romance with Karen was not in the offing, at least a soft bed awaited me in the trailer. I played more unprofitable cribbage with Gibson while acquiring a taste for the jazz pianist Thelonious Monk. I listened to songs like "Tinkle Tinkle" and "Little Rootie Tootie" in the same way you would listen to a fascinating foreign language you were just learning to speak. Gibson also bothered to explain his success as a bookie. "William, it derived from my customers love affair with ephemeral factors from the land of hunches, premonitions, inside tips, and numbers revealed in dreams. Coincidences only prove that a great many things happen, but people continue to lust for the key that opens all locks."

"That sounds a lot like a dig at philosophy."

Gibson permitted himself a wolfish smile and dealt a hand. "I only mean to point out that philosophers are bad gamblers."

I picked up my indifferent cards. "In the movies, bad gamblers get broken legs for not paying their bookies." I let the implication speak for itself.

"Barbaric and unnecessary," Gibson said with a delicate, dismissive wave. "One accepts a few losses in the course of business. Limit the size of bets. Weed out the undesirables and move on. My customers knew full well the consequences of visiting my competitors."

"Enlightened self-interest. That makes you an ethical philosopher."

"*That* made me fourteen million dollars after expenses."

After the Christmas break, Carl stopped by the library to confirm a weekend sail—Friday night dinner with Albert, the usual. I introduced Karen, who heard the sailing talk and recounted that her father rented a boat on the East River and took her sailing under the Brooklyn Bridge.

"You should come with Bill and me," Carl said. "You'll get soaked and probably drunk; extra benefits."

"Wow, thanks," Karen said, then looked at me. "Billy, are you okay with me horning in? You must think I'm taking over your life."

"It's not that special a life," I replied, trying to be cool.

"What horseshit," Carl answered. "It's actually kind of sickening how much 'Billy' loves himself."

"'Decker the Wrecker' here claims he won the Vietnam War single-handed, Karen. First thing he ever told me. Then I read in a newspaper somewhere that we lost. Now I don't know what to think."

Karen clapped and giggled like a kid at a puppet show. I had never seen her radiate such enjoyment. Whether or not she wanted me, I saw how much she wanted to belong. *Shit*, I thought, *she's lonely as hell.*

"I'd love for you to come, Karen. You can be Captain Hook's first mate. Maybe I'll be able to enjoy myself for once."

Carl grinned. "What do you say, beautiful? You and I sail while the Professor here passes out the beer and explains reality."

"Karen can explain reality better than I can," I said. "She's got the numbers down pat."

CHAPTER THIRTY-NINE

"Rock Me on the Water"

Carl's boat was a DuFour 31 sloop, berthing six. A poor man's yacht, he called it. Karen was waiting for us in the marina parking lot, sensibly dressed in long sleeves and a floppy sun hat tied under the chin. I was hatless in a Gator T-shirt and sunglasses borrowed from Carl. A crisp, heady breeze riffled the bay. Morning—as Cat Stevens frequently assured us those days via the radio—had indeed broken in serene glory, putting my petty concerns in their place. Carl and I hoisted the sail. Karen freed the mooring lines from their cleats, hopped nimbly back aboard, and we were underway.

We set a course south out of Hillsboro Bay. The plan was to round the peninsula and head north into Old Tampa Bay. It was as fine a plan as any since we didn't need one. Carl had stocked a cooler with sandwiches and Dos Equis. Karen, to my surprise, flourished a pill bottle containing a fat joint. We fortified ourselves accordingly. Carl could sail the boat by himself but happily took Karen on as his mate. While they worked the sail, Carl expounded upon broad reaches and close hauls. He called the wind an invisible tool. Karen peppered him with, well, a boatload of questions. I quit listening to their words, preferring their music to accompany the DuFour as it delved and rebounded rhythmically in spirited air. Time seemed to offer no friction, no cause for discontent, and for a little while, I quit chasing my desires and opened a book of poetry I'd brought along.

It happened to be the collected works of William Butler Yeats. In one poem, I found the words *man is in love and loves what vanishes*. Not in love with a particular thing, but all of us inescapably in a state of longing for love, casting love's net, and catching maybe nothing, maybe a bounty, all the while caught up in nets ourselves, kept or thrown back by others, unsure either way if we are lucky or not. I looked up to see Karen watching me from the opposite stern seat. Carl was between us at the rudder.

"What book is that, Billy?"

"Poetry; my namesake, William Yeats."

Karen nodded and gazed toward the shoreline behind me. Finally, she said, "Read me one, a short one I can understand."

By chance, I had memorized "Lake Isle at Innisfree," describing, among other things, nine bean rows planted in a mellifluous "bee-loud glade." I gathered my courage and recited it—afterward, a smatter of applause from my shipmates.

Then Karen wondered whether or not Innisfree was a real place.

"If it's real, it's in Ireland," I told her.

"Sounds like a hippie commune," Carl shouted over the wind.

Except that he lived alone, Karen pointed out. Then she mused, "I wonder if you can survive on beans and honey?"

"The Vietcong survived on way less," Carl said, breaking the spell. And soon after that, with Karen's help, he brought us about to the beam reach that would start our return leg back to port.

Winter twilight comes early, even in Florida. The sun fell behind a ragged cloudbank, expressing itself alternately in glints and embers. Carl had secured the rudder and momentarily gone below. Karen came to sit beside me. "Billy, I'm cold and sleepy," she mumbled, leaning against me, resting her head near mine, slipping her hand under my arm to draw herself closer.

Carl came up from the cabin, smoking a joint. He paused in the hatchway to size us up. "Family cruise," he shouted. "Let's keep it that way." He offered me a congratulatory toke as Karen (I assume) pretended to sleep. "When Sleeping Beauty wakes up, tell her she's welcome to come to my dad's house after we dock." He moved to check the sails, then went below again, returning quickly with a light blanket. "Just another fucking day in paradise," he proclaimed, tossing me the blanket. He studied us a moment more, flipped the joint into the bay, then readied the boom for our next tack. I spread the blanket over Karen. She shifted closer until my arm cradled her, then lay her head on my chest. Carl executed the tack, and the

DuFour surged obediently ahead. I watched the shoreline ease by, feathery palms and stands of mangrove, a rusty water tower.

"Amazing," I proclaimed out loud, meaning only to think it, meaning not just Karen, but everything encompassed by my stoned wonder. Karen opened her eyes, looked up, and smiled, seeming to take my utterance as a long-awaited sign. With "Rocket Man" blaring from Carl's tinny transistor radio, Karen kissed me as I have never been kissed before or since—as if the kiss meant to continue the rest of our lives, as if nothing else mattered. My body flooded with chemical shock. Karen tensed as if the shock had passed into her and finally drew back.

"Christ, Billy," she whispered. "I was beginning to think it would never happen." She gazed up at me like an actress in a movie close-up. Then she took my hand in both of hers and held it against her breast. "Is this what you want?" she whispered. "This" might have meant only erotic caresses and where they led, but I somehow knew better. "This" meant *her*. Yes, her body, but also her family, her loneliness, all her unforeseeable wants and needs.

"*You're* what I want," I whispered.

"Good." She didn't say another word, just burrowed a little closer, seeming to give herself over to me like an exhausted traveler to a midnight bed. The sailboat rocked us on the water, Carl and I looked at each other in that predictable male way, and Karen fell incontestably asleep.

At the Decker household, Carl's father appropriated Karen, calling her a "knockout." To my surprise and Albert Decker's delight, she knew the details of her mother's trailer park business: inventory, cash flow, taxes, and revenue per square foot. I joined Carl on the patio, where steaks sizzled while chameleons flitted, indifferent to my knotted stomach. Carl greeted me with an amicable leer. "That poem was a nice touch."

"No touch." I flopped down in a lime-green plastic chair, both too weary and too keyed up to say more.

Carl ticked off a list on his fingers. "Hippie nature poem. Sailboat. Blue sky. Trusty captain. Pot. Beer. What's that shitty Dylan song you like? 'God's on My Side'?"

"Something like that."

Carl pierced a steak with a grill fork and flipped it. "You should be happy as a Mexican jumping bean. What gives?"

"Nothing. This is me being happy."

"Well, she's not my type, but I see the attraction. She's like a cute little elf with boobs. She's pretty smart too. I expect she'll pulverize your soul. But maybe that's what you need."

"Don't you think it's odd that she's in there talking to Albert like nothing happened on the boat?"

"Why not? She landed her fish. It's packed in ice, so what's the hurry to cook it. Right?" Carl flashed an exceedingly wicked grin, then handed me a glass brimming with whiskey and soda.

Both Gibson Levine and Carl had stated the obvious; that I didn't understand women. But after all, Gibson had married Karen's mother, an act of dire expediency as far as I could tell. And Carl seemed to take from women only what lay within easy reach. What did *they* know that trumped what I had learned from those few, sweet days with Wanda Grice?

Albert insisted we spend the night. Karen and I would head back to Gainesville in the morning; Carl would stay behind and do a little boat upkeep. Just before turning in, Karen and I sat alone, listening to Sinatra recall perfumed hair falling free. "Life should always be like this," I pontificated, in fact only caring what life would be like in an hour.

Karen nodded. "I would kill to have a boat like that."

"Money should do the trick; no need for homicide."

"A *whole* lot of money."

"Well, maybe Carl will give you a good deal when he gets a bigger boat."

"Maybe."

I didn't reply. It seemed to me we'd run out the string on small talk.

"Bill, I want you to sleep with me in my bed, not here. Is that okay?"

"Well, I suppose. Up until a few hours ago, I didn't know you liked me except as a friend."

"God," she said, "this is our third trip together."

"That's true." I was never so happy to concede a point.

Only Karen's cleanliness, scant decorative touches, and a kitchenette—certainly not its size—distinguished her dwelling from a room at the Alligator Motel. A few miles from campus, her cottage stood in a row of identical white stucco structures arrayed along the fence line of a cow pasture. From a distance, the effect was like sugar cubes on green felt. After showing me her place, Karen made a point to knock on cottage number one and intro-duce me to her landlord, an enterprising dairy farmer. He seemed like a happy man, happy to meet me, tolerant, fond of Karen, eager to tell her he finally had no vacancies. *Fortunate indeed is the man whose brainstorm is vindicated*, I thought.

While Karen listened to the farmer evaluate the weather, I found myself wishing for a change of clothes—we had driven here directly from Tampa. On the other hand, Karen's bed was only a few sugar cubes away. No, I decided, better to be clean and fresh. We bid a perfect day to the dear landlord, then Karen drove me to the Mango Lodge. She insisted on seeing my room. "Tragic," she appraised good-naturedly, surveying its nonexistent ambiance, then knelt to look through a stack of records on the floor. "These are great; I love Joni Mitchell. Cool. Buffalo Springfield. Can we take these?"

"Sure," I said, agreeable to anything likely to lengthen our time together.

"We have a washer and dryer where I live," Karen offered, pointing at my overflowing basket of dirty clothes. As I stuffed garments in a pillow-case and grabbed my toothbrush, she seemed to watch me with an air of surveillance. I turned and asked her if I'd missed something.

"No, I just think you should come live with me. Right now. We'll both be graduating in a few months. I'm out there going crazy all by myself. I've been scared of guys since what happened to my sister, but I'm not scared of you."

Here was my fantasy, offered up, no strings. And when had I ever heard anyone speak so plainly, so touchingly, of their needs? I stood there—as it were—holding the bag, unable to pronounce a simple "yes."

"I try not to be scary; thanks for noticing. But seriously, what if we get sick of each other after a week? That would be pretty damn awkward. Shouldn't we—?"

"Have sex first? Sex is always okay if people like each other. Right?"

I didn't know. Wanda and I never got far enough along for an answer. And in Don's conundrum, the girl either liked sex or liked you. Not both.

"I was going to say get used to each other's ways."

Karen hoisted herself up on my desk, reminding me of Mr. Pee. And she certainly seemed eager to enlighten me. "Shit, Billy, if people like each other, they *adapt*. We like each other, so we'll adapt, right? Do you want to be with me or not?" Karen brought a smile to the question because she knew my answer.

I showered at the cottage while Karen started the laundry. Afterward, we sat at her all-purpose card table eating grilled Velveeta sandwiches and iceberg lettuce wedges drenched in ranch dressing. We toasted each other with Gallo wine in Cleveland Indian coffee cups. We followed up with a couple of obligatory tokes on a joint, making Karen shimmer in my eyes like the golden gift of the Magi.

While I washed the few dishes and folded my clothes, Karen disappeared into the bathroom, emerging finally in a short blue nightgown. "Too much?" she asked, twirling with nervous laughter.

"Too much what? Desirability? Attractiveness?"

She came over, sat on my lap, and kissed me in the same spirit as that first, incomparable kiss.

"Still not too much, if that's what you're going for."

A few aspects of our lovemaking merit depiction; most merit discretion. I'll mention that Karen's bed was so narrow that we couldn't lie on our backs side by side without risk of falling off. The same danger applied to a passionate shifting of position, causing my attention to wander among peril, ecstasy, humor, and solemn concentration. And I quickly understood one difference between Karen and Wanda. Karen knew what she wanted.

"No," she moaned at one point. "Go back to what you were doing before…" Fine with me, and in any case, everything worked out as nature intended. When we subsided to our "sides" of the bed, I heard Karen snoring softly. I would later learn that she had taken a "red devil" pill—a drug called Seconal, a sedative-hypnotic barbiturate used back then for insomnia. Now it's considered old-fashioned and obsolete in light of Valium, Xanax, and the like. These days, Seconal is primarily used to help with assisted suicides. In the 70s, it was a street drug of choice for people with too much on their minds. Karen and I always slept with my chest to her back, but my warmth and comfort weren't quite enough to eliminate the red pill, so we never had much pillow talk in the afterglow.

Well, there'd been a murder in her family, and besides, I sure as hell wasn't looking for excuses to break the spell we'd conjured together.

That first morning I woke to the smell of cheese toast and Joni warbling "Free Man in Paris," her soaring glissandos undeterred by the tinny speakers of Karen's record player. Karen, dressed in one of my T-shirts, stood by the sink, humming along. The window air conditioner lay silent, irrelevant in early coolness. I savored the moment, feeling ridiculously lucky, like a drunk stumbling into paradise.

"How are you *adapting*, Billy?" Karen called out without turning around. Her voice rang with happiness.

"Pretty well. I don't think I'll go extinct anytime soon."

She came to the bed, climbed up, and collapsed on top of me, smelling pleasantly sweaty and human, better than any scent from a bottle. No tension seemed to exist between us, only easy energy in endless supply. We expended a bit of it, got up, shopped for groceries, rescued a few more of my belongings from the Mango Lodge, then went to the movies: a double feature of *Shampoo* and *The Stepford Wives*.

That day became the template for days to follow. The Buddhists say all suffering is "resistance to what is." Karen and I lived, for a time, without noticeable suffering. After all, what was there to resist? Aunt Miriam had replenished my bank account. The Levines supported Karen. Work and studies posed no significant burden. Worries about taxes or infidelity didn't hound us—no need to hang on for dear life. If we let go, we'd float into a future whispering gently, assuring us that it would take care of itself.

And our bond lessened Karen's fearful memories. She opened for the first time a taped-up box of her sister's clothes—a periwinkle cashmere sweater, a black blouse glittering with small beads, a mustard-colored leather skirt. I sat on the bed, watching as she held them up, smelled them, hugged them. "Shit," she said, struggling with tears. "I wish I could go back and give *you* to Marie."

"And I'd let you if I could, I mean, if it would save her. I'm sorry she didn't cross paths with kind people."

"She did." Karen exhaled a deep sigh. "Maybe you'd be wasted on her. I don't know. Anyway, thanks for volunteering for the experiment. But as things stand, I have to keep you." She smiled, and things were better than ever. I picked up the last of my belongings from Mango Lodge and, at Karen's insistence, called Carl to reveal my whereabouts.

"He knows where we work," I protested beforehand. "Why borrow trouble?"

"No Carl, no sailing. And anyway, he worships the ground you walk on. You must have saved his life or something."

"I wrote him a couple of papers and he thinks I'm Shakespeare or Plato."

"Call him, Shakespeare." Karen's half-serious frown of reproach got me on the phone.

My disappearance hardly hurt Carl's feelings. "Don't worry, Professor, I know where you lovebirds hole up. I followed you home one night, but I figured I'd wait until you stuck your head out from under the covers. I'm heading out to Tampa tonight on business, but I'll come by when I get back. I might have a little surprise."

Carl showed up a few days later with several surprises: a bottle of cognac and three brandy snifters, a turntable, a receiver, and a couple of Polk speakers, offered from what he characterized as his dad's "excess inventory." All on loan, he swore, only to make his visits bearable. As Karen and I sipped cognac (a fiery epiphany), he set up the stereo. When he finished, I put on *Beggars Banquet* by the Stones. Carl lacked an affinity for music, but I knew his favorite song: "Sympathy for the Devil." As it played, he swigged his cognac.

"Wow. So this is where the magic happens," he said, looking around in false wonder. The three of us were shoehorned around the card table, exhausting all the chairs. "Fuck, it's small," he added. "They should pay *you* to live here."

Karen took no offense but did stare at him, trying, it seemed, to size up what lay beneath the profane swagger. Then: "Is this an act, or the real you?"

I expected a belly laugh from Carl, but instead, he put his cognac down and nodded in admiration. "Now that's an ass-kicking great question. The genius here must be rubbing off on you."

"Well," she answered, "we have done some rubbing. But what's your answer?"

Carl considered as he made a show of emptying his snifter in one long swallow. "I'm playing a part no one else has the guts to play, sweetness. But it feels totally natural. Either I'm a damn good actor, or I'm playing myself. Satisfied?"

"Not really. I want to know why you're . . . generous. Most people aren't like that. It just makes me—"

"Suspicious?" Carl put fingers to his head, emulating horns. "What's puzzling you is the nature of my game, right?"

"I was going to say curious. You're no devil. Billy wouldn't be friends with you if you were. Maybe you just want people to like you, or maybe you're a confused saint. But if you're taking over your father's business, I'd watch that generosity. I mean, after tonight."

Carl chuckled, shrugged, stretched. "Don't worry, my dear; I know the difference between business and friendship way better than most people, probably including you. Anyway, I'll own the shop, but I'm not sitting in there running a cash register, that's for damn sure. I have other, *way* bigger fish to fry. You wanna sell stereos?"

Karen chose that moment to pull the bobby pins out of her topknot and shake her hair loose. "No, but I might buy you out someday. I mean, if, let's say, I became the wife of an eminent philosophy professor, I'd need a hobby, right?"

Carl roared and slapped the table. "You two are the best show in town; better than *All in the Family*. It looks like you're going to stay on the air for quite a while." Karen grinned and kept her eyes on Carl, evidence (I fervently assumed) that she was putting him in his place, not angling for a marriage proposal from me. In any case, I had no real chance—or appetite—to clarify the matter. Karen pushed on with her interrogation.

"By the way, Carl; what's the bigger fish you have to fry?"

Carl described his marijuana "business plan" as eagerly as a Little Leaguer describing his first home run. For her part, Karen peppered him with a raft of questions about cultivation, packaging, distribution, and how prices got set in the marketplace, throwing in a few suggestions based on "a couple of finance classes" she had taken. Carl wondered if Karen's chats with Gibson had taught her anything about money laundering and tax evasion. She admonished him to keep me out of his "racket," but otherwise—forgive the phrase—they were thick as thieves.

Carl became a fixture. He never arrived empty-handed, always proffering a gift: a bottle of Grand Marnier or Chambord, or just a six-pack of sweating Schlitz bottles. Occasionally he brandished concert tickets to Johnny Cash or Stephen Stills. Some weekends we sailed. And often, Carl and Karen chattered and guffawed outside in lawn chairs while I labored to finish my master's thesis, which I scribbled in longhand and farmed out to be typed. My subject was: "Deconstructing the Garden of Eden—A Hermeneutic Exploration of Free Will." I suppose it is not a surprising topic for an unrepentant fornicator evicted from a small Southern town by his earthly father. It might, however, surprise you that I argued for a charitable interpretation of God's motives, much as I'd begun to suspect the existence of Ed Shaffer's better angels at work in my exile. In my thesis, I maintain that God sent his best slithering salesman to argue for disobedience, *knowing* Adam and Eve were no match. Without moral choice, his kids would never be anything but goldfish in a bowl, so God granted them free will as "punishment" for their transgression. Further, he provided a world where they could confront suffering and hard decisions, thus keeping the spark of free will alive and lending untold depth to the souls he had created.

In the parlance of my college days, I had my writing shit together, sprinkling in Marxist and feminist tropes for good measure. The Greeks wisely inscribed "know thyself" in the temple of Apollo at Delphi. But knowing *others* doesn't hurt either—professors on your thesis committee being a fine example. Not that I had any idea whether or not free will and God existed. Philosophy predicts nothing and proves nothing. But using my thesis to grapple with my father's childrearing outlook gave my writing a certain convincing flair.

When putting one word in front of the other became more torturous than a forced night march, I'd join my intoxicated companions outside for a beer or a toke. Karen usually wore shorts and a T-shirt, dispensing with a bra. You might wonder—given what happened later—if I ignored signs of simmering sexual chemistry between my companions. I'll answer the question this way: if good sex sufficed, Karen and I would still be together. But it doesn't work that way, any more than lousy sex (Linda and Carl) guarantees a breakup. Maybe I should have seen the writing on the wall concerning Karen and Carl, but to butcher a phrase, "so many lines to read between, so little time."

CHAPTER FORTY

"Gimme Shelter"

"Seven million dollars," Gibson announced. "That's what the government claims I owe them. It represents fully half of my resources. To surrender that amount to them would not only impoverish me but amount to an admission of guilt."

"Fifteen four and a right jack," I replied, announcing the points of my cribbage hand.

"A fortunate score, given your play of the hand."

"No doubt," I conceded. "Anyway, why would the IRS expect you to pay up if you know they're just going to arrest you?"

"They wouldn't. But you see, no arrest would follow. The *federales* long ago extended an offer of immunity through my attorney."

Liquid light sifted in through the blinds—a cloudless February day. The Levine women were running errands, and Bona had the day off. I had the odd feeling that Gibson and I were the only two people in the world.

"You'd still have seven million dollars," I said, belaboring the obvious.

Gibson favored me with his classic shrug.

"I'm living proof of the adage that a smart man who does not learn a trade becomes a rogue. I fear I'm a rogue, William. As such, I cannot relent in my defiance." Gibson's narrow, elegant face held firm. I understood. I hadn't been back to Hopperton since that first Greyhound bus ride. And whatever philosophy was, it wasn't a trade. "Besides," Gibson continued, "the point will be moot before long." He toted up his hand for a run of three, giving me the edge.

"What do you mean?"

Before answering, he walked over to the turntable and put on a record. It sounded classical yet familiar and vaguely exotic. "If we were playing poker," he began finally, "I would say I'm bluffing with a weak hand and very few chips. I am—to use the vernacular—busted. A year perhaps. They tell me I will wind down like a watch."

"What's wrong?" I managed, not wanting to know. Gibson glided back to the table. I felt a pang of horror as if death itself inched closer.

"Nothing interesting. Lung cancer. The two-year survival rate is vanishingly low. The classic, futile long-shot bet. Do you know I only smoked because bookies smoke? Customers expected a cigarette hanging out of my mouth. Part of the costume, you might say. Foolish." He waved his spidery fingers. I waited. "Now, I wish not to be sentimental at the end. I intend to bequeath you my cribbage set and my humidor, but only in exchange for a service. Are you amenable?" He fixed me with mild, glistening eyes.

"As long as you're not asking me to help you kill yourself, I'll probably do it," I said, visualizing Mr. Heffelfinger's ravaged face, "but not because you're giving me something."

"Very noble, if injudicious. Rest assured, I do not intend to kill myself. I'm curious to follow the process to its conclusion. As one places a period at the end of a sentence. Now, you must tell no one of my condition, least of all, Karen. Do you agree?" I nodded, supposing I would find out for myself someday what dying and secrecy had to do with one another. Gibson didn't mention what specific service he required. I imagined myself sailing to the Caymans with Carl.

"Tell me, William, do you know this piece of music?"

"I've heard it, that's all."

"It's a Gypsy tango, quite unforgettable. Its Danish composer conducted an orchestra that played for silent film audiences."

"What's it called?" I asked, relieved to veer away from our mortal topic.

"'Jealousy.' Which, I confess, is my predominant emotion these days. Jealousy of the living. Jealousy of you and dear Karen. I suppose the two of you will marry?" He suddenly sounded wistful, fragile.

"We . . . we've never talked about it."

"Ah. And have you endeavored to divine her inclinations?"

"She joked about marrying a college professor; that's about it."

"The women in this house don't joke. They consider it a waste of purpose. At any rate, and despite my prior admonitions, I give you my blessing. Now, as your vocation seeks the meaning of life, you have naturally sought to know how Karen conceives the meaning of life, have you not?" Gibson sat watching me, his chin resting on the tips of fingers, joined as if in prayer.

"You know damn well I haven't; otherwise, you wouldn't ask me, Socrates. But I get your point."

"At last," Gibson murmurs, beginning to put away the cribbage set and betting dollars and silencing the tango. I followed him to the living room, where he stood and stared at Delilah through the patio glass. "I am averse to her," he mused, "like I imagine I would feel toward a formidable ex-wife. Would you mind going out there and keeping her company?" I could not have imagined a less likely question. The moment felt mysterious.

"Not at all,"

"Good. Please bear with me." He walked away and returned with a book: *Of Human Bondage*. "Read this aloud to Delilah; it soothes her."

The knock I hadn't heard when I first slept in the trailer came that night. Karen crawled into the bed and whispered, "I can't stand sleeping alone. Stay with me, Billy. Please." I sensed her entreaty reached far beyond one lonely night.

"All right." I felt drawn to a future that seemed already to exist, one in which my next words spoke themselves: "Do you want to get married?" Karen quivered or shuddered as if my words had physically struck her. I wished I'd said "Will you marry me?" but she didn't seem to notice the difference.

"We can have a wonderful life," she answered, sliding on top of me and coaxing me to enter her. As I did, she gasped and cried, "I'll always want you to fuck me. Always." I wished she'd added, "And I'll always love you," but that went without saying, didn't it? I mean, we'd said it before, more or less. And besides, clumsy words didn't change the fact that we belonged to each other. I felt unprecedented ecstasy, as if now, and only now, was I losing my virginity. Karen and I were Adam and Eve—not the first lovers, but the first to plumb these exact depths of feeling.

We had crept back into the Garden while no one was looking.

I'm sure now that Karen had forewarned her mother. Gibson's blessing constitutes one powerful clue, and Mrs. Levine's demeanor the next morning strikes me as virtual proof. She served us coffee and kolachke—a Polish pastry featuring a generous glob of strawberry preserves—and took Karen's announcement with disconcerting aplomb. Gibson stood at a distance, arms folded, impassive, a solitary Greek chorus. We sat in the living room, Delilah included. She stretched out at my feet in pursuit of attentive scratches and rubs.

"Well." Mrs. Levine smiled. "This is news." She paused to ask Karen to pass her the half-and-half. "Of course, I have my reservations," she continued, "for several reasons." She didn't name them, apparently finding them self-evident. "But both Karen and Gibson assure me you're a fine young man, and Delilah seems fond of you. You have worked hard in school, it appears, so I hope that bodes well."

"I hope so too."

"We'll be fine, Mom," Karen added. She sat close, holding my arm captive, rocking a little with nervous energy.

"Yes, of course," agreed Mrs. Levine. "But now, Bill, I take it your parents are…?" She paused, waiting for me to fill in the blank.

"They're mad at me," I said. "They don't like my choices. I guess you can understand that."

She gave a small, rueful chuckle. Utterly fake, as I saw it.

"I suppose I can, but I'm wondering now about their … participation."

"I'm on my own, but I'm a responsible adult, so—"

"Karen and I will make the arrangements. Is that all right with you?" Mrs. Levine sipped her coffee. Like the first time I'd seen her, she wore a suit—dark red this time—unusual attire for a quiet Sunday morning at home, given that the office was closed.

"Sure. That sounds good."

"In that case, would you be kind enough to entertain Gibson while I confer with Karen?"

By early afternoon specific arrangements emerged. I believe now that these arrangements already existed, the product of mutual concessions between Karen and her mother. We were to be married in a nearby chapel in a few weeks, around the Ides of March, which Gibson explained to me was not only the date of Caesar's assassination but also the deadline in Roman times for settling debts. I would supply a ring, a suit (no tuxedo), and the best man (Carl). Dorothy Levine would take care of everything else at her expense. Karen professed no interest in a wedding dress. She and her mother would shop for something "nice but sexy." By my estimation, Dorothy was out-of-pocket at most several hundred dollars. Karen preferred to postpone our honeymoon until after graduation. That way, we could go somewhere fabulous—maybe the Yucatán—and take our sweet time. I'm struck now by how preferable it all seemed; how wonderful to be relieved of ceremonial nonsense.

Gibson didn't present a worldly counternarrative, but he did suggest I buy Karen an engagement ring; in fact, the most expensive one I could afford. True to his nature, he didn't proffer any of his dollars to that end, only saying, "I'm willing to revise the odds in your favor at the point you grasp the need to exceed expectations." He made it clear that the point had not yet arrived.

Karen drove me to Gainesville, announcing on the way that a Tampa high school had hired her to teach math next fall. Not that she had to take the job if I objected to living there.

Why not? I thought. What better trail to blaze did I have in mind? And a bigger city would offer me better teaching chances. "Take the job. You can always back out if something better comes along." Karen nodded, radiating contentment. And I had to admit it felt good to have a compass heading of sorts to follow.

She dropped me off at Mama Lo's, then headed back to Hibiscus Shores to shop and plan. Mama Lo's is a barbecue joint near the railroad tracks that separated white and student Gainesville from black Gainesville. Carl was already inside, playing pool. He hadn't bothered to ask why I wanted to meet him. Beer and chitlings provided incentive enough.

I announced my marriage plans over a plate of barbecued goat. To borrow a phrase, Carl chortled with glee. "Shit, Professor, I sweet-talk women, coax them into bed, hang out with them, all that crap. A bunch of them, as a matter of fact. You meet one by accident, make no move whatsoever, and end up hitched. I mean, what is she? Number two score for you?" I shook my head, but without much vigor. Carl held up his fingers, making a careless peace sign. "But I have to admit she's classy. Not one of those girls with big tits sloshing around under a skimpy top."

Carl added his unorthodox blessing to Gibson's, agreed to be the best man, and absorbed my final request with a broad smirk. "Baby needs a fancy ring, huh?"

I waved away the cigarette and kitchen smoke. My eyes watered; my throat burned from the hot sauce. "It's not for Karen; it's for her mother."

"Sure, whatever. You look a little sick. Pressure getting to you?"

"No, I'm great. I'll be even better if you help me out."

"Okay, but I'll tell you one thing: this is the first time a *man* has ever tried to get me drunk so he could screw me."

We walked a few blocks to a hole-in-the-wall jewelry store on University Avenue. Carl knew the proprietor, and in short order, plunked down a wad of bills from his wallet as a down payment on the best (if small) diamond ring in the store that wasn't gaudy. We left with the ring; the proprietor seemingly unconcerned about the unpaid balance.

"We're both criminals," Carl revealed without elaboration. "We trust each other." Maybe, I thought, that applied somehow to Carl and me as well. He also fronted the cost of a suit and rented a Lincoln Continental (subdued offspring of the chrome monstrosity that whisked Don Heffelfinger away), offering himself as our chauffeur. "We're running this little burlesque show by the book," he said with relish.

Over the next few weeks, I watched Karen for a hint of buyer's remorse. If anything, she seemed happier by the day. She gushed over the ring, even making a special trip to the trailer park to show her mother. I finished my thesis, confident of its acceptance. Still, a mild depression afflicted me as I sat alone in the sugar cube cottage. I had overcome everything and acquired a mate more lovely and compatible than I could've imagined. What now? Was I perversely wishing for new tribulations to overcome? And what about my family, my mother?

Shit.

I broke the happy news to Aunt Miriam.

"I'd blame you for being muleheaded if your father wasn't worse. He knows he should never have sent you away. Your mother loves you and misses you, but she always takes his part. So, I guess we're stuck. Anyway, congratulations. I'll mail you a check. Are you sending out invitations?"

"There's nobody to invite but you," I pointed out.

She didn't reply right away, then, "Your mother would disown me."

"Yeah."

"Oh, a little bulletin. Wanda finally popped up in her hometown. Somebody called my detective looking for the reward even after all this time. I find myself admiring such tenacity, as tacky as it is to be so greedy.

Anyway, Wanda is married and has a child. Our informant doesn't know the age or sex of the child. We're dangling a little more money out there to find out. I'll keep you posted."

Karen knew nothing about this crucial chapter. Maybe in a couple of years, when our happiness was rock-solid, I'd tell her. In the meantime, despite her usual pallor, she tanned nicely from hours sunning herself behind the cottage. She wanted to glow against the ivory sundress she picked out for the ceremony and show off the pearls she agreed to wear at her mother's behest. Unlike Sally's dime-store paste, Karen's necklace was real, a rare accident of nature rather than a cheap deception. And this time, I would be allowed to kiss the wearer. A better outcome, yes, but now stirred-up memories caused both Wanda *and* Sally to attend absurd weddings scattered through my dreams. I can't recall the dream nuptials, but I can still summon the actual wedding like an on-demand movie.

Before my wedding day, "chapel" brought to mind a sweet little church, not a room situated inside a business whose primary merchandise was lawn ornaments: giant metal insects, shiny orbs on pedestals, flamingos in wrought iron painted hot pink, whirligigs, and tiered fountains, all bathed in the discordant tinkling of countless wind chimes.

Anyway, to step back, Carl, Karen, and I arrived at Mockingbird Garden and Monument, Inc. (they also sold burial headstones) in the promised white Continental, well and truly stoned on a joint of "Gainesville Green," a cannabis strain of local fame. The "lawn" from which the various ornaments cried out to buyers consisted of bleached white gravel, imitating the effect of snow blindness in the morning sun.

"Wow," Karen exclaimed, peering out in dazed wonderment. "This is wild." She had taken her mother's word for the aptness of the Mockingbird Chapel, focusing instead on looking irresistible. She had succeeded, and to her further credit, embraced the scene as weird pageantry rather than evidence of a poorly laid plan gone horribly wrong.

"We should have the ceremony out here," Carl suggested, pointing at a cluster of lawn dwarfs. "That way, you could have lots of guests."

The idea seemed to tickle Karen, so I kept to myself what I had long suspected and suddenly knew: Dorothy Levine was not a nice person. For a heartbeat, I pictured Gibson Levine doing her in, enlisting me as his accomplice in exchange for his blessing.

"The chapel's probably gorgeous," I offered, straining to overcompensate. "You can't tell a book by its cover."

"I don't care, Billy," Karen cried, twirling once like an actress in a musical. "I have my ring and my husband. I'm good as gold."

"And high as shit," Carl pointed out.

We gawked our way through the showroom, a treasure trove of fairy gnomes, frogs, toadstools, rose begonias in pots obnoxious with glitter, and—another reminder of Wanda—a sizable Buddha which felt like Styrofoam to the touch.

The chapel comprised a pleasant, featureless space with a podium and vases of fake flowers and tinny classical music piped in from somewhere. I saw no evidence of religious affiliation, and it occurred to me then that I had no idea who would marry us and what they might say. There'd been no rehearsal dinner, no rehearsal anything. Now, Gibson and Dorothy stood by, impassive as statuary. A short, shrunken man with a wispy beard emerged from a side door. He wore a loud, plaid jacket at odds with this, or arguably any, occasion. "Which one of you is the groom?" he asked, not seeming to care. Carl stepped back, chuckling.

"Not me, Padre."

I raised my hand like a fourth grader. The minister, or whatever he was, muttered the one-word question: "Rings?" Carl had them and gave a thumbs-up to confirm it. The withered functionary motioned us up to the podium and read boilerplate verbiage about sacred promises. He spoke in a bored, tremulous, squeaky voice which I barely heard, since, other than listening for vows, the inadequacy of the occasion ate up my attention.

On the other hand, Karen gazed at me with joyous devotion, refuting the cliché that women care more about the wedding than the marriage. *What a wonderful person*, I thought. After that, things went fine. We were married in Jesus's name, which came as a surprise since our officiant held no title but Notary Public. Karen and I shared an enthusiastic kiss, followed by a murmur of congratulations, then Dorothy slipped an envelope to the little man and we all filed out. Carl stopped in the showroom to purchase an iron peacock, bejeweled and painted red and blue.

"I need something crazy to remember this by," he whispered.

CHAPTER FORTY-ONE

"It's Too Late"

Tampa, Florida, 1976

aren and I returned to the Sugar Cube and its neighboring field of contented cows to close out our academic careers, march in the cap and gown parade, then slow dance in intimate celebration to the soul-searching voice of Carole King. In late May, two men and a truck showed up, emptied the cottage, and deposited its contents in a nondescript one-bedroom Tampa apartment little more than twice the size of the dwelling we left behind, its one virtue a bigger bed. Now, at least, we could take a roll in the hay without falling out of the loft. Karen busied herself shopping, sprucing up the apartment, and reviewing lesson material for her new job. I beat the bushes, looking for any teaching position related to philosophy, or at least the liberal arts. Two possible markets emerged: adult education and substitute teaching, both of them part-time, both of them shaky propositions. Aunt Miriam had given me money equivalent to a few months of living expenses. Gibson Levine had given me one hundred dollars cash. Dorothy Levine had written a substantial check to Karen Levine, not Karen Shaffer (who, despite this slight, had happily assumed my last name). In short, after a brief financial honeymoon, I would stare self-sufficiency and the task, if Gibson spoke true, of continuing to exceed a Levine woman's expectations in the face.

Now, I see no point in being coy about how badly things went in Tampa, although I cringe to supply the details. To begin with, I bought two bicycles out of Aunt Miriam's money, both snatched from our tiny back patio the second day, the theft made easy because I had chained them only to each other. I remember staring out from the bikeless patio down a slope reminiscent of the one behind Don's house, this time at a rain-gray, rundown urban neighborhood evidently crawling with thieves. I should have been happy as a pig in slop. Beautiful sex nightly with the woman of my dreams. Dreams. I remembered that line from "Dover Beach": *For the world, which seems to lie before us like a land of dreams…*

Seems.

Other than Karen herself, the whole damn scene felt bogus, an extension of a crummy wedding that Carl and Karen had somehow seen as zany fun. And why, I wondered, had Karen and her mother chosen *this* place, *this* neighborhood, free of any noticeable virtue? And why, for that matter, had I acquiesced so meekly to living here? In truth, it felt like another exile. I stood awhile, wallowing in black thoughts. Then I went inside and told Karen about the bikes. She looked up from sponge-mopping the kitchen floor. "That was dumb, Billy," she said, "chaining them together."

With that matter-of-fact remark, she went back to her task. Not irked, not amused, not sympathetic—just busy working. *Christ*, I thought, *I can't be losing bicycles while she's mopping floors and shortly earning a paycheck. I need to get a car and a job.*

First, the car. Since Carl was down in Key West, I prevailed on Albert Decker to drop me off at "the best junkyard in Tampa." I found my Studebaker Golden Hawk in the back of the lot's many acres, mired in weeds. I paid $250, plus $50 for used tires with actual tread (I had to change them myself). While the Studebaker was jacked up, I straightened out its bent shifting rods, probably why its last owner had given up on it. It shifted smoothly then, and the engine, other than being poorly carbureted, sounded good. I stuck the crumpled title in the glove compartment and headed home, buoyed by my renewed gumption.

Then, less than a mile down a straight road with perfect visibility, a station wagon pulled out in front of me. I smacked it with a sickening crunch, but without enough force to cause serious injury. Vehicles pulled around us, no one bothering to stop; just another mishap that they— thank God—had avoided. I stepped out of the Studebaker, less angry than resigned. The crummy wedding, the stolen bikes, and now my bashed automobile belonged to the same losing streak. Maybe luck didn't play favorites, but my misery hadn't gotten the news. A young woman emerged from the station wagon, calling out how sorry she was. She wore a nun's coif but otherwise dressed like a construction worker. "I was driving these men to the mission for their lunch meal," she explained. "I was in a hurry to get there before they closed. Please forgive me." Four men sat in the station wagon's back seats. None of them made a move to get out.

"Sure," I said. "Do you have insurance?"

"No," she confessed. "I borrowed the car; I don't even have a driver's license. What shall we do?" *We.* She trembled with apprehension. She might have been younger than I was.

"Back up your car so that I can pull off the road." No cell phones; no one called the cops. The station wagon suffered a big dent but seemed to run fine. I told the nun not to stick around, especially lacking a license, registration, or insurance. She hesitated, blessed me, and got in her wagon and took off. Not a saint, after all. The men looked at me and waved. I pried my tire free from the right front fender, slicing my hand in the process, just bad enough to drip blood on the upholstery. No one in the stream of passing traffic found my plight worthy of assistance. I cranked the Studebaker; it ran but would shift no further than second gear. Better yet, it began emitting a series of backfires that afflicted it with troubling lurches. At least the road led straight to my apartment. I limped into a parking space far away from our front door and contemplated sharing my disastrous day with Karen. Maybe soon, I decided, but not now. Instead, I bandaged my hand, then called Albert Decker, telling him I found a car that needed work. When, I inquired, would Carl be around? Carl showed up two days later, sunburned from Caribbean sailing, bearing a decanter of brandy. For the first time since I'd known him, his military scalping inched toward a full head of hair. He poured the amber liqueur into coffee cups while I poured out my woes, mishaps, and premonitions.

"Shit, man, you've got the white man's blues, that's all. What's that gloom women get after they have a baby?"

"You mean postpartum depression?"

"Yeah. That's what you'd have if you had a pussy. I mean, hit by a car full of nuns and bums. Wow. Tell you what, I'll have my dad throw a barbecue and make sure he tells Karen how gorgeous she is. That'll cheer her up."

"That's great, but I'll still have a bashed-up piece of crap car and no job." We walked out into the blinding sun. I pointed to the Studebaker, still a secret from Karen.

Carl gave a low whistle. "Man, your old lady would hate that thing even if it was brand-new."

"It was cool in its day."

Carl ignored my lame defense and inspected the Studebaker. "I know a guy; built some custom metal shelves and shit for my father. Old German guy; fought on the Nazi side in the war. Works in a steel plant. Says he can fix anything metal."

"A *Nazi?*" Greta Miller's imperious image popped into my head. Frau Mueller. Or Heffelfinger. Kidnapper of my friend Don.

"No, just a grunt like me who happened to stay alive. Fought in the Battle of the Bulge; a hell of a story."

I babied the Studebaker two miles to the fabrication plant where the German soldier worked, a place called Imperial Steel. Carl, in his new red Mustang, followed, hugging my bumper.

Hans, a towering, gruff man in a black leather apron, came out of the plant with Carl and inspected the Studebaker. He had the same thick accent mocked in the Nazi POW camp TV comedy *Hogan's Heroes.* "Yah," he boomed, "I can fix it. Motor too?"

"Hell yes," Carl whooped. "The whole shooting match. Send the bill to my dad's store. I'll settle up with Mr. Shaffer here."

"Shaffer?" Hans repeated, eyeing me dubiously.

"My father's grandparents were from Germany. And my best friend's mother came over after the war. She married an American GI named Heffelfinger." Hans nodded without noticeable expression. I needed to shut up.

"Listen, Hans," Carl said, "I gotta go. We need the car back in a week, okay?"

"*Yah, Yah. Kein Problem.*"

"Hey, Hans, by the way, can you get Herr Shaffer here a job in your plant? Just for a few months?"

Hans looked me over like a horse he might buy—one he suspected would go lame.

I had no interest in such a job but found myself waiting for the answer anyway. It turned out that Hans did need a helper and didn't exactly say "no" to me becoming that helper. Instead, he stated the obvious. "This place is not for Herr Shaffer."

"No shit," Carl said, motioning Hans out of my earshot. In light of possible help coming my way, I stood by, as meek as a child.

"Hans will take you on as his apprentice," Carl revealed on our way back. "None of them last more than a few months anyway, so he's not expecting you to be the pick of the litter. He just wants to know if you have enough sense not to kill yourself. And don't chitchat with him. He hates that."

Sense enough not to kill yourself. Like that man in my father's plant, Larry. A judge tossed out the suit against my father, but things had gone downhill anyway. My mother and I corresponded regularly, but my father remained a topic we stepped politely around.

"Don't worry," I told Carl. "I don't intend to die in such a stupid way. Besides, what on earth made you think I'd take the job?"

"Two hundred fifty pesos a week, señor, that's what. How much is Miss Karen bringing home?"

"About eleven thousand dollars starting."

"Do the math. You'll be king of the hill. And as soon as I make a college connection through one business or another, I'll be calling you professor for real."

Carl had come by on the next Saturday after our meeting with Hans, driving a remarkably intact old Studebaker and telling Karen he'd taken it in trade for weed, and thought an extra set of wheels would help me job hunt. I thanked him and praised the car as "sweet," inviting Karen to agree.

"It's sweet of Carl to offer it," she allowed, peering sidelong at the car like it was rotten meat.

"I'm sweet as cherry pie," Carl affirmed. "Now, can we go inside and whip up cocktails from the Drambuie and scotch I happen to have in this bag?"

Like in the "old days" (a couple of months ago), the gathering of our little triad had the mood-altering effect of a euphoric drug, making everything bright and funny. As we sat drinking our second round of rusty nail cocktails—Karen now giggling about the ludicrous Studebaker—Carl said, "Hey, I have a favor to ask."

"No, I will not have sex with you," Karen chirped, "even drunk."

"Damn. Well, how about my second choice? A buddy of mine needs help in his plant for a few months, a special job. Pays better than a grand a month. Double your income. I thought about the Professor here. Best part is if he gets a teaching job, he can walk out; no questions asked, no hard feelings. My buddy will hire him on my say-so; done deal. What you think?"

I looked at Karen, hoping she'd speak first.

"It *sounds* good. Is this a legal job?"

Carl bellowed. "Do you think a crooked job would pay such shitty money?"

Karen tapped her nails, considering. "You said we'd double our income. How do you know how much I make?"

"I don't, but I was trying to be nice. For all I fucking know, you'd be tripling your income."

"Hey," I protested. "Don't I get a vote?"

"Sure." Carl smirked. "I vote you take the gig. How do you vote, beautiful?"

"You don't have a vote, Carl. But I don't care as long as it doesn't slow Billy down from getting where he's going."

The Studebaker did a creditable job of transporting us to the Decker house for grilled steaks and more Rusty Nails—Frank Sinatra's favorite drink, according to Albert. He hovered over Karen, complimenting her looks, giving her the inside scoop on cash flow. She basked in the attention, pleased, I thought, to have Albert and Carl as the family she'd married into. I considered Gibson and Delilah a fair trade and hoped Dorothy Levine would stay on her side of no-man's-land. As I sat watching the falling sun tint Tampa Bay, I allowed myself to place a small bet on the proposition that everything would work out.

Monday, in the stifling heat of June, I started at the plant. After signing tax papers in a cramped office reeking of countless dead cigarettes, I looked up to see the leathery secretary grinning at me from behind rhinestone glasses.

"You're a virgin, aren't you? she speculated with a friendly smile. I somehow processed the true meaning of her question and answered, "extra virgin." She gave a raspy cackle and patted my hand.

"You'll be fine," she said. "Just don't be a smart aleck and don't take no shortcuts."

I walked through the office's rear door and got my first glimpse of the business end of Imperial Steel, an enormous, rectangular bay about the width of two football fields and sheltered by a corrugated roof suspended on struts over a bare dirt floor reddish with powdered rust. A hulking collection of machines stood at the plant's center, generating a constant, grinding cacophony punctuated by percussive slams of metal torturing metal, each whomp! driving winces of alarm down to my bones. I had been feeling overmatched by life anyway, and now I confronted the brutal, concrete apotheosis of that feeling. And right on cue my father came to mind, along with the Lake City laborer job he'd arranged for my exile, and its humiliating similarity to my present employment. He had met my defiance with grim amusement, unmoved. One way or another, I could hear him say, fools end up in the same kinds of places.

Groaning inwardly, I looked for Hans. He stood nearby, stripped to a sleeveless undershirt, bent over a drafting table, staring at blueprints. I edged toward him, half afraid of the contempt I expected to mark his first sight of me. But when he looked up, he simply said, "Herr Shaffer, good, I have work for you." I felt an odd relief. Hans saw me as just another tool to be proven useless or useful. This simple proposition, free of emotion, suited me. Maybe I could surprise us both.

"I promise to be careful," I said, "and pay close attention." Hans grunted what I took to be a vague sort of approval. Then he pointed toward a man limping along beside a mobile crane as it trundled a steel plate in our direction.

"He will teach you," Hans said, "then you will do it."

Ace, the limping man, was gaunt and one-armed, pushing seventy by my estimation. He gave me the rundown on the crane's clamps and control box, smoking continuously, only stopping to roll another cigarette. He accomplished this by laying the papers on a truss, filling them with tobacco from a leather pouch, then single-handedly manipulating the raw materials into a tidy white tube.

"Never fuckin' hurry," Ace admonished, a cigarette bobbing and weaving between his blistered lips. "And don't fuckin daydream." I thought I detected his head nod toward his missing arm. In any case, he ferociously spat as he hobbled off, leaving me to contemplate the thunderous crack a jackhammer makes punching holes in slabs of steel.

Hans watched me for a couple of days, his orders delivered with a fatal air, probably expecting me to quit or make a terrible mistake. But somehow, by the third morning, when I showed up on time, not yet injured, not yet having cost the company significant time or money, he simply said, "Here, Herr Shaffer," handing me a list of pieces to retrieve. Hans would never again instruct me except to answer questions. It was as if he told me, "I've held your fate in my hands for two days; time's up."

The men around me joked, shouted, and good-naturedly raked each other over the coals about hangovers and the pussy that eluded them. They didn't seem to fear, as I did, the murderous weight and heat threatening at every turn. They didn't work, as I did, as if they walked on a tightwire with no net. On their breaks they sat outside in the sunshine provided by the open end of the bay and took their raucous turns at a seemingly endless game of pinochle.

As it turned out, I never suffered a single injury. The tightwire I walked—and fell from—was strung at home. Like people say about life itself, it all came down to dust; in this case, the red-orange metallic powder that saturated my sweat-soaked clothes, making my return home every afternoon a renewed ordeal. My condition horrified Karen. Where was the tweed jacket worn by her up-and-coming philosophy professor husband during a pleasant faculty party? She went so far as to shield me with a beach towel as I stripped down on the small concrete landing outside our front door. Even the bag where I deposited my dirty work clothes remained quarantined outside. Since we lacked a washer and dryer, I shuttled back and forth to the laundromat, each trip earning me a distinct look. I'm sure she wondered how she'd ended up with a filthy laborer; I wondered how I'd ended up with a wife so quick to blame. Well, hadn't we both been warned? Gibson had cautioned me outright, and Dorothy Levine's wedding arrangements—whose wrongness I'd sensed but couldn't define—was her way of telling Karen what her marriage was worth. Still, we weren't at each other's throats; we even made ecstatic love. Maybe a good talk—the kind we never found necessary before—would repair everything.

"Are you mad about the dirt?" I asked, starting with the obvious. We lay in bed the night before our first post-marital visit to Hibiscus Shores. Karen seemed to flinch at the question, then answered, "I know I've been grumpy, but I'm not mad. Honestly, Billy, it's not worth talking about." She pulled me toward her, a deep sigh signaling her intent. Relief and desire flooded through me.

"It's only for a little while," I whispered. "I promise."

Karen put one hand over my mouth and the other between my legs. "I know," she whispered. "Now shut up."

Later that night, I dream-watched Wanda breastfeed our baby, her long yellow hair encircling the child like tender vines. "It wasn't your fault he drowned," she consoled. I remember her exact words because I woke up then, awash in guilt for conceiving such a fantasy while lying next to Karen, and for whatever I'd done to the drowned boy, or man, his identity less than a wisp now. My wife slept on, unaware that I sat up in bed to watch her. "I'm sorry I lied to you about the Studebaker," I whispered. I might have mentioned other sins, but that's what I chose to confess. It didn't matter anyway. Karen had taken one of her little red pills.

Noon sunlight glanced off the silvery skin of mobile homes as I sat on the patio with Delilah, sipping a vodka and orange juice. Karen had taken many measurements when we first moved into the apartment; now, she and her mother were shopping for drapes. Drapes meant permanence, didn't they? I savored this comforting thought as I alternated between my cocktail, reading my latest book—*Madame Bovary*—aloud, and rubbing Delilah's scruffy pelt to let her know I was still her buddy. For a couple of weeks, I'd been avoiding Charles and Emma Bovary's story. Charles was a dull country doctor, and Emma was an alluring, romantic woman enamored of wealth and passion, prone to having tempestuous affairs behind her husband's back. Since I'd begun working at the plant, the novel's plot and characters had rung too true. But Karen and I were not book characters, deliberately made ignorant of each other's true nature. To use a term Hermine Delaplaine would trot out many years later, we were *simpatico*. I felt it in my bones, whatever my recent petty misgivings. Now, *Madame Bovary* delighted me again with its masterful depiction of a tragic arc, never mind that the modern reader could see it all coming a mile off.

A tap at the patio glass. Gibson stood there, waiting. I looked for signs of decline—a dimming of the eyes maybe, or graying of the skin—but he seemed unchanged, other than the noticeably muted hues of his shirt and slacks. I left Emma Bovary with Delilah but took my drink. I supposed cribbage was in the offing.

"My naps get longer, William. Soon, I wager, I will be asleep more than awake." In true Gibson fashion, the remark came off as an observation, not a complaint. "Given that trend," he continued, "I remind you now that I bartered a service from you in exchange for my nuptial blessing." We walked to his shadowy study, where he busied himself with preparations for cribbage and music—in this case, the songs of Edith Piaf.

"She was a Parisian street singer, a figure about whom strange myths have arisen: that a miracle cured her childhood blindness; that she slept with a man to pay for her child's funeral. She once remarked she could never refuse a man because she grew up in a brothel. Neither of us, I surmise, has much experience with such accommodation." A joke, by Gibson standards, and a good sign, I hoped.

"How are you feeling, sir?"

"Sir?" Gibson raised an eyebrow. "A relic from another age. Well, William, my good cells are tired of reproducing, and my bad cells are champing at the bit. But that little drama is still off-Broadway. I am still myself and still capable of retaining my dollar bills."

Piaf's irresistible vibrato surged from the speakers. You didn't need to speak French to grasp her yearning. "What do you need me to do?" I asked. I felt I would do anything. Gibson seemed to gather himself before replying.

"In less than a month, I will ask you to do a good deed under circumstances you will find difficult. It's premature to be more exact, but you are certainly entitled to adequate notice." By now, we sat at our accustomed places across the cribbage board.

"Okay."

Gibson pursed his lips. "I expected more interrogation. In its absence, I assure you that you are uniquely qualified to perform the service. Otherwise, I would not ask you."

I considered my unique qualifications and came up empty. "Like I promised, I'll do it." A couple of hours later, Karen and Dorothy returned, having placed a custom order for "lovely drapes." We would presumably return in about six weeks to pick them up, beyond the time of my "service" to Gibson. I felt gears grinding in machinery I could not identify.

"Shit, man," Carl said. "I saw Hans at my old man's shop. He says you're doing pretty good. He just can't understand why in the hell you're there in the first place." We were out having a beer on a weeknight; Karen was home grading papers.

"Same reason he's there, I guess."

"Naw. The old kraut is there to work. You're there to keep the missus happy."

Seekers of ice-cold *cervesas*, warm nachos, and salsa piquant with cilantro packed the little Mexican tavern. We didn't quite have to yell to hear each other.

"She's not happy, so you can kiss that reason goodbye." I sulked across the table. "If I don't get out of there pronto, I'm going to be in divorce court."

"Come on, man. That sounds more like bragging than complaining. You know she loves the shit out of you."

"Wanda used those exact words."

"Whoa, Professor, get a grip. I didn't come here to watch you cry in your beer. Anyway, I'm working on another gig for you. As far as that goes, you could even work in the shop, push stereos out the door. You'd be a natural with your sappy, honest face. Mostly commission, though."

A little drunk by now, I yelled over the crowd, "If you get me a college job, I'll do things for you that you can't even imagine."

Carl slapped a fifty-dollar bill down on the table. "Let's go. The sooner we get out of here, the sooner I can forget you said that."

CHAPTER FORTY-TWO

"Mrs. Robinson"

A couple of weekends after we visited Hibiscus Shores, Karen insisted I take her out for dinner and a movie she'd been dying to see: *Taxi Driver*. She'd selected a restaurant too—the Columbia—famous for its paella and sangria, not to mention flamenco dancing. I relished the prospect. Weeks of steady physical exertion had turned out to be a partial cure for my native anxiety. I felt up for anything. And still another good omen: Karen suggested we go in the Studebaker, just for the fun of it. I vacuumed and washed its upholstery; polished it with turtle wax, the real stuff that doesn't go on without elbow grease.

We drove to Ybor City for our seven thirty reservation. The restaurant took up a city block, its ornately arched entranceway further decorated with flamboyant Spanish-tile murals. Had we simply walked around the exterior, I would've considered it time well spent. Inside, the seating encompassed a fountained courtyard and balconies, otherworldly to my rural Georgia eye. A senorita led us to a table tucked into a quiet corner, a table with one guest already seated—Dorothy Levine.

"Hello, Bill," she said as mild as milk. I looked at Karen, who wouldn't meet my eyes, and took the chair nearest her mother.

"Hello, fancy meeting you here."

"Yes, well, I'm sorry to surprise you like this. I only wish this was a social visit." I froze, understanding everything at once, down to the fact that we'd taken the Studebaker so I could drive myself home. The moment delivered the rudest possible shock, yet it also fulfilled a nagging suspicion. This contradiction, I believe, allowed me to master myself.

"Actually, I'm not surprised. And let's face it, Mrs. Levine, you're not sorry." I turned to Karen. "I didn't know you were such a coward."

Mrs. Levine put her hand on Karen's arm to silence her. "Now, Bill, this was my idea, not Karen's. Men can have explosive tempers. Perhaps you are different, but for reasons you may know, I didn't want to take that chance."

Cruel replies came to mind. The one I settled on—one I may have rehearsed in some dark dream—was this:

"It's terrible you lost a daughter, and it's almost as terrible you're ruining this one."

That hit home, and Mrs. Levine, I'm sure, had not expected to be hit, given her opinion of me. Her mildness hardened into hate, turning her mouth into a red slash, but she had chosen this place to avoid a scene and couldn't very well slap me or scream curses.

Karen stepped in. "Billy, I'm divorcing you to keep *you* from ruining my life." At this point, the waiter approached with elegant glasses of water, creating an awkward, silent intermezzo.

"Yes, you can get rid of me by divorcing me. Stop my evil plans to destroy your life. But unlucky for you, it's still against the law to marry your mother." Had I rehearsed remarks to make reconciliation impossible, I could not have done better. Mrs. Levine, somewhat recovered, resumed control.

"Bill, in the future, you will have to direct your insults toward Karen's attorney. My daughter will stay with me for a week, allowing you to find new lodgings. That seems more than fair. I thought perhaps the three of us could have an amicable meal together and sort this out in a civilized fashion, but I see I was wrong. Perhaps you should excuse yourself."

I nodded and stood up.

"Well, Karen, I think I'll go see *Taxi Driver*. Enjoy your dinner. Fuck you, Mrs. Levine."

Ybor City possessed a semi-derelict quality I had not expected: boarded up storefronts, sidewalk litter, meager foot traffic. It looked like I felt, with only a few going concerns along Seventh Avenue. I called Carl, who met me at a dive bar nearby called The Plank—as in "walking it."

"Tell me you knew about this, Carl, and we're done forever." We sat at the bar, alternating sips of Cuban coffee and well whiskey—no need to shout over anyone here. Only the ravishing bartender, a dead ringer for Chita Rivera, kept us company.

"Not a clue, Professor, I swear. Those bitches covered their tracks like pros."

"What gets me is the drape story. Letting me think everything was cool while they snuck off and cooked up a plan. That's evil. Why do that?"

Carl called for another round, asking the bartender if her behavior lived up to her beauty. I vaguely recognized the words *culo* and *Domingo* in her fiery rejection. Carl cackled and gave her a thumbs-up.

"It's the old biddy," Carl said, returning blithely to my misery. "What else has she got to do but mess with you? Evict some poor losers from their trailer?"

"Okay, but you know Karen. You were just preaching about how much she loved me."

Carl stared off like a sailor assessing the wind. "I may have got that one wrong. *Lo siento, amigo.*" Then, he gave a maddening shrug. "You can't blame people for who they don't love. Face it; people change their mind about whether there's a god, why not about some poor slob they married? Or maybe she just hung on to you until she figured out her next move. Anyway, you should be figuring out why you married *her.*"

"How about I loved her with all my heart?"

"Yeah, maybe. What's that saying from philosophy class? Necessary and something?" I knew what he was driving at.

"Necessary, but not sufficient."

"Bingo."

As we left the bar, I asked Carl what the bartender had said to him in Spanish. "She told me I could kiss her ass on Sunday—my kind of woman."

The Deckers had a good lawyer on retainer. Since both Karen and I had signed the apartment lease, she couldn't legally kick me out. Her lawyer didn't put up much of a fight anyway since Karen wasn't staying there (her belongings disappeared one day while I was at work). At least I had a residence, a job of sorts, and means of transportation. Other than being angry, lonely, depressed, purposeless, and sad, I was okay. When I informed Aunt Miriam, sparing few details, she groaned with disbelief. "Bill, you are about as poor a judge of females as I am of livestock. What shall I tell your mother? That your wife ran off with a Bible salesman?"

"I don't know. I swear I thought life with Karen would be Ed and Maggie Shaffer all over again. That's how sure I was."

"Well then quit being so damn sure of yourself. A guaranteed way to lose at poker is to play every hand. My husband, rest his aggravating soul, never did figure that out. Throw in your cards for a few hands and let your brain catch up with that other part."

Karen called me only once, to tell me she was keeping her wedding ring. Perversely curious to know why, I pretended to fight her for it. "Give me the ring back, and I'll know you didn't marry me for a diamond, which is about how it looks."

"You fell apart as soon as I married you, Billy. It's like you were waiting for the chance. I didn't marry a grease monkey, or whatever you are."

"I'm impressed you figured me out so quick. Or did somebody help you?"

"Insulting my mother won't change anything. You misrepresented yourself, and I'm keeping the ring."

"Keep it. That won't change what *you* are."

"Which is what?"

"Cowardly. A snob. And insincere." I'm not sure what made me choose that third insult. Karen seemed mortally offended by it, bulldozing her way past "cowardly" and "snob."

"Bullshit. I don't have an insincere bone in my body. What I felt for you was real. It just happened to be based on the wrong information. Insincere? Remember when I said I'd always want to fuck you? That's true. Maybe I'll wake up in five years in bed with some guy I wished was you. But outside of the bedroom, I doubt it."

"Maybe you're right. Maybe you're not insincere. Maybe you're sincerely chickenshit. Maybe you're not anything. Or just a bunch of numbers repeating in your head. Maybe I just imagined you. It's beginning to feel that way."

"Okay, Billy," she said, sounding tired of it all. "I'll see you later." Then she hung up. I stood holding the phone, feeling like I'd been body-slammed. Not because Karen and I had split; I had begun facing that fact with mounting relief. But it killed me that our parting wasn't bitter-sweet—only bitter. Self-help books tell us pain is our teacher. I couldn't think of anything splitting up with Karen had taught me except that heartache exists.

A few days later, Gibson called.

"William, Gibson Levine here. I want to first apologize for not forewarning you about Karen's plans. I did know. My wife revels in sharing her plots and ruses. But I faced repercussions I couldn't risk at that time." Gibson sounded a little breathless and hoarse; I wasn't about to criticize him.

"That's okay. It wouldn't have changed anything."

"Thank you. I hoped you would not be sufficiently disillusioned to renege on our little bargain."

"No. I'll still help you as long as Karen and Mrs. Levine aren't around."

"A fair stipulation. As it happens, my wife flies to New York City in a few days, intending to reestablish residence in Brooklyn."

"Wow. How long has *that* been in the works?"

"It has never left Mrs. Levine's mind. But Karen was here."

"Karen's going too?"

"Yes, as logic would dictate."

"What about you, sir?"

"Why I will remain here, all affairs now settled other than a precious few. The park will change hands, the spoils divided."

"Where will you live?"

"A hotel, I imagine. Then a hospital, then a hospice. Perhaps you will visit for some hands of cribbage."

"Of course." No one spoke for a moment. "How's Karen?" I lacked a better question.

"From what little I've seen of her, she is in flux. Still quite fond of you, I believe. You won her over in all but one sense."

"One sense?"

"Yes, her hearing, figuratively speaking. She only listens to one person other than herself. And to that person more than herself. You married Karen, unbeknownst to you, on a provisional basis. The terms did not favor you."

"Yeah. I wish I'd known that sooner."

"I thought I'd make that clear; sometimes I speak around things in my effort to pinpoint them. Again, I'm sorry."

"No, I didn't mean to imply it was your fault. You mentioned you hadn't seen Karen much?"

"She's not at Hibiscus Shores. Her mother tells me she's in Tampa at a seminar related to her profession. A long seminar, apparently."

"Strange she hasn't dropped by to see me."

"Yes, quite odd."

"Anyway, what do you need from me?"

"After my wife departs for Brooklyn, I'd like you to come here and assist me with a kidnapping of sorts."

"What do you mean 'of sorts'? I'm pretty sure kidnapping is a federal crime. Big trouble."

"My troubles are a hair's breadth from being over, William. But to address *your* well-being, I wish to transport Delilah to a wildlife refuge, a preserve. An informal one, but quite legitimate. There will be no paper trail or money changing hands. As you may guess, I wish my wife not to know where Delilah resides. Not to be vindictive; after all, she has already suffered a devastating loss. Rather, I wish to afford Delilah a bit of happiness. She should not be a pet; she should not be property. What I ask of you is to come here and escort her to the refuge. I would do it, but I'm afraid of her. You see, I believe she knows I could have done this sooner and failed her. A nonsensical projection perhaps, but there it is. What do you say?"

"Okay, where are we taking her, and how do we get her there?"

"Oh, not far. Over in Osceola County in a converted cattle ranch south of Kissimmee. The land is reminiscent of the African savanna. The refuge people will supply transportation."

"Mrs. Levine will . . . pitch a fit."

"Yes, but a quiet one. She acquired Delilah through the black market. Legally, she has no right to recovery. I will suggest she purchase a pair of Burmese house cats. She favors that breed."

"Okay, I'll do it. Just don't get me arrested."

"Due diligence, William. Have no fear."

I wanted to consult with Carl before venturing into quasi-criminality but I couldn't reach him at his Gainesville apartment or Tampa home. And Albert Decker was vacationing in Brazil, according to his store. So: sleep, work, brood, the woeful pattern interrupted by one tidbit from the *Hopperton Herald*: Evaline Chiles announced the betrothal of her daughter, Sally, to Milton Fredericks. I knew from Aunt Miriam that Sally had been "seeing a boy forever," her way of saying marriage was long overdue.

According to the *Herald*, Milton Fredericks had a law degree from Emory University and would practice in Atlanta as a member of his father's firm. If I rightly understood the timing of such things, I would be divorced before Sally was married.

And for good measure, while he meant no unkindness, every Monday Hans would size me up and shake his head as if to say, "Why are you still here?"

I didn't know exactly, sure only that no other place had claimed me. When I was a boy, my mother would catch me daydreaming and tell me I was *in this world but not of it*. Which begs the question: what world *did* I belong to? The Levines had chewed me up and spit me out, and still, I owed *them*: legal fees and bizarre obligations. Gibson had crushed me at cribbage. The Levine women had done the same in a game I didn't even know I was playing. Clearly, not my world. My Philco radio had whispered secret knowledge to me. I'd fallen in love with that knowledge, with the idea of secrecy itself. But to what use had I ever put secrecy comparable to the masterful sneakiness of the Levines? No, *my* machinations had rebounded disastrously. Maybe I should migrate to Carl's world, where there seemed to be no need for guile, only confidence and nerve. In fact, now that I thought about it, wasn't a kind of helpless transparency at the heart of our friendship?

As I said: sleep, work, brood. Sleep and work possess obvious value. Brooding is trickier. It fills a hole, burns mental calories, even consoles in its way. But as far as brooding changing anything—you may as well try to facet a diamond with a bar of soap.

Delilah's liberation took place on a Sunday. Carl called me the prior Friday to propose a morning sail.

"Sounds good. By the way, where have you been keeping yourself, Joe DiMaggio?"

"Huh?"

"*The Graduate*, nineteen sixty-seven, Mrs. Robinson. Obscure reference, sorry. Just wondered where you've been hiding, that's all. The law hasn't finally caught up with you, has it?"

"No, no. I've just been . . . nowhere, here and there, you know, gotta keep moving."

"So I'm finding out. Anyway, we can catch up tomorrow. Believe me, I've got a weird tale to tell. I'll meet you at the marina. What time?"

Carl paused as if giving the question deep consideration.

"I'd say, about . . . no, let's make it eight o'clock."

"Okay," I said, expecting Carl to keep me on the line to demand a preview of my story or relate a profane anecdote. But something—some misbegotten grand scheme probably—preoccupied him. He mumbled "great" and hurried off the call. No matter. I couldn't think of anything better for my tortured state of mind than a fine, uncomplicated day on windblown open water.

"Hey, Carl," I yelled. "It's my job to mope." Instead of bustling around the boat, getting it shipshape, he sat on a davit, the sails still wrapped, his head drooping. I speculated on a hangover, but being fit for an outing was as close as Carl got to religious dogma.

He looked up, the usual energetic glow sapped from his eyes. "Karen's at my house," he muttered, distaste—or something like it —in his voice.

"What does she want?" My heart jumped ahead of itself, terrified of every answer.

"The hell if I know," Carl replied with anomalous glumness.

"Listen, Carl; if she stopped by from her seminar to tell you she's moving to New York, I already know. Her stepfather filled me in. Just don't expect me to go back to your house for a farewell toast."

"Fuck," Carl groaned, burying his head in his hands.

"What?"

"There's no seminar, Professor."

"What do you mean?"

"Karen's been staying with me."

"Why? Did something happen to her mother?"

"No, man, Karen's been staying with *me*."

I got it then, just like I'd gotten Mrs. Levine's meaning at that Ybor City restaurant. An enormous puzzle seemed to solve itself in an instant of ghastly clarity. Gibson had once told me that if you don't know who the sucker is in a poker game, it's you. No doubt now which *you* he meant.

"It doesn't matter," I replied, surprised to find I meant it.

"No, no," Carl insisted. "You gotta understand. Karen called me; said she couldn't be by herself. Okay, I said, come on over. When she got here, she said she couldn't *sleep* by herself. She said you and her were kaput forever. She just needed some company until she got over the divorce. Nothing romantic. So, for a couple of nights, we just slept in the same bed together—that's all it was."

"Until it wasn't, right?"

"Yeah."

"I figured, knowing the two of you. The *real* two of you. But, as I said, it doesn't matter. I'm not even mad. The whole thing just makes me sick. *I* make me sick. I got kicked out of Hopperton for being clueless. So I go educate myself only to find I've gotten dumber."

"I'm the dumbass, man, believing that horseshit about her being lonely."

"She probably was. Other than you and me, I don't think she has a friend in the world. Now there's just you."

"Not me, brother. She's heading up North, just like you said. She told me this morning. Things got very unfriendly."

"Why, exactly?" I asked, in search of miseries not my own.

"Why? Because she told me she didn't even like me, and I told her she came over here just to mess things up between you and me. She freaked out. Especially when I told her I was going to spill the beans to you."

I managed to laugh despite myself. "Karen doesn't appreciate being accused of insincerity."

"That's a very professor way to put it, but yeah."

People were trickling into the marina. A family walked by laden with coolers, picnic baskets, and fishing rods. They all talked at once, trumping each other in excited tones. Gulls circled and squawked, sensing the prospect of easy food. Other than the knots Carl and I were tangled in, the day promised perfection.

"Listen, Carl, Karen does what she wants, or what her mother convinces her she wants. She's not Lady Macbeth; she's just spoiled. And you're just as bad. You take what you want. You obey the laws you want to obey. You slept with Karen because you wanted to. No other reason. Now you want forgiveness like I was a priest or something, and I think you expect to get it because you know what a fool, what a pussy, I am. But like I said, *it doesn't matter.* That's my answer. Along with the fact that you and I can't be friends anymore."

Carl stood up and looked at the sky like he was searching for the wind. "I can't believe I convinced that bitch to go sailing with us that first time."

"Actually, Carl, it was one of the best days of my life. Still is. I just read too much into it, that's all. A swallow doesn't make a summer, and a kiss doesn't make a marriage."

"You lost me there, but how about this? Take a week to cool off. We can meet in that dive in Ybor City with the sassy bartender and talk things over. My treat. What you say?"

"Very generous. As usual. But no thanks. Your generosity always ends up costing me an arm and a leg. Karen sniffed that one out; I'll give her that. Kindred spirits, I guess. Anyway, I'm heading out, Carl. My best to your old man."

We left it there, more or less. I drove back to the barren Temple Terrace apartment, groaning—in my father's words—like "a mule-kicked field hand." Tomorrow meant Gibson, Delilah, and, for all I knew, Karen returning from Tampa. Once I got back, I made a beeline for the bottle of Seconal she left in the medicine cabinet. I popped two, fell on the bed in my clothes, and woke up sixteen hours later with a raging headache.

CHAPTER FORTY-THREE

"Ave Maria"

It came to light later that Karen stayed in Tampa to avoid my visit to Hibiscus Shores, and Carl went sailing to avoid her. Gibson took one look at me Sunday morning and saw the futility of cribbage. I waited with Delilah for her new caretakers, reading another excerpt from *Of Human Bondage* aloud, the part where Mildred, having used Philip to care for her until she has her baby, runs off with Phillip's friend, Harry. Delilah seemed unsurprised by the betrayal, her only comment a philosophical flick of her tail. Gibson paced around the living room, checking his watch. The truck arrived around two o'clock. Its crew consisted of a heavyset man with mutton chops and a young woman with a pretty, sun-beaten face already suggesting premature middle-age.

The man, with a loud, *basso profundo* voice, engaged Gibson, sorting out practical affairs. No money would be paid or accepted for Delilah, per se, but travel expenses were another matter. The young woman ventured to the patio and squatted down beside Delilah. "Hello, beautiful," she murmured in a raspy voice. I noticed a pack of cigarettes in her breast pocket.

"Do you work where she's going?"

"My ranch."

"Are you going to sell her?" I watched for her reaction.

"Nope. No selling, trading, breeding. Just a good home. This one could stand to have her teeth cleaned. Otherwise, she's a living doll." The woman answered without indignation, which reassured me.

"I'm not her owner, but Mr. Levine is scared of her, so..."

"And you're not?"

"She's nicer than most people."

"How old are you? What's your name?"

"Bill. I'm twenty-six."

"Same age as me. Most people our age are scared shitless of big cats."

"Delilah's the only one I've known. I guess ignorance is bliss."

"Delilah, huh? I'm Merry."

"Mary Magdalene is my mother's name."

"I'm a Merry Christmas Merry, not the virgin kind."

"As in Merry and Pippin."

"Exactly, a big-ass hobbit; but I prefer 'Hail Merry full of grace.'"

"That's how Catholics pray, right?"

"When we've been bad, we repeat it, like writing 'I will not talk in class' on the blackboard a hundred times." She grinned and stood up. "Well, let's get this show on the road." She snapped a short leash onto Delilah's collar and handed it to me with a grin. "Lead on, Frodo."

I tugged on the leash with negligible force. Delilah looked up at me with soulful eyes.

"Let's go," I said. "Time for a nice walk."

"That's showing her who's boss," Merry commented with a poorly concealed snicker. She gave a firm upward pull on Delilah's collar. The cat rumbled, collected herself, and soon I was leading her through the living room, out the front door, and up a ramp into the back of an unmarked box truck. At the top of the ramp, Delilah peered into the semidarkness, growled, and sat down. Merry, who'd been following, stepped past us and proceeded to the far end of the compartment. Once there, she lay down in the deep bed of straw spread on the truck floor. A moment later, Delilah roused herself and padded toward her. "She's jealous," Merry called. "She's afraid I'll get the best spot. These pussycats sleep about twenty hours a day, so they're picky about their beds." She switched out Delilah's leash for a length of chain, which she affixed to a grommet. "Thorson will stay back here with her. He'll sedate her if she freaks out. You ride up front with me. Should be there in, oh, about ninety minutes."

Before we pulled away, Gibson came around to my window. He touched my arm, his hand trembling slightly.

"I expect a full report, William."

"Yes, sir." He was beginning to look unwell, subtracted from. I wanted to cover his hand with mine but feared he'd feel patronized. "Full report," I promised.

Merry's property surrounded a big frame farmhouse, a barn, and a couple of concrete outbuildings. Other than a truck garden, no crops were evident. Instead, the land stretched out flat and scrubby, green here, parched there. I escorted Delilah to her new home, a sizable chain-link pen situated under a live oak. Exiting the truck, she growled with what sounded like bewilderment, which I addressed with running nonsense patter—my comments on a recent baseball game. Once inside her pen, she drank water, sniffed and pawed at the straw, then lay down and closed her eyes. Two nearby pens housed a female lion and what Merry informed me was a jaguar impounded from a drug dealer. "We have vets who volunteer; nutritionists, naturalists, people like that. Delilah will be happy."

After a tour, she and I headed back to Hibiscus Shores. "You didn't believe me," she said shortly after we pulled out. She waved her cigarette like a tiny wand.

"What?"

"When I promised you Delilah would be happy."

"Only because you *can't* know that. It's an epistemological impossibility."

"Or your doubt is a projection of your experience. Not to be contentious, but as a country girl, I rarely get to use my Duke University education."

"*My* experience tells me you're good-looking. Maybe you're not in any objective sense. But one thing I do know—I didn't project you into existence. If I did, you wouldn't be smoking."

"Shit." She scowled. "We're going to be fighting the sun all the way back. Anyway, maybe your idea of me existed before you did—my gorgeous face, my bad habits . . . everything. Just one more idea floating out there, waiting for you to come along and think it. It's like that song, 'Me and My Shadow.' Except it's you and your ideas. Put them together and you get a world. Or the story of a world. Bad stories mostly if you look at how people live their lives."

"Putting your cynicism to the side, I'm familiar with Idealism. I explained it to my second wife on our first date. It's been around a few thousand years. Not as many fans these days. People want proof."

"So they say. What people actually want is to watch TV and not think. Not that thinking helps you figure reality out. That takes awareness, which is probably the opposite of thinking."

"Drinking green tea, I ended the war."

"What?"

"Nothing; just a bit of pertinent nostalgia. You seem very aware of cigarettes." I batted at a cloud of smoke.

"Yeah, wonderful, aren't they?"

Merry and I spent time together over the next two years until she moved to Washington DC to lobby for animal rights. We weren't a romantic couple, though we did have sex twice. "It's not nothing, and it's not everything," she said of lovemaking. The first time took a while because she "needed to be sure I wasn't grasping at her soul." The second time was for mutual comfort when Gibson and one of her charges—Priscilla, a lioness—died within a week of each other. Merry came to Gibson's funeral with me. Karen was there alone. Maybe Mrs. Levine was still stewing about Delilah; I don't know. Perhaps if I'd been alone, I could have found out. As it was, Karen stared at Merry like she was a ghost and vanished like one herself after the ceremony.

"I figured out why Delilah likes you," Merry said after the funeral as we sat drinking Guinness in a fake Irish pub. "Females, including me, can tell right away you're a softy. It's a sweet quality, very appealing. You're easy to get close to. But that also means it's easy to pick your pocket. That woman at the funeral would put her hand in your pocket again if she had the chance."

"She lives in Brooklyn. I don't think her hand could reach that far."

"Agreed, but current example aside, you do recognize the principle, right?"

"I get it, and since you're so damned insightful, tell me why Karen and I fell in love and you and I didn't. It seems perverse."

Merry considered, tapping her glass with bitten fingernails. "People drink beer when they're in the mood for it. Cheap beer can leave a bad taste, put you out of the mood for a while. Love's probably about like that."

Over the previous few months, Gibson Levine had faded elegantly away, consoled, I hoped, by my assurance that his bet on Delilah's happiness had paid off handsomely. I visited him often, out of affection and, to a lesser degree, from a lack of alternatives. No Carl, Merry only on sporadic occasions, and, once in a blue moon, a beer-drinking night with plant coworkers. Gibson bestowed his cribbage set and Cuban humidor (he kept his dollar bills), insisting I take them from his hospital room as he watched. "William," he said, "even now I find myself unable to leave anything to chance. It's quite amusing, don't you think?"

"Mildly amusing at best," I replied.

Before the end of 1976, Patty Hearst was incarcerated and Gibson Levine was set free from circumstance. The son of Sam continued to terrorize New York City, making sure Karen continued to plague my thoughts. Shortly after Gibson's death, a couple of strangers knocked at my door: moving men delivering a leather sofa, the lovely one from his study that now graces my home in Micanopy. A note from Gibson read as follows: "William—I ask a last favor in exchange for the accouterments I bestowed to improve your cribbage. You will receive a rare thing—a useful work of art—a thing of beauty and substance. I wish it to be appreciated, and you provide its best hope. Please keep it and care for it. With *eternal* regards, Gibson Levine."

Mildly amusing, right to the end.

I quit Imperial Steel in early 1977 (no birthday cake in the lounge; nothing from Hans but "*Sehr gut, Shaffer*") to teach English as a second language, mostly to sturdy-looking, quiet, conscientious Spanish speakers. On weekends I subbed for call-offs at Albert Decker's store, netting a killer car radio setup in return. Worker dependability, Albert lamented, waned by the day, and Carl—well, Carl was a lost cause "business-wise." Based on Carl's purported weed profits and Albert's sparse foot traffic, I suspected the high-end stereo component business might be more of a lost cause than Carl.

Otherwise, I wondered what the hell to do next. I wrote a couple of "slice of life" short stories about unrequited (sappy) teenage love and submitted them on the off chance that I possessed literary genius without knowing it. The least dismissive reply read as follows: *You write passably well, but this particular collection of words goes nowhere fast. Keep trying.*

In other words, my slices of life were lifeless. Did I continue to try? After a dogged, absurd fashion—call it collecting puzzle pieces for a puzzle that did not exist. Those pieces included borrowing other people's lives; repackaging ideas from books; keeping my eyes open, and writing down what they showed me; occasionally being graced by a dawning light.

I possessed no extraordinary zeal, but let me suggest it's harder to give up than you think. The body, as they say, has a mind of its own, insisting you take the next step, even in the dark. Get up, shuffle around for sixteen hours, go to bed. Within that ritual, I wrote things down, saving them for the time a brilliant story would coalesce. I knew by then it probably wouldn't involve the over-the-top absurdities of Delia Wingfoot and a second Civil War. However, I still daydreamed *The Dark Warrior* in my head as a way of keeping Wanda Grice and Don Heffelfinger and my secret radio and dark doings with crossbows and swamps alive. It's a paradox, isn't it? You know you can't go back, but that doesn't stop you from spending half your life scheming to remember the way.

CHAPTER FORTY-FOUR

"Abide With Me"

Tampa, Florida and Hopperton, Georgia 1977-1978

Some years transpire without much notice. The year 1978 would have been such a year had my father not died that August in a head-on smash-up halfway between Hopperton and his workplace. A 1970 Chevy Chevelle struck his Caddy when its teenage driver lost patience with the lumber truck creeping along ahead of him. The Chevelle, a muscle car with well over 400 horsepower, turned the Caddy's massive grill into so much tinfoil. I think now about how long the wreckage and carnage lay inert, waiting for their terrible message to be fully understood, and how every step—discovery, investigation, identification, notification—occurred in slow motion by current standards, human to human, no digital databases at officials' fingertips. The lumber truck driver, or anyone else passing other than a trooper, would need to get to a phone, the nearest one several miles down a two-lane rural highway.

I remember how, when I was growing up, reports of such accidents appeared with such regularity in the Hopperton paper that you thought of them as a weekly feature. To further drive the deadly point home, our high school showed grisly films to scare us out of our recklessness. Yet, there were few posted speed limits beyond the town, no seatbelts, no signs, or double lines to discourage passing. Only crosses and flowers along the roadside from prior fatalities, their meaning lost on most of the living.

Aunt Miriam broke the news to me, the phone jangling before sunrise, a muffled sob buried in her voice, my father's immortality—self-evident until now—brutally refuted.

I sat on the bed's edge, slumped in semidarkness, turned to stone by the evil tidings.

Aunt Miriam seemed to understand. "You don't have to say anything, Bill. I know it's too hard. Just tell me when you'll be here."

"Later today, I guess. I just have to go to Penney's and buy a suit. How's Mother?"

"I can't tell. She says Ed's bound to be happy now that he's with his Redeemer. Since I got here, she sits with her hands in her lap, trying to smile. I hope to goodness you'll tell her you made peace with your father in your heart, take half the blame, give *her* some peace."

"I'll do that; I promise."

"Good. All you bullheaded men have worn me to a frazzle."

I stopped in Lake City for gas and to hose water into the Studebaker's radiator. From the grimy Sunoco station, I could see the now-defunct Alligator Motel, its glass shielded from vandalism by graffiti-covered plywood. My entire past felt like that: no longer inhabitable, a relic of bad decisions. Back on the road, a muggy slipstream battered me through the open window, the sun cooking my left arm. Fearing the Studebaker might overheat, I crept along, playing tag with the foot-dragging semis clogging 441. I reached the Georgia line sweat soaked and apprehensive, fending off the urge to bawl like a baby. Whatever time I got to Hopperton, it would be too soon, and it would be too late.

To ease my reunion with my mother, Aunt Miriam had shooed away the sympathizers and taken the phone off the hook. Casserole offerings still clustered on the porch swing. I walked in without knocking, calling out. My mother emerged from the kitchen, drying her hands on her apron. "Praise God," she murmured as she came forward to embrace me.

"I'm sorry, Mother," I said, not sure what other words would help. When I hugged her, she felt lighter, more delicate than I remembered.

"All shall be well," she recited softly, "and all manner of things shall be well."

"I'll try to believe that; I really will." That was as close to a promise of faith as I could get. One thing had changed since I was seventeen: I refused to lie to my mother.

I suppose she looked older, but the sight of her stepped me across the divide of years as if it were no more than a footbridge; I knew our true affections had survived unchanged. We sat in the parlor, my mother in her accustomed Queen Anne's chair, lovely in a pale blue dress, glowing with sadness. Her hair fell longer now, softer—no more perms. Aunt Miriam had set an untouched glass of wine beside her. Gospel hymns drifted in from the hallway via the same transistor radio that usurped my Philco twenty years ago. I listened to quiet talk between my mother and aunt about funeral arrangements and how kind people had been, especially Mrs. Chiles, who took up the burden of telephoning everyone with the news.

"How's Sally?" I asked.

My mother seemed grateful for the question. "She's in Atlanta, dear, visiting her fiancé. Milton, I believe he's called.

"Oh."

"They expect to marry next June after he graduates from Emory and joins his father's firm."

"Will the wedding be here?" I asked. "Isn't that the tradition?"

"Ordinarily, but in this case, no. It should be quite an affair. Milton's family is Episcopalian." "Milton's family is rich, is what they are," Aunt Miriam amended.

"Have you met him?" I asked no one in particular

"Heavens no!" Aunt Miriam again. "He was here for one blessed day to ask for Sally's hand. As if the Chiles would object. Then he left town in a cloud of dust."

In the old days, my mother would have scolded my aunt for uncharitable thoughts. Now she nodded.

"I wish she'd chosen a local boy. A Baptist or Methodist. But I do pray for their happiness."

"As do I," Aunt Miriam said. "Annabel Chiles brags that he's quite good-looking. I only hope Sally will suit him."

"I think Sally is beautiful," I said.

Aunt Miriam raised an eyebrow. "Is that right? Well, she certainly hasn't heard that often enough. Perhaps since the last time you told her."

I could think of no reply.

"Oh, don't worry, Bill," she said, patting my leg. "I applaud you sticking up for your friend. Very gallant." The word "gallant," however unearned, reminded me of why I had come to Hopperton.

"Mother," I said, plunging ahead with half-rehearsed sentiments, "I wanted to tell you I'm sorry I caused you so much trouble, you and Father. And that I stayed away so long. I was waiting for an apology I probably didn't deserve. You raised me right, but for a while, all I could see were my own selfish thoughts. And I'm not mad you sent me away, at least not anymore. To be honest, if nothing had happened and I'd gone off to college, I doubt I'd have come back to live in Hopperton. I mean, it's a nice town, but everyone here thinks the same way. I like to hear different opinions. Suppose somebody says they like Castro; it doesn't bother me. And people do say that outside of Hopperton. Back here, I had sex with a girl and it was the end of the world. In Florida, I got married and divorced and nobody thought much about it except to say they were sorry or, in the case of my wife and her mother, good riddance."

I paused then. My mother seemed to listen intently, her head slightly bowed. "Did you get married in a church?" she asked as if her fate hinged on the answer. I'd informed her of my marriage, of course, but omitted the embarrassing ceremonial details.

"In a chapel. Karen is half Jewish and half Catholic. But the man who married us did it in the Lord's name." And with no particular point in mind, I added that there were lots of flowers.

She nodded. "We were wrong to send you away, Bill, even if we believed it was right."

"Mother, I love you, but whatever you believed, you didn't send me away for my own good. You sent me away for everyone's good *but* mine."

My mother cast a beseeching look toward Aunt Miriam, who took a long drag off her cigarette, then paused for an enigmatic moment before speaking.

"Mary, I've seen it that way myself from time to time. As much as I know you miss and love Bill, your last ten years with Ed were quiet and peaceful, as you told me yourself. And that's what Ed wanted above all— your happiness, as best as he could calculate it. Maybe he was wrong. Maybe you'd have been happier with Bill around, gossip and scandal be damned. But Ed, God bless him, sized everything up and thought different. He didn't think Bill's happiness was his responsibility, or yours, and I happen to think he was right. But it's hard for a young man to be thrown to the wolves at eighteen. So, I gave Bill money. There, that's my confession."

My mother sighed and took a small sip of wine. "It's not my place to judge, Miriam. Now that Ed's in heaven, I feel the need to forget all mistakes but mine so that I'm fit to join him one day."

Aunt Miriam gave a dry, raspy chuckle. "Well, if you're not, there's little hope for the rest of us stragglers."

That day provided a rarity in human affairs as I have known them: we seemed to forgive each other and mean it. And while I found this phenomenon hard to replicate in later life, at least I knew it was possible. I attended my father's funeral service in my dark suit. The congregation wore white to celebrate eternal life, nicely highlighting my black sheep status. My mother endured the relative ruckus of a Baptist service, in which people sang "Abide with Me" at the top of their lungs. A great many people, by Hopperton standards, Baptist and Methodists alike, showed up at the cemetery to acknowledge my father. An important man had died. And, unless those who spoke about him were excellent liars, a good man in the eyes of his survivors. I suppose all memory carries its distortions, like a shadow, and praise of my father brought this home: I'd been looking at his shadow since I left, forgetting the man upon whom considerable light fell.

Back home, after the burial, Aunt Miriam confided she was returning to Hopperton. "I'll try it here in this house with your sainted mother." We sat on the veranda so she could smoke. Crows fussed in the pines, and heat wavered up from Stagecoach Road.

"What about your hotel?"

"Oh, I'll miss it." She sighed. "But Mary and I are entering our 'old maid' phase together; God love us both. As time passes, she'll need to talk about Ed at great length, and I'll need someone to pray for me at even greater length."

"Hail Mary full of grace," I recited. "Pray for us sinners."

Aunt Miriam chuckled. "Goodness, are you becoming a papist?"

"No. A friend taught me. It seems to fit."

She tapped her cigarette over a glass ashtray shaped like a swan. Her reliable bemusement briefly gave way, and the corners of her mouth fell as if dragged down by force.

"It fits too well. I'm afraid I'm going to be terrible at this—being old." She reflected a moment, then said, "Oh bother. Come back as often as you can, Bill. And try to bring shocking stories with you—if they aren't too grisly."

"Of course. Scandals and salacious stories are my specialties. Speaking of which, when you see Sally, say hello for me. Tell her I'm happy for her."

Aunt Miriam gave an odd laugh. "Don't be a coward, Bill. When you visit, you can say your hellos to Sally directly."

"Won't she be living in Atlanta?"

"Oh yes, but after the divorce, she'll certainly move back to Hopperton."

I left wearing my Swiss watch, with my secret radio wrapped in an old army blanket and stowed in the Studebaker's trunk. Maybe Albert Decker could restore the Philco's faded mystique. My mother gave me our old tin percolator, which she'd replaced with an electric coffee pot. I promised to come back for Thanksgiving. Then murmurs of love, and embraces, and a sense, as I drove off, that I had dreamed my visit. Or maybe the opposite: that I was leaving someplace real for the bewildering dream I was otherwise living.

On the way out of town, I stopped at a new coffee shop called Take Your Sweet Time. Its décor surprised me: neo-deco with shiny metal tables. A thumping disco tune saturated the interior. The two workers wore matching pistachio-green shirts. A young woman, a high school student, I would guess, operated the counter. The man filling orders, mostly soft-serve cones, looked familiar. When he turned to face me as if he felt my eyes, I recognized Bobby Heatwole.

"Well, well," he said with a chuckle, "if it isn't someone more infamous than I am."

If he intended malice, he hid it well behind a genial smile, even offering a handshake. His meekness had vanished.

"And still unrepentant," I said with impromptu bravado.

"Awesome. Tammy's on her break, smoking. I'll call her up front so we can talk."

Bobby brought over coffee and bear claws. He hadn't heard the news about my father yet, having just returned that morning from a business trip to New York City. After extending condolences, he told me how he came to own the coffee shop: a small inheritance and Abel Theroux's weed money. "Abel's in prison for another four years," he confided. "I'm building him a nest egg. He's still got a limp from when your friend kicked him. That was terrible, right? I wanted to kill you both."

"Bobby, I swear I don't know what got into Don. He thought he was fighting the Civil War or the Vietnam War, maybe both. He got it into his head that Abel was there to beat me up. Crazy shit. I had no idea what was going to happen."

"I know. Mother Buddha told me."

"Who?"

"That's what I call Wanda. She vouched for you. I thought you were going to stand up on a table in the school lunchroom one day and scream that I was gay."

"I didn't even know until Wanda told me. She swore me to secrecy."

"Yeah. People don't always keep their promises. Anyway, how's the coffee?"

"Awful. Tastes like shellac."

"Doesn't it? There is some sort of political embargo on quality coffee beans. But people don't know any better." Bobby glanced around at his chattering clientele, mostly younger people, people I didn't recognize.

"Are you still 'private'?" I asked.

"In the closet?" He shrugged. "I won't deny who I am if somebody asks me. Not that anybody does. I run a business, pay my taxes, go to church. Nobody is going to see me holding hands with my boyfriend because I don't have one. I guess you could say I'm a gay virgin. I *have* slept with two women just to find out what sex was like. I've only ever talked to one other gay person in this town. Do you remember Mr. Peebles?"

My reaction was less surprise than a light dawning.

"Remember him? He gave me a philosophy book before I left town which led to my dubious career and possibly my first divorce. But don't take my perverse humor to heart. Next to my father, Mr. Peebles was the hero of my youth. Still is, for that matter. He sends me postcards from California."

Bobby's eyes widened with delight. "Wanda was my Mother Buddha and Mr. Peebles was my Father Confessor. I guess you and I were fated to compare notes."

"Speaking of comparing notes, have you heard from Wanda?" I felt my heart revving up at the prospect of news.

Bobby leaned back, seeming to study me.

"Not for a little while. What do you want to know?"

Now I studied him. "Anything you're willing to tell me."

"Anything?"

"Now you're scaring me."

"Sorry. She's fine, or was the last time we talked, maybe two years ago. Married, divorced, like all you straight people. I called her once since then, but the number was disconnected. East Tennessee, I think. She has a daughter. That's what you want to know about, right?" Bobby spoke in a restless, nervous voice at odds with his previously amiable demeanor. I felt something building in me akin to fight-or-flight panic.

"I'm not going to freak out, Bobby; just tell me." A medium lie.

"She might be your daughter."

"Might be?"

"Well, probably is. Wanda only slept with your friend one time."

"Are you talking about *Don?*" Wanda and Don's versions of their sexual "history," as slippery and shifting as they were, had convinced me nothing happened between them. No doubt, Bobby noticed my mouth hanging foolishly open.

"Yeah, him. Ugh. He made her pity him until she gave in."

"You mean . . . all the way?" I cringed at my words.

"Sorry, but I think so. She told me she might've married you if she knew for sure the baby was yours. Or if you'd acted more like you couldn't live without her. I think she went kind of crazy. She said something like 'What if the baby looks just like the other guy?' I told her I didn't think babies look like anybody at first, but it didn't help."

"*Everybody* went crazy back then. Shit, one day, when I was down in our cellar, I saw skeletons dancing. Maybe you were one of them."

"Please explain," Bobby said with a bemused smile. "This should be good."

"Back then, people seemed to swirl around me like characters in a demented play."

"And I was one of those demented skeletons? I'm honored."

"Not to be rude, but yes, you probably were. As a kid, I had a few— very few—things figured out. How to get good grades, stay on the good side of most adults, you get the idea. But I was a one-trick pony. I couldn't adapt to a little chaos. I rebelled ineptly, made terrible decisions, told lies. Ten years later, I get married, and practically overnight, I'm divorced. What did I learn in those ten years? Well, I did learn how to ride a motorcycle, but I still broke my arm on the damn thing. However, what shocks me most is that my parents had precious few tricks up their sleeves, despite their apparent mastery of life. I baffled them so completely that they had to kick me out or—I guess—face social extinction. Hence, the skeletons."

"That's why I go to church, Bill. Believe in Christ and go to heaven. Simple. What are a few years of hassle compared to eternity?"

"Bobby, I suspect Mother Buddha would tell you to meditate, apprehend dharma, learn to live right, and eventually get off the wheel. Christians say it's what we believe; Buddhists say it's what we practice. I lean towards the Buddhists, but I haven't voted yet. It's funny. I taught various philosophies without ever adopting one. I imagine that makes me a dilettante."

"I worry that if they kick me out of church for being gay, I'll quit believing. Then I *will* go to hell."

After a contemplative pause, I said, "I hear Sally Chiles is getting married."

"It's an arranged marriage," Bobby assured me as if he'd been present at negotiations. "Between the local boys that Sally didn't want and the ones that didn't want her, that pretty much exhausted the supply. And trust me, I get the *good* gossip."

"An arranged marriage wouldn't have to go far to beat the usual way. Maybe Sally's onto something."

"I heard *you* were Sally's chosen one back in the day. What happened?"

"We were tuned to different stations."

"No hand jobs under the bleachers, huh?"

"A handshake at the front door was about it."

Bobby smiled like a sage. "Sally's scared shitless of not being pretty. It's her kryptonite, her 'if only.'"

"That makes sense. And if only I'd found a good job right out of college, I'd probably still be married. And with Wanda, who knows? Women always seem to end up in my blind spot. Anyway, I better hit the road. I'm on my way back to the sunshine state."

"How about another rancid coffee and bear claw to go? It's on the house."

"Okay, thanks. Can I leave you my number and address in case Wanda calls? Tell her I'm not mad about Don, I swear."

"Sure, no problem. Anything for true love, right?"

"I wouldn't go that far, but— Hey, do you happen to know what Wanda named her daughter?" Bobby frowned in concentration.

"Shit, she told me…"

"Was it Delia, by any chance?"

"That sounds right. It definitely rings a bell."

CHAPTER FORTY-FIVE

"Diamonds and Rust"

Micanopy Florida 2017

I t's a Sunday in early October, about halfway between Labor Day and Halloween, almost fifty years to the day since I fell in love with Wanda Grice, forty years since my father died, and almost one year to the day since Carl Decker died. While two men could hardly have lived by more disparate personal codes then Carl and my father, I have come to see one trait they shared at the time of their passing: both men were in the act of keeping a promise. My father's promise, of course, was the one he made to Mary Magdalene Carstairs just after the war, the strict vow that actually mentions death and parting, the one contemporary hearts seem inclined to loosely interpret. Carl's promise—assuring a distraught Olivia he would retrieve a diamond engagement ring lying at the bottom of a Tampa canal—had included a conspiratorial wink in my direction, as if we both knew a search would never materialize.

But it did.

I'm in my kitchen, rustling up some faux Cuban food in my crock-pot: boneless chicken thighs, black beans, onions, peppers, and a liberal sprinkle of *carnita* spices. Carl loved Cuban food, so I am preparing it for the memorial get-together unfolding later today. Linda is bringing cognac. Some subset of Hermine, Natalya, Ramona, and Olivia will likely stop by as well. Culinary duties, unfortunately, provide little relief from recollections of Carl and other confounding events of the last year. Once again,

I find myself taking ten steps back in order to clear the path for a single, uncertain step forward.

Unlike Linda, I don't believe magic or fate had anything to do with Carl's death, although obvious ironies color its circumstances. Either way, the facts are that less than a month after he got out of prison—just after the southward equinox—Carl's body was found floating in the canal behind his house, the autopsy revealing a massive heart attack. He had called me a few days before—unusual for Carl at the time—anxious to discuss the visit Ramona had made to Tampa after learning he was HIV positive. She had scolded him and glossed over his paternity, "kicking my sorry ass," as Carl morosely put it.

"Ramona figured out a long time ago you were her biological father," I told him. "I mean, she can look in the mirror. She'll never call you Dad, but she already keeps her distance from other humans as a matter of principle. I'm not sure what principle, but anyway, she'll soften up. After all, she cared enough to read you the riot act. She'll come around if you're truthful and nice to her mother."

"What about Olivia?" Carl asked, the concern in his voice, if anything, more pointed.

"Olivia thinks adults live in a boring movie," I answered, "so in her mind, we're freaking out about nothing. She only knows that she adores you. By comparison, I'm just an old guy full of outdated opinions."

"Yeah, thanks, Professor. My head is all fucked up from this AIDS bug, and Linda giving me the evil eye, and me wondering if everybody hates me." Listening to Carl, I pictured an undefeated fighter getting knocked to the canvas for the first time.

"Nobody hates you, Carl." *Except for the people you swindled. And maybe Karen for stealing her wedding ring. And Linda and me, but only from time to time.*

"Maybe, maybe," he muttered. I hope not, Bill. I never hurt anyone on purpose who wasn't trying to kill me. And you know I never slept with Karen or Linda when they were married to you; only before and after."

"I know. Just take your pills, sail your boat, steer clear of shady dealings, and you'll be fine."

"Bitcoin isn't shady, dude. It's the future."

"Whatever. Just remember what I said."

"Sure, sure. Listen, I'm coming to see you the minute I get my sea legs under me. We'll straighten everything out over a bottle of cognac. And I might have another surprise."

"Great," I muttered, knowing further preaching was futile. Following a few more forgettable remarks, Carl and I exchanged goodbyes and hung up. After our conversation, I felt like I imagined Delilah felt, pacing back and forth on the Levine's patio. Carl no longer seemed like a friend or enemy, but a black-sheep brother whose flawed charisma was beginning to desert him. *Far more behind than ahead.* A truth not limited to Carl. His call disturbed me, so, to distract myself, I checked the pH of my grape arbor soil and looked for yellowing leaves, a telltale sign of iron chlorosis. Well, at least nature was having a good day. I went inside, poured myself a stiff Jameson and ice, parked myself on my sofa, and listened to The Doors' first album at high volume, waiting for the booze to light my fire. Shit, I thought, as I perused the album cover. Another haunting relic from 1967. And wasn't I becoming a relic myself?

My next call from Tampa came a few days later, when Linda, her voice garbled and shaking, delivered the bad news.

"Carl's dead, Bill. It was that damn ring."

I prickled with icy disbelief, my thoughts smothered by shock.

"And yes, Bill," Linda continued through her sobs, "I know all about Carl and your first wife. Carl dove for that godforsaken ring almost every day after you told him Olivia 'adored' him. Leave it to you to use the word adore. My god. And how in the world did you let yourself get tangled up with me after Carl screwed—what's her name—Karen? Don't you have *any* sense? Did you even *try* to read the signs?"

"Forget signs for a second. What happened, Linda?"

"He . . . he was snorkeling. Maybe held his breath too long. Heart attack. Shit, I don't know. He wanted your diamond ring for Olivia. That's why I chose a sapphire. Sapphires reveal trouble, but diamonds *bring* trouble."

Linda broke down then, and I murmured consolations, ending with my willingness to come to Tampa.

"Okay, come. And I know the ring wasn't your fault. He took it. He told me. And you know what that bastard said just a couple of days ago? He fell in love with her when you three were on a sailboat excursion. Just watching her. You were reading poetry, and he was watching her."

"He told me a story like that over Labor Day. I didn't care much then, and now—"

"I know what you think of my beliefs, Bill, but isn't it *possible* he told me because he had a glimpse of the future and wanted to cleanse his soul? Can't you see that?"

"Well, I can't think of a single mystery I've ever gotten to the bottom of, so yes, it's possible. I only meant to say that I'm not mad at Carl anymore and haven't been for a while. I think he knew that. I hope to God he did."

After we hung up, I called Ramona. After a wrenching silence, she said, "Dad, I'm sorry for you and Mom and Olivia; that's as far as I can go."

"No need to go further, honey. Just be gentle when telling Olivia. I'm on my way to Tampa; hope to get there before dark. I'll call you when I get back."

On the drive over I listened to "Suzanne," Leonard Cohen's hypnotic folk masterpiece. In the song, Cohen's Jesus was a sailor like Carl, but unlike my poor friend, he could walk on water. As the melody's minor key mysteries wove through me, I rehashed my conversation with Linda. Finding the *first* cause of Carl's death, the birth of it, you might say—the moment that opened the dark doorway—seemed crucial to her: maybe a look on a sailboat, maybe stealing a ring. In truth, I could hardly blame her. After all, humans started working their way back to the Reason for Everything since about the time they first entertained thoughts. Without that impulse, there would be no philosophy, no suit and tie career for me in lieu of distilling turpentine. And as the miles to Tampa passed, along with their nondescript pastures, and two billboards warning against hell, and truck stops with the lowest legal price for cigarettes, I found myself wondering what one thing—if any—caused the particular life *I* ended up leading. Of course, I knew better, knew that life was a constantly bifurcating bewilderment of choices. I remembered a story by the Spanish writer Jose Luis Borges whose title translates to "The Garden of Forking Paths." The story portrays life as an infinite temporal labyrinth, the point being that all time tracks, all paths we *might* follow, exist simultaneously. We are most aware of the track we follow, but glimmers of other tracks haunt our dreams.

I sighed. Just arcane mumbo jumbo to distract me. Not bloody likely, I thought, that I would find the pivot point of my life or Carl's death among the litter of events in one universe, much less among an endless supply of them.

Still, even Borges's story had a beginning. I speculated that mine should begin with my secret radio—but what to say after that? How could I possibly get from *there* to Carl obsessed with recovering a diamond ring lost at the bottom of a canal, his boat anchored over the likeliest spot, Carl outfitted in a mask, fins, and snorkel? Would he be Sir Galahad diving for the Grail, his chivalrous heart unable to keep up with its Quest, or just a sad corpse floating in irony and briny water?

About then, the spare, haunting guitar intro to The Doors' "The End" enticed me away from such thoughts. I listened intently for opening lyrics I knew by heart, words about doomed plans and looks never again to be exchanged with a beautiful friend.

I considered Carl in the dark light of Jim Morrison's song. He had *not* been a steadfast, loyal friend. But he *was* beautiful—confident, generous, energetic. And none of his manifold weaknesses, including his spinning moral compass, altered the fact that he loved me. And if I didn't love him, would I be on my way to Tampa?

I sped past the white fences and pristine rolling pastures of Ocala's thoroughbred horse farms. Many of Ramona's possible futures—at least ones involving her handsome attorney—would be enacted nearby. According to Borges, they existed *now*, wearing happiness or misery in all their conceivable costumes. Somewhere, or *somewhen*, Carl and I were murdered in the quarry, our Eastern European assailants driving off to live long and unjustly profitable lives.

Maybe anything. My hands ached from gripping the steering wheel too hard. I felt old and tenuous and consumed with disbelief. Multiverse or not (probably not), in my neck of the woods, only one perilous path showed itself. I thought of Karen's sister Marie tumbled from her path by a slight shove or slipped foot. No wonder people prayed for a compensatory afterlife.

Gloomy thoughts hounded me the rest of the way to Tampa, and when I stepped out of the Studebaker, Linda's greeting didn't help the cause. "The door's fucking open," she called from the patio. As I made my way inside, I felt her gaze stalking me. *Oh shit*, I thought. Not the most nuanced reaction, but it's all I had left in the tank. When I reached the patio, our eyes met briefly across the pool. Then Linda pulled her sunglasses down and raised a tumbler to offer a mock toast. "I'm drunk; bad wife, bad widow." She wore her version of widow's weeds—black shirt and black slacks— in other words, her usual garb. Lacking a helpful reply, I walked over to where she stood, her form backlit by an elaborate, cloud-shredded, rubescent sunset.

"Do you want a hug?"

"Eventually," she said, her speech blurred by the booze. "Prob'ly." I sank into the chair next to her, a matching glass of whiskey already at hand. She sized me up by some metric of suspicion. "I forced this ritual on Carl—the evening cocktail. Not the strongest bond for a happily married couple, but you work with what you have. Didn't you and I have our little ritual back in Gainesville? My brain is a little foggy."

"Sharing a joint, as I recall, contemplating the goats and stars." Linda chuckled in bitter parody.

"They found him floating face down in the channel like a dead fish. Still had his mask on. Still looking for that stupid trinket, stupid asshole."

"Linda, you gave me hell for doubting he saved my life that day in the quarry. I don't doubt it now and haven't for a long time. For me, that buys a certain amount of . . . tolerance. And I remember you looking all day for a sapphire ring lost in the grass. So how about a little mercy?"

"Okay, okay, Saint William. All I know is we're not getting the band back together anytime soon."

Large swallows of whiskey followed. I sat there, trying to summon up a worthwhile comment. "Hey, your Christmas tree lights are out," I ventured.

"Not out, off. Indefinite period of mourning, like a flag at half-staff. These days cigarettes and whiskey work better than magic and wisdom."

Likely true, I thought, but right then, I wanted specific, cold facts.

"Where is Carl? I mean, is he at a funeral home, or—"

"The coroner still has him, checking for nonexistent foul play. We should be able to bury him in three or four days. A so-called man of the cloth will say prayers over him at the gravesite, right next to Albert. It can't do any harm, right?"

"Well, I can come back for the service."

Linda expelled a smoky sigh at my offer, a reaction I mistook for appreciation.

"That won't be necessary," she said, lighting the next unfiltered Pall Mall off her last.

"I don't mind at all."

"But I do."

"Then why in the name of God did you drag me over here?"

"To sleep with me until the funeral. But listen, Bill, I'm not going to have intercourse with you. I'm not saying that was your intention when you drove over, but I was afraid that when the time came, you'd see it as cosmic justice. Better to clear the air in advance. God knows we have enough to answer for already."

Indignation at the absurdity of it all tried to rise up in me, but I knew it would be a waste of enzymes and hormones. "I'll stay if you admit you laid down the sexual law because of what *you* might want to do. Does that seem fair?" I gave her my best *I ain't lookin' for trouble* smile.

Before answering, she took a deep drag and picked a speck of tobacco off her lips. "Yes, I want to you-know-what your brains out, satisfied?"

"No, but I'll stay anyway. For the sake of all concerned."

"Including Carl, I suppose?"

"If he exists anywhere, it's between us."

Linda sighed. "I take it you still don't believe in spirits."

"I believe reality requires something to exist, as opposed to nothing. What that 'something' includes I'm not qualified to say. But if it includes spirits, I wouldn't be that surprised."

"Then you won't be surprised that I already set out some of Carl's clothes for you."

"Seriously?"

"Damn, Bill, you must have the biggest blind spot in the world. I can dry my own tears, thank you, but I can't manufacture a decent man with a warm body, especially at my age. And don't be a prick and tell me it's *my* problem. You've been nice lately."

"Okay, but I'm not for rent. I'll stay as an honorable gesture until the funeral, and that's it."

"More than reasonable, as always." She said it like it wasn't quite a compliment.

I did leave after the funeral, reasonably intact, but with the uneasy feeling Linda expected my carnal warmth to be available indefinitely, a suspicion time has borne out. To be fair, her wishes to platonically visit my bed have been rare. Her phone calls now mostly concern day-trading and her Wicca Facebook group rather than karmic debts or omens about Carl she and I ignored. Her financial "second sight"—however you account for it—allowed her to repurchase our old Gainesville home. She plans to sell the Decker property and move back, thus regaining the affections of the household gods she pissed off to save Carl from his drug buddies. And she will have goats again, a whole herd of them, tended by the Central American women (fleeing from cartels) she plans to hire. It is only from time to time that loneliness goads her (and her Christmas tree) to visit me for my bodily, if intercourse-free, company. And against an overwhelming tide of advice, I have given her what comfort I can. Ramona calls it peace at any price. Hermine calls it congenital stupidity. I call it peace at an affordable price. My father died amid our long, slow argument, and—to use his pet phrase — "only a fool" would risk surviving that emptiness again.

Hermine's opinion in the matter, harsh as it is, didn't arise from jealousy. Neither of us ever demanded monogamy. We sat on Hermine's bedroom balcony one afternoon between Carl's death and Halloween, sipping sweet, icy Auslese and watching white ducks waddle pondward, cheating death as they crossed Gainesville's busy Eighth Avenue. Apropos of nothing, I observed that geese and swans mate for life, but ducks only for a season.

"Interesting," Hermine remarked, lifting a tanned leg to check her toenail polish. "Perhaps you and I sprang from copulations of ducks and swans. We're both more loyal than ducks, more promiscuous than swans."

"You think I'm promiscuous? I'm flattered."

"Olivia tells me you have a Russian mistress."

"Come on, I told you about Natalya."

"Yes, but you didn't say she was *living* with you."

"Olivia is a lousy journalist. Natalya has made herself at home; that's true. Just not in my bed. No sleepovers. Her domestic surroundings are sub-optimal; *ergo*, she has informally confiscated mine."

Hermine stretched while emitting her signature sigh of chronic disbelief. "Don't worry, Bill. I'm not jealous of your Moscow mail-order bride. But tell me, do you have a superpower that allows you to survive being run over roughshod by women?" As the ducks inched across the avenue, cars waited with nary a honk. Automotive patience took the sting out of Hermine's question.

"The thing is, I don't *feel* trampled. On a good day—like today—I feel like my so-called misfortunes are just stories I read. Bittersweet slices of life, lessons learned, turn the page, no real harm done; you get the drift."

"Oh, believe me, I do. Disassociation. You didn't get squashed by a car tire today, so the road's a pretty good place for ducks, right?"

"A fair point, Hermine. Insulting, but fair."

"Thank you. If I've killed your false hopes, then my career as a shrink has not been in vain."

"What about you? Have you given up hope?"

"Alas, no. Hope is harder to give up than either sex or a sense of superiority. Quite a nuisance."

"Speaking of hope, are you familiar with the apple barrel conundrum?"

"No, enlighten me, pray tell."

"Blame Mr. Peebles, my high school teacher, for this one. Imagine you have a barrel of apples to see you through the winter. The question is, do you always eat the least appetizing apples now and save the better ones for later, hoping to make them last, or do you eat the good apples today and risk days without any apples at all?"

"Damn, Bill, I think I'll use that one on my clients. What's *your* verdict?"

"The good apples, of course. Enjoy life until they run out. Then eat something else. There's plenty of stuff to hope for besides apples."

"Unless apples are all you have."

"In which case you ferment the rotten apples into wine and die happy."

Hermine's wine glass caught the sun when she raised it. "I'll drink to that."

Since Ramona was on call the Halloween following Carl's death, Hermine agreed to drive Olivia over to pick up her "alien eggs"—the wine-soaked plums from our Thai dinner—and apply the goop necessary to turn Olivia into a little green teen from outer space. As I told Hermine, Natalya more or less lived with me during waking hours, having reduced her residence to a staging area for belongings and male baggage. For the record, we had sex only once. "We are opposite sex," Natalya pointed out as she unhooked her fashionable purple-and-gold peasant skirt. "We are friends, we are drunk, we try." And having failed to achieve much, we returned to chess and conversation, coffee and vodka. For my part, the bedroom problem wasn't Natalya's musk-scented body or alcohol, but that she offered herself as if she were the cake you bring to introduce yourself to a new neighbor.

Anyway, when Olivia and Hermine arrived for trick-or-treat preparations, Natalya greeted Olivia—her "little dove"—with flamboyant European cheek kisses, then turned to confront Hermine, who stood exuding feline grace in silky, pastel summer slacks and blouse. "You have delicious eyes," Natalya murmured, her accent intensifying the effect. I could swear Hermine blushed, a reaction I had never come close to inducing.

"Hermine's my spirit guide," Olivia explained to Natalya, "that's different from my grandmother, who happens to be a white witch." Olivia bubbled with occult authority and the joy of teenage self-centeredness brought to full fruition. After all, two fabulous women—more like modern goddesses, really—fussed over her makeup and tinfoil regalia. How much more important could one possibly be?

I watched and remembered my last Halloween as a participant: the infamous Harvest Hop, where I confronted Abel Theroux and later tried to kiss Sally by moonlight, scattering her dime-store pearls and possibly our futures as well. Next year's reunion would also mark that episode's fiftieth year. I cringed to imagine myself standing ill at ease among a milling clump of unrecognized Hopperton geezers gabbling in the Southern twang I had shed over the decades. Even so, Carl's death had convinced me to go. Every person at that reunion had half a century of sunrises and sunsets under their belt that had nothing to do with Bill Shaffer. They would be far too busy padding their histories to burn *me* at the stake. Still, people will inevitably ask me what I've been doing for the last fifty years.

Not that much, I'll say. Taught philosophy, got married and divorced, the usual stuff. Right now? I'm dating a psychiatrist, trying to get my novel published, tending grapes. Nothing spectacular. When they ask what my book's about, I'll say, "It's what I call an honest fantasy. Folks from Hopperton are in it. Maybe even you. But not with real names, of course. And some crazy stuff that happens in the book is over the top, but that's writing for you." If my sordid exile from Hopperton comes up, I'll shrug and say, "Sins of youth, who doesn't have them? Water under the bridge." That should pretty much cover things. And whatever Sally has to say to me can't be any worse than the jagged barbs sunk into me over the years by my wives and lovers.

"Hey, Bill," Olivia called. "Check me out." I looked up to see a scrawny, grinning metallic biped with pea soup skin and feelers tipped with sparkling stars, cradling a jar of purplish alien spawns. (I became "Bill," by the way, not long after Carl died. Olivia had discovered the patriarchy.)

"You look adorable as a creature," I replied, my answer met with a frustrated groan.

"Oh my God, Bill, adorable is the *opposite* of what I'm going for." Despite this weird second scolding for using the word 'adorable,' and after patronizing instructions about holding the camera, I took cell phone pictures of the three women. They looked happy; I felt happy, satisfied. Not from "imperishable bliss" found only in poetry, but from having come to this sweet moment in good enough shape to enjoy it.

"We're all three going trick-or-treating in town," Olivia chirped, "in the rich people's neighborhood. Natalya doesn't have to do anything; she's going as a Russian spy." This bit of cleverness seemed to be the funniest thing the three women had ever heard.

"Hilarious," I said. "Enjoy. Are you coming back, Hermine?"

Hermine favored me with a mock pout. "Alas, only to drop off Natalya; early session tomorrow. So not tonight, but soon." That suited me. I had decided to add a Natalya-based character to my book. A little solitude would help me conceive her. Probably a spy.

Natalya didn't visit me the next day. Or the next. My extra strong coffee went begging, and I had no chance to pit my Queen's Indian defense against her chess prowess. And nothing from Hermine, despite her promise to come by "soon." Even Linda failed to call. A bit peculiar, but I went about my business, trying to flog my book to completion, trying to "eat the good apples today." Finally, after three days of radio silence from all my female cohorts, Hermine pulled up in her little red Mazda Miata convertible. I happened to be standing outside, watching the last bit of sun bleed upward into clouds. When I waved, she just shook her head, which I took as the classic tagline of a hard day at the office.

"Bill," she shouted, "do you still keep a stash of weed on your porch?" Micanopy wasn't the kind of town where anyone cared.

"Sure, come on up." Since weed usually led to sex and Natalya was elsewhere, I had high erotic hopes—assuming Hermine could shake off the day's existential dust. She could count on my help with the shaking. As I rolled a crude joint, she sat in silence, gazing into the dusk, a striking departure from her usual running commentary on human shortcomings. Her appearance too was odd—not the typical suit implying a $100 an hour fee, but jeans and a black T-shirt reminiscent of Linda the first time I saw her by Carl's dock. The dim porch light lent Hermine a monochromatic look, her skin pale—a kind of bleached effect. I found her captivating.

"You look like high-concept art." I handed her the joint.

"What you see," she muttered, "is a low-down soul in a high-concept body."

"What happened? Did you insult a suicidal patient?" To be clear, this was already a running joke between us.

"Shit, Bill, I almost wish that was it. No, I slept with Natalya. She's living with me now. And I think we're in love."

I surmise that age, wisdom of a sort, and the familiar ring of her words buffered me against their ramifications. And of course, I'd often rehearsed after the fact what I *should* have said to Karen and Linda. Which all boiled down to me replying: "Okay, message received. Now, I'm going to do what I was planning to do before you came over. Pick cherries. Edit my book. Revel in unkind thoughts no one will ever hear. You're welcome to sit here as long as you'd like. Smoke as much as you'd like." I felt a darkness invading me, forcing me to my feet. I needed to be alone to fight it off.

Hermine reached out an imploring hand. "Bill, I just want you to know I didn't do this out of promiscuity. Remember when we talked about swans mating for life? That's what I'm shooting for here."

"Okay," I said. "I believe you. And it's not like anything can go wrong."

"Yes," she said, sadness and guilt wrecking her try for a grin. "What are the odds?"

CHAPTER FORTY-SIX

"Paperback Writer"

Micanopy Florida 2017

Since the crockpot is self-sufficient, and Linda has not yet arrived with the cognac to toast Carl's life and times, I pour myself a glass of ruby-red Tempranillo and settle down on my left-hand porch to await developments. It's too early for game three of the Astros-Red Sox Division Series, but the mental convergence of baseball and Hermine takes me back to certain long summer days of my youth, when Hopperton boys gathered on a scrubby, rocky field of sunbaked clay to play ball. My cracked Mickey Mantle bat, so heavy I had to choke up six inches to wield it, required a nail and electrical tape to avoid the woodpile. Sliding into a base guaranteed scrapes and scabs. We played until good and dark, disputing every "out" and "safe" call at the top of our lungs, never actually quitting until, about the time the ball turned invisible and stars turned visible, someone's mother (I forget whose) clanged a dinner bell and sent us reluctantly scattering, the game abandoned.

Abandoned.

For a while afterwards, that's how I felt in the wake of Hermine's decision to cast her lot with Natalya and call a halt to *our* lovely game, harshly clanging the bell, bringing to a logical (if devastating) conclusion the years we "played together like children." As I saw things, she had abruptly and conveniently redefined as mere frivolity the lightheartedness she had always demanded. I seethed for weeks at this rank hypocrisy, letting my regard for her sink to a level hitherto reserved for certain pandering politicians.

Ramona offered little sympathy. It was my problem, she said, not Hermine's: I had too high an opinion of people. As far as that went, Ramona added gratuitously, Hermine was no great shakes as a therapist, either. Olivia, of course, took endless delight in the upheaval and lesbian intrigue, and she too thought it was my problem. I hadn't married Hermine; I hadn't bought her an expensive necklace to seal the deal. Only Linda commiserated, even offering to visit and comfort me. Maybe later, I told her, once my foul mood subsided.

"Bill," she said, "I can sense the Hermine story isn't over. Not that you'll win her back, but accounts must be settled. That's how things worked when I was a property law attorney, and that's how things work with destiny."

In short, everyone weighed in, and I saw no profit in raising objections. Instead, I worked on my novel with diabolical energy and finished it within two months. Hermine had inspired me early on to write with a sense of fun; now, she inspired me to lend my prose a savage edge. Once I had tidied up my manuscript, I ventured onto the web and found a site called Writer's Recourse, from which I purchased a list of reputable small presses. I didn't bother with an agent, feeling myself beneath their notice, and resigned myself in advance to vanity publication.

But one rash publisher, a small, "cutting edge" outfit (their term) called Incongruous Press, accepted the book—praising its "satirical naiveté," daring to compare it to *Forrest Gump*. Not, mind you, the feelgood Tom Hanks movie, but the 1986 picaresque novel by Winston Groom, in which Forrest says—just once—that being an idiot is nothing like a box of chocolates. Forrest's tagline in the book concerns the urge to urinate. He cusses, smokes pot, covers Bob Dylan songs in a folk band, and, for good measure, goes into space with an orangutan. Baffled by the comparison, I nevertheless gave my consent with silence, failing to tell my publisher that *The Dark Warrior* wasn't recently conceived with postmodern intent but had started life as a thrilling, entirely sincere, what-if adventure dreamed up by a seventeen-year-old, male, rural Georgia closet liberal in 1967. Of course, it made no literary difference that retired professor William Shaffer tried like hell to stay out of the way of young Bill Shaffer, letting "him" tell his story. Very few readers spend time wondering how the words got there. And I suspect most writers couldn't tell them.

Anyway, if sales figures are any indicator, most people will never read *The Dark Warrior*. My hope now is that it becomes a so-called "cult classic," its fame spreading among hipper circles of the literary cognoscenti. That said, the book will make unique sense to those who have followed the present story, and for that reason, I will summarize it here.

True to my teenage conception, the book's hero, John Freeman Kent, stumbles across the camp where Robert E. Newlee secretly musters a neo-Confederate army to avenge the one defeated a century earlier and thereby reverse the course of history. Also intact is my beloved first line: *My one regret in life is losing Delia Wingfoot, even though I know it was for the best.* And Delia herself remains a golden-haired, crop-dusting, ordnance-dropping aviator whom Kent—home for the summer before his senior year of college—meets and falls for when she performs in an aerobatic thrill show. As a token of his affection, he bestows on her a ruby necklace passed down to him by his mysterious Russian gypsy aunt, Iriama (rumored to be an undercover counterspy). The necklace's delicately chained stone imbues its wearer with the power of second sight, allowing Delia to bomb more efficiently.

Alas, the necklace does not permanently seal the young lovers' bond. Kent loses Delia to another man, a swashbuckling soldier of fortune named Kal Recker. Kent meets Recker in the Great Swamp. Kent is reconnoitering, and Recker is on the run, having escaped from a Georgia prison after being framed by the Ku Klux Klan for a bank heist (the runaway slave ghost who titles my book magically causes Kent and Recker's paths to cross). Recker is no angel, but his underworld connections prove invaluable. He tells Kent that corrupt, racist Georgia politicians and lawyers, along with the Klan, are involved in shielding the new Confederate army from exposure—which explains why Kent's warnings to police and other local officials go unheeded.

Other factors complicate matters. For one, Kent has just called off his engagement to Polly Styles, the local favorite to win Miss Georgia Peach. While Kent remains fond of Polly, differences of philosophy about money and the Negro Cause come between them, not to mention that Polly's barrister father, Nero Styles, raises vicious German shepherds and sells them to the police. Another vexing complication is that Newlee has an illegitimate son by a Nazi *fraulein*, and that son, Benedict Hess, is a classmate of Kent's; in fact, a close friend. Hess reveres his blood father, who writes him lengthy, incendiary, traitorous letters, one of which Hess proudly shows to Kent. The letter, which Hess praises as "a genius manifesto," reveals his father's demented philosophy and hints at violent, albeit unspecified, schemes.

After many cloak-and-dagger subterfuges interweaved with run-ins and close escapes, Kent and Recker confront Newlee and several minions in the Great Swamp. Here, Delia Wingfoot's air cover is useless, and the Dark Warrior, who might otherwise have aided them, battles a malign swamp spirit, the ghost of a slave plantation boss whose right arm transforms into a demonic bullwhip. Newlee is a deadeye archer, specializing in the crossbow. One of his bolts homes in on Kent's heart, but Kal Recker leaps forward, taking the projectile in his shoulder. Just then, Newlee himself is attacked by an alligator, giving Kent and Recker time to escape. The Dark Warrior and his adversary are nowhere in sight. Delia Wingfoot, a skilled nurse before her flying career, tends to Recker's near-fatal wound as Kent visits Benedict Hess, hoping Hess can persuade his father to lay down his arms before rivers of blood flood the Georgia clay.

"Cripes, Kent!" Benedict exclaimed. "I can't betray my father. After this is over, we'll have two great countries in place of a system where some states are enslaved against their will by an illegal government, don't you see?"

"Benny, that's what they said a hundred years ago."

"The Confederacy was unlucky back then, that's all; if Stonewall Jackson had lived..."

"Okay, how about passing along a white flag powwow request to your father?"

"I ... I don't think so, Kent. If you're not laying a trap, then he might treat you as a spy. Either way, I'd never forgive myself. You should go home. Let history play itself out. No offense, but my father is far wiser and smarter than you are. You won't beat him, but you might end up dead. And I would hate to lose you as a friend."

Despite this failed meeting of minds, Kent receives a welcome update from the Dark Warrior via their secret radio connection: The whip-wielding slavemaster's ghost weakened when the alligator attacked Newlee, allowing the Warrior to subdue the malignant spirit—ironically, by way of magic chains.

"I can't kill him," the Warrior shouts with a fierce chuckle, "because he isn't alive. But defeat Newlee, and I can banish him back to from whence he came."

And more news—good and bad. Under Delia Wingfoot's careful ministrations, Kal Recker is quickly recovering. Unfortunately, Kent also learned from his informants that Newlee has moved his encampment to an unknown location.

"It can't be too far," Delia says excitedly. "I'm sure to spot it from the air. Kal can come with me. A second set of eyes will speed things up."

"Great!" Kent replies, "I'm going to go see my old high school history teacher, Mr. Felix. I think he can help us."

Kent shows Mr. Felix the bloodstained crossbow bolt removed from Kal's shoulder, along with a "borrowed" page from Newlee's manifesto—a necessary betrayal of Benedict Hess he profoundly regrets. Mr. Felix is disturbed by the bolt, but even more so by the page's content. During the war, he served as a cryptographer and senses a looming disaster hidden in a madman's code. He tells Kent he has an old friend in Washington DC, a retired jazz saxophonist who takes illegal bets for senators and Supreme Court judges when they want to put a harmless C-note down on the World Series. This man, Mr. Felix swears, has the president's ear. A couple of days later, an insignificant-looking history teacher, battered briefcase in hand, boards a train to DC.

With any luck, Kent prays, help is on the way.

The Dark Warrior stretches to well over three hundred pages, but that's the gist. A cautionary justice prevails, though Mr. Felix is quick to point out that evil is still among us, waiting for hearts to falter. The part of the book most challenging for me to write, its tragic soul if you will, concerns Benedict Hess, who, tormented by growing doubts, goes to his father's secret lair seeking reassurance. He finds his father drunk, infuriated at an underling's incompetence. As the poor minion awaits execution in front of Newlee's mustered troops, Benedict Hess pleads for the man's life, but rather than relenting, Newlee demands that his son perform the execution as an act of loyalty.

We never know what would have happened, since at that moment Delia Wingfoot and Kal Recker, aloft in a converted war surplus Piper

Cub, drop a bomb that detonates where Newlee and his son stand. Later, of course, John Freeman Kent learns of the affair between Delia and Kal. He's upset but "takes it like a man"—to use a phrase rendered disreputable by gender politics. At the end of the book, he sits in a gazebo in his hometown, peace restored, looking at twilight stars and remembering the line that started his reverie: *My one regret in life is losing Delia Wingfoot, even though I know it was for the best.*

But it's different now for Kent. What happened to Benedict Hess and his father renders regrets of the heart trivial. Later that night, he will visit Polly Styles, not to rekindle their romance, but to comfort her after her father's imprisonment for treason. In the novel's last moment, a shooting star streaks across the sky—a kind of astrophysical farewell. Kent stands up and salutes it.

Time to move on, he thinks. *Time to write a new first line for my next adventure.*

As I contemplate Kent's next adolescent exploit, maybe busting a worldwide cheetah-poaching ring, Hermine pulls up in her newest toy, a lava-orange Porsche Carrera. I am surprised to see her so early in the day, particularly given her reluctance to attend what she dubbed "Carl's morbid after-party." She steps out, waving a book, her lime green slacks shimmering in the morning light. She looks especially well put together today, like an actress heading to an audition. When I stand up, she spots me. "My god, Bill," she calls out, "what fever dream accounts for this garish literary hallucination?" She has obviously acquired my novel.

"I just call 'em as I see 'em," I shout back. "And I see from your ride that your late mid-life crisis is still raging." She advances, cackling, shaking her head. We meet on the steps and exchange a friendly, lingering kiss. Then she studies my face as she wipes her lipstick from my mouth.

"You're cooking something intoxicating I can't quite place," she says. "Let's go investigate."

A word of explanation. Although I remain tossed aside for Natalya, Hermine has, shall we say, reacquired an interest in my business. A few weeks after our split, someone knocked on my door with the fervor of a process server. It was Hermine, intent on "reconceptualizing" our relationship. The gist of her proposal, announced right there on my doorstep, was this: we sleep together occasionally; in exchange I quit sulking. "I'm not a lesbian," she insisted, "and I have needs which Natalya cannot fully meet, even though she is a man in a woman's body. And you are clearly disintegrating in my absence."

"I'm disintegrating no faster than the average old fool," I had retorted, masking my pleasure at the turn of events. "Be honest, Hermine. If you want a back door man, just say so." She had then pushed her way in, decrying my "sordid junk heap of a mind." Once we were seated at opposite ends of my sofa, I had explained—taking my sweet time—that "Back Door Man" was an old Howling Wolf down-and-dirty blues tune, re-recorded by The Doors in 1967. I tortured her a little bit further by offering to play her version of choice. She sat with arms folded and legs crossed, one glossy black high-heeled shoe bobbing and weaving in agitation. Finally, she sprang to her feet and fixed me with a steely glare.

"Bill," she said, in a voice tinged with menace and exasperation, "I am heading for your bedroom. If you are as boring in there as you are out here, I fear we are truly finished."

I stood up as if in weary defeat, hanging my head. "You win this round," I growled, "but don't think I'm surrendering." I *was* surrendering, of course, which, I later told myself, was a beautifully Buddhist thing to do.

That anecdote said, sex between Hermine and me is more or less a symbolic possibility these days. To put it plainly, Hermine is smitten with Natalya, not me, and it turns out my libido is unable to overcome this fact. So, it's the kitchen table rather than the bedroom as we wait for other souls to arrive.

Hermine sits across from me, sipping from a cup of whiskey-inflected coffee, affecting shock as she flips through the pages of my novel. She looks tired, her crow's feet etched by an arbor-dappled slant of sun. "I could write a forward to this . . . divulgence," she says, smiling wolfishly, "then publish it as a psychiatric textbook. College students would be forced to buy it and we would become rich. What do you think?"

I shrug elaborately. "I think you overvalue my genius. The book is nothing but a trifling *homage* to youthful sincerity; a mere bag of shells."

"You mean bagatelle."

"That too."

I wait to fend off more acerbic banter, but instead Hermine lapses into silence, her eyes falling. Then she looks up and says, "I honestly don't know if your novel is inspired or terrible, but given what I know of your checkered past, I do recognize its sincerity." As I nod my appreciation, a pained expression clouds her face. "Listen, Bill, "I don't know why I'm telling you this now—possibly the whiskey or exotic Latin American aromas going to my head—but during our years consorting, I kept waiting for an opportunistic, insincere Bill Shaffer to show his face, even after I knew better. I can't say marriage would have suited us, but there's no doubt I strung you along, and I'm owed a comeuppance."

Given her stricken look, I sense Hermine has harbored this declaration for a good while. I am unsure what to say, or even feel. Finally, with what I hope is a charitable smile, I reply, "My first wife Karen cured me of insincerity. And as for comeuppance. you'll have to look elsewhere. I don't deal that particular drug. Too dangerous."

Hermine sighs. "Have no fear, Bill, the world is full of dealers in such commodities. And anyway, don't you Buddhists say our intentions define our future? My bad intentions can hardly hope to escape cosmic justice."

"I'm not a card-carrying Buddhist, but I do believe karma exists. The problem with your logic is that karma is the sum of *all* our actions and intentions, not just a cherry-picked few, which makes figuring out what we're 'owed' a lot harder."

A ghost of her old smile creeps back into Hermine's face. "And doesn't *that* make things conveniently vague, Bill? No, I see now I must put my faith in old reliable—my guilty conscience." Before I can answer she gets up, walks to the window, and peers out. "How lovely it all is," she murmurs, "and none of it is required to pursue happiness. She reaches up and fondles a leaf on one of my house plants perching on the sill. "What is this called?" she asks.

"That's a croton."

"Will it be joined by a certain magic Christmas tree later today?" Hermine still faces the window, but the mischief in her voice is apparent enough.

"I don't know. Linda and white magic have been butting heads lately; theological differences."

"That's regrettable, but at least they have you to counsel them."

"Yes, there's that. Speaking of wives, where's Natalya? Isn't she tired of hiding from me?"

Hermine returns to the table before answering, noticeably amused by my questions. "The little woman may come by once she's assured it will not be just the three of us. She naturally assumes you are plotting to kill her, possibly the two of us together to intensify the poetic justice."

"Makes sense. How about the three of us meeting in a public place? There's a little Italian restaurant that just opened up down the street."

Hermine grins. "You mean like in *The Godfather*, with a gun hidden in the toilet?"

I shake my head. "I just want to convince Natalya to follow a less homicidal train of thought."

Hermine sips coffee and drums her nails up on the tabletop. As I get up to brew a fresh pot, she says, "Here's an idea. Based on all your horror stories, Linda Featherstone can convince anyone of anything. We'll have Linda call Natalya, denigrate you a bit as the disenchanted ex-wife, then assure her you're harmless. And Linda should mention that she's a lawyer and a widow. Natalya is overly impressed by such things."

"Are you serious? They've never even met."

"A call from a strange woman will intrigue Natalya. She thinks life is like your absurd novel."

I laugh uneasily. "This is beginning to feel like one of those old forties screwball comedies where somebody always says 'your idea is so crazy it just might work.'"

"Relax; I know Natalya. And don't forget my professional status as a mental *savant*."

"Fine, but you don't really know Linda, and that's what worries me." Hermine flicked my worry away with a manicured hand.

"And if history is any judge, dear Bill, you don't know her that well either."

Linda arrives bearing cognac and a small, unexpected suitcase. She drops the suitcase in the foyer, hands me the cognac, then greets Hermine with a half-realized hug. I see no sign of the Christmas tree. I do see changes in Linda, however. She is still pale, but not pallid; still thin, but not gaunt. She has let her cropped hair get agreeably bushy since I last saw her a few weeks back. Her blouse is a soft gold rather than the usual black. Better yet, Hermine engages her in small talk as if no tension ever existed between the two women. I am left to ponder the meaning of the suitcase and the larger mystery of Linda's revitalized appearance. One thing is certain: I will not compliment her looks and risk suggesting Carl's absence has improved her lot.

"Bill," she says, turning abruptly from Hermine, "I can't stay as long as I'd like. I'm expected at Olivia's soccer jamboree. Then I'll be with her and Ramona the rest of the weekend." Before I can answer, she glances at Hermine with a smile and adds, "And I see that you have plenty of company."

Hermine shakes her head. "My company is not as plentiful as you might think, Linda. I'm romantically involved with a woman named Natalya, who, if I'm not mistaken, you have never met?"

"No, but I feel like I have. Bill's colorful Russian mistress. Or so I thought until he cried on my shoulder. I was a little surprised by the turn of events, but I'm not at all surprised to see you here."

"Oh?" Hermine says, her voice simultaneously pleasant and poisonous.

"Let's retire to the kitchen and crack open this cognac," I suggest, hoping to divert what I fear is an ominous conversational flow.

"In a minute, Bill," Hermine says, raising a hand as if to block my approach. "I'm anxious to hear Linda's insight into our relationship."

Before answering, Linda turns in a circle. "I like this house," she muses; "not as much as the Tampa house or the Gainesville house, but the twin porches and big windows of this place give it great charm."

"It's lovely," Hermine says, without the slightest pretense of conviction.

Linda stops turning when she faces Hermine. "Bill has probably told you that I believe I'm a white witch. That I worship a Christmas tree. The truth is, I don't know what I am, or how the divine and I are connected. But I do sense certain things. To put it in non-spooky terms, you and Bill have spent years together building a house you never finished. I see the two of you continuing to build that house, even if it remains unfinished."

A brief silence follows. Then Hermine grins and says, "Well shit, Linda, that's exactly right. I wonder if you would mind using some of your verbal magic on Natalya? She thinks Bill is plotting her murder."

Linda stands outside by the arbor to call Natalya, insisting on "absolute privacy." Hermine, possessed by an odd restlessness, scrubs dishes at my sink, an unprecedented behavior providing her a clear view of Linda.

"Can you read lips?" I ask.

"Shut up, Bill."

"Sure, Hermine, but first I need to tell you something remarkable. This is just how we were situated when I fell in love with Wanda Grice—me watching her wash dishes."

"Not remarkable, Bill; barely interesting."

"Come to think of it," I continue, undeterred, "kitchen tables have played a pivotal role in my life. I was sitting at one when I decided to take that stupid job that got me divorced from Karen. And Linda and Carl raked me over the coals at our kitchen table in Gainesville, and—"

"Please, Bill, recognize that you're half drunk—get a grip."

I sink into chastised silence, my attention forced elsewhere, first to the festive doodles of a Miro print hanging nearby, and then to Hermine's workout-firm bottom, and from there, by a slightly guilty-ridden leap, to Linda's naked body lying still in the soft, dim light of a bedroom two short blocks and thirty-five-odd years removed. Red wine and whiskey urge me to pursue this sensual contemplation, but a lifetime of overthinking prods me hard in a contrary direction. Why had neither woman (or any other)—I cast about for a word and what comes to mind is a Biblical term from Reverend Farrior's sermons—"cleaved" to me? Granted, I muse, in the Bible it is the man who must leave his mother and father and cleave to his wife, but surely the reverse applies? Such questions and speculations are not new to me. Like Carl, they are troublesome old friends with whom I never fully come to terms. And like philosophy, so many answers come to mind that the net effect is no answer. It's them, it's me, it's the modern *zeitgeist* or karma, it's chance or destiny, it's an object lesson or the wrong question, it's irrelevant, it's missing the point. And to muddy the water further, I am currently the most significant man in both Hermine and Linda's lives. Does that constitute "cleaving" of a sort?

Get a grip, indeed.

Hermine sways slightly, humming "The Girl from Ipanema," her gaze still fixed on to Linda. The song happens to be the most widely recorded in popular music history, but I keep this jewel of trivia to myself. Instead, I get up and pointlessly check the crockpot. Still crocking. As I'm replacing the lid, Linda reenters, wearing a smile of understated self-satisfaction.

"Well?" Hermine asks, not bothering to look up from dishes which suddenly command her entire attention.

"Natalya is on her way. I loved her raspy accent, by the way. It felt like I was doing a scene in a spy movie."

"Great," Hermine manages, "what did you tell her?"

"I told her Bill had this terrible habit of disparaging and mocking the unseen, but otherwise he wouldn't hurt a fly. I told her about Carl; she told me how she more or less deported her menfolk back to Russia. Then we talked a bit about interior decorating. She wants to see the Gainesville house once I get it refurbished."

Hermine turns from the sink with arms folded and fixes Linda with an apparently admiring stare. "I don't know if you're a good witch, Linda, but you certainly have a gift for drawing people out. I don't recall Natalya ever speaking a furniture-related word in English. Maybe in Russian, but I wouldn't know."

"Different spirits speak to each other in different ways," Linda answers in a tone of a pious certainty apt to goad Hermine into a withering reply. I brace myself for an outbreak of hostilities.

But Hermine only nods as if acknowledging a deep truth, then says, "Your house tour sounds like fun; mind if I tag along?"

We decide to wait for Natalya before lifting glasses to Carl. Three celebrants seem pitifully few, and anyway, Hermine points out, Natalya probably knows "hundreds of exotic Russian sayings about death to liven up the proceedings." Linda prefers to wait on one of my porches, and Hermine concurs, designating the "weed porch." I drag a maple rocker over from the other side, returning in time to hear Linda utter the phrase, "interesting bastard." "Not you, Bill," she says, glancing up with a smile.

"Not that interesting, huh?" I reply.

Ignoring my wit, Linda says, "I'm telling Hermine about Carl. She wonders what I saw in him."

"Carry on then," I say, affecting cavalier disinterest. I park the rocker as far away from the two women as I can, then gaze out with deliberate intensity at the smattering of traffic and gray-bottomed clouds hinting at a twilight deluge. It's a pathetic performance on my part, considering I'm bound to hear every word Linda speaks. And I suppose it's equally weird of Linda to confide in Hermine as if I'm not there.

"See, Hermine," Linda says, "Carl and I shared something that Bill and I did not—a criminal mindset. I see now that's why I chose law and real estate as my professions." Hermine nods silently as she deftly rolls a joint with fingertips unimpeded by long, perfect, avocado-colored nails. "We spent a lot of our time together with me debunking his stupid schemes," Linda continues, "and I suppose you know all about how Bill got this house and, for that matter, how he ended up with me."

"Yes," Hermine says, "I wormed it out of him over many years. All the machinations and bloodline drama. Juicy stuff. I must say he held out as long as he could. As for your bond with Carl, well, I confess that Natalya is a bit of a rogue as well. She's puffed up with her sexual power. Oh, it's real enough, but, as I have warned her, it's a finite and narrow power, given life's complexities. She just tells me I'm jealous and starts taking off my clothes." Hermine sighs, lights the joint, samples it, then adds, "And I suppose psychiatry could be called a form of criminal activity—looting people's minds for fun and profit."

Linda, to my surprise, takes a tepid hit from the joint before replying. "I thought with Bill I would mend my ways, I really did. But certain spirits have forced me to see that all along I wanted an untrustworthy life, a life I could outwit." She returns the joint to Hermine, then sighs. "Do you know how I paid off the house where Bill and I lived? I bribed clerks in the offices of my competitors by offering a cut of my commission. I knew everybody's best offer, everybody's bottom line, everybody's deal-breaker. I rigged the game. I guess most people are honest based on how ridiculously easy it was."

"Well," Hermine says, "treating life as a game is a common failing of smart people, if indeed it's a failing. Care to comment, Bill?" She extends the joint to me, apparently amused beyond telling.

"I'll pass on the pot and the comment," I say; "no comeuppances, no opinions. But I am curious about the dueling epiphanies I was obviously meant to overhear."

"It's called an honesty encounter," Linda answers without turning her head. Arms folded, she stares through the screen at the outside world. "If both parties are truthful," she goes on, "a lasting bond is sealed between them."

"It's 'let's get acquainted' on steroids," Hermine adds, "and given Linda's success in bewitching Natalya, I would be a fool not to give it a shot." If she's gaslighting Linda with earnestness, I can't detect it.

"Well—good," I manage.

"A woman's coming," Linda announces in a low, premonitory voice, "a colorfully dressed woman. I assume it's Natalya."

I look out to see Natalya—indeed brightly bedecked in a filmy gold blouse and black skirt splashed with yellow and purple pansies— approaching the house, her forceful strides imparting a noticeable bounce to her breasts.

Hermine chuckles and says, "That outfit means she's coming to see *you*, Linda; better brace yourself." A cynical cheeriness flavors her warning.

"I'm perfectly fine as I am," Linda replies. "Maybe I'll be lucky and have two honesty encounters in one day."

In fact, no detectable sparks fly. Other than paying conspicuous inattention to me, Natalya seems at ease as she sits on the sofa with Linda, chatting in a understated manner I find pleasantly out of character. Hermine and I stay in the kitchen, tending to food. After gathering together for lunch, our little quartet toasts Carl. I feel the occasion lacks sufficient zest to attract his soul, but who knows? Natalya does offer a Russian proverb about death, loosely translating as "After you die it's too late for doctors." Linda's toast is "Carl, I hope you find your diamond, wherever you are." She delivers her wish, as far as I can tell, with affection free of acerbic irony. I contribute a few words about Carl's love of sailing and his openhearted zest, failing to mention the sad paradox of such a man dying in shallow water. Oddly enough, Hermine speaks last and most memorably, clearly addressing her remarks to Linda: "As you know, I take Bill's part concerning his dealings with Carl. Nor do I believe that Bill's dead friend is in a better—or worse—place. That said, if he does continue to exist, I imagine it is where he was most comfortable in this life—namely, in the wind."

When Linda leaves for the soccer game, Natalya hurries out as well, loathe to be alone with Hermine and me. Hermine stays to help me clean up.

"What gives?" I ask, suspecting there's no need to elaborate. Hermine answers as she continues to ladle spicy chicken into my ancient Tupperware.

"Natalya will probably move on soon. I'm hoping another attractive woman can help me settle the question."

"Ah."

"Yes, *ah*, wiseass. But don't worry, I'll explain my motives to mystical Linda. More honesty, more bonding."

"No worry from this quarter," I say, "just the sympathetic observation that love is a hoot and a half."

Hermine snaps the Tupperware shut with a theatrical groan. "I don't suppose you'd take me back if things go south?"

"Let's not get *that* honest quite yet," I answer. But listen, Hermine, consider yourself entirely in my good graces. Nothing could convince me our time together hasn't been well spent. As someone once said to a man named Coyote, no regrets.

She grants me a wry, sad smile. "It's so you to cheapen my self-abasement with what I assume is a rock song allusion."

"Yes, and it's so *you*, Hermine, to respond with highbrow snobbery.

"Any more endearments to share?"

"Just one more. I love you."

"Well, I should say, after all the erotic trails we've blazed."

CHAPTER FORTY-SEVEN

"Like A Rolling Stone"

Waycross, Georgia, 2017

O ctober has arrived, and I'm on my way to a Marriott Inn for the Hopperton High School fiftieth class reunion as rain falls alike on my Studebaker and the countless, indistinguishable SUVs blowing by me on Highway 441. Bravo, all you hustlers, but I'm in no hurry to get anywhere. I poke along, listening to *the* song coming to me from out on Highway 61.

How does it feel to be a complete unknown? Maybe preferable to being the all-too-well-remembered black sheep. Thoughts zigzag across my mind like tracer bullets in a midnight ambush. I know that Carl would mock this comparison since I've never seen combat or even shot a gun, but there it is, probably snuck into my brain by his ghost. From my Trump victory gloom to my hairline vanity, every mental precinct clamors anxiously to have its vote counted. I had imagined facing Sally would be my moment of truth, but mingling with a clump of crowing Trump voters may be the acid test of the Zen-like composure I plan to exhibit. And just to make things weirder, the Marriott sits on the outskirts of Waycross, the town Wanda Grice left behind when she materialized at Hopperton High like a teen-fiction anti-princess. I won't get any closer to Waycross than an outlying hotel, but that's far closer than I've ever gotten to locating Wanda, a regret made more poignant lately by the fact that I dedicated my book to her. Several copies of that book lie in my trunk, and while they all may return with me undisturbed to Micanopy, you never know.

I arrive at the hotel late Friday afternoon for the Saturday reunion. Time to check in, decompress, stretch my legs, eat a meal in solitude. In short, gather my fractured wits.

The Marriott features a restaurant called The Bubbling Pot. Despite this enticement, I order a turkey club and regard my fellow customers as they eat, chat, or nosedive into their phones. Some qualify as possible classmates, but none of their aging faces spark the least recollection. Then a tall, fit, well-dressed woman approaches. She's about my age, but her hair's whiteness, unlike mine, appears only in frothy streaks embellishing a perfect nut-brown coiffure. Her eyes hide behind fashionable red frames, but I haven't forgotten Sally's slight slouch and loping stride.

"You found me," I say.

"I had the front desk tell me when you checked in. Kind of sneaky, I know, but if you were going to yell at me, I didn't want it to happen at the reunion."

"Why on earth would I yell at you?"

"Because the last time we talked, I told you I hated you, then hung up." Sally stands warily, arms crossed, poised for a getaway. I suspect she rehearsed our encounter as an ugly incident.

"I'm not mad about that. It was one of the two fascinating conversations we ever had, along with our little squabble after I tried to kiss you, remember? Nice to see you, by the way. Are you going to join me? Have you eaten?" This much *I* had more or less rehearsed on the drive up. Sally shakes her head, then sits down gingerly, treating the chair like an expensive concert seat she bought with a counterfeit ticket.

"You look younger than I thought you would," she says in a breathless rush. "Would you order me cherry pie *à la mode* and coffee?" Without waiting for an answer, she leans closer and whispers, "I have to go pee. It always happens when my nerves get rattled."

Shades of Forrest Gump. "Sure," I say. "Good to know." Sally hurries away, and I wonder for a second if she's coming back. I imagine myself consuming the pie and coffee, checking out, and driving back to Micanopy—another lesson stubbornly unlearned. But she's back quickly, if anything more keyed up than before.

"Bill, can we get the pie to go and take it to your room? I feel like everyone here is listening to me. I hope you don't mind. I'm a mess."

"Not at all. I can take these ridiculously shiny shoes off." I've come to the reunion to face down any detractors, tell Sally no hard feelings, and maybe casually catch up on the last half century. But she seems to have a more complicated, fraught agenda—a possibility I should have anticipated given my history with women. As we walk to my room, I give myself a silent pep talk right out of *Siddhartha*: let the river steer the boat.

Upstairs, Sally ignores her dessert, choosing instead to tumble onto the oversized bed with an uninhibited grunt. "This is how I talk to my therapist, Bill. And besides that, Lord, I'm tired. And *my* shoes hurt too." She kicks them off.

"You look well," I say, "and I see you've mastered the art of dispensing with formalities. Do you want a couple of Tylenol?" So much for any working assumptions about Sally.

"No, just water. I've got better stuff in my purse."

"Okay, I'll go get ice." As I trek to the ice machine, I wonder whether Sally goes by Chiles or another last name. Either way, as I remind myself, this beleaguered woman is the same Sally I held hands with as we sang the doxology:

Praise God from whom all blessings flow
Praise Him all creatures here below

Yes, I think, we are all creatures down here, scavenging for ice or diving for diamonds, looking for deities to praise, looking for love, for things to add up that don't add up, acting out purposes buried too deep to discover. Sally on my bed summons to my mind Wanda on hers, searching for music beside piles of dirty clothes; and Karen—for a narrow moment—making room for me beside her; and Linda, pretending to sleep that first morning, offering her naked body like art…

The ice machine rumbles and grinds then dumps its batch of frozen pebbles—hit or miss—into the bucket. Enough pseudo-poetic babble, it seems to say; back to business.

"Thank you, Bill. I've got to rest quietly for five minutes," Sally says when I return, downing her pills and closing her eyes. "Good idea," I tell her, parking myself in a chair. I soon close my eyes, and the name "Sally

Hayes" drifts into my consciousness. Is that Sally's married name? No. I remember now. It's a girl Holden Caufield encounters in *Catcher in the Rye*, the one he calls "the queen of all phonies," although he's so lonely he invites her to live with him in the woods. I don't think Sally Chiles is a phony, and I don't want to live with her. But, because I would like to shorten the space between us, I sit and wait. I hear her begin to snore lightly, and five minutes becomes an hour in which I eat her dessert, feed an exploratory pod or two into the coffee maker, and, as a last resort, watch parking lot vehicles come and go like Michelangelo's women. When Sally finally wakes, it's with a disoriented start. She stares at me in the chair, then looks down to check her modesty.

"You must wonder what happened to me," she says, swinging up to a sitting position, smoothing her skirt.

"No, I assume you conked out from the pills. It's—"

"Not that, what *happened* to me."

"You mean your life? A lot, I imagine."

"Well. I jump around like spit on a hot griddle if that's doing a lot. Not that I get anywhere."

"Putting aside the question of where there is to 'get,' it sounds like *you* wonder what happened to you."

Sally picks at her skirt with shiny red nails.

"And *you* sound just like my therapist. What I wonder is . . . can you please make fresh coffee?"

As I pop in a pod of Southern Pecan, she revisits the bathroom, using the occasion to croon an old Monkees tune from our high school hop days as she performs her ablutions. Sleepy Jean the homecoming queen definitely needs cheering up.

Sally's voice plays hard-to-get with the proper pitch but reminds me pleasantly of Dusty Springfield singing "Son of a Preacher Man." When she comes out, I request "Downtown" by Petula Clark.

"I only sing on the toilet, but at the rate I drink coffee, you may get your wish."

"Sally, that's the first deliberately funny thing I've ever heard you say. Good to know the last fifty years weren't a total loss."

I fear my "total loss" comment is a sardonic bridge too far, but Sally is fixated elsewhere. "Bill, you said something downstairs about your *first* wife. How many wives have you had?"

449

"A couple."

"Were they beautiful?"

"Sure. I told my second wife I wanted to paint her. My first wife was a knockout when she was in the mood. But to my utter surprise, looks didn't carry the marital day either time."

Sally walks to the bed, nodding as if to say she understands perfectly. Then she props herself on fluffed pillows, artificially flavored coffee on her lap, situating herself, it seems, for a lengthy chat.

"You told Miriam I was beautiful when you were here for your father's funeral. Beautiful like your wives? Or was it different with me? Or just bullshit?"

"Different. I was contemplating—or engaged in—sex with my wives."

"You didn't contemplate sex with me?" Sally seemed crestfallen.

"Yes, of course, but only in the vaguest, most adolescent way. You weren't broadcasting on that channel. By the way, you ask questions unthinkable to the Sally I once knew. Those pills must be good."

"I was a professional virgin back then. Now I'm . . . never mind. Are you going to tell me why you called me beautiful?" Sally takes her glasses off and peers as if to read my fine print, hoping for unfiltered soul-to-soul communication, or, more likely, hoping to cow me into honesty. As I try to soldier on, a memory comes to life.

"I called you beautiful—that exact word—to your face, long before I told Aunt Miriam. Don't you remember?"

Sally registers a panicked inner search that comes up empty.

"When?" she asks, trying to scoff. "Back when we were six or seven?"

"No. Before the Harvest Hop; you were Martha Washington. I thought you looked great, full of lively energy—'vivacious' captures it best, I guess."

"You were talking about *inner* beauty, right?" Sally grumps. Clearly an inferior vintage in her eyes. Nevertheless, she can't hide the pleasure of recovering that old, forgotten compliment.

"You're a hard case, aren't you? Look, how could I be objective about your looks anyway? I'd known you all my life. Besides, physical beauty is a crapshoot, except that cheating is allowed."

"What are you talking about?"

"I mean, it's a crapshoot as to whether your face fits the fashion trend. If it does, great. If it doesn't, buy a magazine and imitate a face that does.

450

Voila. Outer beauty. But I don't remember you doing that—trying to be a magazine glamour girl. It makes me wonder what kind of beauty you were going for."

"I would have looked like a clown in all that makeup."

"Well, I'm not about to deconstruct cosmetic oppression, but I don't think the fear of looking like a clown was your problem. You wanted to be thought beautiful exactly as you were, right? Isn't that what we all want? Nothing wrong with that, but it's a lot to ask when your pool of Prince Charmings consists of popular jocks at Hopperton High, circa 1967."

When I finish, Sally shakes her head like the indulgent mother of a pretentious child. "Did you make that little speech up on the spot?" she asks.

"No. Hard-won insight. In addition to being a know-it-all philosophy professor, I wrote a novel—a dystopian fairytale—set in Georgia in the sixties. I had to study you for one of the characters."

"I'm in the book?" she cries with a preschool squeak of delight.

"Well, someone whose circumstances *resemble* yours at the time, a local girl from a good family—"

"What's my name?"

"*Her* name is Polly Styles."

"My God, everyone will know it's me! Am I good or bad?"

"I would say Polly Styles is far more good than bad. She's Miss Georgia Peach of 1960."

Sally's eyes dart back and forth as she searches her memory.

"Was there such a pageant, Bill?"

"I don't know. It doesn't matter. The book is an alternate-reality *fantasy*. And I should warn you that Polly Styles's father is a corrupt, racist lawyer who raises German shepherds and sells them to fascist police."

Sally reacts as if my comment were a bad smell. "Lord, what kind of book *is* it?"

"It's how I looked at the lily-white South when I was seventeen. Sally, I was on my way to becoming a secret left-winger by the time I was ten years old. My parents had given me their old parlor radio which could pick up stations from big cities late at night. Soul music and national stories the Hopperton fish wrapper never covered. Black people were always the mistreated underdogs to me. Something in my genes, I guess. I thought of that radio as my friend. I even gave it a not very original name—My

Secret Radio. It even affected how I look at love; I mean the way people send and receive love on different frequencies. Is anyone broadcasting on our frequency? Is anyone listening to our frequency? Do we believe that only love traveling on our frequency is true love? I even used the radio as a character in my book."

Sally waves her arms. "You lost me after fish wrapper."

"Well, at least you know the depths of my depravity. Anyway, the short answer is my book is a kind of a graphic novel without the pictures. A man tries to start a second civil war and restore slavery. I crush the attempt. Well, my alter ego does, with a little help from the ghost of a runaway black slave, among others."

After a pause, Sally replies, her eyes closing briefly before she speaks. "I used to watch you, Bill, your face pinching up. I knew you didn't like the way people talked, including me. My mother said you were from a good family, and after you found a career, you'd outgrow your foolishness. I thought what *she* thought because, well, I took her word for most everything."

"You thought I was foolish? Without even talking to me?"

"That was my mother's word. I just wanted my dreams to come true. And even though I was afraid of what you might be thinking, *you* were my Prince Charming, Bill, not those loud boys drinking beer at the lake. Now *you* know."

"Now we both know. Finally too old for hide-and-seek."

"Too old for too many things," Sally muttered, unmoved by my distilled insight.

I cast about for a new topic.

"How did Aunt Miriam come to tell you I said you were beautiful?"

"Hold that question," Sally says, heading for the bathroom again. This time she picks Patsy Cline and warbles a bit of "I Fall to Pieces," after which she explains loudly through the closed door that Aunt Miriam despised her fiancé. "She called to tell me you said I was beautiful *and*, by the way, to tell me Milton had been to her hotel with women, most likely prostitutes from the look of them. Then she said I wasn't pretty enough or flashy enough to keep a good-for-nothing Atlanta playboy happy. That's why this whole 'beautiful' thing got my goat."

"I'm sorry," I shout.

Mercifully, Sally returns to the bed—after a brief detour for ice water—before continuing our heart-to-heart.

"I guess Miriam thought I'd call off the engagement, but that horse had already bolted the barn. A big business deal of my father's hinged on the marriage. And I was twenty-eight. What Miriam said changed nothing, except that *now* I was marrying a scoundrel who thought I was ugly. Honestly, to this day, I wish she hadn't told me, even though she was right."

"I guess I'm different; I prefer to know the worst things."

"Is that why you tried so hard to find that girl—Wanda? Your aunt told me she even had her detective looking." Sally props herself up on pillows, holding her knees. I feel, through no fault of hers, like a squirrel stalked by a cat.

"I can't pinpoint my motives back then. Maybe."

"What would you have done if you found her?"

"Try to find out if she was actually pregnant. If there was a baby. And why she told Bobby Heatwole she slept with Don and told me she hadn't. She didn't want to marry me, so why lie?"

"*If?* Didn't she have a pregnancy test?"

"No. My father banished me to snuff out the scandal, the disgrace, not for getting a girl pregnant. He said gossip would percolate as long as I stayed in Hopperton."

"Never mind, Bill, please. I didn't mean to stir up mud from the bottom."

"It's all right; it's good, clean mud. Good for the complexion." Sally concedes a small laugh this time.

"I would have given fifty dollars to hear one of my husbands speak cleverly like that, but to be fair, one of them was decent—the one that's dead, of course. I also had two miscarriages, two mastectomies. And good moments sprinkled in; I won't lie. A wonderful affair, for example. But that was a while ago."

"And yet here you are, trying to figure it all out, trying to get it right. Damn admirable if you ask me."

"You think? Well, when I went into the bathroom just then, and before that downstairs, I took another little white pill. That's where I got the courage to sing and spill my guts. Does that seem 'admirable' to you?"

"It sounds like America these days: anxiety, money, and pills in an endless and very profitable loop. It snags a lot of people. Look, we had well-meant advice coming out of our ears as kids. Lots of generalities: work hard, trust in God, whatever, as if adages would immunize you against the shitstorms of life. Personally, I could have used a couple of cynical truth-tellers to temper my fantasies. But to answer your question, you wouldn't be here confronting me if the pills owned you, so admirable still gets my vote."

"You are kind," Sally says with a tired smile. "You're preachy and hard to understand, but kind. I didn't see it back then. I mean, I did, but I didn't have that name for it. Hopperton girls thought about dreamy boys, not kind boys."

"We non-dreamy boys thank you for your belated recognition."

"See? That's what I mean. You *talk* like a book. Speaking of which, where's the one you wrote? Do you have it with you?"

"Sure. I'll give you a copy." I stand up to retrieve it from my suitcase.

"In that case," she tells me, her voice suddenly quavering, "I have a gift for you." She pivots and springs from the bed with sudden energy, then walks over and kisses me gently, tasting of toothpaste and exuding the tang of recently applied perfume.

CHAPTER FORTY-EIGHT

"Love Minus Zero/ No Limit"

The kiss is brief. A gift, as Sally said, not a prelude. She's high, I suppose, but self-possessed enough to whisper, "That wasn't as hard as I thought." As I sift through the possible interpretations of this remark, she returns to the bed.

"Well, I liked it," I say, tossing my book to the foot of the bed.

"Thank God. I've been carrying that kiss around for fifty years." Sally's face flickers with emotion, but the moment doesn't feel as burdened and weepy as I had feared, so I pose the obvious question.

"Why didn't you kiss me back then?"

"Come on, Bill. You were drunk. It wasn't a real kiss."

With that, I begin to explain how I had feigned drunkenness at the Harvest Hop to hide my motives for quarreling with Abel Theroux, which in turn requires me to revisit Wanda and Bobby Heatwole at the Rialto and theorize why Don Heffelfinger smashed Abel's knee. Don's mention soon morphs into an account of his father's drug-masked illness and the ensuing deceptions and contriving, all culminating in the swamp catastrophe.

"People said you and Don killed his father for money. That maybe you were queers." Sally offers this tidbit in passing as room service arrives with club sandwiches and fries.

"You know, as off base as that rumor was, it did foreshadow something—two men tried to kill me for money. Maybe I'll tell you about it after we eat."

"And maybe I'll burn your book if you don't tell me now."

I pretend reluctance as I describe the quarry disaster, appending a sketch of Carl Decker, including his entanglement with my two wives. I throw in Gibson Levine and Delilah for good measure. Sally dispatches her food with uninhibited gusto, cackling wide-eyed at my account like I'm a stand-up comic dishing succulent gossip. For one sweet patch of time, we have evolved into pals, which, I suspect, is the role nature intended for us all along.

Sally tells a tale, too, one I'm tempted to steal for a short story. Her first husband, Milton, tired of toiling in his father's law firm, picked up what's come to be known as a "side hustle" aiding and abetting a bank client in an embezzlement scheme, *a la* Carl. In Milton's case, what he offered his employers was his fast car—an orange 1978 Porsche 911 Super Carrera—and his willingness to rush deposits from one bank branch to the next, staying one step ahead of auditors who otherwise would notice shortfalls left by pilfered funds, ahead, at least, until a police car tried to pull him over for speeding.

Milton weighed his options. Better, he decided, to make his timetable to the next branch and take whatever medicine his failure to pull over spooned out. After all, he had the resources of a high-powered law firm at his disposal. And Milton did manage to deposit the funds. Unfortunately, the auditors had smelled a rat and, after enjoying a leisurely lunch, returned to the branch they'd just left, where suddenly a $200,000 discrepancy gaped like a sinkhole.

Milton served eleven months of an eighteen-month sentence, during which Sally divorced him for not loving her, his criminal behavior merely the pretext. Not a unique story until you know that Milton found salvation in jail, and after his release enrolled in a Baptist seminary. He started a church and eventually became a successful televangelist, using his incarceration as an object lesson in redemption. He still preaches on air, according to Sally, along with his lovely wife, twenty-five years his junior.

"The thing is," Sally reflects, "I can't say he's a bad guy or a greedy fraud. I've watched Milton's show. It's all love and forgiveness, not hellfire. His gorgeous wife seems quite nice. I'm not proud of how sick it all makes me feel. I even pray about it. But I don't think God believes me, you know? I've even fantasized about calling *them* up and asking them to pray for me. Can you beat that?"

"Well, only if the new wife is having an affair with an atheist accountant and they end up running off together after embezzling every penny of Milton's nest egg. Then you'd *really* know how much love and forgiveness was in his heart."

Sally was not amused.

"Are *you* an atheist, Bill? Please tell me our years in church together weren't a joke." By now, I am lying on the bed next to Sally for conversational comfort. She grabs my hand and squeezes it as if to secure my soul against whatever heresy I might utter.

"No, atheism was Don's department. I do question how Christians often regard God—as an immensely powerful person who doles out favors and punishments according to his whims. I tend to think of God as the repository of all the mysterious laws holding our universe together. Anyway, speaking of Don, I don't suppose he ever graces these affairs?"

"Once, years ago, looking for you."

Sally and I sleep side by side, holding hands. She leaves just after dawn: the reunion—her "baby"—requires hands on care and feeding. I promise to come down after lunch. "It'll be fun," she promises.

"A colonoscopy is fun," I say. "*This* is painful."

The reunion takes place in a vast, hollow cube of space that makes the affair it serves seem puny. Nevertheless, gallant streams of orange and black bunting, along with other icons of spookiness—cobwebbed witches and ghosts—do their damnedest. The cloying side of 60s pop music emanates from an unoccupied DJ's setup: the Box Tops, the Association, the Monkees, Frankie Valli, even Frank and Nancy Sinatra proffering "Something Stupid"—the stuff I sneered at from the Olympian heights staked out by Dylan and Hendrix. Today, oddly, these tunes console me with their effortless happiness. A cash bar is already doing brisk business. Sally comes over, impales my jacket with a name tag, and kisses me on the lips. Her equivalent, I suppose, of announcing I'm under the Godfather's protection. She points to a five- or six-person clump and says, "Go say hello to Tommy and Clare; they're married." Star quarterback and church girl. Sticking with each other—presumably—for decades. I walk over, exchange a few friendly hellos, and answer easygoing questions about what's been keeping me busy. The rest of the group doesn't need to ask each other. Clare is quiet; Tommy is boisterous. They are both healthily stout. As he explains his new riding mower's shortcomings, she fixes her attention on what he's saying, nodding her head in affirmation. A signal, as I see it, that she likes and respects him. And maybe, I think in a weaker moment, she doesn't want to look at me.

After a few more sessions of innocuous cordialities, I tire of hearing about grandchildren; I break free and take Sally aside. "It's not bad," I admit. "Nobody cares a poop about my scandal." She gives me Linda's "you're a dumbass" look.

"Do you think people quit having scandals just because you left? You've moved way down the list. Bobby Heatwole is gay; nobody cares anymore. At least not enough to mention. Somebody's kid here is not their kid, and everybody knows but them. I could—oh, I need to stop doing that, don't I?" She pauses and shows an intimate smile.

"None of us know very much," I say, smiling back.

I'm relaxed enough now to venture a Canadian Club and Coke and sit alone at a table. Pretty soon, I'll head to the room to gird myself for dinner and festivities. I'd like to talk to Bobby Heatwole, but Sally says he's in Manhattan, getting rich franchising a business called JodaSerk, a string of retro-hip vegan milkshake joints. As I'm about to get up, an unfamiliar man approaches me. He's dressed in a nice suit and sports a full, dark beard. Most notably, he looks fit—no overhanging gut, no hobble in his stride. I can't connect him to any of my old classmates; I surmise he's a husband dragged along. Whoever he is, he sits facing me, intent on catching my eye, as if seeking a fellow stranger in a strange land.

"Hello," I say.

"Yes, of course, hello. Have you deciphered it yet?" He seems a little manic, maybe on some spectrum or another.

I play along.

"The meaning of life? Sure."

"No, Shaffer, nothing remotely that pedestrian. I'm referring to the sexual conundrum I posed to you."

My God, it's Don. Of course. Who else would call me Shaffer? Who else, without sentiment, would barge past fifty years to pursue arcane trivia? I take no offense; quite the opposite. I'm deeply touched that he's kept our friendship alive in his mind all these years and now returns to it, unfazed. I struggle to do the same.

"Well, I'll be damned, Don," I manage, downing my drink then reaching for a handshake. Despite his appearance, Don's grip is as equivocal as ever.

"Most likely, but hardly germane. I am quite curious to know since I made a bet with myself."

Do you mean your little proposition about girls who like you or like sex?

"The very one." Don grins and beams like in the old days, his energy overwhelming mine. And yet—he's *brittle*, I think, as if an aspect of him hasn't changed that needed to.

"I'll tell you once you summarize your current state of affairs."

He waves me away like I was a salesman in a mattress store.

"I'm hale and unattached, too long among Union sympathizers, but otherwise content. Now, no more delay. What, dear Shaffer, of your life among women? Do you prefer their lust or affection?"

"Sorry to say I've never demystified the female paradox—either in theory or in practice. I suppose I prefer women happy if you'll excuse the sophistry. Now answer me one: do you still believe the South will rise again?"

"A delightful bit of a non sequitur, Shaffer. You would have been truly formidable in our youth had you known anything. No, I concede that particular war is lost. And I admit it without regret. I've evolved so far as to agree with Frederick Douglass that no slave should die a natural death. Nevertheless, I still cultivate the seed of truth contained in my father's manifesto—that war is essential to human progress—to the extent that I have published my findings in a book called *The Phenomenology of the Civil War*. Mind you, I do not limit my analysis to that singular conflict. I point out that if Picasso's *Guernica* was a great work of art, then the Spanish civil war that inspired it was an even greater one. As I explain, wars are the breaking of long-suppressed and pernicious fevers, a radical curative which—"

"I prefer aspirin and antibiotics for my fevers, Don, but that said, I'd love to read your book. How long ago was it published? I've given up looking for your name online."

"Ah, yes. I publish under my current name, D. H. Mueller, evoking D. H. Lawrence, do you see?"

"I do see. A subtle stroke. But I'm more taken by your title. The term phenomenology suggests—"

"Well discerned, Shaffer; I am a philosopher. Self-taught, mostly. My mother has afforded me every opportunity. She is—"

"She's still alive?"

"Oh yes, she's only eighty-nine. She still cooks for me and supervises my physical regimen. Quite remarkable."

"I would say."

"Indeed, I owe her the balance I maintain between intuition and logic, a state which allowed me to deduce your likely presence at this reunion."

"You guessed I would be here?"

"*Deduced*, Shaffer. You see, I have maintained a lifelong correspondence with Clare Johnson, my high school sweetheart from afar, now Clare Eddleston. She, in turn, keeps in touch with your Sally. More is generally known about you than you might imagine." Don states this with triumphant pride.

"Then you know about my book? From *my* Sally? The novel recently released by a commercial publisher?" A brief shock flits across Don's face; more, I think, from the chagrin of not knowing than surprise at my novel's existence.

"No, I— Well done, Shaffer! A slice of modern life, I imagine, told with compassion. Am I right?"

"Not quite. It's a critique of Southern racism, using caricatures of the people I knew in Hopperton, including you, me, Sally, Wanda, and . . . your father. I guess there's no point in sugarcoating it. Given your network of people spying on me, you'll end up with a copy sooner or later. You might ask Sally to lend you her copy before she burns it."

Don's eyes dart back and forth like he's speed-reading Marx's *Das Kapital*. Finally, he smacks his hand on the table.

"Fantastic! I will read your book as the antithesis of mine and perform Hegelian synthesis. Who knows? Maybe a new book will emerge. I don't suppose you've kept the name Delia Wingfoot in your potboiler?"

"I have. I'm surprised you remember."

Don leans back, his quasi-military posture giving way. "You know, Shaffer, I have contemplated the past unrelentingly, much in the spirit of Proust, to the point that I wonder if my recollection corresponds to anything that happened or whether I've overpowered events with cognition. Do you see?"

"I see—or think I see—you want to talk about Wanda. Have you seen her? Anything you want to clear up for . . . for, shall we say, reality's sake?"

Don emits a slow sigh, the kind he used to give when I beat him at chess. "I'm heartbroken to say I know nothing of Wanda's whereabouts or those of her . . . progeny if any such exist. And alas, Shaffer, while my higher faculties tell me I was once intimate with Wanda—*once*, mind you—my memory will not retrieve the event. Even taking trauma into account, how can that be?" He looks bereft now as he pauses to pull gold-rimmed glasses from his breast pocket, then rubs them absently with his tie.

I answer Don as I would answer no one else.

"I can't say precisely, but we know from quantum physics that a photon's manifestation as either a wave or a particle depends on the observer. A few modern philosophers suggest history itself, including our individual past, concretely changes according to how we 'observe,' that is, remember it. It's possible how you think about Wanda at any given time determines whether or not you were intimate with her. Sometimes yes, sometimes no. You know, like the cat in the box being both dead and alive until you open the box. Anyway, it bears consideration. As they say, the universe isn't more bizarre than you imagine; it's more bizarre than you *can* imagine."

Don's face remains blank for a few moments, then bursts into manic glee.

"*Plastic* history—of course, Shaffer! By heavens, the Civil War may be won after all! I smell a new book, thanks to you." As Don claps me triumphantly on the arm, I hear "Norwegian Wood" begin to radiate from the DJ's speakers, its droning sitar pulsing eerily through the cavernous room. I also see Sally heading our way, clutching what is probably Don's name tag.

It turns out that Don has shown up without bothering to RSVP, a crime against nature in Sally's eyes. Still, she takes a seat and scolds him without real animus, fixated instead on his physical metamorphosis.

"M-M-Mustang Sally," Don manages to stammer out. "My mother has an Aryan perspective on health and exercise, not . . . not to be confused with racial views. She has private thoughts, of course, like anyone, but her insistence on physical glory reflects—"

"You look way *younger* than Bill and me," Sally says, "and the beard suits you."

Don reddens.

"Yes, as . . . as Epictetus said, the beard is a sacred constituent of the true philosopher, distinguishing him from the Roman citizen whose idleness allows the time to shave, thus—"

"Don, old friend," I break in, "at the end of your discourse, don't forget to thank Sally for her compliment."

"Oh, for God's sake, let him talk, Bill. I'm a grown, educated woman. I don't need a chaperone." I smile inwardly; it seems Bill and Sally's "honeymoon" has come to its rightful end.

"Point taken," I say. "My apologies. For all I know, you two have never had a real conversation before, and here I am spoiling the occasion." I brush aside murmurs of protest and continue. "And you have traits in common I could never have mentioned back in the day, or even recognized: you're both very strange and, despite our squabbles, very endearing—my tribe, it seems. Anyway, I'm heading upstairs to make a call and take a nap. How about the three of us sit together for dinner?"

If you must leave a message, Ramona's phone begrudges, *now is the time*. She misses no opportunity to purge the world of nonsense, whereas I believe the world suffers from a dire shortage of it. I leave my message and open the curtains. The naked sky is classically azure except for a retreating mass of rain clouds the color of bruises. A pair of cardinals swoop and flit above the black-tar rooftops, alighting according to judgments impossible to guess. As I'm watching, the phone performs a little musical number—the term "ringing" hardly does the performance justice. I recognize the caller and answer by saying, "Is there never a moment's peace?"

"When you're dead," Hermine says, "soon enough." Hermine is calling from a tattoo parlor. Olivia, she says, wants to speak with me. Emergency. I next hear Olivia's life-and-death, spy-movie whisper. "Listen, dude (calling me "Bill" was a failed experiment), I'm getting a tattoo, but don't freak out; it's a tiny little diamond." This homage to Carl touches me; he is still "Uncle Carl" to Olivia, who sees no need to uproot her affections.

"I won't bother to ask if your mother knows where you are," I say.

"Smart," she says, no doubt smirking. "Anyway," Olivia adds, "Mom is on a date with a doctor."

"She hates doctors."

"She says she doesn't hate this one yet."

After a few seconds of unaccountable noises, she tells me she's outside where no one can hear us. "The *real* reason I'm calling you is—oh my God—Hermine thinks Natalya has a crush on another woman. It's a vibe thing." I should mention that Hermine and Natalia's liaison thrills Olivia beyond words. Now she can brag that she comes from a family of criminals, tragic death, witches, *and* lesbians.

"Is Hermine upset about Natalya? Is she getting a tattoo?"

"No, no, she's my spirit guide and my ride, that's all."

"I see. Well, as Shakespeare said, 'The course of true love never did run smooth.' That's from *A Midsummer Night's Dream*, Act one, Scene one."

"Dude, are you even *listening* to me? Do you want to hear the *best* part?"

"Definitely. Sorry."

"Okay, listen." Olivia's voice lowers even further for the conspiratorial effect. "The woman Natalya is crushing on is your *ex-wife*, maybe."

"You mean Linda?"

Olivia groans at my stupidity.

"Oh my God—yes! Isn't that *crazy*."

"Insane. Did Hermine tell you it was Linda?"

"No, but why else would Grandma visit *them* when she's in town to see *you*? She *hates* Hermine!"

I understand my reaction now will determine whether Olivia has wasted her time in making this call.

"I suppose I should call Linda and talk to her. Sex between her and Hermine could ruin everything. Besides, people that old shouldn't be bothering with sex."

"Stay out of it, dude! I'm just *telling* you. If you do anything, I'll die."

Mission accomplished. "Okay, I'll hold off for now. Anyway, maybe it's fake news."

"Yeah, maybe. I gotta go. The goth lady is ready for me."

"And where on your body will this 'tiny' tattoo reside, may I ask?"

"My middle finger. It's the rage now. Natalya wants me to get a honeybee on the other middle finger. I might. Gotta go. Hermine wants to talk to you. You better not say anything."

Hermine, it seems, wants to peer at me through the lens of reunion angst. I tell her I'm just another brick in the wall, other than Sally's kiss and Don manifesting himself.

"You don't appear traumatized," she says. "I'm a bit disappointed."

"Right now, I'm glad I came, but give it time; my subconscious has lost a step."

"Hmm."

"You sound preoccupied. Anything going on?"

"As if you didn't know after talking to Olivia. What a cynical intelligence that girl has. She comes at you like a blitzkrieg."

"So your devious little experiment to test Natalya has actually yielded results?" Hermine's sigh resonates through the miles between us.

"For the sake of discussion, Bill, let's say you're desperate to have me back."

"Sure, as long as we stipulate I'm not."

"And let's say I'm neurotically fatalistic about Natalya."

"Patently obvious."

"And that Natalya is pining for Linda and imagines herself 'lord' of the manor you sold to save Carl's ass, even though Linda is radically heterosexual and would probably take *you* back before she would consort with Natalya."

"Given what I know, a completely absurd and entirely credible scenario."

"Yes, and as for the widow Featherstone—"

"Okay, what does *she* want? I've been waiting forty-odd years for the answer to that one."

"Just those awful, smelly goats. Now that we're 'honesty sisters,' she exults to me about her new life. She has dismounted from the merry-go-round of futile longing, it appears, and I'm jealous. Hence my so-called 'preoccupation.'"

"*Siddhartha.*"

"What?"

"The book Wanda Grice gave me for Christmas, 1967. Skinny little book, dog-eared now, lives in my kitchen. All about the merry-go-round and a little about how to get off. Not quite an instruction manual, though, even after many readings."

"You want the young woman who gave you the book, Bill, not wisdom."

As if it has been waiting for Hermine to say this, a deep ache stirs in my gut, forcing out my words. "I guess that's why I'm never satisfied with the ending."

"Of course, of course," Hermine says, her tone telling me that she has already moved on to a new thought. "And speaking of Christmas, Natalya will be gone by the current one," she muses, "but on the bright side, holiday sadness will probably bring me a few new clients." As I cast about for some consoling levity, I hear Olivia shouting in the background, asserting her infinitely more pressing needs. Hermine has to go. But before hanging up she bestows a final admonition: "Please, Bill, don't get swept up in some foolish intrigue and forget to come home. I'll never forgive you."

Her voice is uncharacteristically husky with feeling.

I close the curtains and lie down, hoping for a little Buddhist emptiness, but my mind—if you will—has other ideas. *I'll never forgive you,* Hermine had said, meaning, I suspect, *forgive me.* Gibson Levine once told me that forgiveness was my way of giving a faithless universe the benefit of the doubt. Maybe. More likely, I'm just my mother's son. Thinking about my mother somehow brings Karen's mother to mind: Dorothy Levine, two-faced in her pontifical wool suits. Likely passed on by now. Who, I wondered, did Karen listen to these days? Did she know I'd become a philosophy professor and rue the day she sold me short? I shake my head to chase these questions away. They are as empty as they are tempting, and I have enough hollow spaces already.

Better to picture what's going on downstairs, including the possibility that Don and Sally are falling in love. Well, as Gibson was fond of saying, "The only thing truly unlikely is that nothing unlikely happens." On balance, I favor the notion of Don and Sally. Their mating, and the backstories leading up to it, could be elements in a peach of a novel, its pages filled with the sort of romantic triangles from which I've bowed out, or from which I've been booted after losing a two-to-one vote. If I wrote that book, I would hope to avoid the temptation of seeing those three-sided affairs in terms of wins and losses. Lucky or unlucky to have "lost out"—who can say? What I can say is that I'm not infirm, or crazy, or evil. And I feel an overwhelming fondness for the people in my life; the past be damned.

That said, no amount of bravado or philosophy alters the one hard truth I'll never shake, if truth can be said to inhabit a work of fiction: I do regret losing Delia Wingfoot. Maybe she, mother or daughter, will read *The Dark Warrior* and reach out to me...

I have a couple of hours before the fried chicken, cornbread, and green beans stewed in ham hocks, so I close my eyes. Wanda appears, hovering in the chess club doorway when I dream, crowned with shimmering electric hair. I'm thrilled to see her. I call to her, telling her I love the shit out of her and, in the way of such things, remind her to bring her knight and bishop out before her queen. Wanda smiles and begins to sing an old Dylan song about love speaking like silence.

Like silence, yes. Still, I could listen to Wanda sing forever.

Author's Comments and Acknowledgements

Afew years back, I happened to be reading an archived 1967 newspaper from a small Georgia town and came across an article detailing a school-funding feud between two adjacent counties. One county sought reimbursement for taking the other county's high school students, and the second county refused. Ordinarily, the state of Georgia would have funded the students, regardless of the school they attended. However, Georgia authorities saw the transfer as an obvious ruse to circumvent *Brown v. Board of Education* and feared complicity by the state would put federal school funding at risk. I found the conflict between the two counties to be a fascinating unintended consequence of resistance to integration, and its story stuck with me. Another article in the same newspaper lamented how black students would "slow down" white students as integration proceeded. A third article proudly announced a local young man's enlistment in the army and quoted his "hope to fight for freedom in Vietnam." Even though the newspaper articles were less than fifty years old, I felt like I had opened a time capsule.

Not long before reading these articles, I had started a short story about a young man with idealistic liberal instincts in the throes of a divorce from a pragmatic conservative woman. What if the young man, I wondered, had been raised in a small Georgia town like the one reflected in the 1967 newspaper? What would his journey from youth to manhood look like? To satisfy my curiosity, I gave the young man the name Bill Shaffer, placed him in the fictitious town of Hopperton, Georgia, and *My Secret Radio* was conceived.

Of course, there is a fair bit of literary territory between a novel's conception and birth. This fact brings me to my real purpose in making these remarks: namely, to express my gratitude to those who made my crossing of that territory possible. My deepest thanks must go to my wife Carol, whose patient support never wavered, and whose careful, multiple readings of drafts prevented many errors and infelicities.

Other readers also provided invaluable critiques. John Covolo, Mark Cunningham, and Chuck Hiers, all raised critical issues that caused me to rethink and rewrite individual sections. The result was more believable, more authentic characters and greater verisimilitude of event and place. My copy editor, Deborah Dove, steered me clear of many pitfalls and pointed me toward greater logical clarity. My superb book designer, Andrea Reider, and my talented cover artist, Tanja Prokop, created a beautiful vessel for my words to fill. To my friend and fellow writer, Bob Walker, I offer thanks for his enthusiastic belief in my literary talent. In a world quick to blame and slow to praise, Bob's appreciative generosity stands out.

And lastly, to all the fascinating people whose paths have crossed with mine, from family and affection's tribe to lost lovers and potent strangers, from those who cared for me to those who could well have done without me—I extend my gratitude for your influence. And my characters thank you for giving them life.

Made in the USA
Middletown, DE
04 November 2021